P10

VICTOR GOLLANCZ
A Biography

VICTOR GOLLANCZ

A Biography

by

RUTH DUDLEY EDWARDS

LONDON
VICTOR GOLLANCZ LTD
1987

First published in Great Britain 1987
by Victor Gollancz Ltd,
14 Henrietta Street, London WC2E 8QJ

British Library Cataloguing in Publication Data
Edwards, Ruth Dudley
   Victor Gollancz: a biography.
   1. Gollancz, Victor   2. Publishers and
   publishing—Great Britain—Biography
   I. Title
   070.5'092'4   Z325.G64

ISBN 0–575–03175–1

Typeset at The Spartan Press Ltd, Lymington, Hants
and printed in Great Britain by
St Edmundsbury Press Ltd, Bury St Edmunds, Suffolk
Illustrations originated and printed by Thomas Campone, Southampton

To Neasa MacErlean

Do I contradict myself?
Very well then I contradict myself,
(I am large, I contain multitudes).

Walt Whitman, Song of Myself

CONTENTS

LIST OF ILLUSTRATIONS

Following page 110

The Rev. Samuel Marcus Gollancz (*courtesy Oliver Gollancz*)

Johanna Gollancz, née Koppel (*courtesy Oliver Gollancz*)

Alexander Gollancz

Nellie Gollancz, née Helena Michaelson

Hermann Gollancz, later Sir Hermann, as a young man (*courtesy Phyllis Simon*)

Israel Gollancz, later Sir Israel (*courtesy Oliver Gollancz*)

Nellie Gollancz with her mother and other members of the family in the garden of 256 Elgin Avenue. Winifred, May and Victor are standing at the back (*courtesy Florence and the late Hugh Harris*)

Victor in the garden of 256 Elgin Avenue

Victor at Oxford

At Repton

The schoolmaster at Repton with his pupils

Passport photograph, 1918

David Somervell at Repton (*courtesy Robert Somervell*)

Joseph and Helena Solomon, portraits by Solomon J. Solomon

The Rev. Albert Löwy

Ernest and Henrietta Lowy

Ruth shortly before her marriage (*photo Gertrude Lowy*)

Ruth at the time of her first meeting with Victor (*photo Gertrude Lowy*)

The wedding, 1919

The young parents with Livia, 1921

Ruth with Diana and Livia, 1923

Following page 238

The Lowy family, *c.* 1930 (*photo Thomas Fall*)
The Gollancz daughters, *c.* 1930
Victor in the 1920s
Sir Ernest Benn (*courtesy Glanvill Benn*)
Stanley Morison (*courtesy Cambridge University Library*)
Leonard Stein (*courtesy Mrs Sarah K. Stein*)
Brimpton Lodge, painting by Ruth Gollancz
The children dancing in the Brimpton garden, early 1930s
On holiday in Italy
Victor & Ruth at Brimpton, early 1930s
Ruth's painting of the family at Brimpton, *c.* 1940
Victor at a Left Book Club rally, late 1930s
House party at Brimpton showing Sheila Lynd and Molly Pritt
House party at Brimpton showing Jennie Lee, Aneurin Bevan, Madame Maisky, Ivan Maisky and John Strachey
Ivan Maisky, D. N. Pritt and Victor, in the garden of the Pritts' house, near Brimpton
Harold Laski (*courtesy London School of Economics*)
John Strachey (*courtesy Communist Party Library*)
Harry Pollitt (*courtesy Communist Party Library*)
Richard Acland (*courtesy R. Acland, photo Gayfere Street, BBC*)
Betty Lewis, née Reid (*courtesy Betty Lewis*)
John Lewis (*courtesy Communist Party Library*)
Harold Rubinstein (*courtesy Michael Rubinstein*)
Frank Pakenham (*Popperfoto*)

Following page 558

Silver wedding, 1944
Victor at a Left Book Club rally
Victor at Dartington Hall, 1941
Norman Collins (*courtesy Sarah Collins*)
Sheila Bush, née Hodges (*photo Brian Fisher*)
Diana and John Collins (*courtesy Diana Collins*)
In Germany, 1945

ABBREVIATIONS

ASPRA	Anglo–Soviet Public Relations Association
AWP	Association for World Peace
CCC	China Campaign Committee
CCG	Control Commission of Germany
CND	Campaign for Nuclear Disarmament
COBRSA	Council of British Relief Societies Abroad
CP	Communist Party of Great Britain
FDC	Freedom Defence Committee
ILP	Independent Labour Party
JSHS	Jewish Society for Human Service
LBC	Left Book Club
NCACP	The National Campaign for the Abolition of Capital Punishment
NCCL	National Council for Civil Liberties
NEC	National Executive Committee
NPC	National Peace Council
OTC	Officer Training Corps
PA	Publishers Association
SEN	Save Europe Now
TUC	Trades Union Congress
UEM	United Europe Movement
UNRRA	United Nations Relief and Rehabilitation Administration
UNRWA	United Nations Relief and Welfare Association

PREFACE AND ACKNOWLEDGEMENTS

A MEMBER OF Victor Gollancz's staff once recommended that the firm publish Françoise Gilot's *My Life with Picasso*. Highly excited, Victor took the manuscript home and skimmed it, then telephoned his colleague to announce, 'We can't publish this! Supposing someone wrote like that about Beethoven . . . or me!'

On that evidence, it seems unlikely that Victor would have entirely approved of this book. He would, however, have been pleased by its length and by the thought that it might attract, to the things he most believed in, the attention of a new generation. The speed of his disappearance from public consciousness since his death in 1967 has been extraordinary, given the fame (or notoriety) he achieved at home and abroad in his own lifetime. He is remembered mainly as a publisher and as the organizer of the long-defunct Left Book Club, but, as a handful of contemporaries know, Victor exercised his mighty personality in more arenas than that. Two examples: in the late 1940s the German people saw him as a saviour, wrote letters of gratitude in their tens of thousands, piled honours upon him, named streets after the English Jew who cared about them; conversely, in the 1960s, he was the object of obloquy in Israel.

Victor applied to his good works a vigour, iconoclasm and intensity that struck a powerful chord in the public imagination: Bob Geldof without the advantages of modern communications. It was primarily his temperament that doomed so much of his life's work to obscurity: he was too importunate and easily bored to earn a lasting reputation as a missionary in any one cause. He dropped each as abruptly as he had taken it up, to address himself to a new campaign and a new audience: he was an initiator rather than a consolidator.

The causes themselves tended to be transient: anti-fascism in the 1930s; the alleviation of grim conditions in Gemany after the war; the abolition of capital punishment in the 1950s; the fate of Adolf Eichmann in the 1960s. Then there were his methods of reaching the public: short-lived topical books and pamphlets; massive public meetings; innumerable letters to the press; ecstatically received and often brilliant radio and television appearances. And the impact of his personality often counted for more with his intimates, his followers, his readers, than the content of what he was propounding. (In the stalls at a musical performance he would make his flamboyant presence felt by applauding louder than anyone else — behaviour notable at the time, but not noteworthy in the long term.) Yet Victor lives on egregiously in the memories of hundreds of his contemporaries, who love him, vilify him or laugh about him as if he were still there to inspire, infuriate or charm.

Victor wrote four volumes of reminiscences: *My Dear Timothy, More for Timothy, Journey Towards Music* and *Reminiscences of Affection.* In all of them he contrived to avoid those aspects of his career that people most wanted to read about, and concentrated on self-analysis and disquisitions on his past or current enthusiasms. Researchers into Left Book Club days were blocked by Victor's denial that any relevant papers existed and forced, sometimes under threat of libel actions, to accept his sanitized and hence dull account of his role in the late 1930s. He might have loomed large in the memoirs of famous contemporaries, but his own hypersensitivity and quirkiness made that impossible: criticism of Victor in print was entirely his own prerogative. The overwhelming charity of John Collins and Frank Longford in their autobiographies, for instance, enabled them to write about him in his lifetime in terms that he approved, while others, such as David Low, found it easier virtually to avoid mention of him. Even after he died, similar inhibitions afflicted those who feared wounding his family or lacked the will to unpick the tangle of contradictions that made up his character.

When I asked Livia Gollancz, in 1977, if I could write her father's biography, neither of us realized how time-consuming and difficult a project it would turn out to be. Even Livia did not guess at the terrifying extent of the source material or at the staggering range of her father's activities. Certainly she could not be aware that, once committed to research, I tend to resemble a dog with a bone. I did not know Victor: indeed I was rather baffled during an early discussion when Livia said that one of her reasons for having me rather than other interested authors take on the project was that I had never met him. Her instinct was entirely right: Victor could engender enmity or devotion in even the level-headed on the briefest of acquaintance.

Victor's demands almost defeated me. When I took the commission I had a full-time job, and had assumed that I could produce the book in my spare time. It soon became clear that I must choose between the job and Victor. In the firm's offices, for instance, it was necessary to read the file for every book published during Victor's forty years at the helm, for Victor was as likely to have written an illuminating letter to the author of a cookery book as to a distinguished politician. In the Modern Records Centre at the University of Warwick were private papers of Victor's running to many thousands of items, among which clues were scattered about quite unchronologically (so that one might find in a letter of 1957 a vital piece of information on an event of 1907). Nor were the two enormous *Tim* books easy to mine. For Victor had refused (perversely, I felt) to provide an index. Worse, there was Victor's misguided belief that his memory was infallible, as well as his dislike of checking facts, his deficiencies as a reporter, his poor judgement when his emotions were engaged, and his propensities to self-delusion and exaggeration.

It was what Victor called his *mana* (loosely — charisma) that persuaded me to choose him rather than salaried employment. I had become intellectually and emotionally involved with him, fascinated by the different facets that glinted in his writings and intrigued to the point of bewilderment by the wildly different attitudes to him expressed by his contemporaries. In 1979, I became a full-time writer. Since then (after the advance payment had been exhausted) I have often had to shelve Victor when money ran short, in order to work on other books. And because I was determined that the portrait of Victor should be fair, there was a prolonged period during which I tried to make the text reflect the criticisms of the readers of the first draft: my husband, my parents, John Bush, Diana Collins, Jon Evans, Livia Gollancz, Oliver Gollancz, Vita Gollancz, Sheila Hodges, Francesca and Stuart Jeffryes, Gordon Lee, Julia and the late Harold Simons, and Richard Storey. Phyllis Simon, Victor's cousin, commented on the early chapters, Canon Edward Carpenter on my treatment of the Repton episode and Glanvill Benn on the Ernest Benn chapter. At the same time, more important papers turned up, necessitating a great deal of rewriting. David Burnett of Victor Gollancz Ltd made very helpful suggestions on the second draft.

Many readers have voiced strong views, and they have rarely been in chorus: indeed, the more intimately they knew him, the more idiosyncratic their comments, proportionally to Victor's idiosyncrasies in his dealings with them. My debt to these readers is tremendous. They forced me to defend my selection of evidence and my judgements, and picked up many errors. Sometimes I was thrown into despair over a particular passage where A felt I was being hyper-critical, B felt I was being unduly kind and C thought I had got it just right but might have made the same point more tellingly with a different anecdote, but overall I found the arguments and discussions of enormous value and interest.

As the book is being published under the aegis of Livia Gollancz, and because her sisters Julia, Vita and Francesca have co-operated, suspicions of censorship must be allayed. Of course there have been disagreements on interpretation here and there, but all parties have been concerned to get at the truth. All four of Victor's daughters are forthright, and all share an innate and remarkable honesty: none of them ever questioned my right to tell the truth as I saw it. After due discussion, I have at the request of some member of Victor's family or circle omitted perhaps a dozen stories or quotations — always peripheral — that would have been too embarrassing. No one ever asked me to omit anything I thought was important. The more I hear stories of what timorous piety can do to biographies of the recently dead, the more grateful I am to Victor's relatives, friends and, most particularly, to the Gollancz sisters.

Livia has a horror of anything that smacks of flattery, but even she would have to admit that I owe her a special debt. She has given me unrestricted access to all her father's papers and has answered all my questions with total frankness. As my publisher, she has seen the book grow out of all proportion to her first vision, and the production costs mount accordingly; as my editor, she has endured it as a thorn in her side and a cause of overwork for far longer than she could have imagined; and as Victor and Ruth's daughter, she has bravely clenched her teeth at some of my conclusions. She knows it has not been easy for me either. Our relationship has endured great strains and many arguments, but we have trusted each other's integrity throughout. Even at our stickiest moments, my affection and admiration for Livia have held firm. Three of my readers rightly gave her the same unsolicited testimonial: 'Hats off to Livia'.

I must single out some other people. The first is my husband John Mattock, my first reader, critic and editor, who has shared the house with Victor's turbulent personality over many years. His routine question to me on returning home in the evenings was not 'How's the book going?' but 'What's he been up to today?' The other members of my household, Neasa MacErlean and Michael Kersse, never flagged in their support, affection and willingness to listen to anecdotes about Victor, who has not been an easy lodger.

My parents, Robin and Sheila Dudley Edwards, were, throughout the project, involved, encouraging and helpful. Both were fascinated by Victor, and applied their prodigious and very different talents to the manuscript. My mother did not live to see the publication of the book, but she would be pleased that my father worked his way through the proofs on behalf of both of them. If I have at all understood Victor, it is because Robin taught me to revere objectivity, and because Sheila showed me the creative force of emotion channelled through taste and intellect.

Diana Collins, Sheila Hodges and John Bush (her husband) should be thanked as a trio, for they knew Victor better than any other surviving friends and they swapped comments on the early draft. They all went to enormous trouble to help and advise me and lavished hospitality on me during the process. My abiding memory of their joint involvement is of a dinner party when the four of us squabbled about aspects of Victor's character only to collapse into helpless laughter at each outrageous story that someone had just remembered. I regretted very much that the late John Collins was not there to share in the enjoyment. I met him only twice, but I shall never forget the warmth, humour and understanding he brought to bear on his egocentric old friend and inspiration.

Richard Storey, of the Modern Records Centre in Warwick, is the archivist of researchers' dreams, combining professionalism and profound knowledge with an extraordinary readiness to help people in their work. Since I finished at Warwick he has sent me each completed part of his catalogue (drawing my attention to anything he thought I might have missed), has answered my every query and request by return of post, and has read the book both in manuscript and proof. His encyclopaedic knowledge of the archive has saved me from more errors than I dare recollect.

As my dear friend Gordon Lee is fascinated by and wise about what goes on in people's heads and hearts, Victor was grist to his mill, but it can only have been his great kindness that carried him through two readings of the book and innumerable discussions of Victor's quirks. More, an 'Ugh!' in the margin, in Gordon's hand, drew my attention to many infelicities of style.

Many others helped me. I must thank especially Sir Richard Acland, Glanvill Benn, Sir James Darling, John Gross, Sir James Harford, Betty Lewis, Lord Longford, James MacGibbon, Elinor Murphy, Nancy Raphael, Hilary Rubinstein and Graham and Dorothy Watson. Many of my friends have taken an interest, suffered my anecdotal obsession and offered moral support: those deserving special mention are Piers Brendon, Patrick Cosgrave, Susan Chadwick, Marianne Elliott, Marigold Johnson, James McGuire, Oliver Snoddy and the late David Tierney. Elke Hassell typed the manuscript superbly in very difficult circumstances, took a great interest in Victor and became a friend. And of the many kindly Gollancz staff, Margot Charing, Carol Fenton, Harriette Lloyd and Frances Wollen provided me with far more help than I could have reasonably expected, while the late Jon Evans made invaluable comments and suggested the epigraph to the book. To all others to whom I owe so much, my apologies for consigning them, to a brief mention in the acknowledgements. I ask forgiveness of those whom I have failed to mention at all. (Incidentally, in the course of the book I discuss Victor's extra-marital affairs without naming the women involved. Readers may be tempted to make guesses based on the names of those I cite as important interviewees. I enter here a caveat: I have been selective in citing my sources and careful in my acknowledgements; names can be omitted.)

I ask no forgiveness of my readers for the length of the book, which was dictated by the huge spread of Victor's activities and interests as well as by the more bizarre aspects of his personal relationships. Nor do I apologize for my generous use of quotation: Victor had such a horror of being misrepresented that I considered it only fair to let him speak for himself on controversial or complicated issues; a great deal of the source material is at present inaccessible to scholars, particularly that relating to the 1930s and Victor's publishing career; reading between the lines is often crucial; and many of the letters are very amusing. (I have normally avoided the obtrusive 'sic', and have occasionally made trivial alterations in the quotations only where a lapse in punctuation or spelling distorts the meaning or seriously distracts the eye.)

Some readers may raise an eye-brow at my nomenclature: 'Victor' rather than 'Gollancz'. Although I have in my other biographies always used my subjects' surnames, on this occasion I found the convention rang false. Here 'Gollancz' is the publishing firm, and 'Victor' its founder. All those who had even a passing acquaintance with him were required to call him 'VG' or 'Victor'. He has usually been 'Victor' to me in my conversations with his friends and that is how I think of him.

It has been an appallingly difficult book to write, yet I end with no regrets. Victor has done to me what he did to many of his colleagues in publishing or campaigning, expecting me to participate in his every passing enthusiasm, playing the tune to which I danced with no regard for my convenience and driving me to the limit of my endurance. Yet he has opened up to me a much wider world, full of issues that must not be shrugged off, and on which I find him usually to be intrinsically right. And he has never ever been boring.

In addition to those named above, I am grateful to Max Platschek, who translated most German documents for Victor Gollancz, to Becky Smith, who took on the index at short notice and to the following, who gave me information, advice, support or lent photographs. Some of them also gave me permission to quote material.

The late Robert Aickman, Kingsley Amis, the late J. R. L. Anderson, Betty Askwith, Harry Armitage, David Astor, David Baird, Alva, Colm, Deirdre and Eamon de Barra, Chaim Bermant, Pearl Binder, Jane Blackstock, the late Sir Adrian Boult, the staff of the British Library and the British Newspaper Library, Felicity Bryan, Liz Calder, Anna Clarke, Nina Clarke, the late Norman Collins, Sarah Collins, Lettice Cooper, Constance Cummings, Peter Day, Lewis Denroche-Smith, Peter Eastty, Lord Elwyn-Jones, Patrick Forbes, the late Heinrich Fraenkel, Nicolas Freeling, Lord Gardiner, Joanna Goldsworthy, the late Marguerite Gollancz, Lord Goodman, John Grigg, Peter Gronn, John Handfield, Lady Harford, Florence and the late Hugh Harris, Desmond and Jennifer Henderson, Gavin Henderson, the late Lily Henriques, Dorothy Horsman, Graham and Marjorie Hutton, Violet Jackson, Elizabeth Jenkins, Yvonne Kapp, Michael Katanka, the late Arthur Koestler, Paul Le Druillenec, Ed Lewis, the staff of the London Library, Daniel Lowy and family, Jean MacGibbon, Deirdre McMahon, the late T. L. Martin, Queenie Matthews, David Mattock, Walter Meigh, the late Sir Robert Mayer, John Midgley, the staff of the Modern Records Centre at the University of Warwick, F. Morton, Henry D. Myer, the Librarian of New College, the Librarian of the Oxford Union, Richard Pooley, the Headmaster and Archivist of Repton, Helga Rubinstein, the High Master and Archivist of St Paul's School, Sir Alfred Sherman, David Shipman, Oliver Simon, Robert Somervell, Sarah K. Stein, A. J. P. Taylor, Lord Walston, Shirley Williams, T. Desmond Williams, Harry Yoxall, Elizabeth Zass.

The following kindly gave me permission to quote from published or unpublished material:

Allison & Busby Ltd (Duff, *Left, Left, Left*), Professors G. E. M. Anscombe and G. H. Von Wright and Rush Rhees (Ludwig Wittgenstein), John Franklin Bardin, Morchard Bishop, the *Bookseller*, the late Lord Boothby, Arthur Calder-Marshall, D. N. Carey (Geoffrey Fisher), Mark Bonham Carter (Lady Violet Bonham Carter), Winston Churchill (Randolph and Winston S. Churchill), Humphrey Cole (G. D. H. Cole), Collins Publishers (Jerrold, *Georgian Adventure*), Anthony Cox (J. S. Middleton), Sir John Cripps (Dame Isobel Cripps), Brook Crutchley and Arthur Crook (Stanley

Morison), Curtis Brown (Spencer Curtis Brown), Faber & Faber Ltd (T. S. Eliot and Sir Geoffrey Faber), Michael Foot, Lady Glubb (Sir John Glubb), Monk Gibbon, John Grigg, John Hadfield, David Higham Associates Ltd (Eleanor Farjeon, Dorothy L. Sayers, and Edith Sitwell), the *Jewish Chronicle*, Naomi Lewis, Clive Lofts (Norah Lofts), the London School of Economics and Political Science (Sidney Webb), Nigel Nicolson (Harold Nicolson), Oxford University Press (Gerard Hopkins), Trekkie Parsons (Leonard Woolf), A. D. Peters & Co. Ltd (Phyllis Bentley, John Gloag, Rose Macaulay, A. D. Peters, William Roughead, L. A. G. Strong and Alec and Evelyn Waugh), Harriet F. Pilpel (Edna Ferber), Brian Pollitt (Harry Pollitt), Jacquetta Priestley (J. B. Priestley), A. J. P. Taylor, Mrs David Teale (Allen Lane), E. P. Thompson (Edward Thompson), John Updike, Rosalind Wade (William Kean Seymour), Dr Rachael Whear (David Low), Peter Wheeler (Sheila Lynd), Colin Wilson, G. Woytt (Albert Schweitzer), Lord Young.

(Efforts were made to get in touch with all others quoted — or their executors — but in some cases this proved impossible.)

R. D. E.

VICTOR GOLLANCZ
A Biography

CHAPTER ONE

CHILDHOOD

HEARKEN TO ME, you who pursue deliverance,
you who seek the Lord;
look to the rock from which you were hewn,
and to the quarry from which you were digged.
Look to Abraham your father
and to Sarah who bore you.

'Thus instructed,' writes Chaim Bermant, 'the Jew felt that he was not only part of a lateral family of contemporaries — brothers, sisters, uncles, cousins — but of a vertical family stretching back into history and forward into time . . . To be part of a Jewish family is thus to be hemmed in, to a greater or lesser degree, by history, by antecedent and precedent, by the attitudes of past generations and responsibilities to future ones.'

To the young Victor Gollancz, determined to be his own master, and temperamentally disposed to live for the joy or agony of the moment, this constriction seemed insupportable; all its manifestations in his orthodox family circle were equally repugnant. And he was infuriated as much by the political and social conservatism of his environment as by its religious taboos. In late middle age he recognized that it was his struggle against this tradition — embodied in his father — that gave depth and passion to his thinking and emotions, and helped transform the orthodox Jewish child into a fiercely controversial prophet of Christian ethics and individual liberty.

He did not explore the reasons why his personal relationships were to be as often characterized by *Stürm und Drang* as by the charity, tolerance and love that he sought to practise. Nor did he ever recognize how much his extended family had contributed to his becoming a sincere crusader for universal brotherhood.

Victor was born on the ninth of April, 1893, at 256 Elgin Avenue, Maida Vale, a five-storey house in a pleasant middle-class area of north London. His father, Alexander, was a moderately prosperous wholesale jeweller of unimpeachable Jewish orthodoxy and, in his respectability and industry, a model Victorian. The son's capacity for hard work was to become legendary, but the father's, though less dramatically apparent, was just as impressive. Their home was remote from the office (in Duke Street in the City) where Alex worked six days a week, never arriving home before 9 p.m. save on the eve of the Sabbath and other days of observance, and never taking holidays. His ambitions were modest and typical of his community: he wanted his two daughters, May and Winifred, to marry well and be good wives and mothers, and Victor, their younger brother, to have a fine education and become more successful than himself. Meanwhile he was driven by an obsession with the need to provide for them and his wife Helena ('Nellie') in his lifetime and against his death. Even when, in his seventies, his son's success in business relieved Alex of any need to add to his modest estate, his life-long addiction to work was too deep-rooted to break. Too old and ill to work in an office, he was found by visitors to his home examining diamonds and disinclined for social intercourse. If Alex's devotion to his work seems excessive to those of a later age, it was unremarkable in his generation of the family, notable achievers even by Jewish standards, and though Alex, in his desire for a quiet life, might appear dreary, there was nothing ordinary about the Gollanczes. If he provided a conformism for the young Victor to rail against, other relatives provided models for more constructive traits of character.

Victor's grandfather, the Reverend Samuel Marcus Gollancz, appears briefly in Victor's first volume of reminiscences (*My Dear Timothy*) as 'an adorable old gentleman', *chazan* (cantor) of the Hambro Synagogue, whose hobbies were singing tenor arias and carving miniatures. He was a more complex and steely character than Victor ever realized, emerging from his own memoirs as a curious mixture: modest yet self-satisfied, content yet ambitious, ecumenical in practice yet unquestioningly obedient to his tradition.

From the end of the eighteenth century, when European Jews were under increasing pressure to adopt surnames, Samuel Marcus's grandfather took the family name from a small village in Poland. Samuel Marcus's father, Israel, settled in Witkowa, in the Duchy of Posen. Already heavily populated by German immigrants, it was annexed by Prussia in 1793 and Germanification continued throughout the nineteenth century (with a brief hiatus when it came under Russian control between 1807 and 1815). Samuel Marcus, born in 1820, was a product of a Hebrew and German culture which revered

SIMPLIFIED FAMILY TREE
OF THE GOLLANCZ FAMILY

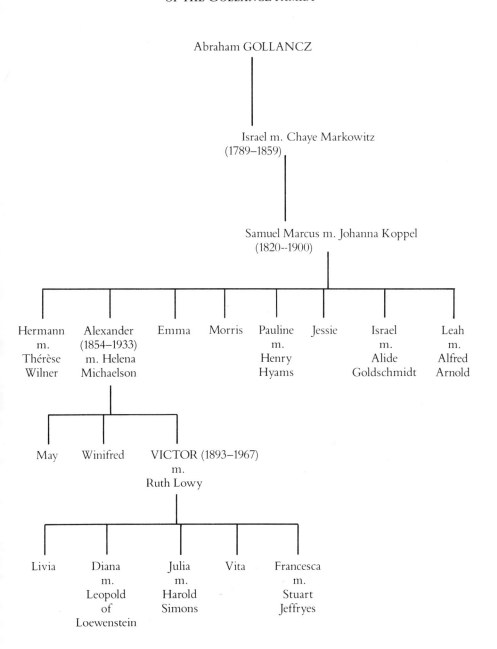

Abraham GOLLANCZ

Israel m. Chaye Markowitz
(1789–1859)

Samuel Marcus m. Johanna Koppel
(1820--1900)

| Hermann m. Thérèse Wilner | Alexander (1854–1933) m. Helena Michaelson | Emma | Morris | Pauline m. Henry Hyams | Jessie | Israel m. Alide Goldschmidt | Leah m. Alfred Arnold |

May Winifred VICTOR (1893–1967)
m.
Ruth Lowy

| Livia | Diana m. Leopold of Loewenstein | Julia m. Harold Simons | Vita | Francesca m. Stuart Jeffryes |

scholarship and made it natural for Israel and his wife to encourage their gifted son's ambitions. At the age of twelve he began the life of a roving student of Hebrew and the Talmud, moving around Germany to sit at the feet of ever more exalted masters. Two of the rabbis under whom he studied — Akiba Eger and Israel Lipschitz — were men of international reputation, whose enthusiasm for their pupil marked him out as a prodigy. Later, his fine voice had him sought after as an assistant in synagogue services, and before he was twenty-one he was advised to move to Berlin to take a doctorate.

Samuel Marcus's natural desire to rise to the top of his profession was frustrated by one of his mentors, the Rabbi of Witkowa, who warned against the temptations of Berlin — citing the case of a youth of his acquaintance who had there been converted to Christianity, thus driving his distraught father into a lunatic asylum. Samuel Marcus, a dutiful son, bowed to the will of his rabbi and his widowed father, and settled for a less distinguished career. By 1850 he was rabbi at Bremen, where he spent what he later recalled as the happiest four years of his life, and where he married Johanna Koppel and fathered his first two sons, Hermann and Alex.

It can only have been ambition for his children that drove Samuel Marcus to follow the recommendation of some English visitors, and apply for a post as cantor with the Hambro Synagogue in the City of London. It was an adventurous step for a man with strong ties of family and friendship in Germany and no knowledge of English. He was asked to read prayers in the synagogue by way of audition and his performance received plaudits from the *Jewish Chronicle*.

> Mr Gollancz combines a musical voice with the most correct intonation. His reading evidences a sound knowledge of Hebrew grammar; and the high testimonials he has from some eminent Rabbis and preachers on the continent certify to his unexceptionable moral and religious character. A reader like Mr Gollancz would be an ornament to the Hambro Synagogue and the Jewish clergy of our community in general.

Other candidates had to be heard, and Samuel Marcus returned to Bremen to await developments. After three months he was invited back to conduct a service again, and was elected unanimously. The *Jewish Chronicle*, offering the synagogue its congratulations on having elected 'so efficient and highly educated a man', had some advice for him:

> It is hoped that on his return he will earnestly devote himself to the study of the English language, so that he may be able to address his Congregation from the pulpit in the vernacular. And we also hope that the time may

come when no First Reader will be appointed to any congregation without being qualified, or with the understanding, that he qualifies himself for the duties of the pulpit.

The *Jewish Chronicle* spoke for the Anglicizers among the Jewish community. On the one hand, there was a deep reverence for traditional learning and a desire to avoid any dilution of religion or race, but with only about 35,000 Jews in Britain at this period, ministers normally had to be recruited from the continent. The Hambro Synagogue had been in existence since the early eighteenth century, serving the needs of the Ashkenazim (Jews of German and Polish origin), who clustered in large numbers in the City. Among them Samuel Marcus would have felt at home. On the other hand, there was a determination to prove by assertion and example that being Jewish was no hindrance to being patriotic Englishmen. Those who settled in England — and Samuel Marcus proved to be no exception — wanted to rear children who, being good Englishmen as well as good Jews, would show anti-semitism to be absurd.

In the spring of 1855, when Samuel Marcus arrived with his family to take up his new position, there were still formal obstacles to Jewish progress, but they were falling fast. It was a time of great optimism in the community. Public schools were gradually opening to its children, and in the year of Samuel Marcus's arrival, Jews' College was founded to meet the need for home-trained ministers of religion. Although Oxford and Cambridge were to remain closed to Jews until 1871, other universities, particularly University College, London, offered them higher education. More important than that, many Jews had been successful in business and some had taken up public positions. In 1858, the Oath of the House of Commons was amended to allow Baron Lionel de Rothschild to take his seat.

Heartened by such examples, prosperous Jews set their sights on the best available education for their sons. The sense of community was strong; the wealthy became benefactors of their poorer brethren, who showed proper gratitude. Samuel Marcus was among them, eulogizing, in his reminiscences, the millionaire philanthropist Sir Moses Montefiore, who occasionally entertained him, and recounting proudly a compliment paid to him on his children by Baroness Lionel de Rothschild. Yet he had his moments of disenchantment: his family's successes were academic, not financial, and he was capable of peevishness about contemporary values. A later poem of his, 'Enlightened Times', included the stanzas:

Who cares for what is just and right
To-day, within our world?
In times which men deem full of light,
With Mammon's flag unfurled?

The millionaire alone commands,
His gold doth cry aloud.
They fawn upon his huge demands —
By wealth the world is cowed.*

Both family reminiscences and Samuel Marcus's obituaries make it clear that, though he had a fierce determination to give his children every opportunity for advancement, his ambitions for himself ceased with his appointment to the Hambro Synagogue. He was to hold the same position at the synagogue until his retirement in 1899, his inadequacy in English precluding him from preaching. He was in any case ill-placed to compete with the new generation of English-born and Jews' College-trained men. Nevertheless, and allowing for normal piety towards the dead, Samuel Marcus's obituaries show him to have been a success in office. His congregation was proud of his scholarship, and delighted in the beauty of his voice and the genuine piety that infused his readings of prayers. If he was not, as Victor was later to claim, 'probably the most distinguished cantor of the 19th century', he was certainly a well-respected and admired one, whose achievements earned him a twelve-line obituary in *The Times* in 1900. His work for charity was well recognized, and he helped found two Jewish charitable institutions — the Soup Kitchen and the Jewish Board of Guardians — as well as being a diligent hospital visitor.

According to a contemporary, Samuel Marcus had 'zealously devoted himself to the study of the Torah, to participation in divine service, and to the practice of charity, the three principles upon which, according to Simon the Just, the world was based.' His orthodoxy was total, even to a fastidious observance of the Talmud injunction that 'Every disciple of the Sages upon whose garment the slightest speck or stain is found deserves death'; he attracted amused attention 'for the extreme orderliness of his attire and the scrupulous neatness of his general appearance'.

The tributes emphasized his modesty, simplicity, humility and 'unworldliness of character', but Samuel Marcus had a toughness and vision that belied his unassuming image. From the time of his arrival in England he coped not only with a new culture and a new language, but with a rapid change in the size and structure of the Jewish

*Translated from the German by Hermann Gollancz.

population. The 35,000 grew by 1880 to 60,000, of whom more than half were British-born, whereafter refugees from Russian and Polish pogroms poured in — almost 150,000 by a 1919 estimate. Fearing the Anglicization policy would be swamped by this foreign tide, many of those already settled tried unsuccessfully to discourage immigration. Others, more alive to traditional loyalties, provided assistance and advice to their persecuted brethren. Samuel Marcus, who had himself benefited greatly from community support, did his best to help newcomers to the East End. (His own synagogue was changing its composition drastically as the well-to-do moved to the suburbs and the new arrivals took their places.) He continued with his charitable work until his health failed. Nor did he confine it to the Jewish needy, having recognized early that Jews should work within the wider community, and that co-operation with other religions was desirable. His orthodoxy did not prevent friendly alliances with members of the reform community, and with Christians.

The Hambro Synagogue had housed the grateful Samuel Marcus and his family in 'a nice house . . . in a very genteel street, No. 15a Bury Street', where he remained for 25 years and fathered six more children, one of whom died in infancy. To educate seven children on a small income was difficult, but Samuel Marcus and his wife accomplished it triumphantly. The boys went to Jews' College, to learn to be 'worthy of the perfectly compatible privileges of their glorious British birth and their still more glorious Jewish faith'. (In Chaim Bermant's view it was 'an uneasy synthesis of English and Jewish culture', producing rabbis with the veneer of Church of England clergymen. Certainly it accentuated the compatibility that already existed between Judaic and Victorian values.) Unusually for orthodox Jews, the Gollancz daughters were also given opportunities to develop their talents. A rich friend in Bremen was permitted to pay Emma Gollancz's fees at Queen's College, in Harley Street, and Leah became a serious student of music.

By 1900, when Samuel Marcus died and his grandson Victor was seven years old, the Gollancz family had reason to be satisfied with its position in the world. Hermann, the oldest, was a rabbi and had just become the first Jew to secure a D.Lit. from the University of London. Israel, the youngest, was a university lecturer in English at Cambridge. Emma, after a time as honorary secretary of the Council of Jewish Girls' Clubs, had gone to Newnham College, Cambridge, until her parents' failing health called her home. The assistance she gave Israel in editing his many books was well-recognized in academic circles and she edited in her own right volumes of the Temple Classics.

(Her *Times* obituary in 1929 referred to her as Israel's right hand.) Pauline was married to a headmaster. Leah, who died in 1895, had before her marriage been a fine pianist and an Exhibitioner at the Guildhall School of Music. Within another five years, Hermann had become Professor of Hebrew at University College, London, and Israel Professor of English Language and Literature at the University of London. Both were on their way to knighthoods.

The two middle sons, Alex and Morris, were comparatively unsuccessful, and had gone into trade. Alex, hunched by curvature of the spine, worked hard to attain a decent living; Morris, crippled and lisping, barely held down his job as a watchmaker's assistant at a pound a week. The contrast with Hermann and Israel gradually grew more marked, and the *Jewish Chronicle*, of which Alex was a devoted reader, glowingly recited all his eminent brothers' achievements. Its obituaries of his father emphasized *their* distinction and their parents' public pride in them, a version of events confirmed by Herbert Bentwich, who recalled in 1930 that Samuel Marcus 'and his clever little wife were proud folk, talking always of the talents of their children, with a special pride in Hermann and Israel, who afterwards justified so amply all their boasts and ambitions.' Hardly surprising, then, that family recollection has Alex and Morris self-conscious about their own relative lack of success and ill-at-ease with Israel and Hermann.

Nevertheless, Alex was devoted to his family and stayed in close touch with his parents and siblings. There was frequent contact with his wife's relatives, too — the Michaelsons and Friedlanders. Intra-family visiting, therefore, opened up a world of richness and achievement to Victor and his sisters.

On their father's side there was of course an emphasis on academic excellence, but the musical tradition — so important to Victor later — was very strong too. Samuel Marcus, even on his modest income, had managed to attend opera performances in Bremen and in London, and talked frequently about the great singers he had heard. Alex shared his enthusiasm, and transmitted to the next generation his father's reminiscences about such legendary performers as Adelina Patti, Jenny Lind, Nilsson, Mario and Tamagno. The musical members of the family were brought up to believe them irreplaceable, and operatic decline inevitable. Morris also adored opera, though he could rarely afford it, and it was one of Alex's very occasional extravagances. On the Michaelson side, too, there was musical stimulation. Uncle Assur lived with his mother and loved to sing ballads to the accompaniment of the lady he loved, Elsie Grant (a gentile he would not marry until his mother died). They used to hold little concerts which Victor remembered vividly.

> The whole complex — Elsie Grant, Uncle Assur, old Mrs Michaelson, leafy St John's Wood, the studio (with the collection of cracked but beautiful Dresden and Chelsea that Elsie Grant used to keep there) and above all the grand piano, for ours was only an upright — fascinated me irresistibly; and I used to adore being taken there when I was still a very small child, not perhaps more than four or five.

Great Aunt Rosetta Friedlander, with whom the children spent holidays in Hastings, had been an inveterate opera-goer and owned an enormous stock of opera libretti. Victor's cousin, Arthur Friedlander, was a professional musician. And Victor's mother could play on the piano such Chopin and Victorian showpieces as 'The Midnight Wedding'. Winifred also played, and Alex contributed to the musical ambience of Elgin Avenue by humming opera arias around the house — though, like Victor, he could not sing in tune. So music was natural to Victor from infancy as an essential ingredient of normal life. In addition to what he heard in the family circle, he was fired with enthusiasm by the band performances in the parks to which his father occasionally took him.

Art was taken almost equally for granted. Grandfather Samuel Marcus's exquisite miniature carvings had been exhibited in Germany and were highly prized within the family; Uncle Assur was a painter; Uncle Morris loved antiques. There were other broadly educational influences. Aunt Minna Michaelson was a great traveller, who talked in his grandmother's drawing room of her journeys, and started off a museum for Victor with a necklace of garnets from the Sahara and a piece of marble from the Parthenon. Uncle Max Michaelson was wealthy, and lived in such grandeur in Sydenham that the young Victor was a nervous visitor there.

Further afield again, Alex had a small circle of close friends with whom family visits were exchanged, and he did not confine himself entirely to Jewish company. He had a few gentile acquaintances, and on at least three occasions brought a clergyman home for Passover. Personalities also varied widely: tolerant Israel, self-sacrificing Emma, romantic Assur, kindly Morris, and Hermann, who had a vanity even more prodigious than his achievements.

All in all then, Victor's sense of beauty had been aroused early by his family, and his intellectual curiosity had grown in fertile soil. No less important for his development was the family's commitment to public service. For them, as for many Jews, philanthropic activity was a matter of course. Both male and female Gollanczes appeared regularly in the Jewish press as modest donors to appeals, or as members of charitable and educational bodies. Israel's and Hermann's careers took them beyond such humble good works. Israel, although his orthodoxy diminished with the years, worked hard for improvements in rabbinical training, but his most important public service was in a secular sphere. In 1903 he was one of the founders of the British Academy and served as its secretary until his death in 1929, while his other causes included enthusiastic support for a projected national theatre. Hermann, both professor and rabbi, produced an endless succession of translations from Hebrew and Aramaic texts, and wrote on Jewish history and theology, but was also an indefatigable social worker and an active member of committees as various as the National Council of Public Morals and the Kinema Commission. Nor was he averse to controversy. With Israel's help, he publicly engaged and defeated Chief Rabbi Adler on a major point of principle — a 'courageous fight . . . against a somewhat reactionary officialdom', remarked his *Times* obituary.

Both Hermann and Israel were vocal in the press on major issues of the day. Israel, for instance, was in 1919 a signatory — with other distinguished Jews like Lionel de Rothschild, Lord Swaythling and Claude Montefiore — of a letter condemning the enthusiasm of Jewish newspapers for 'Bolshevism and its "ideals"', which they repudiated as intrinsically dangerous and 'false to the tenets and teachings of Judaism'. Hermann, even in his old age, broken by the recent deaths of his wife, sister Emma and Israel, and the suicide of his son Leonard, found the strength to enter into a major dispute with the *Jewish Chronicle*. He had written a pompous but well-intentioned letter to *The Times*, wishing it a happy 1930, congratulating it on its role as the 'harbinger of truth', and listing the grave issues confronting the world. He also demonstrated his essential decency and lack of bigotry by expressing the hope that Arabs and Jews should learn to live in brotherhood in Palestine (anticipating sentiments his nephew Victor was later to promulgate). The *Jewish Chronicle* at the time was touchy to the point of paranoia about any undermining of Zionism, and accused him in hurtful and vitriolic terms of 'ridiculous vanity' in speaking on behalf of Anglo-Jewry. His words were distorted so as to make them suggest Jewish and Moslem religious 'mingling'. Hermann's lengthy response was admirably spirited, predictably vain, and justifiably wounded by the gross misrepresentation. When he died, ten months later, the *Jewish World* and *Jewish Chronicle* were ungenerous. (Victor, coming from such an environment, took naturally to publicizing his contentious opinions and was to annoy the Jewish press even more.)

Victor's memoirs are of more value as an insight into the older man, rather than the boy or the youth, for all his efforts to recall accurately the early passions that preoccupied him. The reminiscences of his childhood are so bound up with his resentment of his father's values as to give an illusion of a claustrophobic household, cut off from any bigger world. Yet his belief that public duty went hand in hand with professional success, his aesthetic values, his intellectual curiosity, his messianic streak, his energy — all are traceable to natural genetic inheritance and the nurture of an extraordinary and outward-looking family. His relatives are not alone in receiving scant treatment in his memoirs: the account of his schooldays mentions his fellows and teachers even more cursorily. It is autobiography in the purest sense — an examination of his own feelings, his own thoughts, his own struggles, triumphs and failures. Those inhabiting the world around him are given no more than occasional walk-on parts, without identity or purpose of their own save to introduce him to new vistas, give him presents he liked, or idly divert or irritate him. He showed no curiosity about any of the people he knew in his childhood other than his father, and those who impressed themselves more positively on him later were frequently banished from his memory in all but formal terms. The reasons, insofar as they can be separated out, were fourfold.

There is no doubt that Victor's interest in others was limited by his own egotism. He could love individuals passionately, but only if he believed that they loved him no less passionately in return; apart from the occasional youthful crush, reciprocation was essential to him; he had to feel if anything more important to the objects of his affection than they to him. Once that criterion was satisfied, he was free to attribute to them the other necessary virtues. Many a woman (for most objects of his real devotion were to be women) was alternately touched and embarrassed at finding herself a vessel of purity, goodness, spirituality and beauty — an angel unsullied by attempts on Victor's part to discover what she was really like. In those who did not so lavish affection on him, he had little or no interest. To most of his family he was simply one of six young relatives — certainly of no more import-ance than Hermann's three sons — and this it was in his nature to resent. To his mother, he came second to his father. His father expected him to accept and obey, and Victor's determination to control his own destiny made that impossible. Yet his father put him first, and ultimately it was only his father that Victor tried to understand.

(At the age of thirty-nine, his own master and a successful man, he was able to show his dying father the affection masked for long years by strife and then neglect.

> I asked myself if somehow, without saying anything — for he was shy . . . and would have been embarrassed by a confession — I could get through to him at this very last moment and make him understand what I felt. And so, remembering the love of music that he had inherited from his own father and passed on, for my happiness, to me, I bought a huge pile of gramophone records: forgotten old things that he had heard in his boyhood . . . such as 'Casta Diva' from *Norma* and the shadow-song from *Dinorah* and 'O Paradiso' from *L'Africaine* and the drinking-song from *Lucrezia Borgia*. Hour after hour, until he wanted to sleep, I would play them to him. It was the tiniest of reparations, which he paid back, in his turn, a hundredfold; for a day or two before he died he suddenly muttered to himself, not intending, I believe, that I should hear, 'I never knew I had such a wonderful son'.
>
> He was a Pharisee; he was hide-bound; intellectually he was everything I most passionately reject. Nothing of this will I withdraw. But I understood as I heard him mutter those words, and I am telling you now as the conclusion of the matter, that underneath all the accidentals — I mean everything that his background and environment and all the rest of it had contributed — the essential was what he then revealed: a gentleness, a humility, a gratitude, a willingness to forgive.

Alex had done more than forgive. For Victor consistently and selflessly to give up so much of his time to an individual rather than a cause was extraordinary. Alex recognized this, and in responding as he did, with a declaration of admiration for his son, he ensured that the love Victor had always had for him would be intensified, and that he would pay him the supreme compliment — that of using every talent he possessed to understand him as he understood no one else, and to explain publicly his point of view and his virtues.)

First, then, Victor's egotism. Second, people were more often than not primarily guides through whom he discovered new worlds to conquer. Those relatives who gave him a taste for the wider possibilities of life crept into his memoirs on those credentials. Given his precocity, schoolfellows could not even perform this function, so they were of little importance. Where some might remember childhood mainly by reference to friends and shared pastimes, Victor recalled almost exclusively the solitary exploration of an ever-expanding universe.

Third, there was his intensity of address to the interest of the moment, which led him to change the majority of his friends at watersheds throughout his life. Most of those closest to him at one period were usurped in the next by a new group who shared his latest enthusiasm.

Fourth, hypersensitive to adverse comment, he tended always to reject those who criticized his behaviour in any way. Though Victor, as a clever child, was an object of some pride in the family, his clashes with his father, his wilfulness, his attitude to religion and, later, his failure to live up to normal Jewish standards of filial support, led to criticism of him. He rejected the critics and forgot them. The only Gollancz relative to earn a kind word in his memoirs was poor Uncle Morris, whose distinguishing feature was a horror of hearing anyone spoken ill of. He would mutter shyly, 'Muthn't thay, muthn't thay'. Victor, who said nothing of his Uncle Israel, a man admired and loved by his family, friends and pupils, cited Morris retrospectively as the only perfect Christian he had ever known.

The immediate family fared little better. His sisters are mentioned only with reference to his father's refusal to give them what Victor considered a good education — an early inspiration to passionate feminism. But there were other reasons for leaving them out: the elder, May, however she performed as a sister when he was growing up, was later a woman for whom he had no respect and little affection. She was a naive and rather pathetic hypochondriac, and Victor found her ridiculous. Their paths rarely crossed. Winifred, gifted as a child, became mentally ill as a young woman and degenerated into hopeless schizophrenia.

A more noteworthy exclusion from *My Dear Timothy* is his mother, who is afforded very few words. Victor confessed the reason in 1953, in a letter to his cousin Oliver, who had asked him if unconscious suppression had been at work. The invitation to a Freudian analysis was accepted:

> Conscious suppression, not unconscious. Mother, not father, was at the real root of the trouble at home. Her terribly inhibited sexuality led her to concentrate herself entirely on father (her care of May & Winnie did not fundamentally affect this), and this must have produced in me an Oedipus complex far greater than the normal one — or rather, it turned me against its natural object — as, no doubt, in my tiny subconscious, I felt horribly cheated . . .
>
> I could not say all this. I could talk about father, because I have resolved my relation with him, & now love him. But I have not resolved my relation to mother (I hope I shall before I die): I deeply sympathise with her, and, of course, I'm dreadfully remorseful that I didn't sympathise with her then. I'd give up most things in life to be able, retrospectively, to

do so (or rather, I mean, to have done so then.) I attribute no blame to her
— I mean, she was in no way subject to blame — but I do not love her. And
I cannot speak freely about all that side of things till I do love her.

This admission of Victor's must be taken as correct, for without it,
his revolt against everything his father stood for remains bewildering
in its range and intensity. There was something seriously wrong in
256 Elgin Avenue, far more wrong than he could ever bring himself to
admit publicly, and he, like his sisters, was marked for life by it. At the
root of the trouble, as Victor said, lay the relationship between Alex
and Nellie. The family tradition is that Nellie had introduced some
mental instability, and she was certainly a victim of many neuroses. If
the accidental conjunction of her temperament with Alex's did not
make her peculiar, it must certainly have rendered her condition much
worse. Where Alex was grimly determined to move not a jot from the
values of his upbringing, Nellie's explorations took in mesmerism,
evolution, Ibsen, the subconscious, Herbert Spencer, liberal Judaism,
and telepathy. Or, as Victor put it,

> anything, any idea or theory or movement of thought, that was a little, or
> even a great deal, off the main track; the main track not only of
> conservatism or orthodoxy in the more obvious sense, but also of that
> sane, solid, bourgeois approach that sees every phenomenon in a
> commonsensible or plain man sort of way, with nothing highfalutin or
> mysterious about it . . .
>   . . . beneath a very great terror of life, bound up with sex . . . she had an
> eager, searching, almost radical type of mind, as well as such spiritual
> strivings as could persist in an atmosphere of conventionalised religion.

Alex was 'affectionately contemptuous' of these eccentricities, as he
was of her attempts at writing plays and novels — which, in his turn,
Victor mocked. It says much for Nellie, given her subordination to
Alex, that she never let such ridicule deflect her from her interests. At
the very least, his suppressed derision and her disguised apostasy must
have been a source of tension for the children, betraying as it did a
conflict of values. Alex, the man of absolute certainties, represented
authority. Nellie, eternally questing and unsure, was neurotically
subservient. Yet her influence was the immediately telling one. All
three children began young on their own spiritual and intellectual
quests.

Nellie's most apparent neurosis communicated itself to Victor very
early: she lived in irrational terror that Alex would not return safely
from the office. Her explanation hinged on a traumatic experience,
before Victor's birth, when Alex went to Birmingham and news came

of a disaster to his train. Nellie claimed she had had a vision of him telling her that he was all right, but until his safety was confirmed she was panic-stricken and tortured by the ghastliness of the crash. Victor never knew if the story was a true one, but the grip of Nellie's subsequent terrors was not in question. She was, he said, 'the most terrified creature I have ever known, except, in some dreadful moments, myself.' She was compelled to journey each day to Duke Street to collect Alex, unable to live through the agonies of waiting.

The arrangement was that he would always be in his office by a certain hour; and so her anxiety would be confined to the last few minutes of her pilgrimage — culminating in the breath-catching second when, reaching the Duke Street office at a painful run, she would peer through a window from which a thick yellow blind had been removed for the purpose, and assure herself that — yes, thank God, he was there.

On the infant Victor, this daily reminder of his mother's fears had a devastating effect.

My earliest recollection is of standing on my bed one night in a sort of little boudoir that opened out of my parents' bedroom. It had just gone eight . . . my parents were usually back from the City at round about a quarter past nine. During the last half hour my anxiety had been growing: at eight it had become terror . . . Then, appallingly, the terror developed into panic. I swayed in a horrible dance from side to side, lifting first one foot and then the other: I sobbed dreadfully: I prayed, 'Dear God, dear God, please bring them home.' And then I heard the key in the door. I don't suppose I shall ever again experience the blessedness of sudden relief that I experienced at that moment, and at hundreds of similar moments as the years went by. It was as if the agony had never been. I was no longer alone. I was secure. I went to sleep.

(The 'hundreds of similar moments' included many after marriage to his wife, Ruth. If she arrived home late, or he did not know where she was or when to expect her, he became hysterical. A less direct effect of Nellie's obsession with Alex was, as he said himself, to make Victor fiercely jealous, and that created within him a lasting capacity for jealousy about his loved ones — obsessional in the case of Ruth — which reinforced his insatiable appetite for reassurance and adulation, and his deep aversion to criticism.)

All three children were sensitive, and all three suffered, but in a Jewish family the only son should have been the focus of his mother's attention, and Victor was thus doubly cheated. It was small wonder that he developed a wide range of solitary interests and consolations. He was saved from misery by his aesthetic sense, intellectual curiosity and capacity for unstinting commitment to the interest of the moment. Everything the world could offer was there to be enjoyed to the full. Momentary experiences that might pass others by were throughout Victor's life cherished as 'sacramental'. This early one was typical:

> I remember standing one August, as a boy of six or seven, on the little balcony of my home near Maida Vale, and feeling myself caught up I knew not whither as hussars came riding down from a neighbouring barracks, and the paving stones echoed to their horses' hooves, and the street was afire with the afternoon sun, and everything was silent.

He could be caught up similarly by the density of fog, the feel of rain or earth, the smell of a flower, or the taste of food. Victor was a sensualist in the fullest meaning of the word. Even his passion for cigars he could trace back to delight in their aroma round the park bandstands of his childhood.

Orthodox though his father was, secular ambitions led him to send Victor to non-Jewish schools, the first of which was the Paddington and Maida Vale High School, where he went with his sisters from kindergarten until about the age of ten. Fifty years later, he could still recapture the smell of doughnuts during school cricket and remember how he used to bat: 'I would always rush out, I remember, at the hard rubber ball, however wide it might pitch on the off, and make a swipe at it to leg.'

The school, apart from this, rates only a passing mention, and the ensuing two years at prep school — Oxford House, Sutherland Avenue — left no memories worth his recording, so we must assume his time there to have been sensually uneventful. The out-of-school pleasures recalled from that period were experienced alone: bowling a hoop in a nearby street 'with furious speed', collecting plane-tree burrs, studying the workings of the railways, painting and fretwork (short-lived enthusiasms) and, most important of all, exploring the world of geology and mineralogy. This abiding interest started with the discovery in his mother's bookcase of a small illustrated textbook, and he applied himself to building up a collection of fossils, which he found either in quarries on the outskirts of London, or during occasional summer holidays with relatives in Margate or Hastings. He did not deign to buy them or receive them as gifts 'for the search, the discovery and the careful extraction — cutting round and prising out so that nothing might be damaged or lost — this was the heart of the matter: the third term in a relation between me as a person and the rocks, the holy spirit, which purchase, or previous possession by alien hands, would somehow have robbed of its purity.' His laboriously collected specimens were arranged — each with its own Latin label — in cardboard nests of drawers he had bought at a draper's.

Although opportunities for building up his collection were few, he was able to extend his knowledge of the subject more easily. For all the repression he felt in many areas of conduct, he was allowed a great deal of freedom of movement for a child of his age and time, and at the age of ten he became a regular frequenter of the South Kensington Museum, where he was permitted to work in the geological library and sketch exhibits. He also joined the Geologists' Association. Limited pocket money and the restrictions on Sabbath travel made it impossible for him to go with his fellow-members on fossil-hunting expeditions, but that frustration did not dent his interest, which continued for several years after he moved on to public school.

The enthusiasm was not discouraged at home, but any thought his parents might have had that geology could be his career would have been without foundation: Victor was incapable of any scientific mastery of chemistry, physics, astronomy, botany or zoology, so his potential was severely limited. He knew it himself, but his romantic absorption in the subject continued unabated, joined as time went on by an equal passion for palaeo-botany and palaeo-zoology. 'It was the world's magic past that so compellingly called to me: nostalgic with a nostalgia far surpassing mere homesickness or longing for one's own petty past, I lived starry-eyed in the strange vast aeons that had preceded my arrival on earth.' With so many sources of bliss around him, and the promise of a world full of infinite variety, his childhood was, as he said himself, ultimately more full of joy than pain.

The same temperament, however, could heighten distaste or irritation into an occasion for frightening violence, agonies of fury, or fits of sobbing. By his own account, his lifelong horror of war originated from just such an occasion — and he referred back to it often in broadcasts and in conversation. At the age of six, he came across a commemorative volume for Queen Victoria's Diamond Jubilee, a volume called *Sixty Years a Queen*.

> I was looking through this book one day, round about my sixth birthday, when I came across a couple of pictures that faced one another: on the right-hand page was the Charge of the Light Brigade (at Balaclava) and on the left-hand page was the Charge of the Heavy Brigade. In one or other of them, I don't remember which, a man on horse-back was slashing down with a sabre at another man's head, and the other man's head was — half off. I'm back again now, from half a century later, in the Elgin Avenue drawing-room; or not in the Elgin Avenue drawing-room, because as I

looked *I* was the man with his head off, and the whole of me was an agony of pain and an obscene degradation. It was at this moment that my horror of war was consciously born; a horror that was then, as it has been ever since, a horror as of something that was in the same room with me, that was on the very table in front of me, that was outraging *me*, even though it might really be happening in China or Spain. And a horror not only of war; a horror also of violence, and of flogging, and of capital punishment, and of all the other unspeakable outrages that never fail to produce in me a feeling of personal contamination.

It is, of course, impossible to assess how much the mature Victor was grafting on to his young self a complex response to what was clearly an unpleasant experience, but there is no doubt about the trauma. It demonstrates how imaginative a child he was, not least because the picture was far less horrifying than his memory records. There is no man with his head half off, although there is a graphic depiction of one slashing with his sword at another. Victor's was a morbid imagination. Loathing the horrors of the world, he tended to brood on them. The experience as recounted has another point of significance — Victor putting himself in the place of the victim ('outraging *me*'). It was a technique he deliberately employed throughout his life to give immediacy to his campaigns against suffering. Much later, he talked of how he spent the night before an execution trying to live in the mind of the condemned murderer, and was accused of attributing to his subject the sensitivity that was peculiarly his own. Such criticisms were perhaps unfair: he was going further than others in an exercise virtually of his own inventing. Yet his public declarations on the matter, and his inability to understand the accusations, betray a gap in his reading of human nature. In the spectrum of his universal sympathy, the middle range was often grey, or out of focus, or neglected in favour of the more satisfying extremes.

Over-reaction to the common experiences of childhood was also evident in his attitude to Sabbath visits to the synagogue. Victor was thrown into an early passion of resentment by the walk to his Uncle Hermann's synagogue — a walk made compulsory by the Sabbath taboo on riding.

> . . . there was the forty-minute walk after Saturday breakfast to the Bayswater Synagogue . . .
>
> If I thought that there was the slightest hope of sensationally bad weather, I would get up as soon as it was light and anxiously examine the sky; for there was quite a good chance that if it was really pouring cats and dogs, or was obviously very soon going to pour them, my father would announce, to my — I was going to say 'to my relief', but that is a feeble

expression, for often I would hop from foot to foot in an ecstasy of delight — my father would announce 'No Synagogue today'.

It was a fifteen-minute stroll. Perhaps the mature Victor was subconsciously exaggerating the length of the trip to point up the stupidity of the prohibition on transport, but it is as likely that the compulsory nature of the undertaking greatly magnified the burden of the imposition on the young Victor. It was the first stirring of resentment against the obligations laid on him by a religion not of his choosing. The intellectual rebellion was to follow, as he became older and acquired the vocabulary to challenge every aspect of a faith and practice that seemed to him irrational.

No doubt even a household requiring occasional Church of England worship would have inspired some resentment, but orthodox Judaism meant not only unquestioning obedience to received wisdom, but a remorseless succession of observances and taboos that brought the conflict into daily prominence. Victor has given many thousands of words to it in his memoirs — the forbidden food, the attendance at synagogue on high days and holy days, the ritual prayers, the *goy* housemaid to light the fire on the Sabbath, the prohibitions on writing on that day, on switching on the electricity, on using the telephone — the list was long, and less bearable as he discovered other children free from such constraints. Hypocritical and absurd as they seemed to him, he was yet unable to shed certain ingrained revulsions in later years. He was never, for instance, able to eat pork or shellfish. Nonetheless, he never felt his identity threatened.

> . . . while in one very real sense I felt personally involved, simultaneously, in another and even realer one, I didn't feel involved at all. The thing touched me and didn't touch me at the same time. The reality of my involvement was an accidental reality, not an essential reality. It was the real me that was affected, but not (I knew by every instinct and lived with the knowledge) the realest me.

Hence the channelling of compulsion not into unhappiness, but into anger and occasional bouts of blind rage when his father responded to his intellectual challenge with bland rectitude. Like David Daiches's rabbi father, Alex 'took it for granted that the deep, unmentioned roots of his own faith would spread automatically down the generations.' He had an uncurious mind, a Jewish education and no understanding of the pressures of a Christian society on the next generation. Victor records the phrases his father employed in an effort to stanch the relentless flood of disputation: 'I suppose there *is* such a thing as public opinion'; 'People don't *do* such things'; 'So you see nothing wrong in riding on *Shabbas*. Very convenient!'

The synagogue ritual for the Day of Atonement annually brought their arguments to a head. The all-day fast and the hours in the synagogue were bad enough, but the recitation of the *Al 'Hit* (General Confession) drove Victor to distraction. To admit to robbery, usury, lying and a multitude of other crimes, and so accept the notion of collective guilt (and the implication that he was held responsible for the sins of others) produced in him an intellectual brainstorm. After all that to hear his father's refrain 'Thank God I have never done anything wrong in my life' drove him on occasion to physical violence.

Victor felt only the disadvantages of being Jewish; he relates nothing in his memoirs of his *barmitzvah* (coming of age ceremony), and took no pleasure in Hebrew; and there are but a few hundred words on what for many people was the crowning glory of family life — festivals and the celebrations of the Sabbath. He admits to enjoying only the Feast of the *Succot* (Tabernacles), during which booths laden with greenery and fruit were built outside as the focal point of the celebrations. It was sensuality again, for he relished the rich sights and fragrances, but there was another advantage: Alex constructed no tabernacle, and the family visited others'. That he failed to find pleasure in such traditionally happy family reunions as the Passover *seder* was largely a result of conditions in the Gollancz family. Alex and Nellie, uneasy partners, lacked the gift of making such a celebration moving or joyful. Similarly, Alex failed to convince his son of the merits of male pre-breakfast prayers and the laying of *tephillin* (little boxes containing Hebrew texts) on head and arm. As with his intoning in the synagogue, Alex imbued his words and actions with neither colour nor meaning. To Victor it was so much mumbo-jumbo, and he ceased to participate as soon as he could. It was not all Alex's fault that Victor lumped together the feasts, the prayers and the taboos and found them devoid of spiritual significance. The boy's innate resentment of authority left him peculiarly ill-fitted to partici-pate even in potentially pleasurable events if his father had a dominant role.

The father's tragedy was his failure to transmit to Victor the legacy of Samuel Marcus — a sincere and uncritical acceptance of the glories of Judaism. Indeed, the next generation was prone to condemn Alex's conformity as a literal rather than spiritual interpretation of the tradition; Israel's son Oliver saw his Uncle Alex as the epitome of formal religion and barren orthodoxy. Victor described his father quite accurately as 'a fanatic for the commonplace': nothing could move him an inch from his faith in formal Judaism, the Conservative Party and the *Daily Telegraph*. It may have been that his education at Jews' College made him even more vehement in his support of the Jewish community's values than his father. Of the many letters he wrote to the *Jewish Chronicle*, by far the most proclaimed the importance of observing the ban on Sabbath trading. The only traceable exception to his virtual obsession with the *minutiae* of Jewish life was a letter to *The Times* (much later, in 1926) suggesting that the dates for beginning and ending summer time should be coloured in all calendars.

Alex's reversal of his father's innovative approach to the education of women was to lead to particularly ugly scenes with his son. Alex was determined to rear May and Winifred for marriage and motherhood. He may have felt that his sister Emma's academic training had caused her to remain a spinster. By conventional Jewish standards, Alex's three sisters had failed in their natural function. Pauline and Leah, though they had married, had no children. Victor became aware early that May and Winifred were being trained for nothing, but makes no reference in his reminiscences to the deleterious effects on them as individuals. He is, quite consistently, concerned only with the effects on himself. When he went to public school his dissatisfaction turned into full-blown feminism, but even before that it was another focus for rebellion against his father. There were early political arguments also; while Victor was still at prep school, he had become an enthusiastic Liberal. After all, his father was a Tory, and that early detestation of violence made Victor warm to Lloyd George as soon as he heard of his opposition to the Boer War. He quite naturally cleaved to the party he thought to be against imperialism and in favour of peace.

By the time that Victor, at thirteen, won a scholarship to St Paul's School, the obstinate father was faced with as obstinate a son, and the grounds for argument coincided with all that the father held sacred. Victor was challenging Alex's every view on religion, politics, society and conduct. Alex's reliance on home and synagogue influences to keep Victor on the Judaic straight and narrow had already been shown to be misplaced. Now, with the onset of adolescence, Victor's struggle against paternal authority could only intensify.

CHAPTER TWO

SCHOOLDAYS

VICTOR'S LATER ATTITUDE to St Paul's (in Hammersmith, West London) was characterized by a benign indifference. The institution, the teachers and the pupils figure hardly at all in his recollections, which centre around his independent activities and his own inner life.

Yet St Paul's was a remarkable and happy school, highly regarded by most of its ex-pupils, and it had a considerable effect on Victor's intellectual, if not his emotional, development. As a day school, he said later, it offered none of the public school magic that was to entrance him when he went to teach at Repton. At Repton, though, he was in a position to initiate change and hold centre-stage; he could not have bowed as mere pupil to the fagging, corporal punishment, petty rules, empty ritual and anti-semitism he would have been all too likely to encounter at a conventional boarding school. St Paul's was outstanding academically: it gave him a first-class classical education, brought him into contact with peers brighter than the public school mean, and offered full rein to his developing political views. Perhaps the best advertisement Victor could give these aspects of the school was virtually to omit them from his account of it. It means he found himself untrammelled on his journey to self discovery, and free from the intellectual frustration that would have arisen had he been required to move at the pace of a slower majority.

His account of his first day at school falls short of the laudatory:

Dirty and sordid lavatories have always obsessed me, and I still occasion-ally have nightmares about them. There are Freudian explanations for this obsession which seem reasonable to me; but I derive it in my own case from a visit to the lavatory on my very first day at St Paul's, and the shock it gave my instincts for cleanliness and beauty. Through one of the many doors in a row, with the paint flaking off them, you entered a cubicle of rather grimy roughcast, and sat down on a depolished seat. Below the hole in the seat was a trough of stale water, which ran undivided from the beginning of the row to its end. Lying in the water, or floating sluggishly down from higher up the stream, were lumps of ugly faeces, which emitted a mouldering smell. I didn't like it; I liked it so little that I preferred, during my whole time at St. Paul's, to endure agonies of restraint right up to the last possible minute, rather than visit the horrible *cabinetto*.

Victor entered St Paul's in September 1905 as a Foundation Scholar, entitled to wear a silver fish on his watchguard, and with full remission of fees. There were 153 Foundation Scholars, the number chosen to correspond with the number of fishes caught in the Miraculous Draught, and about a quarter of the school's complement — an indication of its policy of attracting the able. Not that Victor's attendance at St Paul's was dependent on gaining a scholarship. Although he later tended to play down the family's prosperity, his father's income varied between £500 and £1000 a year — far above that of the average professional before the First World War. St Paul's annual tuition fees of £24 9s would have been easily affordable. By offering so many scholarships, and welcoming an unlimited number of Jews, St Paul's had a head start in competing for university scholarships and exhibitions. The teaching was splendid and though athletes were admired, there was none of the philistinism of the classic public school: academic excellence was the goal. (St Paul's made special arrangements for Jewish boys. While morning and evening prayers were being held in Hall, they met in the art school. The venue also for those suffering after-school detention, it was described by a staff-room wit as 'a synagogue in the morning and a penitentiary in the evening'.)

Victor's arrival coincided with that of its new High Master, the Reverend A. E. Hillard, who had taken over from the redoubtable Dr William Walker, creator of the modern St Paul's. The change probably operated to Victor's advantage: Hillard, a rather dry, steady, colourless man, kept his distance from the pupils. Moreover, he taught only divinity, from which Jews were excused, so Victor had virtually no contact with him. A classical scholar, best known as co-author with his colleague Cecil Botting of a famous Latin textbook, he continued the classical bias of the school and made only organizational changes.

The school was organized into clubs rather than houses, and Victor was in 'D' Club, whose head for his first four terms was that stalwart of the Army Class, B. L. Montgomery. Other future notables in the school included G. D. H. Cole, four years Victor's senior, and Harry Nathan (later Lord Nathan of Churt), with both of whom Victor was to be closely involved later in his career, just as his path was also to cross that of several earlier Paulines — Norman Bentwich, Leonard

Stein and Leonard Woolf. That roll-call testifies to the intellectual strength of St Paul's and the prominence within it of gifted Jews. Victor's immediate contemporaries achieved less fame, but many of them were to reach high positions in the civil service, in academic life or in other professions. Victor, clever though he was, had to work hard to excel.

He spent his first two terms in the 'Special' form, reserved for promising classical scholars. In the huge, echoing Hall, he and 33 other boys spent the day on Greek exercises, and were sent home with Latin prep. His first-term reports show great prescience on the part of his masters:

> Has worked excellently well. Perhaps is inclined to think a little too much of simple speed: but when his interest is aroused the quality of his work is of the best. Has good abilities and great powers of work. He has come on fast this term. Translates well: (shows literary appreciation). Very promising.

The classical bias at St Paul's made for a restricted curriculum. Victor's time there was given over not quite exclusively to Latin and Greek composition and the reading of classical authors in the original. French, English and mathematics were the only other subjects studied, and were not taken very seriously. It was a grinding schedule. School hours were 9.30–5.00 every weekday, and the younger boys were expected to do two hours' homework. For Victor there was the added burden of a five- or six-mile walk home on winter Fridays, as the Sabbath 'came in' at sunset. He was accompanied by two much older boys who, from a sense of their own dignity, ordered Victor to walk behind them and forbade him to speak unless spoken to. Victor's involvement in the life of the school stopped with his schoolwork. Even had he so wished, he could not have played games, as they were held on Saturday. There was no outlet for his musical interests at the school, and his father would not permit him to learn an instrument, lest his schoolwork be affected (just as Samuel Marcus's father, almost 80 years earlier, had refused to allow his son to learn the violin).

The organization of the school enabled a bright boy to skip from form to form so quickly as to make few permanent friendships. Victor reached the top form, the Upper VIIIth, at the age of sixteen, having passed through six forms in three years. He had done well at all subjects, even mathematics, which he was allowed to drop at fifteen. He collected several form prizes during these years and his reports were consistently good, if not outstanding, with only an occasional caveat. The only serious criticism during his early years at St Paul's was that his written English needed compression, for Victor, then as later, considered his own prose too good to cut.

In the printed records of the first few years there is only one reminder of the individual: Victor's long fruitless quest for the top Smee prize. Mr Smee had endowed a prize of £17 per year 'for original work of a scientific or practical nature' and this was normally divided proportionally to merit among all the entrants, so that the top prize was only £3 or £4. Victor failed in far more lucrative and prestigious prizes at school (and later at university), but the Smee rankled most. He was an also-ran in three consecutive years. The first time his submission was an enormous drawing entitled 'The Age of Reptiles: A Diagrammatic Sketch of a Typical Landscape in the Jurassic Epoch (Original)', which Victor viewed nostalgically 40 years later.

> It is an extraordinary performance: comically ill-drawn, but done with such obvious devotion, such painstaking attention to the last detail, as really to be rather moving. An accompanying key classifies the various objects in appropriate categories: aves, reptilia, pisces, crustacea, echinodermata, arachnida, insecta, mollusca, and vegetabilia . . . ninety-one items in all. There are pterodactyls in the air, ichthyosauruses in the sea, an iguanodon, among other monsters, on land . . . There are a couple of extensive beaches, with each grain of sand meticulously filled in; molluscs, and a fine assortment of my beloved ammonites, richly cover them. There is an array of cycads . . . with various spiders hanging low from their fronds . . . and there are rocks in the sea, with bryozoa sticking to them. But the centrepiece is a gigantic brontosaurus, with a sausagy neck, a half-witted gape, and an eye no bigger than a grain of my sand.

He won only ten shillings, so he tried again in 1907 ('The Age of Mammals. A Diagrammatic Sketch of a Typical Landscape in the Tertiary Period. (Original).') with exactly the same result. He doubled his winnings the next year, this time transporting to the school his precious fossil collection. Whether this third Smee failure was responsible for, or only coincidental with, his loss of interest in matters geological we do not know, but Victor, who had been reading ever more difficult textbooks, seems abruptly to have abandoned his studies.

Throughout his life, acquaintances found both endearing and annoying Victor's apparently random responses to disappointment, often blaming native perverseness when insignificant setbacks provoked his most explosive expressions of disgruntlement. There was an internal logic to his reactions, however: he could accept defeat at Latin composition, which engaged his intellect, but he had put his heart into his geological researches. The Smee examiners' failure to see their worth was a blow to the inner Victor, a blow still resented when he wrote *My Dear Timothy*.

New enthusiasms were taking over, and, Smee notwithstanding, left little room for fossils. Chief among them was music, which had thus far been an accidental pleasure, to be seized when the opportunity presented itself. Alex provided the catalytic experience when, as a treat, he took Victor to the opera in about 1907.

> He worked hard over that first *Traviata* he took me to, marking some principal arias in the libretto . . . and making me con it: and he kept whispering to me at the performance, sometimes unnecessarily (as 'ballet') and sometimes helpfully (as 'cabaletta', when Melba broke into 'Sempre libera').

Victor found the performance deeply moving and began to frequent the opera alone. Over several seasons, occasional visits became regular, and regular visits grew into attendance at every possible musical event. Each performance fuelled the growing obsession and made him more frantic for the next opportunity. There were opera *libretti* at home, and these were supplemented by his discovery in the attic at Elgin Avenue of *Telegraphs*, dating back a decade or two, which gave cast lists of forthcoming performances. Victor learned off the *dramatis personae* and their interpreters and at night in bed he prepared himself from the *libretti* to hear the operas. His Great Aunt Rosetta donated her large collection, so he had all the classics. He also made lunchtime visits to a library near the school.

At sixteen Victor was an addict and caused his father considerable worry by his fixated ravings, most particularly about Emmy Destinn — a dramatic soprano who, he decided, was the greatest singer of all time. By now, although still bound by his father on matters of religious observance, Victor was largely out of parental control, and had begun a musical round that occupied almost all his spare time. In season, he rushed to the Covent Garden gallery queue every day after school and seat B49 was recognized by the regulars as his.

His first love was Verdi, and he claimed 47 attendances at *Aida* by 1914, but he also became an early enthusiast for Wagner (the cause of many skimped lunches — a bar of chocolate and a banana — at Hammersmith Public Library). He was carried away by the music-drama, and Alex, already wounded by Victor's insistence on Destinn's ascendancy over Adelina Patti, would protest: 'Leitmotiven! Nothing but a lot of repetition.'

Victor was intoxicated by *Tristan*. 'For three or four years, until the curtain came down on all such possibilities in the summer of 1914,

Tristan was half my life: I lived in the anticipation of it, in the experiencing of it, in the remembering.' He even persuaded his sister Winifred to play through the opera from a piano score.

There was far more to his musical life than Verdi and Wagner, although so much time was given to tracking down performances of their work all over London. Of the wide range of opera he heard, he later singled out three great experiences: the 1910 Savoy production of Gluck's *Orfeo* (which he attended three times), *Pelléas et Mélisande* (Debussy having become familiar from the piano-playing of Elsie Grant in Uncle Assur's studio) and Richard Strauss's *Elektra* (advance criticisms of which damned its 'revolutionary cacophony', and so ensured the young radical's sympathetic attention).

The list goes on: Sunday afternoon concerts at the Albert Hall, seasons of the proms at the old Queen's Hall, bands at the White City, and a record shop there where he could have records played for him. Drury Lane, the Old Vic and even the Holloway Theatre figured in his itinerary. He was transported by Beethoven, Haydn and Mozart; he worshipped Berlioz; he was unmoved by Bach. Victor's love of music in his boyhood verged on the mystical, and while his appreciation grew more sophisticated in later years, he was never after 1914 to experience the enchantment cast over him by the singers he heard then. And though he was to admit that Henry Wood was not a great conductor, he venerated him for his education of a whole generation — Victor's generation. Wood

> understood, as by no means every conductor understands, that a concert should be an act of communion, with soloists, orchestra, every member of the audience and the conductor himself participating in a sacrament of unity. Or if he did not consciously understand this; if he would not have put it that way himself: then his simple and unreflecting humanity, and his love of music and respect for his audience, combined to produce an atmosphere akin to that of an early Christian love-feast. We really did love everything and everybody on those prom nights: the music, the performers, our neighbour and Henry Wood.

The communion was marred, in the view of the mature Victor, by his own 'spiritual greed'. So all-absorbing was the search for joy that he revelled in the anticipation of it even more than in the actuality, to the extent that the immediate satisfactions of a performance, even as it was happening, came second to the enticements of the next. There was another level of perversity — the fear 'that by hearing something precious too often I should grow tired of it, and that this would mean not merely to spoil my own pleasure, for the thrill of dawning recognition would be done for if the thing had become too familiar, but somehow to dishonour the music itself.'

This fear used to grip him on his trips to the White City, where he would spend his waiting moments counting how many performances of any scheduled piece he had already heard. Whatever the total, he could never leave, much less stop his ears.

> If *Aida* happened to be included I wanted to keep away but couldn't; and then when I got home I would be seized by a dread that everything had been ruined — and for how little: Covent Garden was one thing, a military band another! — and would go through a kind of ritual counting in an effort to persuade myself that I hadn't really heard the work so often after all. The formula never varied, and was repeated two or three times on each occasion: 'Aida. Heard it nine times at Covent Garden: heard it three times on an MB.' MB meant military band. And I would do the same for other operas.

The neurotic fear dissipated with the gradual revelation that great music could never become stale; there would always be new interpretations to savour. The spiritual greed, the lust for joy and the sweet torment of anticipation stayed with him until maturity. His own later self-assessment concluded that this was a manifestation of his childhood's 'particularly fierce egoism' and it is hard to dissent, or to dismiss the remorse implied by such admissions.

Music was the healthiest of the areas of contention around the family table, but Alex's frequent aside to his wife when Victor was in full flow — 'The boy's *meshuggah* [cracked]' — became more agonized as Victor ran up his social banner. His daily route from Westbourne Park Underground Station took him by a row of near-slums, outstripped in their squalor by those he passed on winter Friday evenings, and he was beginning to find in four writers in particular the ammunition he needed for the running battle with his father.

Ibsen was first: 'The exposure of conventional humbug! The satire against compact majorities! The hatred of compulsion! The warning against betrayal of a self's uniqueness!' Shaw was a 'divine gadfly that . . . goaded us into life more abundant' through a moral passion 'to deliver us from indifference and complacency by putting, with a gaiety that masked his priesthood, "the case against".' Maeterlinck's symbolist dramas touched that part of Victor's imagination that brooded on the dark mysteries of love and death, and Walt Whitman's 'pansacramentalism, his contempt for respectability, and his fellow feeling with harlots and criminals' gave expression to a new philosophy which Victor was determined must be preached to mankind in general and Alex in particular, 'for how could it conceivably happen that the truth should be shown to a man and he shouldn't recognize it in a second?' His father, annoyed and bored by the incessant tirades, amplified his lament: 'The Ibsen and the Shaw and the Whitman and the Maeterlinck — the boy's *meshuggah.*'

There was political argument too. Carried away by the excitement of the 1906 election, he was 'body and soul' with the Liberals, a precocious reader of the *Daily News* and a venomous critic of Alex's conservative *Daily Telegraph*. Lloyd George was his hero, especially after his 1908 People's Budget. Victor stood four-square for anti-imperialism, social reform and individual freedom — and anything else calculated to make his father squirm. Public opinion, respectability, simple-minded patriotism and conformism were anathema to Victor's messianic zeal:

> . . . and with a passion so fierce that I was compelled — really compelled, driven by a force that I couldn't withstand — to rise up in immediate defence of anything or anyone in any way unorthodox, by simple reason of their unorthodoxy and irrespective of what my own views might happen to be about the person or topic in question. There was something missionary in this passion; I had the burning conviction that if for a moment I were silent, if for a moment I compromised or hummed and ha'd or were anything but to the last degree militant, I should be guilty of most shamelessly betraying what, beyond any particular truth or falsity in the matter under discussion, was an overriding truth, or rather *the* overriding truth, at the very heart of reality: namely that everybody was not only entitled but categorically obliged to think, say and do (subject, in the last case only, to his not hurting others) what he himself might consider it proper to think, say or do.

In fairness to Victor, Alex's obdurate refusal to countenance any new ideas whatsoever made him just as much the aggressor. No one could change his views, not even when otherwise all-important family loyalty was at stake. Israel, for instance, semi-orthodox himself, had married a non-orthodox wife, and his memorial service was held in a Reform Synagogue. When he died Alex mourned him, but in his own way. He inserted a death notice in the *Jewish Chronicle* announcing that prayers would be at his — Alex's — house, and in the issue covering the memorial service at the West London Reform Synagogue, it was reported, at the behest of Alex, that he had not attended it. Similarly, when the *Jewish Chronicle* quarrelled with Hermann over his plea for Arab-Jewish co-operation, Alex obliquely but clearly dissociated himself from his brother, in a letter to the editor proclaiming his life-long Zionism.

He might have believed in collective guilt, but not in guilt by association.

Yet though Alex never shifted his own ground, he was tolerant, never directly (as far as we know) forbidding Victor to proselytize, and contriving, in time, to forgive May, who hurt him deeply by becoming a Christian. This counted for little, for 'shun the limelight' as he might, his complete certainty that his views were 'correct' frequently drove Victor into violent rages.

> Sometimes, I am afraid, I completely lost my head. Leading down from the hall of our house to the basement was a flight of stairs, enclosed, in some curious fashion I can no longer visualise, by a sheet of coloured glass. One day in the middle of a furious argument I smashed my fist through this smokily yellowish screen, and the resulting wound spread down to my finger tips and up beyond the shoulder. The remains of it are still visible: a tiny bleached scar just above my right wrist.

He found other ways to take the offensive, including vegetarianism, which he adopted for a few years up to 1911, his last year of school. He abandoned it for reasons he could not later recall, beyond a certainty that it was not out of moral weakness, 'nor from a dislike of making a nuisance of myself and demanding special arrangements and generally upsetting things, for consideration of that kind was no part, I fear, of my attitude to my parents.'

Little consideration was evident in his rejection when he was about eighteen of some of the orthodox taboos. Victor barely mentions his father's reaction, though it must have brought him more grief than anything else. But there was consolation for Alex in Victor's continued academic success, for in his last few years at St Paul's, when boys were expected to do three hours' homework, Victor's routine was to come home from Covent Garden, study for an hour, knock six times on his forehead and thus prepare himself to awaken at 6.00 to finish his work. Nor was this all. He felt that homework didn't really count because it was compulsory, and therefore without meaning, so he was driven to do extra 'real' work. Looking back, he saw this compulsion as a mixture of guilt (an important element in his character), hatred of external authority, and passion for self-direction.

Even allowing for exaggeration in Victor's retrospective estimate of a regular 1.00 a.m. arrival home, it is odd in the context of the times that his parents allowed him to adopt a style of life that was to induce chronic insomnia. Probably they had little choice: he was outside their control, and they were past trying. He writes of lack of money when he was at school, but between pocket money and lunch money, cheap gallery seats and free band concerts, he had enough to render the musical world accessible. Besides he was prepared to go without lunch, queue for hours, and then walk home. In any case, with Nellie so often immersed in a mystical world of her own, and Alex so rarely at home, supervision of the family was minimal. In any case, why provoke the anger of one all too prone to rage at any curtailment of his liberty?

Victor had joined the top class in September 1909 and his teachers saw fit to award him the Winterbotham Scholarship (£35 10s annually 'to the most deserving student in Classics'). That same year he passed School Certificate and began work for a university scholarship. His reinforced sense of individuality was clearly spilling over into the classroom. In July 1910 his Latin master wrote rather sniffily: 'Unequal worker and singularly bad critic of himself: wants rather more "Latin sense". Keen.' His English was noted to be 'Fluent and connected: not very interesting', and his English style not 'as good as his matter'. However, the standards were exacting; though the youngest in the class, Victor came third overall and was runner-up for two Latin prizes. By Christmas he was top of the class, and drew approving comments. 'He is able, and vigorous, and full of interest', and he was urged to concentrate on the classics — an injunction he obviously took too much to heart, as the next report accused him of neglecting his French, and 'sacrificing soundness to effect' in English. The Greek master found him too talkative and the Latin master, though considering him in general a good scholar, thought he had little facility in Latin verse.

It says much for the rigorous standards of St Paul's that Victor should earn critical reports in a year when he again won the Winterbotham Scholarship, and added to it a prize for Latin essay, a prize for proficiency in comparative grammar and philology, and a prize for Latin elegiac verse, in addition to sharing the VIIIth form composition prize and narrowly missing the prize for Greek iambics — worth over £50 in all. But St Paul's success was based on perpetual challenge.

By this stage boys in the VIIIth were expected to translate *The Times* leader into Greek or Ciceronian Latin twice a week. One of the masters, A. D. Knox, impressed Victor with his ability to pick up a leader and read it off straight away in Platonic Greek. Cecil Botting, his successor, was not quite in that league, but he was the only master Victor referred to in his memoirs, where he describes their occasional visits to the opera together, and his helping Botting with the *leitmotiven*. Botting was a tireless private coach and Victor thought him constantly divided between his sense of duty and his capacity for good living. 'He was always torn during the intervals between a desire to absorb my expositions and a sense of duty that kept nagging at him to mug up next day's Homer. He usually chose the latter.' Much of Botting's attraction for Victor was his apparent willingness to listen to musical instruction, but he also scored with Victor by giving all his pupils before departure a wonderful dinner with 'all the appropriate wines'. (At his own farewell dinner, Victor was sick after a very strong cigar, for although he had been introduced to them by a friend of his father, cigars had not yet become one of his main pleasures.)

In the autumn of 1910, Victor was elected to the School Union Society, a school debating club unusual in the independence accorded its officers, who were allowed to run it without interference, and choose their own subjects for debate. G. D. H. Cole had been President in 1908, by which time he was a confirmed socialist, and the minutes show conservative boys in a majority at debates, with a strong radical element running them close in numbers. Victor became a frequent speaker, his first recorded speech including a defence of Dr Crippen. The second was priggish, condemning musical comedy as 'extremely inartistic', degraded and guilty of shutting out better and more serious plays. His political liberalism came into prominence during the first term of 1911. He declared himself for the introduction of the referendum, as it would 'educate the lower classes, and rouse the people from their lethargy', and spoke the following week in favour of British evacuation of Egypt. Two weeks later, he again made an impassioned speech on the losing side against 'more drastic restrictions on alien immigration'.

> Mr Gollancz, in opposing, conjured up a pathetic picture of exiled Russians, leaving their ruined homes and their country streaming with blood, and sailing away to England, their breasts glad with anticipation and their dreams full of the White Cliffs they should soon behold. But lo! the door was slammed in their faces. The day the Alien Bill was passed was a bad day for England, which up till then had been a land of freedom. There was no narrow patriotism in humanity.

Speakers for the motion exhibited xenophobia and flippancy, with an anti-semitic flavour which led to a walk-out by Victor and his class-mate Teddy Solomon. They were prevailed upon to return and Victor duly made his rather touching concluding speech, which seriously taxed the reporting powers of the secretary. He 'pointed out the worldwide influence of Tschaikowsky, Shoppenhauer [crossed out] Goethe and Schiller (phonetic sp!) and other foreigners. Beauty was conceived differently by different critics. The generally accepted stamp of a foreigner "fat podginess and trumpet noses" might be lovely and attractive in the eyes of some.'

Not all Victor's boyhood views were identical with those he held as an adult, but there is a remarkable consistency down all the years. In April 1911 he announced his hopes for universal peace. By now secretary of the Society, he was abused as an aesthete in a debate in October when he declared his support for a current strike, speaking 'of the awful condition of the poor who were without proper food, clothes, or dwellings. The only way you could open the eyes of the public to this state of things was to make them suffer. Peaceful picketing was justifiable because those who refused to strike were traitors.' On this occasion he carried the majority with him.

A week later he was under attack on charges of general negligence, particularly with regard to the brevity of his minutes. Surviving a vote of censure by a majority of 17 to 1, Victor took the bit between his teeth, and his succeeding minutes were so slapdash as frequently to frustrate his biographer. He also introduced the time-saving practice of abbreviating stock phrases, so that a typical entry began 'At a.d.m.o. Thursday November 16th at 1.45pm the Pres. in the chair, the m. of t.p.d.m.w.r.a.c.' And after a long argument, he secured the right to suppress any part of a speech he thought worthless. Victor's behaviour was an amusing early indication of his impatience with routine and his autocratic streak. He remained impervious to criticism which extended even to the *Pauline*, the school magazine, where appeared the following thrust: 'The Secretary, although his minutes are sometimes "scrappy" is a mine of information on music.'

The scrappy minutes yield the information that Victor was in favour of reciprocity between Canada and the USA, thought the works of Charles Dickens overrated, entirely lost the minute-sheets of a meeting, approved of the public school system, thought that 'the great modern problem was relation of old and young' and considered social reform an inevitable trend and impossible to stop by artificial means. His term of office ended good-humouredly, when he 're-gretted his numerous shortcomings as Secretary and trusted that his successor would not have as many votes of censure passed on him as he had had himself.'

Given what we know of Victor's temperament and interests, it is hardly surprising that he was not popular at school. A near-contemporary recalled him as a compelling speaker who would attend the junior debating society even when in the senior, but though he was nice to younger boys, they found him rather superior and dogmatic.

And while he did well, he was not academically supreme — a fact made plain when he failed in 1911 to win a scholarship to Balliol — so he did not merit the respect paid to those whose results were outstanding. Neither his multifarious interests nor his inclinations led to any intimacy with other boys. Very occasionally, in his final year, his classmate T. L. Martin accompanied him to the opera, and he vividly recalled Victor arguing violently with other people in the queue about the relative merits of Puccini and Verdi.

The other major thread of Victor's development in these years is his sexual awakening, which of course brought him joys and agonies of exceptional intensity. His first sexual experience he puts at the age of nine (the same as Rousseau, he noted), and it was unwittingly instigated by the headmistress of the Maida Vale High School. He later described her as small and in late middle age, dressed in black, and less than sexually attractive.

> It was in her study that the experience happened. But no, this is not quite right. It had begun to happen a few minutes earlier — at the moment at which, for some reason I cannot remember, I had been told I was to go and see her. I have mentioned Rousseau. I must make it clear, therefore, that no physical contact of any kind took place between me and the headmistress: that I desired nothing of her, as she desired nothing of me: that no word was spoken by her, and no gesture made by her, which even with my present experience I could imagine to have been remotely sexual, either in origin or in significance: and that it was of the situation and the situation alone — the being sent for by her, with me, the small boy, as the summoned, and she, the grown woman, the headmistress, as the summoner — that my experience was born.

Victor found the experience 'sweet and poignant' and sought to recapture the 'feeling', as he described it, by praying for its return and inventing fantasies to help it along. Every time it recurred, it seemed more intense and although he was ignorant of sex and therefore the feeling's origin, natural instincts soon brought masturbation to his aid.

> The ecstasy it gave me was overwhelming. But I never practised it for its own sake: I should have felt that dishonourable. I am getting into deep waters, but I must put it like this: my surrender at the moment of my summons to the study — for surrender is of course the proper word for it — was how sex awakened in me, sex the bodily aspect of our destiny to merge: I was caught up out of myself, literally in ecstasy: I was loyal thereafter to that ecstasy of surrender: and masturbation helped me to achieve it. Masturbation without the surrender, if such a thing had been conceivable (and I doubt whether the practice is ever possible without

fantasy), would have seemed to me disloyal and disgusting. And if anybody accuses me of highfalutinly dramatising a common or garden tendency to masochistic autoerotism, I shall reply that you explain nothing by labelling it; that my memory is excellent; and that I have been honestly living myself back, these last two hours, into an experience of early childhood.

Innocent ecstasy turned into shame and guilt when he reached puberty, and more particularly with the advent of his first nocturnal emission, which terrified him lest it be a symptom of desperate illness brought on by masturbation. His parents were surprisingly enlightened: news of the evidence on the sheet reached his father, who overcame great embarrassment to reassure him: 'There's nothing to worry about in what's happened to you: it's nature.' The terror retreated, but the guilt remained.

It was precisely a sense of having isolated myself, cut myself off from what I have previously described as joy in communion or communion in joy, that masturbation produced in me after every new act of self-indulgence. . . . Each time, when the thing was over, I felt that some link between me and everything had been deliberately broken by my own act: not merely a precious link but an essential one: and that now, by the breaking of it, the essence of me and of everything was somehow irretrievably spoiled.

Every masturbatory episode produced consequent misery, followed by hope, followed by ritual counting ('I won't do it again after counting twelve'), followed by joy, followed by another lapse and so on. He lived with repeated failure, he says, by suppressing his guilt, yet his reliance on his own will-power to cure the habit was hopeless, since it did not recognize the need for communion with the divine. None of this seriously affected his enjoyment of life until, when he was about sixteen, a schoolmate (with 'big, slightly bulbous green eyes' and a 'malevolent whisper') told him he knew of his filthy habit, which put him beyond the pale for decent people, and warned that he was now beyond salvation, and would 'rot and rot inexorably till he died'. Victor's vague knowledge of sexually transmitted diseases served only to augment this new terror: his reading of Ibsen's *Ghosts* and his mother's warnings about lavatory seats merely confirmed the malevolent prognosis. He lived several months, he estimates, believing himself unclean, diseased, and robbed of any chance of marriage or fatherhood — 'the dream of perfection I had cherished for almost as long as I could remember'. He felt like an outlaw: 'By my own deliberate act, by the way I had contaminated my body (I am describing to you exactly what I felt), I had broken the links that united me with universal living: I was separate, alone, without lot or part in the everything. I had deprived myself, treacherously, of it; I had deprived it, quite as treacherously, of me.'

Music could not help, because he had betrayed it. He avoided it.

Ultimately he nerved himself to visit the family doctor, Richard Armstrong, a man of whom his mother was rather enamoured, and whom Victor despised. Armstrong rose magnificently to the occasion. He allayed all his fears, explained about sex and gave him friendly advice, culminating in an injunction not to work too hard and to replenish his vitality when grown up with a couple of whiskies and soda every day. 'He showed me out. I turned my face to the sun and sniffed the stone pavement. I smiled. Hell was a myth, Paradise the only reality.'

Suspicions of later over-dramatization on Victor's part are dispelled by a reading of a poem composed a few years after the consultation, heralding his later paean to Armstrong — 'dearer to me, on account of one common-sensible action, than that of any other of my many dead friends.' The sonnet, 'To R.S.A.', reads:

> Old friend, I sneered once at your Tory mind —
> I, the young Radical. 'He understands
> To set a bone well with his doctor's hands,
> But not the soul of his own human kind.'
> There came a day for me when I must find
> A friend to tell my fear to — how the strands
> Of innocence seemed snuff'd, & the wide lands
> Of joy forbidden. God, were all men blind?
>
> This one would listen with a mocking eye,
> Laughing at such poor boy's simplicity;
> This other, as I told him brokenly,
> Would frown & coldly censure . . . Should I try . . ?
> Ah well, you understood. I'll do my best
> To thank you with my love. Forgive the rest.

Masturbation apart, sex was not a problem to Victor during his schooldays. He had been romantically drawn at the age of eleven to a girl a few years older, 'but though I wanted very much to be in love with her I was really only in love with her name, which was Una.' Otherwise he remembers only once being stirred erotically before he went to Oxford, and that by an unknown woman in a short skirt. He fell in love with a boy at school but it was a love untarnished by sexual desire, and brought him bodily peace and a sense of cosmic harmony.

I wonder whether homosexual love may not sometimes be purer (purer in heart) than average heterosexual love; and whether to give everything and demand nothing, after the fashion of chivalry, may not more commonly be the mark of it.

. . . No love in my life has been purer, in the sense in which I have already used the word, more selfless and other-regarding, than my love for Gilbert Joyce.

Victor's only memento of 'Joyce' (a pseudonym) was a photograph inscribed 'To V.G., on winning the only open scholarship to New College.' Victor, in his nineteenth year, was older than many of his competitors. Nonetheless, this award was a major distinction that greatly impressed his schoolfellows. During his last two terms in St Paul's, Victor was an important man. He was a prefect, and, as the top classical scholar in his form, should automatically have been Captain of the School, but that position involved the reading of prayers, so as a Jew he was precluded. He continued to work to the St Paul's standard, encouraged to prepare himself for competitive scholarships once at university. He 'set a valuable example of steady and interested work in his subjects [Latin and Greek]', and the English master confessed that he 'writes more sensibly than he did'. He was secretary of the Debating Society, indulged himself to the full in music, and was happy in his love for Gilbert Joyce. Normally casual in his attire, he was more impressive now that success in the scholarship entitled him to wear academic dress. Life was sweet, the only discordant note sounded by another prefect — a 'filthy swine' — who implied that Victor's relationship with Joyce was a sexual one. Even problems at home loomed less large, now he was an independent success and free of religious shackles.

He went up to Oxford in the autumn of 1912, at nineteen-and-a-half, on cordial terms with his parents and with a future bright in academic promise.

CHAPTER THREE

UNIVERSITY

—————————————————

New College, Oxford
23 Dec 1911

DEAR SIR,

You did a very good Essay & got 93 marks for it. General Paper 65 Latin & Greek unseen 50, 61 Latin Prose 70 Greek Prose 65 Greek V 55 Latin Verse 70 —

I think you ought to get one of the University Prizes, but unless you improve are not up to the Hertford or Ireland —

With all good wishes

Believe me
Yours sincerely
W A Spooner.

The Warden of New College was known for his honesty. On this occasion he was also percipient; even nine months of nose to grindstone failed to turn Victor into a scintillating classical scholar. As a contemporary observed, Victor had an outstanding intellect, but as a pure scholar was good, not great. His interests were too wide and his mind too undisciplined, particularly once the tight régime of the school timetable was lifted. By his own account, Oxford for him meant an extension of his knowledge of the cosmos, the discovery of friendship and the working out of how he might 'remake the world'.

It proved fortunate for Victor that he had failed Balliol. Just as St Paul's had been the school for his intellect and temperament, New College was the ideal college. Sir Ernest Barker has written of it:

> If there are three standards by which the merit of an Oxford college may be judged — the quality of its scholarship, the beauty of its buildings, and the prowess of its athletes — all would agree that whoever was first on any of these standards New College was certainly second on all . . . if and when it was not first.

Its foremost asset was the Reverend Dr Spooner: kind, shrewd and loved by his colleagues and his undergraduates. Victor's retention of his letter (when others from dear dead friends were unhesitatingly consigned to the wastepaper basket during clear-outs) speaks of the warm regard in which he was held. In *My Dear Timothy* he paid him handsome tribute, for Spooner in his wisdom gave his undergraduates the loosest possible rein. Victor's persistent avoidance of 'compulsory' lectures might have led to trouble, but Warden Spooner handled him brilliantly.

'Mr Gollancz,' he said to me once, 'Mr Henderson tells me you go to no lectures, and are generally slack in your work. When he's given you a composition to do you turn up with nothing, and explain that you've been very busy. Busy at what? At your clubs and societies, he tells me. Well, I shan't interfere. If you pull off a first, I shall congratulate you. If not, I shall take away your scholarship and send you down.'

That there were remarkable dons goes without saying. More remarkable were their 'bonds of common affection', observed by Barker — affection for the Warden and the college, and for the sense of community thus engendered. Two were pre-eminent for Victor: Gilbert Murray and Hastings Rashdall. New College was acknowledged as the leader in Greek studies, and Murray was then its presiding genius. His successor as Regius Professor, E. R. Dodds, wrote of him:

His lectures were memorable, not merely for the delicate art with which they were composed or the beauty of the voice in which they were delivered, but because they were a communication of experience; it was this which gave them their quite extraordinary quality of immediacy. To hear Murray read aloud and interpret a passage of Greek poetry brought successive generations of his students the intoxicating illusion of direct contact with the past, and to many of them a permanent enlargement of their sensibility.

Murray was not locked in the past; he cared about the contemporary world also. Although Victor regretted his being a rationalist, he applauded his humanitarianism, referring to him (in a letter to his parents) as 'Gilbert the great'. Later they were associated in many public causes, and the relationship was warm, though never close. Hastings Rashdall was also a strikingly good man, who was to have a profound effect on Victor's religious experience at Oxford.

Apart from these two, and Spooner, Victor had little to do with the dons, preferring to spend his time with New College undergraduates. The student body was mainly conservative, but there was a liberal and socialist coterie which provided Victor with his closest friends. He did not go further afield in search of kindred spirits; New College had all he needed.

Bernard Strauss, a couple of years Victor's senior, was his first and best friend there. They had known each other for many years, as their families were close, and Bernard was deputed to look after Victor when he got to Oxford. (His brother, Frank Strawson, was to be a director of Victor Gollancz Ltd; another, Otto Strawson, became a reader for the firm; a third, Eric Strauss, the psychiatrist, had an uneasy relationship with Victor for many years; and a sister, Doris Orna, did occasional translations for the firm.) Bernard was a warm-hearted but serious-minded man from a highly political family, all of whom were fanatical single-taxers.*

Victor's circle also included Ralph Rooper (a pacifist and an open scholar in History), Douglas Jerrold (a sardonic, individualistic, irreverent radical), Ewan Agnew (rich, philanthropic and gentle), J. B. S. Haldane (the brilliant socialist and scientist), Spencer Hurst and Paul Hobhouse. Harold Laski did not become a friend, but his was an influential presence in the college and the Union. They all thrived on endless wrangling over ideas, politics and solutions for the world's problems. Before Oxford, and for some years afterwards, Victor adhered to a serious reading programme to equip himself 'as efficiently as possible, for liberal or progressive world-citizenship.'

> I was eager to understand how the world-machine functioned — how the wheels of the world went round. Wages, prices, production, money, shops, rate of interest, banking, credit, trade, 'business', foreign exchange, gold points, tariffs, employment, supply and demand, entrepreneurs, taxation, middle men, five pound notes — what, in hard fact, did they *mean*, these and a hundred more like them? How did they work out in practice . . . And how, more important than anything, did they all fit together?

As a discipline, economics was not to Victor's taste, but he read widely within it and then explored the solutions — syndicalism, Fabianism, guild socialism and many others. All these were meat for discussion with his friends. 'For the rest, I read anything, in prose or in verse, that rang with the praise of freedom: or sang for joy: or was instinct with a feeling for human dignity and universal brotherhood.'

He was in love with Shelley, William Blake and Plato, all of whom

---

*Henry George (1839–97), an American land reformer and economist, advocated a 'single tax' on idle landowners' rent income, and the abolition of all other taxes. Humanitarian and religious threads in his argument (notably in *Progress and Poverty*, 1879) made it attractive to many Liberals.

appealed to his metaphysical instincts. To his schoolboy pantheon of
Ibsen, Shaw, Whitman and Maeterlinck were added many more —
dramatists, chiefly, for although he read some novelists, his main
interest was in plays, the 'principal vehicle for exposing social shams
and furthering the work of human emancipation'. The post-Ibsenists
were especially important, for their work was complementary to his
other studies, but all theatre with a polemic flavour was attractive to
him, from Ben Jonson to J. M. Synge.

Victor approached such reading in characteristically earnest
fashion, and records his annoyance at Laski's blasé attitude:

> He came round one evening and told me he had been working very hard: 'I
> want to slack a bit,' he said. 'I should like to read one of your plays.' I
> enquired whether he'd like something lightish or heavyish. 'I don't care in
> the least,' he replied. When I'd looked something out that I considered
> suitable, he glanced at it hurriedly and asked for three more. 'I'll bring
> them all back in the morning,' he said.

Despite so many distractions, Victor's neglect of academic work
was yet not total. During the spring and early summer of 1913 (when
his play-reading embraced Greek drama) he was wrestling with his
submission for the Chancellor's Latin Essay Prize — 'A Dialogue on
Socialism'. In the Easter vacation he wrote about his exertions to a
recently acquired non-Oxford friend, Harold Rubinstein, a young
lawyer and playwright he had met at the opera.

> 'Liberalism & Socialism' is getting on — though I'm finding it much stiffer
> than I thought and I am not at all sure that the ideal which I uphold against
> socialism — and also against a lot of official Liberalism — would not seem
> to you and many socialists socialistic. It very often *seems* so to me but I'm
> sure it isn't, and at any rate its something *very* different from the socialism
> of the Fabian Essays and the introduction to 'Major Barbara'. But whether
> its socialistic or not its social.
>
> However these be 'but the maunderings of a mind that can't keep off a
> piece of work in hand.'

It was a substantial piece of work and incorporated Victor's political
thinking as it had so far developed. In *My Dear Timothy* he spends
almost 5,000 words summarizing its argument, which was presented
as a discussion between a young socialist, Sosiades, a liberal,
Cleanthes, and an old conservative, Epiondes. Although Cleanthes
comes out the winner, arguing powerfully in his closing speech for
gradual social reform rather than demolition of the existing structure,
he admits that his programme will take a long time. When it bears

fruit, however, it will be seen 'that it was prudence and not timidity that restrained us'.

Victor later saw the essay as a portrait of his mind in 1913.

> It is the picture of a liberal horrified by poverty: seeing it as a barrier to the development of personality that liberalism longs for: turning to socialism as the only cure: reacting against socialism as itself inconsistent with the liberal criterion of universal freedom: but fighting an antisocialist battle which, in the very moment of attack, is already regarded as lost. For I cannot read that closing speech of Cleanthes, with its clear low note of sadness and even despair, without hearing it as a swan song.

That the battle is lost is by no means implicit in Cleanthes' peroration, and Victor's contention that it is was so much *post hoc* rationalization. He always disliked any allegation of inconsistency in his views, quite correctly claiming a natural progression, but in his eagerness to prove it, he attributed too much farsightedness to the young Victor. In 1913 he was still full of hope for the Liberal party: it was to be many years before he could accept socialism, before he could conclude that the good of the majority outweighed considerations of personal liberty.

He won the Essay Prize, and the university had the piece privately printed. He says modestly in *My Dear Timothy* that he was probably the only contender, but it was a remarkable document for all that. It demonstrates a precocious grasp of contemporary politico-philosophical issues, combined with the scholarship necessary to couch sophisticated arguments in Latin prose.

Yet again, Victor had exercised his penchant for work entirely of his own choosing. The Greek plays were read for fun. The prize was for fun, status and money (of which he was always rather short at Oxford, presumably because any contribution from Alex was pitched at undergraduate adequacy). Victor's tastes were not luxurious, but he ran up substantial book bills, he liked good food, wine and tobacco, and there was the expense of musical performances when he was in London. Spooner himself had helped out with a loan of £50, but Victor was a needy case only by comfortable standards. His Easter holidays had been spent walking through Wales and Devon.

In this letter to Rubinstein, there is a passage illustrative of youthful enthusiasm bordering on presumption.

> [The] spot I was at was lovely — about 3 miles from Bettws-y-Coed. I suppose you know the latter. I think it the ideal place for a Festival Theatre. To spend the summer there walking in the morning, playing tennis and boating in the afternoon and then all going together in the evening to the

theatre, to hear the 'Ring' or 'Agamemnon', relieved by 'You Never Can Tell' and 'Consequences' [a play by Rubinstein] — I can imagine nothing more ideal. It is really quite time that we did have a Festival Theatre in the country. Bernard Shaw was *once* keen on the idea (he talks about the 'Ring' on Margate Pier — of all places! — in the 'Perfect Wagnerite') and I am going to write to him and one or two others and try and stir them up. I believe the money could be raised quite easily.

It was one among many ideas which lapsed, like his plan to have his own play staged — for his creative endeavour in 1913 had run to the composition of a sub-Ibsen drama called *Daughters*.

Daughters must be seen as a form of catharsis. The main characters are the Alex Gollancz family, thinly disguised as Mr and Mrs Chadworth and their children Janet, Grace and John (or Jack, twenty years old, 'tall, straight and magnificently vital, with a high forehead and thoughtful eyes'). Janet is introspective and reads all the time, Grace is going mad from frustration, and Jack intends to be Prime Minister. He champions their right to a liberated and productive life against the hopelessly intransigent attitude of his father. A sample:

> MR. C. (*Very angrily*). You're very clever, aren't you, with your high falutin talk and your mad modern ideas. But I've lived in the world a little longer than you, and I'm not going to discuss with you whether I've brought up my daughters the right way or not. (*Tenderly*). Do you think I'd ever let Grace drudge at hard work when there's no necessity for it? Thank God I know what's the correct thing.

Although he gets wild with anger at such conservatism, Jack is genuinely fond of his father and worried by his overwork and tiredness. His mother seems merely to irritate him. (Rather pathetically, the only significant difference between Jack and Victor is that Jack has a 'deep, rich voice, full of the joy of life' when he sings the theme of Siegfried's horn.)

In Act II, when he is forty, Jack is already Home Secretary and is introducing a Women's Suffrage Bill, which against all expectations fails. (Oddly, Victor in *My Dear Timothy* says it was a bill for the abolition of capital punishment, a lapse made all the more bizarre by his clear memory of the play's feminist message.) Jack's wife, Sylvia, a loyal political supporter, appals him by insisting that their eighteen-year-old daughter Una should not have a career. Desperate to convince her, he announces that in addition to the spinster Janet he has a sister he has not seen in twenty years.

> She got unhappy — and she only half knew what it was that was the matter with her. She took to going with Father to the 'bus in the morning, and

watching the men with their newspapers starting for business . . . Then her mind began to get morbid and unhealthy . . . *She fed on herself* . . . And one night she went away with the foulest-minded man you could imagine . . . We could never get news of either of them again . . . That's the whole pitiful story.

Coup de théatre: the butler enters to announce the arrival of a strange woman, who turns out to be a sunken-cheeked Grace, abandoned by her husband after two years to make a living on the streets. Jack (to whom it apparently does not occur that he might offer Grace a home) takes her back to her parents and Janet, who is still reading. Chastened, Sylvia agrees to allow Una to work for a living.

The action of Act III takes place three years later. Grace is getting madder and Mr Chadworth is weak, bent, tired, lame, haggard, lined, weary, broken and sometimes dazed and bewildered. Mrs Chadworth 'In her every action . . . shows that all her life is centred in her husband.' Una comes in.

The girl of the last Act has developed into a graceful and lovely woman. She is glowing with health, and is filled with a great vitality which is never boisterous. She has the deep and quiet joy of life which is worlds apart from superficial gaiety; and sweet seriousness looks out from her eyes.

She has come to announce her engagement to her father's private secretary: after the marriage they are off to spend their honeymoon in Lord Holdhurst's house in Italy. As Jack in Act I drove Grace to desperation by describing his marvellous life outside the home, Una now does the same, with fearful consequences. She leaves the house 'singing softly, with all the joy of pure womanhood, Wendy's tune from "Peter Pan"', and Grace does something horrifying — presumably to herself — in a room offstage.

'It was not a good play,' said the mature Victor. It was a very bad play, but valuable as an exorcism of 256 Elgin Avenue, and a mine of clues to the Victor of 1913. The situation at home had deteriorated. May, 'of a strongly religious temperament and . . . dissatisfied with orthodoxy' was about to apostatize from Judaism to Christianity, despite all attempts by Alex and Hermann to keep her in the fold. (After baptism she worked for a time in the East End at Dr Barnardo's, and her father, though he did not follow the tradition of sitting in mourning for her, could not bring himself to see her for some years. Victor, giving Alex full credit for his virtues, was rightly proud of his tolerance in leaving her the proper share of his estate.) Winifred was also turning troublesome, and already showing signs of mental instability. Victor's attitude to his involvement was clear from

Daughters. Railing against his father's treatment of them had gained nothing, but there was no suggestion that he considered a brother's responsibilities might go further than that.

The young Victor thought very well of his play, and was heartbroken because he did not have the £80 necessary to stage it. He had it typed and bound, and dedicated it to Ewan Agnew, 'Friend, feminist, and lover of the drama, This play is dedicated in sincerest esteem and truest affection by The Author.' At least one other copy was painstakingly written out in his own hand, bound in leather, and presented to a close friend.

Club and society life was important, and Victor was a member of the liberal Russell and Palmerston, a founder member of the Liberal Club and a speaker at the New College debating society, the Twenty Club. On the literary side there was the New College Essay Society, restricted to eighteen members at any one time, with the ritual recitation of a Latin toast followed by the passing of a loving cup around members and visitors. . . 'but when my own turn was coming to bow, receive the loving-cup, drink, face about, and bow again, I always felt afraid that I should giggle nervously and ruin everything.'

The society was deeply serious; it specialized in such papers as J. B. S. Haldane's on Darwinism, A. P. Herbert's on State Interference, and Bernard Strauss's on Masefield. Victor attended quite frequently and spoke, and, after a couple of unsuccessful efforts, was finally elected in June 1914 on the proposal of the president, Douglas Jerrold. A more frivolous body was the Midwives, so-called 'because we assisted at the birth-pangs of one another's compositions', and one of the few societies in which Victor was closely associated with members of other colleges. It provided some light relief in Victor's daunting intellectual schedule.

'[Christopher Morley] had found a forgotten letter, signed Kathleen, in a blotter at the Union, with a number of crosses and "These are from Fred" as a postscript. The novel we composed on the basis of this fragment, writing a chapter apiece, was a miracle of deduction.'

The Union, however, was the main attraction.

I was constantly there, not only on Thursdays in the Debating Hall, but almost every day of the week in some part of the building or another: writing letters for instance, in what is now the billiard room — one initialled the envelopes and posted them free; and this made me feel very important, so that often, when there was nothing in particular to write about and nobody in particular to write to, I would think up recipients and topics for the mere fun of scribbling my initials . . . But better than anything were the long slow winter afternoons, spent amid the haze of tobacco smoke in the reading room upstairs. The armchairs were deeper than any in the world, the fires like fires in a railway engine . . . I would sit there from lunch till nearly seven, reading, dozing, eating much hot buttered toast.

Of course, there was much more to his Union activity than that. Victor was anxious to be a success, and he worked hard at it. Lord Birkenhead, in his life of Walter Monckton, describes the difficulties of speaking in the Oxford Union at this period.

> . . . the audiences were large, incalculable and merciless. They had become conditioned by [Philip] Guedalla to a form of speaking difficult to imitate, grave in purpose, frivolous in outward appearance, heavily embellished with epigram and paradox. The speaker addressing them for the first time was as one groping through a maze . . . There was something of the atmosphere of a Roman arena, and courage and a constant animal alertness were demanded of those who were to survive and triumph in these lists.

Contemporaries were less taken with it: C. E. M. Joad found the Union depressingly conventional, overserious and terrified by any ideas beyond the ordinary; Jerrold said in his memoirs that he recalled no star orators; and *Isis* reports frequently aspersed the general level of mediocrity. *Varsity*, on the other hand, found the general standard 'wonderfully good', while lamenting the absence of individual speakers to rank with the great of the past — a complaint common to most generations in most such institutions.

The first two Presidents in Victor's time were R. M. Barrington-Ward, later editor of *The Times*, and Walter Monckton, later an influential Conservative minister and confidant of King Edward VIII. (Balliol and New College tended to dominate the Union.)

Faint praise was the house style in *Isis* and *Varsity* reports, but it was never damning enough to stifle Victor — who, indeed, earned his share of bouquets. His debut, in November 1912, was in a debate on women's suffrage. Laski was effective, and Victor 'seemed interesting and well meaning; we shall hear him again.' They did, in January, when Victor 'had the honour and credit of ably winding up one of the best Union debates [on Food Taxes] of recent terms.' The next debate — women's suffrage again — exhibited Victor's 'patience in waiting and power in speaking', and although he spoke 'too fast and too long' the following week in favour of the disestablishment and disendowment of the Church of England, he was 'well worth hearing'. Partnering Harold Macmillan in a condemnation of public schools for being out of touch, he earned an 'eloquent' beside Macmillan's 'brilliant'.

He was elected to the eighteen-strong Library Committee in March 1913, coming sixteenth, improving that to ninth in June. That month, defending the motion 'that War between civilized modern States is impracticable and unreasonable', Victor 'denied that support of the motion was inconsistent with patriotism', and 'made an earnest and quite successful speech'.

By the beginning of his second year, Victor's enhanced status was evident from his promotion up the list of speakers. On 16 October, in defending the government, he was commended by *Isis* for 'really debating', while *Varsity* found his speech 'detailed and fluent'. A week later, he attacked the government's attitude to militant suffragist outrages, and was very loud, fluent and sincere, though *Isis* carped that he was 'not good enough to speak twice running'.

He was 'on the paper' (announced in printed notices) for 27 November, and wore the appropriate full evening dress. He spoke in favour of the abolition of theatre and music-hall censorship, and *Isis* and *Varsity* gave him the attention due to a rising star.

Isis:
[He] declared that he had torn up his prepared speech, as its matter had already been used by previous speakers. It was this, I fancy, which accounted for his being more effective than I had expected. It intensified his always obvious sincerity, and arrested his generally *too* fluent speech. Probably the best speech of the evening.

Varsity:
[He] was horribly pleased at speaking No. 5 'on the paper'. Self-satisfaction is his great danger as a speaker. Otherwise he was really very good, fluent and full of knowledge.

In December, *Isis* ran an assessment of contemporary debaters.

Who is not dull at the Union? Firstly, there are three New College speakers who have treated the House to some genuine oratory — Mr Raju, Mr Laski and Mr Gollancz. All these are naturally fanatic, and the two latter (especially Mr Gollancz) have a rather exaggerated idea of their own importance. But, anyway, they remain as the only three (and the third is doubtful) who really can move the House.

The two journals had charted Victor's emergence over the years from his New College contingent: Bernard Strauss ('horribly depressing', yet 'loudly applauded by Mr Gollancz . . . These two always seem to be enjoying some awful conspiracy'), J. B. S. Haldane ('decidedly entertaining in his lighter moments'), Douglas Jerrold ('the Union's prettiest wit'), A. P. Herbert, and Ralph Rooper, of whom 'much may be expected in the future', although he ultimately fell short of his promise.

The esteem in which Victor was held as a speaker was not matched by his personal popularity. The reporters were broadly consistent in their appraisals up to the summer term: 'Mr V. Gollancz . . . has yet to master himself . . . One is always made strikingly aware of the opposite view by reason of his inability to realise that there is one.' . . . '[He] gave an able and lucid exposition . . . but he should be less monotonous and less certain that every sane man agrees with him.'

Elevated to fifth place in the next Library Committee elections, he was absent through illness for a good part of the second term, but on his return was again first speaker, this time on a motion condemning the policies of the South African Prime Minister, Louis Botha. The following week he advocated 'drastic changes in the Public School system', and

> lamented the impossibility of cross-bench speaking. After rebutting certain arguments already used from his own side of the House, he brought forward three reasons for his support of the motion; the too great length of a Public School career, the absence of co-education, and the monopoly of this education by richer classes. The best speech during this debate, and greeted with well-merited applause.

He spoke once again that term, in favour of 'One man, one vote', but was outdone by Nicholas Davenport, whose speech on the gospel of 'No man, no vote' was hailed as brilliantly witty by both university organs. Victor, said *Varsity*, 'was singularly lacking in humour in his attitude towards Mr Davenport's speech; in fact, we fear this failing is always rather obvious in his speeches. Otherwise, he is quite a fluent and sound speaker.'

Perhaps significantly, Victor had just been defeated for the position of treasurer by Davenport, by a margin of 177 votes to 52. A few days later he achieved the accolade of election to the Standing Committee, and a place on the green benches beside the president's chair. He had forgotten this when he wrote *My Dear Timothy*, but he plays down his Union successes overall:

> my longing [for office] was in vain, for my Union career was not a success. I spoke well — much better, I think, than several of the men who won office: but passionately always, in the heaviest of manners, without elegance or cynicism or wit. My style was a little like Cicero's, or Raju's,

though I never attained the perfection of these masters. Moreover, I was without charm of manner, had little intellectual distinction, dressed badly, and, at the beginning, didn't even know how to dine . . . Most damaging of all, I was socially an outsider.

This last observation was true. Etonians, Wykehamists and old boys of other senior public schools dominated Oxford, and though a number of St Paul's men were there, they could not compete as a clique. Victor, in any case, showed little interest in them. Nor did he have the money or athletic prowess to gain entrée into more prestigious social circles. (His Jewishness was no more than a minor problem, for there was little egregious anti-semitism at Oxford, and Victor, after the St Paul's experience, had no cause to bear a chip on his shoulder.)

Ultimately it was his temperament and personality that denied him popularity, just as it had at St Paul's. His didacticism repelled those outside his small circle of friends, all of whom were interested (allowing for Jerrold's irreverence) in what preoccupied Victor; in return, he had no time for those averse to serious conversation about the issues of the day. While he accepted all invitations, he spent a great deal of his time alone, reading. His emotions were so intertwined with his intellectual preoccupations that he was not easily capable — ever — of small talk. Politically messianic, he must have been an uneasy companion for the Tories who held sway at the Union.

His disposition to anger compounded the problem. Passionate resentment at slights — real or imagined — was always to have a dire effect on his personal relations. Two episodes from Oxford illustrate this.

> Cecil Chesterton and I were both present one night at a meeting of the Fabian Society, which was private — he as the guest of the evening, I an outsider smuggled in by a friend. He made a slimy, smeary, nudging, winking sort of antisemitic speech; and after waiting in vain for some protest I attacked him myself. I was afterwards told that I had surpassed all limits in offensiveness, and that my behaviour had been particularly shocking in view of what was due to him as a guest and of my own dubious status there. I mention the episode, not because I am proud of it (though I really am, rather), but to prevent you drawing false conclusions, in the matter of antisemitism, from anything I may have written in this chapter.

The other episode figures in a sonnet he composed a couple of years after it occurred. It was written in a fit of remorse, and dedicated to Ralph Rooper, probably his second closest friend at Oxford, at a time when Rooper was on ambulance service in France.

Forgive me for it — that unhallowed night
Through which we walked together, long ago,
And spake no word, because I hated so,
Being foul with jealousy. We left the light
And nursing poison, as mean serpents might,
Came out on Shotover. There, far below,
Lay Oxford, our great Mother, in a glow
Of generous warmth. Shame caught us at the sight;

And — God be praised — with pitiful words I tried
To kill the silence. Turning, back we strode
To homeward . . . and at last the Cowley Road,
Magdalen, and our own gate, and your fireside.
I may speak of it now; for hate is dead,
And love, binding us three, rules in its stead.

'Being foul with jealousy' was a state of mind familiar to Victor all
his life. Starting with his anguish over his mother's obsession with his
father, it marred many other relationships. With men it was to be
jealousy at their fame; with his wife, jealousy of any affections on her
part that might threaten theirs — their own children were not exempt.
The 'unhallowed night' expiated in the sonnet seems to have been the
culmination of some triangular drama with sexual undertones in-
volving Victor, Rooper and another. He fought the jealousy once he
had recognized it, but there were always severe limits to Victor's self-
knowledge, particularly during the currency of any passion. The
cause in this case was probably the girl with whom he fell in love (or,
as he put it, 'imagined' himself in love) at Oxford — Joy, Ewan
Agnew's sister, who was 'beautiful . . . like a tall green lily'. This
infatuation was not long-lived. It had not yet begun in his first term at
Oxford when he met his future wife, Ruth Löwy, at a single-tax
dinner in London and 'gazed into her eyes the whole evening . . . I
imagined myself in love with her beauty and goodness — with the
combination of them, I mean: and let me add, for the benefit of
psychoanalysts, that however lovely a woman may be, however
radiant with every glory extolled in the Song that is Solomon's, I can
feel no atom of desire for her person unless her goodness is to match,
and the other way about.'

Certainly the many women over the years for whom he felt love at
varying levels of intensity were distinguished by social conscience and
a sincere concern with the state of the world. The serious attachments
were all to attractive women, who were frequently taken aback by
Victor's public tributes to their pulchritude. His women had to be
both beautiful and good, so if he was attracted by some spiritual

quality, he projected physical beauty on to its possessor. This exercise was unnecessary in Ruth's case (although she could hardly live up to Victor's assertions of her pre-eminence among all women in both spheres), but she was for the moment inaccessible so Victor was free to go back to Oxford and fall in love with Joy.

Joy inspired two poems. They were of equally awful sentimentality, and one serves as an early illustration of an important trait of Victor's — his need to relax into child-like dependence on the woman he loved:

To Joy — after seeing in her album my portrait with a line from 'Peter Pan' written below it.

> Many a name of the sweetest tone,
> Many a name has been given to me;
> Boyfriend's, & girl-friend's, & Mother's own,
> 'Dominus', 'Tootles', & 'Victor G.'
> But voice ne'er sounded so graciously
> As when, on a day, said faëry Joy
> 'This is the name I will give to thee —
> "I want to be always a little boy"'
>
> So now, when at night the winds make moan,
> And my heart is sick for what cannot be,
> When the sun goes down, & I feel alone,
> Far from where men die — ah, then I see
> The brow & the eyes & the hair of thee,
> The hair's soft gold without alloy,
> And I hear thy voice say whisperingly
> 'I want to be always a little boy'.
>
> Is it less happy, the rose full-blown,
> Than when the bud held it tenderly?
> Nay, this is the secret — when we're grown,
> To do great things with a heart of glee.
> The good God meant it so; but see,
> Men have broken their lovely toy;
> And I want to mend it beautifully,
> I want to be always a little boy.
>
> L'Envoi
>
> Girl-princess, woman soon to be,
> Grow up, don't grow old, dear faëry Joy;
> Oh remember this that thou taughtest me —
> 'I want to be always a little boy'.

Clearly, Joy had read Victor well. We do not know if she was drawn to him physically; certainly he was not to every woman's taste.

Though about five-feet-ten and slim, he was balding and round shouldered, and looked much older than his years. He made little effort with his appearance, dressing in shapeless and untidy clothes. His nose was prominent, and he wore glasses for his short sight. Features that were to make him rather fine looking in later life were unappealing in a young man. His successes with women had to be based on the magnetism of his vitality rather than on physical attractions.

When the Joy affair had run its course, Ruth came into view again in the summer term of 1914. He wrote to his parents: 'Harold Rubinstein is staying here the week end beginning June 12th — and so is Ruth Löwy — who is spending the Sunday with me — and I hope more than the Sunday!'

He arranged 'a recherché little lunch party' with five guests — Ruth, Rubinstein, Agnes Murray (daughter of 'Gilbert the great'), Leah Kay (daughter of Klingenstein, Victor's cigar-merchant friend) and Ewan Agnew. He was also 'a bit in love' with Agnes, who was currently embarrassing G. D. H. Cole with her passionate devotion. 'We ate salmon mayonnaise and strawberries and cream and drank moselle cup. Afterwards we went on the river. But Ruth dropped a terrible brick: she wore sand-shoes, apt for Margate. I immediately fell out of love with her: I thought she didn't know how to dress.'

So Victor's heart was whole again, and was to remain so for several years.

The letters about the lunch party constitute the only correspondence with his parents to have escaped his purges. It is dangerous to read too much into so few documents unless they fit an established pattern, but they do show a characteristic lack of concern with the family's doings, and are quite open about his own interest in Ruth. It would have been consoling to his parents that his lunch-party included other Jews. A postscript enquires about the duration of festivities after the wedding of a cousin, as he has an invitation to a ball at Claridge's for the next evening. He sees little chance of success in the recent Hertford scholarship competition (an accurate prediction), and he is short of money again: will they 'for Christ's sake listen out for coaching jobs?'

The 'for Christ's sake' is rather unexpected, being potentially offensive to an orthodox Jew unless used humorously, and one does not associate Alex with a sense of humour. Besides, Victor was contemplating being baptized himself. His interest in Christianity had begun with a reading of the New Testament at St Paul's, when he had been deeply affected by the Sermon on the Mount — particularly the injunction to love your enemies, which he regarded as a considerable advance on the Judaic 'eye for an eye'.

> As to Christ, I thought of him, at this time, as a Hebrew prophet — by far the greatest of Hebrew prophets, it is true, but still 'just' a prophet. I loved and reverenced him as I loved and reverenced Socrates, that other beautiful hero of the search after truth — more intensely, but in much the same way.

'All my thoughts and emotions about religion, in the narrower sense,' he says in *My Dear Timothy*, 'were centred at Oxford on Christianity.' He remembers going just once to 'the cold little orthodox synagogue'. His memory betrayed him here, for after the end of his first term at Oxford he wrote a letter to the *Jewish Chronicle* taking issue with an article condemnatory of Oxford Jewry, refuting from personal experience the allegation that synagogue attendance there was low. He had been involved in an eager discussion among the congregation of changes in the service; the Adler Society was flourishing; and

> most hopeful of all, the synagogue service has been entirely remodelled, so as to meet the spiritual needs of Jews who are at the same time twentieth century Englishmen. . . . Altogether there is an atmosphere of awakening life, of growth, of energy; there is no necessity to struggle against a 'lack of enthusiasm', for the latent enthusiasm is now coming to the surface and showing itself. For it was, indeed, inevitable that enthusiasm, perhaps the most noticeable feature of the 'Home of Lost Causes', which produced Gladstone and Newman, should show itself in the Jewish life of the University, directly that Jewish life was made a living reality by the introduction of necessary reforms . . .

This enthusiasm was short-lived, but he was not yet ready to abandon his religion completely: instead he became involved for a while with liberal Judaism 'which I felt to be genuinely religious and, what was much the same thing, to demand my support as revolting from orthodoxy.' He occasionally visited the rooms of Basil Henriques, the spiritual leader of Oxford liberal Jews (and later famous as a philanthropist in the East End of London), 'though some mixture of gravity, heartiness and evangelism in the atmosphere rather embarrassed me.' A clash with the liberal Jewish theologian, Claude Montefiore, whom Victor found unsympathetic, hastened his final estrangement from all forms of organized Judaism. He examined his reasons in his memoirs:

> As I sit here and reflect about my brief dalliance (it cannot have lasted more than a term or so) with liberal Judaism, there comes into my mind an

image of almost complete dissociation: between me as the one party and liberal Judaism as the other. Nothing really passed between us. I was looking at it, the whole time, quite from the outside: I was in no way engaged. And it wasn't engaged with me either . . .

Oh, let me cut through everything I was going to say after that — all about the coldness and flatness of liberal Judaism, its impersonal ethicism and moralism, my conviction, which was a passionately moral conviction, that I dare not, in loyalty to spirit and truth, but keep it at arm's length as something particularist, alien, hedging off, ununiversal — let me cut through all this and get straight to the heart of the matter, which is this: that I was on my way to the adoration of Christ.

This revulsion at the 'alien' and 'particularist' nature of liberal Judaism was probably inevitable. The liberal Jews, for all their culture, open-mindedness and twentieth-century Englishness, were Jews first, and Victor was Victor first and foremost. He could embrace only beliefs that he had evolved for himself, and such evolution could not flourish in the potentially discordant company of those whose spiritual house was built on foundations of Jewishness. Implications of separateness from the rest of humanity were quite unacceptable to Victor, who was finding himself among preponderantly Christian friends.

The adoration of Christ had not yet crystallized in 1913, but Victor's contemporary speeches confirm his later claim that he was already 'passionately eager to see Jews, Englishmen and the whole world become ethically Christian'.

And when I say ethically Christian, I mean ethically Christian: in politics, in economics, in personal relations, in everything. . . . I burnt with the fiercest conversionist fire, I would happily have worn myself out (and later on, temporarily, did wear myself out) to make the whole world good — poor sinner that I was!

Yet he was not himself living by the Christian ethic.

I was selfish, self-righteous, envious, jealous: spiritually, though not I think physically, greedy; capable of great anger: careless, often, of other people's happiness, and given to judging them. I was marked by these uglinesses hardly, if at all, less disfiguringly than in the old Elgin Avenue days. I knew them to be wrong, for I wanted to be loving and generous; with part of me I *was* loving and generous — not merely because I wanted to be, but spontaneously: and frequently I felt great remorse. But I was spiritually lazy, so far as my own person was concerned . . . I had failed to realise either that to be good oneself is one's best contribution to goodness, or that the price of being good is eternal vigilance in a million minute particulars.

The mature Victor believed himself a much better person than the undergraduate, but for all his egotism and insensitivity, there can have been few of his age so anxious to search out the good and the beautiful and make the world a better place. (Charges of humbug were later to come from those who saw how often he preached what he could not practise, but the imbalance arose not so much from unusual short-comings in his conduct as from his inability ever to resist an opportunity for righteous propaganda. In 1948, thirty years after Ralph Rooper's death in the war, his aunt sent to Victor — 'one of those who has not allowed his youthful ideals to be smirched' — some of his old friend's writings, pointing out the testimonial: 'Victor never committed an insincerity in his life'.)

Christian ethics led him to a closer study of Christ, and the difficulties he had with Christian theology were eased by Hastings Rashdall, clergyman, philosopher, Fellow of New College and Dean of Divinity. (Like all undergraduates, Victor had to sit an examination in divinity, an imposition bitterly resented by the majority. *Varsity* called it a 'blasphemous farce'. It was intellectually untaxing, but Victor's hatred of compulsion led him to apply several times to the tolerant Warden and Tutors for postponement. It was presumably through his divinity studies that he met Rashdall, known as 'the Rasher'.) Where Victor greatly admired Gilbert Murray, it was Rashdall he loved, with a love which remained intact over the years. As a proselytizer tailored to Victor's character, Rashdall could not have been improved on. 'The Socrates of the Cornmarket', he was on the left wing of the church and his divinity lectures concerned themselves with the discovery of truth. He believed that there should be a rational basis to religion, but also understood the place of emotion, and, an ecumenist, he found in Claude Montefiore's *The Synoptic Gospels* more appreciation of Jesus than in many Christian theologians. There was passion behind his fine intellect, and he was an excellent teacher. Above all, he became personally involved with his pupils, offered lively conversation on politics, religion and philo-sophy, and enjoyed life and laughter.

In *My Dear Timothy*, Victor admits to unavoidable anachronisms in his analysis of how he felt about Christ at Oxford: his views had developed gradually over the following four decades. He provides a list of what made Christ a necessity for him, and it can be taken as substantially accurate, allowing for a greater cogency of expression in the mature man.

(1) I have always felt a vast, single, living bliss *behind* everything. I have always been certain it is *there*.

(2) I have always felt a life and a bliss *in* everything — I mean in every particular, in stones and chairs and mantelpieces and paper as well as in what is ordinarily called life: and it is through my meeting with these particulars, living and what are usually thought of as other than living, that I establish communion, feel myself mingled, with the bliss beyond.

(3) There is in me an imperative need, not only to establish communion, not only to merge myself, but also to worship. . . . I have worshipped the vast, single, living bliss beyond — that has been the central fact of my life; and I have worshipped it at once in and through the whole body of particulars, and in and through such single particulars . . . as good deeds on the one hand and stocks and stones on the other.

(4) In religious language, I come to God through the world: in Platonic language I come to the Idea through the particulars . . . it is in the particulars that I feel and love the Idea. And Christ . . . is the Supreme Particular.

(5) I worship the beyond in and through the particulars, but do not worship the particulars themselves. Not the 'ordinary' particulars. I *do* worship the Supreme Particular, as I worship the beyond. I worship Him as very close, very friendly, very accessible . . .

(6) Christ, the Supreme Particular, is, for me, a concrete individual, one Person, with a man's nature . . . our nature is essentially His . . . this is what we really are, the rest being error and misunderstanding. To the extent to which we realise this — to the extent to which we 'believe in' Him, we are in Him. He is each one of us — every man — all but completely released from bondage to error and unreality; to the error and unreality of self-centredness as opposed to communion, of what Blake calls 'selfhood' . . .

And all this being so, worship by a man of Christ as the Supreme Particular is worship both of God and of humanity.

The bliss in and beyond the particular had been with Victor from early childhood, and it stayed with him until his death. Some of those who knew him found it life-enhancing; some found it ridiculous; some thought it affectation; some self-indulgence. The very range of these reactions is an indication of Victor's uniqueness, and his unsusceptibility to simple explanation. What might have been accepted in an artist or poet sat uneasily with the businessman or, earlier, with the schoolboy or undergraduate. A poem (*circa* 1917) refers back to an episode in St Paul's:

> 'I love to see things move!' he cries —
> (A fleck of paper fluttering to the floor).
> His comrades laugh; but in the skies
> God sees Creation, and the void before.

Given such early manifestations of his blissful empathy with the world, his need to worship, and his messianism about Christian ethics, it is clear that Victor was already very far along his own path to Christ.

Yet there were serious theological barriers to his baptism. All Rashdall's liberalism was needed to accommodate Victor's idiosyncratic views on the Incarnation — roughly that historicity was an irrelevance, and that even if Christ were a myth, that myth's embodiment of the ultimate truth meant he had always existed and always would exist. Victor was uninterested in the physical Resurrection, which he thought highly unlikely, but believed in Christ's spiritual resurrection. Nor did he care much about Trinitarianism, but found an acceptable explanation of it in Plato.

> I leaped at Plato's answer in the later Dialogues: 'his last word,' says A. E. Taylor, 'on the problem how the sensible comes to "partake" of Form is that it does so through the agency of divine goodness and wisdom.' Ah, I said, but this is trinitarianism: divine goodness and wisdom is the Holy Ghost linking God the Father, unmanifest, with God the Son, our universe of manifestation: the three being one. But, I went on to say, isn't Christian trinitarianism superior to Platonic trinitarianism? Doesn't it explain what Plato can never explain? For isn't it something actually *happening*, a living, concrete, flesh-and-blood *occurrence*, whereas the other is a cold theoretical construction?

This, he confesses, was so much intellectual play-acting on the part of his younger self; it was not an issue that moved him. What caused him real difficulty was Atonement.

> That Christ atoned or atones, this spoke intimately to me; I responded to its beauty, and, not at all understanding what it meant, yet felt it to be true and important. So I began to study the literature, and was revolted. At the back of everything I read was some variant of the idea that humanity by its sinfulness had outraged God, or God's honour, or the law of righteousness: that this outrage must be made good: that nothing but condign punishment would suffice: and that Christ, by his suffering on the Cross, had given due satisfaction on behalf of humanity, or on behalf of such men or women as might identify themselves with Him by faith.

Victor felt it bad that a Christian God should exact punishment, and much worse that innocence should be punished on behalf of guilt (the theory of collective guilt being one of the unacceptable tenets of orthodox Judaism). Rashdall helped.

> He taught me what is indifferently known as the Origenistic, Abelardian, or Moral doctrine of the Atonement. . . . The Abelardian doctrine is most succinctly expressed, not in anything the master wrote himself, but in a sentence of Peter the Lombard, his disciple: 'The death of Christ justifies us [or makes us just or good by making it easier for us not to sin], inasmuch as through it charity is excited in our hearts.'

Rashdall's commentary on Atonement elaborated this view to Victor's entire satisfaction and during the summer term of 1914 he decided to be baptized. Rashdall made arrangements for the ceremony to take place in the autumn.

It was the outbreak of war that finally ensured a cancellation, but Victor subsequently doubted whether he would have seen it through in any case. He disliked institutions and was unhappy about certain aspects of the Church of England; he was worried about burning his spiritual boats and uncertain of his own motives; he suspected sub-conscious worldly motives for abandoning Judaism, and his occasional experiences of anti-semitism made him wary of formal apostasy. Over and above all this, there was the matter of Alex, 'horribly wounded' by May's conversion to Christianity. 'Could I wound him again still more horribly — for I was his son, not his daughter — without being sure, at the very least without being sure, that my motives were unmixed and that what I had contemplated was inexorably demanded by conscience?'

The summer term of 1914 was Victor's golden time at Oxford, as it must have been for so many in retrospect. It seems churlish to point out that Victor's happy memories of glorious weather omit weeks of rain and wind, including Eights Week, which generated little enthusiasm by comparison with the previous year. In essentials, his recollections of the magic of that time accord with the facts and with the mood of the solitary letter that survives from the period.

Before he could surrender himself to pleasure, he had to face Part I of his Oxford examination — Classical Moderations, the preliminary papers in the language and literature of Greece and Rome to be taken before beginning Greats, which was largely concerned with philosophy. Victor needed to do well in Mods, for the renewal of his scholarship depended on it. To compensate for his academic idling, he attacked the curriculum with his usual ferocity a couple of weeks before the exams began.

> Once I *had* started I hardly slept at all — hardly went to bed, I mean — until, a few weeks later, the last wretched paper was finished. (But wretched is only rhetorical, for I am devoted to the classics — other than Demosthenes, whom I got a gamma for . . .) The *maître d'hôtel* of JCR . . . used to bring me a great pot of coffee before leaving at night for North Oxford. In the morning, after an hour or two's doze in a chair, I would go to the barber at the corner of Holywell Lane and have an electric massage to my head: I had the idea it would freshen me up. When the whole thing was over, the porter of Holywell Lodge expressed serious concern for my health: he thought I looked ghastly.

He took a first, which must have been some compensation for his failure to do well in the Hertford.

With Schools over, the rest of the term was devoted to enjoyment of all the particulars that Oxford offered — animate and inanimate. It is impossible to paraphrase adequately all that Victor found joy in — the New College garden, punting on the Cherwell, cycling in the countryside around Oxford — experiences which inspired a love of England as a physical entity. There was a grassy bank near his New College rooms where undergraduates used to sleep out many nights.

> The bloods drank champagne, which I, of course, couldn't afford; but as pearl changed to rose I would find myself looking at the sky with that freshness of peace which you very rarely feel except when waking in the open air — and then off to play tennis and back to a breakfast in JCR hardly less extravagant than the bloods' champagne: porridge, sometimes, with a lot of brown sugar and cream, followed by a steak and fried onions and glasses of lemon squash. All this must sound awfully gross; but it wasn't really, not in that mood and with that setting.

So much of the joy was in conversation, as described in a poem called *Oxford, 1914*.

> To lie abed, pretending noon is dawn —
> This is the Oxford morn.
>
> To read philosophy — and slumber soon —
> This is the afternoon.
>
> To talk with friends until the break of light —
> This is the sacred night.

His delight in conversation became so intense that 'daytime, for all its beauty, seemed nothing but the pleasantest of interludes in a symposium indefinitely prolonged'.

That summer term also saw Victor's participation in the chartering, along with Laski and others, of a launch in Eights Week. They steamed up and down shouting 'Votes for women' through a megaphone, and Victor, fearful of some terrible retribution from the bloods, hid for a long time under a table in the classical reading room. Even so, he had been very brave. As he admitted himself, Victor was physically timid; indeed, at times during his life he exhibited downright cowardice. The demonstration on the river was his only militant gesture. His feminism was sincere, but he was better fitted for propaganda through the written or spoken word.

In June, the Warden and Tutors decided that in addition to his original scholarship, Victor should have the Longstaff Exhibition for the year 1914–15. He went down to London well content, and took in some music. Accompanied by Harold Rubinstein, at the end of July, he heard Emmy Destinn sing Aida. He counted twenty-two curtain calls and after they had finished, he stood in Floral Street to watch her leave with Dinh Gilly, her husband. She gave Victor a rose, which his mother made into pot-pourri (and later passed on — in a little bogus Chinese teapot — to Victor's eldest and most musical daughter). Five days later was declared the war which neither he nor his politically minded friends had anticipated.

CHAPTER FOUR

SERVING: A SOLDIER?

> New College Lecture Room No VI
> Friday 10 a.m.

MY DEAR HAROLD [Rubinstein],

(I was going to write to someone else first, but feel I owe it to you!) A thousand apologies for leaving your letter so long unanswered, but I've been appallingly busy — for reasons which I will explain in a minute or two. (This letter will be probably both disjointed and stilted; because I am supposed to be taking notes on a lecture on Plato's theory of the 'community of wives', and have to look up at the lecturer every minute or two.) But before I explain them, let me tell you how delighted I was to hear the good news of 'Consequences' in America. But 'clean and wholesome'!!! The critic obviously looks upon you as a typical Hearty Englishman! However, c'est magnifique.

I should love to go North for the premiere of 'Over the Wall'. But the simple fact is that I can't afford it. My financial position is nothing in the extreme, and I rarely spend more than twopence at a time —

I am frightfully busy for several reasons. In the first place, the two University Papers, 'The Varsity' and 'The Isis' have been amalgamated during the war, and I am editing the combined result. Its not uninteresting, financially not to be sneezed at, and gives me a couple of free seats for as many theatres as I like in the vac. By the way, I should be awfully obliged if you would dash me off something — say a 'London Letter' done in a light style. Will you?

Then I have arrears of work to make up, the Union largely to run — there are only three of the Standing Committee still up — and various other activities. So I'm not being lazy!

They've chucked me even from the OTC here, on account of my eyes, so that means I have to give up all idea of anything military. Still, though its pretty miserable, there are compensations.

How is the Doris play?

The eye of the lecturer is on me, so . . . 'We note a curious paradox. If they are not, how can we ascribe seeming to them? That is the puzzle we have to consider' . . .

> Au revoir.
> Yours ever
> Victor G.

This letter was written some time during the Michaelmas Term of 1914, when Victor was trying to make the best of things. In an unsigned editorial in *Varsity/Isis* he succumbed to melancholy:

> . . . those of us who were up last year are the sole survivors of the real Oxford, condemned to haunt, like pale ghosts, the scenes of former life. The Freshers that come up this year, with no knowledge of the Oxford that is gone, know nothing of the joys that once were so powerful here. They, too, live a life subdued and quiet, hushed into the grey tones of an aimless monotony. The great god Pan is dead; and now Oxford is no more.

New College had few undergraduates left in residence; their rooms had been taken by 'far more useful individuals — to wit, wounded warriors who have exchanged the khaki of action for the hospital blue of enforced repose. On my window-sill lies — and will lie until I am in the bankruptcy court — a box of cigarettes, so I get through the window a good deal of accurate information of what may or may not have taken place.'

Few of Victor's friends remained. Jerrold, Lewis Denroche-Smith, Strauss and others had been given commissions. Verses from an anonymous contributor to *Varsity/Isis* in October 1914 illustrate vividly if inelegantly how the town looked to those who were still up.

> I stand amazed; I'm feeling dazed!
>   Reigns everywhere seclusion?
> Have cap and gown *en masse* gone down?
>   Or is it my delusion?
>
> With wild grimace I scan the face
>   Of everyone who passes;
> There's not a soul who's sound or whole,
>   And nearly all wear glasses.
>
> Some knock their knees; asthmatic wheeze
>   Shakes some; some look dyspeptic;
> A groggy heart afflicts a part;
>   Part, spasms epileptic.
>
> Oh passing strange I find the change;
>   The place is looking oddly.
> I find the few whom once I knew,
>   'Clean gone,' like the ungodly.

Victor's unhappiness at having been rejected by the forces emerged in *Varsity/Isis*: 'And what an odd lot we are, those who are left! The blind, the halt, and the maim — the babe and the suckling side by side with the hoary and infirm — and last, but not least, those to whom the War Office in its wisdom has not yet seen fit to issue commissions.

There is not a man among the lot who does not long to be with his friends "on the way to Berlin".'

Physical timidity notwithstanding, Victor's anxiety to get into uniform was as fervent as that of any of his contemporaries. Of the Officer Training Corps he wrote:

> We have signed our papers, we have gone before the stern board of three, we have been medically examined — and now we are either busily engaged in mastering the mysteries of drill, or are moping about disconsolate, watching with envious eyes those who, more fortunate than ourselves, have been accepted for training. And they all seem to be enjoying it . . . it does seem rather hard luck that men should be rejected, for instance, because their eyesight does not reach a certain technical standard, although in every other respect they are thoroughly fit and willing. Responsible positions in the field may be closed to them by such a defect; but surely there are many services connected with the war which do not require a piercing vision, and it seems a pity that such men should be precluded from any serious training. For instance, a private in the RAMC, if stationed in one of the home hospitals, obviously does not require to see as perfectly as a man who has to fire on the enemy in the field; nevertheless, it is impossible to get into the Corps without passing the regular eyesight test. I speak from bitter experience.

Though he had succumbed to war fever, and indeed believed fully by this stage the propaganda about German atrocities, Victor's liberalism and hatred of jingoism prevailed. He wrote a scathing leader about an article he had read assailing everything Germanic.

> Because Germany is at war with us, because her crimes against humanity and decency have been appalling, is that any reason for hurling indiscriminate abuse on her artists — on men who are of those who speak for the world at large, and not for any one particular nation? Nietzsche loathed Prussia; Wagner was a revolutionary; Wedekind is in violent revolt against the loathsome German autocracy and militarism which have caused the war. At a time like this it is our duty to keep our heads sane and clear, and, instead of attacking artists, to think out some method by which, when we have crushed and humbled the arrogance of the German Empire, we may prevent the renaissance of a system which is at once militarist and autocratic, and by which every child in Germany is taught to look upon the Kaiser as a God-sent leader who can do no wrong. When the soul of the German people comes up for judgement we tremble to think of the multitude of sins against decency and humanity which will be laid to its charge. But of one thing we are sure — that there will not be included among them the fact of having produced a Wagner and a Wedekind!

And in the following week's *Varsity/Isis*:

On Monday night a meeting was held to wind up the affairs of the Anglo-German Club. This is really tragic rather than amusing, for the Club was an attempt to realise an idea. I, for one, am proud to have been a member, for the Germans in Oxford were a charming set of men. One of them, dying from wounds in a French hospital, sent to his old college a message that brings tears to the eyes of those that knew him.

Such defences of German artists and undergraduates were courageous in the climate of the time, but Victor was fully in line with current thinking about the reasons for the war, and terms like 'loathsome German autocracy and militarism' and 'sins against decency and humanity' would have drawn nods from any Tory. Where he dissented was in excepting certain elements in Germany from blame, and in his implication that it was brainwashing that had produced in the German populace at large the militarism and Kaiser-worship of which he disapproved. His humanitarianism led him to condemn the white feather mentality:

I said above that nearly everyone had offered himself to the OTC, except those who were prevented from 'family' or other reasons. I have heard rumours of unkindly treatment meted out in one or two colleges to those who are remaining at home for the first-named reasons. I hope that such rumours are untrue; and, in any case, such an attitude is fortunately exceptional. We wish to see nothing in Oxford that can be compared in any way to that week in London during which misguided girls went about presenting white feathers to youths who had not enlisted. As long as Conscription is not introduced into this country, every man has to decide for himself whether or not he shall serve; and that decision once arrived at, it is the grossest breach of good taste to attempt in any way to interfere. It may require a greater courage to stay at home when one's duty to one's home demands it, than to go abroad and serve one's country in a more obvious and active way.

He makes no mention here (or elsewhere in his Oxford writings) of the vexed issue of conscientious objection; his radicalism was still very limited. There were undergraduates well to his left, Macmillan and Laski among them. He thought himself radical, for he tended to measure himself against the prevailing politics of Elgin Avenue and St Paul's. As *Varsity* had said, he was 'fanatical', but that was in the expression of his opinions, not in their substance. His instinct was aggressively humanitarian, but his day-to-day politics normally fitted in comfortably with the Liberal Party.

Most of his friends had been in the same humane liberal mould and they tended to reinforce each other's positions. Victor always liked to gather around himself — for serious conversational purposes, anyway

— those who agreed with him. Later he might play bridge with Tories, and when it came to music, politics did not matter, but intimates had to be political allies.

When he wrote of this period in his memoirs, he dwelt at length on his feelings about the war from about 1916 onwards, but said very little about the 1914–15 academic year. 'I went up for a month or two in the autumn of 1914, and am not at all sure that I didn't become an unofficial sort of Secretary of a bogus Union in a bogus Oxford.'

College records show him technically in residence for the whole of that academic year, and the number of undated letters to Rubinstein from Oxford addresses tends to confirm that. On the other hand, it has proved impossible to trace him in Union or college newspaper records after the first term, so the truth would seem to be that he stayed in Oxford, but lost interest in it to such an extent that his last months there were expunged from his memory. He would not have wished to remember the opinions he held then, in any case — opinions intrinsically conventional until he met the circumstances which were to push him into reaction against even the liberal establishment view.

Where he was discernibly outside the mainstream was in his faith that mankind could progress to a cosmic view like his own. Even while peddling a rather orthodox view of the war, he was putting his case for the betterment of mankind to the 'bogus' Union (which had decided to proceed with informal debates). Opposing the motion 'That there is no such thing as international morality', 'he spoke with a very real eloquence and fire; and he persuaded us that in international morality lay the only hope of establishment of universal peace . . . [Ralph Rooper] was scathing in denunciation of the speakers on the other side. He pointed out that the moral course was in the long run the most profitable.'

It was a dismal affair. Victor tied with another speaker for the best speech of the evening, 'though it must be confessed that this is not very high praise'. There were seldom more than eighty people in the Union Debating Hall, which could accommodate a thousand. The other clubs were similarly depressing. Victor had also now become secretary of the Russell and Palmerston, and indeed addressed the Liberal club in November on 'The War that will end Wars', but the societies were in financial trouble and suffering a grave shortage of members.

His response to the atmosphere was to turn lethargic. Although his scholarship had been renewed in October 1914, he was clearly idling to an unacceptable degree by December, when the Warden and tutors of New College threatened to gate him for half a term unless he performed well in a special examination.

The letters to Rubinstein suggest that he was preoccupied by the desire to play his part in the war, while his memoirs tell us only that 'After a good deal of fumbling at the outbreak of the 1914 war . . . I joined up — with the Inns of Court OTC.' Much effort had gone into this fumbling, before the OTC emerged as a prospect. Previous and later letters to Rubinstein had discussed drama and literature, but in spring 1915 there was only one theme. A postcard from the OU Liberal club reads

My dear Harold —
    Just a line, to let you know that Dunkirk is now very uncertain, as apparently it is being absorbed by the War Office, and may be altogether abandoned. Meanwhile, Mrs Agnew has just written to tell me that E. V. Lucas (and Masefield) are doing work — she does not say of what kind — in France, and advises me to write to EVL, using her name. Which I have done. I'll let you know if anything comes of it.
                                                    Yours ever
                                                        V.G.

This proved too delphic for Rubinstein, whose response generated an explanatory letter.

My dear Harold —
    All my friends tell me that my writing is getting atrocious! The whole story is this. I signed on to go to the front with the Quaker Ambulance — meanwhile learning motoring, etc. Then I got a frantic wire from Rooper not to come, and the upshot of it is that the whole thing is probably going to be abandoned — being absorbed by the War Office. In the meantime, I got a letter from Mrs Agnew telling me that E. V. Lucas and *Masefield* (not Rothschild — my God, Harold, what a pair to mix up!) are doing work — what work she doesn't say — in France, and inviting me to write, using her name. Which I have done, and am now waiting — but it will probably turn out to be Hospital orderly!
    I've also got my eye on something else — which will probably come to nothing!
    Oh, I'm aweary of the war.
    I'm very glad about Ruth L. — but what *on earth* do you mean about bearing up??? You don't mean to tell me that our names were ever tossed about with a hyphen between them!
                                                    Ever yours
                                                        Victor G.
Let me know your plans — I suppose you're trying for some war-work too. Its going on till Doomsday.

(Ruth Löwy's engagement to Benjamin Polack, a school-teacher at Battersea Grammar School, and son and heir apparent to the housemaster of the Jewish House at Clifton College, had just become known. He had joined up on the outbreak of the war and was commissioned in January 1915.)

Whatever happened to Mrs Agnew's plan, Victor's next letter showed the extent of his desperation.

A third, and this time definite, change of plan. The Vice-Chancellor of Sheffield University has appealed to able-bodied Varsity men to go and make munitions, for which the need is appallingly pressing (I could tell you stories . . .), so I am going about the middle of next week with two or three other New College men. (8 hours a day, and £2 a week.) If by any chance you would care to join us — as I should much like — *wire immediately* on receipt of this, and I will get you a nomination. Of course, it is no use disguising the fact that the work will be trying in the extreme; but I honestly think that every able-bodied man whose health can stand it ought to do it.

In great haste
Ever yours
Victor

You only have to
sign on for three
months.

This plan apparently came to nought, but Victor had more success with the Inns of Court OTC, and after a short time forming fours on a parade ground in London, he was sent to Berkhamsted. His account is confined to this laconic passage in his memoirs: '[I] was among the first of my lot to become a lance-corporal: enjoyed night ops, for their freshness and romance and the smell of the country: learned the know-how of cleaning a rifle, but not of shooting with it: got floored in map-reading: was thought fit, after a month or so of this, to lead men into battle, or at any rate home battle.'

A letter to Rubinstein from Berkhamsted Young Men's Christian Association showed rather more pride.

A thousand apologies for not replying to your letter sooner, but I have been terribly busy, working often eighteen hours a day. On the whole I am enjoying myself hugely — I enjoy the feeling of getting up a new subject well, however revolting that subject may be. I am in high favour with my Captain, was made a lance-corporal (unpaid) about ten days ago, and paid LC today. Pretty good promotion, n'est-ce-pas?

In October 1915 he received a commission as Second Lieutenant in the 21st Provisional Battalion of the Northumberland Fusiliers and was sent to Cambois Camp, in Blyth, Northumberland. 'Find it in your heart,' he wrote to Rubinstein, 'to write to me *often*, and let your letters be as severely intellectual as you can make them — I dread complete decay!'

There was little chance of intellectual decay, whatever environment Victor was in. His next letter to Rubinstein included a criticism of his latest play, with its Meistersinger motif and its Henry James overtones, together with reports of his reading of Pushkin, Galsworthy and Gilbert Cannan's *Peter Homunculus*. ('Is there any news of Julia West's translation of the Tchekhoff plays? I'm dying to read them — Tchekhoff is far and way the most delightful of the Russians; he and James are the only people who know how to write real short stories.') Of the battalion personnel he said little, confining himself to his own future prospects.

> I have not been able to write before because we have been living in the midst of alarms and rumours, which, with two doses of inoculation, both of which I took very badly, have pretty well taken up all one's time. We have been asked to volunteer for Garrison Duty in Egypt or India, and the whole battalion has done so. We may go quite soon, we may not go at all; you never know in the army. I shall go out if the Battalion does; tho' I need not, because our medical officer tells me that its a standing wonder to him that with my eyes I even got a home service commission — I could get transferred to another home service unit; but I shall certainly go out with the Batt^n except in the event of conscription. Then there wd be plenty of available men, & I should stay in England

Of his activities at Cambois, he said nothing in his letters to Rubinstein. The relevant passage in the memoirs begins thus:

> Proceeded to Cambois (pronounced Cammus) near Blyth: patrolled the coast of Northumberland: got involved with the barbed-wire entanglements, or fell into the trenches, when inspecting them by night: rather enjoyed this: enjoyed, very much more, popping in from the darkness at intervals and going to sleep on a moth-eaten sofa a couple of inches from an anthracite furnace in a diminutive log-cabin: had little in common with my associates: was extremely and deservedly unpopular.

While, to Rubinstein:

> I arrive in town in time for breakfast on Friday morning (17th) on six days' leave. We must manage to fix something up. What about concerts? Are there any? I'm quite out of the world up here. I shall be pretty full up; by most dexterous pulling of a thousand wires, everyone has managed to gather to London from the four ends of the Earth — Ewan, Hurst, Denroche-Smith, Rooper, Micklem, everybody! Let me know what can be arranged. I leave here on Thursday night.

Everyone, that was, except those in the battlefield, and with them Victor was conducting a regular correspondence of a more intimate kind than with the non-Oxonian Rubinstein. Finding his Cambois fellow-officers antipathetic, he was forced to live on fleeting contacts, in person or by letter, with his undergraduate friends.

Little survives, but what does suggests the tone of the rest. Bernard Strauss wrote to him in November 1915 from the front (whence he had sent Victor a telegram — just before going into action — ending with the words 'GOODBYE LIBERALISM FOR EVER', which Victor had read literally).

My dear Golgotha

Your letter was an inspiration, and a revelation — a revelation (if such were needed) of your nobility of character, and of the real worth and meaning of your Friendship — and it will be an inspiration to me in the long winter months which lie before me. Altho' I have forgotten exactly what I wired on the impulse of the moment, it was never a Goodbye to Liberalism. I think it ran *Goodbye. Liberalism for ever!* — a flaming watchword; no farewell cry of departure. Indeed, as you say, I could not say Goodbye, even if I wished to; for by Liberalism I understand everything worth living and dying for — that is why years ago I once said that you and I were the only two real Liberals in Oxford; to us it was a passionate religion embracing all life's activities, not merely a hotchpotch of political view — γνῶσις not δόξα — it still is. With you, I share the conviction that nothing dies, except what is evil. That is why the thought of Death has no terrors for me: and if I fall, it will be cheerfully and with a good conscience, and with the passionate hope that the sacrifice will not have been in vain — indeed it will not have been.

The letter ended in praise of Winston Churchill's defence of his Dardanelles policy in the House of Commons.

A great man! he will return to his own one day.

Goodnight. Your ever affectionate
Bernard

The nostalgia provoked by such letters must have been hard for Victor to bear in his Northumberland wilderness — harder, perhaps, than for his friends on the Front, who lived with the feeling that they were fighting for an ideal worth preserving. While they were experiencing the comradeship of battle, Victor was engaged in seemingly pointless activity, and instead of *esprit de corps*, he found conflict. Another letter of Strauss's is quoted in *My Dear Timothy*.

My beloved Golgotha,

I have just received your two letters: as I read the first, I imagined for a moment that I was back in Oxford, listening to you declaiming in faultless English with your back to my mantelpiece, with Douglas Jerrold sprawling in an armchair, Agnew with his patient smile, and Jack Haldane and Hobhouse struggling by the window.

Such memories only aggravated Victor's irritation with his fellow-officers, as he later explained:

Oxford had won me with a threefold allurement: she was England, she was youngness, and she was friendship . . . And I had lost all this in the meantime — from the ending of Oxford to the beginning of Repton. I know now that I was myself much to blame for my reaction to the majority of my fellow-officers and for their reaction to me: here was the clash with my father all over again . . . I was eager and naïf: they were jaded and bored, or so it seemed to me. I thrilled to the heat of the sun and the freshness of dew: they thrilled, I thought, to nothing. I hated poverty, and the poverty, above all, that reeked everywhere around us in Northumberland: they struck me as hating the poor, or at least as being terrified of any betterment in working-class conditions that might jeopardise their own. I loved music: they liked musical comedy. My feminism involved an attitude of sexual reverence for women, and I loathed dirty stories . . . they were men of the world. In sum, I reacted to the majority of my fellow-officers very much as a few of my critics have reacted to me — with a mixture of hostility and contempt: and they in their turn very properly dubbed me a prig.

Not long after Victor was seconded to other duties, he wrote a poem 'To certain of my late fellow-officers' which inclines one towards sympathy with them.

> Mean and most vulgar — with no joy in sky,
> Rain, and the smell of grass, and morning dew,
> Flowers, and birds that praise so sacredly,
> And all the gentle things God made for you.
>
> Mean and most vulgar — knowing nought of love
> And the dear friendliness of common life,
> Smiling, that lifts the answering heart above,
> Laughter, that each may fling to each in the strife.
>
> Mean and most vulgar — with this only fear:
> That they who labour but to bring you cheer
> Will rise from their long servitude one day,
> And save your souls, and take your gold away.
>
> But there — life smiles. I would not be unkind;
> So look — I just dismiss you from my mind.

Victor's time with his battalion was mercifully short, but before he left he was at the centre of a drama. His account of it is brief.

[I] borrowed a horse without asking permission in a moment of enthusiasm, never having been on one before: coaxed it down an incline to the ferry you took for Newcastle: didn't know that I had to dismount before the diesel began gasping: was immediately thrown, and brought the horse down on top of me: faced a subalterns' court-martial, the horse being the Colonel's: was found guilty, but can't remember the punishment.

Pencilled and faded notes made by Victor at his court-martial (on the back of his birth certificate) indicate that the charges he faced included obtaining a horse under false pretences, representing that he could ride a horse with spirit, obtaining this horse from a Non-Commissioned Officer, and allowing the horse to lie down endangering the King's Highway. One witness reported seeing him 'careering down the road, and calling for help'. It was wonderfully typical of Victor that he should have opted for a horse with spirit rather than a quiet hack, despite being unable to ride at all: an instance of physical timidity overcome by *hubris*.

The welcome escape route from the battalion opened up in February 1916, when Geoffrey Fisher, Headmaster of Repton and future Archbishop of Canterbury, had an urgent need for a classics master.

My dear Harold,
    Just a hasty line to you — not I'm afraid one of my literary letters! — to apologise for not sending that 35/–. Could you wait a week more for it? For the following reason. I have had the Sixth at Repton definitely offered me, together with a commission in the School OTC. I had a most delightful interview at York last Thursday with the Headmaster, who is a charming man and most keen on getting me. All this has meant a tremendous lot of first-class travelling, wires, telephoning, etc: and a lot more still to come, as I still have to see the Brigadier, on whom the transfer depends. I think it will be alright, as my CO recommends it, but cannot of course say definitely till I've seen the Brigadier. So don't mention it to a soul. You don't mind about the 35/– do you?
                                                    In great haste
                                                    Yours ever
                                                    Victor G.

As Victor was on Home Service, the War Office raised no obstacles to his secondment to Repton, and the Brigadier, unsurprisingly, voiced no objections either. On 8 February, a telegram was despatched to Rubinstein.

REPTON TOUCH CAME OFF HOPE TO BE IN TOWN TOMORROW NIGHT FOR A DAY
OR SO

VICTOR

CHAPTER FIVE

SERVING: A TEACHER!

AS A PLACE I loved Repton as I have loved no other of the places in which it has been my lot to live. . . . The Village was architecturally dull like most Midland villages, but the church with its really marvellous spire, the old Priory buildings and the Hall are clothed in romance for me; and the little walks around — Parsons Hills and Anchor Cave, Orange Ponds and Hundred-Acre, the Shrubs and the Rocks — how charming they were.

So wrote the level-headed historian, David Somervell, many years after he and his companion in arms, Victor Gollancz, had been forced out of Repton.

On Victor, miraculously delivered from the lonely barrenness of his life in Northumberland, the place had a magical effect: it was England, 'youngness' and friendship back again. More than that, it proffered the kind of friendship that Victor was temperamentally attuned to — friendship with himself as *primus inter pares*. St Paul's had shown him little of the public-school spirit. Repton, founded in 1557, had a long history, a great tradition, and a strong sense of community.

In 1916, when Victor arrived, the school was emerging from a period of upheaval. One future Archbishop of Canterbury, the big, eloquent, liberal-minded, generous William Temple had, as head-master between 1910 and 1914, won the hearts of some of his boys, but neglected the bulk of them. Administratively, the school had gone rapidly downhill, and morale was low when, in September 1914, a second future Archbishop of Canterbury, Geoffrey Fisher, came to restore order and the confidence of parents.

In his account of his period at Repton, Victor made considerable efforts to be fair to Fisher, but the headmaster's prudence was as repellent to him as his father's, so he was never able to appreciate the virtues which held the school together at a time of great difficulty. To Fisher, trying to maintain academic standards in the face of wartime staffing problems, this New College scholar with his First in Mods was a godsend. To Victor, Fisher (only seven years his senior) quickly ceased to be 'a charming man' and became 'the old man' or 'the little man'.

The Northumberland pattern of exasperation with his fellows repeated itself at Repton, with a couple of exceptions. In his search for travelling companions on the road to joy and wonder, he was looking towards youth, exhilarating and capable of exhilaration. David Somervell reflected later, 'The first thing to realise about Victor is that he was absurdly young. . . . He was also absurdly clever, absurdly amusing, absurdly childish in many ways, absurdly idealistic in his outlook on life, and absurdly affectionate.'

Within a couple of hours of arriving at his lodgings in Repton, Victor, in his absurdity, was hiding a detested pudding under a bookcase in his landlady's dining room — a subterfuge to which he had frequent recourse, until the occasion when he forgot to remove the evidence later and was exposed by the cat's discovery of a rejected fish.

Victor was tried out with the Lower Sixth, into whose classroom, and lives, he exploded with a lesson in Latin prose. Fisher had given him a set of the class's Latin compositions, but Victor, who had not bothered to correct them, decided to play his first lesson his own way.

> I announced that I'd give a lecture instead — on 'The Comedy and Drama of Latin Prose'. The boys clearly thought me *meshuggah*; but my father had thought it (and said so) so often that I took it for granted. I was tremendously excited. The place had already gone to my head; and now to that climate of enchantment was added a delight in exposition — in exposition for its own sake, in *showing* people things, in coming out with the truth as I saw it. I was born as a schoolmaster during the course of that happy tirade; and a schoolmaster I have remained ever since, though in a number of disguises.

His first class ended with everyone in the classroom roaring a Ciceronian triplicate in chorus, and Victor in a state of intoxicated delight with his new profession. The intoxication expressed itself in a rush of poems about joy, happiness, loveliness and glory. He was looking over the brink of a deeper communion than he had hitherto experienced.

> Till then, for all my friendships, human beings hadn't been much in the picture, or not to my awareness: the communion, the sense of merging, had been with the smell of the grass and the heat of the sun and the feel of the rain: with all natural phenomena, and with the spirit behind them and in them. My friendships had been a matter of contact, often of the closest

contact, but not of merging and being lost. And now it was in and through the boys, above all, that I met the unity.

This was the first new element in my joy. The second argued an interchange with the life of the universe even more mutual than in boyhood.

Greedily, he was reaching out for more contact than could be achieved in the classroom. (In the school chapel, the hymns, 'sung with exaggerated brio by fresh young voices in unison, moved me deeply.') Gaps in the timetable spelt deprivation, so he went back to his lodgings to write to Harold Rubinstein of his enhanced love affair with the universe. He was 'having a most happy time' and looked forward to the great joy of seeing the boys' opening out. 'They are a delightful lot; one or two of them very stupid, but none coarse or vulgar.'

His gusto could not be confined to his own lessons. He gave, on 14 March, his first speech at the Repton School Debating Society, on a motion that 'This house considers that the formation of a Dramatic Society in peace time is desirable.'

> Mr Gollancz then rose and gave us the benefit of his eloquence. He turned his attention to the President, who, he considered, had taken a miserable view of drama. The acted drama is the highest form of art (except the music drama), and one does not go to the drama merely to be amused, but rather to have one's better emotions stirred in the company of other men. In Greece everybody went to the theatre regularly, and the more we cultivate the drama we will approach more nearly the artistic achievements of ancient Greece. He then pointed out how inferior the drama when read was to the drama when acted (hear, hear). Finally, in these days our educational methods are changing; the value of 'making things go' and doing things together is being realised, and consequently societies, literary and dramatic, are really the most vital things in School life.

(Victor's personal preference for reading plays in solitude had been subordinated to his anxiety for communion.)

That same month he announced happily to Rubinstein, 'The muse is active!!!', and soon gave a fuller progress report:

> I am having a far happier time here than ever I dreamed of or hoped. I find my work fascinating — both my classical work with the Sixth, who, if not very clever, are a charming lot of men, & one or two of them already very close friends of mine — & also my English work with a low form. I am reading Keats with these last, & find them not in the least disposed to look on poetry as dull & milk soppy, as I had first feared . . .

The close friends were headed by Leslie Jaques, to whom Victor was drawn by 'his finely chiselled features, high complexion and black curly hair', and even more by 'that loneliness you often feel in young people . . . that makes you gentle in their presence.'

This romantic attachment was the strongest of those he formed at Repton. It was noticed by others, and although Victor himself speculated at length about a possible homosexual element in it, surviving contemporaries dismiss the idea. Jaques seemed merely the apogee of Victor's love affairs with all his close disciples, who were soon taking tea in his rooms and revelling in his mockery of some of their other masters. Those meetings with the boys increased in scale and frequency, as Victor's interest in his colleagues decreased yet further.

He had met his most formidable enemy on the first day. Guy Snape, 'a fine bulldog of a man with a drum-and-drumstick arrangement in his larynx', had made his values clear in an overheard conversation with a colleague. '"It's our solemn duty, mah dear chap," he replied, whacking away at every word with his drumstick, "to instil into the boys such a hatred of the Hun that for the rest of their lives they'll never speak to one again."'

It was an opening line which Victor enjoyed mimicking for the boys, and for his first and best schoolmaster friend, Allan Gorringe. Gorringe and his wife, Moë, a militant feminist pacifist, welcomed Victor, entertained him frequently, and encouraged him to liven things up among the 'morass of high Toryism' in the staff-room — an injunction which made them even more attractive to Victor. Gorringe, gentle — even 'womanish' — was happy to cheer from the side-lines, and offered no challenge to Victor's radical primacy.

David Somervell, whom Victor met at the end of term, was a man of more potent intellect, later to be very successful as a teacher and popularizer of history. Their friendship was more a matter of convenience, mutual respect and relish in the fighting of a common cause. Somervell found Victor a delightful addition to the staff, but had only limited contact with him during that first term, for Victor's mind was totally on the boys and he had been warned by Snape, an inveterate trouble-maker, that he should avoid Somervell like poison.

When term broke up in April, Victor returned to London and the company of the few friends, Rooper and Rubinstein in particular, who were based there. He was involved in a controversy which caused a new upset within his family: Marie Corelli was the unlikely cause. She had written an article for the *Sunday Times* in which she claimed that Shakespeare had an abhorrence of Jews and Germans, and both

Rooper and Victor rallied to Shakespeare's defence. Rooper's letter to the paper drew on textual evidence. Victor's more personal rebuke ended,

> I may add that though I was born a member of the Jewish race, I have no particular sympathy with the Jewish people. My habits of thought, and all my instincts, are Western rather than Eastern, and it is not the Jew in me, but the Liberal, that is offended by a hatred of any race whatever — be they Jews or Indians, or even fellow-countrymen of Goethe and Wagner. Let us loathe, if we will, Jewish legalism and Prussian imperialism — no one detests them more than I; but towards Jews and Germans let our attitude be a little more consonant with that ideal of brotherly love which is one of the sublimest conceptions of the faith which Miss Corelli, I believe, professes.

Impeccable liberal sentiments, but hardly calculated to appeal to orthodox Jewish opinion. The *Jewish World* picked it up and commented:

> We doubt not that the letter from Mr Victor Gollancz which appeared in this week's *Sunday Times* will have given considerable offence to many Jews who read it, and we should not be surprised if the writer intended that it should. In us, however, a perusal of the letter excited deep pity for the poor anaemic-spirited individual who penned it, mitigated, we confess, by a sense of thankfulness that the obvious 'guid conceit' that animates this young gentleman has led him to a candour that at least may be 'useful for future reference'.

It reproduced the last paragraph of the letter, and went on scathingly and at length to denounce him by implication as disloyal, and a fool or a snob.

The following week's *Jewish World* carried Victor's long and eloquent apology for having unwittingly caused great pain to many Jews. He blamed the *Sunday Times* for mutilating his letter, and himself for having expressed badly his plea for universal brotherhood. The *Jewish World* congratulated him on his 'manly and considerate words', and delivered itself of a brief homily on the essential Jewishness of the notion of universal brotherhood.

Victor's fury at having to write the retraction was vented in a letter to Harold Rubinstein.

> You will probably have seen my letter in this week's J.W. rag — if they have published it. Immediately on receipt of my father's letter on Saturday morning — which was really appalling; allowing for hysteria & an obvious desire to work upon my feelings, I could still see in it a great amount of genuine grief, stupid, but there — I wrote him a long letter of what I regarded as abject apology, & despatched it by special messenger. He

amazed me — tho' I fear I had expected it — by not replying a word, but sending thro' my mother (who has been rather wonderful) a statement to the fact that he would consider no resumption of any sort of relations 'til I had removed the original sting by a public apology. I weighed the matter a long time; & came to the conclusion that I had better do so, especially as I heard from other sources that many people — Jews — were seriously offended. Hence my letter in this week's J.W. It is appallingly abject, & I loathe myself for it; but at any rate I have apologised for hurting their damned feelings — without in any way deserting my position. If they interpret it as such in their b— leader, I shall write another letter, & damn the consequences.

I loathe & detest the whole business, & it has put the finishing touch to my antipathy to the whole crew. Northcliffe himself could hardly have produced anything so stupid, vulgar, & malicious as their leader. To have written a letter like that is the most appalling sacrifice to make to my father's feelings — tho' he'll probably not in the least consider it so. I have flatly refused to write a word to the S. Times; & the only people who will read the letter in the J.W. are the people who habitually read the rag — & to buggery with them! (This particular oath, which forgive, is a relic of my Newcastle days!) . . . I'm going to write a psychological novel, tracing a young Jew's gradual revolt from Jewishness.

As Victor by now was financially independent of his father, it is to his credit that he made, through affection, what was to him so intolerable a sacrifice. It illustrates the depth and genuineness of his love of his father, for he abhorred admitting that he had been wrong in anything (except, long in retrospect, in his memoirs and even then selectively and with self-justification). The episode also betrays the insensitivity that so often caused Victor, quite unconsciously, to wound those he loved. No more was recorded of the affair, except a few lines in Alex's favourite paper, the *Jewish Chronicle*, which inserted a tactful reference to Victor's *Jewish World* apology.

Had Victor encountered serious anti-semitism at Repton, it might have tempered his resentment towards the Jewish community, but what little prejudice there was hardly touched him as a member of staff. He was undeniably Jewish in appearance. Somervell recalls a colleague saying, 'he looks as if he'd faint at the sight of a pork chop' — but he was rarely sensitive about it. He had nothing in common with the stage Jews of coarse gentile jokes — vulgarly ostentatious, graspingly mercenary, and clannish — and was himself already a noted *raconteur* of jokes the more sophisticated Jews told against themselves. Thus he was unperturbed when he heard a crony of Snape's remark, 'I don't like our Jew.' Snape's response found a more vulnerable spot.

Waves of laughter came flooding from Pruke [Snape], full of that bonhomie, a bit conspiratorial, that made him so human. 'Ah, mah dear fellow,' he got out on the tide of it, 'ahbsolutely lahmentable!' Then, as if bored with the subject and in contemptuous dismissal: 'The fellow's pahlpably not a gentleman.' I couldn't have understood, at the time, how right he was, for he was using the term in its technical meaning, and I knew nothing of any of that; so I felt rather hurt.

Victor's second term at Repton was made even more joyous than his first, by 'the Paddock, at cricket, on high summer afternoons.'

> The Paddock is a cricket-field . . . at the back of the Priory; it merges into a buttercup meadow, and flows on, watered by streams, to the sky. Hitherward rises a slope; and on it I would lie through those long afternoons in the glare of the sun, with the click of the ball in my ears, and a company of friends by my side, and the smell of the grass in my nostrils, and the yellow and green out beyond . . .
>
> Repton will always mean for me, above everything, the Paddock in summer. Much else was of greater importance: but in terms, not of struggle and of helping seedlings to grow and of making a better world and of the joy that these efforts brought with them, but of a carefree and innocent happiness, the Paddock is my Repton. I had two summers there, and each had its own special quality: the first was dawn and the second was day.

Away from the Paddock, his intimacy with the boys was broadening and deepening. The tea-parties turned into open house, with any pupil free to drop in for a chat or to borrow a book. Such literary afternoons changed character when, after a play-reading, Amyas Ross of the Lower Sixth launched a philippic against the Irish. (The Easter Rising in Dublin was fresh in all memories.) Victor, appalled by Ross's assumption that the race was incapable of self-government and his ignorance of the drive towards it, took him to task. Bob Watson came in with '"hack" points culled from partisan textbooks', and James Darling 'twittered about patriotism and the duty of all good Englishmen to stand by their country: and interjected an attack on the poor, who had somehow cropped up.' Bobby Johnstone reacted wonderingly to Victor's arguments: 'I say, isn't all that *radical*, what you're saying? The radicals are *bloody* people. They ruin the country, and teach the working classes to put on airs.'

> I was flabbergasted. Here was a set of boys, nearly all of whom I knew to be decent and generous, even perhaps great-hearted; and yet not one of them, to judge from their talk, had the smallest degree of sympathy with people less well-off than themselves, or any stomach for an argument that ran counter to their prejudices.

Aldous Huxley, who for a term had been on the Repton staff, had also — though more quickly — been depressed by the boys' opinions, remarking to Somervell: 'Not until I came to Repton did I realise the awful significance of the word *bourgeoisie*.' He fled to Eton. Victor was made of sterner stuff, for 'there and then, without reflecting on consequences, I took my decision. I would talk politics to these boys, and to any others I could get hold of, day in and day out: I would talk politics round the tea-table, politics in the classroom, politics on the Paddock.' By the end of the term the conversations about politics — which as treated by Victor included philosophy, religion and morality — had borne fruit. Amyas Ross, strolling around the Paddock with Victor, 'saw the beastliness of poverty and war with such a sudden and almost intolerable insight as I had experienced myself, so many years earlier, first in the Elgin Avenue drawing-room and then on the train from Westbourne Park.' The others were a tougher proposition: Darling still disliked the idea of equality, while increasingly distressed by the idea of poverty; Johnstone was bothered, but unconvinced; Watson 'blustered'; Jaques was silent.

Victor kept politics out of the classroom that term, not yet being sure enough of his ground, but his conversations outside school hours with sympathetic masters, his extra-curricular dealings with the boys, and his reading were all stimulating him to deeper thought about the nature of education. In that term he wrote an article on 'Public School Reform', and was peeved to have it rejected by the *Daily News*. He had made no effort to improve relations with his colleagues, and was beginning to harbour a deep antipathy to one of the housemasters, Jacky Shearme. 'I could find nothing in that hobbling little figure but the three emotions he specialised in: hatred of the Hun, fear of the radicals, and distrust of the working class.'

Hatred of the Hun among his young friends also troubled Victor, but he loved them and thought they could be saved.

> Not a single opportunity did I miss of being with my friends during the remainder of that July: not a walk, not a service in Chapel, not an hour on the Paddock. And when the end had really come, and the photograph of our little play-reading group had been taken in the porch, and they had said good-bye, I sat down and began wondering what it would feel like — this is exactly how I thought of it — to see nothing really alive all those miserable weeks. Couldn't I prolong things a bit?

To that end, he ran over to James Darling's house and arranged that, when he left with some other boys at 6 o'clock in the morning, they should all go into Derby for breakfast. 'I had the feeling that, if only for a few hours, I had got the better of fate.'

Enemies on the staff, and undisguised emotional dependence on the boys: it was small wonder that Fisher was perturbed. During the holidays, while at work in Lloyd George's Ministry of Munitions, Victor received a warning letter from the headmaster.

'I must write a line to you,' it ran, 'to pull you up in the path you are pursuing before it is too late.' Friendliness between masters and boys was, of course, all to the good; but there was a certain line that should not be passed, and a certain dignity and reserve that every master should maintain. I had not maintained it; and he wanted to save me from finding out for myself that such a course of action did not pay. I had to realise that there were two distinct classes in a Public School — the teachers and the taught; classes having constant relations with one another, no doubt, but distinct and separate none the less. The 'popular' master was suspect, and rightly so, by his colleagues and the more thoughtful among the boys. 'If I did not think that parts of your work have been valuable, I should not have troubled to write to you. Yours sincerely, G. F. Fisher.'

The letter worried Victor. Was he suspected of playing for popularity? Had he been wrong in thinking his affection for his pupils was reciprocated? He wrote for clarification, and it arrived a fortnight later.

I refuse to write long letters from the tops of Welsh mountains. I will give you two instances of what I mean. You had some boys up to dinner last term, and borrowed the prefects' room gramophone to amuse them with. You also went with a lot of boys to Derby on the last morning, and gave them a feed there. This sort of thing will never do. Yours sincerely, G. F. Fisher.

Victor, deeply relieved, dismissed Fisher's strictures from his mind. He would not be bound by unacceptable class distinctions — a view he held still in 1952.

. . . that business of 'teachers' and 'taught' — 'there are two distinct classes: the teachers and the taught' — how insensitive it is, how arrogant, how mechanical, how contrary to what, when there is a genuine 'teacher' about, is really seen to be happening! For in true education there are no teachers and no taught. There is an interchange: the master learns as he teaches, the pupil teaches as he learns. Both give, and both receive. The master gives his wisdom, the boy gives his freshness: and they react on one another, this wisdom and this freshness, and transform one another.

In enunciating later a principle to which he was already committed before he returned to Repton in the autumn of 1916, Victor was forgetting still that what came easily and naturally to him was difficult for his less gifted colleagues. Darling, who himself became a highly respected and successful headmaster, recalled Victor as 'a genius of a schoolmaster', and his opinion of him is borne out by many sources. That genius, his carefree intimacy with the boys, and his overt contempt for many of his colleagues made their job more difficult, and made the boys think less of them. He had truly, as he put it himself, a *mana* (charisma), and he used it to the pupils' benefit, but for those colleagues lined up against him this *mana* was threatening. The housemasters, and particularly Shearme, were uneasy at the extent to which the newcomer was winning their own boys away from them. Victor made a resolution to stop disparaging his colleagues to the boys, but he could not often live up to it.

He was offered a permanent job at the Ministry, but chose to return to Repton, his convictions intact and even strengthened by Fisher's rejected warning. Fisher, conscious of Victor's pedagogic gifts, now promoted him to the Upper Sixth, where Ross and Darling awaited him, with Jaques to follow. Among the other boys in this small class were Harford and Manoukian, destined quickly to become equally intimate with Victor, who had decided that he need not confine himself to the syllabus, particularly once the end-of-term Oxbridge scholarship exams were out of the way. So though he continued teaching Latin prose, his best efforts were reserved for a series of lectures on Greece, and its drama, literature, philosophy and religion. The boys responded well and discussion became intense, with classes running over time and Victor 'heady with elation'.

Somervell, writing about it almost thirty years later, said:

> He took charge of the Classical Upper Sixth — it was a rather particularly good form by Repton standards — and he just took them by storm. There happened as between Victor and these boys, what I have never seen happen anywhere else, education not by mimetic drill but by direct communion or inspiration. Toynbee has some profound pages on the difference between these two modes of education, the ordinary and the extra-ordinary. . . . We call both education, but they are really two different things; and the latter of the two is not only a rare but a disturbing phenomenon. When you see it you either like it or dislike it very much, and most people will — perhaps rightly — dislike it.

Much later, James Harford recalled

> the influence of the most vivid and vital personality of all my experience then or since. . . . His impact on the classical sixth at Repton was cataclysmic, messianic. He seemed to be the incarnation of all the godlike elements in the spirit of man.

VG's presence exuded energy, goodwill and gusto. He was of middle height, already a little inclined to fat, with a large smooth face of an interesting pallor, small black moustache, and small dark eyes with an expression of the most restless and alert intelligence. He had bad sight and always wore glasses. He spoke in a very clear animated voice, with a range of tone which included an excited bantering falsetto which was quite irresistibly comic. Although he was constrained to wear khaki uniform a great part of the time, he was the most unmilitary figure one could conceive.

Notions of discipline and status were completely foreign to Victor's nature. To us he was an undergraduate among undergraduates — a fourth year man among 'freshers'.

They were fascinated by his brilliance and magnetism, which made Latin composition 'alluring and exciting'. More potent still was his opening up to them of the ideas of Plato and Aristotle, 'woven into a rich and exhilarating revelation of the possibilities of men's nature and the means by which a corrupt society could be transformed and the common man freed from the bonds of ignorance and materialism. Victor . . . was a philosophical radical, and libertarian ideas pervaded his outlook, his conduct and his teaching. All the resources of his striking and abundant personality were made available to us, and the warmth and brilliance of his spirit blazed down on us like the sun at midday.'

For Harford, Somervell and Gollancz were in many ways complementary. 'On the one hand adult, mature, factual, dated, temperate, traditional, English: on the other, youthful, sweeping, generalised, heady, exuberant, Graeco-Jewish.'

Darling, also writing in old age, recalled how no teacher except Somervell had till then 'touched my imagination or awakened any enthusiasms'.

Gollancz altered all that.

In a classroom he was electric. He would sweep into the room, usually late, with a disreputable gown under his arm and plunge straight into a fluent outpouring of whatever had been latest in his mind. No matter if this had little to do with the nominated subject of the period. Plato's *Republic* gave him full scope for anything. There was an exciting freshness about everything which he taught and he treated us more like undergraduates in a tutorial than as schoolboys in a class. His mind ranged from China to Peru and from the prophet Isaiah to his pet aversion, Lloyd George.* It covered

*Darling anticipates here. Victor's disillusionment with Lloyd George developed slowly, and only hardened into a sense of near-betrayal in 1918, when Lloyd George not only failed to exhibit the required enthusiasm for the League of Nations, but advocated a crushing retribution on the Germans.

in the process the glories of the age of Pericles, the Italian painters and the music of Wagner for which he was in the process of an enthusiasm. It was impossible not to be carried away by him but he welcomed argument and disagreement. The tremendous range of his intellect may have been his greatest quality, but it was the enthusiasm which carried all before it, and enthusiasm is the one indispensable quality of a good teacher. Suddenly our eyes were opened to the whole range of human intellectual endeavour as well as to Socrates, Plato and the Greek tragedians. He helped us to write Latin prose as though we thought in Latin, trying to express the sense rather than to translate the words. He gave us Literature, and Poetry and Art and Music.

Both Harford and Darling emphasized in their memoirs the highly emotional state of the boys Victor was teaching, most of whom expected to die in the war. As Harford pointed out, it was no surprise that the atmosphere was overcharged, and 'the thoughts of youth deeper even than is usual'. Victor, said Darling, 'did give us something exciting to live for and enjoy'.

Possibly Victor's greatest enthusiasm was for the ideals of education itself. One lecture to his class is reconstructed in *More for Timothy*: an examination of the Platonic search for perfect Beauty and hence God, and its achievement through education. It incorporated Victor's thinking on how a teacher should teach. The aim of education 'is not to inculcate — to fill a vessel so far empty: but to "convert" — to turn the soul round, that our eyes may see the light. That is done through liberation of the pupils' souls from all impediments, for "the souls of men and women are divine".' A teacher 'does his pupils the best service when he helps them struggle free'. The modern concept of education is based on the premise that the child needs to be tamed. 'You see the result in a world of masters and slaves, of greed and stupidity, of bloodshed and strife — and yet a world, for all that, in which decency, nobility even, are always breaking through.'

> There is only one way in which an older man can help a younger so to free himself; and that is by fostering his sense of joy . . . by remodelling education so as to make it a means for releasing all those stores of spiritual and intellectual energy that lie hid in a child, we shall be doing more than we could ever do otherwise to render manifest that men and women are truly created in the image of God.

It was Victor's answer to Fisher, delivered instead to the Upper Sixth. The power of his *mana* can be seen in the number of his pupils who became schoolteachers, for Victor's enthusiasm for this highest calling of all, was communicated to them at the most crucial time.

Victor delayed discussion of contemporary affairs with the Upper Sixth until he had laid the intellectual ground-work through examination of the Greek world. When he felt they were ready, he set them an essay on poverty. Most put in a disappointing performance, and Victor was troubled by their 'vicious snobbism', but in the ensuing argument it became clear that 'they were reaching out, nearly all, for the good, and it was only because they were ignorant of undeniable facts, and hadn't learned how to think, that their "good" was so questionable.' And so, from then on, began 'the second or classroom phase of our "movement" at Repton'. Every day there were political or sociological discussions of 'passionate sincerity and fierce argumentativeness on the boys' side and of elation on mine'. The session he remembered best arose from an essay on the question whether, knowing the universe would end tomorrow and nothing would follow, they would do something tonight that could harm no one but they had always thought wrong. For Victor it was a means of getting down to 'ethical bedrock': he was delighted by the morality they demonstrated. Yet the assumption, for the purposes of the argument, that there was no after-life led to more trouble with Fisher. Victor wrote to Rubinstein in fury:

> Fisher has come forward with an amazing accusation that I had influenced ('it appears to me' he said in effect 'that you must have influenced') a boy to conceive doubts of the Divinity of Christ! An amazing accusation, without a thread of truth in it (except, perhaps, in so far as I had made the boy *think*) which I made the nasty little man withdraw.
>
> Also, last night I had it out with him on the subject of the correspondence of the holidays, about 'too great friendliness. . . . ' I found his mind tiny & cold, & his views on education deplorable . . . I shall hope to be at the Ministry after Xmas — my hands are too much tied here . . . But the boys are a joy — & I'm not going to allow any miserable little pedantic parson of a schoolmaster to make me alter my attitude towards them. . . .

Victor's motivation to go into the ministry was purely negative. The attractions of Repton were too positive to be ignored, 'pedantic parson' notwithstanding. A poem he wrote around this period summed up his reasons for staying.

ON BEING INVITED TO GO INTO THE MINISTRY OF MUNITIONS

Sit here forever, talking steel
And helping slowly to amass
A safe reserve of zinc and brass?
    What think you I should feel,

Who have heard the cheering madly flung
From myriad throats when Repton wins;
Who have known the place where joy begins,
Where every soul is young?

So he stayed, and hurled himself into the saving of the young from those he found contemptible. He took his battle regularly into the debating society, where his influence permeated the speeches of his pupils, and where he was constantly available to back up their stumbling attempts to purvey his message. The motions were connected with the vital issues: humanities versus sciences, the state's duty to the poor, women and the vote. David Somervell supported Victor in his espousal of guild socialism, a creed of 'infinite possibilities', and the alliance went beyond the debating chamber into the classroom:

> It was, of course, inevitable that I [Somervell] should go into partnership with Victor. He was a friendly soul with an expansive temperament. His boys were, in a sense, already my boys. He consulted me about everything, and I identified myself entirely with 'the experiments'. If I had seen danger ahead I should still have done so, but I did not; nor did anyone else. The headmaster . . . gave us his blessing, and the housemasters made no open objection. Far the most important of them was old Harry Vassall, chairman of the O R Society and right hand man of three successive headmasters. I remember him saying to me in the early days, 'This is one of the best things that has happened in Repton in the thirty years I've known it.'

The chief experiment was the establishing of a civics class, scheduled to begin after Christmas. This was not to be limited — like such classes in America — to the study of institutions. It was to tackle the great issues of the day, the great ideas, 'the great movements that were battling everywhere around: imperialism of this sort and that; militarism and a League of Nations; capitalism and socialism, competition and co-operation.' Those issues that 'would shape the future of the world'.

As worked out by Victor and Somervell, enrolment in the class, to be held in leisure time, would be voluntary, with an undertaking to attend weekly for at least a term. 'We went down to see Fisher. David was bland, I was eloquent. Quite a series of interviews followed. In the end, just as Christmas was looming, Fisher laughingly agreed.'

Both Victor and Somervell are very hard on Fisher in their

memoirs, seeing as duplicity his acquiescence to experiment: he would benefit from successes yet remain free to distance himself from failures. In fact, Fisher was being rather brave. The divisions among the staff were widening, and were exposed in the debating society in December. The motion that 'in the opinion of this house the dismemberment of Germany is absolutely essential for the future peace of Europe' established battle lines between the proposer — Snape — and the opposers — Somervell and Victor. Snape contended forcibly that peace could be ensured only by tearing militaristic Prussia 'away from the German body'. Somervell insisted that the Allies were fighting 'to change the mood of Germany, not to dismember her body' which latter course Victor condemned as creating 'a perpetual spirit of revenge and hatred'.

The motion was defeated in the Upper House (composed of those who had spoken in the society at least once, and therefore dominated by the Sixth) and carried in the Lower. The seeds of division had already been sown. Snape hated Somervell and Somervell hated Snape, whom he always considered the only wicked man he had had close contact with. Snape resented Somervell out of professional jealousy and also 'because I [Somervell] was everything that he was not. I was a gentleman by birth, a public school man, a personal friend of the headmaster, easy going, casual and amusing, a man who never seemed to work hard or take anything seriously but none the less "got away with it".'

Politically, the more radical Victor was more abhorrent to Snape, but his Jewishness, and the fact that he was 'pahlpably not a gentleman' at least disqualified him for the worst of Snape's social jealousy. Victor, for his part, made efforts to like his main enemies; Shearme, who rarely challenged Victor publicly, and Fisher, who tried to hold the centre, became objects of loathing. When Somervell saw the proofs of *More for Timothy* he took exception to Victor's retroactive tolerance of Snape, but Victor was not exaggerating his own charity. He was touched by Snape's devotion to his physically handicapped child and helped throughout his time at Repton to coach the boy, and he and Snape, once their enmity had brought Victor down, exchanged friendly letters. Snape was the most vociferous enemy of the 'experiments', but it was all above board. More dangerous were those who refused to come out into the open; those who were better regarded within the school than the rather ridiculous Snape; those who silently resented Victor's obvious contempt for them — a contempt made clear in a vilificatory sonnet (almost certainly aimed at Shearme):

> Poor pitiful old man . . .
>   Do you ever bow your head in shame, before
> Souls that are free & generous as the wind?

Victor's attitude to the war now differed considerably from that he had expressed in *Varsity/Isis* in 1914. In the interim, the right-wing views of his fellow-officers and staff-room colleagues had driven out the last vestiges of his hard line on Prussian militarism and left a thoroughgoing liberalism. In *More for Timothy* he explained why he had not believed the Germans to be solely responsible for the outbreak of war. Most of the blame lay with the 'personal egotism and greed' of all humanity, the nationalism of all countries and the clash of capitalistic imperialisms.

> Why, then, did I want to win? Because — oh, because I didn't like the idea of being conquered: because I loved England: because the war, having happened, was *there*, and you must choose between the belligerents: because I hated nationalistic war-mongering, and though there wasn't very much in all this talk about Prussian militarism — hadn't others been militaristic too, and how, for the matter of that, had we built our own Empire? — still there was *something* in it, still the militarism of Germany, as Germany had developed, was almost symbolic of barking lieutenants and bullying sergeant-majors and uniforms and obedience and everything else I found loathsome or ridiculous. At its simplest: an Allied victory would give far more hope to the world than a German one.

(By Snape's standards, such a view was no doubt insufficiently patriotic, even though Victor was not challenging the premise that a British victory was desirable. His view of how that victory should be imposed on Germany was out of sympathy not only with the right-wingers among his colleagues, but with many stalwarts of the Liberal party, and these divisions were to deepen during the military catastrophes of 1917 and 1918. At the end of Christmas term 1916 he was content: the civics class was being set up and the boys were enthusiastic, and although he had decided that voices other than his own should be heard in the class, he could be confident that his views would triumph.)

At this period, a good deal of his spare time was taken up in planning a book called *The Making of Women*, a project first mooted at Oxford. It had taken him some time to find a publisher, but eventually Stanley Unwin agreed, provided Victor would take 300 copies. The star among his contributors was the feminist Maude Royden, Ralph Rooper's aunt, and the book was intended mainly as a plea for a moderate feminism.

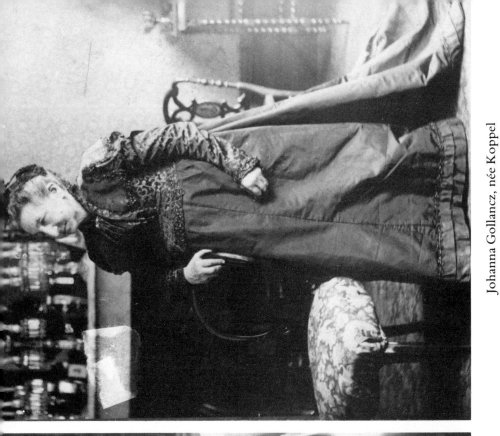

The Rev. Samuel Marcus Gollancz

Johanna Gollancz, née Koppel

Alexander Gollancz

Nellie Gollancz,
née Helena Michaelson

Hermann Gollancz as a young man

Israel Gollancz

Nellie Gollancz (sitting, third from left) with her mother (second from left) and other members of the family in the garden of 256 Elgin Avenue. Winifred, May and Victor, *l. to r.*, are standing at the back.

Victor in the garden of
256 Elgin Avenue

Victor at Oxford

At Repton

Above: The schoolmaster at Repton with his play-reading group

Right: David Somervell at Repton

Below: Passport photograph, 1918

Above: Joseph Solomon by Solomon J. Solomon

Above right: Helena Solomon, née Lichtenstadt, by Solomon J. Solomon

Right: The Rev. Albert Löwy

Ernest and Henrietta Lowy, née Solomon

Ruth shortly before
her marriage

Ruth at the
time of her first
meeting with
Victor

Right: The wedding, 1919

Above: The young parents with Livia, 1921

Left: Ruth with Diana and Livia, 1923

This was Victor's first contact with publishing, but he had already shown his anxiety to get into print. When his friend Ewan Agnew married a woman to whom Victor was much attached, he had a collection of his own poems privately printed and dedicated to the couple. Joy is the theme of most of the eighteen printed poems: joy sought, joy achieved, joy temporarily lost. Some are specifically hymns to the Creator. Others are concerned with the indirect worship of God through his creation. All are a homage to feeling, to emotion, to the particles that make up the world.

Yet Victor was not immune to frustration. He was not easily content with a life that yielded him only a measure of the experience he wanted. Though his Repton disciples brought him much happiness, they could not fill his every waking hour, and there were times when other worlds beckoned. After his return to Repton from the Agnew wedding (which he had enjoyed hugely: the chief bridesmaid was like a goddess), he wrote to Rubinstein 'I'm very busy, & faintly bored — not in my work, but because I pine for London & the people there. These Snapes . . . & Slimies [Somervells] — my God, awful. Even the Gorringes are become quite deplorably dingy.'

Such splenetic outbursts were usually to signal new ventures; Victor's energies demanded fresh outlets. From 1917, his writing and editing plans were growing apace.

> I hope you will send me as detailed a criticism as possible of my introductory essay, which Ralph has, I think, handed over to you. I am anxious for it to be as good as I can make it.
>
> I am also writing a little volume of lectures on the Republic of Plato, which I hope Macmillan will publish.

The Plato project did not come to anything, but the feminist essays did.

Victor's plans for the book were not fully realized, however; it was a much slimmer and less ambitious volume than he had anticipated, and though the reviews were moderately enthusiastic, he was not satisfied. In several letters to Rubinstein he urged him to use his influence to have it reviewed by leading feminists, to 'wangle some Jew (!) stunt in the Jewish Chronicle or somewhere', and to bring it to the attention of his correspondents — 'e.g. the Löwys'. It went into a second edition, but failed to create the stir Victor had hoped for, largely because it was too moderate in its central thesis — that extreme feminists were wrongheaded in appreciating no distinctions between men and women. An educational programme was outlined that would fit girls for earning their own living, while the endowment of motherhood was recommended to ensure that their options remained open. Victor's eloquence was restrained until towards the end of his summing up: 'We live at present in the shadow of the capitalist and his press, we are dragooned by bureaucrats, and we train up our sons to bow the knee to every piece of respectable hypocrisy. Feminism, if it really stands for the freedom of women, must stand for the overthrow of this rotten structure. It can only fully achieve its purpose by helping on the triumph of the wider policy of progressive humanity . . .'

Despite the attacks on capitalism, Victor was still a committed, if idiosyncratic, Liberal. A 1917 letter to Rubinstein gives the flavour:

> I'm dining with R B R [Rooper] & some people called Burns, who are carrying on a vigorous Liberal propaganda in the newspapers, & want me to take part. I've just finished 'New Worlds for Old' which I've never read before, & don't think much of — too Webbite — its extraordinary how he can't keep 'officials' & 'the machine' from slipping in, against his obvious desire. On the other hand, B. Russell's 'Social Reconstruction' is a wonderful book — & I'm getting more in sympathy with Guild, as I get more out of sympathy with State, Socialism. Who publishes Orage's book 'National Guilds'? And is that the right title? I've ordered it at the shop here, but they don't seem able to trace it.
>
> I hope you read your 'Nation' every week — its worth a thousand of your decayed 'New Statesman'.

His flirtation with guild socialism lasted for some years until it was discredited. Otherwise his dislike of any idea that smacked of totalitarianism kept him in the Liberal camp, despite all disappointments, until the 1930s. What he preached to the Repton boys was his own mixture of religion and politics — a combination of Christian ethics, mysticism, belief in the perfectibility of man, and advocacy of social equality and individual liberty. It was Utopian, but it was not socialist in the commonly understood sense, yet his relentless eloquence, his immoderacy of expression, the fervour of his converts, his alienation of his colleagues and the events of 1917–18 combined to make him seem a dangerous radical.

The civics class began undramatically, with a solid series of lectures, mainly by Victor and Somervell, on such issues as national and international reconstruction, parliamentary reform, the position of women and the future of the Empire. It was a great success, with more applications for membership than could be accommodated, and its influence penetrated even the staid pages of the *Reptonian*, where an anonymous letter asked that the *Nation* be made available to boys, and an editorial in May criticized public schools — including Repton

— for paying insufficient attention to the purpose of education, defined as '*to teach a man that he is a rational part in the scheme of the existence of things, and to fit him out to play his part as such.*' The most senior and most distinguished of the housemasters, Harry Vassall, was as approving of the civics class as he was of Victor-Somervell experiments in general, and most staff observers were neutral at worst. This latent support, had it been mobilized by the leading spirits, might have helped avert later trouble.

The original intention had been to seek out a broad range of lecturers, but, in the event, occasional contributions from William Temple and Hooton (a liberal social-credit enthusiast on the staff) were the only variety in an otherwise unrelieved diet of Victor's and Somervell's respective brands of liberalism. They did invite Snape to give two lectures on Conservatism, but this attempt to demonstrate open-mindedness backfired. Snape, whose early attempt to sow dissension between them had failed, was making no efforts to disguise his mounting antagonism to their joint scheme. He was a powerful presence in the no-man's land of the debating society, but in the civics class he was effectively on enemy territory. Somervell records:

> He accepted the offer with transparent insincerity and before the time came exhausted his ingenuity in trying to pick a quarrel which would give him an excuse for backing out and putting the blame on us. In this he failed, and so the lectures were delivered. They were quite amazingly bad. We had expected at least a fluent and vigorous display of jingoism and sentiment, but presumably he was embarrassed by our own presence. At one point (or perhaps more than one) Gollancz failed to restrain his facial expression, and an electric dialogue between the two interrupted the lame and stumbling discourse.

Victor, in his account of the episode, blames himself both for attending the lectures and, having turned up, for infuriating Snape as he did. Whoever was at fault, it was an unedifying consequence that two masters should quarrel acrimoniously in the presence of a large number of their pupils, and it ensured even more bitter enmity from Snape.

That the development of the experiments went on unchecked had a great deal to do with the personality of the leaders among the boys, who, in Somervell's words, combined enthusiasm with respect-ability. Harford, Jaques, Holdsworth and Darling were all natural gentlemen who knew where to draw the line. Holdsworth was a talented athlete who became a teacher at Harrow; Jaques became an Eton schoolmaster; Harford was first a teacher and later a colonial governor; Darling became a pioneering headmaster at Geelong

Grammar School in Australia. (He and Harford were eventually knighted.) They were all deeply influenced by Victor, but they had no desire to revolutionize society; their essential steadiness freed Fisher and their housemasters from anxiety. When Harford proposed that they should found a journal, Fisher was agreeable.

A Public School Looks at the World — or the *Pubber*, as it was better known, came out first in June 1917. It had been founded, James Harford explained in his editorial, 'in the belief that the study of politics . . . is the most absorbing study in the world.'

'It will be very good, I think,' wrote Victor to Rubinstein, urging him to buy it on publication.

Harford's very moderation was questioned in the *Manchester Guardian*, which, in a broadly approving review, found fault with his apparent implication that politics is a study to be enjoyed rather than the means of attaining a better society. Perhaps smarting from this criticism, he wrote an article on 'Sin', affirming that 'the happiness that man is to seek is an active, a creative, a vigorous, a splendid thing. It must be perpetual struggle and effort, perpetual love and work for others.'

It was high-minded stuff, and high-mindedness was the hallmark of the journal. In the first two issues, Manoukian wrote about the rights of small nations (specifically Armenia), Benn Levy, the future playwright and Labour MP, recommended the reform of women's education, Ross's article 'Psychology and Politics' considered that the politician should 'aim at Plato's ideal of the perfect combination of intellect and emotion', and Holdsworth appealed for the cultivation of taste, for 'to the Creator, who takes pleasure in what He creates, a world devoid of taste is a world devoid of value, interest, and all that can make it worth creating.'

The former and the present headmasters gave their *imprimatur*; in the first issue Temple supported widespread educational reforms, and Fisher (in his Speech Day sermon, reproduced in the second) called for self-sacrifice in war and in peace to bring about a better world governed by Christian principles and brotherhood. Victor and Somervell shared the burden of full and regular notes on current affairs, and were models of objectivity and moderation. There were book reviews and poetry, including a sentimental offering from Victor:

THE CINEMA

I love to go where humble people, weeping
At some poor tale of innocence and woe,
Watch breathlessly, or feel their hearts a-leaping
At old heroic deeds of long ago.

I love to sit, and, turning to my neighbour,
  Ask of him, questioning, some trivial thing,
And see him, wearied with much sorry labour,
  Smile, and then make a kindly answering.

I love to think that these are all my brothers,
  With hearts as warm and friendly as my own,
And others everywhere, and countless others,
  And no man going through the world alone.

Under Harford's editorship, the two summer term issues were a success, both financially and critically. Victor was elated, for in addition to the *Pubber* and the civics classes, he had, as he put it to Rubinstein, 'with the aid of Slimey & another man . . . prepared a vast bombshell for the little man Fisher, in the shape of a great scheme of reconstruction for the classical side of the school, making it really liberal (& I hope Liberal — anti-George) & humane. If it goes through, I really think it will be something rather epoch-making.'

'The little man' responded very positively to the suggestions (which Somervell drafted) for providing most of the senior boys with a syllabus including classes in modern history, world history, general principles of science, and political science and economics. It was he who juggled the time-tables so as to allow seven hours a week for these innovations, which were to take effect at the beginning of the Christmas term.

So . . . the term ended, for me [Victor], in a mood of quiet exaltation. Everything was going so wonderfully! I had a vision of innumerable Pubbers, of a Civics class everywhere, of curricula increasingly humane: of an England saved by schoolboys from poverty and an earth purged in classrooms of war. But I was sorrowful, too, at the thought that Jim Harford and Holdsworth, and so many others, would be leaving for ever. Most schoolmasters, I suspect, or at any rate most sensitive ones, are saddened by the feeling of self-division, of losing a precious part of one's own person, that I experienced then. No longer to participate in the development from seedling to plant, from bud to flower! There are few lonelinesses like it.

They were not the first of Victor's boys to leave. Manoukian had joined up before the end of the summer term and was killed shortly afterwards. Harford, Holdsworth and Jaques went off in July. Again, Victor found the good-byes terribly painful. He had established the custom of holding gatherings in London for boys on holiday from school, or army camps. High-minded or not, the closeness of death made them hunger for light-hearted entertainment, and Victor, his youthful priggishness about musical comedy forgotten, shared their pleasure in revues and shows like *Bubbly* and *Tails Up*. They went to the same ones over and over again, and celebrated their reunions with champagne and a good dinner. Their favourites were Leslie Henson and Jack Buchanan, and Victor entered into the spirit of the thing with impersonations of them. Harford thought him the most entertaining person he had ever met; his anecdotes were excellent, and his mimicry succeeded through sheer verve. To young men training for war, Victor's *joie de vivre* was infectious and vastly cheering. It was, said Harford, 'incredibly un-English' to boys accustomed to English reserve, who saw their quondam schoolmaster rolling on the floor with laughter. Some of the evenings ended in 36A Dryden Chambers, a set of rooms he shared for a while with Ralph Rooper and Adrian Boult after his parents' wartime move from London. (Boult remembered his holding a party for eight to ten boys on one of the nights they coincided there.) So contact was maintained for a time between old boys and present pupils.

Victor's openness with the boys can be gauged from a few surviving letters to James Darling (not even one of his special favourites). For a schoolteacher in 1917 to address a pupil as 'My dear Jimmy', refer to a fellow-teacher as 'Slimey', and sign off 'Love from Victor G' was a breach of etiquette to confirm Fisher's worst fears. Financially Victor was better off than ever before, for in addition to his Repton salary he was being paid to work for Seebohm Rowntree on the Reconstruction Committee,★ so he could afford to indulge freely in frivolous and expensive evenings with his young friends.

He returned to Repton towards the end of September, refreshed and optimistic, his thirst for outside experience slaked by his work for Rowntree. (He had even been sent on a short trip to Ireland to investigate the effects of land and housing acts.) The civics class had attracted attention outside Repton: even Eton had taken up the idea. Amyas Ross, Victor's first convert, was now the acknowledged leader of the movement, and editor of the *Pubber*. As a House captain, he

★The Reconstruction Committee, set up in March 1916, was designed for a job much like that William Beveridge was to do a quarter of a century later. It was given ministry status in July 1917, and proponents believed it would prepare the ground for a new British spirit and outlook, as well as for an administrative reconstruction of social and economic policy using the apparatus of wartime control. Rowntree, the great humanitarian and tireless worker for social justice, was dropped from its Advisory Council in 1918, but kept in touch for the rest of its short life. After the war, the coalition government ignored its work and dismantled the wartime controls as quickly as possible.

began his own experiments, or 'stunts' as they came to be known, and through them he transformed the ethos of Priory House. Ross, wrote Somervell, 'was fanatical about the welfare of the House of which he was head, and which he took over after a year and a half of disastrous mismanagement on pseudo Prussian lines. His ideal was of a jolly community of friends and equals of all ages and dignities, inspired by a vivid interest in the things that really mattered.' Through his inspiration, even the most ordinary of the boys were caught up in the study of politics, literature and art. The effect on the morals of the Priory boys was remarkable. A House notorious for widespread homosexuality and masturbation became famous for chastity.

Ross's achievements stemmed from an imaginative humanitarianism allied to a compelling personality, but there was, as far as the future of the experiments was concerned, another side to the coin. As well as 'very able and almost savagely sincere' he was by now fanatically left-wing and a champion of the Russian Revolution. With the moderate Harford generation gone to war, Ross stood head and shoulders above his fellow-pupils, and while the enemies of the experiments found their suspicions confirmed, the neutral sceptics took alarm. The political climate from late 1917 to spring 1918 provided ample scope for controversy between the 'smash Germany' jingoists and the proponents of a negotiated peace, deemed 'pacifists', a term close to 'traitor' in some minds at the time.

There was public evidence of resentment early in the term when a letter in the *Reptonian* attacked Victor and Somervell by implication in a condemnation of their 'movement for turning Repton into a collection of little prigs'. No one could have doubted that they were behind all the political activity, with the greater part of the credit or blame attaching to the more charismatic Victor, who had set Ross off on his independent, more Bolshevik path and had also injected the mystical elements. Ross's *Pubber* was full of Victor-inspired religious feeling, and Ross's own article in the November issue on 'The Best Life' spoke of God as the Ideal Life: 'man, to realise it, must be swallowed up in God's personality.' That was uncontentious, but two other articles were not. First there was Darling's view — that patriotism was worthless if inspired by narrow capitalist self-interest, but noble if in its supra-nationalism it was based in love of humanity. An attack on this piece was deflected by a rumour of Fisher's pleasure in it; he had apparently found it suitable for a Repton pulpit.

Ross's second article enjoyed no such patronage. 'State your Terms' examined the government's apparent reluctance to do so, which it attributed to either serious divisions among the Allies, or the government's fear of admitting that rather than fighting for right and universal peace, its objectives had been self-aggrandisement.

The reaction bore Shearme's stamp. He persuaded the less-than-clever football captain to write to the *Reptonian*, complaining of the 'cosmopolitan influence' vitiating the 'healthy patriotism' of the school. This obvious dig at Victor's Jewishness was rejected by the journal's censor, Somervell, but future issues of the *Pubber* carried the disclaimer: 'Nothing that appears in this paper is to be taken as expressing the opinion of the school as a whole.'

In an effort to pacify the patriots further, the *Pubber* faction asked one of their number, Brownjohn (with whom they were on friendly terms) to write a letter to the journal challenging its 'heresies', so that they could reply. Brownjohn sent in six pages of rhetoric about 'poisonous weeds of pacifism', virtually accusing the heretics of shirking through cowardice. Somervell and Gollancz composed what was both an answer and a parody, and showed it to Brownjohn, thus making a dedicated enemy of him also. Fisher banned both letters from publication.

The next *Pubber* editorial, a committee effort, affirmed the paper's commitment to 'the great ideals for which England first entered the war', cited *The Times* in support of its views on magnanimity in victory, defended its right to criticize the government constructively and held out an olive-branch by declaring that its policy — except in matters of detail — was that held 'in common with the vast majority of Englishmen'. In the correspondence column Fisher showed his approval: 'No one will suppose that I agree with all your views: with some I violently disagree. But the impartial reader of your editorial will not fail to note how closely you anticipate the spirit and even some of the details of President Wilson's speech to Congress on December 4th last.' The Headmaster could hardly have given them more support without placing himself in their camp.

Meanwhile, the changes in the Sixth-Form curriculum had been greeted enthusiastically by that respectable organ, the *Reptonian* (which Victor despised). It observed with wonderment that, although the restructured and broadened time-table was 'great', the pupils were still unsatisfied. Societies had suddenly become so numerous as to be 'absolutely bewildering'. In addition to the comparatively recently founded philatelic society, music club and civics class, there had now sprung up a poetry and a religious club. With all this at his disposal, and the *Pubber* (which, it noted, had been favourably received by the 'Great Press of England'), 'the modern Reptonian should not be uneducated'.

All these attempts to dampen down controversy came to nothing early in the next year. Apart from a minor clash between Victor and Snape over the morality of reprisals, the debating society had thus far been a rather humdrum forum, but in the spring term, the fiery Ross took over the presidency from Darling. On 19 February there was a debate before an audience five times the normal size on the motion that 'in the opinion of this house it is disgraceful that Conscientious Objectors, whether genuine or not, should be disfranchised.' Any doubts that passions were bound to run high are dispelled by the recollection of a contemporary ('The Boss' is Fisher):

> . . . with a singular unimaginativeness . . . the War Office called up a boy precisely on his 18th Birthday, or at 18½ if he had Certificate A. During the winter of 1916–17, the average expectation of life of a subaltern on the Western Front was supposed to be three weeks; and I can well remember boys who had been thus arbitrarily called up at any stage of the school term, coming round the bedders on their last night at Repton and shaking hands with everyone, knowing, as we also knew, that in the following term, at the voluntary intercession services in Chapel on Friday evenings, we might hear their names read out by the Boss in the O R casualty list for that week. Moreover, the war showed no sign of ending; and in the spring of 1918 the Allies seemed to come perilously near defeat. Inevitably, therefore, we were living under strain. Of course, we were not conscious of this all the time: but the Boss must have felt it far more deeply than he allowed himself to show.

Such was the emotional context of the debate. Somervell recalls that 'Both sides armed for a trial of strength, and a trio of masters emerged on either side . . . Powerful Scropites [Snapeites] sent well drilled contingents of small boys to pile up "patriotic" votes and the patriotic majority was sure to be overwhelming in the lower house.'

Ross opened the proceedings with a speech guaranteed to infuriate the opposition — contending that genuine conscientious objectors were morally more courageous than those who fought. Others in the debate (speakers included Victor, Somervell and Snape) were equally intransigent, and a master, the Rev. Mr Agard-Butler took the palm, when he said 'on behalf of himself and all other Reptonians that it was a disgrace to Repton that the motion had been permitted at all, that in the days when he was at Repton the proposers would have been ducked in the horse-pond, and that it would be a crying scandal if the motion were passed in either house.'

The motion was won in the Upper House by 12 votes — which was to be expected — and lost in the Lower by only 20 — which was not. With feelings running high, Agard-Butler's advice was taken: one of the young supporters of the motion was thrown into the river. Others were subjected to gross bullying. A protesting deputation went to see Fisher. There was a long, hard wrangle. Though Fisher valued the success of the experiments, he was deeply concerned at the turmoil into which they were throwing the school. Somervell and Gorringe, fighting for the experiments' survival, prevailed. Somervell's account:

> Remedies were tried. A masters' meeting and a meeting of the whole school each to listen to a forcible lecture from the head on our divisions. Blame was apportioned, four fifths to Snape and Co, one fifth to us. Penalties were inflicted — in inverse proportion. Gollancz was temporarily suspended from addressing the Civics Class, the Pubber was provided with a second conservative editor. As it happened the fifth — the last — issue was in the press, and the conservative editorial . . . was the joint work of Fisher, myself and a conservative boy who had long contributed our Military notes and was not the new editor.

The bewildering consequence was two contradictory editorials. The first assailed Lloyd George and the Versailles declaration, which put an end to any possibility of peace by agreement. The second defended the Versailles decision as the only sensible one. This compromise, uneasy as it might appear, looked workable, and the credit for it goes jointly to Somervell and Fisher. That was not how Victor saw it, however. He wrote to Rubinstein:

> We have passed through a most acute crisis here. There has been great resentment against the Liberals on the part of the reactionaries for some considerable time, & the matter came to a head when a motion objecting to the disfranchisement of COs was carried by a sweeping majority in the Deb. Soc. It was a great occasion. But next day reprisals followed — duckings in the Sternyard, sousing of fags who had voted for the motion etc. Their perpetrators were congratulated in form by Snape. Huge row — Snape told off violently by Fisher — attempt of reactionaries to get rid of me — perpetual interviews — I eventually win. But I doubt whether I should survive another crisis of the sort. A great number of housemasters tacitly sympathised with the perpetrators, saying that it was a public disgrace that such a motion should have been debated at all!
> It's an awful business, trying to break the circle of reaction! But my disciples among the boys are beyond words splendid.

Meanwhile, Victor and Somervell had been working on a book, finished a week after this letter and published a few months later, called *Political Education at a Public School* and dedicated to Harford and Ross. It was a plea for the study of politics as the basis of public school education, and although the name of the school was omitted, it consisted mainly of a detailed description of the experiments. Undaunted by their (unmentioned) setbacks, the two authors ended on a note of optimism that was soon to prove misplaced. Yet even Victor knew he was playing a dangerous game. He wrote to Rubinstein during the Easter holidays that 'I'm just a little bit torn in the matter of Repton policy. The number of genuine liberals of the finest type we are turning out is amazing; on the other hand, if I persist in my present policy I can't possibly get a permanency, & I love the place so I don't ever want to leave it. The very thought of next term, with the sun & the grass & the cricket-field, makes me feel like a lover about to see his mistress!!!'

Political judgement was never Victor's strong suit. Somervell was more reliable, but in March the allies had allowed Amyas Ross an initiative that sealed the fate of the experiments. He came to an arrangement with the proprietor of a radical bookshop, specializing in revolutionary literature, to co-publish the *Pubber*: issue five included the words 'Published by the Repton School Book Shop, Ltd., and Henderson & Sons, 44 Charing Cross Road, S.W.1.' To the sophisticated, Henderson's, known as 'The Bomb Shop', was a joke. To others, it was a Bolshevik outpost.

Somervell and Victor had weathered parental complaints. Had they been aware that they had also come under the scrutiny of the War Office, they might have held back, but they were not and so did not. A file on Repton had been building up within the War Office for a considerable period; it is thought that allegations of 'pacifist' activities had been brought to their attention by a Snapeite boy and one of the masters. Victor was in the most vulnerable position, not only because he was seen as the leader, but because he was nominally at Repton to help with the OTC, with regular duties of drilling and training (at both of which he was hopeless and a joke among the boys).

The Bomb Shop was the last straw. The War Office put pressure on Fisher. Victor, living in Dryden Chambers and enduring an OTC course at Chelsea barracks, received a letter from the headmaster three days before the beginning of the summer term. It told him he was sacked, and all the experiments suspended. In their ensuing interview, called at Dryden Chambers at Victor's request, Victor, by his own account, characteristically shrugged off the catastrophe: imagined or impending disaster was always much more upsetting to him. 'I remember that he was embarrassed, and that I was gay. I remember feeling that I rather liked him. I remember two, but only two, of his sentences: "I have supported you consistently for a year and a half" and "David Somervell is the most obstinate man I've ever had to deal with."' The civics class was suspended for the duration of the war and the *Pubber* was suppressed. After weeks of argument with Fisher, Ross, in feverish state, left the school at five o'clock one morning for the milk train. Somervell, having refused to sign a pledge of silence on all political matters, also left the school.

When the reality hit Victor, his mood changed drastically. He wrote to all his old allies, and the 'distraught' letter to Harford ran, 'I'm of course utterly forlorn — life for the time has lost every bit of meaning.' He was much cheered by the many condolences he received from boys and masters, including Snape. Victor drew on these letters when writing *More For Timothy* and then jettisoned them (as he jettisoned the diary of his first two or three terms at Repton). Those he quotes from speak of the vitality, the morality, the hope and the enjoyment the writers had gained from him and his innovations. He did not exaggerate his own impact on the boys: Darling and Harford, reflecting in the tranquillity of old age, were still full of gratitude for Victor's expansion of their horizons. It was the sure knowledge of a profound success in a good cause that preserved the events at Repton among Victor's happiest memories. In summing up, he made a great effort to be fair. After his rather disparaging treatment of Fisher throughout, he concluded '. . . as I try to leap the gulf, and to look at things, not as a boy of twenty-five, but as a man of sixty, a bit of fineness suddenly obliterates everything else: he gave us our chance, and few others would have done so. My major emotion, accordingly, is one of gratitude. I am rather surprised about this.'

In the summer of 1918, Somervell and Gollancz were writing *The School and the World*. In deference to Fisher's wishes, the school was again unnamed, but the book provided further justification for the teaching of politics in public schools, and tackled the questions raised from the first book by reviewers and others. Discussing the curtailment of the experiments, they blamed their own failure to canvass general support and involvement among the masters. They did not give sufficient weight to a point Harford made many years later: the senior boys' feverishness as they prepared themselves to go to war turned quickly into virtual rebellion — open, in Ross's case — which was intolerable even to the well-intentioned Fisher. Victor's reflections on his personal performance:

> Unless you have annihilated your selfhood, depersonalised yourself — and become more of a person thereby — your *mana* is a bad *mana*, because you have appropriated to yourself a little fragment of God's prerogative. The 'glow' is, partially at any rate, *your* glow: in the best case, power and pride

have been at work — whether consciously or not makes comparatively little matter — on what might have been God's glow . . . The upshot of it all is that you are interfering with people, or, again in the best case, sharing God's interference; and only God has the right to interfere . . .

This doesn't mean . . . that you shouldn't advocate what you believe in with all the conviction you feel — with the glow aforesaid; but you must so have prepared yourself, by quietly laying yourself open to God, as to be reasonably satisfied that you have partially succeeded in what should always be your aim (reasonably and partially being as much as any human being can manage): namely, not to impose yourself, but to let God do his work with your humble co-operation. I had not so prepared myself all those many years ago . . . and so, while my *mana* was a good *mana* in the sense that, as I still believe, everything I advocated was good, it was a bad *mana* in the sense just explained.

In 1952, the less metaphysically-inclined Somervell wrote a mature analysis of the affair and Victor's part in it, which was never published.

Repton was a birdcage and in 1910 it imported an elephant named William Temple. In 1916, undeterred by this experience, it imported another elephant named Victor Gollancz.

Now these two young men — they were both young, Temple just thirty and Gollancz not long past twenty — had a very great deal in common. Both were, by Repton standards, giants, as their subsequent careers were to prove. Both were natural-born and incorrigible evangelists, with an incredible facility of exuberant and effective speech. Both were God-intoxicated men. . . . Both of them were, or regarded themselves as, socialists, with an idealistic socialism of their own which was all mixed up with their religious beliefs and ethical standards and had really very little to do with the socialism of politicians and economists and less still to do with the 'socialism' of trade unionists which is simply capitalist profiteering the other way round. Both adored Plato, Shelley, Blake and Beethoven. Both were spiritual beings encased in delightfully homely exteriors, with waist measurements that 'belied their souls' immensities'. Temple has been many times compared with Mr Pickwick, and if Mr Pickwick had been a young Jew he would have looked exactly like dear 'Golly'. And that brings us to the further point that both, along with their sky-scraping spiritualities and first rate brains, were emphatically jolly men, loud laughter, vigorous, good companions, and withal in some indefinable way childlike and one might add comic. Thus they were both of them extraordinarily attractive to boys. Boys were staggered by their spiritual and intellectual gifts, but that alone would not have done the trick. What was so intoxicating for boys was to find that these same spiritual and intellectual giants should at the same time be just 'Billy' and 'Golly', sources of endless amusement and inextinguishable laughter.

. . . Gollancz was a very Jewish Jew and Temple a very Aryan Aryan (whatever that may mean). But the differences were less than you might suppose . . . [yet] the two stories worked out very differently. Yes, a difference of circumstance.

Before Temple was elected headmaster he wrote a letter in which he said that he approached the problem of the public schools 'as a revolutionary'. . . But no sooner had he got to Repton than he found that he was a headmaster, responsible for an *institution*. He had his own Geoffrey Fisher inside him, and the revolutionist went down before the G.F. . . . So in a very short time he found that he had made a mistake in coming to Repton at all. But he loved it, just as Gollancz did; loved the boys and their charming discipleship. He made many of them think about religion and love God as they would never otherwise have done. But there was no revolution.

Gollancz has not told us that he approached the problem of the public schools as revolutionary, but there is no need for him to tell us, for he evidently approaches everything as a revolutionary. He was not head-master, and was not responsible for the 'institution', and it is apparent that he dislikes all institutions. He is essentially an anarchist. With Temple, Jesus and Caiaphas were inside the same skin. In the second episode they were certainly not! There was a very good, if slightly comic, Jesus, and a very good Caiaphas too. They came into head-on collision, and *what fun* it all was! Jesus was sent packing, and Caiaphas lived happy ever after.

Both Temple and Gollancz left an awful mess behind them. Put the elephant into the birdcage, and what can you expect? Poor Fisher had to tidy up both the messes and I suppose he did it very well. Repton relapsed into the useful insignificance from which it had momentarily emerged. But both episodes had none the less been extraordinarily well worth while. There had been in both episodes a positive outbreak of 'education'.

That piece was written for Victor, who was delighted with it. He had relied heavily also on the long account of the episode which Somervell wrote in 1918. What he did not see was what Somervell had written in the 1940s in his private reminiscences, where, after giving the history, he asked himself why had he helped Victor and Ross even when he disagreed with them. His answer was that he was standing for a principle, and with a curious mixture of integrity and cantanker-ousness sacrificed his post and his prospects for it; in spite of its occasional follies, the movement was right.

. . . do I still seriously think that the movement was a good thing? Well, what I *now* think — if you really want to know — is that it doesn't much matter one way or the other. I think that education is just a lot of dodges for keeping people occupied and out of mischief while they are growing up and that it does not much matter what dodges you employ. Each boy will in any case become what his heredity and his home environment have predestined, so why bother? But in 1918 I thought differently . . . and went down with my flag flying.

Perhaps wisely, Somervell did not convey these more cynical ideas to Victor, even when he offered his comments on the typescript of *More for Timothy*. Victor, who had just lavished about 50,000 words on a loving description of two fulfilling years, would not have taken it kindly. James Darling, all of sixty years after the Repton experiments, was concerned at their undimmed importance for Victor.

> The thing that worries me about the Repton episode and him is why it mattered so much to him in later life and why he remained so emotionally upset by it. My nearest approach to an answer is that he regarded Repton as his war effort, a poor substitute for the offering of his life as so many of his friends had given theirs . . . In my experience the age-group of those who were 18–23 in 1914 never recovered from the loss of their friends, a great generation sacrificed, though they reacted to the loss differently. It was worse for those who couldn't share the same experience and perhaps this explains Gollancz's fury at having his own contribution rejected.

There were other elements: Victor, still smarting years after his exile from Paradise, was temperamentally bound to justify himself at length, and the Repton experience was not just highly charged emotionally — it set him on a course for life. At Oxford he had toyed with the idea of going into business as a logical extension of his researches into how the cogs of the world operated. He fell into schoolteaching by accident and discovered the satisfactions of converting apparently unpromising human material into workers for his truth. His father had never listened, and his peers at Oxford were either friends who already shared his principles or else beyond the reach of his powers of persuasion. At Repton he discovered his *mana*, and his success had been more than he could have dreamed. When he was sacked he realized that schoolteaching was effectively closed to him: 'I decided then and there that I would somehow or other slide into "political" publishing, with the reservation that, at the age of forty-five, I would enter national politics.' For Victor, the experience that precipitated such a momentous decision had to be interpreted as a success.

CHAPTER SIX

FINDING A DIRECTION

THE SENSE OF desolation was still strong in Victor when he wrote to Rubinstein in June 1918 bringing him up-to-date with the news.

> It was wonderful seeing the Walküre again — house absolutely crammed on both occasions. I've also seen 'Figaro' and 'The Magic Flute'; and 'Aida'. Nothing else — except an act of Tosca and do. of Butterfly. But I find I'm not in the mood for such things — I frankly prefer 'Yes Uncle' with a Reptonian. What is any art without the mental background of human companionship? It is only as a symbol of that that anything gives one happiness — drama or music or books, or even the green grass in summer. Of course the break with Repton has been a ghastly thing for me.

He had changed a good deal from the solitary schoolboy. Henceforward, unless he was concentrating on some piece of work — reading or writing particularly — he was to be miserable if alone. Yet it is difficult to assess how much individuals mattered to him. There is no doubting his genuine affection for many of his Oxford friends. No record survives of his immediate reaction to Bernard Strauss's death (in December 1917) or Ralph Rooper's (in May 1918), either in publications, correspondence or poetry. He himself says in *More for Timothy* that he gave more thought down the years to his pupil Manoukian (killed in September 1917) than to either of them, and his last book, *Reminiscences of Affection*, contains, among the many pages relating to friends, only indirect reference to Rooper and none at all to Strauss or Paul Hobhouse, another Oxford intimate among the fallen. It would be wrong to infer that he did not suffer by their deaths. He had letters from Rooper and Strauss included in *War Letters of Fallen Englishmen* (published by his firm many years later), and, in 1950, in his own anthology, *A Year of Grace*, he dedicated the section on freedom to Strauss. When they were mentioned in correspondence he wrote of them in sad and affectionate terms; but there is no indication of deep personal pain or mourning, even from one much given to expressing his emotions on paper without embarrassment. Grief for the departed, given Victor's vital nature and concern for the now and all the tomorrows, had perhaps only little space in his heart. Turning his attention always to the suffering of those yet alive, he had no need to sublimate his feelings for the dead.

Of his other close Oxford friends, he virtually lost touch with Spencer Hurst, occasionally ran into Denroche-Smith at musical performances and had little other than formal association with Haldane. Jerrold, who became a publisher, was to remain in contact with Victor on and off throughout his life, but not as a close friend — indeed, there was to be a breach that lasted almost 24 years. Ewan Agnew, for whose marriage Victor's poems had been privately printed, died in 1930, but though Victor wrote affectingly in *The Times* of his gentleness and sweetness, he had had only slight contact with him in the intervening years. (Harold Rubinstein was a special case: he and Victor married sisters and so the two families were very close; Rubinstein was to be the Gollancz libel lawyer and an ally in some of Victor's causes.)

Most friends of the moment were associated with a contemporary enthusiasm — a not uncommon pattern, but one which in Victor's case was very marked, the more so in view of the early intensity of the relationships. Oxford friends were fellow-spirits in sensuous enjoyment and allies in the liberal crusade. Of the Repton cohort, Gorringe was dead, and Somervell, the subject of many tributes in *More for Timothy*, he saw only rarely after the 1920s; of the all-important boys, only Benn Levy — a second-ranker in Victor's heart — had much to do with him after the war, and then only because Levy moved in political and publishing circles. Those who lived to consider the reasons for their decline in his overt affections are in two minds: perhaps he had frozen them as adolescents, and failed to come to terms with their independent development, or perhaps he was disappointed in the way they had turned out. A letter he received around 1919 from some of his favourites — drunkenly questioning his motives and influence on them — may have set up its own reaction in his subconscious.

Over the years, he would respond with a warm letter to any of the old boys who initiated a correspondence, but do little to sustain the relationship. Harford and Darling were rarely in England, so geography played a part, but that was not so in the case of Ross. To Victor (in *More for Timothy*) Ross was saintly and inspired, but their dealings had been so limited that he got the date of his death wrong by about ten years.

His father, so important in his childhood, is virtually absent from his voluminous reminiscences about later life, although there was still inevitably a good deal of family contact during the Oxford vacations.

The main source, apart from family memories, for what was happening to the Gollanczes from that time is the *Jewish Chronicle*. Alex was continuing to act predictably. In May 1914, in a report headed 'Votes for Women', he was mentioned as seconding a motion to allow lady seatholders a vote at United Synagogue meetings. His wounded response asserted that he had been concerned only to encourage the ladies to take an interest. 'I emphatically repudiate,' he wrote, 'the least semblance of a political colouring in our proceedings . . . Had I known that my views might have been misconstrued — as they seem to have been in certain quarters — I, for one, would not only not have seconded the resolution but I should have abstained from voting altogether.' In November 1916 he was calling for the erection of facilities for Jewish soldiers at each large military base. '"A Jewish Hut for Jewish soldiers" — how full of import — where Jewish soldiers could fraternise amid Jewish surroundings, and where divine service could be held, when circumstances permit; in a Jewish atmosphere.'

The same year saw letters to the paper from Winifred. The family memory is that she had fallen in love with a Protestant whose religion made him unacceptable. The turmoil that resulted, so soon after May's conversion, is nowhere mentioned by Victor, although Ruth Gollancz told one of her daughters that Victor had once had to spend a very unhappy couple of days alone with Winifred when she was in a state of some mental distress. Her *Jewish Chronicle* correspondence shows her to have been far more intelligent than May, while sharing her struggle to establish spiritual values of a totally different order from Alex's. In September 1916 she was distressed by a letter from her cousin, Hugh Harris, which defended pacifism on theological grounds. Winifred's long rebuttal was a passionate affirmation that 'my country right or wrong' was a sentiment impeccably Jewish as well as English. In laying aside 'self' and fighting for his country, an individual was 'fighting for something higher, he is fighting for his country . . . he is fighting for his God.'

If the sentiments were akin to Alex's, the language had much more in common with Victor. Her next letter, a couple of months later, was also on a subject dear to Alex's heart — the keeping of the Sabbath. Primarily concerned to ask tolerance of those too tired, after a week's work, to go to the synagogue, she yet again came to an orthodox conclusion: 'But one thing seems to me certain, that those who can should make every effort to attend some synagogue in order to preserve our places of worship for those who cannot but would attend. And then hopefully we may look forward to the day when once again we can all journey in joyous throngs to the House of God.'

By this time Winifred was already living away from home, attached to an institution in Sussex called The Girls' Heritage. Her next letter, in January 1917, was a fervent denunciation of the prevailing methods of teaching children about orthodox Judaism — 'which aims at stuffing as many facts and as much so-called knowledge into a child's head as possible, and which is content to leave the rest, the child's thinking soul . . . to take care of itself.'

If that letter struck Alex as heretical, the next — and last — must have worried him more. Published in September 1917, it was in response to a recent written sermon in the paper, which had included the sentence: 'those who are pleasing in the sight of God are often intolerable in the eyes of man.' Winifred believed, and argued at length, the untruth of this precept, regretting the unavailability of anybody with whom she might discuss such topics, since as 'a "young person" myself (of an exceedingly hopeless kind!) who has every wish to be pleasing to God, and no wish whatsoever to be despised and rejected by fellow mortals, I feel I should like to be instructed on the subject, and by no one better than your anonymous preacher, if he will be so kind.'

This sad distress-call indicated a real feeling of isolation in her intellectual and emotional struggles. Her need for help could not be met within the family. The Christian May could hardly counsel the Jewish Winifred, even had she the intellectual equipment so to do. Alex, with May a renegade and Victor non-practising, was now a factor in the religious struggles of Winifred, and anyway lacked the flexibility of mind required. Nellie's devotion to Alex excluded any support for those with whom he was in conflict. Victor was too busy and there is little to suggest that he was interested. Contemporaries have no recollection of his ever talking about his sisters (although he used to joke about his father's orthodoxy, relating such pronounce- ments as that provoked by a question of Victor's: 'I could murder, but I could never eat pork'). There was no stringent separation; a letter to Darling in 1917 mentions that he had been to a revue with his sister. What is clear is that he had as little to do with his family as possible. May was too dim, Winifred too distressed and the atmosphere at home was no more to his taste than ever it had been. Furthermore, his parents had moved to Hove (near Brighton, Sussex), and Victor could not bear to be away from London. A letter to Rubinstein in the summer of 1917 concluded 'I've not — as you might, mightn't you, have so beautifully guessed? — been in Brighton.'

Winifred's love apparently died in action, tipping her over the edge. Family folklore has it that Alex put her in a hospital because she was becoming a nuisance and bombarding people with letters. Whatever finally precipitated her committal, it certainly occurred not long after her last letter to the *Jewish Chronicle*. She was pronounced schizophrenic, her condition deteriorated, and after several years she ceased to recognize visitors and then to have them. Alex, ever assiduous in his family responsibilities, paid for her upkeep in the private wing of a Colchester Hospital and left her an annuity in his will.

Victor's remoteness from these travails must be seen in the context of his youth and temperament. His Jewish obligation to put family first ensured that he would — in reaction — tend to put them last; his kindnesses and generosities had to be voluntary. He did the minimum for his family consonant with retaining his parents' affection, for, thoughtless as he could be, he was incapable — as he showed in the row with his father over the *Sunday Times* letter — of breaking his parents' hearts. That concession apart, he virtually cut all ties with the Gollanczes at large. Pride in the name and in the achievements of his successful uncles was conventional and therefore repellent to him. (An exception was his response to sweet approving letters from his diffident uncles Morris Gollancz and Assur Michaelson, who received affectionate answers and occasional gifts.)

With his parents away in Hove, Victor lived on for a few months in Dryden Chambers. After that it was hotels, and money became important. Courtesy of Douglas Jerrold, invalided out of the army and now in the Ministry of Food, Victor had been put in charge of organizing kosher food rationing. It was, he told Rubinstein, 'a fat £400 a year billet; but I think the WO will soon remove me, and send me to a labour battalion in France, or a garrison battalion in Egypt, or something like that.' His premonitions proved correct, as Jerrold explained in his memoirs:

> . . . the War Office discovered that he had got, as punishment for his misdeeds, a better job, and, quite unofficially, a Colonel came to see me. 'We are determined,' he said, 'to stamp out this Liberalism.' It seemed to me rather a large job for the War Office to undertake in the middle of a war but the Colonel was adamant. He felt, he explained patiently, that if Gollancz's good fortune became known in other schools, all the masters anxious to get jobs in government offices would start defending the Russian Revolution, whereas if . . . 'But surely he's not fit for active service,' I asked. 'Oh, certainly not,' the Colonel replied (he evidently felt that it would spoil the tone of the fighting if Gollancz were associated with it), 'but we thought perhaps Singapore . . . it's very hot there now,' he

added meditatively. I made it clear, having received Tallents's instruction, that the Ministry would raise no objection if our official was required for military service, but would certainly protest if any attempt were made to use his nominal military rank as a second lieutenant in the OTC as a weapon to secure his transfer to some less useful civilian post. The Colonel felt our attitude unpatriotic and unhelpful but clearly had expected nothing better; he had heard, he hinted darkly, that he was unlikely to get much assistance from us. 'Why should you,' I asked genially, 'since this is the Ministry of Food and not the Spanish Inquisition?'

All Victor's attempts to stay at the ministry were unsuccessful. It was not so much that he objected to a Singapore posting, more that he was enjoying life in London, with Repton friends and an undemanding if tedious job that left him plenty of time for reading. He borrowed £50 from his Ministry boss, Sir Stephen Tallents, purchased a pistol and a solar topee, and set off with a draft of the Manchester Regiment in a state of excitement about seeing some of Europe and 'the blazing and sun-drenched and glamorous and fabled and immemorial East'. He was appalled by the lavatories on the train, but fell in love with Italy. On the journey he finished his share of the second book he was writing with Somervell (*The School and the World*), and demonstrated some increase in maturity by getting on well with his military colleagues. 'They called me The Sheep; they said I looked like a sheep when I laughed.' The boys had taught him to scoff at his own physical peculiarities and equipped him to get on better with the unsophisticated. He was much less of an intellectual snob than he had been three years earlier.

The trip and therefore, in a way, Victor's war, was a fiasco. From Taranto he sailed first to Port Said where, 'attracted by a callipygian book-jacket' (Victor was ever stirred by an attractive female bottom), he read and was horrified by his first pornography. An uncomfortable journey through the Suez Canal was followed by encampment in the desert near Suez, where his night blindness caused him to lose his way until he was rescued by a little Arab boy. After a long voyage across the Arabian Sea to Bombay, then to Colombo and Singapore, he encountered there a climate as hot as the Colonel had promised and a feverish stomach complaint that landed him in hospital for weeks. In December 1918, by now, as he used to claim proudly, the longest-serving Second Lieutenant in the British Army, he was invalided out and despatched back to England by cargo-boat. Victor later made a virtue out of his inglorious wartime career, but he had made serious attempts to get into active service. The 1915 letter to Rubinstein ('I am in high favour with my Captain, was made a lance-corporal [unpaid] about ten days ago . . . Pretty good promotion, n'est-ce pas?') may or may not have been tongue in cheek, but his failure in Northumberland had stung his pride. The boys' mockery at his lack of military bearing finally put paid to any ideas he may have entertained of impressing the army on its own terms, so he had changed to a posture of despising the whole military ethos.

He wrote to Rubinstein from Hove in February.

> Mon cher Harold —
> Me voici revenu — invalided with Gastroptos (does your Greek carry you so far?) I await a medical board; meanwhile lack of sheckel keeps me down in this appalling place. We must contrive to meet somehow soon, however. What are you doing with yourself these days?
> Me with an abdominal belt — rather comic, n'est-ce-pas?
> > Write
> > Yours ever
> > Victor G.

He could have returned to Oxford to take his degree, but that had no appeal. Victor wanted to get on with life. There was nothing seriously wrong with his health: his main complaint had been wrongly diagnosed as the dropping of the internal organs, whereas it was merely nervous dyspepsia. His fever occasionally recurred for some years after the war but it was never serious enough to lay him low. He was not long without a job — there can have been few twenty-six-year-olds with his qualifications available at that period. He had edited one book, had been co-author of a second, and another joint effort was about to appear. He had some civil service experience, and was exceptionally well read in politics and economics, extremely literate and obviously exceptionally intelligent. More than that, he had great faith in his own abilities and was a powerful seller of himself. Very soon he was back in London, working close to William Wedgwood Benn as secretary of the Radical Research Group, a body set up by Sir Donald Maclean's Independent Liberals (the 'Wee Frees'). His antipathy to Lloyd George had intensified, and he was chiefly charged with the production of questions to harass the coalition government, and general briefing for Wee Free politicians. Jerrold was privy to his complaints: 'Victor's final disillusionment took place, he told me, when he prepared a careful series of notes for one distinguished legislator, on a Budget debate, only to hear him, after floundering hopelessly for a quarter of an hour, wind up with an eloquent peroration calling on the Government to take immediate steps to "float the funding debt."'

It was not a well-paid job, but Victor had other plans anyway. He persuaded the Oxford University Press to let him edit a series of short books designed to supply 'a guide for all through current problems and events'. The series covered a wide range, including Sir Harry Johnson on *The Backward Peoples and our relations with them*, Emile Burns on *Modern Finance* and Victor himself on *Industrial Ideals*, a competent introduction to everything from the Soviet system to profit sharing. It was concise, clear and free of propaganda and must have tied in well with the work he was doing for the Wee Frees, but there cannot have been much money in that either.

With Dryden Chambers no longer available as a base, Victor lodged

SIMPLIFIED FAMILY TREE

OF THE LOWY FAMILY

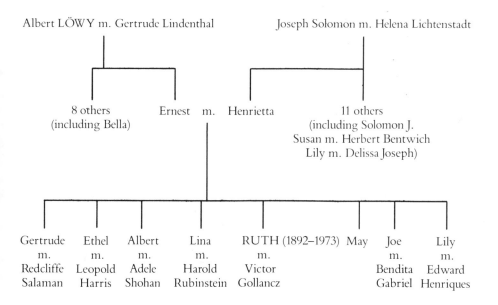

with Douglas Jerrold in the Colvilles — 'one of those derelict London quarters, full of cats, broken bells and decaying stucco, where, a hundred years earlier, revelry and popping champagne corks had sounded by night. . . . Everything about it was deep, dark and dusty, and if you hooded your eyes you could still see its splendour.'

He was not destined to remain there long. Early in April, he was invited to a dinner party by Ruth Lowy. (The family had dropped the umlaut in response to anti-German feeling, just as Hermann Gollancz's sons had changed to Gollance.) Ruth's fiancé had been killed in 1916 and she had not seen Victor for five years.

Ruth came of a family as distinguished as Victor's. Her grandfather, Albert Löwy, had been born in Moravia and educated on the Continent, but in 1840, at the age of twenty-four, he came to London. A Hebrew scholar, he was a co-founder two years later of the West London Reform Synagogue, where he served as a minister for fifty years, and was even more renowned than his friend Samuel Marcus Gollancz. By his wife Gertrude Lindenthal, a minister's daughter, he had nine children (one of whom, Bella, was editor of the five volume English translation of Graetz's *History of the Jews*).

Ernest, the eldest son, was a successful stockbroker, famous on the stock exchange for breaking the top hat tradition before the First World War. He walked in one day wearing a straw hat, which was seized and smashed, as were its three successors. Ultimately he wore down the opposition and attracted imitators. He was an engineer *manqué* who spent most of his spare time in his workshop, and collected model engines from all the English railways. There was a working steam railway at the bottom of the garden of his Holland Park home. (His feel for engineering was passed on to some of his children, including Ruth, who in later life always carried a tiny screwdriver in her handbag and was the family handyman.) His unpretentious conversation consisted largely of anecdotes and puns, and while he took an active part in Jewish philanthropic activities, he had little interest in the philosophical aspects of his religion. He and his wife Henrietta were as much a contrast to each other as were Alex and Nellie Gollancz.

Henrietta Solomon was one of twelve children of a prosperous leather merchant, Joseph Solomon (born in England of Dutch extraction), and his gifted wife — born Helena Lichtenstadt (of Prague and then Vienna). Historians of the family describe Helena as highly cultured and rather bohemian, and within the large family inherited artistic abilities were encouraged. The pianist Susan abandoned her career to marry Herbert Bentwich and herself bear a family of twelve, including two distinguished professional musicians. Lily was a talented painter (who married the architect Delissa Joseph), and one brother was the popular painter of portraits and biblical and classical scenes, Solomon J. Solomon, RA. Henrietta, the youngest, played the piano, sang a little, and also painted, but later became too much involved in a variety of intellectual and political pursuits to give much time to the arts. Her enthusiasms, like Nellie Gollancz's, included theosophy, but she was best known for her activities on behalf of the Pankhursts. She and two of her daughters went to prison for the suffragette cause.

Although Ernest was sympathetic to Henrietta's suffragette activities, they had little else in common. Intellectually they were poles apart. After the birth of their eighth child, Henrietta had had enough, and banned all sexual activity. Their involvement with their children while they were growing up was minimal; like many Victorian and Edwardian children, the two boys and six girls grew up seeing almost nothing of their parents beyond a nightly fifteen-minute visit, wearing clean clothes provided by the nurse who brought them up — Miss Slade.

In a *Times* profile of·Ruth in 1964, the Lowys were described as 'a warm, tough, emancipated and abundant family, rich in painters, musicians and liberal campaigners' and she was quoted: 'Nowadays they would have called us Beatniks'. Her sister, Lily Henriques, disputed the attribute of warmth, for as a child she experienced little parental love, and the gaps in age between the children prevented any one of them from being intimate with more than one or two siblings. Each child spent a few years in the nursery, progressed to work with a governess in the schoolroom, and then went on to a school. Lily (eighth child, sixth daughter) knew little of Ruth (fifth child, fourth daughter) until she had grown up, for the age gap was exacerbated by Ruth's reserve. In Lily's view, Ruth was cold and rather spoiled by her good looks, her popularity as an athlete at St Paul's Girls' School, and her all-round ability.

Whatever the deficiencies of Lowy family life, it was a stimulating environment for the children as they grew into adulthood. The girls were especially fortunate for their time. They were introduced to, and encouraged to participate in, political and philanthropic activities, and were expected to continue their education after school. None of them was intellectual: Ruth's generation of Lowys put their artistic ambitions before books. Gertrude, the eldest, trained as a professional photographer and the next sister, Ethel, studied architecture. Ruth, after an academic year at Wilmersdorf, spent three years at the Slade from 1909 to 1912. There she was friendly with Isaac Rosenberg (her mother and Aunt Lily were paying part of his fees), and he drew her as a pre-Raphaelite Sleeping Beauty. She also showed her excellent critical sense by purchasing for £5 a picture from her fellow-student, Stanley Spencer. Until the outbreak of war she rented a studio in Chelsea, but although a talented painter, she lacked the single-minded drive to become a serious artist and the creativity to be experimental. War work took over, much of it spent in teaching officers to drive. When Benny Polack was killed she decided that she must find some means of earning her living. Her father's wealth was limited and fluctuating, and Ruth was not a woman to marry without love for the sake of security. She was a considerable craftsman in drawing, so architecture was an obvious choice. In 1917 she had the distinction of being one of the first four women admitted to the Architectural Association. Her eye for meticulous detail was evident in two drawings in the *Architect* and the *Architects' Journal* in 1919. The Director of the AA recalled her as an exception among female students in her competence at calculations: he described her as 'a perfect wonder' who 'could do anything'.

Ruth was an unusual and self-contained woman. A year older than Victor, she was now twenty-seven, and reputed to have declined several proposals of marriage. All her life she remained a rather enigmatic presence beside Victor, efficient where he was inspired, calm where he was excitable, practical where he was creative, careful where he was extravagant, prosaic where he was hyperbolic. Yet, if she was his antithesis, she was, through her single-minded loyalty to him, the essential complement. A feminist, she was attracted by Victor's support for the suffragettes and his then uncommon respect for women's intellect and creativity. However much he flirted, he never saw the female as a plaything. And to that was added his life-force: his massive exuberance, his sensuality and his passion, all of which she must somehow have sensed in the early days through his rather shy exterior.

Ruth's unflappable self-confidence was evident in the way she set about renewing her acquaintance with Victor. He had not met her since the afternoon on the river in Oxford when he had been aesthetically repelled by the sand-shoes she wore (presumably a manifestation of her bohemianism). She had since observed him several times from a distance while he was based in Dryden Chambers in 1917. Victor's account of their reunion was published 49 years later:

I accepted the invitation, [to dinner] but got the wind up as time slipped away: not at the prospect of being captured, but because I was socially shy. I waited till a minute to midnight — the morning of the event — in an agony of indecision; then telegraphed 'Very greatly regret have to go at a moment's notice to China' and felt marvellously free. But Ruth must have thought I was exaggerating (she often thinks this), for I got a note the next morning to enquire if a week-end at Hurley, where the Lowys had a cottage, might be feasible in May . . . I accepted, and sent no subsequent telegram.

Victor's experience of women had been very limited. He had met few girls since adolescence but had fallen temporarily in love with most of them. No doubt his relative poverty was inhibiting: the Lowys lived in a style to which he had never been accustomed, and Victor loathed being put in a position of inferiority. Ruth cannot then have known how susceptible Victor was, though she was to learn during their married life that his readiness to fall in love was not just an adolescent trait. In the circumstances, it was inevitable that he should be bowled over by a woman who so comprehensively met his criteria of goodness and beauty. It was his good luck that Ruth was prepared to make herself available, and not easily put off. In dealing with the wary Victor she showed that combination of practicality and sensitivity that was to underpin their future relationship. Having bound him to another engagement without rebuking him, even by implication, for backing out of dinner, she showed no false pride in adjusting herself to his unpredictability. Two notes survive to show the method she adopted in handling Victor. The first, as prosaic as all her written communications, was dated 7 May.

> We are leaving for Hurley by car about 5 o'clock Friday afternoon. Could you ring us here at Park 95 before 9.15 am any morning & let us know if you can fit in with this arrangement.
>   Yrs
>   Ruth Lowy

No phone-call came, so she telephoned on the 9th and left a message: 'Miss Lowy rang up and would like you to ring up Park 95 about lunch time. If not the address is The Haven, Hurley and the Station is Maidenhead.'

One way or another, Victor arrived and 'within an hour of my arrival was in love, for good and all, with . . . my Ruth.'

The Hurley house-party was followed by a few weeks of courtship. They were greatly assisted in overcoming Victor's shyness by their proximity to the same bus-stop.

. . . during the two or three weeks that elapsed between the first and the second of my visits to Hurley I would execute a manoeuvre dictated, in equal portions, by passion and pride. I would arrive at the bus-stop a good ten minutes before she'd be due, barring exceptional precipitancy — and the idea of the ten minutes was to look after that: would do a run towards each bus as it started: would slacken and miss it: would walk slowly away: would do my run again — and *da capo* till she appeared. So we met, more or less accidentally, every morning; and what did I care if the bystanders thought me *meshuggah*, or a policeman looked suspicious? For the rest, we went a lot to the ballet, particularly when Karsavina was dancing: and one night, just as the wedding-march had started in *L'Oiseau de Feu*, silently — the words are beautiful, and endless custom has not staled them — we plighted our troth.

The second weekend at Hurley was in early June. There, they put their commitment into words, and Victor quickly rang his father with news of his engagement. Alex, overjoyed that Victor was marrying a Jewess, was ecstatic that she came from a family so 'solid' — well established in England and socially, culturally and financially respectable. With all these unexpected blessings to be grateful for, it hardly mattered that the Lowys were not orthodox Jews.

The wedding was fixed for 22 July 1919 — an early date, considering that Victor's job with the Wee Frees was to end the same month. He was without capital, but his optimism was boundless and his network of contacts in politics and publishing was growing. Victor, recalling many years later what he thought of as the poverty of their early married life, reveals his material standards. Lowy, he says, had recently lost a lot of money and could give them very little: only £500 (about four times the annual unskilled wage) for household equipment and £500 in a marriage settlement. Rich Uncle Max Michaelson, instead of the £250 hoped for, sent a metal freemason's dish on which they could raise only £1. Victor was so poor that he had to defer paying the £37 for Ruth's engagement ring for a year. Victor's memories of poverty were as exaggerated as they were romantic. In 1931 he assured a needy author that he understood his condition, having lived 'on about five pounds a week during the first two years of my married life'. In fact, within months of the marriage, he was earning £500 a year working for the Rowntree Trust — writing a comparative survey of minimum wage legislation around the world — and in April 1920 his salary was raised to £600. Ruth was bringing in a small income working part-time in the library of the AA. Much to the displeasure of her director, she had given up her studies a year before qualifying.

Like Victor, Ruth believed that a feminist could put family first: there was no question of her continuing with her architectural training. In view of the way their married life was to be conducted, this was very fortunate. In the service at the West London Synagogue (where her father held office, and where Victor found her 'indescribably beautiful in cloth of gold with white lilies'), she took upon herself 'the fulfilment of all the duties incumbent upon a Jewish wife', but she seems to have realized at a very early stage that she was taking on much more than that — the duties incumbent upon the wife of Victor Gollancz. From the very beginning, and throughout their married life, Victor was completely dependent on her emotionally and practically. When he needed her she had to be there. If he rang home from the office he was upset if she was not there to talk to him. If she went out without him he would work himself up into an anxiety neurosis akin to those his mother suffered over his father. She was vital to bolster his self-esteem, participate in his enthusiasms, control his wilder excesses and at all times reassure him that she loved him more than anyone else. She was also essential to cut his hair, chauffeur him (he never learned to drive) and organize the running of the household and its finances. From home to Oxford to the army to Repton, and back to the army again, his bodily needs had been catered for. Even at Dryden Chambers there was a valet. Yet his inability to look after himself was not a simple matter of inexperience. With his hands he was, as he said himself, 'a nincompoop'; the recalcitrance of inanimate objects drove him to outbursts of frustrated rage. He was hopeless with personal finances, and however much he earned, Ruth curbed his expenditure by doling him out modest pocket money. (Frugal herself, she recognized Victor's need for comfort and occasional luxury. During their engagement, she endeared herself to him further by encouraging him to spend a couple of pounds on the last available seat to hear Emmy Destinn sing Aida once again.) She was an excellent organizer, gardener, driver, dress-maker; she could soothe Victor and sort him out when his collar-studs' failure to co-operate drove him into a screaming fury.

Victor was a full-time career for Ruth, and she recognized the fact. In return for putting up with his demands, for the disruption caused by his explosive temper, and for his jealousy and egotism, she gained enough to make her satisfied with the bargain. Victor had the passion for life that she lacked. He introduced to her a world of excitement, incessant crisis, agonizing fears and ecstatic joys. If she could reach neither his heights nor his depths, she could participate in them far enough to feel her own existence more fulfilling and more fun. She

loved him and could not but be affected by his devotion to her, which
he expressed privately and publicly, sincerely and often hyperbolic-
ally, until he died. Extolled as the most beautiful and best woman in
creation, she could endure with only occasional pain his frequent
flirtations and two infidelities. It seems to have suited her to live with a
man whom the slightest incident could drive into a tantrum, a sulk,
wild exhilaration, shouts of laughter, anxiety or remorse. Ruth could
appreciate music, if not at the same pitch of intensity as Victor. Victor
could appreciate art, if not at Ruth's level of expertise. Socially he was
dominant; she was content with second place. Intellectually she was
his inferior, but that was unimportant — indeed advantageous — for
Victor could not have endured living with competition. Ruth
provided the ballast, Victor was the life-enhancer.

They began their married life in a flat in Campden Hill Square but
moved within the year to Ladbroke Road, where Livia Ruth was born
in May 1920. They were living in modest prosperity, with good
furniture and sufficient domestic help to enable Ruth to continue with
her part-time job. In December they set off for a belated honeymoon
in Rome, initiating a lifetime's practice of getting away together from
domestic responsibilities. It began disastrously, for her father had
insisted that they carry the minimum of money and leave him to
arrange for the bulk of it to be available at the Bank of Rome. Victor
fretted all the way lest the arrangement fail. True to form, when the
cashier announced that no money had arrived he first fell into a rage
and then, recognizing this as a major disaster, became calm. For a
couple of days they lived on bread, olives (for which he had a passion)
and cheese. When the money came through they devoured enormous
steaks. Victor, 47 years later, could still describe several of the meals
they had in Rome, but he could recall even more clearly the music that
was rehearsed in the Opera House near their hotel and the accompanying chorus of birds. These sensual pleasures survived the relative lack
of success of the honeymoon by Victor's standards. His own
explanations for its qualified failure were that they were short of
money and had not yet learned how to live together. The first is yet
another indication of his need for comfort: having to endure a
second-rate hotel, and denying himself full access to the opera — this
was a real deprivation. The second is a sign that Ruth had not yet
entirely adapted herself to Victor: there is little evidence that he ever
made many concessions to her.

The straitened circumstances of the Roman holiday may have given
impetus to Victor's next career decision. He had toyed with the idea of
politics: Wedgwood Benn believed he had wanted to be another

Disraeli, but was kept out of politics by financial necessity. He now postponed such ambitions for several years and reverted to his Oxford decision to go into business and his post-Repton scheme to make that business publishing. In his mentor Wedgwood Benn he had an admirable contact, for his elder brother Ernest controlled Benn Brothers Ltd. Victor, in addition to his work for Rowntree, had been editing Benn's Grey Book — a Wee Frees publication for which he was paid £100 in April 1921 — and had impressed Benn with his ability to work hard and produce results. Wedgwood introduced him to Ernest and, on 16 February, Ernest offered him a job as manager of the works-magazines department with an overseership of the books department. His diary goes on:

> 22 Feb Interview with Gollancz who comes to try & squeeze up the terms offered to him. I promised to confer with my fellow directors. He still impresses me very favourably.
> 23 February A conference with Shapland & Hughes re Gollancz & Works magazines. Decided to meet Gollancz halfway.
> 1 Mar Victor Gollancz home for the night to discuss the new works magazines department. He impresses me as a distinct acquisition.

By 1 April 1921 Victor had joined Benn Brothers.

CHAPTER SEVEN

PUBLISHER: THE YOUNG TURK

SIR ERNEST AND I undoubtedly misunderstood one another. He ran a chain of 'trade' papers, with a few 'trade' books hanging on to their coat-tails: and Sir Ernest's idea was that the books should be freed from the coat-tails and, in greatly increased numbers, should go their own way. I, on the other hand, while happy to do what I could in the matter, had no intention of confining myself to *Modern Gasworks Practice* and *Automatic Telephone Systems*. Moreover, our social and political ideas were not of a piece. I was much as I am now: while Sir Ernest was a proselytizing money-man (as well as a teetotaller), and was just finishing an exposé of his creed, entitled *Confessions of a Capitalist* . . .

Apart from the occasional dismissive comment about Ernest Benn, that was almost all Victor ever put in print about their six years together, though in private he often enjoyed ridiculing him. Benn himself, though not above making jibes at Victor occasionally in later years, displayed generosity in his main public reference to Victor's period with the firm: 'Mr Victor Gollancz . . . came to me to manage this department, and I had the benefit of his outstanding genius for the next six or seven years, until the clash of opposing philosophies made it wise to arrange a separation.'

Political differences were not a problem when Benn and Victor first met. Benn's father, the first baronet, had been a Liberal MP, and Benn himself was a philosophical liberal of the old school who, like Victor, had worked hopefully for the Ministry of Reconstruction. He even shared his antipathy to Lloyd George. Although experience of bureaucracy and disillusion with his old party were beginning to make Benn doubt the efficacy of moderate state intervention, in the spring of 1921 he was still a liberal and, like Victor, a crusader by instinct. Benn Brothers had been founded by his father to publish the *Cabinet Maker*. Other trade publications had followed and, from the turn of the century, when Ernest Benn took control, growth accelerated. From a base of a dozen or so such magazines as *Gas World*, the *Fruit Grower* and the *Electrician*, the firm drifted into publishing technical books for each specialized public. Benn wished to expand further, but he had no ambitions in the field of general publishing. His main reason for hiring Gollancz is explained by his son Glanvill:

[He] . . . was much interested in good industrial relations. *Space*, the Benn house journal, was already well-established. He had half-formed plans for putting the firm's publishing expertise at the disposal of business firms who might be considering producing similar house magazines. VG seemed the ideal man to further this idea and duly joined the Benn HQ then at 6 & 8 Bouverie Street.

As this idea was still nebulous, Benn had decided to give Victor a second responsibility. Concerned that editors of journals were allowing themselves to be distracted from their proper work by book production, he had set up a separate book department, in whose operations Victor was now to assist. Benn had worries about the timing of the appointment: '1 April — Gollancz started at an awkward moment. My decision to go to America makes it a little difficult for me to throw myself into his new department, but he will be able to fill his time up in the books department & this may work out better in the end.'

Back at Bouverie Street three months later, he investigated progress in the department — where Victor had not been treading water.

18 July . . . if we go on adding to titles . . . we shall gradually build up a big & I hope remunerative business. Gollancz had done absolutely nothing in connection with the works magazines for which he was appointed, but in the three months that he has been here established his suitability for a managership of our books business.

26 July — Began discussions with Gollancz as to an agreement with him to take over & run the technical books department.

2 Sept. — Completed lengthy negotiations with Gollancz & signed a 5 year agreement with him to act as manager of our technical books dept.

The diary does not record the salary agreed, but it is clear from other evidence that the lengthy negotiations had secured Victor more money and considerable freedom of action. Benn was true to his individualist principles. No autocrat, he recognized Victor's talents and gave him the maximum of responsibility and the minimum of interference. Although Victor was bored by technical books, they provided excellent training and he knew he had to make a success of them before he would be permitted to branch out. By December 1921 his department needed its first salaried traveller and in 1922, having convinced Benn that art books were semi-technical, he began (with the help of the art director, Cecil Hughes) the production of sumptuous volumes aimed at wealthy collectors.

Expansion was so rapid that in March 1923 Benn and Victor decided to make the department a separate company, Ernest Benn Ltd, with themselves as Chairman and Managing Director respectively. Glanvill Benn paraphrased and commented on the reasons as recorded in his father's diary:

> . . . partly for financial reasons (from accountancy and taxation considerations books and periodicals are two different species) and partly in order to give VG a personal commission interest and shareholding stake in the new company, for which he was so largely responsible. This was typically friendly of EB, a gesture of confidence in VG's abilities and an opportunity for him to build up his personal fortune — a gesture for which he did not give Sir Ernest credit in later years.

Benn's action was also a reflection of the new political creed he was beginning to develop. America had had a profound impact on him: he now rejected outright any form of collectivism and was fast becoming a full-blooded advocate of *laissez-faire* individualism. In letters to *The Times* from 1921 onwards he developed this philosophy and drew attention to any developments — particularly totalitarian — that threatened personal liberties. A consistent man, he believed in providing others with the profit motive, and personally generous, he liked to reward hard work and achievement. Benn had no cause to regret his decision to set up the new firm. On 4 December 1923 he wrote in his diary:

> On Friday we had a board meeting of Ernest Benn Ltd the new book company which is really doing great things . . . the first half year . . . fully justified our highest hopes, the profit appears to be between 4 & 5,000 & reflects the greatest credit on the genius of Victor Gollancz, who is alone responsible. Gollancz is a Jew & a rare combination of education, artistic knowledge & business ability . . .

Ernest Benn Ltd was a staggering success — 'the first great publishing sensation of the post-war years, with the turnover rising from £2,000 on foundation to £250,000 seven years later.'

To assist him with the growing burden of work, Victor returned Douglas Jerrold's favour and recruited him from the Treasury.

> [I] read a little, but even that was hardly sufficient to differentiate me [Jerrold] from the run of young men looking for jobs. Ernest Benn felt as puzzled about it as I did. To this day I remain one of his few unsolved problems. Was I really putting the bread into his mouth or merely taking it

out? I could always see this legitimate but irritating inquiry in his eyes when we met, and his rather pleasant but unrevealing smile seldom reassured me. The spectacle of a young man of apparent intelligence, who was neither an artist nor a poet but still not a business man, filled him with good-natured irritation. Gollancz took a different view. I was there, as far as he was concerned, for that very reason.

When it came to recruitment, Victor was always to display a preference for the *tabula rasa*.

Benn never got over his mistrust of Jerrold, whom he found too much the civil servant in his approach to publishing, and Jerrold failed, as so many others were to fail, to live up to Victor's expectations. But for a few years he was a useful lieutenant, whose cynical eye and acerbic pen add a great deal to our knowledge of Victor's time with Benn.

We worked in Bouverie Street, passing to our dingy offices through a corridor decorated with faded photographs of deceased chairmen of gas companies, some of them with a tie and others with a collar. It was not an inspiring milieu. All the partitions were glass, there were no carpets, and very little business. There were no bells, or at any rate, none which could be heard over the roar of Gollancz's voice shrieking for orders.

Jerrold arrived believing that authors wrote books, publishers published them and booksellers sold them.

And that, of course, is as it should be. The terms on which a publisher does business pre-suppose this division of functions, but alas, it no longer [the late 1940s] has any basis in reality, and only those publishers who themselves are manufacturers of books or who sell direct to the public can make a regular living with any comfort. Victor Gollancz, who has a genius for money-making, was intuitively aware of this profound truth even before it became true, and did his utmost for three years to dissuade me from experimenting with general publishing of the old-fashioned kind. Instead we manufactured art and technical books; tools of trade on which we were able to put a price bearing no relation to the cost, because, as our sales-manager used to say, 'they have *got* to have it'. We published the first books in the English language on automatic telephones, on synthetic rubber, on cotton cellulose, on low temperature carbonization, on hydrogenation, on cellulose esters, and on scientific agriculture according to the Rothamsted formulae.

It was primarily Jerrold's job to ferret out subjects and authors from universities or technical and industrial research institutes. With money plentiful, science and industry innovative, competition unrestricted, and the Benn trade papers to give publicity to Benn books, this staple crop could hardly fail. Victor himself preferred to concentrate on his art books, on which he made a great reputation and a financial killing. He travelled widely in Europe (he even had a Paris office for a short time), buying art and art-related books from German, French and Dutch publishers and selling Benn books in return. The speed with which he built up the list was astonishing. The spring 1924 catalogue of books on fine and applied arts was 32 pages long (itself handsomely printed on expensive paper): it described almost seventy books on oriental art, woodcuts, painting, sculpture, engraving, typography, ornament, drawing, ceramics, decoration, furniture, textiles, stage-craft, illustrated books, metalwork and architecture. Six or seven guineas was the average price of each superb volume, with limited editions in specially fine bindings costing up to twice as much.

> The essential thing about an art book [wrote Jerrold] is that it shall have nothing to do with art. It is either a tool of trade for the collector and dealer or it is just nothing at all, from the sales point of view. The authors of successful art books are provided by the Government in the persons of the officials of the Museums. The illustrations also come largely from the Museums. The skill of the publisher is shown in the collection of his mailing list and the quality of his reproductions, which must be beautiful in themselves and at the same time bear some resemblance to the originals. To make a really beautiful colour plate out of a piece of porcelain, lacquer or jade is not too easy, unless you know the trick. Gollancz did. He employed a miniaturist to paint each object in the appropriate light against the appropriate background. The rest was easy and the results spectacular.

The books were largely geared to collectors of the objects illus-trated. Jerrold, assuming that there must be a cultured market that loved beauty for its own sake, suggested early on to Victor that they should reproduce real paintings and sculpture, or publish books illustrating the culture of an epoch, a race or a religion. ' . . . I can still see the look of horrified despair on his face, and hear the howl of anguish which passed his lips. To say that it passed his lips is indeed a grotesque understatement, for it echoed round the office. I inferred without waiting to be told that the proposal had not got what another of our colleagues called "a good commercial smell about it".'

Another story of Jerrold's gives an amusing account of Victor's working practices and his sense of fun:

> The only art book, if it could be so called, for which I incurred any responsibility was a monumental work on dogs by Mr Edward Ash, that well-known and enthusiastic authority. The book came to me through a chance call of the author's at the office as the result of which I in due course

received one of Gollancz's famous Napoleonic notes beginning, 'I have to-day commissioned the most important work on dogs which has ever appeared'. As a great privilege I was to be allowed to 'produce' it. The months passed by, and 'the most important work' grew more and more so, in its author's eyes, as its length expanded, but less and less so in Gollancz's eyes, as the bills mounted up. When the final reckoning came it was found that the book, although acclaimed as a notable success, had actually made very little money for the publishers. By then 'the most important work which has ever appeared' had become, in Gollancz's office memoranda, 'your book on dogs', and I was the culprit. Gollancz, however, was well repaid by fate for his spiritual desertion of his erstwhile distinguished author, for Mr Ash, it appeared, was a regular concert goer, and Gollancz was always meeting him. Having an uneasy conscience, he felt compelled to conversation, and they had at least a dozen talks on dogs and their habits in the foyer of Covent Garden and at Queen's Hall. And each time Gollancz reported the meeting with a grimmer face. 'There's something wrong with that fellow,' he said finally. 'I simply can't understand it. He doesn't even seem interested in dogs.'

For the author of 'the most important work on dogs which has ever appeared' it certainly sounded odd, but I thought no more of the matter till one day, at the height of the Covent Garden Opera season, Gollancz came into my room laughing uncontrollably. 'The mystery is solved,' he said. 'It isn't Ash.'

'What on earth do you mean?' I asked.

'Well, it just isn't. He was quite rude to me last night. He told me that he couldn't imagine why I always rushed up to him and started a conversation about dogs, which he detests, as he's a cat fan, that he does not write, and that, finally, his name is not Ash.'

It was indeed poetic justice. The idea of Victor leaving his wife and his friends time and again, perhaps even foregoing a drink, in order to make laborious conversation about dogs with a complete stranger, still makes me laugh almost as much as it made him.

On a visit to New York in September 1925, Benn was 'delighted to find how good a reputation we have won with Gollancz's art books', but the boom could not last. There was a finite number of collectors' items, and once the obviously attractive subjects had been covered, the hazards involved in more speculative areas became unacceptable; it was difficult to see scope for expansion. Victor was already burning his fingers on an ambitious Shakespeare project: Harley Granville Barker was editing the plays from the point of view of their stage performance. This time the books themselves were to be the collectable item, and they were lavishly illustrated and superbly printed. One edition was limited to 100 copies at 12 guineas each, the other to 450 copies at 4 guineas. The series was launched in 1923 and abandoned in 1926, after seven volumes had appeared. Half the edition was unsold and the whole venture accounted a failure. If growth was to continue, it was clear it must be in the field of general publishing. Benn had acquired Jarrolds in 1921 (it was sold to Hutchinson at a small profit two years later), and as its Managing Director, Victor had gained useful experience of a fiction list. He was uneasy about the risks involved in moving further into strange territory, but Douglas Jerrold was keen and was allowed to begin the general list with H. A. L. Fisher's *Modern World* series, Harold Laski's on *Political Thought*, and a series of biographies edited by Philip Guedalla. The great success of at least some of these was enough to establish Ernest Benn Ltd as general publishers, and the acquisition in 1926 of Fisher Unwin, with its *First Novel Library*, provided a further base from which to expand. Jerrold noted Victor's initial lack of enthusiasm for his experiments and put his own interpretation on it. 'Gollancz saw himself as the conductor of an orchestra, determining the tune and the tempo. When a book he did not like made money, he had a feeling of resentment. Even where he liked a book, he was indifferent to its success if he had not himself planned it.'

Douglas Jerrold was not imagining things. These observations about Victor were to be borne out time and again in his running of his own firm. It can have been of no consolation to Victor that the two biggest successes of his general publishing list at Benn were due to Ernest Benn himself, who was responsible for acquiring the smash hits *The Intimate Papers of Colonel House* and *The Letters of Gertrude Bell*. As a rule, Benn left Victor to his own devices, but he occasionally exercised his prerogative as head of the firm. *The Letters of Gertrude Bell* had been all but formally rejected when Benn, a close friend of Miss Bell's father, insisted it be published. His gleeful account in his book, *Happier Days*, does not mention Victor, but by implication damns the bulk of his staff of Ernest Benn Ltd. Referring to his over-riding of the 'experts', he wrote:

> It will be the common experience of any normal enterprise, quite outside the book business, that when that order of things happens, trouble is apt to come upon the scene. There is nothing as annoying to managers and editors as interference by the 'old man' up above who, down at the very bottom, is regarded as a fool, and only gains a little in degree of worth as one moves up through the grades of staff. For this reason *The Letters of Gertrude Bell* were badly produced, on poor paper; two thousand copies only were printed and bound in two volumes at £1. 1s. per volume, and the experts waited hopefully for the inevitable remainders, and the writing off of a loss. Nothing of the kind happened: we sold many thousands of the

£2.2s. edition, and many more thousands of a single volume, and to this day the pundits are puzzled to be sure of the particular quality which carried the work to such success.

Victor's other serious error of judgement at Benn's was to turn down (against Jerrold's advice), *Gentlemen Prefer Blondes*, 'but that was not a case of failing to appreciate a masterpiece, but of failing to see a good joke.' Such lost opportunities were rare. As Victor's interest in general publishing grew, he showed himself to have quite as much flair there as in other areas. Between them, he and Jerrold planned the hugely successful *Benn's Sixpenny Library*, a series with 'the revolutionary aim of providing a complete reference library to the best modern thought written by the foremost authorities of the day at the price of sixpence a volume.' Early volumes included David Somervell's *A History of England*, and *The Mind and Its Workings* by C. E. M. Joad. Like the sister series, *Benn's Sixpenny Poets*, the idea in many ways anticipated Allen Lane's Penguins.

The move into fiction began slowly but the tempo accelerated and the range widened. Within a couple of years Ernest Benn Ltd could boast a stable of novelists that included Dorothy L. Sayers, Ethel M. Dell, E. Nesbit, Phyllis Bentley, Robert Hichens and H. G. Wells, for whose *The World of William Clissold* the firm paid the enormous advance of £3,000. The non-fiction list also continued to expand rapidly, and the firm developed a reputation for brilliant advertising. Ernest Benn wrote in 1943 (retrospectively doubting the efficacy of advertising): 'I believe I am entitled to claim to be the father of modern book advertising. When Mr Gollancz was my manager I went in for full pages in the *Daily Herald* and double columns in the *Sunday Times*, and I was, I believe, the first publisher to enter the advertising market in so vigorous a fashion.'

Whoever was the father of the practice, Jerrold claimed credit for the conception of the idea. Certainly the first such advertisement appeared when Victor was abroad, a display bringing to public attention G. P. Gooch's *Germany*, which title was spread in bold capitals across two columns. Predictably enough, Victor was 'more than indignant' when he returned, but when the technique proved effective, he adopted and improved it — giving it, in Glanvill Benn's words, 'pulsating life and vigour'.

As Jerrold describes it, Victor eschewed simple eye-catching announcement of new publications in favour of telling the public what to read. The messages' style owed much to current advertising of consumer goods: '"Be careful. On Friday the most important book of the century is coming out. You will look a fool at dinner if you haven't got a copy and read at least the first few pages." . . . [This] shifted the appeal from the book as food for the mind to the book as an elementary social necessity to people who wished to be considered well informed. But it was the big type that made it possible; the novelty and the noise.'

The tactic worked, but it 'was like Haig's tanks on the Somme. It had achieved a surprise but could not be relied upon to do so again.' Victor, says Jerrold, spotted this at once. He equally quickly spotted that a prerequisite for selling books was good reviews, and that one way to guarantee good reviews was to have the ultimate reviewers recommend the books to you for publication. Gerald Gould, fiction critic of the *Observer*, became a reader for Ernest Benn Ltd in 1926, and when the books he had selected were published, inevitably — and honestly — he praised them. The quoting of reviews helped to sell books and simultaneously to promote reviewers, who enjoyed the publicity themselves. The days of the unsigned review were numbered. Victor was among the first to see the potential of this system for improving business. Others followed, and there were rumblings in the trade about unethical practices.

About Victor's gifts as a publisher there was no dispute. Both Jerrold and Benn, writing at a time when they had little liking left for him, used the word 'genius', and neither man was ever lavish with superlatives. His successes and his innovations were legion and his mistakes few. Philip Unwin, who had come to Bouverie House with Fisher Unwin, found the atmosphere stimulating and exciting. 'On the business side there was the shrewd paternal figure of Sir Ernest . . . Victor Gollancz was in the first flush of his publishing genius.' From the outside it must have seemed that the winning combination of Benn's backing and Victor's flair was set fair for lasting success. That it was destined to be short-lived was because of Victor's temperament. However much rope Benn gave him, he remained the master, and Victor resented having to seek ratification of courses of action that he knew to be right. Publicly, all seemed well. When the now prosperous firm moved into Bouverie House, and laid on a subsidized gourmet lunch for seniors and privileged juniors, Victor was on his best behaviour in the presence of Benn. In his absence, Victor would dominate. Glanvill Benn used to attend.

> Unless Sir Ernest was there too, VG would do most of the talking, telling Jewish jokes as only he could, or holding forth earnestly about the always unique merits of his latest favourite book . . . Intellectually he was well ahead of the 8 or 10 others who might make up the company at lunch. Inevitably resulting in the numbers sometimes dwindling down to

himself, Douglas Jerrold and perhaps one of us new boys, for whom he had undisguised contempt.

If the new boys suffered Victor's disdain, some of their seniors, including Ernest Benn, found him personally objectionable. Until he arrived, the firm had reflected Benn's own civilized, reserved and rather austere personality, but now Victor had brought life, vigour, energy, excitement, emotion and fun into the firm. On the debit side were his arrogance, wilfulness and explosions of bad temper. Neither his virtues nor his failings could be easily ignored by anyone: the noisy expression of his moods bothered even the neighbours. In 1961 he received an anonymous letter:

> Hearing your still pompous and bragging voice today on the radio programme 'Desert Island Discs', I am reminded of your early days with Ernest Benn Ltd, when, although not with the same firm, but in the same building, we found it necessary even in the hottest weather, to close our windows against your shouting and bullying voice.
>
> Surely, whatever your faith, you must realize that more good can be done in this world by quietness and patience, than by all your storming and raging, and your attitude that everyone else is an inferior and has to be bullied.
>
> Never will there be peace in the world whilst men like you exist.

Benn found it unpleasant to be called in to resolve 'an ugly squabble' between Victor and an author, and Victor's young secretary, Dorothy Horsman, was at first in awe of his temper and his habit of hammering on the desk when emphasizing a point. His treatment of the chairman also shocked her: where others were respectful, Victor would rush to his door, knock perfunctorily and 'charge in'. She found a way of coping, having been trained by her experience of a violent father to consider men intrinsically unreasonable. Victor would spend a great deal of time and effort choosing a particular quality of paper for a book, only to reject the mock-up out of hand when it was presented to him — 'Take it all away!' — if his mood was wrong. Horsman learned that this was the very moment when he would delegate responsibilities otherwise strictly reserved for himself. 'New paper? What does that matter? Get new paper!' Although she rebelled occasionally, she came to see his virtues, and to find amusing those absurdities that rendered him by turns exasperating and disarming to his colleagues. Glanvill Benn had little reason to remember Victor other than resentfully, but he enjoyed being in his office as Victor pleaded with a demanding author over the phone. Victor had had his old-fashioned telephone specially equipped with a long cord so that he could stamp

around his office while using it. For the watching Benn, the moment
when Victor got the cord entangled round his legs while continuing
his passionate appeal over a bad telephone line was as good as any
comedy sketch.

Though Victor made some concessions to Ernest Benn, he showed
scant regard for his feelings once he found himself secure. When he
threw a party on the firm's premises for literary London, the guests
were in evening dress, there was a singer and accompanist, and alcohol
(never provided by Benn) was in lavish supply. It was a great success,
but Dorothy Horsman observed Benn frowning on the sidelines. His
son Glanvill was hurt when Victor and Ruth did not give him — a
junior member of the firm — so much as a smile.

In private, Victor denigrated Benn as he had denigrated Fisher:
Benn, like Fisher, was in a position of authority, and denied him *carte
blanche*. In a letter to Ruth in the mid-1920s he wrote: 'I've been having
a series of troubles with the incredible little E.J.P.B. (he is *really* NASTY
— very!) but I don't want to bother you with them . . .'

Benn's more charitable reaction to Victor emerges from his diary.
In January 1927, reviewing the previous year, he showed his
ambivalence.

> *Victor Gollancz* is another story. I spend alternate periods of 3 months each,
> hating him & loving him. His business ability is tremendous, his energy
> abnormal & he has made a great thing of E.B. Ltd. We have backed him
> with about £80,000, more real money, I suppose, than any publisher ever
> had before. The combination of my finance & his flair has produced the
> biggest thing in publishing history. I doubt whether he has any sense of
> responsibility or obligation in respect of our money & that is the weak
> spot. I foresee some sort of partnership in which we take preference shares
> for the bulk of our money, & he gets a permanent interest in ordinary
> shares . . . The development & growth of E.B. Ltd is the feature of the
> year. Every circumstance seems to have been kind to us. Most of our
> books have been successful showing how good is the judgment of
> Gollancz. The Intimate Papers of Colonel House & Wells' Clissold, two
> very big speculations, were both received with acclamation & both made
> money. The combination of Bouverie House & good books & good
> advertising has put us right in front & almost every week brings us the
> offer of another business. In the middle of the year Edgar Greenwood
> offered us his technical books for I think £7,000. I passed him on to Jerrold
> & the price came down to £5,000 & then Gollancz took him in hand &
> bought the business for £3,500. This was followed by Steads books a
> smaller but more important deal & then in September Fisher Unwin came
> along. It is too early to speak with certainty but my feeling is that we have
> done a very good stroke of business.

As the firm expanded, so did Victor's commission. After a couple of years with Benn he was able to live in the conditions necessary to him: comfort with occasional luxuries. His family was also growing: his second daughter, Diana Ruth, was born in December 1921; his third, Julia Vittoria, in July 1923. On a weekend in Paris in 1924, Ruth persuaded him — not without difficulty — to go with her on holiday to Florence. Victor was torn

by a hideous conflict between an essential laziness, an almost ecstatically breathless delight in ease and comfort, and an obsessional drive not merely to work but, as I had been in the habit of calling it in my schooldays at St Paul's, to work 'extra'.

So when my wife kept pulling me to Florence I fought against the temptation for several days, hanging about indecisively, standing by the hour at the entrance to Cook's near the Madeleine and then walking away again; for the obsession to be back in London, to be watching the orders, to be building up the list, had me in its grip. When at last I found myself in the *wagon lit* . . . I was furious.

This time, however, there was a good hotel and enough money, and Victor thoroughly enjoyed the holiday: henceforward, more often than not he was the instigator of their trips abroad.

In 1925 the family (Vita Vittoria, the fourth daughter, was on the way) moved to a house of their own, 42 Ladbroke Grove, complete with six bedrooms and a servants' sitting room. They had had a nanny since 1922. The house cost £4,000; Victor raised a mortgage of only £2,850. Time not money was the reason for Victor ever to deny himself a concert, now they were so well-to-do. Gradually, he was becoming a figure in the literary world; Ruth dressed and behaved as his consort. They had not yet made many new friends, and for a few years their closest association was with members of Ruth's family, for some of whom, at first, Victor showed great warmth.

> I love four daughters of one race
> Right well (do they, do they love me?)
> Dear Lina for her sympathy,
> And Maisie for her brooding grace:
> Sweet Lily for her laughing fun:
> But Ruthie best, for we are one.

Only the passion for Ruth lasted. For a time, Victor valued Lina (by now married to Harold Rubinstein) for her kindness: when Ruth was away she would invite him to their home. May and Lily had the virtues of young womanhood. On their side all the Lowys were conscious of Victor's emotional unpredictability, appreciating his uncertain temper. He could add immeasurably to the pleasure of a family reunion, or he could wreck it. After two disastrous Passover *seder* nights at the home of the Lowy parents, Lily — now the wife of Edward Henriques (with whom Victor never got on) — took over the festival and invited all the family except the Gollanczes. Thereafter, Victor and Ruth organized their own celebration.

Victor's changing moods also impinged on his own household. He adored Ruth, and sent loving letters when they were parted, often even from the office to home, but he frequently inflated petty domestic irritations to the point of bursting with his own rage. Whatever the provocation, Ruth was never seen to lose her temper, accepting gracefully Victor's demands on her time and attention. Through it all, she coped with pregnancies, motherhood, and the burdens of running a large house to high standards. Although Victor was fond of his children, his involvement in their early upbringing was intermittent, and he chafed for a while at the lack of a son. His disappointment when Vita was born was intense and ill-concealed. Harry Yoxall, junior to Victor at St Paul's, was at Dymchurch, in Kent, for a summer holiday in the mid-twenties.

> My boy, then $1\frac{1}{2}$ years old, was being pushed by his nurse in a go-cart along the front, with my daughter ($4\frac{1}{2}$) walking beside, when Victor met them.
> The little boy was admittedly beautiful, with gorgeous golden curls . . . Victor, fed up, I suppose, with his quiverfull of . . . girls, began raving about him, paying no attention to the little girl. 'What a lovely boy he is,' Victor exclaimed, 'what gorgeous hair. How lucky' (to my wife) 'you are to have him.' Whereupon our little girl burst into tears, saying 'The nasty man doesn't like me.' For once, according to my wife, Victor was taken aback and put in his place.

With time, he became resigned: and he bore up bravely when Francesca was born in 1929, and gave her 'Benvenuta' as a first name.

Victor's emotional immaturity verged sometimes on the infantile, as when he tried to eat into the limited time that Ruth could devote to her daughters. There were strong echoes of his own childhood, when he had felt deprived by his mother's obsession with his father. Ruth was 'Mummy' as well as 'Ruthie', and he was often 'Tiny Boy', 'Tiny b' or simply 'B'. Once in the twenties, when she went away for a short holiday with Livia and Diana, a pathetic letter pursued her, bewailing Victor's desperate loneliness, claiming a constant headache, and begging her to return. It was followed by another more reasonable in tone: 'B. hastens to tell his darling Love, so that she gets it at the same time as the other letter, that his head's a good deal better. But he's still *very* lonely!!'

In another letter of the same period: 'My darling darling Ruthie, may we go away for one of our lovely weeks abroad? I've suddenly got an immense desire for the lovely freedom of a week with Mummy in picture galleries, with drives & lunches & reading after dinner in a lounge with a band playing. When shall we go — to Rome or anywhere?'

Ruth occasionally questioned his behaviour, and he could be made aware of his own selfishness. Several of his letters promise better behaviour in the future and plead for forgiveness. One from Germany follows details on book business with

> My darling, I haven't been able to finish the poem. But here's the skeleton of it. I was feeling that it was good that I had gone away, in spite of my (& I know your) loneliness, because it helps one to see things in perspective & to know how much I love you & the children, & I thought that

> > . . .
> > When the long days have run their span
> >
> > . . .
> > You'll welcome me, refashioned man.
> >
> > As once, with faint mysterious smile
> > You welcomed me in Leicester Square,
> > Or when the darkness closed us in
> > By Hurley's river, & we were
> >
> > Bound by a kiss
> >   (to beget & bear & bring up the children happily)
> >
> > Dear lover Ruth, so merciful,
> > So true & loving kind to me,
> > Forget the unworthy thing I am,
> > Remember what I hope to be.

Other letters underline his recognition of his childishness, one giving the encouraging news that he is managing alone and feels 'quite grown up!!'

The strains on Ruth were compounded by her fertility, which forced her for a long time to restrict sexual intercourse. Victor's metaphysical and aesthetic approach to sex posed a serious problem. It is well expressed in the account of his first sexual encounter with Ruth at Hurley after their engagement: 'We went off to a field when we got back, and made physical love to one another in the blaze of a low sun. My manhood was bursting its bounds, and we all but became as one flesh. The "all but" is attributable to the atmosphere of our homes and to the power of our traditions. A beauty was murdered by our reluctance.'

Explaining his views in his memoirs, he described birth-control as a vital contribution to the eradication of world poverty.

> But contraceptives mean wilfulness, planning, preparation: they shackle freedom — I don't mean this bit of freedom or that, but freedom generally, the freedom that's about in the world, and glorifies existence. They interfere with the waywardness of spirit. So they spoil, not necessarily any individual act of intercourse (for perfect union, with or without contraceptives, is always possible), but the whole general scheme of things — the meaning, not so much in events, as between them. And when, by manipulating a contrivance, you stop something reaching its goal of which rushing to a goal is the essence, you are damaging integrity — again I mean integrity as such, over and above particular instances of it; for you are deliberately making a thing deny its own nature. There is little difference in this respect (though a great deal in respect of physical satisfaction) between the use of contraceptives and *coitus interruptus*; and I believe that the injury to nerves which commonly results from *coitus interruptus* is not only the aftermath of physical frustration, but derives also (if you can separate the two) from a shocked perception of spiritual impropriety. In both these cases, those of *coitus interruptus* and prevention by contraceptives, as well as in that of masturbation, you can imagine God saying 'What a waste!'

Abstinence seems to have been the only method available to Ruth, until the opening of the Marie Stopes Clinic in 1927, when spermicide became available and she resorted to it. A letter of 1926 tells of attempts to confront the problem of sexual frustration.

> My darling darling Ruth, I adore you. When I'm alone like this, I know that, though I worship your body, its not your body that I most truly love, but all the best things that have given me joy, that are now all concentrated in you — my lovely smell of grass, & shining street on cold clear nights, & hot sun. Oh my darling Ruth, will you always think, when I'm irritable & worried & not sweet to you, that that's not the real I, but the real I, in his heart, is always always tender to you. God bless you, darling.

Victor was a passionate man, but Ruth ('my lover with the body like Botticelli's Venus in our Uffizi'), was so much the focus of his adoration that infidelity was unthinkable. Uxoriousness is a Jewish trait, and Victor had it in abundance. Not for many years did he talk himself into justifying adultery. Despite the selfishness evident in some of his letters to Ruth, this devotion shone through.

When not writing love letters or bemoaning his loneliness, Victor

made efforts to be 'Papa'. The occasional letter would be conscienti-
ously devoted to reports on those children Ruth had left behind or
enquiries about the health of those with her. Loving messages were
sent to 'darling Poo [Livia]' or 'darling Didi [Diana]' and Vita and Julia
were the apples of their father's eye, but if he was out of sorts and not
feeling 'grown up', they were forgotten.

Victor's five-year contract with Ernest Benn Ltd was due to expire in
April 1928. He started negotiations in December 1926. Although both
he and Benn were later to give the chief reason for their rupture as
political and philosophical differences, these were only a small
element in the equation. At Benn's Victor wanted to earn a great
reputation and a lot of money, so he had put politics temporarily
behind him and did not discuss them in the office. Benn, on the other
hand, had become increasingly politically-minded and the leader of
the Individualist crusade. In 1925 he published *Confessions of a
Capitalist*, which sold a quarter of a million copies in thirteen editions.
Based on a telling of his own success story, the book made the case for
the entrepreneur. It is one of the funnier of the many paradoxes of
Victor's life that Benn, whose *laissez-faire* capitalism was the polar
opposite of everything Victor was to stand for publicly, should have
given him the opportunity to become the entrepreneur *par excellence*,
for the opportunities and rewards he found with Benn would have
been almost impossible to come by elsewhere.

Victor began early discussions about a new contract in order to keep
his options open. The decision for him was a simple one: stay for more
money and prestige, or leave and set up his own firm. Benn found
Victor's financial and other demands excessive but valued his talents
and energy. He had reservations about what he felt to be the *avant garde*
fiction and drama Victor was introducing to the list. Both men were in
some doubt as to the most advantageous outcome of the negotiations,
which reached their peak in August 1927.

On 11 August Victor sent a pessimistic telegram to Ruth (who was
away on holiday with the children): 'FORGIVE NO LETTER DELICATE
NEGOTIATIONS PROCEEDING ARRIVE SEVEN FRIDAY PROBABLY
THIRD CLASS — B'

On 20 August *The Times* carried a report that on the previous day,
at an extraordinary general meeting of Benn Brothers, 'resolutions for
increasing the capital of the company to £250,000 and making a bonus
issue of Preference shares to existing Ordinary shareholders were
confirmed. A. R. Pain, E. G. Benn and V. Gollancz have been
appointed directors of the company.'

This concession was not enough to satisfy Victor. On the morning of 29 August, the matter was settled, and his telegram ran: 'BREACH FINAL GOD BLESS YOU ALL — B'. Ruth responded magnificently:

> My dearest Love
>   . . . I send you from the very depth of my little heart my blessings & love & strength for the future — Be brave & of great courage & God will give you victory as he has given me Victor.
>   If you would like me home for the week-end don't hesitate to let me know —
>   My mind was with you all this morning wondering how things were going. This scrawl is all over the place because my heart is so full of love for you & it has upset the bumping a bit
>   My very sweetest smile & my very deepest love for little Victor
>   from his little Ruth

Benn made his assessment on 5 September 1927.

> *Gollancz goes* This has been a year of new buildings & strikes & upheavals & I have come down to Aldeburgh to think over the last of them, the rupture with Gollancz. His agreement expires next April & ever since last Christmas he has been discussing new terms. These have included the alteration of the name of the firm to Benn & Gollancz & remuneration to match. For 1926–7 Gollancz earned £5,000.
>   The more we discussed the wider became our differences & the end of it all is that we agree to part. The partnership is an unnatural one. First there is the fact that V.G. must be 'boss', he is a natural leader & in his own interest he should set up for himself. Only so can he acquire any real financial sense. Operating with our money it is impossible to restrain the desire to expand — he would ruin us in time. Next there is the difference in tastes & points of view. The exotic, modern, Jewish flavour must prevail in anything he does & that is not my real line.

Victor was at his worst during his years at Benn. He was young; his arrogance was out of control; he was hungry for success and money; he was greedy for Ruth and jealous of his own children. Intent on his own career, he had neither time nor energy for public causes or people in need. He had not entirely forsaken his search for goodness and beauty, even if he expressed it only in the occasional contrite letter to Ruth. It was a matter of priorities. In order to do what he really wanted — to publish propaganda that would improve the world — he needed first to become a resounding success. Setting up his own firm would give him total freedom to publish what he wished, once he had financial security. He had already demonstrated the necessary entrepreneurial gifts, but he had a few more years to put in serving Mammon before he could serve God or the common good.

Ruth supported him in his decision to go it alone, and there were promises of financial backing from family and friends who recognized his ability. The only opposition came from Alex: 'What,' he said, 'leave Benn's? *Benn's?* Don't you know how solid Benn is? And such money you are getting!'

CHAPTER EIGHT

PUBLISHER: THE INDEPENDENT

THE STORY OF Victor Gollancz Limited — its rapid success, shaking the book world, and its sustained prosperity, leaving it one of the most stable publishers in England — has been told in detail by Sheila Hodges in her history of the firm.* The business itself comes into the present biography only insofar as it sheds light on Victor's propensities and preoccupations. Virtual financial impregnability was a precondition to his later crusades, and until it was achieved, he was committed to establishing a successful general publishing house, a process that occupied most of his energies for five years.

He had been undecided for most of 1927 about abandoning the security of the Benn umbrella. His desire for independence warred, during the long negotiations, with his reluctance to risk penury, but by making unacceptable demands on Benn he pushed himself towards the decision to break with him. Simultaneously, he sought, and gained, widespread informal promises of moral and financial support. His initial timidity was in stark contrast to the courage he displayed once the die was cast; it was not his style to build up a business slowly from a modest beginning. Fredric Warburg, nine years later, faced the same central problem that Victor had to resolve.

> An established firm needs no policy. It has its own authors, its prestige, its contacts. New books are attracted to it by a force accurately describable as publishing gravity. It can get along almost, but not quite, without effort. A new firm needs a policy because its authors are few, its prestige not yet earned, its contacts still to be made. Without a policy it may never emerge into sufficient prominence to have a chance of success. A policy, a personality, an aura of some kind is the first essential of a new publishing house.

From the moment Victor made his decision, it was inevitable that the aura of his firm would be one of energy and excitement. Burying any doubts, he brought his *mana* to bear on those whose help or

Gollancz: The Story of a Publishing House (Victor Gollancz Ltd, 1978).

money he needed, convincing them utterly that he would succeed. Those who knew his work at Benn's needed no persuasion. Staff were willing to leave with him; printers and bookbinders promised him long credit; authors he had encouraged and publicized studied their Benn contracts for loopholes; and the *litterati* urged him on.★

Even those who had little time for him personally had faith in his talent. He was promised money by Lowy relatives who believed he had a sound commercial future. On this occasion Victor did not despise the Jewish network: the firm was funded largely by Jewish money. Harry Nathan, who had been a few years senior to Victor at St Paul's, and was now a well-to-do solicitor and a prominent Liberal, found several backers among Jewish businessmen, including Lord Melchett. Others came from the prosperous circle around Ruth's family. *Persona non grata* with most of his own relations, who were in any case not rich, he could not look to them for support.

For a new publishing firm Gollancz was financially solid. At the time of its incorporation, in December 1927, it had a nominal capital of £60,000 made up of 55,000 £1 Ordinary Shares and 100,000 Founders' Shares of one shilling each. Only 40,000 £1 shares were subscribed at first, with six shillings a share paid up. Along with the £5,000 from Victor's Founders' Shares, that gave a cash resource of £17,000. (The £28,000 available to call on if necessary was never needed.) Victor himself purchased 5,000 Ordinary Shares over the next few months. It was a much healthier position than Jonathan Cape's in 1920, when he started on cash reserves of £7,000, but Victor's anxieties required a substantial safety net. His contradictions where money was concerned are illustrated by his method of increasing his stake: he had the nerve and confidence to invest more heavily than necessary in his own firm, but fears about future catastrophe made him loth to hold shares that he might suddenly be required to pay up fully, so he contributed the full £5,000 as soon as possible.

The terms of the agreement between Victor and the firm gave him not only managerial control (his title was Governing Director), but additionally — on the basis of his Founders' Shares — absolute voting control. The agreement was drawn up by Nathan and it was a graphic

★The editor of the *Observer*, J. L. Garvin, sounded one warning note. While recommending warmly that he go ahead, he thought the new firm should be called 'The Victor Publishing Company', leaving the surname out lest its foreignness repel. Victor, as antipathetic to apparent moral cowardice as he was drawn towards self-advertisement, had no time for such pusillanimous advice. In this biography, except where ambiguity might result, the publishing house is 'Gollancz' while the founder remains 'Victor'.

demonstration of the faith his backers had in him. On his side he offered his talents and accepted restrictions on his freedom to leave the firm. On their side they gave him *carte blanche* to run the business as he wished, £1,500 a year fixed salary, and a commission of 10% on the company's net profits.

In the two months between the break with Benn and his actual departure from Bouverie Street, Victor set in train plans for the acquisition of the authors, money and staff he needed. Like most publishers setting up on their own, he did not scruple to recruit writers from the firm he had just left. As he wrote to Dorothy Sayers in 1933, 'I never try and entice authors away from any publisher except Benn: but in his case I make every possible effort to get anyone I want away from him, for I told him I should when we had our final little argument.'

He wrote personal letters to Benn authors he hoped to capture. No copies are available, but the trust he had engendered and his gift for communicating his excitement are clearly shown in this response from Susan Glaspell, the American novelist, in mid-October 1927:

> Dear Victor Gollancz:
>   Writing as you did makes your adventure seem adventure indeed, and that is always something in which we all may partake to the measure we can. Life goes on swiftly, and so adventure is right, for something less than ourselves is the ultimate blasphemy, while the energy to form new, and at the highest — well that is the God we find ourselves unable to give up.
>   Ernest Benn Ltd is to me but a name except in so far as it is a place from which have come occasional letters, signed Gollancz, which make me know what I have tried to do has been seen and felt. In relations with publishers I have before this had pleasant experiences, never before this quite different feeling of understanding from the source . . . Your letter gives me a warm sense of things going on, and so I am grateful, and, I need not add, hopeful . . .

Victor's response would have won the heart of any writer.

CONFIDENTIAL

26th October, 1927

My dear Susan Glaspell,
    Ever so many thanks for your letter. The understanding which it shows is very precious to me.
    I became a free man a few hours ago, so that I am now in a position to write to you about your work. I don't need to tell you that not only do I hope to publish, under my own imprint, all your future work, but I am desperately keen on publishing 'Brook Evans' in my first list. I hope to have some very good things and some very distinctive names in that list,

but you will know that I am saying nothing but the bare truth when I tell you that I would sooner have 'Brook Evans' than any other of the publications which I have in mind.

If you are going to let me have this honour, it will be for Curtis Brown [her agent], of course, to make certain that there is no commitment to Benn in the matter. I do not believe that there is such a commitment. You told us that you were glad we wanted the book, but further than that you never went, and morally, as far as my side of the thing goes, I have no doubts at all. I think I am entitled to say to you in very great confidence that, while the publication of your books has been my greatest single enthusiasm during the past few years, this enthusiasm has had to meet very considerable opposition on the part of colleagues who have not had the same sympathy as I with the gospel you teach. I could put this more strongly if I wished to, but I think you will understand.

I have talked to Curtis Brown about all this, and have told him that I hope that arrangements can be completed in such a way that I may announce 'Brook Evans' when sending information to the press about my first list, which I hope to do in December. I shall, of course, not actually publish any books until well into the New Year.

May I say here about my immediate plans. I am going at once into a temporary office for a couple of months in order to form my Company and complete my first future publishing programmes. Then early in 1928 I shall move into more permanent offices and start practical publishing work.

Again with many thanks for the letter, which I shall treasure,

Yours very sincerely,

Victor Gollancz

Benn had no legal hold on Susan Glaspell, but he had on certain other authors Victor coveted. When Dorothy Sayers requested her release from a contract she said was signed 'as an expression of my confidence in Mr Gollancz and of my appreciation of his kind and generous attitude towards my work', Benn wrote back that he had spent a great deal of money advertising her *Unnatural Death* only because there were two novels to come. Benn's standpoint was reasonable, but he expressed himself in terms so dry in comparison with Victor's that he found himself holding authors against their will.

To Benn, Victor was behaving in an ungrateful and underhand manner. To Victor, Benn was an enemy to be given no quarter. Glanvill Benn concluded that Victor was one of those who could feel only resentment towards a mentor, and Victor had endured six years as protégé and subordinate: the accumulated humiliation ruled out any acknowledgement of Benn's kindness. Yet he behaved well where other publishers were concerned, and his consequent reputation for honourable dealing did much to compensate for some of his more unpopular initiatives.

In addition to his personal attractions to authors who had come to value his taste, percipience and charm in handling them for Benn, Victor was an excellent prospect for other important writers by reason of his boldness. He achieved a certain notoriety later as a cautious man with advances and royalties (cheese-paring, in the view of many authors and agents), but he had the strategic sense to offer big money to established names, an unrivalled eye for a winner amongst unknowns, and the all-important advantage of being a genius at publicity. His ability to generate good commercial ideas himself was also evident from the 1928 list, which included the staggeringly successful omnibus of *Great Short Stories of Detection, Mystery, and Horror* (which Dorothy Sayers was contractually free to edit), George Birmingham's Bible quiz book and Harold Rubinstein's *Great English Plays*.

So profitably had he used his last few weeks at Benn Brothers that only nine days after leaving he could write to Guedalla:

> Any chance of the Palmerston Papers being ready for publication in late Spring rather than Autumn? Things are shaping with fair rapidity and I now see something of a Spring list in sight. But I only want to publish a Spring List if I can get some good names in it, so as to carry a decent first advertising display. Otherwise, I'll wait for my first Bumper Autumn List. Spring would be a great advantage as it would obviate the necessity of living on capital for nine months.

Even though Guedalla's book was unavailable before summer, through energy, inventiveness and cajoling, Victor had a first list of thirty books in proof at the end of December. Hitches and set-backs brought out the best in him. When Glaspell's American publishers demanded that *Brook Evans* be held up to allow simultaneous publication in the summer, he wrote to her pleading 'sentimental' reasons for having in his spring list a book 'typical of the kind of work for the publishing and pushing of which I have fought for five or six years'. And her New York publishers were begged to

> please let me publish in the spring. I have often told you of my feeling for Miss Glaspell's work and you know therefore how much it would mean to me sentimentally to publish 'Brook Evans' with my very first batch: but it would also mean a great deal to me commercially because I want for my start-off in April the biggest possible number of things which I can afford to advertise on a really lavish scale, and 'Brook Evans' is one of them . . .

. . . I wonder if you could stretch the point as a favour to me at the start of my business — a favour which, whether or not the occasion ever arose for me to return it in kind, would always be the occasion for my gratitude.

As so often with Victor, his pleas to the men of business failed, but his appeal to the author succeeded. She bullied the Americans into acquiescence and on 19 April 1928 Gollancz brought out *Brook Evans* as their first publication. Another 63 followed in the course of the year, and after only eight months' trading, a dividend of $7\frac{1}{2}$ per cent was paid to shareholders.

Although friends and investors helped through recommendations, the acquisition of the early books was almost exclusively Victor's work. He had no editorial help. When he left Ernest Benn, and contrary to the expectations of both Benn and Jerrold, he had no job to offer his old friend and lieutenant. Jerrold was bitter, and the bad feeling was intensified over the next decade by professional rivalry (from 1929 Jerrold was a director of Eyre & Spottiswoode) and political antagonism, as Victor moved left and Jerrold right. To on-lookers, it seemed that Victor was betraying Jerrold, but there were reasons for his apparent callousness: Jerrold lacked the kind of commercial flair that Victor admired; his impious outlook and cutting wit often caused offence; he was fractious when in pain from his war wound (a shattered arm); and the intelligence and vehemence with which he expressed his political opinions would have been disastrous in a firm whose destiny was to propagate the opposite view.

An ideal alternative seemed to hand in the person of Leonard Stein, who had agreed before Victor left Benn to invest in his firm and become his partner and deputy chairman. Stein was a man of exceptional intellectual achievement. Five years Victor's senior, he had been a Balliol and University scholar, had taken a First, and had been President of the Union. (Victor once referred to him in a letter, before they got to know each other well, as 'the horrible Stein'.) During the war he had reached the rank of Staff Captain and thereafter had worked as political secretary to the World Zionist Executive. Victor had come to know him well as his publisher at Benn Brothers, and Stein respected Victor's qualities. Also, in 1927, they appeared to be at one politically: Stein was a Liberal candidate. But Stein's fiancée, introduced to Victor in 1927, disliked him on sight and found his manners abominable: when they visited his house, he met them in the library in shirt sleeves, ignored her, and produced some French erotic books for Stein to look at. She did not know Victor well enough to realize that his enjoyment was without prurience. Afterwards, she questioned Stein's decision to go into partnership with Victor, but he assured her that it would work out well: 'there's nothing about him I don't already know.' When Stein's work for the Zionist Executive got in the way, he and Victor agreed amicably to postpone his appointment until 1930. Victor was happy to go it alone for the first couple of years. Quivering with urgency himself, he communicated to his tiny staff and those outsiders on whose co-operation he relied a feeling that nothing in the world was more important than bringing about the greatest publishing sensation of all time. The manner of the move to new premises set the tone. A lease on the Covent Garden offices of a bankrupt publisher, Williams & Norgate, extending back from 14 Henrietta Street to 30 Maiden Lane, had been signed, and Victor found the delay in the evacuation of the building unendurable. As Sheila Hodges described:

> At last he could bear it no longer. He told the two secretaries to pack the files and letters into cardboard boxes and tie them up with string. When this was done he hailed a taxi, had the boxes and two typewriters placed inside, and instructed the driver to take them to No. 14 and to wait for him. Then he and the 'staff' gathered up everything that was left — typing paper, envelopes, odds and ends of pens and pencils — and walked to Henrietta Street. As they approached the front door Victor strode ahead, shoved the door noisily open, planted his armful on the first table he came to, and marched straight on to the room at the far end of the office, which was to be his for the next seventeen years.

Victor's determination to trample over obstacles provided an example for the staff. Dorothy Horsman, who came with him from Ernest Benn as his secretary, turned herself into an efficient production manager within months. Agnes Rasmussen made a similarly speedy transition from secretary to sales manager. (Victor's feminism was put to the test when he became an employer, and came through with flying colours. He expected of women absolute efficiency, commitment and professionalism in what were commonly regarded as men's jobs.) Edgar Dunk of Williams & Norgate came with the building and adapted rapidly from working in a dying firm to being *de facto* company secretary in one about to be born. They and the others who arrived gradually did not openly question Victor's assumption that the inconvenient, dingy offices should remain undecorated and the bare boards uncarpeted. After all, he himself worked happily in a room lit only by a sky-light and described by a colleague as 'bleak and charmless as . . . a by-election committee room'.

Three other directors were on the board at its inception — Stanley Morison, whose typographical genius had been harnessed by Victor in some of the books published by Ernest Benn Ltd; Frank Strawson, Bernard Strauss's brother and a close friend and substantial investor; and William Farquhar Payson of the New York publishers, Payson & Clarke. In theory they were all to be active in the direction of the firm. In practice this idea proved to be a non-starter. Victor ran the company as a kingdom and he wanted no barons. In the first year or so he occasionally consulted his co-directors, but the sham was soon dropped; both he and they recognized that he wanted only assent to his own decisions. Payson & Clarke withdrew their investment and their representative in 1932 when it became clear that the anticipated co-operation between the two firms would not work. Strawson, nominal company secretary, contracted tuberculosis and left the duties to Dunk, content to act as a cypher. Morison was interested in design, not policy, and the enlargement of the board after a year to include Ruth Gollancz brought no challenge to Victor's supremacy. She attended board meetings and undertook some design work (it was she who painted, to Morison's rough design, the VG colophon that hung outside the office) but her chief contribution was organizing Victor and acting as his hostess.

Although Morison severely limited his involvement in the firm, it was he who, next to Victor, played the most distinguished part in its tremendous impact on the book world. Victor knew that he wanted arrestingly designed advertisements and books; Morison had the skill to translate Victor's ideas into compelling reality. The famous Gollancz yellow jackets were the finest achievement of two brilliant men of complementary talents, who shared a disposition to shock people into attention. Morison's best work for Victor was done in the early years. Their mutual respect never warmed to friendship and they were to draw further apart as their politics diverged in the 1930s, with Morison finally resigning from the board in 1939. Their relationship was a stormy one. They often laughed together, but Morison was not prepared to be brow-beaten by Victor, and when he was shouted at, he shouted back. Yet while there was a major role for him to play in putting the firm on the map, he too caught the sense of excitement and gave of his best.

The new venture soon achieved a fame that brought a steady stream of established authors and unsolicited manuscripts to its door. Perceptive readers — Gerald Gould (who had followed from Benn), Ralph Strauss (also a reviewer) and Jon Evans — picked the winners, and Victor planned the publicity campaigns that were to turn unknowns like A. J. Cronin and Eleanor Smith and modest sellers like Daphne du Maurier and Phyllis Bentley into household names. It was his showmanship — visible even in the green ink 'V.G.' signature to his letters — that took English publishing from what Warburg in a purple passage describes as the 'pony-and-trap' period into

> the automobile epoch. Chief among the internal combustion engines was Victor Gollancz, with a very high horse-power. With the foundation of his firm . . . the revolution may be said to have begun. Then we saw the shape of things to come. Instead of the dignified advertisement list of twenty titles set out primly in a modest space, there was the double or triple column, with the title of one book screaming across it in letters three inches high. The forces of modernity had been loosed, the age of shouting, the period of the colossal and the sensational had arrived. It was not to die down till World War II checked its frenzies. Though Gollancz was the great innovator and the lettering of his advertisements the biggest and blackest of all, his competitors did not lag far behind.

The competitors might copy him (Collins and Heinemann were the chief culprits), but they had the persistent problem that Victor's innovativeness and publicity instinct kept him always several jumps ahead. His reputation spread quickly. 'On the continent,' Enid Starkie told him, 'I am told that you are the one publisher today of any nationality who has genius.' Such praise could only serve to boost further his happy reliance on his own instinct for the potential bestseller, and his readiness to lavish advertising money where a publisher less secure about his own judgement would hesitate fatally. When he spent money he spent it on a grand scale. In his first year or two, rivals could console themselves that he would burn himself out. Then, as bestseller followed bestseller, authors deserted them or grumbled that they would sell better with Gollancz. Envious eyes were cast at the annual parties in glamorous surroundings, where obscure Gollancz authors could rub shoulders with London's literary lions, where Ruth dazzled their guests in magnificent gowns (by Motley the theatrical costumiers as often as not), and where on one occasion the chief ornament on the table was an ice-swan filled with caviar. Privately the Gollanczes entertained and were entertained frequently. From the slow social beginning of the 1920s, when they were grateful to meet the famous at the soirées of Robert and Sylvia Lynd, Victor and Ruth were themselves becoming distinguished members of London literary society. By the early 1930s even the most optimistic competitor could no longer dismiss Gollancz as a flash in the pan. The rules had been broken. He published books at the times of the year normally left fallow; he backed newcomers extravagantly; and he dominated the Book Society choices and recommendations. Nor did he endear himself by his obvious contempt for the conservatism of the old guard, his lack of interest in befriending them as individuals, or his distaste for cooperating as a member of the Publishers' Association. ('I refuse,' he shouted to a colleague, 'to be manacled by fools.') Communal efforts to curb him proved futile. He delighted in flouting publishing conventions and often enjoyed the resulting consternation. His belief that he was right and his contempt for his critics made their attacks bearable, even when he was accused of sharp practice and unethical behaviour. To an author upset by reviews, he wrote in 1931:

> Isn't the thing to do when one is unfairly attacked (whatever the nature of the attack, literary or whatnot) to be angry for half-an-hour, and then to forget all about it, and go on with the next thing? I am, at the moment, suffering from a concerted attack by a big group of publishers, apparently solely because I advertise my books! I have been subjected to this sort of thing ever since I started, though the method has constantly changed: first of all I was going broke, then I was stealing other people's authors: now it is that I am being successful, but only because I am advertising, which apparently is immoral . . . You no doubt saw the article in last week's *Bookseller*, which is part of this definite, concerted, almost official movement. The article is, of course, not merely technically libellous, but very wickedly insulting, and quite devilishly contrary to the facts (the actual fact being that, in spite of every kind of blackmail, I have always refused to allow advertising and reviewing to have the slightest connection with each other); and when I first read it I was furious, and actually went so far as to ring up my solicitor, and tell him to get out a writ for libel. Then the whole thing seemed so horribly undignified: if these little men want to be stupid and nasty, why should one bother oneself with them. . . ?

Yet the ethical criticisms were not entirely baseless. Publishers with their noses out of joint were not the only ones to find Victor's advertising methods questionable. J. B. Priestley, whom he knew well, was aggrieved when an advertisement for Louis Golding's *Magnolia Street* claimed it as 'the biggest hit' since *The Good Companions*. His own *Angel Pavement* had sold far more — 130,000 copies. 'Frankly,' he said, 'I consider your advertisement rather unscrupulous, and I think you will find that a good many of your fellow publishers will object to it, though, of course, I bear you no malice.'

Victor's 'distressed' response explained that it all depended on what one meant by 'the biggest hit'.

I should have thought that in the case of books everyone would understand this phrase to imply a very big and immediate success made either by a 'first' book, or by an author whose sales have previously been comparatively small. In this sense *The Good Companions* was a colossal 'hit', and so, for instance, was *The Forsyte Saga* in its one volume form: and just as I don't imagine anyone would think of calling anything of Galsworthy's after *The Forsyte Saga* a 'hit' — although at least one of the subsequent novels has, I believe, sold considerably more than *The Forsyte Saga* — so I don't believe it would occur to anybody to consider *Angel Pavement* a 'hit' in this sense . . .

As to what other publishers think, this has never concerned me, and never will. I think you will agree that the only thing which should concern us is what we think about our own emotions . . .

I need not add that I shall, of course, honour your wishes in the matter, and not use that expression in the advertisements again: and I am very glad that you wrote so frankly to me. Let me, please, be as frank and say that you must not use the word 'unscrupulous' to me.

Priestley responded in a blunt but friendly way, agreeing that Victor's interpretation of 'hit' excused the advertisement, but 'it does not seem to me a usual interpretation! . . . I hasten to withdraw, not "unscrupulous", which I never said, but "rather unscrupulous", by which I meant "careless" rather than anything else. There is, of course, far too much wild advertising of books, but that is the fashion, and there is no help for it. Let me conclude by hoping *Magnolia Street* has all the success it so well deserves.'

Victor's response, disputing various figures given in Priestley's letter, was equally friendly and said all was well, but the exchange did little for their rather uneasy friendship.

The publishers continued to seek some means of putting the upstart in his place. Maurice Richardson attended a formal gathering called by the Secretary of the Publishers' Advertising Circle in 1935.

Luncheon was held in one of the gilded mosaic masonic halls in the Holborn Restaurant. After the waiters had left, the doors were locked and the secretary got up and began to waffle about desirable and undesirable publicity techniques. He was cut short by Charlie Evans, the well-known managing director of Heinemann, a genial fellow not unlike C. B. Cochran. 'Let's get down to brass tacks,' he said with a wave of his cigar. 'We all know what we're here for. How can we down VG? Anyone got any suggestions?'

There was a faintly embarrassed silence. A foreigner might have thought he was calling for a volunteer Sparafucile or hit-man . . .

Nobody had any practical suggestions. Michael Sadleir of Constable, with an expression of weary anguish on his handsome, ravaged features, treated us to a diatribe on the vulgarity of our times as compared with the gracious nineteenth century. He had recently completed his researches for

Fanny by Gaslight, his novel of the Victorian underworld. 'We live,' he said, 'in an age of plugged music, plugged films, and now plugged books. So let us combine together and take vast spaces ourselves and go on taking them, page after page, until we drive him out, out into outer darkness, out, out, out.' It might have been Dr van Helsing planning the exorcism of Dracula. Less than enthusiasm was shown for his proposal. Some of the smaller, specialist publishers shook their heads vigorously. 'Gollancz has got no back list,' they consoled themselves. 'He won't last.'

Soon after this the meeting broke up in desultory confusion.

Victor was never dishonest: that is to say, he kept to the terms of contracts; his counting-house's accounting methods were beyond reproach; he paid royalties promptly; and he was incapable of bribing a reviewer. Yet he often verged on the casuistical. Often he persuaded authors to take small advances or a lower scale of royalties than they were used to in order to leave more money available for advertising. If the early advertisements then failed, by his own criteria, to yield results, he dropped them. He never understood the irritation of authors and agents at this manoeuvre, and was shocked at an attempt to secure his guarantee of a stipulated level of advertising for a particular book.

> It is difficult to explain briefly just why this idea of an advertising guarantee is so abhorrent — and none the less so in the case of a book about which one is extremely enthusiastic. Somehow or other a wrong atmosphere is created: one feels that one is doing what one is doing, not for pleasure, or for the workmanlike handling of a book, or anything of that kind, but because one is compelled to do so: and that produces a sense of irritation and annoyance, and altogether the wrong kind of feeling. Take the case of O'Flaherty. As you know his sales in other hands have not been big: but I think I have got something almost great in *The Martyr*, which I published on Monday last, and as the result you will find a complete double column devoted to this book alone in this coming Sunday's *Observer*, and a half double column in the *Sunday Times*. You know every bit as well as I do that there is no other publisher in London who would risk this on a book: I do it in this case partly for pleasure, and partly because I think that, in the long run, it will be good business. But I feel pretty certain that, if there had been any guarantee of advertising (such a guarantee could obviously not have been on anything like that scale) I should not have splashed the book in this way, but should have confined myself to necessities of the guarantee.

Then there were the novelists (like V. S. Pritchett) who came from other publishers and were themselves classified — for the purposes of advances and royalty scales — as 'new novelists', on the grounds that Victor had never heard of them before, or that their sales were yet low.

Victor's self-justifications were so exhaustive that few were prepared to argue the matter through. They either accepted that he was a law unto himself or they transferred to another publisher. He was even proud of his unpredictability. To Liam O'Flaherty, he wrote: 'I admire *Skerrett* immensely, and am very proud to be publishing it. I feel the happier in liking it so much, because so often (by some piece of perversity) when I take on an author "blind" I dislike the first book he offers me.'

Verbal agreements were another problem. Victor did not like them, but they occasionally evolved during conversation. If disputes arose later, Victor (who believed his memory to be infallible), was always able to argue righteously and powerfully for his version of events. It was the very knowledge that he was telling the truth, as he genuinely saw it, and that he would build his argument on the foundation of that truth, that wore out the opposition. He was always entirely sincere.

A problem that arose over *Magnolia Street* was a classic. The agent, Ralph Pinker, wrote on November 1932 that Louis Golding was labouring 'under rather a strong sense of grievance' because Victor had failed to pay a promised bonus. The response was six and a half pages long. 'I am very sorry to put it that way,' it commenced, 'but in view of the first paragraph of your letter of November 24th, it is no good pretending that I am not myself now "labouring under rather a strong sense of grievance" against Louis Golding.' But for the manner in which the book had been handled, sales would have been poor, and he had advertised it more than any other London publisher would have. Basing his argument on his own recollection of the bonus discussion, Victor went on to present Pinker with an elaborate explanation of why in his view, 'the conditions under which a bonus would be payable had not come off' and therefore he would not pay it. He concluded: 'I have long since ceased to feel the shock which the present kind of business used to give me. But I feel it again now. That Golding should "labour under rather a strong sense of grievance" against *me* — this, I swear, would have profoundly shocked Golding himself six months ago.'

Golding went to another publisher, and Pinker, like other agents, learned to avoid the verbal agreement that only Victor understood. Golding became for Victor another example of the ingratitude of authors. 'I have noticed,' he wrote four years later, 'in the case of some authors a tendency for them in the long run (not, of course, in the first flush of success) to feel a slight *grudge* against the publisher under whose aegis they have become a best seller for the first time. The psychological basis is clear: "After all *I* wrote the book: he merely published it — and made money out of me." I hope you won't let any feeling of that kind remain in the back of your mind: analyse it, it is unworthy.' The psychological basis for Victor's position was equally clear. *He* published the books; they merely wrote them. When in their ingratitude they demanded more money, higher advances or royalties bigger than he wanted to grant, it was out of a failure to recognize the scale of his contribution. As long as best-selling authors assured him of their devotion and gratitude, he acted as often as not with generosity. He never had a cross word with Daphne du Maurier for instance, who was loyal and rather uninterested in money, but demands from less amenable people upset his *amour propre*.

Had Victor not made strenuous efforts to contain his impatience, Gollancz would not have been a success, but his hypersensitivity to criticism frequently goaded him into writing angry letters. One such was a response to an author who lodged a standard complaint: two bookshops visited had expressed ignorance of his book, and the Gollancz traveller had clearly been failing in his duties. 'I am not merely astonished,' wrote Victor

> but also (forgive me, but I really can't help it) very much irritated that an experienced author should write to me in the terms of your letter of September 28th. We deal kindly and gently with the common pheno- menon of the beginner who comes along and tells us that he has enquired in bookshop after bookshop, and that while everybody else's books have been shown his are obviously being ignored by us. But, frankly, to hear the same kind of thing from an author of standing in these busy days is really too much.
>
> Why on earth should any author imagine that, having run the very heavy financial risk of undertaking the publication of a book, we should want to discriminate against it?

When Helen Ashton wrote a cross note accusing the firm of carelessness, and saying it made her sorry she had renewed her contract, Victor responded to her 'extraordinarily unfriendly' letter with:

> I am sorry that you feel sorry that you have renewed your contract. We *immensely* like publishing you and should regret very keenly indeed any severing of the connection: but we are the last people in the world to keep an author against his will and if you really feel that we have been careless and would like to change your Publisher, we should not wish to hold you to your contract against your will.

To Victor's surprise and distress, Helen Ashton informed her agent that the contract was effectively cancelled. Later, he would often dictate his furious letters and wait 24 hours before instructing that they be posted. (Many Gollancz files are enlivened by intemperate correspondence marked 'Not Sent'.) But in the early years, he failed to realize that he was unusual in his capacity to work off his rage in minutes. Unless the cut was very deep, he had virtually forgotten his anger by the time the recipient opened his post.

Natural tactlessness was another problem. In 1928, he took over from the solicitors and the offending author — Humbert Wolfe — the handling of a complaint from Robert Graves and Laura Riding. Wolfe had failed to name her as co-author when discussing a book they had written together. Always a believer in the personal touch, Victor played his best card:

> Dear Mr Robert Graves,
> (You probably do not remember it, but we met in the early days of the war in some little restaurant in Soho. Ralph Rooper, who was one of my most intimate friends, being the other member of the party.)
> It is clear from your letter that some condition of serious friction exists between you and Humbert Wolfe . . . I give you my word of honour that I haven't the smallest doubt whatever that in the matter of the omission of Miss Riding's name he was innocent of any intention whatever to hurt. Miss Riding would, I am sure, be the first to admit that your own name is so much the more famous of the two that it is not unnatural, however regrettable the carelessness, to refer to the book under the name of the more famous collaborator. [Several long paragraphs follow.]
> Forgive me for the length of this letter and for appearing priggishly in the very unusual role of peace-maker. But I know Wolfe well; and I felt I might presume on that meeting with a common friend years ago, to give you my very definite assurance that Wolfe, whatever his faults, is utterly incapable of consciously wounding anyone.

Riding responded with a lengthy exposition of the grievance against Wolfe and, *inter alia*, accused Victor of rudeness in writing to Graves alone. She suggested he drop his 'wrongly inspired peace-making efforts'.

Victor's dignified reply promised to desist and concluded: 'You almost hint, from your reference to "the masculine" contributor, that I am an anti-feminist. It may amuse you to know, therefore, that (a) the whole of my wife's family went to prison in 1913. (b) I, myself, had to keep in hiding at New College for three days because of a protest I made publicly on the river during Eights Week.'

Anger and insensitivity were more than some of his authors could bear, and they voted with their feet. Victor, who was able to say in 1932 that he had a reputation for getting on well with his authors, was four years later admitting that he had lost quite a number by being frank about their books. Frankness also about the idiocy of their complaints, refusal to admit that his memory could be defective ('How dare you,' he shouted at an agent once, 'I am incapable of error!'), and general high-handedness caused trouble with agents too. But his outrageous behaviour was forgiven by many when set against his genius and charm. Graham Watson, who knew him better than any other agent, recalled him as having a contradiction in every provocative twist of his nature.

> Because his heart was in the right place and his faith was in the angels and he was twice the size of life, he was always prepared to pervert every aspect of logic and reason to his own contrary ends. If it suited him to call the moon red on Tuesday, he would expect you to welcome his subsequent pronouncement that it was black on Wednesday. Occasionally, when one boiled with rage at his inconsistencies — people were wrong in thinking that his abrupt changes of belief arose from studied insincerity — he would spot your irritation and, with an immediate change of mood, would charm you back to good humour with a self-deprecatory Jewish anecdote, a giggle of delight at the success of his story and a twisting up of his face which made him look like a monkey.

Above all, he brought exhilaration and laughter into the lives of many of those he dealt with. At the very least, people enjoyed telling stories about his latest capriciousness, and the rampant egotism was more often amusing than enraging. 'My dear Savage,' he wrote to an agent (who was querying a shortfall in a royalty payment to Theodora Benson), 'I have now managed to find the paper. What I promised, in an extremely drunken fit, was that I would make the advance £150 if she began the novel with the sentence "I *am* so glad to see you, Victor." Here is the other £31.9.9.'

At his best, he was unsurpassably deft in dealing with authors. They loved extravagant gestures like telegrams reading 'CONGRATULATIONS ON REALLY SUPERB NOVEL CONSIDER IT MUCH YOUR FINEST WORK'. Far more intelligent and better read than most of his competitors ("ee reads, I mean VG,' said an aged publishers' traveller. 'They don't — publishers don't, you know!'), he gave authors a sense of their own dignity. 'Let me say,' he wrote to Neil Bell,

> that when I said that you should ignore the critics I said it as seriously as anything I have ever said in my life. I have seen author after author pretty nearly ruined by paying too much attention to the critics instead of doing his own work in his own way.
>
> While, therefore, I always feel bound to point out to an author any

criticism which I feel, or which my reader feels . . . nevertheless, the last thing I should wish is that the author should take the slightest notice of this criticism unless he himself agrees with it. I state my own feeling: it is for you to consider whether there is anything in it or not.

And again, to Margaret Iles: 'The thing for you to do is, for the time being (if you can afford it!), to write your best work without any question of its immediate popular appeal: you will then establish yourself, and one of these days you will hit on a theme which you really want to tackle but which also proves popular at the same time — and you will find then that you have already established the *basis* for big sales.'

He fought strongly against the growing trend among American publishers to edit manuscripts and insisted consistently on the paramountcy of the author's integrity. Gollancz gave advice on cutting and provided an editing service if required, but there was no unseemly meddling. Victor's excellent readers gave frank advice and Victor himself, when enthusiastic, was an inspiration. 'You have really sent me home dancing,' wrote Eleanor Farjeon. 'It is so exhilarating to have somebody "see" your book as you've seen it, and going one better on his own. You have left in me a sensation of wonderful satisfaction, and I have been working twice as eagerly since I saw you.' And the poet Humbert Wolfe, to whom Victor behaved with immense personal generosity, could say sincerely ' . . . my dear Victor, no author has ever been luckier in his publisher, no man in a friend than I am in you.' 'I was elated, grateful, and really touched by your charming letter,' wrote Gerard Hopkins. 'One of the great joys of having you for a publisher is that one does get from you such sincere and warm appreciation.'

What made Victor's success with individual authors even more impressive was that he frequently had to simulate an interest in the field in which they worked. Immensely successful for over a decade as a publisher of plays (*Journey's End*, with its monumental sale, made his name), he had to conceal a growing boredom with the *genre*. He had always preferred to read plays rather than attend performances, although his staunch support of the Stage Society in the late 1920s earned him an invitation, in 1929, to stand for election to its Council. Late that same year he admitted to having virtually given up going to the theatre, and he was reading few new pieces. The same trend was evident with poetry, which he published only sporadically — often as a favour to friends. One of his poets, ascribing to Victor an interest he did not possess, wrote enthusiastically to him in 1934:

. . . you must have noted how several publishers have timidly been issuing series of 'new' poets. I have heard them say, without any enthusiasm, 'we must publish some of these fellows' because 'this new-fangled poetry is in the air'. They haven't believed in the 'new' poetry and the people haven't really wanted a poetry that was like a puzzle and had no music. You are different: you put it to the test of yourself, your own judgment and enthusiasm, and I have long thought that you could, if you would, start a revival. The Bloomsbury group have been having it all their own way, sneering at Humbert and at anyone who dared to say a thing simply and musically. The ages are against them. They have no real following, except among the critics whose books outnumber the books of 'new poetry' they celebrate.

Victor soon gave up the struggle with critics and the buying public. With worthy political books to subsidize, he abandoned the publication of poetry to others, and the Gollancz play list dwindled. His position on contemporary fiction (bar detective stories, which he loved) was not much different, although novels were so essential to the firm's prosperity and standing that Gollancz remained a force on the market even while Victor's best energies were being spent on the Left Book Club. To Gerard Hopkins, praising his *An Angel in the Room*, he remarked that 'what especially delighted me was that here at last is a novel of intellectual distinction, which hasn't even a passage of nastiness. I was saying, only a few days ago, what a pity it was that nearly all good modern novels are "nasty" and the bad ones "nice".' With thinly disguised indiscretion, in 1935 he wrote to Elizabeth Bowen, '*Please destroy this letter as soon as you have read it*: for I am going on to say that this is one of not more than half a dozen contemporary novels that I have really enjoyed during the last ten years.' No doubt this made Bowen feel special, but such confidences were counterproductive, for ultimately there was gossip in the literary world that he had lost interest in much of general publishing.

Yet Victor was always prepared to suffer financially rather than dilute the quality of his list. Arthur Croxton, the journalist and theatrical manager, was paid an advance of £150 for his reminiscences, but the manuscript did not live up to expectations. 'Let us put it (very crudely),' wrote Victor, 'that, for better for worse, our publications have something of a "high-brow" flavour, and (again for better for worse) Mr Croxton's book does not fit into that category. It is a good, honest, breezy book of popular reminiscences.' Victor let Croxton keep the advance and the rights to his book, but the experience confirmed his growing reluctance to pay a penny before he saw a manuscript. He had burned his fingers in 1931, when the memoirs of the famous actress Lillah McCarthy, for which he had paid £750, arrived on his desk. He wrote in anguish to her agent:

> I eagerly took it home, and settled down to it the day it arrived. I finished it (though this is hardly the word) in a state of quite ghastly apprehension, and with (literally) cold sweat standing out on my forehead . . .
>
> . . . I would almost say that I have never read so bad a book; and the trouble is, that it is bad from every point of view. It is not merely, to my mind, intellectually contemptible; it is also devoid of any sort of interest, even for the most 'low-brow' reader . . .
>
> . . . It is now obvious, in fact, that the whole of Lillah McCarthy's success must have been due to her beauty, and that she could never have had any brains at all . . .
>
> . . . And then the incredible *clichés*, and bathos. It really seems hardly conceivable that an adult woman, in the year 1930, could begin a paragraph in a book 'I always say "It never rains but it pours"' — or take the last paragraph of all (following on an unbelievably grotesque eulogy of the late Lord Melchett, who really couldn't have been more highly praised by the authoress if he had been God the Son, or even God the Father) beginning 'Life is like that, everything passes' and ending 'God's in His Heaven, All's right with the world.' No, no, no, Moore.

The critical balance between general quality of publications, nicely judged promotional expenditure, size of print runs and personal taste was maintained by Victor through his gut reactions. To many rivals he was some sort of pantomime demon, but the rules of business applied to him as much as anyone. What Benn saw as his 'flashy propensities' — the lavish advertising and entertaining — were not extravagance. The firm's annual parties generated publicity and goodwill. The advertising was never wasteful. Victor's instincts regarding the efficacy of each advertisement or stunt were as good a yardstick as any, although he laid claim to objective science in that regard when he wrote lengthy defences of his decisions to authors and agents. Unnecessary or unproductive outgoings were strictly controlled. With Morison's help, book production costs were kept low through standardization. Unpunctuality and time-wasting were never tolerated; staff were subjected to memorandum after memorandum instructing them to save string and brown paper, to switch off electric lights immediately they ceased to be necessary, never to use office stationery if scrap paper was available, and in every conceivable area to economize. Wages were low, and surroundings generally recognized as Dickensian. Yet those whom Victor considered deserving were given substantial Christmas bonuses, and anyone in real need was treated with considerable generosity: he would haggle over paying a packer an extra two shillings a week, but would think nothing of giving him £50 to help him over a bad time; an underpaid secretary who left because of pregnancy might have her wages paid for a year. Sickness or misfortune rather than comparative wages in the trade was the successful bargaining counter. He governed his staff as an autocrat, but his régime was tempered by the kindness of his heart and his natural propensity to behave like a Victorian paternalist. In the same way, an author in trouble, remembering Victor's tireless negotiations to minimize his advance, would often be surprised at his open-handedness with a loan, or even a generous and unasked-for alteration to the contract. All this was less inconsistent than many observers realized, tying in as it did with Victor's horror of compulsion. He resented paying money he was required to pay but was happy to pay when he did not have to. A correspondence with his old reader, Russell Green, in 1945 illustrates this complex. Green and Victor had never got on well. Green was too careless, irreverent and frivolous, and showed himself a poor psychologist when he put to Victor (years after he had ceased to work for the firm) the suggestion that he might be granted a bonus. He wanted to buy an annuity and avoid a penurious old age, and drew attention to his services in recommending bestsellers in earlier days. The first letter stressed his real need, and thus permitted Victor to overlook the reference to the justice of Green's claim. The second was unfortunately expressed.

During our genial interview some days ago, you enquired why I do not write a best-seller. I replied with a feeble 'tu quoque'.

By an effort of delayed-action 'esprit d'escalier', I realised that my reply should have been:– 'No, my dear Victor, I cannot write best-sellers. I merely select them!'

By that I mean, precisely, that my recommendations of Cronin and Newman and Eleanor Smith (to take three examples and neglect the rest) *alone* poured into your coffers at least

THIRTY THOUSAND POUNDS.

And what was *my* reward?

THIRTY SHILLINGS!!

Your Prophet in Highgate Cemetery would (if I may coin a phrase) 'turn in his grave' if he could hear of this supreme example of 'surplus value' . . .

In brief, no question arises of 'charitable gift', but merely of 'deferred pay'.

Yours ever,

Russell Green

*In the same order of ideas, it recurs to me that only once in my twelve years loyal and strenuous service did you pay me the Xmas Bonus paid to all the rest of your staff.

Green had asked for a minimum of 100 guineas without prejudice to Victor's ideas on a maximum. His plight was too serious for even an infuriated Victor to ignore, but his appeal to justice rather than charity must have considerably reduced the sum he received.

We are willing to make you an ex gratia payment of £100 but simply because, as you gave me to understand, you are in real need of it. You must let me be frank and say that, if anything would have prevented us from giving it you, it is the extraordinary letters which have accompanied your request. We employed you as a reader at a salary which you considered suitable and, while our reader, you recommended certain books to us which turned out successful. (I omit any mention of those which perhaps didn't turn out successful. Nor can anybody say how many best sellers of the finest water you allowed to go.) To base on that fact, and years subsequently, a claim to receive some further sum of money is in the last degree grotesque. And allow me to tell you that you don't begin to understand the theory of surplus value, quite apart from the fact that Karl Marx is *not* my prophet, nor ever has been.

Frankly, we all find your letters very irritating — and I for my part not because of their poor intellectual quality, but because of their bad art.

Yours nevertheless ever,
V.G.

My board, who is here as I dictate this letter, instructs me to add that we want to hear no more of this nonsense in subsequent years, please.

Russell Green was too well acquainted with the true role of the board to respond as if they were the donors.

My dear V.G.,
A thousand thanks!
A noble gesture!
Your cheap
R.G.

Had his early success ever tempted Victor to change his naturally cautious ways with money, a serious legal action in 1931 — over a first novel that turned out to be autobiographical — put paid to any such danger. Henceforward, every manuscript was read for libel by Harold Rubinstein, who received in return a modest fee and access to enough manuscripts to keep him reading happily at home every evening. (And long after Gollancz had abandoned the *genre*, Rubinstein's plays were published, because Victor could not bear to hurt his feelings.) Even that precaution could not eradicate the bogey completely, and occasionally the firm had to pay out money on completely unforeseen libels. It was a problem Victor never learned to take in his stride, specifically because it was both unforeseeable and unquantifiable. Against legal advice, he settled a number of cases out of court when the odds were good that the firm would win the case.

He summed up his position in November 1933 when another suit threatened.

> This is just to let you [Rubinstein] know that I want everything done that can possibly be done at any stage to settle the matter rather than that we should have to fight it . . .
>
> I have a real horror of anything like a legal fight, because of the horrible uncertainty and the incalculable factors . . .
>
> To put the thing in the most extravagant, and no doubt grotesque, form, what I mean is this: if the 99% probability of the outside cost in the case of a fight were £500, and one could settle the thing for £1,000, I should prefer the settlement of the £1,000.

This terror of legal proceedings inhibited Victor from publishing some books he felt to be both artistically worthy and capable of helping mankind. He was never stodgy, and when he began his own business he intended to be a pioneer in literary publishing. It was he who introduced Colette to English readers. In 1928, despite a severe case of nerves about being sent to jail (which led him to take the unprecedented step of asking his co-directors to vote on an issue before they knew his opinion), he published Isadora Duncan's *My Life*. His courage was rewarded by large sales and useful publicity. A young writer, Gamel Woolsey, who 'had hardly hoped to find a publisher understanding and courageous enough', sent the manuscript of her *One Way of Love* in October 1931. Gerald Gould reported it to be 'of a quite unusual sincerity and beauty', but added a caveat:

> To come now to what may be the possible objection to publication, though at the same time it is in my view the most striking and original element in the book. The actual experience of sexual love is described with a naturalness and completeness, an absence of false sentiment on the one side and of prurience on the other, which I have rarely, if ever, known equalled. It is a really quite astonishing performance, and is bound to make a great impression on any honest mind. But of course this involves an amount of plain speaking which the English public might boggle at.

Victor, enthusiastic in his turn, wrote to the author:

> I have read your *One Way of Love* with very great pleasure. It is an exceptionally beautiful piece of work, and I should like to publish it . . .

I think I ought to warn you, however, that in publishing this novel you are running a certain risk. It goes, I believe, farther than any book freely published in England during the last twenty or thirty years, in its absolutely frank description of physical love . . .

Not only does your treatment seem to me completely devoid of offence, but the frankness seems to me absolutely essential to the theme. If I were the author, I would not alter a word of it: nor do I believe that any person of decent mind could possibly find anything that you have written objectionable. Unfortunately, however, that section of public opinion which cries for bannings and prosecutions is not of decent mind: and that section may very well cause trouble.

In other words, I think I ought to warn you that you are running two risks. The first is that the book will be banned by the circulating libraries and many of the booksellers: and that I think is a serious risk (in fact such banning is, I think, almost certain). The second is that you and I will be prosecuted, and even incarcerated. That, I think, is only a very slight risk indeed, and one that I am prepared to take.

It was a brave decision, for it was less than a year since Jonathan Cape had had to destroy all copies of Radclyffe Hall's *The Well of Loneliness*, judged by magistrates to be disgusting, obscene and 'prejudicial to the morals of the community'. Although Cape had been spared jail, it had been technically on the cards. Victor decided to write a foreword which would anticipate ignorant abuse and discourage legal action. Gould approved the idea and the content, although he retained

a faint, instinctive doubt whether the interposition of the publisher between author and public is wholly wise. So far as I can find any reasonable cause for this, it is, I think, a fear that you may attract upon yourself an amount of public and personal hostility which may, in the long run, do harm, and which, even in the short run, may conceivably divert attention from the particular literary merit of the book in question.

The four page foreword, which Gould thought 'quite perfect', spiritedly attacked the sniggerers as well as those who believed no book should be published that one would not give to one's adolescent child. It concentrated on the argument that it is unseemly 'to set down for all to read the most intimate experience of physical love' — a question of manners rather than morals. Although it was, he said, an honourable point of view,

I profoundly differ from it: for if 'life is worthy of the muse', why consider unworthy what is, for the normal man or woman, one of the most beautiful and pleasurable aspects of life?

The fact of the matter is that deep down in the minds of those who feel like this is the old sense of sin — the old feeling that sex is shameful. I believe that the freeing of humanity from this obsession is, after the abolition of poverty and greed (with their sequel in war) the most urgent task that confronts us: and such a book as this seems to me to be one among the things which may contribute towards this end.

Losing his first libel case made Victor lose his nerve. The book had been printed and bound when, in February 1932, he wrote to the author:

This letter is as embarrassing for me to write as it will be, I am afraid, for you to receive. I have delayed sending it because I hoped that I might alter my mind. But I am afraid that I can't do so.

As you probably saw, I was involved in an extremely unpleasant libel action over a book entitled *Children Be Happy*. The book was a perfectly 'proper' one — and was, in fact, far more reticent on many questions than has often been customary in the case of school stories: but the remark of Counsel in Court, which was widely quoted, led to the widespread impression that it was a 'dirty' book. The whole case was given very great publicity — for instance, the *Evening Standard* featured the thing on their front page.

Although the case is happily and satisfactorily settled, it undoubtedly had the effect, for the time being, of focussing upon the firm the attention of what Mr Jonathan Cape called 'smut hounds', and I have been most strongly advised that, if I publish *One Way of Love*, some sort of action is far more likely than it would otherwise have been. I feel that, under these circumstances, I can't go ahead with the publication.

Please don't think that I have, for a single moment, changed my opinion about the book. It seems to me completely devoid of offence for decent minded people: but, of course, one always knew that there would be very many who would at any rate pretend the opposite: and while before I was prepared to take the risk, I don't feel prepared to do so now.

You will understand that this decision is not only, to put it melodramatically, a blow to my pride, but also represents a serious financial loss, as the book is not merely 'set up', but an edition of 1,500 copies is actually printed. I mention this, not because it can affect your own feelings, but to show that, even from the purely financial point of view, it was not a decision that I could come to lightly.

The author was understanding but hoped for eventual publication. Two years later, a colleague of Victor's recommended publication with a couple of minor modifications, but Victor refused to take the risk. It was another example of the extremes of Victor's courage and cowardice. Had the libel action not intervened, he would have taken a gamble, for moral and literary reasons, that few publishers would have entertained. That action had brought to the surface those neurotic anxieties that often paralysed him, so that he ended the episode acting more timidly than was necessary.

Those who found themselves in righteous conspiracy against the forces of reaction frequently took gleeful refuge in mockery of the law. Gerald Gould produced at a party a poem on the arbitrariness of the obscenity rules, and the guests, Victor to the fore, were happy to roar in chorus:

> You may say bloody but may not say bugger;
> You may say bottom but may not say balls.

When it came to actions unrelated to matters moral, even Rubinstein missed the occasional dangerous passage. In 1935 the firm had to pay damages because one Frank Otter had been described in a book by Owen Rutter as having died a bachelor, thus implying that the Plaintiff 'was an immoral woman who had lived with the said Francis Robert Otter as his mistress and that she had falsely and dishonestly attempted to pass herself off as the lawful Wife of the said Francis Robert Otter'. There were several other expensive cases during the 1930s, and so it was not surprising that the lawyers retreated into a caution that annoyed many authors. Printers were so worried that they plagued publishers with queries about the libel potential of their manuscripts. The co-author of a detective story found to his delight the pencilled note '*libel?*' against the following sentences in the proofs:

1. 'We've got your blessed Tory leader Baldwin to blame for the mess we're in'
2. Re the Czechs. 'Why can't Hitler leave the Sexes alone?'
3. 'Pity Hitler don't kill himself'
4. 'Hitler . . . the grotesque maniac'
5. 'Hitler . . . the damned old archer'
6. 'Gout, a once derided complaint now made respectable by the Prime Minister'.

It was July 1939. 'I take it,' the author wrote, 'that somebody else, and *not* your solicitors, was responsible for these notes, of which No. 5 in particular gives me great pleasure. . . . There is, by the way, a parrot in the book named Victor who changes his sex and lays an egg. I trust that Mr Gollancz will not feel himself libelled by this: it is a fictitious parrot and bears no relation to any living person.'

Part of Victor's occasional over-caution came from his difficulty in sharing responsibility. Morison, who could have given much more than technical assistance, had early become irritated at Victor's lack of consideration. In a letter to a friend on 3 December 1928 he wrote

I am sorry that I have not been able to visit you in Vermont. I had the intention of joining my partner, Mr Victor Gollancz, in a business visit to see New York publishers, and I had hoped that he would be able to leave at a reasonable time; but after one postponement and another, he hit upon December as a convenient time; and I must say that it is not the first time that I have found one man's convenience my poison.

In the event, Victor had to cancel the trip, because he would not travel without Ruth, and she was pregnant with their fifth daughter. It is very doubtful in any case whether he could have left the firm to its own devices for the duration of an American trip. His staff might keep things ticking over during his regular holidays or long weekends in Paris, Venice or Rome, but without a full-time responsible partner he could rarely afford even a week or two away at a time. When Leonard Stein arrived in January 1930, it was intended that he fill that gap. Contracted to give most of his working time to Gollancz, he was paid a commission on profits as well as a salary of £1,000 a year, and settled in to work on a project Victor had already turned over to him — *War Letters of Fallen Englishmen*. He was to go through about a thousand letters sent in by members of the public in response to an appeal to the press, then to filter material from colleges and schools and finally to consult what Victor called the 'innumerable privately printed volumes'. The impetus behind the book was Victor at his best: he wished to convey the humanity behind the face of war. He had hired Laurence Housman as editor in a purely consultative capacity. Stein's role was suitable to a bright young editor and it occupied an enormous amount of his time during his first six months with the firm. From then on, he found himself with almost nothing to do. He knew little about publishing and Victor did nothing to teach him. Stein sat in a tiny, seedy office that he hated and waited for work. The two partners communicated occasionally through 'Mr Gollancz — Mr Stein' memoranda, but for the most part Victor ignored him completely.

Stein's resentment fuelled a growing dislike of Victor; they were an appalling combination. Stein was the epitome of the *Jewish Chronicle* ethos. A fervent Zionist, he was loyal and observant of his tradition and his religion, yet in his manners and reserve he was just as intensely English. He was horrified by Victor's treatment of his staff. He flinched at Victor's outbursts of rage and at the generally emotional manner in which office affairs were conducted. 'His heart', he told his wife, 'bleeds for suffering humanity, but not for the individual.' Where others forgave Victor's accesses of fury because the thrills compensated for the spills, Stein saw only a complete disregard for the rules of gentlemanly behaviour. Victor's method of making things up after a tirade of abuse against a female employee — to embrace her and tell her she was beautiful — was not calculated to appeal to his new partner. Nor was his more general familiarity with the staff. They called him VG, and he gave his favourites pet-names. Dorothy Horsman, one of the few women to keep Victor entirely at arm's length, put his behaviour down to attention-seeking, ignored his moods, and got on with her job. (Though even her calm efficiency could be broken through. Morison was the delighted spectator when she once hurled at Victor — one by one — the large pile of order books she carried.) Stein had no job into which to retreat, and he was too conscientious to go on drawing a large income for acting as under-worked editor and occasional high-level messenger.

In mid-1931 a compromise was attempted with the drawing up of a separate list and catalogue for 'Leonard Stein publisher with Gol-lancz', but it came to nothing. Stein had neither the contacts, nor the expertise, nor the flair nor the power to make it work, and even he was beginning to be drawn into open rows with Victor. The final breach came at the end of 1931. Stein left the firm, became a successful barrister and never spoke to his former partner again. In January 1932 he wrote to 'The Secretary':

> You will remember that I have an agreement with you for the publication of a second edition of my book on Zionism. In the circumstances which have now arisen, it will probably be more agreeable both to you and to myself that I should make other arrangements. I shall be quite prepared to release you from the agreement, and shall be glad if you will let me know, on your side, whether it can be regarded as annulled.

The freezing reply exceeded his in formality: 'Messrs Victor Gollancz present their compliments to Mr Stein, and with reference to his letter of the 18th January are quite prepared to release him from the agreement of the publication of a second edition of his book on Zionism. That agreement may, therefore, be considered to be annulled.'

Although Stein had been unable to lighten Victor's load, expansion continued merrily: 1930 was so successful that the company suffered embarrassing liquidity. During the course of the year the board had increased Victor's salary by £500 and his commission on profits had gone up to 20 per cent. The net trading profit, before directors' fees and income tax were deducted, amounted to £24,000 as against £18,000 in 1929. The policy of the company was to put into cash reserves 'every penny which we felt it would be feasible to deal with in this way, without running serious risks of the super-tax bogey.' It was even more galling for Victor to pay unnecessary tax than to vote large sums to passive shareholders, some of whom, while pleased with the handsome dividends, developed qualms about Victor's dictatorial conduct. Edward Henriques, Ruth's brother-in-law, asked in March 1931 that Victor clarify at the next shareholders' meeting aspects of the 1930 report, which had offered less information than the year before. He wanted information about the financing of Mundanus, a subsidiary company set up in September to publish novels in paper covers. (A success in publicity terms, the series died within two years. It was a clever idea, but Victor had not thought it through, so it lacked what Allen Lane brought to Penguin in 1935 — what has been called 'a homogeneity, a cohesive policy.') Henriques was curious too about investments, directors' fees and a number of other matters of detail.

Victor's answer was courteous, detailed and frank, and satisfied Henriques completely, but it also made it clear that he preferred to answer such questions on paper rather than discuss them at the Annual General Meeting. He had no wish to have his decisions debated publicly, and, before long, the shareholders got the message and stopped attending AGMs. They accepted whatever dividends Victor decided to pay them and left him to get on with running the business. Those who knew him well must have been aware that he resented their very existence. Harry Nathan was never really forgiven for helping to put the firm on its feet, perhaps because he was vocally proud of having done so. Like his fellow shareholders, he was an unhappy reminder to Victor that there were claims on his gratitude, and, although he controlled the company, Victor felt it keenly that others owned a large part of it. (Yet he could turn this misfortune to his advantage when it suited him. In the course of a serious dispute with Bernard Strauss's sister over the quality of one of her translations, he explained that the claims of friendship had to be balanced against 'my duty to the Firm which is, as you know, financially only in a very small degree mine, and of which I am, in effect, nothing more than a Trustee.') In private, he objected strongly to others profiting hugely through his talents and hard work. He used annually to calculate how many times over they had recovered their money, and bemoan the unfairness of their yet having a claim on future dividends. The problem was compounded by his conviction that any good year would be followed by a bad one. Keeping down dividends was justified by dark warnings of booms about to end and bubbles about to burst. His fears were sincere. Occasional moments of euphoria never lasted long; anxiety was always uppermost. That anxiety almost always had the positive effect of spurring him on to even harder work and it never manifested itself in public, where his image was one of massive confidence. ('I value my time at one hundred pounds a minute', he wrote to a journalist in 1928.) Typical of the personal publicity he attracted are these extracts from a *News Chronicle* profile of March 1932, part of a series called 'The New Generation':

> When London literary parties talk of 'Victor' or 'VG' they mean Victor Gollancz, one of the livest wires in British book publishing.
>
> A fine scholar, an acute business brain, a practitioner in the unusual, a man of zests, and lightly slashed with genius. A force in literature, whose heart is in politics — Russian flavour.
>
> Thirty-nine, but looks forty-nine — burly head dominated by its bald dome, eyes brown, rather small, humorous, shrewd. Likes to smoke a pipe and pace about while he talks.
>
> Gets through work like a destroyer through sea (his is virtually a one-man business), guts a 75,000 words MS in 45 minutes, sleeps five hours every night and 20 minutes in office armchair every afternoon, often works from 9.15 a.m. to 1 a.m. next day, but believes he could do four times as much work quite easily . . .
>
> The thrills of publishing? Finding a manuscript of remarkable quality even though it be, commercially, a failure; planning, months or years ahead, a large scheme such as the Outline of Modern Knowledge. He believes the interest in books, whether for better or worse, is more widely diffused than ever, and that the tendency will be towards lower prices — a slow approach to the four and sixpenny novel and the seven and sixpenny biography. The cocktail novel has waned — but who can say for how long? The long novel vogue he had thought would end months ago — but it still goes on. Even his alert eyes cannot see the public's mind far ahead.
>
> AMBITIONS: 'To help one day in the building, nationally and internationally, of a more decent economic system.'

Pressures on his time were seriously hampering Victor's ambitions to move beyond straightforward publishing, and it was being borne in on him that a firm with only one senior figure — however hard-working — could not keep everyone happy. The problem that arose with his much-valued Susan Glaspell was an example. She had been delighted with his brilliant handling of *Brook Evans*, which had sold more copies before publication than any of her previous books throughout their entire life. Thrilled, she had looked forward to meeting him on his promised American trip. When that did not materialize, she was understanding, happy with his continued intelligent appreciation of her work. When she arrived in London in November 1931, she wrote to him of the pleasure it would give her to talk things over with him. Victor, who in normal times would have given her a memorable lunch and sent her away feeling cherished, was preoccupied. When in February her agent, Laurence Pollinger, told him she no longer wished to sign a three-novel contract, Victor wrote:

> I have thought over what you told me during the last few days and thought over it rather unhappily.
>
> A horrible suspicion has entered my mind that Miss Glaspell's change of front (if I may without offence call it so) . . . may indicate some feeling of hurt on her side that I have not shown her more attention while in this country. I have myself had a rather guilty feeling about this: but as you know I have had very special calls on my time in one way or another ever since Miss Glaspell has been here. She arrived in the middle of that libel action (now happily settled), which right up until Christmas took up three-quarters of every day, and caused me very great worry and anxiety. As soon as that was out of the way I got gastric 'flu, which left me very low indeed and came just at the time when we are busiest here preparing the accounts for last year. On the top of this there came further great anxiety and pre-occupation, involved in coming to certain internal decisions of which you are aware.
>
> I say all this so that you yourself should not think that I have been wilfully guilty of discourtesy to an author whom, as you know, I immensely admire and respect.

Although Pollinger was sympathetic, the good relationship with Glaspell had gone beyond saving. Victor's very success in making authors feel he was out of the common run made him vulnerable. When he concentrated on them, showed a perceptive grasp of their work, treated them as valued friends and threw his publicity machine behind their books, they thought him a prince among publishers. When his attention strayed, or he seemed to be giving more space to rivals, their disappointment was often proportional to their erstwhile delight. The steady nurturing of a large stable of authors did not in any case come naturally to him. He had his favourites — ideally pretty and talented young women who were also big sellers, though no combination of credentials guaranteed consistent attention. In the case of Glaspell, Victor failed because he had been over-stretched, but there were also unnerving rumblings of discontent from other writers. Ford Madox Ford had been annoyed at Victor's failure to meet him in Paris in December as he had promised. Victor's apologetic response, though it had soothed Ford's irritation, indicated the extent of his necessary abnegation of responsibilities. He explained artlessly that his worries over the libel action had made him forget to cancel all his meetings in Paris. It was one thing to lose a writer because of argument, but to lose them because of neglect was another. Most worrying of all were signs of dissatisfaction in A. J. Cronin, whose first novel, *Hatter's Castle*, had been the smash-hit of 1931. Cronin's wife had stuck a pin in a list of publishers and the typescript had gone to Gollancz. The readers had spotted it as a godsend and Victor had done the rest, throwing everything he knew into a March launch that made Cronin rich and famous overnight. Cronin was grateful but canny, and Victor was made uneasy by his acquisition of an agent, A. D. Peters. In February 1932, with his recent preoccupations fading, he had time to bring his anxiety to the surface. (No apology is made for reproducing the correspondence at length, as it demonstrates so clearly some of Victor's strengths and weaknesses as publisher and man.)

> My dear Cronin:
> I am seriously worried about our relations. I was worried before our interview about *Three Loves*: I was more worried after it: and I am still more worried to-day.
> Before the publication of *Hatter's Castle*, and during the initial sales of that book, all was as well as one could imagine: we met with reasonable frequency: you were cordial in your appreciation of what I was trying to do for the book, and you were kind enough to discuss with me your future projects. I am not conscious that, on my side, there was anything lacking: I think that any publisher would agree that I did the very utmost that could be done for *Hatter's Castle* . . .
> Then, at some point or other, something seems to have gone wrong. I made great efforts to see you at reasonable intervals, but was not allowed to do so . . .
> Then, at our interview here at the office, after I had read *Three Loves*, you will recollect that I *first* ventured to make some purely *artistic* criticisms of the book: secondly, I expressed some doubts as to the magnitude of the sale, and coupled with this expression a tentative suggestion that you might care to consider some reduction in the very big advance — making it clear that, in any event, I accepted the book on the terms laid down in the agreement. I then said that I was sure that you would not connect in any way this suggestion with my *artistic* criticisms of the books: and was surprised and, to put it frankly, hurt, when you sat back in your chair and roared with laughter and said: 'Do you expect the man who has written these two novels to believe that?' That you should be able to say this to me after what I felt to have been real evidence of goodwill on my part, seemed to indicate yet more clearly that something had gone wrong between us.

Other worries were expounded, including Cronin's willingness to take literary advice from his agent, Peters.

> All of this leads me to feel that I have offended in some way, and that I have done this offence many months ago. What is it? In the whole of my life in

publishing (a matter now of about eight years) I have known no case in which relations between an author and myself, having begun as cordially as ours did, have gradually practically ceased altogether. Or is it perhaps that you feel that relations between an author and his publisher ought to be on a purely formal footing — all business matters being transacted through an agent and the publisher's part consisting simply of receiving the manuscript in due course, and publishing it as best he can? This is, of course, a perfectly tenable point of view, but I can't think it a wise one.

Forgive me for writing at such length, but I am really unhappy about the situation, and I feel I must be at fault in some particular or particulars of which I am unconscious.

'My dear V.G.,' responded Cronin,

I am awfully glad to have your letter. I was actually on the point of writing you to say that, although I had obviously disappointed you, you might perhaps let us rally back to our old footing. For I will say that I've been very unhappy at your silence and have contrasted this mentally with the corresponding phase last year when your frequent letters were to me such a source of encouragement and delight.

Now, I'm going to be determinedly honest in this letter so please do believe me when I emphasise that I am acutely conscious of all that you have done for me. I'm fully aware that — where six other publishers might have sent me back the manuscript of 'Hatter's Castle' with a polite refusal *you* accepted it — and by most lavish (and for a first novel, unheard of) publicity secured for it a remarkable success. But if you imply that this success has gone to my head, that my gratitude has evaporated into thin air, then really — you are mistaken. For heaven's sake, V.G., don't think I'm that kind of fool who lies back in his chair and roars with laughter, saying: 'I! *I* who have written these two books — ' If I were like that I'd poison myself on the spot. The fact is that I was horribly nervous during that particular interview and in trying to conceal it gave you no doubt a completely wrong impression of my state of mind. . . .

You see I was then terribly depressed. Your reception of *Three Loves* was the biggest disappointment I've had in my life. Because that book represents a struggle between a natural impulse and a series of inhibitions set up by reviewers it cost me simply torture to write. I do know that certain people like the book . . . but you were the person I wanted to like it; and when you told me frankly that if it hadn't been for *Hatter's Castle* you wouldn't have been disposed to go ahead and publish this . . . I did feel like dying.

Please understand. I *hate* flattery but I am on the other hand terribly sensitive of the view of anyone whose opinion I really value. It was for the identical reason that I hesitated to approach you when the book was still unfinished. I was seething with ideas (*and trouble*) but I was too diffident to bother you. Once at luncheon I did botch through a certain plot for you and was conscious of it for long afterwards. I felt, candidly, that you wanted the finished product — or nothing . . .

Let's wipe out the whole sad misunderstanding and start afresh. I've been struggling for the last six months but now I feel that I've found myself. I have more enthusiasm and confidence than before I sat down to write the first word of *Hatter's Castle*. But I know I'll never get anywhere if I'm at variance with my publisher. And this honestly has made me very unhappy. I have the most cordial feeling towards you and I hope that you may one day entertain a vestige of this for me.

'My dear Cronin,' came the reply, 'I can't tell you how delighted I was to get your letter. I am terribly rushed to-day, and haven't time for more: I will write to you more fully to-morrow or Monday: meanwhile, I didn't want twenty-four hours to pass without letting you know how happy your letter has made me.'

That was the first of many such misunderstandings and reconciliations. Victor learned to curb his frankness, but Cronin, once his fourth book, *The Citadel*, had outstripped in popularity even *Hatter's Castle*, ceased to question his own talent and concentrated more on the small print of contracts. Neither man really liked the other and despite their ostensibly sincere exchanges, they had good reason for mutual mistrust. Certainly Victor was privately unenthusiastic about Cronin's books. They stayed together for decades for commercial reasons: Victor in particular could not afford a rupture. On this occasion such a rupture would have been caused as much by neglect (which was bad business) as by insensitivity (which he could do little about). He needed badly to find a partner who could help to keep the authors happy.

He found him at the *News Chronicle*, working as assistant to the Literary Editor, Robert Lynd. Norman Collins was twenty-five and had worked for three years in the Oxford University Press. Victor wrote apologetically in October 1932 to the *Chronicle*'s editor, Tom Clarke:

Since I started this business I have been looking for a partner: and as I approach forty the matter becomes imperative. As you know, I made one attempt, which was not a success: and now I want to make another.

For some time it has been becoming more and more apparent that Norman Collins is my man. I have sounded him, but nothing final or definite, as I felt I must write to you first. Will you find it in your heart not to hate me, please, and to give us both your blessing and tell me to go ahead.

Clarke responded graciously: 'If Collins goes, it will be a great loss to the paper and to me personally, but I feel I have no right to stand in his way.'

To Lynd, a personal friend, Victor enlarged on his excuses and spoke of Collins as 'that very rare thing — a *young* man (which is what I want) with most, if not all, of the qualities for which I am looking. Also, I believe he will be able to get on with me: and there are not many men who can get on with me in an office.' Lynd, urging Victor to cheer up, wrote that 'while you have struck me a Jack Doyle blow, I don't blame you for delivering the blow. I suspect that I should have done the same thing in the same way.'

Victor happily set about fixing the details of the generous agreement. Collins's three-year contract made him assistant managing director at £1,000 a year, with $2\frac{1}{2}$ per cent of the profits and permission to continue his burgeoning career as a novelist. Even before he arrived he was fêted: at the firm's fifth anniversary dinner the menu, framed in typically jovial style, celebrated his acquisition. When he joined a month later, in January 1933, he was excited about his new career, and Victor was euphoric.

CHAPTER NINE

HISTORY AROUND HIM

VICTOR SET OUT to make the partnership with Collins succeed, for he had no wish to remain a prisoner of his business. From the moment Collins joined he was given work appropriate to his status, business ability and knowledge of the literary world. Collins's sense of the ridiculous made Victor's excesses seem comic rather than irritating, and he greatly admired his gifts — particularly his demonic energy. 'Victor', he said in an interview many years later, 'exuded a greater dynamism than any man I've ever known. Even to see him coming through the front door was like a tempest coming in. He sat down in a chair; the chair creaked. I remember going in to see him one day. He was sharpening a pencil; it was like any lesser man hewing down an oak tree. Everything Victor did was done like that.' For the most part Collins found stimulating the air of perpetual crisis that hung over the firm and, a natural hard worker, he was happy to put in the long hours expected of him.

Not that the relationship was ever entirely easy. Victor almost immediately despatched Collins to America on a book hunt, and there bombarded him with cables couched in a style vehement enough to shake the nerve of any tyro. Collins took a risk and bought Hervey Allen's *Anthony Adverse*, bringing it home to Victor in trepidation. Victor — convinced that long novels were fading in popularity — was horrified by the size of the book, and refused even to read it on the grounds that he was too busy, rebuking Collins for his impetuosity and bad judgement. Collins turned to Gould for help and was greatly relieved when Gould's assessment of the work accorded with his own. Although Victor held off publication until the novel became a smash hit in America, he then launched a brilliant and imaginative publicity campaign. Slow to take off, sales ultimately reached almost 150,000 copies, and when success was guaranteed, Victor celebrated by issuing an advertisement in the form of two cartoons of himself and Collins. The first showed the dejected Collins being reprimanded for buying *Anthony Adverse*. The second had Victor congratulating him on the publication of the tenth edition. ('Mr Gollancz is immediately recognisable,' commented the *Advertisers' Weekly*. 'His business is so personal a one that it would be no bad idea if his portrait were regularly associated with the firm's advertising.')

This public vindication was a sign of how highly Victor had come to value Collins — partly for his skill in adapting himself to Victor's style of running the firm. An onlooker remarked years later that Collins had become so devoted 'that he not only began to think like Gollancz but speak like Gollancz and even look like Gollancz', and Percy Cudlipp dubbed him, retrospectively, 'Norman Collancz'. Though there was never any likelihood that Collins would change his politics to match Victor's, he certainly adopted his literary standards and some of his manner. His letters to authors were modelled on Victor's. He exhibited the same concern for their literary integrity and in his turn attracted encomia, while he could be very sharp with authors or agents who got above themselves. Victor found him an able lieutenant, and Collins gained in confidence. Victor published, and tried to be kind about, Collins's novels, even though privately he disliked them.

During the thirties, despite the inevitable rows (and the absence of any real mutual affection), the partnership worked well and, when required, Victor backed Collins up. He was given a seat on the board and made deputy chairman in 1934. It helped that Victor was becoming busy in other directions, though delegation came very hard to him. Collins was amused at the performance every time Victor went on holiday.

> On the last day before he went he would be in a very benign mood. 'Now, Norman. I'm leaving it all to you. Buy any books you think worthwhile, and if you've got to pay a bit more, then don't worry. Pay it.' Then he would go home and make a phone-call from there. 'Norman, I didn't mean that you should be reckless with money. You mustn't throw it about.' The following morning would bring a phone-call at 9.00 as Victor was about to leave London. 'Norman, I was a bit worried about your reaction to what I said last night. You mustn't be too cautious. I mean if a really good book comes up then you must be prepared to pay over the odds.' Later in the day would come a call from Dover. 'Norman, I didn't mean you should be reckless.'

Victor did his best to overcome his mistrust of anyone else's judgement and his jealousy at Collins's success. A correspondence in March 1938 with Phyllis Bentley, one of Victor's best-selling and most prized authors, tells much about the relationship. Bentley to

Collins: 'I have just looked at the Observer. What a lovely advertisement of *Sleep in Peace*! Thank you!'

Victor to Bentley: 'With reference to your note to Norman Collins, I should like you to know that, busy though I am in a hundred directions, I still not only personally decide how, when and where to advertise all our books, but also personally dictate the advertisements, lay them out and correct the proofs.'

Bentley to Victor: 'I was amused but pleased to have your little note about your personal care for the advertisements this morning. When I sat down on Sunday to thank the firm of Gollancz for the grand advertisement of SIP in the Observer, I hesitated to whom to address it, but thought you would probably be away, performing a wider duty of an international kind. But it is good to know that the master-hand is still on the wheel! As you know, I have always thought that there is no publisher in London whose eye for a book is as eagle as yours, and though I seem to be mixing my metaphors, my opinion remains firm . . .'

This crossed another letter from Victor to her: 'Norman Collins, having seen the carbon of my letter to you, thought you might misinterpret it and think it curt and even angry! My intention was, of course, the very reverse. I was anxious to let you know that I should regard it with horror that *anybody* except myself should attend to the publicity work for your novels.'

Collins to Bentley: 'Just a personal line from me to thank you for your letter which was a very welcome one to receive. It is Gollancz, as he has explained, who actually does the advertisements, but I knew the letter was meant for the firm . . .'

One job Victor delegated to Collins was outside his competence — the acquisition of failing or stagnant firms in order to expand the list and make savings on paper, packing and other overheads. Victor himself had tried and failed on at least four occasions, and so did Collins in his turn. His conclusion was that many publishers were wary of Victor and knew they could not work with him. Victor found this incomprehensible, but had to settle for other means of expansion. He was on good terms with the agent Michael Joseph of Curtis Brown — a source of many excellent books — and when Joseph decided to become a publisher Victor was happy to back him. Michael Joseph Ltd was set up as a subsidiary of Gollancz in 1935. Gollancz invested £4,001 4s. 0d., and Joseph, Victor and Collins were directors. The firms shared premises, packers and accountants.

Robert Lusty (later Chairman and Managing Director of Hutchinson), who began his career with Joseph, later remarked that one could hardly imagine a more contrasting pair. 'Victor was fiery, impetuous, dogmatic, arrogant and excitable; Michael was cool, persuasive, charming and rather cautious. They shared only a considerable vanity.' Joseph, although he ultimately built up a highly successful publishing house, could not meet Victor's over-demanding financial targets and they failed to see eye to eye on many aspects of publishing. He affronted Victor also by accepting 'low-brow' manuscripts. Collins remembered Victor one day trembling with rage as he came in brandishing a new Michael Joseph publication called *Pink and Blue: an anthology of babyhood*. '"What will he do next?" Victor cried. I replied, "How about *Black and Blue: an anthology of childhood?*" He was not amused.'

For his part, Joseph found Victor's interference and criticism trying, and after three years he bought him out when Victor attempted on political grounds to censor a Joseph book.

Victor's early recognition of Collins's competence left him free to look beyond his normal work and make decisions about where to channel his energies, and, by the early thirties, his wealth provided him with a secure base for his endeavours. He and Ruth were able to buy a country house, good furniture and pictures, and their taste was excellent. They were never extravagant, and they bought sparingly, but major purchases appreciated in value. Nor were they inclined to ostentation; even had they been able to afford them, the trappings of wealth had no appeal. Their attractive house at Brimpton, in Berkshire, part-Queen Anne and part-Victorian, was modest enough for a family of their size and range of acquaintance: it could sleep twelve at a pinch. They collected pottery (then un-fashionable), gouaches and other small pieces, but for aesthetic and sentimental reasons — not to impress. Ruth was in full charge of the family finances, keeping accounts, taking decisions on any out-side investments and containing Victor's generosity. She kept him on a tight allowance and held charitable donations to a realistic level. She was a good businesswoman. When her brother Albert, for whom Victor had found a job in 1927, wanted to set up his own printing firm, Gollancz family money provided much of the capital for the Favil Press, Ruth sat on the board, and the venture showed a useful return. Her personal tastes were austere: if she went abroad without Victor, she would stay in a modest hotel and, when he joined her, transfer to an expensive one. She dressed very well and necessarily expensively in public, to please Victor, but she made clothes very professionally for the whole family. The children were brought up knowing that each would in time have to earn her own living.

Outside his office, Victor demanded and got comfort — good hotels, food and wine, first-class travel, a chauffeur, fine cigars and what was alleged to be the biggest, woolliest overcoat in London (which he did not replace until it was too shabby to wear). He took a sybaritic joy in drinking champagne in the garden in spring or eating occasionally in the best restaurants in Europe. Yet he could equally well derive enormous pleasure from a local cheese in an Italian village, or from the taste of water after eating an artichoke. He was not a gourmet in the accepted sense of the word. As his friend Harry Walston observed, Victor could greatly enjoy a rice pudding, but it had to be a first-class rice pudding served in comfortable surroundings. He was always deeply wounded at snide remarks about his daily lunch in the Waldorf or the Savoy Grill, and defended the practice by pointing out that his meals when alone consisted of a plate of cold beef and mustard pickles eaten in twenty minutes. Both he and his detractors had a point. His meal was simple, but he could never have contemplated eating it in a second-rate restaurant. When entertaining, he used the fashionable Ivy. Victor's inchoate guilt about what, in a lesser man, would have been self-indulgence, intensified in later years, but he was able truthfully to justify his standard of living on the grounds that he could not work as hard as he did without such luxuries, for without them he was miserable. Ruth knew that he kept up his work-rate by recharging his sensual batteries in his leisure time.

Music provided the greatest relaxation and with regular attendances in London and short music-packed trips abroad, 1926–36 was a rich decade, dominated in opera by superlative Wagner performances, by 'a galaxy of Verdi performances [that] shone, as a whole, only less brightly than the pre-war ones, for all the lack of a Destinn or Caruso' and by the happy discovery of the wonders of Mozart's operas. He adored the voices of Lotte Lehmann and Elisabeth Schumann, found Yehudi Menuhin a revelation and loved Schnabel as a man and as a pianist of genius. Bruno Walter became his favourite conductor, because 'he had a gift of communication, of sympathy with his audience that almost made one feel one was conducting oneself.'

Salzburg was Victor's musical Mecca, and for several years he made the pilgrimage, but he found time also for detours to Milan, Palermo, Siena, Berlin, Vienna or wherever a musical performance beckoned, and several times a year he attended the Paris Opera. His account of their 1931 holiday shows his priorities and some of the problems Ruth faced in living with him. They had decided that on their way to

Salzburg they would spend a week at Lake Como, which boasted a waterside restaurant (meals outdoors gave Victor intense pleasure). 'But I did not like the atmosphere; the puritanism in me overcame my love of luxury.' So they went to Verona, found it too hot and, having sweated horribly at an open-air performance of *William Tell*, took a car to Merano, where it was dead season and they were virtually alone. Victor found it adorable and they stayed there a fortnight.

> In the early morning, before breakfast, I would walk barefoot on the hotel lawn, to feel the dew between my toes. For lunch we would sit alone at a little table on the veranda. In the afternoon we wandered in the cool shade of the pines down the long Tappeiner Weg, or in the cobbled and arcaded streets; and at tea-time we paraded in the square for the town band, in the company of half Merano and (in patent-leather shoes) Sir Thomas Beecham. We would gladly have prolonged our stay there till winter, even at the cost of missing Salzburg. We did in fact miss three or four performances.
>
> Once we had decided to be off I was in a frenzy (characteristic, I am told) of impatience. I kept urging the chauffeur to go faster, but he insisted on slowing down every time he approached a pair of railway lines, pointing, when I protested, to *Halt wenn ein Zug kommt!* We arrived late, rushed to the Festspielhaus without washing, and were allowed to stand at the back. Lotte Lehmann was singing 'ein sonderbar Ding' just as we got in. But the journey had been too much for my wife, who nearly fainted, and was given brandy in the women's cloakroom . . .

Victor also decided whether they went on holiday alone or accompanied. Sometimes he wanted to take friends at his own expense, and usually the recipients of this bounty were attractive young women. One was Viola (daughter of J. L. Garvin), a poet and for a time Literary Editor of the *Observer*, and a friend of both Gollanczes. (She received much generous moral and financial help from them in her later penurious years.) Ruth did not mind her company, but she would have preferred to be without Sheila Lynd. Victor fell in love frequently, but he had only three major extra-marital infatuations and Sheila (whose Irish name of Síghle he preferred and mispronounced Sigle) was the first of them. He had met her in the late 1920s through her parents, and had found her 'of an eager beauty . . . of a wit and gaiety and intelligence that touched the mind.' Sheila's mother Sylvia was anxious for her two daughters to marry well, and Sheila had been engaged to a man both well-born and with a promising career. When the engagement was broken Sylvia asked Victor to give Sheila a job. He created a position for her, reading manuscripts, interviewing those whom Victor did not want to see himself and finding books. The tone of their relationship by January 1932 is indicated by the close of his formal letter offering her the job.

> The office hours, to which it would be necessary, in the interest of what is called discipline, to adhere to somewhat strictly, are 9.30 to 6.0 on the five real days of the week, and 9.30 to 1.0 on the bogus day: and we go so far as to allow three weeks holiday. These arrangements are usually subject to a month's notice on either side.
>
> Finally, if I may be so gross as to mention it, I should be glad to provide you with pocket-money at the rate of £200 (two hundred pounds) per annum, payable monthly, and, as you might guess, in arrears . . .
>
> Please let me know whether we are to get the band ready for Monday.

Victor found his daily contact (in the office and often over lunch) with Sheila's gaiety and wit insufficient, so he took her on holiday three times. Though Ruth 'would far sooner have been alone with me' she acquiesced, because of her 'beautiful charity, or . . . sane common sense, in sexual matters.' As he said unequivocally in his memoirs, he did not have an affair with Sheila. Even had she been willing, her parents' close friendship with the Gollanczes would have ruled it out. In any event, he was not yet reconciled to infidelity, though still suffering from abstention, much of the time, from sexual intercourse (the spermicide method had failed in 1928). He confined himself to dalliances so open and revelled-in as to provoke J. B. Priestley's remark that any adultery was pure compared to Victor's flirtations. (He once embraced the distinguished novelist Pamela Frankau in a taxi and, when rebuffed, took refuge in 'You do love my Ruthie, don't you?')

Ruth kept him loyal by granting him total freedom. Sylvia Lynd was very shocked when Victor and Sheila travelled in communicating *wagons* to join Ruth in Venice. Sheila called him 'Darling Boss' and showered gratitude on both her benefactors. She was early admitted to a game played by intimates — the elaboration of the mythology surrounding the Gollancz family's familiar, Colonel Moses. Livia has written his short but definitive biography.

> My parents first met Lieut.-Colonel Moses, V.C. (nearly), retired (quite), when he was scootering about on the beam that ran across the ceiling of their bedroom in Campden Hill Square, where they lived immediately after getting married. He is billions of years old, and only failed to be awarded the V.C. after the Zulu War, when it was found that he was fighting on the other side. In shape he resembles my father's nose. He came originally on his little scooter, but later acquired an aeroplane, and is rarely seen without his top-hat. His greatest friends are commas. As my father

took much delight in drawing his picture, Moses tended to proliferate on such places as the office walls, restaurant bills, and in country-house guest books.

As the holidays were tailored to Victor's needs, so too was his home life. His precious time should not be interrupted by troublesome domestic concerns. To the younger children his was an occasional though a powerful presence. When not otherwise engaged, he would discharge his duties as *paterfamilias* on Friday evenings and at Saturday or Sunday lunch. The Friday suppers were attended and enjoyed by all the girls who were over eight or nine, and Victor always gave a blessing after candles had been lit. He had begun to adapt aspects of Jewish ritual to fit the Gollancz family life. He liked the custom of fixing a *mezzuza* (a box containing verses in honour of God) to the door of his home; he loved presiding at *seder* nights; he gave thanks every year on eating any first fruit; and later he was to consecrate one of his houses and conduct Jewish wedding ceremonies after the register office weddings of two of his daughters. None of this indicated any change in Victor's attitude to the practising of the Jewish religion. He opposed unsuccessfully Ruth's routine Saturday attendance with their daughters at the children's service at the West London Reform Synagogue. For Ruth, although she gave in to Victor on most things, remained loyal to her own religion.

The lunches with the children were a more secular affair. On his best behaviour, he held centre-stage as an entertainer. He would recite 'with as much inflation as possible' Edmund Burke's celebrated *paean* to Marie Antoinette; 'a lot of gurgling and giggling' ensued if he missed the pudding with a thread of treacle delivered from a great height — with 'Papa' standing on his chair; rough-and-tumble games of football ended with Victor, more like King-of-the-Castle than goalkeeper, defending the garage doorway against all his daughters; he would imitate a mechanical man's stiff walk and reward with a penny the child who mimicked him best; mock rage could be provoked by pulling on his tie, or another penny prize earned by catching him as he raced around the house; less boisterously, Sherlock Holmes stories and sometimes the Sermon on the Mount were read aloud until his work and the children's strict routine intervened and they all returned to their normal activities.

Even for small children, Victor's *mana* worked. Those few weekly hours with them left an indelible impression. He communicated to them his childhood interest in fossils and on holiday they built up a creditable collection of their own. Yet he found it difficult to communicate with them individually and often took refuge in

incessant teasing of them on the grounds of their notional physical or
intellectual defects. What began as a joke would sometimes go on so
long as to cause real hurt. When they were old enough to merit more
exposure to him they were aware that he was a tense and often difficult
person to be with. He could never relax without stimulation. While he
enjoyed throwing himself single-mindedly into games, demanding
conversation or attending musical performances, he was incapable of
simply sitting round engaging in desultory chat. His explosive temper
could be very frightening and his swift changes of mood meant that he
determined whether an occasion would go well or badly.

In later years the girls appreciated that Victor was in a peculiar
position in being one man in a household of six women. In some ways
it made for family harmony; Victor's jealousy of men would have
augured ill for his relationship with a son. In other ways it served
merely to reinforce the natural law: that Victor merited more
consideration than anyone else. If, for instance, he wanted absolute
quiet while working, everyone lowered her voice. When he and Ruth
took Livia, Diana and a chauffeur abroad, it seemed sensible that
Victor and Ruth should use a first-class hotel, the girls stay in a
second-class establishment, and the chauffeur be lodged less elegantly
again. This arrangement had the dual virtue of economy and training
the girls in independence, but it also reflected Victor's need to be alone
with his beloved Ruthie. Holidays abroad with both parents were
however exceptional. The children expected to be left with their
nurse, Miss Woods ('Woodsie') when Victor and Ruth had their two
or three weeks in Italy or Austria, took their quite frequent short
breaks away, or went to Brimpton for weekends during the school
term to entertain house guests. And the children had their regular
seaside holiday with Ruth.

With their mother at Victor's beck and call, the children saw rather
less of her than they or she might have wished. However, she found
enough time to talk to them, to demonstrate maternal affection and to
awaken in them an interest in art and architecture. As small children,
the younger ones lived under Woodsie's inexorably disciplined
régime, which kept them further away from their parents by sending
them to bed at six. There was even corporal punishment until Ruth
found out and banned the practice. Ruth's attitude to Woodsie's
deficiencies was pragmatic. As she explained later, she felt that if you
found a nurse who was 75 per cent satisfactory, that was the best you
could hope for. Obviously, she was in no position to risk domestic
upheaval by chopping and changing staff, and like Victor she greatly
disliked firing people. Victor was largely unaware of what went on in

the nursery. On one occasion, visiting the place in the middle of the night in search of a biscuit, he found there a small daughter on a similar errand, who, frightened, concocted a lie to explain her presence. He told her the following morning, as he explained in a letter to Woodsie,

> that I could not understand why, when I came in, she was obviously in such a panic of fear, as I had never done anything to make her frightened of me. Then she said in a very low voice, 'When I heard someone coming I thought it was Woodsie'. Dear Miss Woods, this is really quite awful. There is nothing in the world so bad for a child as fear . . . Fear like this leads to every kind of suppression, every sort of lack of frankness, and may well have the gravest possible psychological reactions on a child in after years. You are an unmarried woman: but I must say frankly that the havoc fear of this kind can make in the sexual life of the grown-up person can be quite disastrous.

Urging Woodsie to stay with the children but to mend her ways, he posted the letter after he and Ruth had left for a holiday on the Continent. (Victor handled all domestic-staff crises in the same way. A contemporary letter to his chauffeur, complaining about his strong tobacco, constant sniffing and bad manners with strangers, concluded: 'I do not wish you to discuss this letter with me, or to mention it to me in any way.' If he did not like it, he could get another job.) It was typical that Victor in his genuine worry about the child did not think of the obvious explanation: that she was frightened not by the absent nurse, but by the present father.

That Ruth could accept the restrictions Victor placed on her contact with the children was not just a feature of her realism but of her own attitude to motherhood. As an elderly woman she once told a sympathetic journalist that while she respected her daughters, '"pride in one's children is a sin, leading to possessiveness and the temptation to shape their lives to one's own needs." Remembering the birth of one of her children, she said something extraordinary. "Looking at her for the first time," she said, "free of me after nine months, I could only think of one thing to say to her, and I said, 'Goodbye'."'

As a young girl, Ruth had early sought an unusual degree of independence: as a mother, she sought constantly to give her daughters opportunities to stand on their own feet and develop their individuality. Though at times some of them resented this apparent detachment, most were retrospectively grateful. But the logic behind Ruth's position was not known to others, and she was sometimes criticized behind her back for putting Victor first by so very wide a margin. Intimates at least appreciated that coping with him took up not only most of her time but virtually all her emotional energy. Her occasional efforts to carve out more of a life of her own came to nothing, because they caused him so much distress. She confined herself to occasional good works in support of causes in which they both believed. A letter to her from Victor, dated about 1931, begs forgiveness for having caused a scene because she had had lunch with a male friend. (The letter probably related to Ruth's only flirtation — with the strikingly handsome Reeve Brooke, who much admired her. At her behest, their private meetings were limited to lunch once a year.)

Around this time Ruth abandoned any personal ambition, unrealistic anyway as their social commitments grew and she had to organize a husband, children, ten staff, dogs and two homes, both of which were used increasingly for entertaining. She accepted Victor's friends and made them hers, acting indeed as a consistent point of contact through all Victor's changing enthusiasms. His personality and achievements brought into her life large numbers of agreeable, important or diverting people. The Brimpton garden gave her scope for creativity. For a while three gardeners were employed, but it was Ruth who added the touch of magic that made the outdoor beauties of Brimpton a joy to visitors. She collected seeds while abroad and found ways of making the exotic complement the homely. She could nurture the most unpromising specimen to full glory, and she harnessed Victor's aesthetic sensibilities to produce blasts of colour that took away the breath of observers. ('Did you ever see the dahlias at Brimpton?' asked Robert Lynd suddenly and quite incidentally in one of his columns.) And when he had time, Victor would take a deep interest in the garden's progress. He commissioned a stone seat from Eric Gill and in surviving memoranda from his office to the head gardener he showed considerable knowledge about the names and care of plants, and the usual sense of urgency about the need to make all improvements at top speed. Brimpton became a wonderful setting for summer weekend parties and Victor's lavishness as a host and infectious *bonhomie* made for memorable gatherings. He had the gift of communicating to others at least some of the intense sensual pleasure he found in nature, well illustrated by one of the very many passages on the subject that appear in his reminiscences. He was extolling the unexpectedness of a garden:

> I am not thinking of what you might call the ordinary new things that are suddenly blooming after a week's interval but have been forgotten about since last year: all the purples and blues, for example — the veronicas, and grandiflora geraniums, and tradescantias with paint-blobs of gold, that are

everywhere round me as I stroll about lazily, unable to begin the day's work: but I have seen, with a stab of quite different surprise, a many-branched clump of sweet-william. Its tufts of strong hair are still almost entirely green; but on five of them a single white flower, all crumpled before unfolding, brings the colour of July to my eyes and its smell to my nostrils. And on one of these little white packets a lady-bird is resting.

One of his guests recalled mornings when Victor would be up at dawn to walk barefoot in the dew. 'The sluggards who slunk down to breakfast around 8.30 were made to feel very poor fish at not being equal to the spiritual ecstasy of summer dawns.' Another remembered Victor rushing to seize from a tree and noisily crunch into an apple that had had the sun on it for some hours: that, he explained, gave it a special magical taste. His intoxication with the senses awed and moved his friends, made them see through new eyes what they had previously taken for granted and more than compensated for the egotistical behaviour which was part and parcel of him. Rose Macaulay, to whom Ruth and Victor were very close for some years (she was one of those who entered with delight into the Colonel Moses mythology) summed up one weekend:

A line to bless you! What a *lovely* week-end. I can't forget the garden full of glasses & bottles & toads & music & trees & the moon coming up, and that elf-like child dancing on the sward; and all the lovely day — the garden, & the river, & the tree I sat in, and the onion-potato salad & the chicken & the salmon squash, & the raspberries, and those heavenly tunes playing, and R and V, and everyone . . . so nice, & dancing on the grass, against the background of delphinia.

Even the Emperor Haile Selassie, whom the Gollanczes entertained when he was in exile after Mussolini annexed Abyssinia, was driven to rapture:

To the lady Gollancz, wise in kindness and motherhood, and the eternal youth of beauty, Greetings.

I thank her for her wonderful weekend and shall carry back to my country the memory of her garden and its flowers and birds and her home with its music and pictures and good words. In my country there is no such peace; and our slaves are less willing than her own; nor are our courtiers willing to participate in the gardening and the publife of beer and darts.

To her most wise and dialectical husband kind in all things including the cigar and the brandy, also Greetings.

Ras Tafari,

Emperor (until the present) of the Abyssinians.

At first, those invited were mainly from the literary world: the Lynds, the novelist Alan Thomas and his wife Elsa, Rose Macaulay, the cartoonist David Low and his wife Madeline, the Goulds, the Collinses, Benn Levy and his wife Constance Cummings, and a sprinkling of Gollancz authors. These mingled with a few Lowy relatives and old friends like Reeve and Dorothy Brooke and Otto and the Frank Strawsons. It was noticeable though that most of the guests even in those early days were politically aware and liberal or left-wing in sentiment, for at all times Victor enjoyed vigorous discussion on current affairs with those who broadly shared his attitudes.

At the time of the Brimpton purchase he was going through a rapid change in his political outlook. Publishing had filled his thoughts during the twenties. In his memoirs he records that he walked every day to his office at Benn's during the General Strike, but could not remember whether he called himself a socialist then. If he did, it was a misnomer. He had been greatly attracted by guild socialism during its heyday, had 'thrilled' to the Russian Revolution and had helped to establish the 1917 Club, but liberalism was still dominant when he started his firm a year after the Strike. The only political book in his first list was *Liberalism and Some Problems of To-day*, co-edited by Harry Nathan.

From the moment he became an independent publisher he wanted to disseminate political propaganda, but he was hampered at the beginning by his own confusion of mind. In February 1928, he told Alexander Werth, translator of *The Diary of a Communist Schoolboy* (a revelation of 'the new spirit in both Russian life and literature'), that he was probably more sympathetic to its doctrine than Werth himself, but in October he showed the limits of his sympathy with the Soviet Union when he was asked to pay royalties on a Werth translation of the diary of Tolstoy's wife.

> If . . . I can be assured that remuneration will really go to the Tolstoy family and remain with them, I shall . . . be happy to remunerate them suitably; but if, on the other hand, the money is to go to the Soviet Government, not a penny piece will I pay. Why should I? The Soviet Government publishes the works of English authors in translation without paying these authors a penny. Why should, then, the English publisher pay the Soviet Government anything for the translation of a Russian work?

In the same month he asked the journalist Henry Nevinson to edit an anthology (ultimately called *England's Voice of Freedom*) in praise of liberty, to feature Shelley, Blake and John Stuart Mill. 'My very pessimistic view is that we are at the beginning of a new period of attack on liberty of every kind, and that the publication of such a book as I have in mind may do its little something to stem this movement.' He published it at a very low price to get it read as widely as possible and was deeply disappointed when it fell 'flatter than the ghost of a pancake'.

In 1929, his need to clarify his political philosophy was made more urgent by the hopeless divisions within the Liberal Party and, more particularly, his anxiety that the economic crisis would inevitably lead to war brought to the fore his hatred of killing and suffering. In the same year he published *Journey's End*, a play about the futility and waste of the Great War, and wrote to Gould asking if he had read a recent Gollancz-published novel about a conscientious objector:

> . . . if you did, and if you felt as I felt, that the man had said something very much worth while, and had said it extraordinarily well — you may care to know that the book has been absolutely ignored by the press — I believe there have only been two reviews in all and those inconspicuous ones. If you did like the book, therefore, you may care to do something about it.
>
> You will understand that I am writing for political rather than for commercial reasons — in fact as the result of just having seen a young militarist on my staff standing at attention in my outer office during the two minutes' silence.

In the same year again he devised *War Letters of Fallen Englishmen* as a contribution towards peace. His attitude was summed up in a letter of September 1930 to Lady Rhondda, editor of *Time and Tide*, whose reviewer had implied that the book whitewashed the horrors of war.

> I think you will agree that two and only two impressions remain in any sensitive mind after reading the book —
> (1) The impression of an overwhelming horror of the stupidity and futility of the whole business.
> (2) The impression of what one reviewer has called the amazing 'spiritual grace' of men faced with the last unimaginable disaster.
> The War was utterly foul: man after man who fought in it showed almost unbelievable beauty of mind and spirit.
> . . . I will add that both Mr Laurence Housman and myself (who was responsible for the initiation of the book) are pacifists to the point of extreme bitterness.

He could see that pacifism alone was not enough; his antipathy to capitalism as a philosophy hardened into a conviction that, by encouraging greed, it made men worse and so was responsible for war. The Liberal Party could no longer offer anything to counter the attractions of socialism, which Victor had started to study seriously. When, in September 1929, Benn Levy said of a Gollancz novel that 'I find a page of it far harder to read than two volumes of "Das Kapital",' Victor's defence ended

> Incidentally, I equally differ from you on the question of the dullness of *Das Kapital*★ — in my view about the fourth most enthralling volume of the world's literature.
>
> Yours ever quand même,
Victor
>
> ★It combines all the attraction of
> a   an A+ detective story
> b   a gospel
> c   you must guess

Gradually, Victor was moving towards socialism, but contradictions were evident. He was a supporter of the League of Nations and in accord with the notion of collective security, yet his pacifism made him close his eyes — like so many of his contemporaries — to the impossibility of making the League effective without military muscle. Like Lloyd George (with whom he was in some respects back in sympathy), he believed that disarmament was the answer, and he published with approval a book on *Scientific Disarmament* in 1931. Yet he had little optimism that the message of the book would receive the necessary support. 'I believe,' he wrote in March to Victor Lefebure, the author, 'the modern world is far too careless to bother about saving itself.'

The burden of work for the firm, and a reluctance to commit himself before he was certain, held Victor back for a time from becoming a campaigning socialist. In May 1931, however, he suddenly made up his mind. The Labour government, which had been in office since 1929, seemed to offer hope for a recovery, through radical action, from the economic depression. Unemployment was rising sharply and there was pressure on the pound. Victor was frantic to be allowed to help: business had to go into second place. To the Prime Minister, Ramsay MacDonald, he wrote to announce his desire to 'take an active part immediately in Labour politics: by this I mean, not merely that I wish to contest a seat at the next General Election (which I do) but also that I wish to devote as much time and energy as possible to working for the Party.' He explained his history, and his original intention of going into full-time politics at 45. Now, at 38, he had revised his plans: he wanted to devote his 'considerable surplus energy' to the object he had 'at heart'. 'I am not an *arriviste*. I have always hated poverty, oppression and war: and I want to be allowed to use the energy which has been given to me to do my share in ridding the world of them. Will you see me?'

MacDonald saw him in July and welcoming overtures were made by the Labour Party organization. The following month the government collapsed when the cabinet split (over the wage cuts and other economy measures proposed to halt the slide of the pound). On 24 August 1931 MacDonald became Prime Minister of a National government which the following month introduced a harsh emergency budget and suspended the gold standard.

This was a crushing blow to Victor, who sided with that wing of the Labour movement that rejected and expelled MacDonald. His parliamentary political ambitions now temporarily dead, he was left with the burning desire of the old schoolmaster, to explain to the 'intelligent man in the street' what was happening. To Pethick-Lawrence, now out of office but Financial Secretary to the Treasury during the Labour government, he wrote on 31 August describing the 30,000-word book he would like written in a week. 'There would have, of course, to be a certain amount of historical background, and then a really clear picture of the thing, below the surface, so to speak — so that, when the time comes, the voter may really understand something about the gold standard, inflation, bankers' conspiracies, flights from the pound, over-production, credits, and the rest.'

Although Victor was delighted with what Pethick-Lawrence produced, and got it out in time for the October general election, it had little effect. Shortly after the National government won their crushing victory over the Labour Party proper, Victor wrote sadly to Pethick-Lawrence, who had hoped for sales of 100,000. 'I am extremely sorry to say that *This Gold Crisis* has done badly. It was practically boycotted by the booksellers, who are always Tory; and the advertising produced little result. I suppose this is all part and parcel of the general *débâcle*. The most tragic part of the whole business is that the public doesn't appear to want to know.'

Victor's despair did not express itself in inaction. As he had set out to tackle the Repton boys' ignorance, so he determined to educate the public. He knew there must be a thirst for information marketed in the right way; he had proved it with his first-ever omnibus of new material, *An Outline of Modern Knowledge*, inspired by him and edited by William Rose. Over half a million words long, it sold 70,000 copies in the eight-and-sixpenny edition. If he believed in a book, he was prepared to find time and take financial risks for it, producing unlikely successes. G. D. H. Cole, the most prolific of socialist writers, was the author of a bestseller, *The Intelligent Man's Guide through World Chaos*, retailing at five shillings for 672 pages of facts, tables and diagrams.

Throughout 1932, with the Labour Party split, the Liberals weak and the National government unable to cope with mass unemployment, domestic events drove most middle-class intellectuals remorselessly towards socialism. Even those unhappy with the dictatorship of Stalin saw in the much-trumpeted progress of the Soviet Union's Five Year Plan (begun in 1928) a radical alternative to the failures of capitalist societies. Simultaneously, the clear indications that the Disarmament Conference would fail because of French intransigence in the face of German demands for parity, the League of Nations' impotence in the face of the Japanese invasion of Manchuria, and the electoral successes of the Nazis added to the general disillusion, and made more urgent the search for alternative methods of saving western civilization from collapse or war. Victor showed less enthusiasm for communism than the more radical of the intelligentsia in 1932, but he eschewed doctrinal squabbling. In a year when he chose to commission Cole rather than his communist alternatives to write *What Marx Really Meant* and to edit *What Everybody Wants to Know about Money*, he also published the Marxist-inspired *The Coming Struggle for Power* by John Strachey, a recent convert from Labour to the Soviet view of planning. Fully committed to socialism himself, Victor was anxious to unify the left rather than align himself with any camp, and to entice towards the common socialist cause all men of good will whose minds were open.

In October 1932, he was faced with a letter in the *Daily Telegraph* whose signatories were headed by William Temple, Archbishop of York (the other Repton 'elephant'), protesting against the absence of Christian instruction from a successful Gollancz publication, *An Outline for Boys and Girls and Their Parents*, edited by Naomi Mitchison. After a correspondence with Temple he wrote to him:

> I should like to publish a book entitled 'Christianity and the Crisis' . . . but my general idea is that the book should start with a discussion as to just to what extent Christianity should take any active part in national and international 'politics', and then should go on to a specific consideration of such topics as poverty, unemployment, disarmament, international relations, Russia, etc . . .
>
> Will you edit such a book?

When Temple, mollified and cordial, refused on the grounds of lack of time, Victor put the proposition to a less eminent but more radical cleric, Canon Percy Dearmer of Westminster Abbey, who agreed. A follow-up letter showed Victor's hand more clearly:

> I should explain that I am perhaps a rather peculiar kind of publisher in that, on topics which I believe to be of vital importance, I am anxious to publish nothing with which I am not myself in agreement . . .
>
> Now the book I had in mind . . . must have two main characteristics:
>
> (1) it must be 'official' in the sense that among its contributors must be a considerable number of high dignitaries of the Church, and there must be an introduction by a very high dignitary indeed . . .
>
> (2) Having started out from the position that Christianity is not solely a religion of personal salvation, but must essentially concern itself with politics, the book should then definitely go 'all out' for immediate and practical socialism and internationalism.

He had been perturbed by suggestions from churchmen that the book should be free of propaganda and that contributors should not include extreme pacifists. Fearing that 'the Church *as a church* could not conceivably come out in favour of genuine socialism and antinationalism', he thought of scrapping the project, but Canon Dearmer was able to reassure him and it went ahead. In the same month, November 1932, asking the publisher and writer Leonard Woolf to edit a book which came to be called *The Intelligent Man's Way to Prevent War*, Victor showed how fast the educator was becoming a skilled propagandist.

> The crux of the book, from my point of view, is to be found in the last section. ('International Socialism the Key to Peace'). In saying this I don't mean that I want the other articles to lead up tendentiously to this final section. On the contrary, I want each of the previous articles to be written by somebody who believes that the most important thing for peace is the particular thing dealt with in his own section. But I want the reader to go away, having finished the book, with the impression that, while all the things dealt with in the earlier chapters may be good and vitally necessary under present conditions (and must therefore be vigorously worked for), ultimately the most important thing of all is the working for international socialism. You will understand, therefore, that from this point of view it is even desirable that, though everyone associated with the book must be, of course, 'liberal-minded', the other sections should not, if possible, be written by people definitely associated in the public mind with socialism. For instance, someone of the *type* of Gilbert Murray or Cecil* would be best for the chapter on the League . . .

Looking back on that period twenty years later, Victor re-

*Lord Robert Cecil, whose work for the League of Nations was to win him the Nobel Peace Prize in 1937.

membered his vitals being gripped by the passion 'to make people *see*' that if capitalism persisted, this kind of crisis was inevitable.

> . . . There are days in a man's life when his duty seems quite beyond question, and he never stops to ask himself 'Might something else be better?' This is how I felt about things then. Pacifism was asleep in me, biding its time: it could hardly have seemed relevant to what alone I regarded as actual — namely how, when every moment was precious, I might use such resources as had been granted me to prevent, or help in preventing, another war. To *prevent* — once again that was everything. The possibility of joining a pacifist movement, and working actively in it, never entered my head: if it had, I should have rejected it as a betrayal. I had other fish to fry and the frying of them absorbed my whole attention . . . when I have at last made up my mind to do a thing, I go obsessively at it to the exclusion of everything else.
>
> Then came 1933. For all that I have just written, I don't think I had ever really faced the possibility that Hitler might come to power. We had been at Salzburg for the festival, Ruth and I, the previous summer, and had idled a little at Munich . . . on our way back to England. Arrived there, I found the manuscript of Edgar Mowrer's *Germany Puts the Clock Back* on my desk: I rejected it as far-fetched and war-mongering. And yet I ought to have been convinced by what I had experienced at Munich itself. Strolling one afternoon to the *Alte Pinakothek* we had passed the Brown House. Guards, with steel helmets and bayoneted rifles, were standing on the pavement; and as we hurried away I had a feeling of naked contact with filthiness that I had never had before and have rarely had since, except when reading of executions.
>
> But when I opened *The Times* on that January morning I didn't doubt for a moment what was coming: I knew that war, some time or other during the next ten years or so, was all but inevitable. Franci was only three or four then, and I saw very vividly the London of eleven years later; and before the month was out I had bought Brimpton.
>
> And now what I had felt to be my duty as a publisher took a new turn. Before, it had been a question of enlightening people, in a general sort of way, about the causes of war: now it was a question of preventing a war that was just around the corner. Sense of urgency gave way to maddened feverishness: no more than a split second, now, in which to pull up one's feet from the quagmire!

Hitler's accession to the Chancellorship of Germany not only concentrated Victor's mind on political publishing; it also forced him to relax his instinctive mistrust of dictatorial communism and to re-examine his attitude to Jews. His first decision was to stop subsidizing books without a political purpose. Up to now he had been prepared to make a loss on books with a literary or spiritual quality that appealed to him. One of the first casualties was his friend Edmond Fleg, a Franco-Jewish writer whose *Moses* and *Solomon* Victor had published with pride.

> I simply see no way of publishing the book without a loss: and . . . I can't contemplate a loss.
>
> I am more and more specialising in long books published at very low prices, designed to convert people on a big scale to socialism and pacifism. My heart is above all in this work: and I want to continue with it, and increase it, as long as I possibly can. Now, each one of these books represents a very big risk of loss: so far I have been lucky, but if two or three of these future books went wrong (and they very well may) I should find myself in a very difficult position. That means that in the case of books that are not directly on this subject (even in the case of a book like yours which tends to the same end) I have to look very carefully at the question as to whether or not it is likely to involve a loss . . .

Having established his financial priorities, and having installed Collins to deal with much of the day-to-day work, Victor's next step was to establish himself more firmly as a vehicle for the dissemination of radical books attacking fascism or capitalism — even books entirely uncritical of the Soviet Union. Justifying to himself the decision to peddle Soviet propaganda was not easy. Three years later he told Stephen Spender that he had contemplated retiring into the country for a couple of years to write a huge book in three or four volumes about the betrayal of liberalism by those who refused to accept that communism was its logical outcome. 'In those days,' said Victor, 'I used to say that I was a Communist because I was a Liberal.' He later denied fiercely that he was ever a communist, and essentially this denial was correct. It is better to describe him, in his own words in private correspondence, as 'no more than a "fellow-traveller"' — though 'an immensely admiring and sympathetic one', who was from time to time 'carried away'.

The Soviet brand of communism was the only model available, and Victor, along with men like G. D. H. Cole and H. N. Brailsford, had reservations about the application to Britain of the Soviet model. They called themselves international socialists, a public label useful to Victor during the thirties, when to call oneself a communist — even in a Utopian sense — implied allegiance to the British Communist Party, and he had no intention of allowing himself to be ideologically hamstrung. Yet, thinking the new Soviet society superior to any capitalist alternative, he concentrated on its virtues and sought to repress his doubts. From 1933 to 1939 he steered an uneasy course between his qualified admiration for the virtues of the Soviet Union and his ineradicable passion for individual liberty, and it was often only self-delusion that carried him through. It helped that he wanted to appeal, through his political list, to every variety of left-winger and to persuade all radicals to make common cause. That need was a powerful incentive for him to maintain his independence of any *bloc* so, in the early days at least, he exercised caution in praising Russia, and expressed his political position by donning red shirts and trumpeting his socialism.

His evangelism grew even more sophisticated during 1933. On the one hand he was happy to publish open communist propaganda, and used his new contact with the Soviet Embassy to commission a series to be written in Moscow and called *The New Soviet Library*. On the other, his intellectual integrity made him unhappy with covert propaganda. To a prospective author of a history text-book on the post-war world he explained:

> You are, from my point of view, the ideal author: because I want the thing done with the utmost degree of impartiality — but I also want my impartial author to be of radical mind. I really do mean that I want the book to be as impartial as it can possibly be made: but the author's radicalism will give me the guarantee that if any tendency does, in spite of all efforts, get through, it shall not be a tendency in the wrong direction.

There was no need for such fine distinctions on political books, under which banner he would publish works of intrinsic merit that might help to make war less likely. The works he initiated himself were naturally designed to reflect as closely as possible his own viewpoint. In March 1933, he asked Brailsford to write a book proving that war was inevitable under capitalism and exposing, *inter alia*, the arms traffic. Brailsford was reluctant, and Victor appealed:

> Wherever I have been going during these last two or three weeks I have come up against an attitude among the older people which has really horrified me. The thing has been very vividly in my mind all night because of what occurred at a small party that I was at last night. A distinguished editor was doing all the pre-1914 stuff, with all the old meaningless abstractions and 'idealisms'. However badly 'France' had behaved, if there was an outbreak between 'France' and 'Germany', 'England' must come to the aid of 'France' if 'England' didn't want to be completely destroyed . . .
>
> On the other hand, there is no doubt at all that there is an immense anti-war feeling among younger people. Apart from the universities, even at the public schools boys are beginning to complain that they spend hours a week in bayonet practice, but are given no instruction whatever in the real

causes of war. I believe myself that if one could catch up this floating goodwill among the younger people, and give it the necessary basis of sound *knowledge*, there might be some salvation. Explain to them now authoritatively and convincingly that the whole mad business is a function of capitalism, and there won't be such a danger that they will be hood-winked and used when the time comes.

I do most passionately believe that the publication of a book on the lines sketched out in my previous letter is a paramount duty, and that you are the man to write it.

Please consent to do so.

Brailsford replied:

The main difficulty is (1) my deep scepticism as to my whole political orientation — in short how far am [I] a Communist & if not, why not? So (2) while this perplexity lasts, I incline to concentrate on some positive scientific work . . .

But you give me reasons that appeal to me why I should interrupt it.

If I do the book, I think it will be a rather broader subject than you suggest — the necessity of Socialism, with the argument about war as a main part of the case.

In essence, Brailsford was echoing Victor's constant dilemma, but for this present purpose at least Victor had seen his way clear, and he persuaded Brailsford to write *Property or Peace*. His determination to expose the culprits overcame his normal anxieties. As a political publisher he not only often spent money lavishly without hope of return, but he took risks with libel that few others would — entirely at odds with his normal practice. His criterion was whether or not a libel would be 'of great public importance'. Fenner Brockway's *The Bloody Traffic*, an exposé of the arms trade, frightened Rubinstein with its potential for a criminal libel suit, and even after expurgation few printers would touch it, but Victor's nerve held. Yet George Orwell's *Burmese Days* was turned down a few months later, though Victor's readers thought it brilliant. (He eventually published it in 1935, after Rubinstein had worked on it.)

As well as the socialist/communist issue, Victor had also to come to terms with the Jews. A long correspondence of February 1933 illustrates that in one respect he had changed little since childhood. S. M. Lipsey to Victor Gollancz Ltd:

I have read a book published by you, *Down and Out in Paris and London*, by George Orwell. On its merits or otherwise I have no desire to comment. But I am appalled that a book, containing insulting and odious remarks about Jews, should be published by a firm bearing the name 'Gollancz'.

As a Jew it is to me inexplicable that one of the most eminent and honourable names in Anglo-Jewry should bear the imprimatur of a publication wherein are references to Jews of a most contemptible and repugnant character.

I feel bound to enter a very earnest and emphatic protest.

Victor to Lipsey:

I detest all forms of patriotism, which has made, and is making, the world a hell: and of all forms of patriotism Jewish patriotism seems to me the most detestable.

If *Down and Out In London and Paris* has given a jar to your Jewish complacency, I have one additional reason to be pleased for having published it.

Lipsey to Victor:

You are entitled to your views on patriotism but you are not entitled, as a Jew, to publish a book which contains insidious and lying references about Jews.

The hell which you think patriotism is making of the world, is, in my opinion, nothing to the hell into which the world would be plunged by the indiscriminate publication of books tainted with racial inaccuracies.

Apparently your publication of *Down and Out in London and Paris* is a cause of peculiar pleasure to you. I leave you with this pleasure whilst I adhere to my old-fashioned Jewish patriotism . . .

P.S. As there is an issue of importance involved in our letters, I propose sending a copy of this correspondence to the press.

Victor to Lipsey, copied to the *Jewish Chronicle*:

With reference to the post script of your letter of the 10th February, you are clearly unfamiliar with the law of copyright. I wrote to you a personal letter, and gave you no permission whatever to publish it: the copyright in letters lies with the writer of them: and if you should publish my letter in any way I shall immediately instruct my solicitor.

Lipsey wrote back, assuring Victor he was not intimidated and accusing him of lacking the courage of his convictions.

Victor to Lipsey:

I don't know why I waste my time with you, who appear to be as ignorant of psychology as of the law of copyright . . . If you kept your eyes and ears open, you would know that my father died a fortnight ago, that he was an orthodox man, and, therefore, any expression of my own views at this particular moment in the Jewish press would be, not only in the worst possible taste, but also cause great pain to my mother. If you imagine that, apart from that, I have the faintest objection to the publication of my views, you are comically mistaken.

Far from either repudiating or expressing regret at the views which I expressed (in answer to a quite unsolicited letter from yourself), I repeat that there are few things that nauseate me more than that brand of national or racial patriotism which is always ready to shout out in protest directly there is any word of criticism of the nation or race. Egoism or selfishness, under a thin disguise, are at the bottom of the feeling which prompts such protests: and these are the things which made the world, as I said, a hell for four years, and will shortly, in all probability, make it a hell again. But why should I teach you to think aright?

That ended the controversy, for although Lipsey rejected Victor's arguments, he decided against publishing the correspondence. His reason was that Victor had revealed that he possessed 'one exemplary Jewish trait, respect and love for one's mother, which, in my view, transcends all your abuse, your distorted opinions, your barbarous thinking. Appreciating, as I do, the unexpected discovery of at least one Jewish trait in you, I shall be indulgent.'

Even by Victor's standards, these letters were a choleric over-reaction, giving a clue to his state of mind immediately after his father's death. Although he had kept up contact with his parents and sisters over the years after his marriage, the brunt of visiting and writing had fallen on Ruth and the children. Alex had gone on obsessively arguing against Sabbath trading until he was too ill to hold a pen, and he must have been distressed that in this, as in all other Jewish practices, his son ignored his views. (Benn, not a Jew, had operated a five-day week: Victor was peeved that custom required him to make Saturday a half-day.) The sense of guilt that led Victor to give time and consideration to the old man on his death-bed, and the fundamental reconciliation thus brought about, must have had profound emotional repercussions. It is noteworthy that, in the firm's files, only this correspondence with Lipsey mentions his father's death — and unwillingly at that — while numerous letters make excuses or seek sympathy for his own illnesses or misfortunes (January and February letters bemoan a recent minor car accident). Victor already knew how the Nazis regarded the Jews, and his sense of fellow-feeling with the oppressed was normally strong, yet the traumatic episode with his father had apparently resurrected old antipathies. 'Detestable' Jewish patriotism was very much bound up with his younger rebellions. The confusion did not last long. Five months later, the man who had been earlier untroubled by the embarrassing anti-semitism of Dorothy Sayers was writing thus to L. A. G. Strong about his latest novel:

Why do you make the only completely detestable character in the book a Jew — when obviously as his identity is only casually revealed there can be no kind of aesthetic reason for doing so? Surely, when you have to choose a name and a set of characteristics (in quite an isolated way, so to speak) for a 'vile seducer' you are being anti-social in the true sense by choosing the name Levy and the characteristics 'oily', etc — because you are aligning yourself with all that meaningless and deliberate prejudice which is at the back of every kind of reactionary movement . . .

In the same month he was preparing to publish *The Brown Book of the Hitler Terror*, a volume compiled by The World Committee for the Relief of the Victims of German Fascism. Published in August, it produced clear evidence that the Nazis had lied in blaming the Reichstag fire on the communists, in order to find an excuse for suspending civil liberties. It gave information too about the consequences: 500 murders, including 43 Jews killed for being Jews, and the institution of concentration camps, in which 60,000 people had already suffered cruel treatment. The innocent revelation by Victor on the cover of the book that Einstein was the president of the committee (which he was not, although he approved of its findings) gave the German Government the excuse to put a price of £1000 on Einstein's head. Einstein, already in Belgian exile, had to flee for his life to England and then America amid enormous publicity. Victor, distraught at the implication that he had endangered Einstein's life through culpable thoughtlessness, penned a lengthy self-justification: he had been misled by the committee (which had been infiltrated by communists — the first dramatic case of such manipulation of Victor). The book sold well, and achieved much in terms of education of the public, though it could not penetrate those ears that were unwilling to hear. Douglas Jay, who in September 1933 based an uncompromisingly anti-Nazi leading article in the *Economist* on the *Brown Book*'s evidence, later wrote:

> The whole book, including the treatment of the Reichstag fire, only confirmed in my mind the view of the Nazi leaders, which I had derived from *The Times*'s Berlin correspondents . . . in post-war years when apologists for Baldwin and Chamberlain have argued that nobody could have understood the Nazis' intentions fully before 1938 and 1939, I have noticed that these apologists become sceptical when I reply that it was all perfectly clear in 1933.

Victor was put in a quandary by the reaction to the *Brown Book*, for, while to the left-wing at least it was a confirmation of the evils of Nazism, he was fearful of stirring up anti-German feeling. He never wavered in his distinction between good and bad Germans (Adam von Trott, hanged in 1944 for his part in the plot to kill Hitler, was a visitor to Brimpton in 1933), and much though he loathed Nazism, he felt it important to explain first how Germany's post-war sufferings had created the conditions in which Hitler could flourish, and second what the Nazis stood for, in the positive as well as the negative sense. With that aim in view he had commissioned the distinguished journalist Vernon Bartlett to write *Nazi Germany Explained*, and, as in the vexed case of Isadora Duncan, solicited board members' opinions on whether it should be published. It was extraordinarily difficult for them. The Disarmament Conference was collapsing in acrimony. In the view of Frank Strawson (expressed in a memorandum by Collins), Bartlett's book was necessary because

> (1) it will 'soothe hysteria' (2) it will be 'good for the firm' (because of the preponderance of 'Left' books at the moment) (3) because it will be a useful summary of events. As regards the larger political issues involved Strawson recoils from the idea of an armed intervention by France (which he regards as the ultimate result of the present attitude of Europe) and he feels that anything to avert this certainty is desirable, more particularly as the Government in Germany which he sees likely to follow such French intervention can only be a Capitalist one.

Collins agreed broadly with Strawson, Morison was unenthusiastic but did not care enough to oppose publication, and although the company secretary (the life-long Conservative, Edgar Dunk) felt that it was too early to explain Hitlerism, he would not, given the possibility of war, oppose publication. Victor went ahead and the book had some success, even being used as a school text-book. Four years later, Victor wrote in embarrassment to Bartlett asking if he could cease to make it available.

> My conscience has for a long time been rather guilty about that book. When I asked you to do it I was in what I now regard as a politically muddled state of mind: I had the feeling that by publishing *The Brown Book of the Hitler Terror*, and causing hostility to Germany thereby, I might have been responsible for stirring up hatred and war. I did not then feel what I have now felt for a very long time — that the Nazi regime is definitely and inescapably committed to war, and that the only thing to do is not to 'interpret' the Nazi regime to the British public but to show it up for what I believe it to be.

Though it took him a couple of years to reach the conclusion that the Nazis wanted war, from late 1933 Victor was in no doubt that their anti-semitism could only escalate. One of the attractions of the Soviet

Union was its apparent freedom from anti-Jewish prejudice. In November 1933 he rebutted an allegation by St. John Ervine in *Time and Tide* that Stalin had removed practically all Jews from government, citing five names in evidence to demonstrate that, 'among other outlandish notions cultivated in the U.S.S.R, was the idea that human personality and not "blood" should be the test of worth.'

In the days before anti-semitism became a force in the Soviet Union, it seemed best explicable as yet another side-effect of capitalism — a thesis elaborated in *The Intelligent Man's Guide to Jew Baiting* by the communist sympathizer George Sachs, published by Gollancz in 1935. Germany seemed to prove the point. Jewish commentators who were later bitterly condemnatory of Victor's post-war sympathy for the Germans could not have known how emotionally affected he was by the horrors of Nazism. He read newspapers and journals omnivorously and accumulated files of clippings telling the story of Jewish degradation and suffering on an ever-increasing scale. Gollancz books in 1934 included Fritz Seidler's on the persecution of the Jews — *The Bloodless Pogrom* — and in April 1935, Victor's feelings of outrage and distress had reached new levels. To the novelist Hilda Vaughan he wrote:

> I am enthusiastic about *The Curtain Rises* — except for its stage Jews. Really, Hilda — short fat fingers covered with gold rings, cigars, biting the ends off them (the cigars) with sharp dogs' teeth, mildly sinister atmosphere, collections of antiques, pictures, and women, and even — incredible — 'I will produce your play if you will sleep with me, damn you'. I get the vision of the late William Heinemann, or dear little round, kind witty Max Schuster, or, for the matter of that, myself, asking the women authors who have sent us in manuscripts to come and see us, biting off the ends of cigars, and then leaning across the table and saying, 'I shall lose money on it — but I will publish it if you will sleep with me'. And then, when the dear lady refuses — 'get out!'
>
> Three or four years ago these little comedy touches would, I suppose, have amused me: but one looks at things rather differently now, when one thinks of tens of thousands of Jews being starved, insulted and tortured in Germany and elsewhere — thinks of them with horrified and impotent sympathy, not because they are Jews, but because they are fellow creatures.

Her reply was friendly but intransigent. It concluded:

> . . . his race is a matter of indifference to me, who have met good & bad, charming & detestable people all over Europe and of every race, including my own and yours . . .

But I feel sure that you will agree — at least when the indignation aroused by the present iniquitous happenings in Germany has cooled — that *as a matter of principle*, it would not do for me to offer to rewrite a novel of mine because it contained a character offensive to my publisher on racial grounds . . .

Victor responded:

I am sorry, but if you will forgive me for saying so, you both miss the point, and misunderstand my own attitude. There are, of course, quite as many unpleasant Jews as there are unpleasant people of any other race or nationality: and, except when they are corrupted from their childhood on a gigantic scale, there are quite as many good and decent Germans as there are good and decent people of any other race or nationality. When I say that you misunderstand my attitude, I have in mind particularly what you say about Germans. While I loathe and detest the Hitler *régime* and Fascism anywhere, so little do ! dislike Germans as such that I have, not merely before the Hitler affair but ever since, always used any influence I may have had in favour of friendship . . .

After elaborating on his complaints:

You think, my dear Hilda, that you are in no camp. But, as a matter of fact you are. I would not dream of suggesting that you are consciously anti-Semitic: but that you are unconsciously so I have not, after reading this novel, the very smallest doubt. Anti-Semitism is, indeed, an extremely subtle and pervasive thing, and one may catch it without knowing that one has caught it.

The connection with Hitler is a very simple one. Anti-Semitism is one of the two or three foundations of the Fascist State in Germany: it has led to abominable tortures, miseries, and outrages: and it is spreading with extreme rapidity beyond the boundaries of Germany. Anyone who fans that flame, however unconsciously, must be regarded as being, however unconsciously, in that camp: and I regard it as fanning that flame to put two Jewish characters, and two only, into a book, and to make them *both* ugly and unpleasant.

I shall not, I know, persuade you that I feel as I do not because I am a Jew but because I regard this kind of racial prejudice as satanic . . .

Hilda Vaughan offered to release him from his contract and he refused: their mutual respect was enhanced by Victor's acceptance of her right of artistic judgement, and the episode ended with a reassertion of their friendship, Victor asserting that there 'was *never* the slightest *personal* feeling' in anything he had said.

Victor published Hilda Vaughan's novel, recognizing the impropriety of literary censorship, but where political books were concerned, his liberal instincts sometimes clashed with his sense of mission.

Until the mid-1930s most left-of-centre books were acceptable to him; never characterized by narrow dogmatism, he interfered with authors as little as possible so long as they criticized capitalism and fascism. His exercise of direct censorship on one notable occasion in 1934 arose from moral scruples.

In the manuscript of *Peaceful and Bloody Revolution*, an investigation into how socialism could most efficiently be achieved, Raymond Postgate came out against the use of lying and murder — but on wholly pragmatic grounds. Victor had commissioned the book; both men wanted socialism. But though he claimed to be 'a trifle "redder"' than Postgate, Victor could not stomach his simple dismissal of violence as inefficient. A 'Not Sent' letter to Postgate demonstrated that, though events had caused Victor to abandon his nominal pacifism, he was a long long way from accepting violent means to a desirable end.

> . . . the moral issue must be raised.
>   . . . whether I like it or not, these categories are paramount categories. I am far from being unsympathetic with the various materialist conceptions of morality: but I can't myself believe them. The immediate recognition of the vileness of robbing a blind beggar, or beating a child, or of the goodness of some generous action, seems to me to have nothing whatever to do either with my animal ancestors or with the practical advantage of the race.
>   I believe that violence is not merely bad (irrespective of the ends for which it is used), but so horribly bad, that a book such as this ought not to go out without somebody proclaiming, somewhere or other in it, that it *is* bad: and it is, I suppose, the object of this letter to make that proclamation.
>   You will find it easy, of course, to tie me up in knots. You will say 'You can't have it both ways: if you take this absolute view of good and evil, then you must eschew violence under all circumstances and for whatever end.' Well, tie me up in knots. All I can do is to agree (and I have an illustrious example in a prophet of my race) that I am not consistent. In the very last resort I would try my best to employ violence (I don't know whether I should succeed): that is to say, if I felt absolutely certain (and I think I feel rather more certain than you) that ultimately socialism cannot be achieved except by violence, defensive or offensive, then I should advocate it: because the alternative would be a world so horrible in its despotism, slavery, greed, poverty, and war, that any method (yes, I realise the contradiction) would be justified in sweeping it away, so that something better might take its place. But, while advocating violence in such circumstances, and even trying to be violent myself, I should always say in my heart, 'God forgive us'.

This letter had been designed to act as a preface to the book, with Postgate replying in print. Perhaps recognizing that his final paragraph was too fraught with caveats, Victor had crossed it out, and in the event he decided to abandon the whole letter. He wrote the next day to Postgate saying he could not publish the book and told him to keep the advance.

> On a second consideration, and as a result perhaps of trying to formulate my own ideas, the uneasiness which I felt when I read it has become something worse than uneasiness. I just can't bear the *taking for granted* of violence and all the rest of it which hangs over the book. Nor do I feel that modification is really possible — because what I dislike resides in the atmosphere of the whole book.
>
> The fact is that I feel unwilling to publish it both as a publisher and a socialist.

This war between morality and pragmatism was the essence of Victor's personal torment during the 1930s. Intellectually, he craved the certainty of Marxism. He had the energy, the commitment and the resources to preach a course of action that might save mankind, and in the face of Nazism, that course had to be a practical one. International socialism was fine in theory, but increasingly, more and more attention had to be focussed on the nearest thing to heaven on earth — the Soviet Union. Although he never confined himself to communist books, it was clear that from late 1933 he was stifling his dislike of state socialism, and eagerly seeking justifications for the system of government which seemed manifestly a vast improvement on the chaos he saw in the western world.

Yet by temperament he was a moral absolutist and, additionally, his terror of being trammelled by a rigid ideology held him back from a final espousal of Marxism. His reasons seemed clear later:

> . . . marxists generally, and most ex-marxists as well, understand very little about ethics. I will go further, and, at the risk of appearing to trail my coat, will confess that, in spite of his brilliant insights and the fruitfulness of his analyses, I have never thought of Marx as a real socialist — by reason, but not only by reason, of this very attitude of his towards capitalism (the view that capitalism and therefore the profit motive was 'historically necessary').

That was from the perspective of 1953. It was a view he could not have articulated twenty years earlier, when most reservations were pushed into his subconscious. A more accurate retrospective expression of how he stood with communism, even at his moments of greatest enthusiasm in the late thirties, was his statement that 'for about fifteen months I was as close to the Communists as one hair to another and that for every minute of those months I was billions of light years away from them — as I have been all my life.' Yet he strove hard to overcome his reservations. In a letter of January 1935 he wrote triumphantly to the editor of *The Music Lovers' Miscellany* of another obstacle surmounted. 'I was talking to a young Communist recently and attacking the more rigid Marxist view of art (though I am very nearly a Marxist myself). Mozart's name cropped up in the course of the conversation: whereupon he said very excitedly, "But you're wrong on your facts: Mozart has just been accepted in Russia."'

Had Victor been less honest, and had he had less sense of the integrity of his own personality, he would have swallowed his scruples and accepted the authority of the Communist Party of Great Britain (CP) — although neither they nor he would have thought it expedient that he become a formal member. As it was, his independence and contradictions annoyed friends and foes alike and, not for the first or last time, he was seen by many as a humbug. His resistance to whole-hearted acceptance of the philosophy he was theoretically so close to seemed to communists at best an opting out, and at worst a selfish refusal to advance the only cause that offered any hope. To non-communists, his readiness to swallow pro-Soviet propaganda was intellectually contemptible, and certainly, although he had been quick to see the essential evil in fascism, he was a long way behind others in showing any real critical sense where communist totalitarianism was concerned. In fairness to him, it was only those of dispassionate and remarkable objectivity who could simultaneously appreciate the potential horrors of the two systems and live with that understanding, while Victor was a crusader — and a crusader needs a cause. The propaganda made available to him by communists and well-meaning fellow-travellers was astute and innocent by turns, and paid lip-service at least to the moral values Victor cherished. His adored Sheila Lynd (whom he had failed to convert to socialism) was only one of many he admired who joined the CP through a desire to lessen the sufferings of mankind.

It was inevitable that Victor should take at face-value most of the information that flooded in about the new spirit abroad in the Soviet Union. Enthusing in February 1934 about *Russia Reported* by Walter Duranty, he wrote that 'it is the most convincing account of the victory of the Soviet over the collectivisation of farming that I have yet read.'

He hoped for much from his projected *New Soviet Library*, which was devised in mid-1933 with the help of Tolokonsky of the Soviet Embassy. Victor believed that it was to be an official government series designed to explain to the English-speaking world the nature of Soviet society. Heady with excitement, he had to be convinced by

Tolokonsky that a general introduction by Stalin was 'impracticable'. It was thought that Maxim Gorky might fill the breach. All twelve volumes were to be published together in January 1934, and to cover a range of subjects from *The Soviet State and the Solution of the Problem of Nationalities* to *The Cinema*. A star volume was to be that on *Soviet Justice*, contributed by the Public Prosecutor, Andrei Vishinsky, and the *Industrial Revolution* was to be covered by Bukharin (prosecuted by Vishinsky in 1937 and executed). Victor's innocence was untainted by any understanding of the politics of Moscow, and for him the fiasco of the *New Soviet Library* merely indicated that the 'new spirit' did not exclude bureaucratic inefficiency. Between the Embassy, the Moscow translator, and the Soviet Press and Publisher Literary Service (Prestlit), confusion, procrastination and contradiction reigned from the inception of Victor's 'beloved series'. He kept his temper with the offenders over the missed deadlines, the financial and copyright wrangles, the unexplained changes of author and the total inability of his Moscow contacts to live up to promises.

The correspondence is a graphic and rather pathetic illustration of the extent to which Stalinist control of information could hoodwink the most sophisticated intellectual. At a time when the Webbs were responding to their 1932 visit by compiling their Utopian volumes on *Soviet Russia: a New Civilisation?*, it was not surprising that Victor and his like-minded colleagues saw not a glimmer of menace behind the façade. He asked no questions as to why volumes arrived with the authors' name to be filled in later. Equally, when Vinogradoff, a Russian Embassy official, and the Moscow agency both denied that the Soviet government had had anything to do with the works, Victor explained artlessly that, were they to check with Tolokonsky, he would confirm the basis of the agreement: an '*official government series*'.

No one around Victor was asking any questions either. Norman Collins distanced himself. He did routine editing on the manuscripts if required and left to Victor's political adviser (Emile Burns of the CP) what he called 'points in higher Communist doctrine'. Sheila Lynd, by now a fanatical communist, reported in September on a conversation with Vinogradoff, and suggested that it was time Gollancz sent a representative to Moscow to buy books. 'Luckily anti-feminism is also dead in that country.' Her hint was not acted upon, for Victor had already decided to see the Soviet miracle for himself. In July he had written to his contact in Prestlit:

> I am very anxious indeed to come to Russia, partly, of course, as a matter of general interest, partly to investigate publishing conditions (I was

amazed at the astounding speed with which the English edition of the Moscow trial evidence was brought out) and partly in order to find good Russian books for the English market, as I am convinced that before very long we shall, if we handle it aright, be able to obtain a good market here for Russian books, and I am anxious to take the initiative in finding this market. This visit of mine to Russia is, at the moment, merely a dream, as it is very difficult for me to get away from London for the necessary length of time: but I mention the matter now in case I might be able to come suddenly. It is just conceivable that I might be able to get away at the end of this July.

No response to this overture was forthcoming, for the agency was concerned at the time to keep contact to matters of business. Victor's frustration grew, as his series was obliged to limp on to the market with four less than seductive volumes: *Supply and Trade in the U.S.S.R., Foreign Trade in the U.S.S.R., Health Protection in the U.S.S.R.* and *The Soviet Theatre.* His tolerance was tried too far in November 1934, when a minor misunderstanding elicited a peremptory telegram from Moscow. Justifiably annoyed, Victor wrote listing his grievances and threatening to pull out of the venture.

During the next few months the series died from lack of material. The arrival in autumn 1935 of Vishinsky's manuscript could not save it, for even the loyal Emile Burns found his book disappointing, and Victor did not publish it. Burns recommended that future books on the Soviet Union be written by English specialists with prefaces by Soviet leaders 'to add tone'. Victor had no idea that the political climate in Moscow guaranteed books of unsurpassable dullness and caution, but although his enthusiasm for the Soviet system was undiminished, there was little option but to follow Burns's advice. A much-cherished book on communism and Christianity, ultimately edited by John Lewis under the title *Christianity and the Social Revolution*, was delayed in its late stages of preparation by the withdrawal of all the promised Russian contributors. Henceforward, Victor avoided commissioning work from the Soviet Union. If suitable manuscripts came his way he took them, but for the most part he relied on British or American sympathizers to explain Soviet society.

The frustration did not stop there. Victor delighted in attacks from the right, but exploded when a reviewer in the communist *Daily Worker* attacked as misleading and commercially-minded the blurb on a Gollancz translation of a Russian novel: 'What precisely is the point of being offensive to a man who, according to his lights (however dim they may be), spends a great deal of time and thought (as your associates can tell you) in trying to devise books likely to be of value in certain directions.'

Episodes like this typified the strain Victor was enduring. Much of what he published met with disapproval from some of those he believed should support him. He remarked to G. R. Mitchison that only about once in six months did he get the feeling 'that the show here is not completely useless'. There were few who approved his eclectic approach to left-wing publishing, and it was hard for Victor to carry on with his thankless and often loss-making labours. Nevertheless, he persisted throughout 1935 in his idiosyncratic way, publishing anything that might push public opinion in the direction he favoured. It was Gollancz that produced, within a couple of weeks, the results of the broadly liberal League of Nations Union's unofficial referendum, which showed a large majority of the British people in favour of collective security backed up by armed intervention. It was Victor who commissioned a rush book by Emile Burns, two days after Mussolini's invasion of Abyssinia, to explain it as an inevitable consequence of imperialism. Yet a month later he was lamenting to Konni Zilliacus the difficulty of getting help from the Labour Party to distribute Zilliacus's *Inquest on Peace*, which had been written to help them in the general election of 14 November.

Victor was deeply frustrated by his inability to reach the public with the majority of his campaigning publications. His broad-church approach made him an object of suspicion to political parties; the press usually ignored political writings; and the booksellers' resistance to left-wing books as unsaleable could rarely be overcome. It was only by expensive advertising that he achieved the success he did, and in 1935, even that seemed threatened when J. L. Garvin refused to publish in the *Observer* his advertisement for three books he felt to be of particular urgency. Victor had investigated the possibility of setting up his own bookshop, but could find no suitable cheap site. His main channel of distribution, the Workers' Bookshop, had produced in May 1935 a scheme for a Left Book Club that would disseminate appropriate books from any publisher's list. Gollancz was the only firm to show interest, and the scheme failed. It was to a modification of this idea that Victor directed his attention after the Conservative landslide of November 1935.

CHAPTER TEN

THE ORGANIZER

VICTOR'S GENIUS FOR synthesizing, implementing and publicizing the ideas of others found its most notable expression in the Left Book Club (LBC). Quite apart from the Workers' Bookshop scheme, there was political precedent in the Progressive Book Society, a short-lived co-operative set up in the late 1920s to foster discussion groups around the country, and trade precedent in the Book Society, thriving on the distribution of volumes at full price. Years later, Victor claimed the credit for inventing members' discounts, but he would have had to go round with his eyes uncharacteristically closed to be unaware of the reduced-price book clubs already doing good business in America and Germany. It is true, however, that without Victor the LBC would never have come into being, with all its repercussions on the country's social and political life, and that without the LBC, the British publishing establishment would have dragged its feet for years over the institution of the modern book club.

As the *Bookseller* said in February 1936, Victor had already been instrumental 'in making books about Socialism "respectable"', but he had made virtually no headway with communist-inspired works, and this deficiency in the dissemination of ideas he now felt bound to put right. Italy had invaded Abyssinia in October 1935, and was proving impervious to the feeble sanctions imposed by the League of Nations; fascist bellicosity promised a European catastrophe; the new National government under Stanley Baldwin promised no strong leadership to deal with domestic or foreign problems; and after years of internecine strife, there was no sign that unity on the left was any closer. For Victor, the only hope for future peace lay in the example set by France and Spain, where socialists and communists had sunk their differences in a Popular Front and were ready to fight elections as a credible opposition: a similar course in Britain, he felt, would hold out hopes of a British/French alliance with the Soviet Union to resist Hitler and Mussolini, while at home it could do much to eradicate the social injustice that fuelled Mosley's fascist New Party.

Victor's conception of a Popular Front embraced all opponents of government from dissident Tory to communist — an objective for which there was small support. There was, however, considerable left-wing backing for a socialist–communist United Front, an idea to which the CP was deeply committed and the leadership of the Labour party implacably opposed. Victor therefore saw his immediate political priority as that of persuading the rank-and-file members of the Labour and Liberal parties that they had much in common with those further to the left. Therefore, communist literature must be brought to a wider reading public, and through an organization that had a broad appeal.

The moment when the LBC germinated from a vague idea into a specific project came in early January 1936. Sir Stafford Cripps, prominent Labour MP and a recent and enthusiastic Marxist convert, invited Victor and John Strachey to lunch, to discuss the possibility of founding a weekly paper to promulgate socialism and oppose fascism. That the meeting produced no concrete plans (though *Tribune* was launched a year later) no doubt boosted Victor's impetus towards immediate personal action. Strachey, the most influential English Marxist writer of the 1930s (and a Gollancz author) seemed an ideal ally. Although he was a communist, the wise men of the CP had refused him a party card, recognizing the usefulness of his nominal independence. As they left Cripps, Victor proposed to Strachey that he co-operate in selecting books for a Left Book Club, and together they decided that Harold Laski, Professor of Political Science at the London School of Economics and probably the most influential teacher of his generation there, should be the third selector.

They were a formidable trio: Laski the academic theoretician; Strachey the gifted popularizer; and Victor the inspired publicist. All three had known a lifelong passion for politics and all had swung violently left in the early 1930s. Only Victor did not describe himself as completely Marxist, though he was objectively indistinguishable from the real article. The three, through a longing for all-encompassing solutions to the problems of the human condition, were natural followers of a philosophy that admitted no doubts. Laski once explained that his journey to Marxism had given him 'an increasing confidence in its will: the paradoxical sense that a fighting philosophy confers an inner peace unobtainable without its possession.' Having gained that inner peace, they all showed themselves to be dedicated proselytizers, and won, individually and collectively, the hearts and minds of thousands of young people in pursuit of Utopia.

In choosing his co-selectors, Victor (a Labour Party member) had this deep-running community of ideals and attitudes as the chief criterion, followed by intellectual respectability and an appearance of political breadth. Strachey was under Communist Party direction. Laski was an influential member of the Labour Party's National Executive Committee who contrived meanwhile to hold the conviction that inadequacies in the British democratic system would stymie the introduction of socialism, and he shared Victor's doubts that the classless society could be brought about without revolution. In pursuit of the Popular Front goal, they committed themselves inevitably to a period of nimble, and taxing, ideological footwork.

Strachey was excited by the idea of the Club. Seeking a guarantee of a reasonable income, he wrote to Victor on 10 January that 'it might become something really influential if one made it a principal charge on one's interest'. Victor wished to harness Strachey's enthusiasm as cheaply as possible, so he offered him just the normal reading fee of two guineas a manuscript. Laski, offered only one guinea on the good socialist grounds that, unlike Strachey, he had a job, kindly refused any remuneration.

From the outset Victor displayed a typical combination of parsimony and generosity. To make the Club as effective as possible he was determined to keep wages and royalties to the minimum, thus freeing funds for advertising or organization. The frequent allegation that the Club was but a cunning entrepreneurial device to make yet more money in the name of anti-capitalism had no validity. Victor was not prepared to risk bankrupting Gollancz and was reluctant to spend an unproductive penny, but in the drive to make converts he gave his money as freely as he gave the time that he could otherwise undoubtedly have used to make himself rich.

The first advertisements for the LBC appeared in left-wing and liberal journals and newspapers in February and March 1936. Interested readers sent their names and addresses to Gollancz and received in return a twelve-page brochure which commenced:

> The aim of the Club is a simple one: it is to help in the struggle *for* World Peace and a better social and economic order and *against* Fascism, by (*a*) increasing the knowledge of those who already see the importance of this struggle, and (*b*) adding to their number the very many who, being fundamentally well disposed, hold aloof from the fight by reason of ignorance or apathy.
>
> That the success of this aim is of terrible urgency at the present time,

when the world is drifting into war, and when Fascism is triumphing in country after country, needs no emphasis.

Membership involved a commitment to buy at 2s. 6d. (12½ pence) monthly, for a minimum of six months, a book chosen by the three named selectors. 'It is felt,' said the brochure rather ingenuously, 'that these three together adequately represent most shades of opinion in the active and serious "Left" movement. . . . Under the ruling of the capitalist profit motive' there had been little incentive to push sales of left books; hence the need for the LBC. 'If success on a grand scale could be achieved, it might eventually be possible to issue books at such a price as would bring them within the financial possibilities of the million. This may sound high-flown; but the almost incredible circulation of books in the Soviet Union is before us as a glorious example.'

Victor hoped to have, by May, the 2,500 members necessary to start the club going. In the event, the number was 9,000. In a matter of a few months he had personally planned in every detail the way in which the LBC would operate; he had brought it to public attention; he had organized his slender staff resources to cope with enormous but unpredictable demands; he had wrung from printers, binders and booksellers agreements that made possible a revolution in the book trade; he had set up a steady flow of manuscripts; and he had devised a *Left Book News*, free to members, edited by himself, to appear monthly and, with time, to become a political journal. Onlookers were staggered by his daring, his confidence, his speed and his disregard — yet again — for publishing conventions. The *Bookseller*, while praising his energy and ingenuity, drew attention to some of the inevitable casualties of his stampede. The booksellers were up in arms, because although Victor had forestalled major criticism by arranging that LBC books be obtained through bookshops, enormous publicity had been given specifically to the Workers' Bookshop, and LBC members had been encouraged to give it preference as a supplier: 'Mr Gollancz talks in almost every letter about collaboration with the bookseller, but in the only things that really mattered he has steadfastly refused any kind of collaboration whatever . . . Surely he should be the first to agree that pocket Hitlers are out of tune with popular feeling in this country?'

Threats of a boycott came to nothing, as Victor was in a position of strength, but in favouring the Workers' Bookshop for reasons of politics, efficiency and philanthropy, he made unnecessary enemies. More seriously, he increased the suspicion that the LBC was communist-inspired. It does not take hindsight to see that he got the balance of left-wing interests wrong from the Club's inception. Sixteen years later, he wrote that

> nine considerations impelled my activity: (1) we must prevent war; (2) we could do it only by uniting as many nations as possible in opposition to Hitler; (3) in view of Germany's geographical position, if of that alone, the Soviet Union, France and Great Britain must be the core of any effective combination; (4) no such unity was conceivable unless these peoples and their regimes learned to understand one another; (5) no such unity was conceivable, either, without unity at home — a unity of all anti-fascists, from communists at one extreme to a section of conservatives at the other . . . ; (6) domestic unity was demanded, also, by the need for preventing such a triumph of indifference, or even of pro-fascism, here in Britain itself, as would encourage Hitler to strike; (7) this triumph could be further obstructed by (a) the indifferent becoming anti-fascists, and (b) anti-fascists growing keener, more active; (8) the prerequisite for such a change was a greater understanding of what fascism meant by way of internal bestiality and external aggression; and (9) to effect this understanding, an exposé of fascism must be supplemented by an exposé of its opposite — of the socialism that has for pith and marrow, or alas! (as I must now say) ought to have, the ideal of international brotherhood.

So the primary purpose of the LBC was to demonstrate to the widest possible section of the British people the nature of the fascist threat and the need to unite against it. Yet by the polemical language of his brochure, the political complexion of the selection committee, the tie-up with a communist bookshop, the joint selection for the first choice of two communist books,★ and the domination of the first issue of the *Left Book News* by Strachey, Laski, Sheila Lynd and Ivor Montagu (a leading apologist of the Soviet Union), the Club acquired a reputation for extremism from the start. For all that Victor stressed in his first editorial that his aim was the mobilization 'of all men and women of good will', and promised a 'liberal' June Choice (*Hitler the Pawn*, by Rudolf Olden), his propaganda alienated from the outset all Tories and most Liberals and anti-communist Labour. Bereft of other friends, Victor was thrown into the arms of the Communist Party.

A 'left-inclined' *Bookseller* columnist stated the critics' case:

★*France Today and the People's Front*, by Maurice Thorez, General Secretary of the French Communist Party and *Out of the Night: a biologist's view of the future*, by H. J. Muller — an argument for using genetic selection in a socialist society.

. . . No democracy can hope to succeed unless its people are well informed, intelligent and interested . . .

For this reason I say learn the facts. Learn both sides. Arrive at a balanced opinion. And for this reason, too, I say to Mr Gollancz, that he has done his cause a disservice by appealing to hatred instead of to reason . . .

If Mr Gollancz believes that 'Left' politics are the only ones which will save civilization he should have the courage of his belief. He should assume that for any thinking man there can only be one solution *once he has learnt the facts* and studied the problems they raise.

To my mind the whole angle of his attack should be altered. The campaign should not be a campaign of the 'Left', but a campaign of Reason and Justice, a campaign for Happiness and Security, a campaign for peace amongst men. I should say that even the name itself is a mistake; for to the unconverted the word 'Left' simply means a policy directed by hate with the sole purpose of destroying middle-class prosperity and killing or starving middle-class families.

The objects of the campaign should not be the pitifully inadequate ones of resistance to Fascism and anti-Semitism, but the far more fundamental ones of resistance to the doctrine of force, of support to the ideals of responsibility to and for one's fellow men. It should be the policy of justice and good will as against that of despotism and hatred.

This observer could not have understood how ironic such recommendations were when directed at Victor, the instinctive campaigner for peace and goodness, whose desperation had driven him into association with those who had contempt for pacifism and the Christian ethic alike. But Victor was anyway in too feverish a state to heed such counsel. By the time the Club was launched, Spain and France had Popular Front governments, and to achieve a similar end he was prepared to compromise on the means. Hitler's occupation of the demilitarized zone of the Rhineland exacerbated the urgency. The CP was the only major party to show enthusiasm for what Victor was trying to do, and so earned from him a greater willingness to trim his personal principles than would otherwise have been the case.

Temperamentally needing his intimates to be in fundamental agreement with him, Victor sought the company of those who shared the beliefs into which he had, of necessity, persuaded himself: that the communist vision was in harmony with his own, and that the Soviet Union's infringements on personal liberty were merely a temporary and necessary stage in the development of a perfect society. His resistance to propaganda was low, and diminishing. In the month when he set plans for the LBC in motion, he could still enthusiastically endorse Stephen Spender's proposal to include, in his *Forward from Liberalism*, a defence of idealistic as opposed to opportunistic liberalism, integral to an attack on the 'orthodoxy' of communists. But though Victor might approve of Spender's approach in theory, in practice he was seeking justification for the Soviet *status quo*. Of what A. J. P. Taylor has called 'the most preposterous book ever written about the Soviet Union', he wrote to Spender in February:

> I am glad you are going to tackle the Webbs' book on Russia — an amazingly fascinating work. I had intended, as a matter of fact, to suggest your reading it in order to remove your misconception of the undemocratic nature of the Soviet regime, as the chapters dealing with this question are, to my mind, much the most important in the book . . .

By March 1936, Victor was already so anxious to oblige the helpful CP that communist censorship of all political manuscripts became overt. Where Emile Burns in previous months had tended to correct 'errors', Sheila Lynd, with all the enthusiasm of a recent convert, eschewed all pretence. Reporting on a history of the Paris Commune of 1871, she wrote: 'This seems to me an excellent, very detailed history of the Commune, by an author of — until the very end — unobtrusively correct opinions . . . ' (The book was despatched to Burns to make appropriate alterations and deletions; it was Victor who suggested that the communist historian Dona Torr write an introduction. It was in a suitable form to be an LBC choice in 1937.)

That same March, Victor had a brief correspondence with the CP secretary, Harry Pollitt, that indicates the closeness of the relationship. Victor was impatiently awaiting the arrival of a book by the party's leading intellectual, Rajani Palme Dutt, on *World Politics 1918–1936*. 'Dear VG,' wrote Pollitt,

> Hope you like the review of 'Yellow Spot' in the Daily this morning.*
>
> I have just had a letter from RP Dutt's wife. She is very worried over the delay to Dutt's book. I am afraid I am a little to blame. I had to instruct Dutt to leave all his work and go to Lausanne for some important conversations with Nehru. He went [*sic*] collapsed and had to be taken to Hospital, where he still is. I understand only the last chapter has to be done, and he will do this immediately he is physically fit . . .
>
> So I bow my head for your insult to come as it is really my fault.

'My dear Harry,' began the reply, 'OK — I am sure the other matter was for the time being more important than the book.'

For Victor to accept so quickly the rigidity of the CP — a party far more slavish than its European counterparts in its unquestioning obedience to Moscow — was made easier by his appreciation of the

---

*Yellow Spot was a Gollancz Book on Nazi persecution of German Jews. The 'Daily' was the *Daily Worker*.

qualities of its employees and many of its adherents. Pollitt was able, forthright, decent and full of compassionate understanding for the problems of the working classes from whom he derived. Those intellectuals employed by him with whom Victor had close contact — Burns and Dutt — were, like Pollitt, dedicated, ill-paid, selfless and idealistic. Where Victor and Strachey could be mocked publicly as 'Café Communists', no such charge could be levelled at the luminaries of the CP. Conscious that he failed to measure up to them in terms of self-denial, Victor was the more readily blinded to the fact that they also denied themselves scepticism, intellectual curiosity and concern for personal liberty. There was too the seduction of being treated by the Soviet Ambassador and the CP as a political leader of real importance.

As he consorted with his new friends and eagerly read panegyrics to the Soviet Union, Victor suspended what was left of his disbelief. A staff memorandum of April 1936 ran:

> I have detected a certain absence for some time now of the old spirit which used to animate the Staff, and which I am informed was the wonder of the visiting American publishers . . . This absence of the old happiness causes me personally a great deal of unhappiness.
>
> I think that we may get back to the old position by a little more leadership: and I have decided to make Miss Dibbs general leader and supervisor of all the female staff on the main floor, except Miss Lynd's department and such staff as is definitely attached personally to Mr Collins or myself. Under this arrangement, Miss Dibbs will have no *specific* duties except her present ones: but it will be her *general* duty to see on the one hand that everybody is keen and happy, and on the other that everybody does their work with proper efficiency . . . She will, in fact, be occupying the position which is occupied in a Russian factory by the leader of the factory Soviet.

With Victor proving so pliant, his activities were viewed with approval from CP headquarters in King Street, conveniently just around the corner from Henrietta Street. Strachey wrote to Dutt in May rejoicing at the initial success of the Club, expressing his and Victor's hopes that the *Left Book News* could ultimately become 'the long planned weekly paper' and seeking approval.

> As you may have heard, there were all sorts of rows and intrigues about the starting of the Club. Consequently, it has many imperfections, the chief of which is, of course, its restriction to Gollancz books [something unlikely to have pleased, for instance, the communist publisher Martin Lawrence]. But my feeling, with which Harry concurred, was that the great thing was to get something going. Gollancz has his defects, but he is a man of intense

energy and drive, and he has put this thing over in a way which, I am sure, nobody else could have . . .

Dutt was encouraging. 'The Left Book Club is a brilliant piece of organizing work all through; and its success and scope, so far from being injured, is probably the greater because it is recognized by the public as an independent commercial enterprise on its own feet, and not the propaganda of a particular political organization.'

Victor was distracted from the extent to which he was being manipulated by the extraordinary growth of the LBC (3,000 more joined within two weeks of the launch) and the work that generated. In the *Left Book News* of June he wrote excitedly:

> . . . it is not too much to say that the Club has already begun to take on the characteristics of a genuine *movement of the masses*. The initiative came from ourselves: it was we who had to launch the thing, but we launched it in response to what we believed to be a mass demand, and already . . . the wish of the masses themselves is beginning to take control. That is the history of every genuinely democratic movement.

Evidence of this was 'the wholly spontaneous demand' for the formation of local study circles — a demand that put further burdens on the tiny staff as yet allocated to LBC duties, while reinforcing Victor's conviction that his work was truly worthwhile. The exhilaration of a success beyond the most optimistic forecasts stimulated further his unequalled appetite for organizational detail, but he was already in trouble on the policy front. In July, when the *Left Book News*'s regular Ivor Montagu article on the USSR was headed 'The Land of the Free', Victor was worried about allegations that the Club was communist, and by Labour Party disapproval. To Strachey he wrote that there was a need to be 'wary and Leninist'. He was 'rather alarmed to discover how many of the writers were on the extreme left. Taking the list up to July (1937) and going back to the beginning of the club, the only choices that are not by members of the CP (more or less) are . . . three out of fifteen . . . I think we certainly ought to remedy this. . . . ' Strachey was sanguine: his view was that conciliation of the Labour Party would cost the allegiance of many club members. There must be no deviation from the 'United Front position'. Victor reassured him that he had no desire to 'alter the line. . . . On the contrary, I want to strengthen it. The matter is a purely tactical one: our whole aim must be to win the maximum number of members and frighten the minimum.'

A tactical move (suggested by Laski) was to request Clement Attlee, the Labour Party leader, to write a general book on Labour policy. Victor had also decided to leaven the communist diet by commissioning G. D. H. Cole to write *The Condition of England* (against Strachey's advice).

Strachey was in matters of policy a less than objective adviser, and Laski was too heavily engaged elsewhere to give Victor consistent, day-to-day help. Of the three, he was the outsider. Victor says in his reminiscences that he and Strachey had been fundamentally different in their condemnation of capitalism (morally wrong for Victor, inefficient and historically doomed for Strachey). In the late thirties such differences were made unimportant by their common concern, through which they developed an occupational friendship. Victor found Laski intellectually unsympathetic and less than single-minded in his attitude to the Club. He frequently failed to read manuscripts and had a tendency when he did to confine his remarks to 'first-rate' or 'reject'. That was merely irritating; more upsetting were his occasional assertions of independence. As early as June 1936, Victor felt obliged to write apologetically to Palme Dutt about Laski's unsatisfactory review of his *World Politics* in the *Left Book News*, explaining that Laski had been given the job instead of Strachey because 'it would have looked too much like a family party'.

Strachey thought Laski's review 'deplorable'. (In fact it praised most of Dutt's book, though doubting his conclusion that the British working class could be roused to force an anti-fascist Anglo-Soviet pact.) Other than that, Strachey felt 'the line of the books and of the *Left Book News* has been . . . pretty well as good as it could be.' With that kind of advice coming from his intimates, Victor was encouraged to maintain his editorial and publishing policy unchanged, making only the occasional gesture to non-communist opinion.

To the politically unsophisticated, the committed line of the LBC was not clearly apparent. Unless it was unavoidable, authors, reviewers or journalists were diplomatically styled 'socialist'. The rank and file would not have realized that Dr John Lewis, an ex-Presbyterian minister appointed in November 1936 to organize the groups, was, like his assistants Betty Reid — later his wife — and Sheila Lynd, a dedicated communist (he joined the party in 1939); that Burns, Lynd or Lewis read all political manuscripts to detect deviations; that almost all policy decisions were discussed with CP officials; that the 'Educational' books — devised as a Left 'Home University Library' — were commissioned from Marxist or communist writers, scientists, historians and political scientists instructed to give 'the right approach' without seeming polemical. 'The treatment', wrote Victor in a typical letter, 'should *not*, of course, be aggressively Marxist. That is to say, the thing should be written in such a way that, while the reader will at every point draw the right conclusions, the uninitiated would not be put off by feeling: "Why, more of this Marxist stuff!"'

The sophisticated and well-informed were more suspicious. When Victor wrote to Cole in great distress, in December 1936, that the selectors had decided that his *Condition of Britain* would have to be an 'Additional' book rather than a choice, because it was a reference book rather than a 'readable *picture*', Cole said in his hurt response: 'If now you publish the book, not as a club choice, I suppose you realise that the effect for me is that of a violent slap in the face. You must see that, I think. It is also liable to lead, rightly or wrongly, to the conclusion that, as far as political books are concerned, only Communists, or semi-Communists, need apply.'

Victor answered that such a conclusion would be false:

> We are, indeed, terribly anxious to get as many non-Communist books as possible for the Club: this was one of the reasons why we commissioned Attlee to do a book on *The Labour Party in Perspective*. We have also just accepted for early publication a manuscript which came in and which is quite violently anti-Communist [George Orwell's *The Road to Wigan Pier*]. I assure you that any suspicion of the kind is *completely* unfounded. The very idea of the Club is to be a sort of reading 'Popular Front' by representing every point of view.

This was a half-truth. Cole's book had genuinely been found stylistically unsuitable and Victor was anxious for more non-communist books. He published several that were simply anti-fascist or of a non-contentious nature, but where they touched on British foreign policy they had to call for a United Front (Attlee's was an exception) and only rarely would he permit them to make any criticism of communism in general or the Soviet Union in particular. The speed at which the Club was growing in membership and scope seemed proof that his way of running it was the right way.

The first LBC rally was held in the Albert Hall on 7 February 1937, when its membership was just under 40,000. The *Left Book News* (now the *Left News*) was over thirty pages long. 'Additional', 'Supplementary' and 'Topical' books were available as extras and the 'Educational' category was at the planning stage. Weekend schools had begun, provincial rallies were being arranged, and, most significant of all, there were already between three and four hundred discussion groups nationwide — organized, assisted and encouraged by the efficient Lewis and his able team. The burden of the whole venture lay squarely on Victor, whose inventiveness and energy never flagged, and who

Above: The Lowy family, *c.*1930, on the front steps of 12 Ladbroke Terrace. *L. to r.*: Edward Henriques, Redcliffe Salaman, May Lowy, Lina Rubinstein, Ruth Gollancz, Lily Henriques, Albert Lowy, Leopold Harris, Henrietta Lowy, Adele Lowy, Ernest Lowy, Gertrude Salaman, Ethel Harris, Victor Gollancz, Harold Rubinstein, Dita Lowy, Joseph Lowy

Right: The Gollancz daughters, *c.*1930. *L. to r.*: Vita, Julia, Francesca, Diana, Livia

Victor in the 1920s

Sir Ernest Benn

Stanley Morison

Leonard Stein

Brimpton Lodge by Ruth Gollancz

On holiday in Italy

The children dancing in the Brimpton
garden, early 1930s

Victor & Ruth at Brimpton, early 1930s

Ruth's painting of the family at Brimpton, *c.*1940

Victor at a Left Book Club rally, late 1930s

House party at Brimpton: Sheila Lynd furthest left, Molly Pritt centre

House party at Brimpton, *l. to r.*: Jennie Lee, Aneurin Bevan, Madame
Maisky, Ivan Maisky, Victor, Julia, Francesca, Ruth, John Strachey

L. to r.: Ivan Maisky, D. N. Pritt, Victor, in the garden of the Pritts' house,
near Brimpton

Harold Laski

John Strachey

Harry Pollitt

Richard Acland

Betty Lewis, née Reid

John Lewis

Harold Rubinstein

Frank Pakenham

harried members mercilessly to recruit and expand the club's activities.★ He read the stream of letters that came daily from members, answered some of them personally, insisted on seeing copies of the answers he delegated to Lewis's department, and was responsive to the most trivial complaints and suggestions. He wrote lengthy editorials for the *Left News*, personally organized the rallies down to the smallest detail, read all important political manuscripts, and generated a whirlwind of ideas for books. He attended formal meetings of selectors and informal meetings with likely allies, and entertained at Brimpton a stream of left-wingers that included Pollitt and the Soviet Ambassador, Ivan Maisky. And in addition to this, though he delegated more to Collins, he continued to do what another might consider to be the full-time job of running Gollancz. Laski in his Albert Hall speech paid Victor a gracious tribute that was if anything an underestimation.

> We recognise, and John Strachey and I, above all, have reason to recognise, how much this Club, all that it is and all that it is going to be, owes to your organising genius and to your enthusiasm. (Applause.) Yours was the idea that gave it birth. Yours was the enthusiasm that brought it to maturity. It is the habit of new organisations at some stage of their life to crucify their founders. Mr Chairman, I think it therefore only right that before the stage of crucifixion arises we should confer upon the founder of this Club the sainthood that only after crucifixion will ultimately become his own. (Applause.)

The applause of the 7,000 members present (5,000 more had been refused tickets) was rewarding for Victor. The rally, he wrote in his March editorial, 'was indeed a wonderful occasion; and I think that everyone who was present felt that something really new and valuable had arisen in the political life of our time and country.' The packed Hall, draped with banners proclaiming such slogans as 'Understanding For Action', 'It's Right to be Left' and 'Learn and Lead!' was an intoxicating environment for speakers unaccustomed to mass audiences predisposed in their favour. It was an occasion made more emotional by the wider context — the outbreak of the Spanish Civil War, and the Moscow trials of Stalin's opponents.

Victor, as chairman, had opened by explaining the meaning of the LBC 'in the political life of our time'. The three principles were first,

> the democratic idea . . . the appeal to every man and woman to be politically responsible . . . members of the Left Book Club . . . pride

★For a detailed though slanted account of the organization, growth and publications of the LBC, see John Lewis, *The Left Book Club* (London, 1970).

themselves on being propagandists, when they are sure about an idea or a fact . . .

The second fundamental idea of the Left Book Club is knowledge. A sense of political responsibility at best is only worth half its true value, and at worst is positively dangerous, unless it is combined with political knowledge . . .

But we want knowledge not only of ideas but also of the facts . . . Unless we have this knowledge we are not properly equipped to play our part, to shoulder our responsibility, in changing the world . . .

The third and last fundamental idea, as I see it, is the idea of unity — (applause) — that is, the unity of people having knowledge and having responsibility . . .

The LBC was the antithesis of Fascism. Fascism is an artificial conglomeration of featureless individuals, driven by the external power of monopoly capitalism. Our Left Book Club is a natural unity of responsible and self-moving men and women. (Applause.)

The Left Book Club, therefore, is a united body . . .

Now, I ask you: what is more necessary at the present time than the kind of unity about which I have been speaking? We have, unfortunately, lived so long in an atmosphere of horror that many of us, I am afraid, have grown used to it. And over and above that, we all of us have difficulty, for more than a moment at a time, really to visualize, to understand, not in terms of an amusing newspaper report, but in terms of the day-by-day agonising life of our fellow men.

I wish I were able to bring home to you just what I mean by this necessity for vivid realisation. I wish that all of you sitting here could . . . see out of your seats into the rot and starvation of a mining village; that you could see into a room where five or six people live and love and bear their children and die; that you could see further afield into the underground hangars of Hitler; that you could see into concentration camps where men are beaten, and go mad, and at last commit suicide; and that, above all you could see, here and now, into the bombed horror of Madrid and all the foulness that Franco and his allies have let loose on Spain. (Applause.)

Now if we were all agreed upon the measures to be taken to right these hideous wrongs, we could right them. But nevertheless, obvious though that is, there are some people who seem to think that there is something not quite *comme il faut* about the whole idea of unity — never mind what sort of unity, never mind unity for what, but simply any kind of unity. Such people seem to me to be a species of twentieth-century devil-worshippers.

He was obliged to address himself to a 'very delicate and ticklish point: the relationship of the Left Book Club to those two proposals which are known as the United Front and the Popular Front.' The United Front, or Unity Campaign, was backed by the CP, the Independent Labour Party (ILP) and the Socialist League (the intellectual Marxist wing of the Labour Party). At the October 1936

Labour Party Conference, Communist Party affiliation had been rejected and a policy of non-intervention in Spain affirmed. To the far left, this was a double betrayal, and in the case of Spain a refusal to provide arms to the democratically elected government, while Italian and German arms were available to Franco's forces, was a sell-out to fascism. The split in the Labour movement intensified when Pollitt (CP), Cripps (Socialist League) and James Maxton (ILP) spoke on the same platform, in support of their Unity Manifesto, calling for a united front against 'Fascism, reaction, and war, and against the National Government.' The ILP had already broken from the Labour Party, whose National Executive Committee now disaffiliated the Socialist League.

In the light of this clear opposition from the Labour Party to any association with the CP, Victor was concerned to keep the LBC formally distanced from the campaigns of which Labour disapproved. He admitted that all three selectors were 'wholeheartedly' in favour of the United Front and the Popular Front, but denied that the Popular Front was LBC policy.

What we say is rather . . . that in the Left Book Club we are creating the mass basis without which a true Popular Front is impossible. ('Hear, hear' and applause.) In a sense, the Left Book Club is already a sort of popular front that *happens to have happened*. It is a body of people who happen to have come together and happen to agree on a number of vital topics. Sooner or later, in their various organisations, it is absolutely inevitable that they will act on that agreement.

This brings me on also to the next question, which is: 'Are you a new political party?' The answer is emphatically 'No.' Rather are we a body of men and women of all progressive parties, hammering out our differences, coming to agreement, and then acting in our various organisations.

My feeling is this: if we succeed on a big enough scale in creating this mass basis, then all objections to a Popular Front, from whatever quarter, necessarily and automatically vanish. (Applause.) . . .

Now if I have made myself clear, you will not misconstrue me or think I am describing this as a Popular Front meeting when I say that the whole idea of the Left Book Club is reflected in the composition of our platform this afternoon. (Applause.) We have here Professor Laski (applause), who since I first knew him at Oxford before the War (we are living in such an atmosphere that I had almost said before the last War) has devoted himself unswervingly to the Labour Party. We have Mr Acland, one of the Liberal Party Whips. (Applause.) We have Mr Strachey (applause) whom some people allege to be a Communist (laughter and applause). We have Mr Pollitt, who certainly is a Communist (applause). We were to have had with us this afternoon, as you know, Sir Stafford Cripps (applause), and it is really with tremendous disappointment that I tell you that he cannot come because he has influenza. Sir Stafford, as you know, has been in a thousand fights for peace and the working man . . . And then we have my very dear friend, if he will allow me to call him so, Pritt, who has also been a tireless worker for peace and freedom . . . Now Pritt, as you know, is a member of the Executive of the Parliamentary Labour Party. I do not know what his views may be on the question of the United Front and the Popular Front, which his party has boycotted, but I know he clearly has no objection whatever to the sort of unity I have been putting before you; otherwise he would not be on the platform. Nor for the matter of that, has his leader, Mr C. R. Atlee, who has sent us a message as follows:

'I am very glad to have an opportunity of sending a message to members of the Left Book Club.

'It is of the utmost importance that there should be as wide a circulation as possible of the views of those people who, though presenting the problem from different angles, are united in a conviction of the need for changing the present system of society. Socialism cannot be built on ignorance, and the transformation of Great Britain into a Socialist State will need the active co-operation of a large body of well-informed men and women. For this reason I consider the success of the Left Book Club to be a most encouraging sign.'

Attlee's was the cautious message of a cautious man — strikingly different in tone and sentiment from those of other luminaries. Campinchi, President of the French Parliamentary Radical Group, ended his telegram: 'Against egoism, against blindness, against tyranny let us close our ranks; and forward! Tyranny passes. Liberty is eternal!'; General Miaja saluted the club 'in the name of the already heroic people of Madrid, who are fighting for the liberty of Spain and the spiritual liberty of the world, and will never be Fascist.'; Wilfred Macartney, communist and author of a Gollancz book,★ sent greetings from 'the Left Book Club authors and members now in the International Brigade in Spain. We are sure that if democracy has ever to be fought for in England the Left Book Club will supply an army corps of grand fighters' (it was no wonder that the collection Victor organized for the International Brigade raised £400), and Jawaharlal Nehru's telegram read: 'Greetings to Left Book Club on occasion rally for world peace and against fascism. People of India stand wholeheartedly for world peace and against menace fascism. They have suffered long enough under crushing imperialism. For them and others there can be no world peace so long as imperialism and fascism hold sway. Trust your rally will help in organising forces against these enemies of peace and national and social freedom.'

★*Walls Have Mouths*, an account of his experiences in an English prison, was a sensationally popular LBC choice.

Victor made much of Attlee's message, as he made much of his agreement to write an LBC book (his uninspiring *The Labour Party in Perspective* was the August 1937 choice), but Attlee's wary support for the rally was only a tiny sop for the moderates. Of those booked to speak, D. N. Pritt, Pollitt and Strachey were communist, Cripps and Laski Marxists. Only Richard Acland was not extreme, and he was virtually isolated in the Liberal Party because of his dedication to the concept of the Popular Front. A. J. Cummings of the *News Chronicle*, surveying the rally, wrote a report headed 'LEFT WING CAPTURES YOUTH: NEW DEVELOPMENT IN POLITICS'. The 40,000 members, he said, were

> all undoubtedly vigorous human cells for the propagation of the new religion . . . There can never have been so large a proportion of young men and women at any political meeting in the Albert Hall. This may not be a portent, but its significance is apparent.
>
> Though the 'platform' had a faint tinge of the Popular Front, I was left under no illusion about the inspiration of the club and the kind of appeal it makes to seekers after knowledge. It is very Left indeed.
>
> The name of Mr Harry Pollitt, the Communist leader, brought a bigger cheer than that of any other politicians; and when he approached the microphone to say his piece the audience rose at him as if he were one of God's chosen.
>
> It was Mr Pollitt who declared without any beating about the bush that the Book Club had revealed the existence in this country of 'a hunger for Marxism' . . .
>
> . . . My final impression of this remarkable gathering was that it betokens a formidable as well as a novel development in British politics. The influence of the Left Book Club movement on the newly-formed United Front and, through the United Front, on the Labour Party itself, may soon be plain enough for all to see.

A leader in the same issue emphasized the point.

> The success of the Left Book Club . . . is a very remarkable social fact. It is possible to disagree decisively with some of the doctrines expounded in its publications; but hardly possible to ignore the portent of such a meeting as yesterday's when men like Mr Pollitt, Mr Pritt, and Mr Acland spoke together on a common platform at a moment when the United Front has been repudiated by Labour and the Popular Front by the Liberals.

Victor's ambition to assist in bringing about a Popular Front movement that would attract the broadest possible range of anti-fascists, from the wilderness disciples of Winston Churchill to the ideologue cohorts of Harry Pollitt, was a pipe-dream. A paradox made it so: that the LBC was 'very Left indeed' attracted hardworking communists to recruit members and organize groups, while ensuring that only the unusually independent-minded of the soft left and no Tory wished to be associated with it. Victor, as its leader and driving force, was both vital to its success and damaging to the Popular Front cause. Without Victor the LBC could not survive; with him it perforce followed his line and became more and more a communist front. His editorials and correspondence from early 1937 bespeak the suppression of some of his most fundamental instincts and cherished beliefs.

There was, of course, nothing unexpected in his ready acceptance of Stalinist propaganda concerning the Moscow trials, despite the disquiet widely evident among socialists. Strachey, Montagu and he dutifully and sincerely reiterated the absolute need for the Soviet Union to root out Trotskyite fascist conspiracies. But, publicly at least, Victor never so much as hinted at a qualm about the executions that followed the trials, and he gave space in the *Left News* to justifications of them. What moral agony this must have caused him one can only guess at. For some years from the late 1920s he had been first an executive committee member, then a vice-president, of the National Committee for the Abolition of the Death Penalty, and though he had been too busy to do more than lend his name and give some money, it was a cause that he cared about deeply. On this issue he compromised by omission. On another, he simply reversed his previous position. Writing in March 1937 in the *Left News* he explained why he was not a pacifist:

> I profoundly believe that in the present phase of world history pacifism is not merely mistaken but one of the most dangerous forces which anti-fascism has to face; but while if it came to a fight with International fascism (with the British Government — dare we hope it? — on the right side) I might well find myself shoulder to shoulder with any number of reactionary Imperialists and bitterly opposed to a few (I hope) pacifists, I should always be aware that the pacifists were nevertheless of my kidney, and the Imperialists very much the opposite.

He recommended to his troubled members a book that would help convert them to collective security — *The Citizen Faces War*, by Robert and Barbara Donington, both ex-pacifists.

Perhaps even more poignant was the *volte-face* evident in his 'delighted' response to a proposal for a book, *The Civilisation of Greece and Rome*, which set out 'to break down the vicious habit' of regarding as timeless masterpieces the literary products of those class-divided societies. One chapter was to criticize the suitability of 'the class

THE ORGANIZER 245

literature of antiquity as a cultural training for the dominant class in modern times'. One wonders if Victor knew that Plato was banned in the Soviet Union.

The greatest casualty was truth. It was one thing for Victor to expunge from manuscripts what he believed to be inaccuracies: it was another to suppress what he knew to be true. A letter of February 1937 to Webb Miller was honest about the painful course he had chosen.

> I feel distressed, and indeed almost ashamed, to write this letter, but the fact is that after reading those two chapters last night, I feel I can't publish them.
>
> Please don't imagine for a moment that I think you have exaggerated in any way: and you make it clear on the last page where you put the ultimate responsibility for all this horror. At the same time it is absolutely inevitable that a great number of passages will be picked out from those chapters and widely quoted, for propaganda purposes, as a proof of 'communist barbarism'.
>
> I share to the full your detestation of war: I am in deadly fear of it, and have been in deadly fear of it since 1912. In the event of a war in which we were involved, God knows what would happen either to my brain or my character. But nevertheless, (indeed, for this very reason), I regard the support of the Spanish Government against the insurgents as the most important thing of all in the world today. That is why I feel I can't publish anything which, by giving occasion for propaganda on the other side, will weaken that support.
>
> You may think that this is playing with truth. It isn't really: one must consider ultimate results . . .
>
> Forgive me, please.

That same spring he was shaken by an appeal from Pollitt to suppress August Thalheimer's *Introduction to Dialectical Materialism*, scheduled for publication in May. By that time, he told Pollitt later, the Club was already losing its independence and becoming 'almost insensibly' an organ of the Communist Party.

> My first big pull up, I think, was the Thalheimer episode. What was the situation? Here was a little theoretical book of very slight importance, by a man who had had a row with, or with whom a row had been had by, the Communist Party of the Soviet Union (or of Germany — I forget which). It was a very elementary theoretical book, and . . . I found myself unable to appreciate the earth-shaking differences between this little book and official theory . . . But be that as it may, the book in any case was a trifling one, and a mere 'additional'. But you begged me★ . . . to withdraw the

★This may have been the famous occasion when Pollitt pleaded: 'Don't publish it. Not when I've got to cope with the old bugger [Stalin], the long bugger [Palme Dutt] and that bloody red arse of a dean [Hewlett Johnson, the "Red Dean" of Canterbury].'

book after it was announced . . . because 'the club is now so closely identified with us . . . that if you publish it it will create a most serious impression on the other side . . .'

Although that had offended all his ideas of intellectual integrity, Victor had yielded and there was a storm of criticism

and it was said all over the place that here was proof positive that the Left Book Club was simply a part of the Communist Party. And then, when I got letter after letter to this effect, I had to sit down and deny that I had withdrawn the book because I had been asked to do so by the C.P. — I had to concoct a cock and bull story to explain the substitution. I hated and loathed doing this: I am made in such a way that this kind of falsehood destroys something inside me.

Such moral problems did not frequently crop up, for great care was exercised in the choice of writers, and as the bias of the LBC became known, informed agents and authors knew which manuscripts would prove acceptable. Victor was open about his prejudices. To the creator of Mass-Observation, Tom Harrisson, who was trying the considerable patience and generosity of both himself and Collins, he wrote in March: 'You are really a most extraordinary person — though no doubt none the worse for that. But if you don't look out you will have the ghastly fate of ending up with the POUM★ or the Trotskyites'.

To Victor's orthodoxy Fredrick Warburg owed much of the success of Secker and Warburg, which he had founded in 1936. He provided a publishing haven for the rest of the anti-fascist left, from liberals to anarchists. To him would go, in 1937, Orwell's *Homage to Catalonia*, turned down unseen by Victor because it recorded Orwell's service with the POUM. Orwell's dislike of orthodoxy had already posed a major problem in December 1936, when his *Road to Wigan Pier* proved to be one-half superbly valuable propaganda about the social conditions endured by the working class, and one-half embarrassingly frank and satirical criticism of the British Left. Victor could not bear to reject it, even though his suggestion that the 'repugnant' second half should be omitted from the Club edition was turned down. On this occasion Victor, albeit nervously, did overrule the CP objections in favour of his publishing instinct. His compromise was to publish the

★ *The Partido Obrero de Unificación Marxista* (the United Marxist Workers' Party), a small revolutionary party which preferred workers' control to the existing Spanish Popular Front government and was denounced by the main body as 'Trotskyite' — by now a useful catch-all term for all left-wingers opposed to the Soviet brand of communism.

book with what Orwell's biographer, Bernard Crick, rightly calls 'an extraordinary introduction', full of good criticism, unfair criticism and half-truths. 'Pot calling kettle black' is Crick's observation on Victor's reminder to LBC readers that Orwell was writing as a member of the 'lower-upper-middle-class', and it would apply equally to Victor's analysis of Orwell as a man of contradictions — an extreme intellectual and a violent anti-intellectual; a frightful snob and a genuine hater of every form of snobbery.

Victor warned that the second half was contentious and claimed, wrongly, that it was really written from the standpoint of 'a devil's advocate for the case against Socialism'.

> As to the particular question of the Soviet Union, the insistence of Socialists on the achievements of Soviet industrialisation arises from the fact that the most frequent argument which Socialists have to face is precisely this: 'I agree with you that Socialism would be wholly admirable if it would work — but it wouldn't.' Somewhere or other Mr Orwell speaks of intelligent and unintelligent Socialists, and brushes aside people who say 'it wouldn't work' as belonging to the latter category. My own experience is that this is still the major *sincere* objection to Socialism on the part of decent people, and the major *insincere* objection on the part of indecent people who in fact are thinking of their dividends. It is true that the objection was more frequently heard in 1919 than in 1927, in 1927 than at the end of the first Five Year Plan, and at the end of the first Five Year Plan than to-day — the reason being precisely that quite so direct a *non possumus* hardly carries conviction, when the achievements of the Soviet Union are there for everyone to see. But people will go on hypnotising themselves and others with a formula, even when that formula is patently outworn: so that it is still necessary, and will be necessary for a long time yet, to show that modern methods of production *do* work under Socialism and *no longer work* under capitalism.

Yet he gave some ground to Orwell's attacks on socialists for arrogance, dogmatism, narrowness and sectarianism. This whole section was 'a challenge to us Socialists to put our house and our characters in order', and Orwell was right that socialists should appeal to generous instincts.

> What is indeed essential, once that first appeal has been made to 'liberty' and 'justice', is a careful and patient study of just *how* the thing works: of *why* capitalism inevitably means oppression and injustice and the horrible class society which Mr Orwell so brilliantly depicts: of *the means* of transition to a Socialist society in which there will be neither oppressor nor oppressed. In other words, *emotional* Socialism must become scientific Socialism — even if some of us have to concern ourselves with what Mr

Orwell, in his extremely intellectualist anti-intellectualism, calls 'the sacred sisters' — Thesis, Antithesis and Synthesis.

What I feel in sum, is that this book more perhaps than any that the Left Book Club has issued, clarifies — for me at least — the whole meaning and purpose of the Club. On the one hand we have to go out and rouse the apathetic by showing them the utter vileness which Mr Orwell lays bare in the first part of the book, and by appealing to the decency which is in them; on the other hand we have so to equip ourselves by thought and study that we run no danger, having once mobilised all this good will, of seeing it dispersed for lack of training leaders — lance corporals as well as generals — or even seeing it used as the shock troops of our enemies.

Victor's decision was justified by events. *Wigan Pier* came out in March and was attacked by Laski in the *Left News* and blackguarded by Pollitt in the *Daily Worker*, but it was probably the most successful of all LBC choices — debated in groups all over the country by members who normally had little to say. The introduction which appeared only in the LBC edition came to be an embarrassment to Victor: he was furious when an American publisher unwittingly republished it many years later. It must in parts have raised a smile in those who knew him well: of Orwell's much-discussed contention that the middle classes thought the working classes smelled, he wrote: 'I admit that I may be a bad judge of the question, for I am a Jew, and passed the years of my early boyhood in a fairly close Jewish community; and, among Jews of this type, class distinctions do not exist — Mr Orwell says that they do not exist among any sort of Oriental.'

Harry Pollitt was about the nearest Victor came to knowing well a member of the working classes, but he would have been deeply wounded by any suggestion that his experience of working-class life was limited to books or views of slums through the window of his train to school. There was a naive directness, an absence of self-consciousness amounting to lack of imagination in some of his services in the workers' cause. When the Workers' Bookshop got into financial difficulties, Victor offered to use his free lunch-times to work on their accounts. He would set off in his chauffeur-driven car clutching his packet of sandwiches to work energetically at a job of elementary book-keeping, and return happy in the knowledge that he had done another bit for the working classes, while blithely unaware that his mode of transport might raise the hackles of those he was serving. Similarly, he brought to the attention of *Left News* readers the magnificent LBC recruiting work accomplished by the same chauffeur. (The car was a second-hand Packard. Victor's time was precious, and he was unable to drive.)

To Tom Harrisson he wrote in justifiable rage at unfair accusations of swindling:

> As I write this letter I am getting angry and shall say something that I have never said before, and I hope I shall never say again — and it is this: that if by the time you reach my age you have worked as hard for the working class movement as I have done, you won't have done badly. And let me tell you that not when I was your age but very much later — considerably after the war — I had a damned sight less to live on than you have got.

Harrisson's answer was contrite. '. . . I appreciate the work you have done for the working class. I am not working for exactly the same ideal. But I am working. Money in itself is no damn use to me, & I am as happy as hell on 25/- a week. I know that you have lived on very little (I've thrived on a year at £4). This money I so urgently need is to pay others . . .'

It is unlikely that Victor saw the irony in Harrisson's thriving on an income considerably less than Victor's had been at a time when he considered himself poor. It was Harrisson who had pointed out to Victor that the six-month deadline on a November 1936 LBC competition was unrealistic: those qualified to write the required 60,000-word first-hand account of unemployment were often handicapped by lack of privacy during the day and the expense of artificial light at night. The deadline was extended, but no manuscript came up to publishable standard.

Naiveté was accepted by friends as an endearing facet of Victor. He could be taken in, more than most, by the communists. Writing of Cambridge, where the Marxist proselytizers were at work, in the *Left News* of September 1936, he addressed the question of recruitment to the cause.

> We feel that there ought to be some method by which a rivalry could be achieved between towns and districts, similar to the 'socialist competition' between factories which in Soviet Russia has replaced (for the benefit of all) the greedy and individualist 'push' to 'get on' which is the stigma of our capitalist civilisation . . . one convenient example may be given of what we have in mind.
>
> In the university town of Oxford there are roughly fifty-three members: in the twin and rival university town of Cambridge there are about three hundred and twenty-four members. We can think of no legitimate reason for this disparity: that is to say, we do not believe that there is a bigger body of Left Wing opinion in Cambridge than in Oxford — in fact, if anything, we believe the reverse to be the case.

Why, then, the difference? Clearly because far more active effort is being put into the enrolment of new members at Cambridge than at Oxford.

Victor's trust in his communist friends grew (bar occasional misgivings) with intimacy. As Victor described it retrospectively to Pollitt, it came about because of their growing contact, 'my joy in working with people of your type, and the force of your own personality.' Restrained candour and familiarity were the order of the day. Thus Pollitt could admit freely the financial problems that beset him. When, in February 1937, Gollancz gave a £100 advance for a book by a party employee (explaining the Stalinist purges), Pollitt wrote:

> You remember the cheque I gave you back for [J.R.] Campbell's book. Well here is the authorisation from Johnny for the one hundred pounds to be paid over to me.
>
> I am in a jam to pay wages to day and I wonder whether you could let me have the money some time this morning in pound notes.
>
> Sorry to trouble you Victor, but you know how things are and it will be a big help to me to day.

Of course he traded on Victor's innocence. In March 1937, Victor, Strachey and Burns had a discussion about the future of the LBC. They agreed that all groups should ideally have 'one or two good Party members'; that 'not only these but also existing Party convenors and prominent members should be given the right line' from the centre, through district committees; and that Burns should be 'quite privately' co-opted on to the selection committee, giving his opinion before the formal weekly meeting. This innovation made no difference to the selection policy, but it strengthened links with the CP. Victor was indeed receiving letters from party members 'pointing out the advantage of sandwiching in between books by party members books by others', but he can have taxed himself little about what a 'good' party member might see as his duty in an LBC group, being confident that no conflict of interest could arise. If Victor was deceived, he was in many respects fast becoming a deceiver himself. He was not by nature given to more than trivial distortions, like telling (or getting his secretaries to tell) white lies when appointments or commitments clashed. The lies might grow if he was in a tight corner, but were usually the result of self-deception rather than conscious dishonesty. During the early years of the LBC, however, his preoccupation with ends, and his association with others similarly disposed, had a temporary but serious corrupting effect. His suppression of what he knew to be true was bad enough; much worse were signs that he was adopting some of the tactics of his communist mentors in his manipulation of propaganda. Thus in February he gave Burns advice on what should be done with a manuscript on trade unionism written by a communist, John Mahon.

> As it goes on the thing becomes very much of a Left Wing exposition; and *particularly on this subject* this is to be avoided. What is wanted is not a Left Wing exposition but an apparently impartial exposition from a Left Wing pen. It is not really very difficult to do this — all sorts of devices will occur to you. For instance, one can say: 'The Right Wing point of view was: on the other hand, the Left Wing declared.' In other words, both points of view can be represented in such a way that, while there is a grand atmosphere of impartiality which no one can attack, the readers inevitably draw the right conclusion. As part of this difficulty, the CP crops up rather too frequently. There are, of course, places where it must be mentioned in this form: but there are also cases in which some such phrase as 'Left Wing' could be substituted, to tactical advantage.

To a mixture of dishonesty and self-delusion, with the latter probably predominating, can be ascribed his assertions in the *Left News* that the LBC was 'essentially democratic'. It would have been more correct to describe it as essentially despotic with a veneer of oligarchy. The despot was benevolent and therefore receptive to reasonable petitions from the masses. He had a circle of advisers chosen entirely by himself whose advice he took or discarded at will, but for practical purposes, he ruled alone. When seeking a sub-editor for the *Left News*, he specified that the successful candidate 'must combine initiative with absolutely immediate and unquestioning obedience to my instructions, however foolish they may seem to him.' In the same spirit, he dealt evasively but firmly with an attempt at the conference of LBC convenors before the Albert Hall rally to set up a national council, elected by convenors, that would have some influence on club policy. Neither that nor later attempts to democratize the structure of the LBC had any effect whatsoever. *Left News* reports gave no hint of any disaffection and Victor turned the unaired argument on its head in his explanation of LBC policy on groups.

> . . . each group is working out its own plans, with the very minimum of interference from headquarters. We have in fact purposely confined ourselves to an occasional hint as to a useful line here, or a possible development there; and we have even gone so far, when asked by a group convenor to lay down definite plans of campaign, as to refuse to do so, and to suggest that these must be decided upon by the members themselves.

To the March rallies in Manchester, Glasgow, Cardiff and Birmingham, Victor brought what was known as his 'Club speech' and a largely unaltered panel of speakers. The immense popularity of the meetings was only one sign of the apparently limitless potential of the LBC. As the *Bookseller* remarked, Victor had managed to infuse into the Club 'something of the spirit of a crusade'. Pollitt, in his *Daily Worker* column, spoke of the rise of the LBC as one of the most 'magnificent' achievements of the Left in years.

> Gradually, those seekers after peace, democracy and socialism are being brought together. Gradually they are moving from the position of asking questions to that of finding a common way forward.
>
> These men and women are not Communists. But for the first time in many years they are realising that politics are their own most urgent concern.

Only the *Daily Worker* among the press could be relied on for unqualified approval of the Club's activities, and Victor returned the service in rhapsodic style. In April 1937 the CP organ published his long article, 'Why I read the *Daily Worker*' — afterwards reproduced as advertising material. He praised the paper's accurate reporting of foreign news, its powerful scrutiny of home affairs, and its respect for its readers' intelligence.

> Strachey's column, Dutt's Saturday articles — these are expositions and surveys that, however much we may disagree with a point here or a point there, can stand on their own even in the company of stuff on which months of labour have been expended. What a pleasure to read articles in which events are explained in the light of a consistent theory — instead of the hugger-mugger, rudderless drifting to which one is accustomed in so many papers! . .
>
> . . . perhaps most important of all, the *Daily Worker* is a genuine paper of the masses . . . in its directness, its going straight to the point, its absence of humbug and artificiality and bogusness, it is characteristic of men and women, as opposed to ladies and gentlemen. For my own part, who meet a lot of ladies and gentlemen and find a lot of them exceedingly tiresome, I find this quality extraordinarily refreshing.

After touching on the crucial role played by the paper in defence of civil liberties, he concluded by applauding its 'magnificent optimism', which made the reader realize that the fight against war, poverty and fascism could be won. With a large enough circulation for the *Worker* 'Britain could be changed out of recognition — and, united with France and the Soviet Union, could change the world.'

The day after this appeared, Victor began his long-planned trip to the

Soviet Union. He and Ruth went at the invitation of VOKS (the Society for Cultural Relations with Foreign Countries), of the British branch of which Pritt was chairman and Victor a member. The Soviet Ambassador came with his wife to the London docks to see them off on their Soviet boat and gave Ruth 'a superlative bouquet. It comforted us a lot on the voyage, which was a hideous one.'

Victor arrived in Moscow in a wholly uncritical frame of mind. Alfred Sherman, a perceptive if hostile critic of the 1930s' far left, has summed up the views held by Victor and his fellow enthusiasts:

> The composite image was of a new civilisation, moving with history, putting into practice the frustrated aspirations of Western socialists and liberals: making the best use of labour and resources by planned economic development; giving full scope to scientists, artists, and intellectuals, and bringing art to the people; reshaping international relations along rational lines and resisting fascist expansion, which the Western democracies seemed to lack the will or ability to halt. Where the question of political terror was concerned, the image was diffuse; some regarded it as a necessary evil, some deprecated it, others preferred to ignore or deny it. What characterises the expression of faith in the Soviet Union which abounded in books, articles, and the testimony of returning delegations, is that their authors were projecting their own aspirations and frustrations onto the Soviet scene of their own beliefs and hopes. If the Soviet paradise did not exist, it had to be invented, to substantiate their socialist faith. It was not so much that they were deceived by Soviet propaganda as that they deceived themselves with the aid of Soviet propaganda.

To be convinced fully, Victor needed the evidence of his own unsceptical eyes and ears. He and Ruth arrived in time for May Day, and during the twelve days or so they spent in Moscow and Leningrad, they received, as a contemporary profile put it, 'the honours due to a friendly power'. Shortly after their arrival the literary agency, Prestlit, gave a reception in their honour, attended by officials of the People's Commissariat of Foreign Affairs, VOKS and publishing houses, writers and pressmen. During their stay they were handsomely entertained by Victor's most prized Russian author, Alexei Tolstoi, and were reported by the *Moscow Daily News* to have 'visited the House of Pioneers and Octoberites, where Mr Gollancz made a short speech to the children. They have also inspected the Bolshevo Labor commune, the Central House of the Red Army, the Central House of Children's Art Education, the Museum of Children's Books and the Stalin Auto Plant, and attended performances at a number of theatres.' Towards the end of the visit a reception was given for them by the Chairman of VOKS.

Victor was carried away by his experiences into an enthusiasm to match that of such earlier pioneers as George Bernard Shaw, Sidney and Beatrice Webb and John Strachey. He gave to a *Moscow Daily News* reporter before he left a prepared interview that must have pleased his hosts:

> I came here in two capacities, as a man and as a publisher. I came here as a man after an extraordinarily long period of strain and overwork; I needed a holiday badly, which I had failed to find in other travels in the last four years.
>
> I thought that by coming to the Soviet Union I should really release my mind from all pre-occupations and worries by seeing something so fresh and new that it would take my mind off everything else . . . As to impressions. My biggest impression has been the feeling of real, genuine classlessness which to me has been extraordinarily refreshing.
>
> Candidly, I didn't expect to find it so. Theoretically, of course, I knew it was so, but didn't expect to see it in such a short time, to feel it as a living thing. . . .
>
> For the first time I have been completely happy. . . . Although there are dangers, which the magnificent Red Army which we saw on the Red Square will prevent, there is a feeling that here is a peace of good on such a vast scale, that while here, one can forget the evil in the rest of the world, and feel that whatever dangers of war and collapse there may be, ultimate peace and reconstruction will triumph. . . .

His third main impression had been 'a sort of spring-time feeling . . . that pre-history is over and history is just beginning.' Whereas in his travels in the Far East and Europe he had found in every city he visited 'an underlying sense of decay', in the Soviet Union he felt himself 'in the first stages of a new civilization, with an unimaginable power of development and construction.' And, after describing a few moving experiences of his visit, he summed up: his expectations had been greatly surpassed and he would now be able to carry forward the work of interpreting the Soviet Union to the British people.

Sidney Webb was among the appreciative readers of this encomium. In the course of correspondence with Victor about the republication for the LBC of *Soviet Communism: A New Civilisation* (now with the concluding question-mark dropped), he wrote: 'We were much interested to read your valedictory address on leaving Moscow, which was so immeasurably superior to anything in that line that the distinguished poets and novelists and other "literary gents" have perpetrated under like circumstances.' Victor was duly gratified: 'Very many thanks for what you say about my little interview in the "Moscow Daily News". This was not the usual facile compliment: I have, as a matter of fact, been completely rejuvenated and re-orientated by my visit!' And to an author he spoke of it equally glowingly — 'amazing that place, such an upsurge of life as you could hardly believe.'

He had been active enough before his rejuvenation: now he was consumed with a passion for activity. From the boat, the *Cooperazia*, he cabled to Sheila Lynd asking that Burns read a manuscript 'from special point of view' and have his report awaiting him on arrival. (Her transmission of the message translated this as 'report on from the Party point of view'). Back in the office, Lewis recalled, 'he gathered the entire staff together to hear his enthusiastic and infectious account of what he at that time *did* see as a "new civilisation".' (In November 1937, invited by *Cavalcade* magazine to nominate a man of the year, he chose Stalin, who 'is safely guiding Russia on the road to a society in which there will be no exploitation'.)

He needed his enormous reserves of energy. In an 'Anniversary Self-Criticism' in the May *Left News*, written shortly before he went abroad, he had declared that he and his colleagues were acutely aware of doing only a small part of the work they ought to be doing. Having realized the Club's potential, they now lived in fear of failing to take full advantage of it: 'we must follow up and consolidate every development and seize every opportunity' by better organization and intelligent recruitment of staff. Members should play their part in the new aim of bringing numbers up to 100,000, which would make the Club 'the most powerful body of educated opinion that any country has ever had'.

CHAPTER ELEVEN

A POWER IN THE LAND

ON AN ORGANIZATIONAL level, Victor's achievements and those of his dedicated staff were truly awesome, although of course without the eager and devoted work of active rank-and-file members, LBC headquarters would have been helpless. It was unfortunate that several of the most dedicated employees and many of the activists were, inevitably, communist, for they exerted an influence out of all proportion to their numbers. Faced with the advancing forces of fascism, and with the uninspiring leadership of the Labour Party more concerned with domestic than international problems, many of the most informed and selfless saw no hope anywhere but in the CP. Naturally, for those who threw themselves into the LBC, their primary purpose was to make converts.

In the year leading up to the Club's second anniversary, its development had been encouraged by almost uniformly threatening news from the world's trouble-spots. Even arms from the USSR could not halt the advance of Franco; in renewed hostilities in China, Japan was getting the upper hand; Austria had been incorporated into Germany; Sudeten German unrest was growing and looked set fair to offer Hitler an excuse to invade Czechoslovakia; there had been three upheavals in the French government; new Soviet trials indicated to believers that the Trotskyite menace was even greater than feared; and Italy had joined the German/Japanese Anti-Comintern★ Pact. At home, the pedestrian Stanley Baldwin had been replaced by the equally bland Neville Chamberlain, who had embarked on a policy of fascist appeasement that led to Anthony Eden's resignation as Foreign Secretary. Churchill, Chamberlain's most effective critic, was particularly unpopular with the left because of his record in the South Wales coalfields, his conduct during the General Strike, and his intransigence in the face of agitation for Indian self-government.

★The Comintern, Communist International or Third International was the Soviet-controlled association of national Communist parties. In 1935 it had abandoned its policy of non-cooperation with moderate socialists in favour of support for anti-fascist popular front movements.

In his desperation to oppose the forces of evil and apathy that he saw all about, Victor massively stepped up his firm's financial contribution to the operation of the Club. In May 1938 he wrote to J. B. S. Haldane, his New College friend, who was now an aggressively communist scientist and an LBC author, that

> the Left Book Club, with its 50,000 individual members operating through 5,000 agents, not only has overheads disproportionate to those of any publishing business, but is also now, of course, an expensive political organisation — and all the money has to come from somewhere. We spend £12,000 a year on advertising and general publicity (absolutely essential in order to keep up the increase in Club membership): £3,000 a year on the free 'Left News': and about £5,000 a year on Dr Lewis's department (which involves huge circularisation, travelling expenses, etc.) for the local groups. These three items alone amount to £20,000 per annum. The total number of books in a year is between 500,000 and 600,000 (i.e. an average of about 48,000 a month multiplied by twelve months): and if you take into consideration the authors' royalty and the booksellers' discount of 33⅓rd per cent, you will find *the three items alone* that I have mentioned themselves amount to something like 1/4d of the 2/6d.
>
> And we haven't begun to consider the colossal overhead expenses (an army of girls working on the cards alone), or the manufacture of the books themselves! The fact is that at the end of the first two years of the Club's existence there is a very considerable loss. *But this is absolutely confidential*: from many points of view it is less dangerous that we should be considered to be making huge profits than that we should be known to be making a loss.

(There were no separate LBC accounts, so it is impossible to determine whether Gollancz made or lost money on the Club overall. Certainly, Victor was quite prepared to subsidize it heavily.)

Time was as vital a contribution as money. During the second year of the Club, Victor spoke at the great majority of the 65 or so provincial rallies held (mainly at weekends) throughout England, Wales and Scotland. Strachey and Pollitt were his most frequent co-speakers. Others included Laski, Pritt, John Lewis, Marjorie Pollitt and, at most of the spring rallies, Hewlett Johnson, the 'Red Dean' of Canterbury. Johnson's account of his own visit to the Soviet Union had so impressed Victor that he persuaded him — with little difficulty — to discourse on its wonders to the LBC.

Neither the rallies nor Victor's ingenious membership schemes could push up recruitment to the level he had hoped. In May 1937 it was 44,800; at its peak in April 1939 it reached 57,000. Its growth was limited by a number of factors, the most important being the cost of membership, the intellectual demands of its literature, its domination by middle-class intellectuals and by the Communist Party, and the hostility it engendered in the Labour and Liberal parties and the trade unions. (Although the bulk of membership was Labour rather than communist, it was the latter who had the high profile.) There were many low-paid, uneducated but intelligent people involved in the Club, and there were many discussions on LBC books in factories and mines. For men like Les Cannon, the future trade-union leader, it acted as a 1930s equivalent of the Open University (and helped to convert him to communism), but to most of the non-communist working class it was an irrelevance. For all Victor's searching for books that would appeal by dealing movingly and readably with social and economic problems at home, books on developments abroad and Marxist interpretations of the world took priority. The selectors were too steeped in the company of intellectuals to understand the gap between most of their books and people they hoped to attract. (What, one wonders, were the non-intelligentsia supposed to make of this passage in Laski's *Left Book News* review of the November 1936 choice — Strachey's *The Theory and Practice of Socialism*: 'I think he has simplified unduly the problem of pricing in a socialist community; he has not squarely met the orthodox economist's challenge so much as turned its flank by adopting different postulates from which to reach his conclusion that, at bottom, the problem really is (I do not think it is) straightforward. I believe myself that his account of dialectical materialism makes the epistemological difficulties far easier in appearance than in fact they are; and I would even suggest that his statement of the economic interpretation of history would give the reader the sense that a Marxian clue yields itself more easily than the professional historian would admit'?)

Victor's publishing experience made him rather more alive to the problem than were the other two. He had severe doubts about the suitability of the January 1938 choice — Professor Hyman Levy's *A Philosophy for a Modern Man*, originally entitled *Dialectical Materialism* — but Laski was enchanted by it and his judgement prevailed. (He was not attracted in any case by the idea of lowering standards to achieve mass membership.) Victor offered an easier alternative that month for those who felt unequal to the reading task Levy set. He also tried with his 'B' membership to cater for readers who would prefer to purchase the committee's choice only every second month, and even endeavoured so to time the choices that they received the less high-brow selections. The 'C' membership went further again, but both special categories ultimately accounted for only 10 per cent of the roll.

The limits of Victor's empathy with the masses are suggested by his comment on the launch of the 'B' scheme: 'it does seem to me incredible that anybody cannot find time to read one book of this nature a month'. It was in the expansion of Club activities, not membership, that planning and effort paid off. By May 1938 there were over 900 groups operating in Britain and Ireland and a few more scattered in Paris, Brussels, Zurich and further afield in South Africa, Australia, New Zealand, Ceylon and Canada. Copyright law made it necessary for the many American readers to get their books indirectly, and Indian censors came down hard on anything considered to be communist propaganda. (The Club was so famous by 1938 that the Dewan of Travancore was warned by the Agent for the Madras States that attempts being made in India to start a Left Book Club like that run by 'the publisher and British Communist sympathizer Mr Victor Gollancz' were 'of considerable potential danger'.)

More remarkable than thousands of people meeting regularly to discuss LBC publications was the number of activities that developed alongside those meetings. The historian Stuart Samuels describes the social as well as the intellectual needs met by the Club in his account of a possible day in the life of a member (adorned, presumably, with the bright orange LBC badge whose border carried Victor's watchwords, 'KNOWLEDGE UNITY RESPONSIBILITY', and on which Norman Collins had passed the ill-received observation that it resembled a bottle-top). The member's day might in theory

> consist of waking to find his Left Book Club monthly selection on his doorstep; attending a Left Book Club Russian language class; going to the local Left Book Club travel agency to arrange for a Left Book Club tour to the Soviet Union; spending the remainder of the morning selling Left Book Club publications in the town marketplace; attending a Left Book Club luncheon, organized by some local businessmen; then going to the Left Book Club Centre to play ping-pong and to relax reading left periodicals; selling Left Book Club pamphlets and leaflets for the remainder of the afternoon; in the evening attending a Left Book Club discussion meeting, followed by a Left Book Club film-showing on Spain and a one-act play performed by the local Left Book Club Theatre Guild group; chalking a few slogans on the way home; reading his *Left News* and then dozing off to sleep, secure in the knowledge that the Left Book Club was Not So Much a Book Club, More a Way of Life.

These and many other developments often originated from a spontaneous suggestion sent to Henrietta Street by an ordinary member or group convenor. However busy he was, Victor continued daily to read all correspondence, note members' complaints or ideas and comment on the replies sent to them. He expressed in the *Left News* his distress that his staff were too over-worked always to reply as fully as he would wish, and tried to remedy the problem by augmenting Lewis's slender resources. Lewis did a magnificent job in his *Left News* pages dealing with groups' activities and in his meetings with convenors, building up a network in which every good idea was passed on to all. Methods of putting members in touch with each other were streamlined to be swift and efficient; groups were given constant guidance on how to attract new members and improve the quality of discussion; and individuals were enrolled in LBC-run political education classes to train them as effective leaders. The first summer school he organized at Digswell Park in Hertfordshire in August 1937 lasted for two weeks and for £5 offered full board and a range of distinguished lecturers including such intellectuals and public figures as Cole, Dutt, Burns, Pritt, Harrisson, Strachey, A. S. Neill, Professor Joseph Needham and Sir Walter Layton, supplemented by sport, music and the making of a propaganda film. Victor attended for one day and four evenings, and 'came away so refreshed by the spirit shown by everyone there, and so eager to get on with the work of the Club, that I felt the only thing I could decently do was to cancel my holiday, which was to start on the following Monday.'

Lewis was essential to the success of the Club. Although he could not carry through all Victor's myriad instructions (the Christian groups, for instance, were not a conspicuous success and the Junior groups never really got off the ground), he accomplished more than could reasonably have been expected of anyone. Like his key staff, his communist sympathies made him willing to work absurdly hard for small pay. He was older than Victor, had a sense of his own dignity and refused to accept high-handed treatment. 'John', says his widow, 'was not a Norman Collins.' Yet he got on surprisingly well with Victor. Rows were relatively rare, and if there was little affection between them there was considerable respect. In his book about the Club, Lewis wrote that his was 'an exacting job that was enjoyable because of the intensity, the pace and the thoroughness with which everything was done, and above all because of the zest with which VG would leap at a new possibility, seize on your suggestions if he liked them, or compel you to explore some new idea of his own.'

Lewis's department was expanded during 1938. Betty Reid ran the office, and Sheila Lynd was one of the four organizers. Like the general publishing staff, the groups department accepted Victor's vagaries, his impossible demands and his abrupt changes of mood as a small price to pay for the adventure and the fun. Pressure on space made it necessary to move the department a few doors down Henrietta Street. A room was equipped with a big armchair so that Victor could take there his afternoon nap in greater comfort and peace than in Number 14. Until he settled down to his first siesta no one had realised that the lift shaft was just beside the room. The ensuing tantrum was among Victor's more memorable.

In their organizing and spurring on of their charges, the groups department were trying to make individuals perform what Victor in the spring of 1938, aware that recruitment was now slow, proclaimed to be their primary role.

> While remaining *learners*, while getting more and more of our fellow citizens to become learners, we must also be *teachers and missionaries* on a grand scale. There are tens of thousands, millions, perhaps, whom for one reason or another we cannot get to join our club, but whom we can *begin* to turn from ignorance, laziness, indifference or selfishness, to active and intelligent citizenship . . . To those members who call for action, I say that this action — the action of a mind in scattering the mists from another mind, so that the other mind may see straight and clear — is of a potency beyond that of any other: a potency well recognised by all Fascist and reactionary regimes, for they fear it as the devil fears holy water — and indeed it *is* the holy water in our ritual of education.

Active LBC members responded to the clarion call. Every issue was clear and any member suffering from doubts had others to persuade him out of them. There was little evidence of disgruntlement with their leaders. A poem current among adherents gently mocked a trio generally held in affection and respect by their troops.

> Forced to make the choice themselves,
> Our rude forefathers loaded shelves
> With Tennyson and Walter Scott
> And Meredith and Lord knows what!
> But we don't have to hum and ha,
> Nous avons changé tout cela —
> Our books are chosen for us — Thanks
> To Strachey, Laski, and Gollancz!

Unity over selection of books held up rather better than might have been expected of three such confident individualists. On the major areas of policy they were in agreement. Mass membership was clearly not a realistic possibility, and there was no dispute with Laski about keeping up the overall intellectual balance of the list. Nor was there any schism over the desirability of Stalinist purges on manuscripts that showed signs of Trotskyite deviation. This frequent chore reached its peak of absurdity when Victor received a suggestion from J. R. Campbell that an American author 'might well leave out' of the bibliography of his pro-Stalinist book the works of Trotsky, Radek, Eastman and Kerensky. Having first dismissed the recommendation, Victor had second thoughts. To the American publishers he wrote: 'I can well understand the author's desire to make it as complete and scientific as possible, and of course he gives the warning that many of the books are bitterly Anti-Soviet: but for all that I don't like the idea of an innocent person picking out, let us say, a book like Eastman's and drawing hopelessly wrong conclusions from it! But this is clearly a point that the author must decide.'

The selectors were also united in their anxiety to have more non-communist books, but their well-known prejudices and the mistrust felt for them in most left-wing circles made that an objective increasingly difficult of achievement. Even the eminent Cole, who provided one of the exceptions to the rule in the Club's second year, was pressed to make alterations to fit Burns's notions of propriety. Victor and his colleagues were uneasily aware that the Club's image was under widespread attack.

The left-wing *New Statesman and Nation*, never uncritical about the Soviet Union, had featured from April to June 1937 an often savage correspondence, in which the triumvirate was variously attacked for reluctance to publish other than communist or near-communist books; for cornering the market in Left books; for offering such rich rewards in captive sales that authors were tempted to engineer their conclusions to gain acceptance; for threatening the future of other Left publishing houses by canalizing demand; for tying that demand to a capitalist concern; and for having a membership composed of 'intellectual sheep' led by 'dictator Gollancz'. (Warburg capitalized on the controversy by placing a full-page advertisement for Left books including a Trotskyist gloss on world revolution and André Gide's account of his recent disillusioning visit to the USSR.) Victor's defence cited Cole, Strachey, Attlee, Cripps, Spender, Orwell and a few others as proof that the Club encouraged a wide range of viewpoints, but for those who watched its publications closely — particularly the 'Educational' series — it was a narrow list of exceptions that proved the broad rule. Strachey's two fighting letters were little more convincing. The second contained a lie: 'we do not dream of refusing to select a book simply because we do not agree with its conclusions'. The only other published letters defending the Club were from a communist publisher, a communist bookseller and a rank-and-file member of unknown loyalties. It was poor publicity.

Worse was the announcement by the instigator of the correspondence, J. Allen Skinner, that several left-wingers were contemplating a rival book club 'not tied to any single political party'.* Although the idea came to nothing, it was an alarming indication of the strength of opposition, outside its ranks, to the selectors' conduct of the LBC.

Laski was particularly alive to the need for some means of associating the Club in the public mind with the Labour Party and the trade unions. It was at his suggestion that in July 1937 the selectors approached Hugh Dalton, Chairman of the party's NEC, and offered to issue two special numbers of the *Left News* to coincide respectively with the September Trades Union Congress and the October Party Conference. Each issue would contain four 15,000-word articles on aspects of Labour policy and otherwise carry only the usual Club announcements. The issues were to go not only to LBC members (reaching an estimated reading public of a quarter of a million) but also to the book trade, and through the groups to every relevant association or organization throughout the country. To their chagrin, Dalton turned the offer down. According to Laski, Dalton's grounds were fourfold: the *Left News* was consistently critical of Labour Party leadership; the balance of LBC books was too 'Left' and many favoured the United Front rejected by the party; the selectors were unlikely to correct that balance; and party leaders were too busy to write the proposed articles in the time allowed. Dalton, claimed Laski, had said he might view the offer differently if the *Left News* gave monthly as much space to 'official' Labour as to Strachey, if the balance of publications were similarly adjusted, and if two or three 'official' members were added to the selection committee. The selectors had agreed to his first proposal, rejected the third and contended of the second that the balance was already correct. Negotiations were broken off.

Laski's account was written more in sorrow than in anger. It concluded with a justification of the selectors, who had to put the unification of working class forces before loyalty to the Labour Party leadership, and an exhortation to the membership, who must assist the Labour Party and discuss Attlee's book seriously. Not that the Club was 'an organ of any group or party on the Left. It exists to promote a certain body of ideas which, as they are victorious, will destroy war and fascism. We may be communists like Strachey, or

*A Socialist Book Club set up shortly afterwards by the husband of Christina Foyle, founder of the Right Book Club, failed ignominiously. The Right Book Club itself, like the politically similar National Book Club and the Liberal Book Club, had modest success.

members of the Labour Party like Gollancz and myself. Within the Club, our loyalty must go first and foremost to the general idea we serve. We must use its resources, as our judgement best indicates, to see that the idea has the speediest possible triumph.'

From the standpoint of the Labour Party leadership, the Club was at best an irritant, and at worst a serious threat. The *Left News* urged Labour-inclined LBC members to join the party and a trade union and try from within to win them over to radical policies and support for the Popular Front. It did not help that Victor was known to be close to Stafford Cripps, whose United Front activities had so annoyed the Labour Party that its disaffiliation of the Socialist League had been followed by a ruling that SL membership or appearance on a platform with a communist was grounds for expulsion from the party. (The League dissolved itself in May but some of its proponents continued to support the Unity Campaign as it fizzled out over the next few months.) Nor was it conducive to good relations to have Strachey blatantly exhorting LBC members to 'unceasing work' to win converts within the trade union movement and thus mobilize the block vote against the policies of the leadership. Orthodox trade unionists, moreover, were unlikely to appreciate a conclusion like this to a review by Sheila Lynd of the 'Educational' book, *Trade Unionism*: 'Mr Mahon concludes by posing the question to the reader: is the "official" Trade Union policy, which is still one of co-operation with the ruling class, a safe or sound one; or is the left-wing policy — which recognising the State as an apparatus in the hands of the enemy calls for increasingly persistent, clear-sighted and united struggle against it — the policy to pursue?'

The large minority of the LBC members within the Labour movement who were as far to the left as the selectors might make valuable practical contributions to the work of their local constituency parties, but they were generally regarded in rather the same light as the Militant Tendency more than forty years later — dangerous zealots. Dalton's rejection of the selectors' offer reflected the views of the vast majority of his colleagues. Laski's attack made the hostility a matter of public controversy. An anonymous columnist in the *Bookseller*, surveying the dispute from the sidelines, summed up without hysteria the case for the Club's critics.

> . . . let us have some plain speaking about the latest Thunder on the Left. An extraordinary amount of perfervid indignation and bunkum has been aroused by the Labour Party's declining to supply 'copy' for the *Left News*. In last week's *New Statesman* Dr Hugh Dalton replied to the Left Book Club's accusations of aloofness, sectarianism and general inefficiency.

Very reasonable, Dr Dalton's letter was. I am becoming rather tired of the self-righteousness of the Left Book Club apostles. Let us be outspoken.

The *Bookseller*'s correspondent respected Victor, admired Laski and gave the Club credit for being the most 'original and vital development in book publishing in a decade'. But it was a profit-making capitalist venture undeserving of 'sanctimonious . . . political reverence'. Ostensibly democratic, the Club was yet controlled by an oligarchy of three near-communists, and the Labour Party was right to say 'No Association without Representation'. LBC members should be given responsibility; profits should be devoted to communal interests.

Laski, who made nothing from the LBC, would certainly have had a justifiable grievance against the attribution to him of mercenary motives. Strachey, whose Club books and journalism brought in a tidy income, would have found it difficult to convince his critics that this was truly incidental to his driving passion to convert his readers to his faith. Victor was not prepared to admit publicly either to making or losing money on the Club. The consequence of his secrecy was that people believed what they wanted to, and that although overall he may have lost financially by the Club, his detractors forever believed it to have been a gold mine.

In his other criticisms, though, the *Bookseller* columnist was nearer the mark, though his idea of giving members representation on the selection committee was wholly unrealistic. Victor could no more have been effective within a democratic Club than he could have been a patient participant in a Gollancz workers' co-operative. 'The Club is myself', he once proclaimed in response to a suggestion that he should employ someone to run it.

The selectors retired hurt from their dispute with the Labour Party, and efforts at mollification were made through the *Left News*. Strachey's article on the October Party Conference, applauding its decision to campaign for arms for Spain, was more constructive than usual. Overall, though, there was no dilution of the obvious communist inclination in Club policy. In December the *Left News* announced joint publication by Gollancz with Lawrence and Wishart (whose orthodox communist books were now discounted to Club members) of a journal called *The Modern Quarterly*, designed to contribute to 'realistic, social revaluation of the arts and sciences', under an editorial board glittering with academic talent sympathetic to communism. Still more intransigent was Victor's encomium in April 1938 for *The Week*, an invigorating mixture of fact and fancy edited by *Daily Worker* columnist Claud Cockburn, which claimed to take its readers behind the scenes. It was made available to LBC members at a reduced subscription rate.

It was not only the 'official' Left that was alienated. Luminaries of the ILP (which the CP labelled 'Trotskyist'), sent their manuscripts to Warburg, and Victor had a bitter conflict with the revolutionary socialist Raymond Postgate, with whom he had been on very bad terms ever since refusing to publish his *Peaceful and Bloody Revolution*. Reluctantly forced by the misdeeds of an author to communicate with Postgate in December 1937, Victor explained that he could give no publicity in the *Left News* to Postgate's monthly publication, *Fact*, 'a concern which, in the present international situation, is shortly to publish "an objective examination" of the Trotsky–Stalin controversy. . . . I am well aware that you will reply that I am a Communist hack, but I am quite indifferent to that accusation.' It was an unfortunate statement to have to make to an editor whose board included Stephen Spender and G. D. H. Cole.

Victor was embarrassed rather than distressed by the obloquy poured on his activities by virtually every organization to his right. He felt morally justified in his conduct of the Club, and his wife, staff, co-selectors and advisers were available to back him up. His main intellectual dilemma continued to be this: only orthodox communist authors could be relied on to see things his way, while diplomacy and his need for good books forced him to commission others from time to time. H. N. Brailsford, whose socialist philippic, *The War of Steel and Gold*, had deeply impressed Victor when he read it in 1914, was contracted in 1936 to write for the LBC *Why Capitalism Means War*. Brailsford's independence of mind proved more of a problem than anticipated. By September 1937, when the typescript arrived on Victor's desk, Brailsford had become the object of vilification from Palme Dutt and others for his trenchant criticism of the Moscow trials, and the focus of a controversy in the *New Statesman* correspondence columns. The manuscript reflected his socialist anti-totalitarianism by including what Victor saw as a 'violent anti-Soviet tirade'. He pleaded with Brailsford to cut as much as he could of his criticism of the Soviet Union in the interest of averting war. Brailsford was uncompromising and Victor sought counsel from Burns: 'The situation is, of course, exceedingly delicate: a false move might stir up a disastrous hornets' nest again.' Burns's advice was emphatic: even with further modifications, the offending chapter could not be published. Victor dictated a decisive letter to Brailsford, turning the book down: 'Although I am afraid you won't believe it, there is no question here of political pressure, or anything of that kind. As I have said before, I am a completely free agent, and under the orders of no person or party. It is simply that — if you will forgive me for putting it in so pompous a way — I cannot act against my conscience in this matter.'

That letter was not sent. Two months later, Brailsford had still had no decision and requested information: Victor had no option but to commit himself. He could not publish the book because 'I feel that, by being the instrument through which that chapter is given publicity, I am, to put it pompously, committing the sin against the Holy Ghost.' Intensification of the fascist threat meant that

> the Soviet Union is in a war situation: that in that situation it is not only justified but impelled to take every possible measure that can prevent the faintest chance of disloyalty or disruption within: and that therefore *in this period* the dictatorship of the proletariat through the Communist Party must be not only maintained but increased. Your last chapter implies that these very measures are really working on the side of war, rather than peace.
>
> I am well aware that this decision of mine may have very damaging repercussions, and I have weighed this all up. I shall, I know, be accused of arbitrarily refusing to publish things with which I personally disagree. I don't believe this accusation can be sustained: so far as the Choices of the Left Book Club are concerned, as Laski, Strachey and I disagree among ourselves on many points, it is perfectly clear that we all disagree in some degree with what is said in a great number of the books. So far as those books (other than Choices) are concerned, for which I take sole responsibility, I disagree in some degree or other with at least fifty per cent of them. But the point is that in no case have I been or can I be responsible for the publication of anything which I believe will do positive harm to the one thing — peace — which in my own way I am trying to work for above everything else.
>
> I know that that is a novel view of the job of a publisher: but it has always been my view. I dare say I take myself too seriously . . .

The file is incomplete, but a letter from Victor to Laski two months later tells its own story. It should be read in the knowledge that Laski had stated in the *Left News* only a few months previously that the selectors welcomed 'reasoned criticism' of the Soviet Union but not 'Trotskyite attacks' which constituted 'a declaration of war on that country'. That principle meant one thing to him, and another to Strachey and Victor, who, if it was politically feasible, always expunged from otherwise unobjectionable texts any remarks that might give aid and comfort to Trotskyites. The fact that Laski made a

stand on Brailsford when the dispute was brought to his attention
suggests that he was normally kept as far as possible from contentious
issues, and was left in ignorance of the extent of CP power in the Club.
Victor wrote to Laski that he had made up his mind to take the course
that did the least damage. He argued strongly against the book, which
he was convinced was dominated by pacifism, a creed whose dangers
Victor appreciated because of his own temperamental sympathy with
it. 'I suppose there is no man in the world who hates even what might
seem to be the most trifling violence or infliction of pain more than I
do. I have even been so very sensitive as to walk back three or four
miles in the country in order to kill the crushed worm that I have
noticed in a lane.'

The argument against publication was further weighted by the use
that anti-Soviet propagandists would put it to, but if non-publication
would mean losing Laski 'I haven't a second's hesitation, so we will
publish — and I feel, so far as I personally am concerned, be damned!
— and there is an end of it.'

Strachey accepted the inevitable and Brailsford thanked Victor
warmly for his generosity. He felt cheated, though, when Victor
decided to publish in August ('the depths of the holiday season'), and
years later told Kingsley Martin that 'Victor buried it in oblivion'.
Sheila Lynd wrote a skilful review in the *Left News*, praising the
book's virtues while pointing out its errors in such a way as to placate
any troubled members.

That episode did not seriously damage the unity of the selectors.
Victor had often before found Laski infuriating: his casualness in
dealing with urgent manuscripts was a byword, but Victor could not
afford the luxury of openly venting his annoyance. With intimates it
was different. From the time of the February 1937 rally, when Laski
had addressed Victor sixteen times as 'Mr Chairman' — pronounced
'Che-ahman' — Laski was referred to by that nickname in the office.
That was just friendly ridicule, but other correspondence suggests a
deeper resentment. Laski had reported on a manuscript in his usual
terse manner: 'Interesting things in it, but it is, I think, not really
profound or left enough for our members.' Victor rather gilded the
lily when he wrote about it to Strachey.

> When it came in about six weeks ago I sent it to Mister Chairman to read.
> After a week or so he turned it down with a two word 'reject': on the same
> half-sheet of notepaper were rejects in similar terms of two other books. I
> had an idea that he hadn't read it, and so sent it to another reader (politically
> intelligent, but not one of our definitely political readers — as a matter of
> fact, my best general reader [Jon Evans, whom Victor kept on full-time

despite his active involvement in the ILP]. He writes: 'In spite of its faults the book is a very sound, fascinating and comprehensive survey of its subject and well worth Left Book Club publication.' I think, therefore, that you had better read it — particularly as its subject is rather up your street.

Almost twenty years later, Victor remarked in a letter that he thought Laski intellectually dishonest. 'He was always "fudging" a reconciliation between two mutually inconsistent points of view.' There was some truth in this, for Laski had had to 'fudge' to go as far as he did in advocating co-operation with communists — a symptom of his preoccupation with reconciling intellectually his passion for liberalism on the one hand with socialism on the other — an attempt not unlike Victor's own until he gave up the struggle and accepted the communist re-interpretation of the word 'liberty'. Curiously, in the same letter, Victor wrote a criticism of George Orwell (whom he saw as an interesting contrast to Laski) that had some validity when applied to Strachey and Victor himself:

> I should not myself have said that his intellectual honesty was impeccable. I hope you won't think I am being stupidly paradoxical, and that you will understand my meaning, if I say that, in my opinion, he was too desperately anxious to be honest to be really honest. Did he, I am trying to say, give full play to those doubts, hesitations and searchings about the truth which are the lot of all of us, but which so many try to stifle? Didn't he have a certain *simplicité* which, in a man of as high intelligence as his, is really always a trifle dishonest? I think so myself.

It would be unfair to allege that Victor stifled his doubts for more than relatively short periods during his life, but he certainly did so for much of 1937 and 1938. His reaction to Gide's tortured non-Trotskyite account of Soviet illiberalism was a case in point. He wrote to Ruth in September 1937 that at dinner with Frank Strawson, his wife and his brothers Eric and Otto, there had been 'fierce but friendly argument about USSR — Frank very badly shaken by Gide's latest book. I did a little to unshake him. Have *almost* decided to write a book on Liberty.' The therapy for counter-productive doubts was always to hand: Victor's exhausting schedule, and news from abroad that kept him at a high pitch of emotional intensity. Spain and China were the two key issues. The Spanish question proved so divisive in national politics as to distract attention from Germany. Of the books on the civil war published by the LBC, the most influential was Arthur Koestler's *Spanish Testament*, which came out in December 1937 and was followed up in January by the author's speaking tour to groups.

Koestler's experience as a prisoner of Franco expecting imminent execution gave his book and his talks an immediacy that added feverishness to the LBC's support for the Popular Front forces. The reaction of his audiences had a dramatic effect on him also. He had been briefed to speak in support of the Popular Front. Although he was a communist, he was unhappily aware of the ruthlessness displayed by the Soviet-backed Spanish communists in their treatment of their rivals on the left. He was touched by his audiences' eagerness about Spain, which was untroubled by any appreciation of the complex truth. He responded honestly to the recurring questions about the POUM — now 'officially' denounced as agents of Franco — by saying that he could not agree that they were traitors. Every time he was met by a 'short embarrassed silence'. Thus began his serious disillusionment with communism. Later he prevented the reprinting of the first part of *Spanish Testament*, which included propaganda accounts of fascist atrocities, supplied by the Comintern.

Victor was better informed than his members, but was equally uncomplicated when an issue better kept clear-cut was being muddied. The December and January *Left News* were virtually given over to Spain, and in January Victor urged upon members their paramount duty 'to arouse British public opinion, by every means in their power, in support of Republican Spain.'

> Italy fell without a blow, Germany almost without a blow: Austria after a very brief, albeit heroic, resistance: but Spain still fights, Madrid still stands impregnable, and week by week the 'final' offensive of Franco fails to materialise. This resistance, and the manner of it, show us that whatever may have happened or may still happen in this country or in that, eventually the *malaise* of fascism cannot win against sanity — if only all decent men and women will play their part.

Every one of the 750 groups must arrange Spanish meetings, and individual members

> must themselves feel that every day that passes without some piece of activity is a betrayal . . . 50,000 people, each influencing many others: those others in turn influencing their friends — the result would be a public opinion so overwhelming that any Government that dared to ignore it would at once be swept away.
>
> In the first month of the New Year the Left Book Club is strong enough to undertake this work: and this is the work it was founded to do. If I felt that, after nearly two years' preparation, members would fail to shoulder this responsibility, then I should feel that the Club had failed. It must not fail: on the contrary, we must see to it that now, and during the next few

months, we triumphantly justify our existence. This is the first big chance
for us to prove that we are, each one of us, missionaries for civilization.

The members were unable to change the Spanish policy of the
National government, but they responded enthusiastically to the
challenge. When a National Spain Conference was held in the Queen's
Hall on 23 April 1938, of the fourteen or so organizations represented,
LBC Groups came third in numbers of delegates, close behind
representatives of trade unions and the Labour Party. Meetings and
rallies beyond number were organized; large sums of money for
medical relief were collected; orphans were looked after; and the Club
even launched a food ship. Victor drove himself and the members
relentlessly to more and more activity and he spoke and wrote with
urgency and feeling. Yet, in *More for Timothy*, he recalled an
ambivalence in his attitude to the civil war. 'I tried to pump up
enthusiasm — within myself, I mean — for the International Brigade:
but my heart was cold. There was nothing in me, not a trace, of the
"Thank God we can now have smack at 'em" sort of feeling that elated
so many anti-fascists in those days. I saw the dead and the dying too
vividly.'

Over China, his enthusiasm was untrammelled. Edgar Snow's *Red
Star over China*, the October 1937 Choice, was a moving account of
the Long March of 1934–5, during which Mao Tse Tung led his
200,000 revolutionary followers in a strategic withdrawal (with
fighting most of the way) from the power base of Chiang Kai-Shek's
nationalist army to greater security in the north-west. It was a paean of
praise to the heroism and tenacity of the communist forces, and
painted an idyllic picture of life in the districts — called Soviets —
which they controlled. Well-disposed readers adopted a new people,
and, as a United Front against Japanese attacks had been agreed in 1937
between communists and nationalists, the Chinese as a whole merited
support against foreign invaders. When Snow's book was published,
Japan was swiftly gaining the upper hand, and stories of atrocities
were beginning to emerge. In the October *Left News* (a special Chinese
number) Victor's editorial displayed sincere personal identification
with the Chinese:

I am writing on the afternoon of Wednesday, September 22nd, after
reading the lunch editions of the newspapers, in which it is reported that
Nanking has been duly raided by Japanese warplanes today, as promised.
'The city was subjected to terrific and systematic bombardment' says the
Evening Standard. 'Nothing is so far known of the casualty figures among
the 400,000 people who remained in the city.'

The attack was expected yesterday, Japan having threatened to wipe out the city at noon on that day. Here is a quotation from yesterday's *Evening Standard*:–

'But noon came and went. Several hours later the Chinese capital still awaited the attempt of the raiders to lay it in ruins.

'A Japanese spokesman was asked when the attack would begin. "We may prefer to keep the capital in suspense," he replied.'

★   ★   ★

We have grown accustomed to an excess of wickedness: but in all that record, as it unrolls its evil length back to 1918 and further, I can think of nothing that surpasses in villainy this cold and calculated mass-murder, or in sadistic cynicism the words: 'We may prefer to keep them in suspense.' This Imperialist and Fascist villainy moves indeed: while our minds are still so full of Spain that it might seem that they could hold no other thought, the agony of a whole vast continent puts in its claim.

At the time he wrote this editorial, he was deeply involved in setting up the China Campaign Committee (CCC), to supply information about China, arouse public sympathy and support for the United Front, and raise money for medical and refugee services. Lord Listowel, the Labour peer, was president; Victor was chairman; Margery Fry, a well-known worker for humanitarian causes, was vice-chairman; Dorothy Woodman was the highly effective honorary secretary (a position she filled also on the Committee for the Relief of the Victims of German Fascism, on which Victor served). Other members included Kingsley Martin, editor of the *New Statesman* (who lived with Dorothy Woodman), Ruth Gollancz and the national organizer, Arthur Clegg, who to Victor epitomized both the campaign and 'the quiet, unpretentious, devoted middle-class section of the left-wing England I knew.'

Victor had been useful to the Victims of German Fascism Committee; he was vital to the CCC. Through his LBC machinery he was able to give China publicity that made it a close second to Spain in the left-wing consciousness — lecture tours, guidance for groups holding China meetings, space in the *Left News*, collections and appeals for money. LBC headquarters temporarily offered a bounty of half-a-crown to Spanish or Chinese relief when any member recruited another. The CCC drew on Victor's skills and within only four months of operation had organized hundreds of meetings nationwide; had distributed over three-quarters of a million pamphlets and leaflets; had persuaded isolated groups of workers to take economic sanctions against Japan; had held a successful art exhibition (organized by Ruth) on behalf of the International Peace Hospital in Shansi and was planning another; and had directed thousands of pounds towards the hospital.

Victor's devoted work over more than three years was later rewarded with the Glorious Star of China, and of all that he achieved during the thirties it was the humanitarian dimension of his CCC work that he later remembered with most pride, as he remembered probably with most affection among the friends of his 'political' days Professor Shelley Wang, a CCC campaigner, and the eight-year-old Plato Chan, a precocious artist. Both had a gentleness and sense of beauty that greatly attracted the Gollanczes, who responded with the great kindness they often showed the vulnerable and invited them to Brimpton. Wang was allowed to stay there alone when he needed peace to finish a book for Victor. Ruth organized an exhibition of Plato Chan's paintings.

LBC assistance was warmly appreciated in China. Edgar Snow —grateful to his 'enterprising and brilliant publisher' — collected messages of support for the second Albert Hall rally from Mao, Chu Teh and Madame Chiang. The clamour for tickets at the January rally led Victor to hire the Queen's Hall for an overflow meeting, with speakers shuttled by car between the venues. Victor, Acland, Strachey and Pollitt repeated their previous year's success. Christopher Addison, a Labour peer and the party spokesman on agriculture, was a valuable recruit to the platform, although his presence implied no diminution in Labour hostility to the LBC and he concentrated on the common ground of Spain and China. Sir Charles Trevelyan, the educationalist, Soviet apologist and former Labour MP 'aroused the audience', wrote Victor, 'to a high pitch of enthusiasm with a really superb piece of oratory, devoted mainly to the Soviet Union as one of the chief planks in the peace platform, and as our hope for the future.'

> Enthusiasm had been rising steadily all this time, but it was to reach its climax when Paul Robeson appeared (and I have never heard him sing more finely), and when Harry Pollitt came on to the platform after his speech at the Queen's Hall. Greater applause could never have been heard in the Albert Hall than that which greeted these two. But when Harry Pollitt had finished there was still a surprise: the Dean of Canterbury, after closing the Queen's Hall meeting, had joined us, and I ventured to call on him to make a few concluding remarks. Whatever their opinions, I don't believe that there was a single person in the hall who was not profoundly impressed by the dignity, sincerity and passion of the Dean's speech: and when he ended with the words 'God bless the Left Book Club' I confess that I for one was deeply moved.

Recalling in 1952 how the acclaim of the multitude at his many appearances had gone to the Dean's head. Victor remarked: 'The applause by members of the communist party and fellow-travellers, when they hear something they want to hear, is indeed like nothing on this earth. The reception of a Churchill as the saviour of his country is like the scratching of a cicada in comparison.'

He did not dilate on the effects of the applause on himself. Certainly, as he stoutly maintained his public fiction of being Labour rather than communist in his loyalties, he denied himself the delirious approbation the comrades gave the Dean, who had reached the conclusion that in addition to its other perfections, Soviet Russia had more religious spirit than anywhere else in the world. Yet Victor was both the founder of the LBC and an enormously popular speaker. Malcolm Muggeridge said he was greeted by his members with the acclamation due to a führer. It was an extraordinary experience for a man who had not known fame as a public speaker until his mid-forties: as a prophet he had come into his own. His *mana* was affecting tens of thousands. During the spring of 1938 there seemed to be no limits to the ability of the LBC to fill halls and mount demonstrations on behalf of Spain, China — or Austria.★

When Eden resigned, there were three big London meetings in opposition to the appeasement policy of the Chamberlain government. The LBC gathering drew far larger crowds than those organized by either the Labour Party or the League of Nations Union. The platform boasted the usual familiar faces, two independent MPs, two communist scientists and a handful of 'progressive' clergy. Victor held that the government must be driven out of office and replaced with a 'decent' alternative, which would 'unmistakably declare its intention, shoulder to shoulder with the other peace-loving powers, to resist Fascist aggression', refuse to go to war for sectional, class or imperialist interests, and promise sweeping domestic reforms. The spread of knowledge among as many men and women as possible was the aim, and to this end, the Queen's Hall was booked for an April meeting of 'non-members', chaired by the Dean, at which Victor,

★There was a limit, however, to the market for books on this last subject. Victor was anguished when he received a plea to publish a book by a refugee, Frau Alix Koenig, who desperately needed an income as a precondition of naturalization for herself and her family. He wrote to Harry Fomison: 'The trouble is simply that *I just can't publish twenty or thirty books on Austria*. It is literally a fact that they have been coming in on me — finished books, half finished books, chapters, synopses and the rest — at the rate of two a day ever since Vienna fell. The circumstances of practically all the people are the same as Frau Koenig's . . . We'll give her £50 as an advance, but there will be no obligation to publish. I'll pay the £50 to the company and recover it if we publish.'

with Acland and Strachey, fought through a barrage of abuse from fascist hecklers and won many recruits. Most of Victor's spring and summer effort, however, was directed towards the imbuing of his existing members with the missionary spirit and extra engagements up and down the country were slotted into his already overcrowded schedule.

Victor's state of mind throughout was dominated by a combination of desperation about the 'crisis' of ever-imminent war and a conviction that he had evolved an instrument which, used correctly, could turn aside the catastrophe. It is easy with hindsight to judge his hopes unrealistic, but in the context of the period, to an overstretched and emotional man meeting warmth, commitment and applause whenever he spoke, the chance seemed real enough to change the course of history and save Europe from carnage. Even a more level head might have been turned by encomia from foreign leaders of the calibre of Nehru and Mao, by first-hand accounts of the popularity of the LBC with the International Brigade, and by news of the proliferation of LBC groups around the world. Strachey, after a visit to Spain, seemed as intoxicated as Victor, writing glowingly of the founding of the LBC as a world event, giving heart to fighting men in Western China and on the bleak plateau of Teruel. A common body of ideas was beginning, he declared, to form a network of men and women of every nation, creed, colour and race, who must multiply their members until they formed 'an irrefragable steel mesh' which would bring peace to the world.

Hoping now to reach the millions, but keeping his face set against any lowering of the intellectual content of the Club books, Victor came up with the '"Twopenny" Strachey'. Some of Strachey's books had already had a seminal influence on Club members. *The Theory and Practice of Socialism* (again a euphemism for communism), published in November 1936, had explained Marxism in a simple accessible way. Lewis had trained a corps of group leaders to run study courses on it, and it had become the Club bible. Originally written for the Educational Series, Strachey's new polemic, *Why You Should be a Socialist* was, Victor considered, 'crystal clear' and 'so persuasive as to be, indeed, unanswerable.' He published it in May 1938 in paper covers at twopence, and called on members to secure the sales such a price demanded — 100,000 to break even. Within two days of publication orders had reached 150,000; ultimately over 300,000 were sold. Letters flooded in describing dramatic conversions thus effected. There were two other twopennies that year: one on Spain and the other Haldane's *How to be Safe from Air Raids*. They too reached a much wider audience than the normal Club book.

To sell as many pamphlets as they did, individuals had to undertake a great deal of time-consuming door-to-door selling. Free leaflets were Victor's next innovation. Two were issued in 1938: *The Hitler Menace* in September argued the urgent necessity of standing up to Hitler over Czechoslovakia; *There is a Grave Danger*, in November, alerted the public to the possibility that the British government might grant belligerent rights to Franco. Both were written by Victor in the direct and compelling style of his advertising copy, and called into play his skills in layout and typography. Two million of the first were distributed and ten million of the second. Again the active Club members cheerfully bore the burden of passing on the message to the public, and as ever, the majority were active communists or sympathizers. They could not know that their leader was beginning to suffer doubts about the part they played in his organization.

CHAPTER TWELVE

SQUEEZED BY IDEOLOGY

UP TO THE middle of 1937, Victor's worries about LBC communists had been mainly to do with presentation. For instance, in May 1938 a member wrote to urge that groups be dissuaded from using the word 'comrade', because it upset liberals, and Victor replied:

> We discourage it whenever we possibly can — just as we discourage the singing of the 'Internationale' at our meetings. It is exceedingly foolish to annoy the Liberals. Between ourselves (this of course is confidential) this mistake was made at the end of the great Spain Conference at the Queen's Hall, when, although Wilfrid Roberts [a Liberal MP] was in the chair, the 'Internationale' was sung. Roberts was exceedingly annoyed.

Two months later he was confronted with stark evidence of subversion.

The LBC Digswell Park Summer School in July/August had been on the surface another triumphant success, but Victor had discovered there that the communists viewed the Club as a device for party recruitment rather than as an organization deserving support for its own sake. He found out at much the same time that the LBC Theatre Guild was threatened with take-over by the communist Unity Theatre group, who hoped to curb its adventurousness. The Theatre Guild, with its 250 amateur groups, was run by the dedicated John Allen, whom Victor greatly admired. It was one of the Club's major achievements and a source of great pride for Victor. He protested strongly to Burns about these transgressions, which had forced on him truths he had preferred to ignore; for the first time he had met incontrovertible evidence that not all communist activities were directed towards the common weal, and he feared he might lose control of his Club.

This was only one of a number of problems that was bedevilling Victor's summer. There had been an announcement that Odham's Press was considering launching a rival book club with a social democratic bias. Hugh Dalton, G. D. H. Cole, R. H. Tawney and Sir

Walter Citrine, the General Secretary of the TUC, were tipped as selectors. Victor's editorial in July offered friendship rather than rivalry to the venture, in somewhat barbed terms. He made the usual vehement defence against any implicit suggestion that the Club was failing in its duty towards the Labour Party: 'myself a member . . . I have never sought to conceal [that] I regard the electoral victory of the Labour Party as a political objective of supreme importance.' His protestations had a hollow ring. He was under heavy assault again in the press. *Forward*, a Glasgow socialist weekly, carried from June to August a series of familiar attacks on communist domination of the Club, and made reasonable suggestions about widening the selection committee to include people like Brailsford, Bertrand Russell, Kingsley Martin and C. E. M. Joad. 'Why', it asked, 'should the book reader always have his books selected by the Holy Trinity of Gollancz, Laski and Strachey, the Father, Son and the Holy Ghost?' Victor's answers were intemperate and ill-judged. The first concluded with the remark that in such a varied list he was surprised not to find the name of Trotsky — a jibe that drew the embarrassing response that Trotsky's *History of the Russian Revolution* had been published by Gollancz some years previously and lavishly praised at the time by Laski. Was Trotsky now banned by the LBC? 'Is it to please the "Daily Worker" and the Communist Party?' The anonymous columnist drew Victor's wrath further upon him: 'Now not even Gollancz will deny that the Left Book Club is under the control of the Communist Party.' Victor's choleric response drew attention to the libel actions being pursued by his firm. (His dislike of legal proceedings did not prevent him from suing some right-wingers who made wild attacks on the Club for, among other things, being financed or run by Russia: all proceeds went to charity.) The implicit threat did not trouble *Forward*, but to a dispassionate observer the letters from Victor would have seemed both evasive and bullying, serving only to confirm the widespread suspicions about the Club. Had the observer known much of Victor personally, he would also have guessed that his anger had some origin in unease and guilt. Accusations with truth in them often elicited ill-reasoned bluster, as if by the language of outrage he could better convince himself of their falsity. The day on which *Forward*'s scornful dismissal of his threats appeared was the day he wrote to Emile Burns complaining of communist subversion.

Only three days later Victor was dictating an editorial describing the LBC's greatest *coup* — a close alliance with *Tribune* in support of a Popular Front of all opponents of the National government. That concept had been gathering support throughout 1938, but it was no more popular with the Labour leadership than had been the now defunct United Front, with its emphasis on working-class solidarity. Cripps was again the outstanding figure of the campaign, backed notably by Aneurin Bevan, George Strauss and Ellen Wilkinson, all Labour MPs and members of the editorial board of *Tribune*, of which Cripps was chairman. He and Strauss had had to invest heavily in the paper to save it from collapsing along with the United Front whose mouthpiece it had been. When he decided to throw *Tribune*'s weight behind the Popular Front movement, the editor, William Mellor, objected. Cripps, by August very close to the LBC selectors, added Victor to his board (on which Laski already sat) and, urged on by the LBC triumvirate, fired Mellor. A two-page LBC section was incorporated into the paper and a young *Tribune* journalist, Michael Foot, was offered the editorship. When Brailsford, who had been a founding member of the *Tribune* board, heard that Foot had refused the job and intended to resign in protest against the 'brusque' treatment of Mellor, he tried to dissuade him. About Victor he wrote that 'like you I distrust him and am highly critical of the Left Book Club. (I have reasons drawn from personal dealings with him.) But why capitulate in advance? I assume that you would enjoy full editorial discretion. In that case the worst to fear is that VG would make things difficult for you at Board meetings.'

Foot was not dissuaded and the editorship went to H. J. Hartshorn, a fellow-traveller. *Tribune* was set on a pro-communist course; Strachey became a regular contributor and Victor frequently wrote for the LBC pages. It was no wonder that he filled columns of the *Left News* with praise of *Tribune*, which now answered the need for an LBC weekly paper — impossible to produce for reasons of finance and his own shortage of time. His explanation of what the alliance would mean indicated that for practical purposes he had given up on 'official' Labour and was openly plighting his troth with the rebels. Hailing the drawing together of the LBC and the organ of 'a really militant section of the Labour Party' — a new stage in the mobilization of progressives — he adjured his members to order *Tribune* 'without a moment's delay', and strive to treble its circulation by Christmas.

Five days after the editorial was written, Kingsley Martin, no great fan of Victor's but an admirer of his campaigning work, wrote to tell him of yet another scheme for a Labour Party book club, this time slavishly modelled on the LBC organization. Martin had been invited to be a selector and passed full details of the proposal on to Victor, who wrote to Strachey about it. The terms of his letter suggest that he had been stung into his more traditional position of hard-left righteousness. The 'cover' names for the selection committee demonstrated to him that the 'manoeuvre' was on classical lines. 'The Coles, Tawneys and Attlees [he must have been particularly peeved since the previous month he had welcomed a suggestion from Attlee's secretary that he might publish his collected speeches] can be paralleled again and again among the SRs and Mensheviks★ between February and October.' The right course of action was for the CP 'without anything like a disastrous public statement' to mobilize itself behind the Club. Pollitt should be shown Martin's letter and 'advised of every development immediately'.

> Moreover, he may see some way of mobilizing the party behind the Club's autumn campaign at the B'ham congress, without, however, doing anything which can give them a handle for saying 'you see it *is* the CP'. Do you think there's anything to be said for having Acland on the Selection Committee? We could then say Laski (LP executive) VG Labour Party (!); Strachey, working closely with CP; Acland, Liberal. . . . See what Harry says.

It was only for a couple of weeks that Victor was safely back under the direction of the CP. The following month came the Czechoslovakian crisis. Publicly, Victor at first followed the predictable course: writing his leaflet opposing any sell-out to Hitler; calling with such urgency on group convenors to distribute it immediately that half a million leaflets were on the streets on the day the printers delivered them; and making final arrangements for nationwide rallies that committed him to speak in over thirty different locations between 23 September and 16 December. Less publicly, but in his capacity as founder and guiding spirit of the Club, he wrote personal letters on 25 September to Churchill, Eden, Citrine and Attlee. To the first two he wrote representing the point of view 'of an overwhelming majority of people on what is called "the Left"':

> First, we are desperately anxious that Hitler should be made to understand in absolutely unmistakable terms that there will be no more surrender — for only in such understanding do we see a last faint hope of peace: secondly, if war comes, we wish to see it waged with the utmost efficiency and determination.
>   The confidence we have that this is your own point of view is one of the things that give us hope at the moment.

To Citrine he added that 'we would wholeheartedly support any steps whatever that you and your associates might think it wise to take

★The Socialist Revolutionaries and the Menshevik Party dominated the provisional government of Russia for the seven months preceding the Bolshevik revolution.

in pursuance of these objects.' He also acknowledged Citrine's dislike of the LBC and explained he had allowed communist involvement because of their awareness of 'the menace of Hitlerism'. To Attlee he made the Popular Front case urgently and specifically.

> During the last two or three days there is a really desperate feeling among people to whom I have spoken, both in the Labour and in the Liberal parties, that civilization may literally depend on the drawing together *during the next two or three days* of those elements in the nation that are opposed to still further surrender. (I understand that at last the Cabinet seems determined to stand firm: which makes it all the more important that they should be strengthened in this resolve.)

This was the only chance of preventing immediate war. The Liberals might be prepared to approach Attlee if they could be sure of not being 'definitely rebuffed'. Would Attlee send Victor a message stating if he was willing to consider some kind of alliance? His letters had no effect. He was influential as a propagandist, not as a behind-the-scenes political fixer.

His public statements were clear-cut. Privately, he was in a state of turmoil. In *More for Timothy* he says that the intensification of evil over the preceding months 'suddenly spoke to me and said . . . "Nothing in the world is strong enough to withstand all this evil but goodness: and the essence of goodness is to be good for the sake of goodness, and not for the sake of withstanding the evil."'

> I looked within. I am not going to catalogue what I found there — the faults of conduct, the weaknesses of character, the sins of commission and of omission, and the rest; for I want to avoid, if I can, being smug in reverse. Everything boiled down to selfishness or egoism in one form or another. And I knew this: if I tried to be better myself, if I tried to be, humbly and not wilfully, a channel for goodness, I should be answering evil with a directness not otherwise possible, with an absoluteness that evil itself could not sully . . .
>
> I did try, in ordinary feeling and conduct, to be a little more generous, a little more considerate, a little more courteous, a little more loving, a little more sympathetic, a little less self-righteous, a little less hot-headed and prone to anger and I tried, above all, so to accept the offered grace that I might become the sort of person who no longer had to try, but was better — because he was better: because he was purer in heart.

There is no evidence that those who had dealings with Victor after Munich noticed any sudden change in his behaviour. Yet he certainly believed that from that period began 'within the limitations of my human and personal weakness' his life-long struggle to be a man who *was* good as well as *did* good. That was in his private capacity; circumstances outside demanded that he temper his new perception with an element of compromise. Looking afresh at the activities of the LBC, 'I saw . . . something rather wicked about it, mixed up with a great deal that was good: an element of Hitlerism, almost, in reverse: a degree of contamination by this thing it was fighting . . . some breeding of evil passions, as well as of noble ones: and a certain encroachment of the mechanical . . . on the spiritual. And I was both frightened and ashamed by what I saw.'

Victor gives little space to the LBC in his memoirs. Unable to face up to his adjustment of moral absolutes to the exigencies of the moment, he gives a rather misleading picture of his association with the CP in all his later writings, for publication or not. He did not lie: a man who wished deliberately to rewrite history would not have left myriad incriminating documents in his own files. What he did was admit to what he could bear to acknowledge, obliterating the rest from his consciousness. The process began haltingly when he wrote in an editorial for the *Left News* on 22 September 1938 that he did not know whether Chamberlain might, by standing up to Hitler, make war inevitable or, by appeasing further, bring about 'a morally shattered world'.

Victor's intellect and emotions were in favour of standing firm, but his instincts were pacifist. He still believed the Club must support the Popular Front, but he knew too that he had compromised too much with the CP. These conflicts showed. His editorial argued for stopping the fascist menace, but begged that in the event of war there should be 'no trace of the wrong sort of war feeling — nothing but sympathy with and compassion for the peoples of the fascist countries.' He distorted the truth yet again in his denial of the routine allegations against the Club — allegations made 'in spite of the fact that of the three Selectors two are members not of the Communist but of the Labour Party, and that the third is a member of no party at all' — yet he accepted that in the event of a war 'anti-fascist democrats would be fighting, and rightly fighting (and I intend to say this, for all the sneers of the Leftists) in the same ranks as anti-democratic imperialists.' He ended with the call to spread enlightenment before it was too late: 'I now plead with you this September day of 1938, as I have never pleaded before, to work with all your heart and soul to forge the Left Book Club into an instrument of enlightenment which will help — if I may use words which, however worn they may be, carry with them a desperate appeal — to save civilisation.'

Parts of the editorial must have raised eyebrows in King Street, but there was no serious alarm. The strategy for the future of the Club had already been worked out. Strachey wrote about it to his friend Robert Boothby, an anti-appeasement Tory MP, a few days after the Munich agreement to transfer the Sudetenland from Czechoslovakia to Germany. The LBC base was to be broadened, he explained. Cripps and two Liberals (clearly Acland and Roberts) had been asked to join the selection committee. The Club was to be renamed 'Left Book Club and Anti-Fascist Association' and would ultimately be known simply as the 'Anti-Fascist Association'.

> If we succeed in rapidly changing the whole character of the LBC; making it a body of the left centre, instead of the extreme left, and not limiting it to people who will read books, I do not see why the Club should not become one of the mass bases (the Trade Unions being the other) for fighting the pro-fascists. It *could* be an enormous educational propagandist force, comprising men of all parties, bent simply on giving us a core of several hundred thousand politically educated people who *could* not be swayed by fascist-manufactured mob emotion into betraying this country as the unfortunate people of Britain have been cajoled into doing in the last few days.

Strachey was hoping for an anti-fascist alliance right across party lines, and he assured Boothby that the CP would do everything to help make this possible. Almost immediately after writing, he set off on a four-month visit to the USA, where Laski had also gone for the October to May academic year. Having agreed certain reforms with Victor, they had left him to run the Club alone at a time when he was in a state of great uncertainty. He had reacted to Munich, he admitted later, with 'a mixture of shame and relief, with the relief predominating; how unfair we were to Neville Chamberlain!' Although his contemporary pronouncements showed no desire to be fair to Chamberlain (whom Victor deemed likely to allow Britain to go fascist if he had the chance), his attitude to the fundamental purpose of the Club was undergoing a metamorphosis. On 19 October he wrote in a 'Private and Confidential' letter to Leonard Woolf:

> I see a future more and more dominated by lying propaganda, mass hysteria, violence, unscrupulousness and hatred: and I believe the most important thing of all is to preserve, so far as they can be preserved, tolerance, the open mind, freedom of thought and discussion, and so on. I have myself for many years held the view that these things (for which I have always cared more than for anything) were not ultimately possible in a capitalist society: and I have therefore been prepared — though with

extreme reluctance — to defend the suppression of these things in the Soviet Union, on the ground that a socialist society cannot be brought into being except by means of a dictatorship, and that in this case, therefore, 'the end justifies the means'.

I feel doubtful now whether that point of view was ever right: but whether it was or not, my own ideas on the subject have been altered by the new situation in which we find ourselves. I believe that here and now, without any compromise, these 'liberal ideas' have got to be immediately defended and preserved. If this cannot be done, I see the extinction of everything decent in humanity.

Would Woolf write for the Club a book on the defence of Western civilization?

The following day Victor wrote for the November *Left News* an editorial of almost 7,000 words called 'Thoughts after Munich', which dealt more circumspectly with the same theme. It was the most revealing public statement he had ever made — though it was not entirely frank. Munich, he confessed, had 'produced, at any rate in me, something of what I imagine happens to a man on his death bed: the most ruthless self-criticism, and a determination to achieve an honesty as great as is humanly possible. As a result, there has been a strengthening of beliefs already held, but some shifting of emphasis.'

The LBC had been set up as an '*educational* body' with 'two positive goals — the preservation of peace, and the creation of a juster social order: and one negative one — defence against Fascism.' It had not been intended as a political party, but action through political parties had been encouraged. Now there was a real possibility that groups might be taking action in such a way as to damage the Club. He gave three recent examples. The first was a report to him the previous day about a group almost entirely composed of 'extreme "Left Wingers"', who neither read nor discussed Club books, preferring to chalk slogans in the streets. The second was a letter received two days previously from a group convenor in the North of England, expressing deep disappointment at a recent speech of Victor's in which he had urged the necessity of thinking rather than merely shouting slogans. Thought, said the convener '"wasn't good enough"'. He said 'that they were looking to me for leadership: that perhaps I was tired as well as disappointed (disappointment seemed to me rather a mild word about the world position at the present time!): that thought without action was sterile: and that, among other things, the Left Book Club ought to set up a wireless station for broadcasting to the German people.' This convenor had shown complete misunderstanding of what the LBC meant. The greater the crisis the greater the necessity for thought.

He was in favour of broadcasting to the Germans: he had himself spent all the night before Munich preparing with others a 'memorial' urging that if war came the first action should be an air-drop over Germany of millions of leaflets explaining the real meaning of war. But, he emphasized, it was not the job of the LBC to do more than urge that others organize broadcasts.

His third example of action potentially damaging to the Club was a letter from a leading London group asking for the 'easiest' type of book henceforward in order to push membership to the million. That would be to sacrifice education to propaganda.

> Let me say immediately that I take my full share of the responsibility for those developments in the wrong direction of which I now see a danger, and which I am terribly anxious to prevent. Passionately believing in certain ideas, I have allowed myself, I think (I mean, of course, in my capacity as director of the Left Book Club, not in my capacity as a member of the Labour Party or as a speaker on non-Left-Book-Club platforms), to become too much of a propagandist and too little of an educator. I would go further and say that my eagerness to express certain ideas has, in the rush of day to day work, tended to overlay what I hope I have never forgotten: namely, that only by the *clash* of ideas does a mind become truly free, and that no mind not free can have that utter conviction which will render it immune to any assault of passing circumstance. I repeat again here that I am speaking solely for myself, and not for Laski or Strachey: but, speaking so, I think it right to add that in my view the publications of the Club have tended to concentrate to too great a degree (though by no means exclusively) on two or three points of view, and to forget that any author has a place in our ranks, provided only that his work is of value in the struggle 'for peace and a better social and economic order, and against fascism.'

Lying propaganda was rampant and strengthened fascism: it was vital 'to preserve what is menaced by this evil'.

> No one knows better than I how partial is our democracy, how circumscribed is our own freedom. No one is more bitterly resentful than I that the freedom of the unemployed man is the freedom to rot in unemployment. But for all that the spirit of our civilisation is something totally different, so far at least, from the spirit of Fascism: and I believe myself that, as a result of Munich, the importance of preserving this spirit is overwhelming.

The LBC should have no truck with Nazi-type propaganda. One of its main tasks ahead would be as 'a bulwark of truth and scrupulousness and respect for other people's opinions, and of the most complete freedom of thought and discussion.' The end rarely justified the means, and certainly did not now, when anti-fascist values must be defended with the utmost vigilance.

> I want to say one word more in this connection, and I say it with great hesitation, because it must necessarily sound pharisaical. I have always believed that the Christian doctrine of 'Love your enemies' (at any rate in the obvious meaning of these words) is something too difficult for human nature. But while I do not believe there can be love, I do believe that there can and must be an absence of hatred. There can be no member of the Left Book Club who hates and detests Fascism more than I do: I hate it as a Jew, but I hate it infinitely more simply as a man, who sees everything decent and human being trampled underfoot by it. But, hating Fascism, I do not hate Fascists: and just because hatred, not only of ideas but of persons, is a mark of Fascism, and just because Fascism has been so immensely strengthened, I believe it to be necessary, if we are to fight Fascism, that there should be no hatred of persons in our hearts.

Reverting to his theme of the necessity for *thought*, he produced examples of the menace posed by fascism, regretted that pacifism would not work and pleaded again for the principle of collective security: 'With three provisos: first, private profiteering in armaments, that most disgusting of immoralities, must be utterly suppressed: second, the *emphasis* should be on the fullest possible protection from air warfare, for otherwise fear must always paralyse our diplomacy: and third, and most important of all, we must beware and beware again that in the process of achieving "preparedness" we do not actually achieve Fascism.'

Simply to re-arm was not enough. Thought was necessary to prevent the country from going down the path of 'so-called "patriotic" imperialism' or gradually accepting with equanimity a war against Hitler. War would mean years if not decades of 'agony and degradation and stupidity: and in countries in which a reactionary Government was in power at the outbreak, it would mean the immediate introduction of some form of Fascism or semi-Fascism.' What was needed was collective rearmament combined with a positive peace policy. This was described in detail and included the strengthening of democracy at home; planning to abolish 'working-class degradation'; the establishment of close commercial relations with the Soviet Union; a world-wide propaganda campaign in praise of democratic ideas; the end of colonial exploitation and the granting of Indian independence.

I believe that the discussion and rapid spread of such ideas can win overwhelming support in this country, and so lead far more quickly and far more effectively to Mr Chamberlain's overthrow than mere repetition of slogans such as 'Chamberlain must go'.

★   ★   ★

To sum up, the Club must at all costs retain its educational character: it must, in the balance of its publications, in its group activities and its meetings, be a stronghold of truth and of the free and enquiring mind: and it must regard careful and patient *thought* as its most urgent task — such thought leading to immediate and determined action by members in the organisations to which they belong.

To that end he hoped to broaden the selection committee and better to balance 'negative' (i.e. anti-fascist) with 'positive' (e.g. Leonard Woolf's proposed book) Choices. The LBC house would be put in order with books by Lord Addison and Ellen Wilkinson. 'Let me say this in conclusion:

When we started the Club two and a half years ago we started from nothing. Now, in the new world of after-Munich (for a new world it is) we have a colossal task before us: but we start out on that task with a huge membership, with a nation-wide and indeed empire-wide machinery of groups and area committees, and with two and a half years' experience of failure and success. We start out, I say: for I want our work in the future to be so much better and more effective than it has been in the past, that in the years to come we may look back upon the autumn of 1938 and see it almost as a new Left Book Club that then arose. And if we avoid an easy optimism on the one hand and a cowardly defeatism on the other, and if above all we guard against the peril of self-deception, we may and will still play a part, and a great part, in saving the world from the two scourges which I bracket together as the most terrible mankind can know — war and Fascism.

The immediate tasks facing Victor were manifold and many of them mutually contradictory. To save the Club from being simply an organ of propaganda would mean problems for his relationship with the CP. Overt support for the Popular Front would increase the hostility of the Labour Party. Bringing in new selectors would threaten his personal control at a time when it seemed vitally important to preserve his freedom of action. And at a moment when he desperately wanted to pour money into the Club he was faced with an appalling slump in the market for the general list that had kept Gollancz prosperous, while generous donations to refugees had seriously depleted his own financial resources.

It all called for clear thinking and a consistent strategy, yet despite his measured prose, Victor was depressed, frightened and uncertain. Foreign news was uniformly appalling. In the first three weeks of October alone, Germany had occupied the Sudetenland, Japan had withdrawn from the League of Nations on being declared the aggressor in China and had won two more major victories there, and the French Popular Front had fallen apart. Victor was overworked, in the middle of an emotional crisis and bereft of his most trusted political adviser. In that state, he kept himself sane by stepping up his work to ever more frenetic levels, clutching at straws of optimism, taking decisions one by one as they were forced on him, and acting impulsively rather than consistently. Woolf, for instance, wrote towards the end of October to say that the book Victor wanted would necessarily deal with some topics of 'acute controversy among different sections of the Left and I daresay some of my opinions would be much disliked by a good many members of the Left Book Club. I assume that I should have complete freedom in the expression of opinion within the law of libel and obscene libel.' Still in the mood that had precipitated his editorial, Victor responded with a concession unparalleled in Club history — an absolute guarantee that the book would not be censored. Having sole power in the absence of the other selectors, he spoke for them also. Yet less than three weeks later, he was trying to remove implicit criticism of the Soviet Union from a book on propaganda.

Though the sole arbiter of LBC policy, there is no evidence that he made any overtures to the three putative new selectors. Certainly Richard Acland was never approached, and he was the most attractive of the three prospects. Of an impeccable Liberal background, he was an inveterate campaigner for any variety of Popular Front. (His LBC Topical book, *Only One Battle*, had been published late in 1937.) In November, under his leadership and with loyal support from local LBC members, a sensational Popular Front victory had been achieved in a by-election at Bridgewater, when Vernon Bartlett, journalist and broadcaster, won as an Independent Progressive with the backing of the local Labour and Liberal parties, and with crucial help from the LBC. Even more important, Acland — though a passionate crusader — was privately a mild-mannered and courteous young man who treated Victor with the deference that ensured a successful relationship. One can only conclude that Victor opted for absolute freedom of action rather than a public relations exercise which would have been unlikely to impress opponents of the Popular Front. Neither was any change made in the Club name.

However much Victor now emphasized the primacy of education over propaganda, his most important energies over the next few months went perforce into the case for anti-fascist unity. Yet in correspondence there was a new detachment evident in the tone he used in speaking of the communists, towards whom his feelings had become decidedly ambivalent. His natural dislike of intellectual subservience — shut out of his consciousness for so long — returned. His daughter Livia, now eighteen and a member of a communist-dominated student group, found that Victor had eavesdropped outside the room at their home where the group was holding a meeting. Later he congratulated her on her questioning of aspects of party policy. The process of disillusion was speeded up at Christmas 1938, when on holiday in Paris he faced up to reading a verbatim account of the Moscow trials 'and saw the world, for some terrible hours, as an executioner's puppet-show.' Frank Pakenham, who met him during his journey home, never forgot the horror which Victor evinced in describing what he had learned. And only a couple of weeks after returning, he responded to criticism from Pollitt of his editorials by explaining that no longer would he allow the Club to peddle the party line. Henceforward, though he would work for common aims with the CP, discussion and consultation would have to be 'in an atmosphere of real freedom on both sides'. In the *Left News* in February he went so far as to admit of 'certain barriers against full intellectual freedom in the Soviet Union'. The 'ordinary Soviet public' was unable 'to arrive at the whole truth with a full knowledge of the available facts . . . nor is it encouraged to express opinions running counter to those generally prevailing.' Still, the great mass of Englishmen were 'at the mercy day by day of lying propaganda' and if the Soviet Union's restrictions were truly necessary to preserve 'the priceless gains of the Revolution, and to bring finally into being that society in which every man will be completely free . . . then the price is one that emphatically has to be paid.' However, his conclusion that the idea of intellectual freedom should be cherished was not calculated to win applause in King Street.

Though he wavered at times, Victor's new resolution was evident in his publishing policy. For instance, in the spring of 1939 he disapproved of the political aspects of George Orwell's novel, *Coming Up for Air*, which included a parody of an LBC meeting. Orwell believed 'that some of Gollancz's Communist friends have been at him to drop me and any other politically doubtful writers who are on his list.' Yet to Orwell's surprise, Victor published the book as it stood in June.

It was not easy for him to make gestures of independence; he needed the help of the CP to win support for the version of a Popular Front that Cripps was now trying to sell to the Labour Party — a version which deliberately made no mention of co-operation with the communists. Victor had written of it early in January 1939 to the Dean of Canterbury:

> The next two or three months are, in my view, the definite turning point, which may well decide things one way or another. While the reactionary influences at Transport House are increasing and hardening against any kind of Popular Front that would sweep away Chamberlain, on the other hand the tide is rising with immense rapidity in the constituencies. Wherever I go I find our local groups really live centres which are bringing everybody together to a constructive anti-Chamberlain effort.

Three weeks later, Cripps was expelled from the Labour Party. He had written for the NEC a lengthy memorandum advocating a Popular Front. Only D. N. Pritt and Ellen Wilkinson supported it. His expulsion followed his circulation of the memorandum to constituency parties. That evening he enjoyed a great ovation at the Queen's Hall, at an 'Act for Spain' meeting chaired by Victor, who had begun to organize it only six days earlier when news from Spain suggested that Barcelona was likely to fall to Franco. He had succeeded in packing the Hall, almost filling the overflow meeting at the Kingsway Hall (where relative failure was primarily attributed to bad weather ruling out the planned sandwich-board parades) and collecting a group of speakers that in addition to Cripps consisted of Alfred Barnes (Labour MP and Chairman of the Co-operative Party), Vernon Bartlett, Aneurin Bevan, Isobel Brown (one of the most effective of all activists and fund-raisers for Republican Spain), Lady Violet Bonham Carter, Will Lawther (Acting Chairman of the Miners' Federation of Great Britain), A. D. Lindsay (Master of Balliol and unsuccessful Independent Progressive candidate in the October Oxford by-election), David Low, J. B. Priestley, Wilfrid Roberts, Ellen Wilkinson and Ted Willis (Chairman of the Labour League of Youth). Barcelona fell next day, but Victor believed that the meeting had nevertheless been a hopeful occasion, for the platform had been 'truly *national*' and thus pointed the way ahead — united action to bring down the government.

Bevan had taken the opportunity to express his support for Cripps: 'If Sir Stafford Cripps is expelled for wanting to unite the forces of freedom and democracy they can go on expelling others. They can expel me.' Cripps was a tough fighter, determined to press on regardless with his campaign, and the Queen's Hall approbation must have given him heart. He set up a committee to launch a six-point National Petition calling for united action by 'the Parties of progress', to replace the National government with one committed — among other ends — to a Peace Alliance with France and Russia, control of armaments and an end to colonial exploitation. In this effort to challenge the Labour Party leadership through an appeal to the rank and file, Victor was among Cripps's most devoted helpers. On 8 February he wrote to the Dean: 'As you may have guessed, I have been up to the eyes over the whole Cripps situation (my connection with it, of course, is private) — attending all-night conferences, and the rest of it. On top of all my other work, this has put me behind very badly.'

The Dean, at Victor's behest, had written a pamphlet called *Act Now: An Appeal to the Mind and Heart of Britain*. Its central thesis was that Christianity demanded socialism. Victor thought it magnificent and felt the opportunity too good to miss of extending the argument to include the Popular Front.

> I am enclosing a roneo'd copy (it is now being printed) of the petition that Cripps is launching. Wouldn't it be a good idea to add a postcript — definitely *calling* it a 'postscript' — and to say in it that, just as you have finished writing the pamphlet, this petition that Cripps is launching comes into your hands? I should make it clear that you had no part in the matter at all. With a great air of ingenuousness, you might then say that you are not a politician, and don't know exactly what practical points or difficulties may be involved in Cripps's suggestion for unity between the Liberal, Labour and Co-operative movements: but you do know that, in general, unity against Fascism is a good thing, and anyhow the six points appear to you to be exactly the kind of programme to which the country could be united at the present time. Then you might print the whole petition.

The Dean was a helpful man. Unusually, Victor himself reviewed in the March *Left News* what came to be known as the 'Twopenny Dean', concluding:

> There is a very interesting postscript. The Dean explains how, when he had finished the pamphlet in an isolated part of Wales, the Cripps Petition came into his hands. He explains that he is not a politician and does not know what practical points and difficulties may be involved in Sir Stafford Cripps' Co-operative movements; but he does know, he says, that unity of some sort against Fascism is urgently needed, and that the six points which Sir Stafford demands of any government that is to win our allegiance clinch completely the Christian and scientific principles for which he has been pleading, and provide a basis for their practical and immediate application. He then prints the six points of the Petition.

Two million copies of the Dean's pamphlet — rather than the ten million Victor hoped for — were sold, but by the time it came out Britain and France had recognized Franco's government and Bevan and Strauss had been expelled from the Labour Party for continued support of Cripps. (Wilkinson and Pritt chose the party rather than exile with their colleagues.) The Popular Front campaign was fatally enfeebled. By the imposition of harsh discipline, the party leadership, strongly backed by a trade union movement antipathetic to extra-party co-operation, killed it off over the next couple of months.

As early as March 1939, Victor must have realized that the Petition Campaign was a hopeless cause, but he continued to fight for its objectives. In a pamphlet, *Is Mr. Chamberlain Saving Peace?* ('The Penny Gollancz'), most of which he wrote on 23 March, he analysed the government's recent conduct of foreign policy in detail and in a manner calculated to appeal to anti-fascists of all parties.

> It may well be that owing to a mistaken policy pursued for many months, a genuine People's Government, in place of the existing one, is not an immediate possibility: that is one of the desperate tragedies of the present situation. But if we cannot have a People's Government, we can and must have a government of men, whatever their party, that will co-operate *whole-heartedly* — that is the test — with the Soviet Union: that will stand four-square, without the slightest havering of 'appeasement', to Fascist aggression and so will, please God, prevent war altogether: and that will, if war should, nevertheless, come as a result of Fascist madness, prosecute it to a successful, but not vindictive, conclusion — a conclusion which indeed must mean, and must be fought to mean, the liberation of the German and Italian peoples.
>
> In such a government, neither Mr Chamberlain nor Sir John Simon [the arch-appeaser] could have a place.

The pamphlet was highly topical and hence had a brief life, for on 30 March Chamberlain — frightened by Hitler's dismemberment of Czechoslovakia in contravention of the Munich agreement — took a stand and, with France, pledged support for Poland if its independence were threatened. After this demonstration of strength, he continued to procrastinate on negotiations with the Soviet Union, for which he felt distrust and distaste. The central argument of Victor's pamphlet remained valid, and his energies were concentrated on a desperate attempt to mobilize public opinion along its stated lines. Pollitt, Pritt and Strachey (who had returned in February) were still appearing on LBC platforms up and down the country, as were the usual collection of speakers — to whom had now been added as regulars Bevan, Strauss and other Cripps supporters.

Victor's hope of attracting star speakers across ideological fences proved vain. The Tory anti-appeasers fought their battles alone. The Labour Party were unimpressed by modifications to LBC policy. Ernest Bevin and Herbert Morrison had both bitterly attacked the Club, and the party leadership remained hostile. The rival book club, the Labour Book Service, had finally got off the ground. More threatening still, the Labour Party leadership — annoyed by the Club's ability to attract far larger audiences than it could itself and seriously worried by its strength in a number of constituencies — looked set to take action against the Club. Having purged the leading Cripps supporters they were in fighting mood. The national agent, G. R. Shepherd, wrote in March to borough, district and local Labour parties about complaints made to the NEC concerning 'embarrassing activities' of the LBC in constituency Labour parties. If the Club or its groups spread propaganda against the party, or further embarrassed it in the constituencies, it would be necessary to make membership of the LBC incompatible with membership of the Labour Party:

> Since Groups of the Left Book Club are not entitled to affiliation to constituency Parties, joint political activities with them should not be entered into, especially when these are in the direction of a so-called 'Popular Front' with any other Political Party. Constituency Parties are also urged to protect themselves against proposals emanating from Left Book Club Groups on the additional ground that many members of these Groups are not members of the Labour Party and are certainly not Socialists.

The editorial in the April *Left News* dealing with this new menace was signed by Victor and Strachey. It put forward the predictable defences, and pointed out with justice the impossibility of enforcement of the threatened ban without organized raids by Transport House agents on houses of party members: 'these are the fantastic absurdities to which the frenzied sectarianism of Transport House appears to be leading it.' Their conclusion was that this attack would lead to 'an immediate and enormous strengthening' of the Club as a bastion of civilized values. The lengthy article concluded:

> The present course of action of Transport House, of which this attack on the Left Book Club is but the latest, if perhaps the most extraordinary, phase, has caused heart-break and despair to many thousands of the very finest men and women of the Labour Party. To them we would say this: resist the temptation to chuck everything up, or go back to cultivating your gardens, to throw in your hands — fed up with politics. Above all,

remember that the Labour Party is, in essence, a body of magnificently devoted men and women, who need your continued co-operation.

The attack made upon us is the greatest compliment which the Left Book Club has ever had paid it. Let us be worthy of that compliment.

Do not let us underestimate what the Left Book Club has already done. We have only to double our present size to become irresistible. If we do not realise that, it is clear that our opponents do. Let us realise that as clearly as they do . . . Our answer to every attack must be and will be — recruit, recruit, recruit. Every man or woman won for the Left Book Club is a soldier trained in the cause — in the cause, not only of antifascism, but of a strong and triumphant Labour Party.

It was indeed a tremendous compliment, but that was small solace. Only two MPs still within the party — Pritt and Wilkinson — would appear on LBC platforms, and there was now no hope that less radical colleagues would join them. Even though the announcement that the government intended to introduce conscription united all shades of left opinion against it, it was not enough to heal the divisions. The third LBC annual rally on 24 April 1939 graphically demonstrated both the strength and weakness of the Club.

Victor had worked desperately to widen the platform, but Pollitt's presence meant yet again that no member of the Labour Party could appear. Cripps was now free to join Pollitt along with Acland, the Dean, Wilfrid Roberts and Strachey (with Paul Robeson in support), but the only other new faces were Sir Norman Angell, the veteran rationalist and campaigner for international understanding and holder of a Nobel Peace Prize, and the speaker on whom Victor pinned great hopes — David Lloyd George, now a leading defender of the principle of collective security and a voluble critic of appeasement. Victor had paid dearly for Lloyd George's appearance, having cemented good relations with him by a huge advance for his self-justificatory *The Truth about the Peace Treaties*. Its publication had coincided with the slump in the book market and Gollancz lost about £5,000 on the deal. (That loss, combined with the heavy spending on the LBC, had made Victor deeply worried about the firm's finances.)

The rally packed out the Empress Hall, which seated 11,000. The *Left News* report was written by Cedric Belfrage, author of the February 1938 Choice, *Promised Land*, an 'inner history' of Hollywood — showing what happened to art under capitalism. (He was deported from the US in 1955 after appearing before the McCarthy Committee, accused of having been a Communist Party member in 1937.) He found in the occasion 'the atmosphere of a true religious revival'. Lloyd George came well up to expectations in his attack on

Chamberlain, and described the LBC as 'one of the most remarkable movements in the political field in two generations'. He was present, he said, because he believed 'this method you have inaugurated—instruction and enlightenment — is the only way you can save civilisation.' Victor was able to announce that the Club now had 57,000 members and 1,200 groups. By his estimation, it had distributed over two million books, almost half a million pamphlets and fifteen million leaflets. He collected more than £600 for a Club crisis leaflet fund, much of which went immediately towards a *Save Peace* pamphlet arguing for a British-French-Russian collective security agreement. 1,750,000 copies were distributed within a few days — a triumph of organization.

Neither that nor the brilliant success of the rally as an emotional event could conceal Victor's impotence regarding national political developments. It was not a fact he could accept, for his only shield against despair was the conviction that, with greater effort and through the power of reasoned propaganda, the Club would yet succeed in averting cataclysm. In speeches and *Left News* articles over the next few months he begged his members not to give up the struggle because they had seen so many of their causes lost. 'If I am right', he wrote in June, 'in detecting a widespread feeling of apathy, weariness and disillusion on the Left, then, and if these things persist, the next few months may seal our fate.' They had a moral duty to mobilize public opinion both to stop Chamberlain moving 'in a fascist direction' and to force the signing of the Anglo-French-Soviet Pact favoured by a broad spread of politicians. On the home affairs front the selectors promised powerful ammunition: a horrifying autobiography, *These Poor Hands*, by a South Wales miner; a book about Jarrow, *The Town that Was Murdered*, by its MP, Ellen Wilkinson, who had led the hunger march from there to London three years earlier; and *Tory MP* — an analysis of the background and voting record of every one of the 400 Conservative members of the House of Commons. The latter, published in July, hardened into personal enmity the dislike many Tories had long felt for Victor, as it handed a useful electoral weapon to their opponents. In July also, the LBC had ceased to provide material for *Tribune* (widely known as *Cripps's Chronicle*) on the grounds that the Club was becoming too much identified with the paper. Having thus in the same month performed a very useful propaganda service for the Labour Party and asserted his independence of its expellees, Victor nourished some hope that the party leadership might be disposed to smile on him. He could reasonably feel also that the feeble performance of the Labour Book Service proved that the LBC was worth wooing.

The previous year he had toyed with and discarded as likely to fetter him the idea of seeking a Labour seat. Now his parliamentary ambitions had resurfaced. With Cripps, Bevan and Strauss in limbo, Victor had few supporters among Labour MPs. In his publishing capacity he had had with Pritt, one of his closest friends in the Labour Party, a lengthy dispute over a book Gollancz had commissioned from him. There were faults on both sides; each felt he had a grievance. But though Victor contrived to keep the friendship going, Pritt was very sore. Victor's main hope, then, was Wilkinson, who wrote in mid-summer 'I shall be only really happy when we are engaged in fixing up a nice safe seat for you. It would be fun.' 'Ever so many thanks,' replied Victor. 'Wouldn't it be a good idea if you fixed up a meeting between Herbert Morrison and me — asked us both to dinner, or something like that?'

It is unlikely that Wilkinson ever took the risk of introducing Victor to Morrison, one of his most implacable Labour Party foes. Anyway, a Commons seat was not high enough in his priorities to make him press the point at such a time. There was an increasingly realistic possibility of a pact with the Soviet Union, and in devoting most of his own and the Club's resources to help bring it about, Victor, publicly at least, suppressed his post-Munich hesitancies about the theory and practice of communism. The Dean's panegyric— *The Socialist Sixth of the World*— was to be the October choice, and it was important again to court communist opinion. It was a severe blow to Victor that this policy was threatened as a consequence of one of his own actions — the guarantee he had impulsively given to Leonard Woolf eight months earlier. Woolf's manuscript had caused heartsearching among the selectors, now at full strength with Laski's return from America. 'We all feel', wrote Victor to Woolf on 22 June,

> that there are certain phrases in the book (I do not think more than half-a-dozen) which can very easily be dragged out of the context and used by reactionaries and, indeed, fascists as propaganda against the Soviet Union. We believe that these can be modified in such a way that your point is not put the smallest bit less strongly, while any possibility of distortion by fascists, etc., is obviated. It is simply a question of a word here and a word there, and sometimes, perhaps, *introducing* a particular qualifying phrase which you actually use elsewhere, and the inclusion of which in the sentence itself would prevent the possibility of the wrong kind of propaganda.

On other points, the selectors were discordant: Victor thought the book 'exceedingly valuable', despite a 'certain hostility to the Soviet

Union'; Strachey found it 'definitely not a good book', and liable to harm the LBC; Laski held the middle ground. Would Woolf be prepared to discuss with the selectors the possibility of making a few alterations?

Victor went on to make, at considerable length, gloomy pro-gnostications about what would happen to the LBC should Woolf's book be published unaltered. His fears included the arousal of 'intense hostility', a serious split in the Club, and up to 10,000 resignations from communists and near-communists. It would in any case, he assured Woolf, be technically impossible to publish until early in 1940, though that was irrelevant, since 'we all feel (and believe you will agree) that whether or not the book is modified it would be a disastrous error to publish it until the Soviet pact (if we get it) is reasonably firmly established. However the book is modified, it is obvious that opponents of the pact can dishonestly use it as propa-ganda: and we mustn't provide them, in the situation as it is or may be during the next few months, with that opportunity . . . '

'I must say', replied Woolf, 'that your letter rather astonishes me — not least that you now propose in any case to postpone publication of the book for over seven months.'

I am not hostile to the Soviet Government, but I knew that any criticism of that Government or its policy is interpreted by many people as hostility, and it was for that very reason that I put the matter quite plainly to you before we signed the agreement. Now what I foresaw has happened, and because I deal in a book of which the subject is tolerance with tolerance both in the USSR and in fascist countries, I am accused of 'hostility' to the Soviet government. But that is precisely the subject which in your letter to me and in our conversation you asked me to deal with. I claim to be as good a socialist as any member of the selection committee of the Left Book Club and to be equally desirous with them of the success of the Soviet Union. For the Soviet Union as a socialist state I have like you an affection (though not for Governments and governing cliques — which is a very different pair of shoes). It is just because of this that I think it essential to point out errors in policy which, as I explain in the book itself, seem to me fatal to the ultimate aim of socialism or communism. That is the main object of the book and of course it will be treated as lèse-majesté by people whose attitude towards socialism or communism is the same as that of the Tory to the British Empire.

He was prepared to listen to suggestions and alter anything he was convinced seemed hostile, but would not tone down or alter the main argument of the book, 'on the ground that now is not the time to tell the truth because of the delicate international situation or because what one says may be used for propaganda by one's enemy. Everyone has been saying that on one side or another since August, 1914.'

Victor's reply gave rather unconvincing reasons for the delay and insisted that the differences between them were few.

> On the question of 'hostility', this is a point on which, I believe, you will agree it is very difficult for us to judge of ourselves . . . every now and again — perhaps half-a-dozen times in the whole — there was a phrase which made me want to say: 'How he detests them!' I think it right that everyone should detest intolerance: but I do believe that unconsciously this detestation leads you to detest something more than the intolerance itself.

Woolf wrote again, making it plain that he was unimpressed by the excuses for the delay. 'There wasn't', Victor assured him, 'the smallest suggestion that the book was being postponed because of its probable unpopularity with members . . . I see from your letter that, to put it bluntly, you don't believe me about the necessity in any case for postponement: but I assure you it is a fact.' Meanwhile, he told Strachey,

> Woolf is cutting up nastier and nastier. And he is very anxious to have that discussion as soon as possible. When can you get your memorandum done by? Then we can reckon three or four days for Laski and myself to prepare our points, and then we will have the bloody meeting.
> I am beginning to dislike the book! If Woolf gets any nastier I shall break the contract and refuse to publish it!!

Woolf did not further endear himself by his next letter, which began:

> 'To put it bluntly', as you say, I do not believe in the necessity for an indefinite postponement of my book — nor does anyone with any publishing experience to whom I have told the circumstances — nor in fact did you yourself until Strachey had read the MS, otherwise you would not have put it in your spring list.
> As an author I am not interested in speculations regarding the imaginary influence which my book will have on international negotiations or the membership of the Left Book Club; I am interested in two things only: (1) that the book shall be published within a reasonable time and that it shall not therefore be indefinitely postponed until it is just out of date and all the edge taken off it, (2) that I am paid for my labours within a reasonable time . . .

He politely demanded specific information on the likely date of publication. Victor, who was indeed lying about the technical reasons for holding it up, could only fall back on the unanswerable defence that 'no one but myself has any experience whatever of the problems connected with fitting in Left Book Club choices.' The postponement had nothing whatever to do with Strachey's attitude: 'Neither he nor anybody else has put any pressure of that kind on me — I shouldn't have listened to it if they had.' He ended with a postscript: 'I cannot really believe that you mean: "As an author, I am not interested in speculations regarding the imaginary influence which my book will have on international negotiations."'

Though Victor was prevaricating about postponement, he was being truthful about his own attitude to the book. Nonetheless, he was piqued when Woolf denied the effects its publication might have on Anglo-Soviet negotiations or LBC membership.

> I do not at all take the view that a book, when read by a quarter of a million people . . . can have no effect on international relations. To admit such a thing would make nonsense of all my principles as a publisher: and it seems to me also to make nonsense of a great part of the case for democracy.
> . . . I do happen to know my Left Book Club members. I do not think my estimate of ten thousand was at all exaggerated.

The correspondence was becoming wearisome to both and was suspended once a meeting was agreed for 24 July. Three decades later Woolf recalled:

> I refused to budge, and the discussions went on for two or three hours, becoming more and more difficult, as warmth increased on their side of the room and frigidity on mine. The book was published unaltered and unmodified . . .
> That evening when I got up to go, I felt that I had not ingratiated myself with my three friends, all of whom I liked very much, both in private and public life. There was a slight cloud, slight tension in the room, but I am glad to remember that, before I went out, an absurd little incident entirely dispersed them. On the wall opposite to where I had been sitting was a picture which through the long, rather boring and exasperating, argumentative discussion I had frequently looked at with pleasure and relief. In gratitude to the painter, when I said good-night to Victor, I asked him who had painted it and added that I had got a great deal of pleasure by looking at it. I could not have said anything to give Victor more pleasure or more effectively relieve the tension, for the painter was his wife. I left the room, not under a cloud, but in a glow of good-will and friendship.

The meeting had done nothing to dispel Strachey's bitter hostility towards Woolf's book on the grounds that it misrepresented Stalin's dictatorship, which was, Strachey argued, reluctantly maintained only to suppress subversive capitalists and other enemies of the

working class. He assailed the book in the *Left News* in November
1939, the month in which it was issued as a Choice.

The technical obstacles to such early publication had suddenly
evaporated in consequence of a series of events which caused a sea-
change in Victor's political outlook. Up to late August, the Soviet
Union had remained in his eyes the one reliable bastion against
fascism: on 23 August the Russian and German foreign ministers
signed the Molotov–Ribbentrop non–aggression pact. Hitler launched
the long-feared attack on Poland and in Britain there came at last unity
between most of the right and the left. On 3 September, when
Germany ignored an ultimatum to pull out of Poland, Britain and
France declared war. In the horror of that moment, Victor found
himself allied with long-standing enemies and lined up against
erstwhile reliable friends.

CHAPTER THIRTEEN

RETREAT FROM MOSCOW

'AMID THE WELTER and chaos of the international situation,' John Strachey wrote in April 1939, 'the position of one great power remains constant and clear. The speeches of the leaders of the Soviet Union do not change from appeasement to firmness and from firmness back to appeasement again overnight.' For all his developing scepticism about many aspects of Stalinism, Victor continued to share Strachey's view until the news of the Molotov-Ribbentrop Pact burst on him. Then, as he put it later to J. B. Coates, something snapped in him. Rightly convinced that Nazism could be defeated only through the help of the Soviet Union, he had shut his eyes to that country's cruelties and repression during the mid-thirties. After Munich he began to face the truth, but where possible gave the Stalinist régime, implacable foes of fascism, the benefit of the doubt. Emotionally, he saw the Pact as a complete betrayal of his huge moral investment in selling the Soviet Union to the members of the Left Book Club. Intellectually, he could appreciate that the Chamberlain government bore a mighty responsibility for its failure energetically to pursue an Anglo-Soviet pact. But morally he could not countenance, for any reason, Stalin's accommodation with those whose intrinsic evil was beyond question.

Kingsley Martin concluded that Victor was 'at heart relieved' by the break with the communists, and in that judgement there is a measure of truth. Along with the bitterness came the freedom of being answerable now only to his own conscience. During 1939 he had been conducting a fundamental re-examination of his own philosophy. The profound religious instinct which had found its strongest expression in his relationship at Oxford with Hastings Rashdall had been in abeyance in the twenties and early thirties, and then, from 1933 onwards, sublimated in the fight for a Utopian socialist paradise that would overcome evil. Although later he claimed (and indeed believed) that he had never wavered from Christian socialism, there had been little evidence in the 1930s that he saw Christ as relevant to contemporary politics. After Munich, however, the Christian element in his beliefs reasserted itself as his disenchantment with pragmatic *voltes-face* grew. In mid-July 1939 he wrote to an American author, Melvin Rader, 'I have been talking to one or two people here about the desirability of founding some informal association of men and women who are pledged uncompromisingly to three things —

1. The abolition of production for private profit.
2. The preservation of the spirit of scepticism.
3. The preservation of Christian ethics.'

For his communist friends, Victor's new emphasis was an irritation. There had grown within the headquarters of the LBC itself an atmosphere of distrust. Sheila Lynd, from 1937 Victor's political assistant, was scornful of his heart-searching, and his other close friend, Betty Reid, patiently assiduous in pointing out the errors of his ways. When the Pact was announced, Victor made the depth of his pain and anger clear to his intimates. Publicly he kept it quiet, as he wrestled with the crisis facing the LBC and Victor Gollancz Ltd now that war was imminent.

Contingency plans had been laid during the summer for evacuation of the whole Henrietta Street publishing operation to Brimpton, although in the event, the packers, messengers and a few ancillary staff stayed in London. In the meadow adjoining the garden a hut had been built for the office staff to work in, and lodgings made available locally. Less than three weeks after the Pact, the new Brimpton headquarters, with its skeleton staff, was working efficiently.

It was less straightforward with the LBC. The business side could be run from Brimpton, but no firm plans had been made for the policy and conduct of the Club in wartime. Sheila Lynd, John Lewis and Betty Reid had continued throughout the summer to develop plans for autumn rallies, speaking programmes and general LBC education activity. Those plans needed revision in the light of the Pact, and any such revision required Victor's collusion — which was not forthcoming so long as they were prepared to hold discussions with him only on the basis of Stalin's infallibility. His priorities were to save the Club from internal haemorrhage, to keep within its ranks both supporters and opponents of the Pact and, concomitantly, to avoid any CP takeover of Club policy. Pending a meeting with the book selectors he sent a letter to Club convenors promising a statement later. In the interim no utterance or activity of any member, convenor or group was to be taken to represent the official view of the LBC. The promised statement did not arrive; the selectors were split. Laski was if anything even more uncompromisingly hostile towards the Pact than Victor, while Strachey justified it as a holding operation, consistent with an Anglo-Soviet pact of mutual assistance, towards which the government should be urged. Indeed, such urgings should be the prime purpose of all LBC political activity. Should he prove to be wrong in his assessment and should 'the Soviet Union . . . go into benevolent neutrality to Germany', he wrote on 25 August to Boothby, 'my whole political position would be shattered. I should have to reconsider everything.'

When the selectors met, Strachey made no converts. The policy adopted was one of inaction. Without unanimity among the selectors, and with the political situation changing daily, there was no solid basis for guidance of any kind to the membership.

This negativeness shocked Lynd, Lewis and Reid, especially when they found themselves unable to influence Victor's stance in any way. To Sheila Lynd he announced his intention of personally running the groups from Brimpton, and offered her a job as his sole assistant. Having consulted Harry Pollitt, she turned it down. Betty Reid, offered the job in her stead, took the same course. Both refusals upset Victor, and both women wrote at length to explain their position. 'I may', said Lynd, 'be partly responsible for your present hostility and suspicion in having let you get away with a complete misunderstanding of my conversation with Harry last Friday.

> In the first place you clearly think that the Party prevented me and Betty from coming to Brimpton; in the second I now believe you are nursing the idea that I have affronted you by questioning your courage . . .
>
> . . . I certainly never meant to give the impression that either Harry or I questioned your courage. We understood the practical reasons for which you proposed to run the Groups from Brimpton, and disagreed with them, because we think that in wartime it is more important to *display* courage than common sense. I really thought I had made this clear last Friday, but you must have taken my words in exactly the opposite way to which they were meant.
>
> Secondly, the question of Brimpton: as you know I never wanted to go, and did not think the Groups should be run from there. I went to ask Harry if I *must* go. He strengthened my conviction that the movement could not play an important part if it were run from Brimpton, and left me free to decide whether or not I should go there. Since the Party did not instruct me to go, I was free to refuse and did so. Betty took the same line without consultation with me. . . . Since Friday, you have more than justified our decision that it was unnecessary for a party member to help with the Groups at Brimpton, for you have shown that you don't want a political assistant, but a short-hand typist to type your letters to the Groups.

If I was hostile, as I know I was, when I gave you this decision last Friday, it was not Harry but yourself who made me so: I am sick of putting up with lectures on the stupidity of the Soviet Government, and scoldings for not believing they have gone into isolation.

Since then, as perhaps you don't realise, I have been too angry to sleep . . . since the beginning of the Groups we have worked at building them, regarding it as our main Party work, using our position in the Party to win greater understanding of the importance of the Club. We understand the Groups and the way the Club must work as well as you, and have hitherto worked with you in everything the Club has done. We have been regarded as officers of the Club. But when the situation becomes critical, we find that we are not officers, but office boys — and office boys who are not to be entirely trusted in the building, just because they are Communist office boys . . .

Betty Reid, in a far longer letter, some of which was devoted to a defence of the Soviet action, took the same line, more gently expressed. For her a vital priority was to mount an LBC anti-Chamberlain campaign, but she was also deeply distressed that the long effort expended on developing the educational work of the club should be abandoned. The denial of any lead to the membership was not just negative, it was 'a very positive weakening of the progressive movement'. The problem Victor had to face was not that she, Lynd and Lewis gave their first loyalty to the CP, but that they were loyal members of the LBC 'precisely because we *are* Party members'. They wanted the Club 'to be true to its aims and what it has always preached' and by failing to consult them and by refusing to act, Victor had changed the whole *modus operandi*. His implicit demand that he be given political loyalty was unacceptable. The LBC would become increasingly difficult to hold together if it continued to be 'entirely dependent on one man (leaving aside the Laski Strachey Myth) who may at any moment decide that the whole thing has been wrong, that it should be shut down . . . that it should be swung behind the Government . . . and in fact that the whole organisation is dependent on your individual judgment.' Surely between them they could reach agreement on some form of activity for the Club and avert the 'terrible disaster' of its collapse. 'A political leader (and whether you like it or not you *are* in that position) who doesn't lead but follows events is a danger in time of crisis.'

Her plea for some kind of action, even of a modest and non-political form, was echoed on 2 September by John Lewis, the day before war between Britain and Germany was declared. Neither had guessed that the period of uncertainty might be so short. More importantly for their understanding of the LBC's workings, neither they nor Lynd had realized the crucial role played by Laski and Strachey: although Victor was undoubtedly very close to being *de facto* dictator, either of the other selectors could do untold damage by resigning. In this respect, periods of uncertainty, crisis or potential dissension left the Club in the hands of a paralysed and mute triumvirate.

The tension eased with the outbreak of war, for most of the communists with whom Victor was associated welcomed it — convinced still, like Strachey, that Stalin would wish for a German defeat in the West. Pollitt rushed out a pamphlet called *How to Win the War*, in which he declared that 'to stand aside from the conflict, to contribute only revolutionary-sounding phrases while the fascist beasts ride roughshod over Europe, would be betrayal of everything our forbears have fought to achieve in the course of long years of struggle against capitalism.' The *Daily Worker* followed suit, and Victor, horrified though he was by the approaching carnage, found a sort of truce with the CP possible. Indeed, as he later recalled, several of his communist friends had been so eager for war in the hours leading up to its declaration that they had dubbed him '*Munichois*' for the doubts he expressed. Yet he was determined henceforward strictly to limit CP influence in the LBC. When John Strachey put himself forward as London-based groups organizer in Lewis's place, both Victor and Laski politely but firmly declined. Victor gave his reasons:

. . . it is simply the fact that in the peculiar circumstances administration and the direction of policy would necessarily be one.

If you were up there in London dealing with the Group correspondence and seeing Harry Pollitt every day — as inevitably you would be seeing him — nothing in the world could prevent the whole thing gradually taking on the King Street tinge, and I believe more than ever before that we must avoid that. I fundamentally disagree with your remark that the Club must be either Communist or anti-Communist . . . if it were true the Club would be really meaningless . . .

Although I am immensely conscious of all your work for the Club I have, and I am sure you will agree, borne the major part of the 'heat and burden of the battle'; and I cannot abdicate now from its general direction. I have always consulted you and Harold before making any major decision and every such decision has been unanimous: and, of course, this will apply to the future every bit as much as to the past. But I do feel that I must keep the day-by-day direction in my hands: and the day-by-day direction could not be in my hands, if you, up in London, were doing the Group correspondence.

However, he was responding to pressure to keep the LBC active in wartime. Along with the pleas of Lynd, Lewis, Reid, Strachey and others had come a very persuasive letter from Emile Burns. Lewis and Reid, who had been given a month's notice on 8 September, were reprieved a few days later. On reduced salaries they were appointed for an experimental period of three months to give informal help and advice to the groups from London. They in turn promised that they could be implicitly trusted to work for and with Victor, who was to meet them for discussions on his days in London.

This stay of execution was a sign of renewed buoyancy after weeks of pessimism exacerbated by a serious summer slump in the book market. The preferment accorded Reid and Lewis brought about a complete breach with Sheila Lynd, senior in length of service and convinced of her own superior efficiency. In her written castigation of Victor, she accused him of sacking her because he imagined her to be a more committed party member than Betty Reid. His lengthy and dignified defence made it clear: the real reason was the impossibility of rational discussion with her. His letter ended sadly: 'although I feel at the moment . . . as angry with you as you feel with me, in a day or two I shall think of you as I have for the most part thought of you. But I have little hope that you will reciprocate.'

He was right. He had loved Sheila Lynd for most of the 1930s; the estrangement was to last for seventeen years.

The September issue of *Left News* consisted mainly of a long statement by the three selectors called 'The LBC in War Time'. The clear duty of Club members was to exert themselves 'to win the war and defeat Fascism'. Additionally, they must continue the fight for the values for which the Club stood — liberty, respect for other people's personality, and toleration. This meant open-minded discussion among all shades of anti-fascist opinion. The importance of education, working towards a more just post-war society, was emphasized. The selectors declared their optimism about the Club's future: 99 per cent of resignations had been for such unavoidable reasons as war service, and there was hope that the decline in membership could be stemmed and even reversed through recruitment drives and energetic work by the groups under John Lewis's direction.

More significant for those concerned with the development of Victor's thinking was the brief editorial in October. Setting goals for post-war Britain, it moved on from economic freedom and the socializing of means of production, distribution and exchange to a call for political, cultural and intellectual liberty, with genuine political democracy and complete freedom of opinion and its expression.

Every citizen should be encouraged to form independent judgements on the basis of all the facts. This must be a society 'characterised by a respect for what are called the Christian virtues — justice, mercy, forgiveness, charity, kindness and tolerance — and by a contempt for ruthlessness, pride, cruelty, arrogance, hate, revenge and the pursuit of power.' Members and groups should direct their mind to this:

> Economic planning in the genuine interests of the whole community is the *sine qua non* of a decent society. It implies rigid control. By what technique can that control be harmonised with the widest possible freedom? Or, put in another way: how, in the new society, can we not merely preserve but immensely increase all those gains for humanity symbolised by the names of, to mention only four, Socrates, Christ, Voltaire and our own Shelley?

Devout members of the CP read this editorial as an attack on the Soviet Union. Its publication virtually coincided with the Moscow directive to change the party line on the war. Pollitt fell victim to the shift. Though he confessed his error in initially supporting 'an imperialist war', he was fired in November from the general secretaryship and replaced by Raji Palme Dutt.

The truce was over, and the LBC became a battleground for pro- and anti-war factions. The selectors were once again divided, with Strachey's old loyalties winning against his intellectual doubts about communism. For the membership, it was a period of enormous confusion, made worse by the publication in November, as a Choice, of Leonard Woolf's uncensored *Barbarians at the Gate*, followed in December by the Red Dean's encomium, *The Socialist Sixth of the World*, which itself coincided with the Soviet invasion of Finland. All Victor's appeals for open-mindedness fell on deaf ears at both extremes of the ideological divide: many showed their displeasure by resignation. Of the several letters that Victor quoted in the January 1940 issue of *Left News*, two suffice to give the flavour. The first was from a bookseller: 'We are asked by Mr — to cancel his membership. We do not propose to repeat the terms in which he gave in his resignation, but they were to the effect that if he wanted any anti-Soviet filth he would prefer to join the Right Book Club.' The second came from an LBC member: 'I wish you to accept this as intimating my immediate resignation from the Club. I do *not* want to receive on any account *The Socialist Sixth of the World*. After the Russian attack on Finland with all its brutality, a book praising the aggressor, even if written in all good faith before the attack, would be nothing less than nauseating.'

'MEN OR SHEEP?' ran one of the rubrics in Victor's editorial that month. Noting that many of the resigners had written to say that they owed everything, politically, to the Club, which had made them 'eager and active citizens', he went on,

> the question I want to put to them is this: *do they realise what they are doing?* For the sake of a self-righteous gesture — in order, one might almost say, to save their own souls — they are weakening the organisation to which, on their own showing, they owe so much; and if their attitude were that of even a large minority, as it fortunately is not, they would end it altogether — end an enterprise which by its books, its meetings, its discussions, its vast mass distribution of such publications as the 'twopenny Strachey' and 'twopenny Dean', has converted literally hundreds of thousands to socialism.

Gnawing away at Victor as he penned his pleas for tolerance must have been the consciousness that, in its first three years, the LBC had done little to stimulate an appetite for contrasting views — especially where the Soviet Union was concerned. In the December *Left News* Laski had supported, and Strachey denigrated, the war — a display of impartiality that impressed some and maddened others. Victor's editorials doggedly propounded freedom of opinion, no doubt to the approbation of the majority, yet his postbag was filled with abusive letters, and some of them, he noted sadly, smacked of anti-semitism. It was an unfortunate coincidence that the two pro-war selectors were Jewish.

For several months Victor tried to square the circle. Then came evidence that CPers were turning some groups into 'Stop the War' propaganda organs. More distressing was his growing conviction that John Lewis's anxiety for impartiality within the Club did not match his own. On 19 February he wrote to Betty Reid:

> For some considerable time I have been becoming more and more alarmed at the handling of the Club from Henrietta Street: on several occasions I have tried to explain my feelings to Lewis, but it has always ended in unpleasantness, with the result that for three or four weeks I have not raised the matter with him. On the last occasion on which I raised it, in not at all a sharp form, Lewis got very angry and said to me: 'Do you want to rule out anyone who speaks from a communist point of view?' He must have known this to be a parody of my point of view: but the fact that he made the remark in relation to my criticism shows the direction in which he was going.
>
> I know very well that you *both* think that I am over-suspicious: that I wrongly suspect 'plots' on the part of the groups to dominate the Club from a communist point of view or from a one hundred per cent pro-

Soviet point of view, or whatever it may be. Well, none of us can be sure that we are being objective: but it is my job to come to conclusions on the evidence as I see it.

When I reappointed Lewis I made it clear that I did so on condition that the groups were run as *genuinely* 'all-in' bodies: that in fact every possible effort should be made to correct any undue bias in one direction or another.

I believe that at one time this was honestly Lewis's position: I believe that he still *thinks* it is his position: but I am becoming more and more convinced that no genuine attempt whatever is being made to run the groups on these lines . . .

I believe that a very simple thing has happened. Under the growing stress of events, Lewis, though not a member of the Communist Party, more and more not only takes the communist point of view, but adopts the whole communist idea of propaganda for that point of view.

Lewis, Victor felt, was taking no steps to balance communist-dominated programmes. The Liverpool LBC, for instance, had booked Strachey and the Dean to speak: with both against the war, this made the platform indistinguishable from the Liverpool Communist Party. Unless Lewis did more to honour the spirit of his probation, he would have to go. 'It would be a thousand pities, both for personal reasons and also because it would create a stink in the Club: but I am *absolutely determined* that the Club shall be run in the most genuine possible way as a genuine educational body, representing all points of view. And I am not in the least prepared that it should *appear* to do this, while really, through the groups, pushing the Communist line.' Considering that both he and Laski opposed the line of ' "Stop the imperialist war" ', it would be 'fantastic' to run the risk of the Club being used as a communist propaganda organization.

No accommodation was possible. In April 1940, pleading economic necessity and the inevitable decline in the volume of Club work, Victor gave three months' notice to John Lewis. He wanted Betty Reid to stay, but her loyalties to Lewis made such a compromise impossible. At the end of May Victor and Lewis failed even to reach agreement on the terms of a formal valedictory letter to the groups, yet there was no personal enmity. Both Reid and Lewis were given testimonials which spoke of their 'devotion to work, keen social sense, power of leadership, single-minded enthusiasm for any work in hand, and, of course, complete integrity.' Victor made the proviso that his references should not be used in applications for jobs connected with the war effort. 'I do not mean for a single second', he wrote to Reid, 'that I think you would do the tiniest thing to the detriment of the country in its struggle against Hitler: but as I have given up trying to understand what CP policy really is my conscience would not be clear if I did not make this reservation.'

For the LBC, the departure of Lewis spelled the end to serious attempts to give help from the centre to the few hundred remaining groups. Down in membership to under 36,000 (the bulk of resignations were due to war conditions) and shrinking remorselessly, the Club ceased to be a political organization of moment. Victor kept his promises during 1940, publishing books by communists and non-communists and encouraging open debate on the rights and wrongs of the war. Nor was his constancy based on *raison d'état* within the Club's hierarchy, for from April — after the German invasion of Norway and Denmark — Strachey, appalled by the *Daily Worker*'s 'revolutionary defeatism' and insistence that there was in principle nothing to choose between the German and British régimes, broke with the CP. The three selectors were now of one mind and Victor would have been free to use the *Left News* as a pro-war propaganda sheet. His conscience and his political instinct acted against such a course.

Throughout 1940 he sought to woo CP members from the party line through his long, private correspondence with individuals, in letters to the press and with a pamphlet, published in May, called *Where Are You Going? An Open Letter to Communists*. The latter was not offered through the LBC network: Victor confined himself to announcing its existence in the *Left News*.

The pamphlet had been written in April 1940. Victor feared with good reason that the CP was moving away from the straightforward 'defeatist' line — that in an imperialist war the enemy is at home, and that it is the duty of the working class in each country to attack its own bourgeoisie and so bring about an international socialist revolution — and towards an identification of Britain as the real enemy. (There was good evidence that French communists were being encouraged to commit sabotage.) The *Daily Worker*, having reported as an atrocity the laying of British mines in Norwegian waters, had virtually ignored the German invasion. Both Strachey and Victor attacked the *Worker* in the correspondence columns of the *New Statesman*, and Victor took up the theme in *Tribune*.

Where Are You Going? was an appeal addressed, 'with the utmost earnestness of which I am capable . . . to those rank and file members of the Communist Party with whom I worked with such harmony in Popular Front days, when, however great the difference between their philosophy of life and mine which progressively revealed itself, so many of our immediate practical objectives were, or seemed to be, identical. Especially do I address those who were converted to Socialism by our Left Book Club work, and who may then or subsequently have joined the Communist Party.'

The pamphlet clearly and simply analysed the changing trend of CP propaganda at home and abroad and its consequence: ordinary CPers were being duped into working for a Nazi victory. Their loyalty to the USSR must not take precedence over their duty to Western civilization, 'one of the greatest of achievements of the human race'.

Laski found it 'first-rate' and the argument admirable, but he was critical of its pleading tone.

> You convey the impression of being on the defensive. I think one ought quite openly to say that the CP has deserted international socialism for support of the USSR, and that the consequence of that desertion is that it asks consciously for the defeat of the Labour movement in the whole of Western Europe. It is the duty of Communists to show us what it has to offer in exchange for this. So far we have had nothing but the catchwords of revolutionary utopianism. You treat them as friends who have accidentally gone astray. I can't take that kindly view. Dutt & Co don't go anywhere accidentally.

'Far from considering them "friends",' responded Victor, 'my own feelings are so bitter that I have to catch myself up almost every day, in order to remind myself of the sincerity of so many of the rank and filers whom I know. If I were writing for my own pleasure, or writing, so to speak, about them, of course I should adopt a very different tone: but surely the whole point of the pamphlet is that it is an open letter *to* them?' His targets were those — especially the young — on the borderline, or thinking of joining the CP.

Although he realized the futility of presenting his case to hard-line CP associates, there were two senior communists to whom Victor sent copies of his pamphlet — Harry Pollitt and Ivan Maisky. There was a brief correspondence with King Street.

> 9 May 1940
>
> My dear Harry,
>   You will not, I am afraid, believe it, but it was only after a torment of indecision night after night that I could bring myself to publish this. But eventually I felt I had to.
>   Do you remember one afternoon in your room, after you had returned from Spain? You said: 'Hitler may bomb every village in this country to pieces: the war may go on for ten years: but the British working class will never submit to him.' I know you think now that that kind of attitude showed a wrong balance: but you *did* then sincerely feel it (I shall never forget that afternoon in your room).

Well, I feel as passionately that everything will go if Hitler wins: and that this is *at the moment* the only issue. I believe that the danger of an absolutely smashing defeat is appalling unless we nerve ourselves to resist. And that is why I feel I simply dare not keep silent. I had decided to say nothing at all, until April 10th [the day after the German invasion of Norway and Denmark]: but the 'Daily' that day was too much for me.

> Yours,
> Victor

15 May 1940

Dear Victor,
Who was it who said 'Methinks thou dost protest too much.'? That's how your letter strikes me.

> Yours,
> Harry Pollitt

17 May 1940

Dear Harry,
I didn't say, did I, that you protested too much when you said what you did that day about the working class reaction to a conquest of Britain by Hitler?
I should have thought that even the blindest today must see that that is the issue.

> Yours,
> Victor

20 May 1940

Dear Victor,
Thanks for yours of the 17th.
What I said that day, will prove to still come true, even if you have written a fourpenny pamphlet.

> Yours,
> Harry

24 May 1940

Dear Harry,
If that happens in the sense in which you meant it, you will find no more staunch supporter than I. I may even write another fourpenny pamphlet to say so.

> Yours,
> Victor

Victor's friendship with Maisky, the other recipient, had stumbled over but survived the Pact. As late as 10 May Victor was referring to him (in an argument with Albert Inkpin, the Secretary of the CP Russia Today Society) as 'my friend the Soviet Ambassador'. He had several times explained to his friend that he found Russia's desire to protect herself no worse 'than that by which most great powers have normally been actuated. . . . Sycophancy is not necessarily the best friendship.' But Maisky could not afford to remain friendly with Victor once he went public with his attacks on Soviet policy. To Victor's warm note he replied politely but curtly. The Gollanczes' names went off the invitation list of the Soviet Embassy for all time.

Victor was rapidly to discover that a supposed traitor attracts far more obloquy than an open enemy. In welcoming his resignation from the Russia Today Society (on the grounds of its distortion of the truth about Germany and Scandinavia), Inkpin concluded, 'Of course, it is natural that you should protest your friendship with the Soviet Union. If we were to be influenced by such protestations we should be as stupid as you are opportunist — which we certainly are not.' A schoolmaster active in the LBC put it more violently: 'So you have crossed the Rubicon and it is Civil War in the Left Book Club . . . you have joined that band of infamous traitors, fit only for the nethermost circle of Dante's Hell.' Pollitt wrote a review of *Where Are You Going?* in which he implied that it had been written to curry favour with 'the authorities'.

Amid the vicious denunciations there were enough kind comments about the pamphlet's worth for Victor to feel that it might be having some effect. It is impossible to know whether it changed any minds. Inevitably, it found fertile ground with those already in sympathy with Victor's viewpoint, similarly forced by circumstances to rethink their attitude to the Soviet Union. Those agile enough to stay with the official CP line on the war were probably beyond persuasion. It must have been all the more galling for Victor, as the letters of lament and vilification piled up, to face the truth: that he had been supremely effective as a propagandist during that very period when he had been gulled. Now that he was at last fully his own man, and free of CP influence within the LBC organization, the Club was much weaker and his influence greatly reduced. The majority of LBC members were getting on with the business of helping the war effort, but the vocal minority stubbornly maintained that it was their leader rather than themselves who had proved fickle. 'No one, in my view,' Victor wrote to one of his members at the end of May, 'can think clearly, who hasn't had a Marxist training,

but I think also no one can think clearly who hasn't come through a Marxist training, caught it up into the whole of his intellectual equipment, so to speak, and realised that Marxism is only part of the truth. Professor

Salvemini, [a famous Italian liberal and author of a 1936 Choice, *Under the Axe of Fascism*] in his inimitably witty speech at the last Left Book Club Summer School but one, said, in my view very profoundly, 'Any young man, or any man who has been thinking a year or two about politics, who is not a Marxist, is a knave: any old man, or any man who has been thinking about politics for several years, and who remains *simply a Marxist* is a fool.'

That was an argument easily dismissed as 'unscientific'. There is no evidence that it made any converts.

The well-publicized war within the LBC drew a great deal of press attention. Right-wing papers were quick to play it up, and some of those on the non–CP Left felt that Victor had it coming. 'Gollancz has grown a beard & fallen out with his Communist pals,' George Orwell had reported in April to Geoffrey Gorer, 'partly over Finland etc, partly because of their general dishonesty which he's just become alive to. When I saw him recently, the first time in 3 years, he asked me whether it was really true that the GPU★ had been active in Spain during the civil war, & told me that when he tied up with the Communists in 1936 he had not known that they had ever had any other policy than the Popular Front one. It's frightful that people who are so ignorant should have so much influence.'

Ignorant of certain facts or not, Victor had a clear memory of the anti-fascist principles underlying the LBC's foundation and growth. Recognizing that many of his readers had not wrestled as he had with the implications of Munich and the Pact, he asked them, once they had absorbed *Where Are You Going?* to put themselves a simple question: '"Was I right in all I said and thought from 1933 to 1939? And if so, is the present Communist position (or, to avoid any exaggeration, the present tendency) a logical development in changed circumstances of what was at least *my* old position — or am I running the terrible risk, if I follow it, of bringing about the very catastrophe which I struggled so whole-heartedly and for so many years to prevent?"'

Fear that that catastrophe was now imminent caused Victor to amend the editorial policy of the *Left News*. After the invasion of the Low Countries on 10 May 1940, the replacement of Chamberlain by Churchill and the formation of a National government, he could no longer leave the Club members in the dark. With the May issue of *Left News* he sent out an appeal in his official rather than his personal capacity: members were exhorted to fight for the survival of Western

★The Soviet Union political police, a contingent of whom operated in Spain. In Catalonia, they carried out a purge of Republican 'heretics'.

civilization. The civil war within the LBC was admitted, and instances cited of CP-dominated groups refusing pro-war speakers a hearing. Under no illusion that he could have much more than a marginal effect, he nonetheless determined to throw his full weight behind Churchill, for whom he had a great deal of personal admiration. He did not wish to confine himself to conducting debates with communists; he wanted a proper job. Accordingly he turned up at the Labour Party Conference in Bournemouth in mid-May. On his return he wrote to Attlee, enclosing a copy of the appeal to the LBC members as an earnest of his reliability.

> I really can't go on fiddling away at publishing in this desperate crisis. Can you give me a job in which such qualifications as I have might be turned to advantage? I ought to be of some use in the present situation: I suppose I built up a publishing business more rapidly than had ever been done in this country, and I am able to work for very long stretches with no more than three or four hours' sleep at night.

He received a courteous note promising to make enquiries. He approached Herbert Morrison for a job in his Ministry of Supply, and was advised to try the Ministry of Information. Harold Nicolson, Duff Cooper's parliamentary secretary, had already suggested his name there, but, he explained, there was a difficulty: 'there are few jobs here worthy of your administrative experience and . . . I do not suppose you would like to be used solely for propaganda purposes. Anyhow I can tell you the matter is being considered favourably.'

Whatever the deliberations, no real job came out of them. Kenneth Clark, Controller of Home Publicity, wrote in a friendly manner to say he would hope to seek Victor's advice from time to time. He was occasionally given the opportunity to write propaganda articles which were glowingly praised. That was the limit. The wing of the Labour Party now represented in positions of authority had been the butt of Victor's scorn before the war, and his conversion had been too recent to eradicate their deep distrust. Such friends as he had in the party were either junior or, in the case of Stafford Cripps, now a special envoy to Russia, unable to make use of him. 'It seems fantastic', he lamented to one of his authors, 'that in a desperate crisis like this I can't be turned to proper account.'

It was personally a tragedy for Victor that he was denied the opportunity to spend himself in the service of his country. (In January 1941 he even suffered the humiliation of rejection by the Home Guard.) In fact, it is hard to imagine how he could have fitted successfully into a government ministry. He just might have made a brilliant Minister of Supply, gloriously flouting the rules in the manner of Beaverbrook, but it is difficult to see him as a successful temporary under-secretary.

He continued to devote the best part of his energies to his own campaign, fighting CP and pacifist propaganda, striving to have the men of Munich purged from government, and pressing the Labour Party to work for an accommodation with Russia and a socialist economy — which would, in Victor's view, be more efficient. The non-fiction list of Victor Gollancz Ltd was dominated by publications designed to have the war won Victor's way. A Manifesto was published in *Tribune* in July and reproduced in the *Left News*. Composed by the editorial board (Aneurin Bevan, G. R. Strauss, Raymond Postgate — now the editor — and Victor), it gave what he described as 'the correct political programme' for socialists, and marked Victor's formal alliance with the powerless left wing of the Labour Party. 'The people of Britain are awake at last', it began. 'They are awake to the perils of the situation and to its possibilities. . . . There is universal agreement about two things. One, an unshakable resolution that the war must be fought through to final victory; and two, a conviction that to do this new ways will have to be found.'

The draft programme of action included the granting of self-government to India; the purging from government of the appeasers; the democratization of industry; and the creation through the Local Defence Volunteers of a People's Army. Was it Victor, one wonders, who drafted the recommendation that a new corps of executives be brought into the civil service 'wherever it appears that the red tape of established civil servants is impeding the war effort'?

Although a few of the measures outlined were in time put into effect, *Tribune* was not taken seriously by the mainstream of the Labour Party. Victor's ambitions were shackled by his idealism and complex conscience, which kept him apart from those who compromised with the realities of power. That had been true of him in the thirties. He would never fight a seat for Labour, let alone gain office. The disqualification was compounded from 1940 onwards, as his preoccupation with a heterodox Christian socialist philosophy gradually divorced him also from most of the Labour far left. From 1940, the Christian message began to claim a prominent part in many of his speeches and articles. In *Time and Tide* on 1 June, for instance, an article on the evils of fascism ended thus:

> As the war intensifies, let us be on our guard against the temptation to hate the German people. In spite of everything we may be called upon to hear or

see or suffer . . . indeed, not in spite of it but because of it — let us repeat in our hearts the greatest words that have ever been spoken on earth: 'Father, forgive them, for they know not what they do.' It is to preserve alive the spirit of those words that we are fighting; if we hate, Hitler has half conquered us already.

On balance, however, his public pronouncements and the firm's publications still concentrated on aspects of the *Tribune* Manifesto and their practical application. If many of them were too extreme for the likes of Herbert Morrison, they yet avoided attacking mainstream Labour, directing their venom instead against the Tories' pre-war record, and advocating socialist means of ensuring victory. The wartime Gollancz political publications, in their yellow jackets, may not have greatly affected the conduct of the war, but they planted a seed that was to sprout to remarkable effect in 1945.

Guilty Men, by 'Cato' (Michael Foot, Peter Howard and Frank Owen), was the first and most famous (or infamous, if you happened to be an ex-appeaser) in a series called 'Victory Books'. In its assault on Chamberlain, Halifax *et al* as the men responsible, first, for the war and then for Britain's unpreparedness and the military defeats to date, it established, in Angus Calder's phrase, 'the left-wing myth of the 'thirties in its classic form'. It was brilliant polemic, and neatly ignored the pre-war splits in the left and the Labour Party's record of voting against rearmament measures. At Victor's insistence, after he had taken advice from Rose Macaulay among others, it concluded with three paragraphs in block capitals stressing that with men like Churchill, Bevin and Beaverbrook now in control 'all that is within the range of human achievement will be done to make this island "a fortress"'. In all his propaganda publications, Victor went to great lengths to comb out any defeatist influence. He had been rattled by the discovery that *Tory MP* had been used to good effect by Dr Goebbels' *Völkischer Beobachter*.

Guilty Men, although W. H. Smith and several wholesalers refused to stock it, sold 220,000 copies (many from news-stands) and made secure Victor's position as the most hated and most admired publisher in Britain. His occasional trifling venture into more generally accepted propaganda — for instance, the publication of a eulogistic biography of Churchill — counted for nothing with the right wing of the Tory Party, who saw him as at best a socialist and at an uninformed worst a communist mischief maker, for all that he might put out Victory Books like *Enlist India for Freedom* or *Churchill Can Unite Ireland* (published at a time when Victor privately admitted he could not bear to think about Ireland, so bitter was he about her neutrality).

For a man of almost pathological sensitivity, Victor showed considerable courage in setting himself up for brickbats from right and left. The CP missiles hurt the more, hurled as they were by many he had known well and regarded as friends. Until John Strachey disappeared into the RAF late in 1940, he could at least share the pillory as a fellow turncoat, but from the start it was Victor, understanding so well communist theology and the minds of its proponents, who constituted the more tempting target for CP zealots. He had considerable and growing skills as speaker and writer; he had the *Left News* as a platform as well as the resources of the publishing firm; and above all, he had the stamina, the will and the tenacity to sustain a barrage of public criticism against CP policy. During 1940 and 1941 Victor was by far the most formidable enemy of King Street. Much though they had disliked *Where Are You Going?*, their resentment reached new levels during the controversy that followed the fall of France in June. To several of the LBC CP members who wrote to Victor immediately afterwards, the surrender of Pétain and his colleagues proved the truth of the Moscow line: in an imperialist war, the capitalists will prove to be traitors. That argument seemed to unbelievers to sit uneasily with the 'Stop the War' policy. It also ignored, as Victor pointed out in both the *Left News* and the *New Statesman* in July, the fact that the French Communist Party, by campaigning against the war, had undermined the resistance to Hitler just as harmfully as had the fascists and the weak-kneed right, until it was too late and their spirited defiance was answered by execution or the concentration camp. Accusing him of having perpetrated a 'despicable lie', Sheila Lynd wrote to the *Worker*:

> Mr Gollancz says he 'notes a tendency' on the part of Communists to call him a traitor to the working class. This is just part of the tendency — noted by Lenin — for Communists to believe that 'facts are facts'.
> I am quite sure that everyone who enthusiastically worked to build the Left Book Club as a great organisation for working-class education heartily deplores, that the Left News has been steadily turning since the war began into an anti-Communist and anti-Soviet news sheet.

His moderately phrased riposte missed its mark, and her comment on it demonstrated yet again the depth of her own sense of betrayal:

> . . . it used not to be the policy of the Left News to give respectability to attacks on the Soviet Union commonly made in the capitalist Press by repeating them — even alongside expressions of the Soviet point of view. Mr Gollancz admits that the Left News has recently, on various occasions,

accused the Soviet Union of an anti-working-class foreign policy, but apparently he doesn't regard this as a very serious accusation to make. I do.

A few days later John Lewis followed up with an article in the *Worker* in which, dealing with the Pétain government, he bewailed the harsh treatment in France of anti-fascist refugees, 'which Mr Gollancz approved'.

Of all the accusations and calumnious distortions levelled against him by his old allies, this one hurt Victor most. Once again asking Betty Reid to intercede, Victor spoke of the allegation as 'a damnable lie, and a lie exceedingly damaging to my political reputation and my political future' and threatened a libel action unless an apology was made. He had very good reason, for he had, in fact, been vocally angry at the French policy of wholesale internment and had even contributed to a fund for these refugees the balance of an LBC account held over from the Spanish food-ship fund. Even more distressing was the implication in Lewis's article that Victor equally approved the blanket internment of aliens in Britain. He did not, and had fought it from the start, particularly as it was applied to anti-fascist refugees whose release he had campaigned for. In the week before Lewis's article was published, Victor had received a letter from Paolo Treves, a refugee Italian socialist, thanking him for all his letters 'and above all the kindness you showed my people and myself during my internment. I feel certain that your powerful intervention helped a great deal to hasten our release, and I'm profoundly grateful to you for all that.'

There is little surviving correspondence to do with refugees, but what there is makes it clear that Victor, often helped by Ellen Wilkinson, worked very hard on their behalf. Before the war he had managed to get some political and Jewish refugees into Britain. At Brimpton, from 1938, the family was augmented for four years by a boy whose German refugee parents could not afford to support him, and from 1940 by the daughter of a member of the Free French. Victor had given money, counsel and in some cases jobs to the destitute. When they fell victim to internment, he wrote countless letters of intercession, advised relatives, gave handouts and repeatedly called for the restriction of the policy to those genuinely considered as potentially subversive. It was to be the house of Gollancz that published books like *Help Us Germans To Beat the Nazis*, actually written in an internment camp, and *Anderson's Prisoners*, a condemnation of the draconian thoroughness of the Home Secretary, Sir John Anderson, whose system was later liberalized by Churchill. Dealing with individual cases was time-consuming, often thankless and rarely successful, but, however busy he was, Victor always found the time and energy to help in whatever way he could.

To John Lewis, in an effort to force a retraction of the *Worker* allegations, Victor was able to cite the call in the *Tribune* Manifesto that alien anti-fascists in internment be released to fight, a *Tribune* piece of his own in April deploring death sentences on French communist saboteurs, and his use in *Where Are You Going?* of the phrase 'refugee-harrying reactionaries'. Long and wearisome neg-otiations led to Lewis's sending a letter to the *Daily Worker* retracting the offending sentence and its implications. The *Worker* refused to print it. In the August issue of *Left News*, in which Victor had handsomely given Lewis five pages to defend the policies of both French and British communists, there were a few paragraphs from Victor headed 'A Libel', concluding:

> I do not propose to institute proceedings for libel against the *Daily Worker*, for two reasons. First, because I am advised that it would be impracticable to dissociate Dr Lewis from the proceedings: and, as he has endeavoured to do all the reparations within his power, I am unwilling to penalise him, apart from the claims of a long-standing friendship. Secondly, an inter-Left dispute fought out in the Courts would be utterly loathsome.
>
> I content myself, therefore, with putting on record Dr Lewis's withdrawal and apology, and with pointing out that the *Daily Worker*, having published a particularly grave libel, then refrained from publishing a letter of withdrawal . . . No further comment is necessary on this sordid and contemptible affair.

In August he had again to consider a libel action, this time against *Truth*, an organ with anti-semitic leanings. In an article headed 'Contrast in Patriotism', by Henry Newnham, the following para-graph appeared:

> I was reading early this week the official list of our casualties during the Battle of France. I noticed among the names of other members of the 'ruling class' those of the Duke of Northumberland, the Earl of Aylesford, the Earl of Coventry, Lord Frederick Cambridge — all killed in action. I did not notice any names like Gollancz, Laski, and Strauss, from which I draw the conclusion that what happened in the last war is being repeated in this. The ancient families of Britain — the hated ruling class of the Left Wing diatribes — are sacrificing their bravest and best to keep the Strausses safe in their homes, which in the last war they did not don uniforms to defend.
>
> '. . . then shall our names
> Familiar in their mouths as household words
> Harry the King, Bedford and Exeter, Warwick

> And Gollancz, G. R. Strauss, and Laski —
> Be in their flowing cups freshly remembered.'

Strauss, who had been too young to fight in the First World War, but whose brother had been killed in action, took out a libel suit and won substantial damages. Harold Laski, having been in America during the war, had no case, but his brother Neville, a leading member of the Jewish Board of Deputies, had fought in Gallipoli, Sinai and France, and he too sued successfully. 'I very much dislike the idea of bringing a libel action in this matter,' explained Victor to Harry Nathan.

> Although this doesn't, of course, affect the libel in the very least (for I 'volunteered' and 'donned uniform' long before conscription), I was never actually at the front . . . My military career, therefore, having been an inglorious one, I don't want to go into Court and make a fuss about it . . .
> There is also the financial consideration. Strauss is a very wealthy man, and I imagine Neville Laski is also: I am not . . .

'Rich' to Victor, always implied someone with enormous capital. Although for part of his life he earned between twenty and thirty times the average wage, he could never be shaken from his conviction that he was but comfortably well off. High wartime taxes cut into his net income, but he could have afforded any realistic legal fees. Although in any case he hated libel actions *per se*, his real reason here was, as it always had been: an anxiety running so deep that he would go to almost any lengths to avoid the uncertainty of legal proceedings, which in his imagination were set to beggar him. He contented himself with a published apology from *Truth*.

His only defence against libel, then, was bluff — no protection against the venom of the *Daily Worker*. During the late winter (when the *Manchester Evening News* in its innocence was describing him as a known communist), the *Worker* attacks reached a crescendo. Two episodes in particular provoked their fury. One was a debate against Pollitt at the Oxford University Social Democratic Club in mid-November, in which, according to the *Cherwell* reporter,

> Gollancz, round-faced, side-whiskered, looking rather like a plump rabbi who has strayed in on a party in Keats' Grove. . . . revealed himself an admirable speaker possessed of brilliant debating skill. Every point was rammed home. No apologist for the Churchill government, he stripped Communist policy of its popular propaganda and revealed it as naked sabotage of the war effort. No People's government as conceived by the Communists could be achieved without revolution, and while the revolution was in progress, Hitler would strike. A brilliant Continental

Communist, rejoicing in France's military setbacks, had told him that they would lead to the overthrow of the French ruling-class and a worker's revolution: the force let loose would sweep the German army back behind the Siegfried Line. *This was three weeks before France's final capitulation.* In short vivid sentences Gollancz derided the idea of simultaneous revolutions by peoples against their rulers as fifty years out of date; its expositors thought in terms of the barricades. In a rich voice occasionally rising to a squeak, contrasting oddly with Pollitt's north-country bellow, he recalled the cry of Stop the War uttered by *The Daily Worker* at a time when Hitler was broadcasting his Peace Offer, that he might have time to prepare for his western offensive; the communist story that England intended to violate Holland's neutrality; and, after France had fallen, the hostility to Tom Wintringham's Home Guard Camp [Wintringham was ex-CP] at Osterley, and the bitter opposition to the transfer of fifty destroyers from USA when they were essential to help the efforts to save England from starvation. Even the shelter policy was conceived to lower morale rather than to improve conditions as the writings of genuine opponents of the Government's shelter policy revealed. In all, Gollancz made a profoundly interesting speech, and the smashing blows he delivered to hecklers revealed both his ability and the strength of his case.

Such an exceptionally well informed demolition job was an embarrassment to the CP. The *Worker* had not caught its breath when, in the November issue of the *Left News*, Victor's lengthy editorial redefined the aims of the Club as victory in war and progress, social and political, at home and abroad. This did not, he emphasized, imply that there would be uniformity in Club books or the *Left News*:

under pressure that was always distasteful to us we made that mistake in the past, or came perilously near to making it, and it will not be repeated . . . Freedom of expression and the independent mind are, in the final analysis, among the supreme possessions for which we are fighting, and it must be one of the main purposes of the Left Book Club to foster them. But experience has shown that, in an organisation such as the Left Book Club, neutrality on the life and death questions of the day is impossible: in practice there must always be a 'tone'. And the moment it became clear to ourselves what that tone was going to be, it seemed right to make it clear to others.

All that was bad enough as far as the CP was concerned. And the communist books and articles that were published were regularly balanced in the *Left News* by searing articles pointing up their deficiencies. Now came Victor's suggestion that the LBC be renamed 'The League for Victory and Progress'. To the right-wing press this was a good joke. 'Is His Face Red?' carolled William Hickey in the

Daily Express, happily chronicling the widening of the split between the Club and the CP. The article crowed over the fact that the current Choice, *Marxism and Democracy*, by Lucien Laurat, included violent attacks on the Soviet Government — attacks from which Strachey and Victor had both disassociated themselves. 'To face *more* than two ways at once is a neat trick, even for a successful publisher.' *Truth* found it even funnier, and composed a pathetic piece of doggerel commencing

> Victor for Victory!
> Pardon, Gollancz.
> One valedictory
> Kick in the pants.

John Lewis did not find it funny. In an article on 3 December in the *Worker* called 'Why Has the Left Book Club Failed the People?' he spoke of the days when the Club had 'an historic mission to fulfil and a progressive role to play'. It collapsed because of 'two mistakes in political understanding and two organisation defects'.

> On the organisational side the club was, of course, a one-man dictatorship. This was its strength while that one man thought in substantial harmony with the real trend of events. But when events ran past him, Mr Gollancz was not in a position to be checked by anyone, even by the membership he himself had brought together.
> Hence the political mistake of one man is able to wreck a great organisation.

Had the selection committee been a broad one, and its chairman 'ready to serve and not to dictate to the movement, the Club would be alive and growing still . . .'

> But Gollancz could not tolerate the thought of 'his' movement moving, even by its own conviction, in a direction contrary to his own. The full weight of the choices and Left News was directed for a whole year to swinging the Club into the path of 'Victory,' in spite of Mr Gollancz's attempt to appear impartial. It did not succeed because the membership was too well educated by the books to be misled . . .

Victor and Strachey had both failed the Club and 'the wider movement' in the hour of crisis, primarily because of their bourgeois failure to wage the class war. 'I suggest to Mr Gollancz that when he starts the new "League of Victory and Progress", he inscribes on its banner the famous slogan of Mr Batty, the founder of that strange and passing phenomenon "The Socialist Book Club", "There is nothing left about *my* Book Club."' And in the *Worker* of the following day,

Pollitt referred to the 'spate of pernicious dope being peddled around these days, in which the most pitiful corruptions come from Transport House and the House of Gollancz.'

To the disappointment of the *Worker*, Victor's post-bag from the loyal rank and file persuaded him to keep the LBC's name as it was. 'Many people will regret', it commented,

> that this extremely apt jingoistic title has been dropped by Messrs Gollancz, Laski and Strachey, who have now become war-to-the-knifers and bitter-enders. The reason for not making the change is stated by Gollancz to be as follows:–
> 'The Editorial in which the suggestion was made has achieved its purpose. With, in the main, the best intentions, but from a variety of intellectual and (especially) psychological weaknesses, certain men and women have adopted a policy which, if successful, could result only in the enslavement of the working class. They call themselves "Left" and honestly believe themselves to be so; but by their actions they have objectively ranged themselves with the extreme reaction.'
> This has such a choice application as Gollancz on Gollancz that comment would spoil it.

Victor's paragraph had concluded: 'Henceforth it will be impossible for anyone to imagine that the word "Left" in "Left Book Club" has suffered a similar degeneration.' It was wishful thinking: in response to *Worker* comments and the latest flow of CP resignations from home and abroad, he was whistling to keep his spirits up.

In a desperate attempt to get through to CP members, he proposed a debate between Strachey and a CP spokesman. The party accepted the challenge, but demanded that the speaker be Laski rather than Strachey and, when this was rejected, claimed a moral victory. Victor became increasingly alarmed by the subtlety of CP propaganda. Since the summer of 1940, the party had been organizing a 'People's Convention Movement' with the stated aims of securing a People's government and a negotiated peace with Germany. D. N. Pritt was its leading proponent, his brilliance reinforced by his standing as an MP. (Never a member of the CP, he was unswervingly loyal to it.) On 12 January 1941 the Movement held a conference, attended by 2,000 delegates, claiming to represent over a million people. Many of those represented had no idea that the CP was behind it, and saw it as a genuine pressure group for a sensible peace. Victor was appalled by the unexpected success of the conference and set out to expose it as a cover for communist revolutionary defeatism. In a few weeks he put together what was to be called *The Betrayal of the Left: an examination and refutation of Communist Policy*.

Largely a compilation of articles from the *Left News*, it included chapters by Strachey explaining the need for American aid (which the CP had relentlessly opposed), and the truth about the People's Convention, analysing the nature of totalitarianism and finally espousing the social democratic alternative to revolutionary social-ism. George Orwell explained how fascism had developed on a democratic base, and the need for the Left to come to terms with the virtues of patriotism. 'A Labour Candidate' (Konni Zilliacus) con-trasted Pollitt's premature pro-war pamphlet with Palme Dutt's late-1940 defeatist *We Fight for Life* and Laski contributed a lengthy preface. The bulk of the book came from Victor. His first chapter was a slightly amended version of *Where Are You Going?* The others covered the policy of revolutionary defeatism, a programme of action for 'Victory and Progress' and an epilogue on political morality. Addi-tionally he contributed linking notes between chapters, and two sets of correspondence, one private and one already published in the *New Statesman*. The private letters had been exchanged with Hewlett Johnson, into whose well-intentioned but naive head Victor had vainly tried to rub the truth about the People's Convention. His *New Statesman* adversary had been Professor Hyman Levy, whose *Philoso-phy for a Modern Man* had so perplexed non-academic members of the LBC in January 1939.

The dispute between Levy and Victor had begun on the issue of whether the French communists had or had not contributed to their country's defeat. Ultimately Levy tied himself in knots, approving of revolutionary defeatism while promising to fight to the death against Hitler. Both Johnson and Levy represented the kind of CP supporter Victor most feared and most wanted to reach: honourable people blind to the truth. Johnson was being manipulated by those cleverer than him; Levy was determined to force every fact to fit the Marxist and hence the Soviet mould.

The most effective of Victor's pieces was the 'Epilogue on Political Morality'. In his analysis of how lying and hatred could become second nature in a communist who joined the party out of a sincere concern to do good, he showed a deep understanding touched with 'There but for the grace of God go I'. He concluded with a *peccavi*, free of the excuses he drummed up in later years when the truth became too painful to remember.

> Looking back, I think I erred more as a publisher than as a writer or speaker, and more by omission than commission. I accepted manuscripts about Russia, good or bad, because they were 'orthodox'; I rejected others, by bona fide socialists and honest men, because they were not. It was in the

matter of the Trials that the inner conflict was greatest . . . I published only books that justified the trials, and sent the socialist criticisms of them elsewhere.

I am glad to remember that, when directly challenged by questioners at public meetings, I always spoke my mind, giving the pros and cons as honestly as I could; but I did not strive officiously to speak it, preferring to avoid awkward topics when the choice rested with me alone.

I am as sure as a man can be — I was sure at the time in my heart — that all this was wrong: wrong in the harm it did to people from whom one was keeping some part of the truth as one saw it; wrong in the harm it did to oneself (which was important, not because it was oneself, but because oneself was part of humanity); wrong in the harm it did to Russia, because that country, in which there is so much greatness and still more hope, can only be injured by a sycophancy that treats her as a spoilt child instead of as an adult with errors and crimes as grievous as our own; and wrong above all in the harm it did to the sum total of truth and honest thinking, by an increase of which we can alone find the way forward.

He ended on a note of great generosity, having just heard of the suppression of the *Daily Worker*. Despite its recent conduct, no socialist would ever forget 'that the men responsible for it have acted throughout, according to their lights and as they saw their duty, in the service of the greatest of all causes: the emancipation of the working class, and, through it, of humanity.'

Stanley Morison found the epilogue

a good piece of near-papistical writing, because it is so aristotelian. I may say for myself that it has always been upon the doctrine of truth that I have been obliged to separate myself from the Communists. I admire your admission that you have erred as a publisher. I agree that you have (and who has not?) sometimes taken the easier rather than the more difficult course. I do appreciate however that it was not easy for you to break off association with members of the Party . . . I shall be very surprised if they reciprocate all the sentiments of the final paragraph of your epilogue.

One can almost hear Victor's resentful howl of '*de haut en bas*'. It must have rung even louder when he read the letter from the Secretary of the Labour Party, J. S. Middleton, with his comment that 'Any doubts one had regarding the Political morality of the Communists were completely dispelled at the period when we were all classified as "social fascists" — that was enough for most of us, and it was deplorable that you and other colleagues continued to be misled . . . However, the "Betrayal of the Left" should go far to enlighten many others still lingering with their delusions.'

Others were much more kind. 'Your prose has the clarity of Wells and Shaw. You devastate the enemy,' wrote J. L. Hodson, not one of Victor's sycophantic authors. Koestler described it as 'excellent' in every respect; reviewers were appreciative and Victor received a number of letters from new converts in the Club and outside it. (The defunct Additional books category had been revived on an occasional basis in order, in February, to accommodate *The Betrayal of the Left*, which Victor felt morally unable to make a Choice.) It was later to be regarded as a crucial book in left-wing historiography: at the time it was far and away the most devastating indictment anyone had produced on the CP, precisely because the majority of its contributors understood the compulsiveness of that reassuring creed.

The *Daily Worker* might no longer be in existence, but Victor was still under attack. Even before the publication of *Betrayal*, Pritt had found an opportunity to discredit Victor with inspired mud-slinging in the House of Commons. In the debate on the suppression of the *Worker* on 28 January, he imparted the information that it had never had large individual subscriptions except possibly from 'that hysterical person Mr Victor Gollancz'. The unfairness of that took Victor's breath away, for his contributions had been relatively modest and had ceased months before the Nazi-Soviet Pact. He despatched explanatory letters to newspapers, but the statement (in expurgated form) had been widely reported, and its effects proved impossible to dispel. Unabashed, Pritt accused Victor in March of having alleged that Hitler was making use of the People's Convention in internal propaganda. Hewlett Johnson was identified as the unwitting originator of this misleading accusation, and in one of his letters to Victor he wrung his hands over the dispute. 'It's terrible to me to see such men as you and Pritt at war. Of course it always has taken place: I was prepared for it through my knowledge of the early days of Christianity.'

In the case of the Pritt machinations, Victor's behaviour did indeed approach the saintly. Having heard that Pritt's son was ill, he wrote to Mollie Pritt offering to visit him.

> The split with Johnnie has been very distressing; disastrous though, in my opinion, his 'line' and activies are . . . I have not only tried to avoid all personalities, but have succeeded in doing so: I have on no occasion made any sort of personal attack on him. But he has not reciprocated this attitude — just as he had not reciprocated similar attitudes on the part of others [such as the Elwyn Joneses] who had been friends and who had tried to avoid a personal break.
>
> I say this not even in the most indirect way to attack Johnnie in a letter to

you, but to explain why I have been silent so long but am writing now. After a public outburst against me considerably more than a year ago (Stafford was there — it was before he went to Moscow), Johnnie showed me that he wanted to have nothing whatever to do with me. But I was so distressed by what Pearl and Elwyn told me yesterday that I felt I must just drop you a line.

Her heartrending reply confirmed that Pritt was consumed with bitterness against all those who had once been his friends but now disapproved of his politics. She was reduced to utter misery, cut off from all social contact with the people she had loved and nursing a son dying of cancer. Victor could do little other than send books to the child and arrange to see Mollie in Pritt's absence. The breach with Pritt was never to be repaired.

During the spring and early summer of 1941, there was a further change of emphasis in the *Left News*. While the People's Convention debate continued (with Pritt being given space to defend it), Victor's other major preoccupation — the relationship between socialism and ethics — became manifest. In the symposium he initiated, John Strachey argued the materialist case for socialism. Richard Acland, Liberal MP but socialist, and leader of an informal organization called Forward March, wrote with revivalist fervour on the relationship between socialism and morality. Marxists, philosophers and clergymen joined in the debate along with rank-and-file LBC members. What some criticized as an unduly academic discussion, Victor justified as a contribution to the war effort. Victory, he said, would not come about unless Britain fought with a 'revolutionary dynamic equal, not to say superior, to that of the Nazis.' It would be the reply to evil with good that would defeat the enemy, and this could be brought about only by generating a whirlwind of international socialism at home and abroad. In June 1941, and out of key with many of the protagonists, he came down in favour of socialist ethical absolutism. Socialism must be presented

> not primarily as something more efficient than capitalism, nor as the inevitable next stage in historical development, nor as something by which wages may be raised and unemployment abolished (vitally important though these things are), but as a method of so organising society that *all men* may lead the life of liberty and equality and fraternity which we feel to be absolutely good, whatever may be the ultimate causes of our feeling it.

After quoting 79 lines of Shelley's vision of freedom, Victor went on to commend the Christian ethic, to be elaborated on in a new series, *From the Christian Left*, inaugurated by Mervyn Stockwood. Socialists had much to learn from Christians, even if they did not believe in God, and *vice versa*. 'What are, indeed, equally wanted among socialists to-day, if the struggle is to be won, are three things: a passionate love of humanity, a prophetic call to men of goodwill, and a hard examination, in the light of the best available scientific knowledge, of the means by which the desired society may, at last and in our day, be brought into being.' Further to feed the whirlwind, he inaugurated in the same month a twelve-page regular supplement called International Socialist Forum, edited by Julius Braunthal, a socialist refugee who had been a distinguished journalist in Austria. The main purpose of the Forum was as a vehicle for socialist refugees, to evolve agreed peace aims, and so guard against another Versailles. Writers included must be socialists committed to defeating Hitler, and hold 'personal opinions which are the result of their own thought, not dictated opinions.' In other words, no communists need apply. It was a wrench for Victor to make this exclusion, and his discomfort showed in the fervour of his defence of the policy to a critic, Philip Jordan. Nonetheless, he was exhausted from the hopelessness of any dialogue with the CP.

On 22 June 1941 Hitler invaded the Soviet Union. Churchill made a broadcast that night, and Victor's joy at his offer to give 'whatever help we can to Russia and the Russian people' outweighed his concern at Churchill's equation of the evils of Nazism and communism. It soon became clear that Stalin would accept the proffered help with both hands and, on 12 July, Stafford Cripps signed in Moscow an Anglo-Soviet agreement pledging mutual assistance and no separate peace. On that day Victor was half-way through a three-day session dictating 'at fever-heat' a 25,000 word article for the *Left News* entitled 'The New Situation'.

CHAPTER FOURTEEN

MEANWHILE . . .

IN 1936 VICTOR had ceased to be primarily a publisher; he was never again consistently to devote himself single-mindedly to the firm. Yet there was enough energy left over from public issues for him to give his business what others might reasonably consider to be a full working week. Authors of whom he was fond, or on whom he depended for his prosperity, rarely had to complain of neglect, while others found his interest erratic and chafed at his unpredictability. The writer Edward Thompson, who had had a row with Victor at Ernest Benn, brought a book to him in the late thirties. He had wanted Victor to publish *You Have Lived Through All This*, 'not merely because I thought you were the publisher who would issue it swiftly but even more because I wanted to be associated with you because I admired the dangerous course you had taken . . . ' Distressed at the lack of advertising and the small sales, he wrote in July 1939:

> You are one of the most famous, and most closely studied men in England, and everyone knows you are putting your whole life into your ideas and their propagation. I too care about what I consider civilisation and right ideas. I have had chances, and have refused them, to make money; and like you, have tried to remember what a mess the world is in. When a leading publisher who was dining in an Oxford common room some weeks ago remarked, 'Gollancz is not interested in publishing', I understood what he meant. You are regarded as a man who subordinates everything to his ideas.
>
> Well, that's that. My book has been dead from the moment that it appeared, and I am sorry.

Naturally Victor had an answer — the press was to blame and he wrote a persuasive letter in his own defence, but Thompson's original conclusion was an accurate reflection of how Victor was widely if often unfairly viewed. There was no publisher in England (nor, quite probably, in America) who could promote a book as successfully when his heart was in it. Therefore, when his interest was not engaged, and a book was published without that extra effort on his part, authors felt let down and he was accused of leaving their books to sink or swim. 'When I came to you last year,' Norah Lofts wrote in August 1939,

> I tried to explain to you that I needed positive and energetic publishing. I had been with Methuen during a period when internal upheaval and changes of policy had made them unsuitable people to do the building up which I needed. I need it still. The work is there, not bad of its kind and I have the chagrin of seeing it go down the drain for lack of faith or effort or energy upon your part. That the stuff is both readable and saleable Knopf's have amply proved. If you weren't prepared to give it a chance you should not have taken it on at all.

No soothing answer this time: Victor was too outraged by the slur on his professionalism. 'I am afraid I must reply with a *tu quoque* — and say that, if you hadn't confidence in our ability to handle your work to the best advantage, you shouldn't have come to us.' She took her work elsewhere and became a bestseller.

There were some authors with unspectacular but steady sales whom Victor nurtured like a mother — Elizabeth Jenkins, Lettice Cooper, Theodora Benson, Betty Askwith and Liam O'Flaherty were cases in point — because he thought them talented, or charming, or both. Others, less favoured, left him. Impatience was one of the keys to both his successes and his failures as a publisher. It added urgency to the most mundane task, but it also detracted from his performance of many of the dull chores vital to the establishment of permanent prosperity. Where Longmans and Macmillan were virtually impregnable financially by virtue of their educational lists, Victor had failed to invest the time and money required in that area, and Gollancz's venture into education during the thirties was too half-hearted to get off the ground. Other publishers found security in reprinting classics that were out of copyright, but Victor needed the excitement of live authors and new books. The firm was therefore more precariously based than some of its serious competitors: to keep its profits up it depended on regular new books by such authors as Daphne du Maurier, A. J. Cronin or Dorothy L. Sayers, along with the bestsellers that Victor found or created from year to year. The non-fiction list had many commercial successes and almost as many losers. The LBC had sold millions of books, but the overheads had soaked up most if not all of the profits. The Workers' Bookshop collapsed in the early summer of 1939, owing Gollancz about £10,000. And by the time war broke out, the temporary slump in the book market and the immediate decline in LBC membership made Victor for a time deeply worried about the firm's prospects.

There was in fact no danger of its folding. Victor combined adventurousness with caution to an extraordinary degree, something made evident over succeeding decades when so many other independent publishers went out of business or were taken over. He was an astute businessman; in the interest of security his cash reserves, for instance, were always unusually high. As the firm had turned in large profits year after year, Victor had annually crushed all pleas for increased dividends, announcing in sincerely gloomy tones that next year was bound to be a financial disaster. He could not have predicted the profitable times ahead when he and Ruth decided in December 1939 to hold an enormous party. The decision was taken against a background of moral, intellectual and emotional upheaval, when a pre-Christmas book boom did little to assuage Victor's worries about the phoney war — generally considered as proof of the military ineffectuality of the Chamberlain government. In a magnificent display of perversity designed to raise morale, the Gollanczes sent out innumerable invitations to a 9 p.m. to 2 a.m. party at the Café Royal. 'Any kind of clothes', said the invitation, as a gesture to the exigencies of war. That the guests accepted in the appropriate spirit was evident from the report of the *Manchester Guardian* on 26 January, 1940.

> Probably the most remarkable London party of the war-time was given last night at the Café Royal by Mr and Mrs Gollancz. It was particularly characteristic of the times and the occasion. There were about four hundred guests in every variety of morning and afternoon dress and uniform, except a few, which included Mr Maisky, the Soviet Ambassador, who was in evening clothes. The peerage and Parliament were there, editors, authors and authoresses in serried ranks, publishers, literary agents, players, dramatists, average adjusters, artists, poets, architects, civil servants, military and naval men, cinema folk, and Irish singers were in the crowd. Nearly every shade of English political opinion, except perhaps the extremist Left, were jostling one another. 'How many parties are at this party?' one bewildered guest was asking after many rencontres.
>
> Although nearly everyone there detested Russia for its invasion of Finland and its new imperialist policy, it was expressive of Mr Maisky's personality that his friendships seemed untouched. He and Mr Low, whose cartoons on the Soviets show his sharpest edge, had much to say to one another. After the party had gone on hours some people suggested dancing, and the resourceful host — Mr Gollancz, by the way, has now a beard a little reminiscent of Mr Sickert's — had the carpets cleared away and the floor was soon lively with figures in ball dress, sweaters, and tweeds, office suits, studio clothes, and every kind of collar except white ones. It was the most Continental Balzacian party probably that the Café Royal had ever had.

'What a marvellous and lovely *party*,' wrote Rose Macaulay to the Gollanczes; 'an oasis in the wilderness — at times one felt it must be a mirage, but it wasn't! . . . I do think it was a splendid idea — so did everyone. If you really want *gratitude* for a party, this is the time to throw a party, there's no doubt . . . You looked so lovely, Ruth (I don't mean V didn't — don't get me wrong, will you?).' Victor certainly entered into the spirit of the occasion. 'I didn't get a chance the other night to thank you for the party,' wrote Arthur Calder-Marshall. 'Just as I was coming up to you, you glode [*sic*] on to the dancing floor with your wife and there was such an ecstatic look on your face I hadn't the heart to interrupt you.'

With the party over, Victor was compelled gradually to scale down his attacks of professional pessimism. It soon became clear that the war was bringing enhanced prosperity to Gollancz. Bar a couple of poor spells, throughout the war the public could not get enough books. And under the unfair paper rationing system devised in March 1940, which favoured publishers with a high consumption in the very recent past, the decline in LBC sales from the huge to the simply large stood Victor in very good stead. (This did not stop him assuring Wren Howard of Jonathan Cape in March 1942 that he had used an abnormally small amount of paper during the reference period.) Additionally, unlike many other publishers, Gollancz suffered no bomb damage, except broken windows, in either London or Brimpton.

Indirectly, they had their share of troubles. In September 1940, when their binders, Leighton Straker, were hit during the blitz, Gollancz lost three-quarters of a million printed sheets covering about 700 titles. Three months later, the Southampton printers, Camelot Press, were also bombed, and the greater part of the Gollancz paper stocks went up with the building. Victor reacted well. It fascinated colleagues, who had on countless occasions seen him in a fury at minor setbacks, that he took news of major disasters calmly. He found such problems exhilarating: plans for ever smaller typefaces, paper purchasing coups and other makeshift solutions came readily to him. He was probably right when he claimed that he would react calmly if told he had lost all his money. He omitted to mention that he became furious if he thought anyone's error or greed had cost the firm £5. Unfortunately for those who worked with him, little things like that were very much part of publishing life.

As the *contretemps* with Lynd and Reid had shown, Victor was very vulnerable to the accusation that he had moved his headquarters to Brimpton through cowardice. On 19 February 1940 he wrote to complain of a report in the *Star* that Heinemann, Methuen and Hutchinson had all returned to London, that the others would be coming back shortly but that Gollancz was still away.

> As a matter of fact we have never been away from town in the ordinary sense since a week after the commencement of the war. Ever since then we have had in our London offices the staff (packing, carriage, despatch, telephone, trade counter, Left Book Club headquarters, etc.) that are necessary for efficiency there, and we have had at Brimpton, near Reading, staff (e.g. counting house) that can operate with equal efficiency not in London. I myself am at the London office most of the week.
>
> I should be grateful if some little paragraph could be published in the same feature pointing this out, but not, so to speak, as if it came from me.
>
> I fear that the former paragraph may give the impression that our London office is closed, and almost the only publisher's office that *is* closed — and that that may have a bad effect on authors.

That was misleading. The firm operated from its large hut at the foot of the Brimpton garden, in almost every important respect, and Victor visited London only two or three times a week. There were two excellent reasons not to return to London. The first was the convenience of Brimpton, where the facilities proved adequate for an increase in staff from the commencement of the sales boom. The key people had all moved there — Norman Collins, Edgar Dunk, Dorothy Horsman. Bravado would have been the only reason for a return to Henrietta Street. The second reason was that Victor was physically a coward. When he went up to London, Norman Collins rather cruelly remarked, 'it was like anyone else going over the top'. He worked commendably hard against his cowardice, trying to get a war job, and, after the phoney war had ended, visiting London as often as he did for reasons of business and public duty. In May and June 1940 he fell prey to the invasion rumours, going so far as to bet Negley Farson that Hitler would be in Britain within weeks. Until America came into the war and victory was assured, Victor lived in constant fear, not just of accidental death, but because he had heard he was priority target Number 7 on the Gestapo Black List in Britain (the list was in fact alphabetical). He went to a doctor and demanded and was given a lethal opium capsule. He was nervous too about his children — vulnerable by reasons of their Jewishness — and thought of sending some of them to Canada, but the U-boat danger put paid to that idea. All in all, the constant threat to his and his family's safety placed a strain on him during the dangerous periods of the war.

At Brimpton, the Gollancz staff coped efficiently with the change in surroundings and practices. There was no change of tempo: Victor was there too often for that to be possible. He was not easily resigned, either, to the inevitable inconveniences of war and geographical separation. In an angry moment late in October 1940, he despatched the following to the *News Chronicle*, with a covering note to his friend Gerald Barry, the editor, complaining additionally about the inefficiency of the railways:

> The telephone let-down is becoming a major scandal.
> The offices of my publishing business have for some time been divided between London and the country. The smooth working of the arrangement depends on telephone communication between the two offices, and this is becoming intolerable.
> So far as I can make out, whenever the country office tries to telephone the London office, then, always, if there is a period of 'alert' in London the country office is told 'indefinite delay' or 'restricted service'. This is fantastic. My packers and porters work consistently during periods of 'alert', only going into the basement shelter when the danger is imminent: why then should it often be impossible for the country office to get the London office during a whole day when there may be almost continuous 'alerts' in London — but perhaps not a single aeroplane over the capital?

Walter Holmes of the *Daily Worker* swooped joyfully on this heaven-sent indiscretion.

> The ineffable Mr Victor Gollancz has a letter published in the News Chronicle complaining, if you please, that 'alerts' interrupt telephonic communication between his offices in the country and in London.
> 'The offices of my publishing business,' he explains, 'have for some time been divided between London and the country.'
> This is fact. Indeed, I think Mr Gollancz must have been one of the first to raise the dust on the outward trail from London in those somewhat nervous days of September, 1939. But, so far as I know, the personal safety of Mr Gollancz and the profits of his business were the only great national issues involved . . .
> The innuendo obviously is that the telephone service shows less courage than 'my packers and porters'. Mr Gollancz seems unaware that telephone workers carry on their service not only during alerts, but raids, at the risk of their lives.
> His ignorance is inexcusable, but I fancy some members of the telephone service will take steps to cure him.

The Union of Post Office Workers duly informed *News Chronicle* readers that telephonists worked when bombs were not falling in their locality and that interrupted service was a consequence of cable destruction. Victor wrote to Barry enclosing a response: '*Please* put it in — it is essential that I should clear my Labour reputation, so to speak!':

> I have written privately and in detail to Mr T. J. Hodgson, general secretary of the Union of Post Office Workers, in reply to his letter in a recent issue: but please let me publicly express my dismay that my letter should have been construed as an attack on the Post Office *workers*. The last thing I would wish to do would be to attack them or any workers. I was attacking, of course, what seemed to be a settled policy of the *authorities*. For, whatever the explanation, the fact remains that it has been virtually impossible to phone from the country to London whenever there is an 'Alert' in the latter city.

His letter to Hodgson contained a more convoluted explanation: 'I perhaps expressed myself badly, because it was so obvious to me, after my experiences, that the trouble *was* due to a policy of the authorities that worked automatically, that I imagined it would be obvious to everybody else.' He satisfied Hodgson, but Walter Holmes used the controversy to good effect in a column on the appalling conditions under which telephone operators were working. It was a clever piece of morale-lowering propaganda, contrasting the incompetence of the Government-appointed 'big men' of the Post Office with the heroism of the exploited telephone workers, whose sufferings were described in detail. 'Those', he ended, 'are the telephone workers at whom the Gollancz-gentry curse.'

Similarly, Victor was incapable of letting the firm's publishing programme take the line of least resistance. Only a small proportion of books could be kept in print, but he was still hungry for books of political importance or good sales potential. Non-fiction authors were still often requested to write within a week a topical book for which he saw an immediate market. Fiction authors were still begged for new manuscripts. Although he had enough backlist big sellers to use up his paper allocation ten times over, he chafed at any drying-up in the flow of new ones. However busy he was elsewhere, Victor never lost his delight in taking a promising manuscript through every stage from acceptance to publication. And to keep his firm in the public eye, make authors happy and publicize his own particular enthusiasms, he kept up his advertising throughout the war when there was no real commercial need for it. Such was the shortage of advertising space in newspapers that he entered into a long-term contract with the *Observer* to take a half column every week at the top of the leader page. The VG column was a feature of the paper until after his death.

'I have been getting into despair', he wrote to Phyllis Bentley in October 1940, welcoming the news that she had finished a book, 'about the literary silence of all my "big" novelists. Sayers seems to have abandoned detective novels altogether (and I used to sell forty thousand of her at 8/6) for religious pamphlets . . . ' (He need not have fretted: he was to sell almost 300,000 copies of her play about Christ — *The Man Born to be King*.)

> Cronin (who now lives permanently in America) wrote to me two or three months ago to say that, what with income tax and the probability that sales would fall off in England, it didn't seem worth while to write another novel for the English market (although I had another letter from him a few days ago in which he said he was writing one and it would be ready in the spring): Daphne du Maurier is having a physical baby. All this at a time when the flow of manuscripts is the merest trickle, and when in any case one simply cannot begin to sell novels by unknown authors or 'small' sellers.

Victor wrote such letters according to his mood of the moment, exaggerating the ups and downs in his life. Some people took him too seriously. Typical was a doom-laden letter to Palme Dutt, in pre-Pact days, about the Workers' Bookshop. To those who knew the true state of Gollancz and the temporary nature of Victor's fits of pessimism, it would have been obvious that he was simply trying to avoid paying Palme Dutt a small pre-publication advance. Dutt was horrified and regretted having even asked for the advance. Victor, back in a happy frame of mind and feeling generous, answered 'But really, we can quite well manage that £25 — it isn't as bad as all that: and I would like to pay it, please.' Similarly, when war broke out, Victor immediately tried to reduce royalty levels on books already commissioned, and then as quickly changed his mind.

To most individual authors such changes of mind were merely perplexing. To agents, his capricious and frequently dictatorial conduct was annoying in the extreme. In time, a few of them grew fond of him and saw it as part of the job to accommodate his moods, handle him carefully and woo his friendship. Graham Watson and Herbert Van Thal were to become close to him and a few female agents had flirtatiously successful professional relationships with him. Ralph Pinker, whose agency crashed in the 1930s, experienced his generosity at its most breathtaking: Victor lent him money freely over many years to help him make a success of his businesses (mainly in scrap metal). But for the most part, Victor was a permanent fly in the agency ointment. Those who took their job most seriously recognized his genius in dealing with particular kinds of books, and the *cachet* attached to being a Gollancz author, and so put up with him while grumbling about his consistent cautiousness with advances and his refusal, almost without exception, ever to pay out any money to an author until the day of publication. To Victor, agents were parasitical nuisances put on earth solely to foment ingratitude among Gollancz authors.

Agents were growing in power and influence throughout Victor's career as a publisher. Had he been prudent, he would have contained or disguised his hostility, but he found it almost as hard to keep quiet about his antipathies as about his enthusiasms. In the summer of 1940, he included the following in the text of a public speech on victory and progress:

> I was talking on Monday to a literary agent — stupidest single section of the community. This man had been, up till three months ago, a fervid Chamberlainite; but he spent the last weekend sweating his guts out to prepare, with two or three others, a damning indictment of the Chamberlain gang which he wanted me to rush into print. He even asked me to lend him (literary agents being mean as well as stupid) some of the old Left Book Club issues.

That paragraph may have ended up as the oratorical equivalent of a 'Not Sent' letter, but its message came through often enough in Victor's indiscretions and in his sometimes violent treatment of offending agents. He always preferred to deal directly with authors behind their agents' backs, and many an agent who thought he had an unanswerable case on some contractual haggle with Victor found in his next post a letter from the writer he represented telling him not to pursue the matter. Victor could, of course, use the back door only with those authors whom he classed as 'intimate friends'. Spencer Curtis Brown, for instance, was driven to distraction by Victor's ability to persuade Daphne du Maurier that he was in the right — and Brown in the wrong — on almost every issue. Of course agents were by no means always above reproach. Some played an ambivalent game that created difficulties between author and publisher. A few — William Roughead of A. D. Peters in particular — tried to forbid Victor to make any contact with their authors, a directive which Victor rightly regarded as intolerable. Most merely asked him to stick to the widely accepted etiquette that governed author/publisher/agent relations: that the publisher maintain close contact with his author, but discuss financial and related matters only with the agent. Victor regarded this as both an impertinence (especially where longstanding relationships were concerned) and an insupportable constraint on his freedom of action: he continued to negotiate directly whenever he felt he could get away with it.

In December 1940, there was an A. D. Peters/Phyllis Bentley/ Victor correspondence, illuminating not simply as an example of his way with troublesome agents, but in its unprecedented revelations about the state of Gollancz and Victor's own canniness and caution as a businessman. (Predictably enough, he hated being called 'business-man'.) Victor had received in November the manuscript of Bentley's new novel — *Manhold*. He had published her at Benn and when she came to Gollancz, their joint talents turned her into a bestseller in 1932 with *Inheritance*. He had as much admiration for her professionalism as a writer as for the social conscience she evinced in her stories of the industrial North. He sent a routine letter to Roughead proposing a new three-book contract, and was aghast when Roughead replied on 9 December quoting Bentley's instructions:

> 'If anything happened to the firm of Gollancz — which heaven forfend! — I should wish to be free to choose my own publisher, I should not at all like to be handed over to some firm not of my own choice. I therefore think that Gollancz's terms should be accepted for one book only. I hope, however, that you will make it very clear to him that I have not the slightest intention of leaving him.'

Victor fired off a holding telegram to Bentley: 'DELIGHTED WITH MANHOLD WHICH I RANK IMMEDIATELY AFTER INHERITANCE AND TAKE COURAGE [her previous novel] STOP HOPE TO WRITE FULLY IN A FEW DAYS STOP AT MOMENT OWING TO DAMAGE TO SOUTHAMPTON PRINTER AND TOTAL LOSS OF PAPER THERE AM UNDULY PRESSED STOP MANHOLD NOT AFFECTED AS BEING PRINTED ELSEWHERE'.

Two days later he despatched to her a letter marked 'STRICTLY PRIVATE AND CONFIDENTIAL'. It ran to about 2,500 words, beginning with an account of his great distress at a conversation with Peters himself and the letter from Roughead. Peters, he alleged, had said Bentley's fear was about the possible death of Victor rather than about the disappearance of the firm. He had then said it was 'hardly fair to ask for a reduction of terms, while still asking for a three-book contract.' The possibilities were that the firm might go bankrupt or that he might be killed and it be taken over. The first was a 'ludicrous' idea: 'we are in as strong and stable a financial position as any firm in the country, and I dare to say in an infinitely *more* strong and stable position than all but, say, three or four other firms.' Plunging into an orgy of frankness that indicated the depth of his fear of losing Bentley, he overwhelmed her with a torrent of facts and figures, for her eyes only. Only £13,136 had been called up on share capital, leaving over £30,000 available at any moment. On that base plus ploughed-back profits had been built a publishing business with one of the biggest turnovers in the country. (This was rather an exaggeration. He so much kept his distance from his competitors that he had little idea of how they were doing financially. In the 1940s, according to David Higham, Victor estimated the turnover of Longmans at a tenth of its actual figure.) Cash reserves were more than £30,000 and money in the bank over £22,000. Assets had been written down since the business started. Business was booming.

He then addressed himself to explaining how the firm would survive his death.

> I have made careful arrangements for it to be carried on by a group of keen and eager young people, all of whom have worked with me for very many years, and all of whom know my methods and, so to speak, flavour perfectly. Far from it being probable that the business would go down, after my death, it is quite likely that the reasonable youth of the people who are going to carry it on will increase, not diminish, its success.
>
> When any sort of strong personality (if you will forgive me for saying that — but it is well to write frankly) has been at the head of a publishing business, it has invariably been said that if he dies the business will go smash. . . . These fears have never been realised.
>
> I am sure that you will see how really vital, from my point of view, all this is: if this goes through, then I am quite certain that Peters will try a similar thing with other authors . . .
>
> As I told Peters, I am perfectly ready to pay you the £1000 advance, though naturally I should prefer to pay the £800, for the reasons that I have already given you. (I should regard the £1000 as bad war time finance, but better publishing than making a one-book contract) . . .
>
> I do hope you will let me have a line setting my worries about all this at rest . . .
>
> I have purposely made this letter very business-like. But if I may be sentimental for a moment, let me add this. I regard 'Inheritance', as I think you know, as the nearest approach to a great novel (in the real and permanent, not publishers' sense) that I have published — and all your works in the same *category*. I should absolutely hate a Phyllis Bentley novel to be on another list *so long as VG Ltd existed* — whatever might have happened to VG in the flesh.

It would have taken an A. J. Cronin to resist such a letter. Bentley sent an immediate telegram putting him out of his misery: 'YOUR NICE LETTER RECEIVED CONTRACT SHALL BE AS YOU SUGGEST WITH ALL MY HEART . . . ' Her explanatory letter was full of reassurance.

I have never felt the slightest inclination to leave VG Ltd — except once for a brief period when I felt you were growing rather excessively political. But my allegiance stood even that test, for I knew I should be miserable to see my books on any other firm's list . . .

You need not fear that I should leave the VG firm in the event of the disaster of your death without giving a fair and reasonable trial to the new management . . . I have an attachment to the firm which is founded on strong feeling as well as on business — I have not forgotten, and am never likely to forget, your early encouragement and the faith you showed in my work. I should be immeasurably disheartened and discouraged while writing a novel if I felt that it would not pass through your hands . . .

She had wanted the one-book contract in order to preserve her independence in the event of the firm being taken over by another. A brief letter explaining her contractual protection against that eventuality would have been sufficient to allay her fears. From one point of view most of Victor's letter was unnecessary labour, inspired by an overwrought imagination and a passion for self-justification. Such over-reactions were sometimes alienating; more often, they bound people to him. In opening his heart with abandon he complimented and disarmed the recipient; in showing his vulnerability he inspired affection and protectiveness; and in bombarding them with information he left them overwhelmed and unable to argue. His effusions were rarely a waste of time. It was usually only when they were dictated in anger rather than anxiety that they were counter-productive.

Roughead entered a protest against his writing to Bentley, which Victor happily dismissed. In a letter to Bentley he enclosed their correspondence, suggesting that she write to Roughead ridiculing his attempt to come between author and publisher, pointing out that her position had been misrepresented and taking exception to the misleading tone of Roughead's letter agreeing to Victor's proposed contract. She for her part blamed herself for most of the confusion and rebuked Roughead very mildly. Soon after, Victor airily announced that he had just agreed, in conversation with Negley Farson, a contract for his new book — with royalty and advance levels no agent would have accepted without protest. Roughead registered a further protest. 'It only makes things awkward for us. Please don't do it again.'

'My dear Roughie,' wrote Victor.

Don't make me feel quarrelsome with you, please! *Of course* I must write to authors about anything I like at any time — especially as I am an *intimate* friend of both, and knew one, and was intimate with the other, before you were either.

And you brought it on your own head, you know — so much so that I wonder that you don't 'forget it'!!! (a) you put up a proposition as if it *emanated* from *Phyllis Bentley*, whereas I couldn't help feeling, from my knowledge of her, that it couldn't have originated with her. (b) I demurred most strongly: instead of taking up my demur with her, you wrote straight away saying that 'a one-book contract it must be'. This wouldn't do at all; *of course* I had to write to her — in the interests of both herself and me.

Drop it! But I couldn't for a moment agree to what you suggest in this letter . . .

Merry Xmas and happy New Year!

From the Ministry of Food, where A. D. Peters himself was doing his war work, came a reasoned letter regretting the argument, which he had inspired.

I really don't want to quarrel, or have time for it. But I felt it necessary to register a protest. Of course we don't want to prevent you from keeping in touch with your authors — even if we could. But that is a very different thing from trying to settle contracts with them instead of with their agents. In the case of Farson, I told you what he wanted, and you said you would write to me. You wrote to him (or spoke to him) instead. Was it because you thought you could more easily persuade him than me? In the case of Phyllis Bentley, you received a letter from me, and replied, not to me, but to her. The fact that you may have known both of them longer than I have has nothing to do with it, as you know very well. When a publisher and an agent are negotiating a contract, they are controlled by the same kind of etiquette as prevails in the legal profession. Whatever representations a publisher has to make, on business questions, should be made to the agent, and it is the agent's duty to put them forward to his client. Only when a publisher can show that the agent has failed to do so, has he any justification for going behind the agent's back.

And you, my dear Victor, know this as well as I do.

All good wishes for 1941.

As always with Victor, the matter cut both ways. An undefended author often got a deal worse than an agent would have secured, but some occasionally got better treatment than they would have through a pushy agent. Victor was capable of great spontaneous generosity when an author laid himself (or, more commonly, herself) open to exploitation.

In the case of Negley Farson (which, wisely, he did not try to justify) he had behaved badly. Theirs was a relationship which displayed Victor's contradictions to the full. He often beat Farson down below the terms an agent might have got for him. On the credit side was the patience and intellectual effort he put into encouraging

Farson through his bouts of alcoholism, suffering his public exhibitions of drunkenness, heaping praise on his work when praise was
badly needed, and personally editing certain manuscripts with a
consummate skill that gave a difficult author confidence in the
importance of his own work. On balance, Farson gained more from
Victor's generosity as a person than he lost from his tightfistedness as a
publisher.

There was a tremendous warmth between them, expressed in
countless loving letters, and each appreciated the other's passionate
desire to use his abilities to the utmost. Farson attracted Victor's
compassion because of his human frailty, recurrent self-doubt and
justly grateful recognition of the immense amount of attention Victor
paid him.

In his appeal to Phyllis Bentley, Victor had been vague about his
plans for succession, full as the letter was of unasked-for detail about
other matters vital to Gollancz's survival. The actual state of affairs
would have hardly borne a searchlight. Victor had almost no senior
colleagues. Dunk and Horsman were good at their jobs, but they were
given no encouragement to involve themselves in management or
policy-making: they were expected simply to run respectively the
counting-house and the production side with total efficiency and
dedication. On the editorial side there was Jon Evans, the firm's chief
reader, who after a shaky start in the early days of the firm (when
Victor had complained to his father about his bad time-keeping) had
earned the right to work from home and report weekly on enormous
numbers of manuscripts. His contribution to Gollancz was invaluable, but he was geographically removed from the centre of
decision-making. Then there was Sheila Hodges, who had been
recruited in 1936 as a vastly overqualified roneo-operator and who had
by now risen to be Victor's secretary. Her intelligence, knowledge of
the way Victor's mind worked and obvious talent for publishing made
her a serious prospect for future advancement, but she was as yet
young and untried. There was only one contender to run Gollancz
without Victor — Norman Collins.

Although Victor was an appallingly bad delegator, his LBC preoccupations and his respect for Collins's efficiency had given his young
partner scope to wield power within his own territory. Even at the
height of his LBC preoccupations, Victor still kept his eagle eye on
day-to-day concerns like advertising, jacket design, the fixing of print
runs and so on. But Collins was a highly efficient sales manager, who
additionally carried a heavy burden of editorial responsibility for the

less glamorous authors, and supervised the organizational work of the LBC to the letter of Victor's instructions. While the groups staff dealt with policy and planning, it was Collins and his helpers who dealt with all the mechanics of distribution.

Victor and Collins were in uneasy proximity in the Brimpton hut; the preoccupations of the late 1930's were no longer there to distract Victor; the pair were essentially incompatible anyway; the boss was seriously considering the matter of succession: given all this, Collins's days were numbered. He became the focal point of Victor's innate jealousy of any male competitor. He was too able, too confident, too supercilious and much too prone to delivering witticisms of a kind which hit at Victor's *amour propre*. Collins was able to dilute his fundamental dislike of Victor's arrogance with a deep admiration for his remarkable qualities and a delighted amusement at his absurdities. Forty years after they parted company, Collins could still choke with laughter over particular Victor stories. One of his favourites concerned an occasion in the 1930s when Victor became worried that he was becoming fat and unfit. He determined that he would run around the Ladbroke Grove block daily in the early morning. On one of the few occasions he went out, he collided short-sightedly with the milkman and came home bleeding. Victor had very sensitive antennae for others' reactions to his stories about himself, and Collins was incapable of affecting grave sympathy when he found something funny.

The famous beard was a case in point. 'There was a perfectly shocking period', Collins wrote in a seventieth birthday tribute to Victor,

> when Gollancz grew himself a beard and looked like something pretty dubious out of Conrad. He was taking his appearance seriously in those days and I think I offended him when he asked what he should do with the beard. Should it be longer? shorter? bushier? pointed? or even with two points like von Tirpitz's? The advice I gave him was that he should cut it off and give it to the Nation.

(The beard did not survive long: even Victor's kindest friends could find little to say in its favour. Edmond Fleg's brilliantly tactful criticism probably brought about its removal: '*Tu n'as pas l'air de simple bonté qu'auparavant.*')

Collins omitted from his profile Victor's fortnight of cold silence after his joke. Victor was incapable of firing someone directly, and he determined — as he had with Stein — to force Collins's resignation. Picking rows and then ignoring him for long periods were the predictable tactics. As Victor remembered the relationship later: 'We were not very successful with one another . . . I thought him a good businessman but not a superlative one like myself (how wrong I have turned out to be!).' Recalling that Sheila Lynd had denounced him after the break over the Pact as being 'as bad as Norman Collins', he went on:

> It was indeed the business side of him that Sigle was referring to in her outburst; for while no one could have been more scrupulous in his dealings, the Tolstoyan was being submerged in the man of commerce. Something else, too, was drawing him towards the moderate Right. I objected to his writing novels, which I felt to imply a lack of concern for the firm: this was unreasonable of me: and the effect was, in a subtle way, to estrange him from my politics.

As Victor's *post hoc* rationalizations went, this was more accurate than most, for it was true that he and Collins had moved in opposite directions during the 1930s. But the real source of trouble was Victor's jealousy at Collins's competence as a publisher. He had to go. The novel-writing issue was the one which Victor used to make his partner's life impossible. Even those in the firm who disliked Collins for his superior air freely admit that he worked exceptionally hard and never let his extra-mural endeavours interfere with his job. Victor's denial of his right to write in his spare time was the more outrageous given his own expenditure of energy on just that activity. After a year of angry argument, Collins bowed to the inevitable and resigned, to pursue a spectacularly successful career in radio and television. Sheila Hodges took his place on the board, and though Victor from 1941 complained that he was short-handed, he was again undisputed master and a happier man.

It might have been expected that Victor would suffer from boredom in the country, but in fact he found working there highly congenial. He had his family and staff around him, and plenty of company. He played quite a lot of table tennis with the staff in the Brimpton conservatory (as he had done in Henrietta Street) — for, despite his almost total lack of physical co-ordination, it was a game at which he was 'nifty and agile'. (His accountant, Walter Meigh, recalls visiting Brimpton and being lured into a game. As Meigh's superiority became apparent, Victor adopted the tactic of thumping the table with his bat before either of them served. Meigh's concentration went and he lost the game. Victor did not suggest another: he was content.) Additionally, he had a mass of political work to occupy his spare hours, and regular visits to London, where he could occasionally see friends who could not get down to Brimpton. Friendships did not fade as a result of diminished contact. Rose Macaulay experienced one of those extravagant gestures of affection he so much enjoyed making. When her flat was bombed out in May 1941, she wrote to the Gollanczes: 'I am desolated and desperate — I can't face life without my books — all my lovely 17th and 16th and 18th century library, my Oxford Dictionary, my all. Incidentally, all my MSS and notes were gone, for my Animal Book and my current novel, my typewriter and wireless. I have no clothes, no nothing. I feel like jumping into the river . . .' Victor immediately arranged for the purchase and despatch of the full and hugely expensive *Oxford Dictionary*. It made her as happy as he had hoped: 'how grateful I feel, and how I love you both! I begin to feel I can live again. The OD was my Bible, my staff, my entertainer, my help in work and my recreation in leisure — nothing else serves. Bless you a thousand times for angels!'

There was no taint of 'purchasing affection' in Victor's desire to share his material good fortune with his friends. When the mood took him, his joy in life's good things was a bounty freely dispensed. As he bounced with excited anticipation of Macaulay's joy at the sight of his present, so he adored lavishing on his friends the best food and drink available. He was entirely capable, if a friend was also one of his authors, of beating him down over an advance one day and the next spending enormous sums of money on his entertainment. Because he was better off than most of his friends and more given than most to great outbursts of generosity, he was normally the giver rather than recipient of splendid hospitality. He wanted no material return: his reward came from seeing the delight of others in what he had provided.

Only people perpetually alive to Victor's insecurity and insatiable need for reassurance could become intimate friends. His vulnerability was neurotic. What another could shrug off as thoughtlessness pierced him to the quick. An example was the occasion when a member of the LBC groups staff dashed off on leave from the office without saying goodbye and thanking him for an unexpected cheque. She wrote to apologize and received the following:

Dear Miss——,
At first I felt, not anger, but grief: in fact, the whole weekend I was in a state of misery. But on Monday, by one of those strange twists that occur, my grief turned to fury. I therefore do *not* forgive you: I never felt less forgiving.

It was a sentiment of which Victor would have felt terribly ashamed afterwards, as he would of many of the outbursts of anger that peppered his correspondence, where the dark side of his nature is disproportionately represented. Such letters always have to be read in the light of the knowledge that Victor really did feel more deeply than others. His explosions, his lamentations and his exultations were in proportion to the degree of his emotion. He could go in seconds, and for what to others seemed trivial and often ludicrous reasons, from the heights of elation to the slough of despond. While, through the sheer impact of his personality, he had it in his power to make others feel happy or sad, his hypersensitivity gave them a frightening reciprocal power.

Victor was too much of a child to be naturally cut out for the job of father, but he was spared a great deal because of the way in which Ruth brought up the girls. As children, for the most part, they enjoyed what attention he gave them, and in retrospect were grateful for the money that was lavished on their schooling and wider education, and for the cultured and interesting background in which they grew up. They took happily to Colonel Moses, who was an important channel of communication, and accepted the nicknames Victor gave them and invented dozens of variations. Letters to parents and between siblings are almost impenetrable to outsiders, so larded are they with the family vocabulary, the family jokes and innumerable esoteric terms of endearment. Even one of the Gollancz dogs — and there were four at different times, to which parents and children were very attached — had several names. As the children reached adolescence, shared political and moral values became another link with their parents. Yet by 1940, there were problems in the relationship with the three eldest (Vita and Francesca were only 13 and 10 respectively). Livia, for instance, in her teens in the late 1930s, had become very left-wing and detected inconsistencies between her father's new socialist principles and his style of living. Victor was deeply galled when she fiercely criticized his taking a box at Covent Garden for six weeks and drove him, through her passion, to cancel it. (In later years she regretted this, as it meant he could not follow his plan of catching a final act after a long working day.) They became estranged and although they were politically in agreement on essentials after the Pact, their strong personalities clashed with disastrous regularity. After she had finished her studies at the Royal College of Music, she worked for a little while for the firm before leaving home to become a professional horn player: from early in the war she was to have a successful career in several orchestras, and although Victor was proud of this, they saw little of each other.

During the same period, all was not going smoothly with Diana. In her case, the difficulty was rather with Ruth, who was something of a puritan. (Ruth was later to cause Victor worry because she lived up to her socialist principles and herself preferred to use the National Health Service rather than, like him, private medicine.) She disapproved of cosmetics, which Diana began to use heavily, and, a simple person herself, found Diana's natural sophistication antipathetic. Victor was fond of this pretty and funny daughter, but the omens were not good. Four of the five girls emerged from their senior schools (Livia: St Paul's; Julia: St Paul's and Badminton; Vita and Francesca: Badminton) with a sense of duty to the wider community, whereas Diana's formative years had been spent at Dartington, which instilled no such sense. Nor did she acquire it at art school during the war.

Julia, whose talents were mathematical rather than literary, received from her parents less attention and affection than did the others. What had arisen partly through her bad luck in being the child in the middle of a large family became permanent. She grew up having little in common with Ruth and Victor, and was never at ease with them. On leaving school in 1940 she worked in the firm for more than a year before going on to Reading University to study domestic science. She could never accept the exaggerations that littered Victor's normal accounts of office life. At meals with him and Ruth she used to intervene to correct him and this provoked him to fury or tears. She was glad to leave home.

It was still Ruth who was the fulcrum of Victor's life. His pride in her beauty and utter emotional dependence on her never faded. But sexually, there were serious problems. Intercourse was very restricted, because Ruth's determination to avoid another pregnancy had put her off sex. For Victor this was a distressing deprivation and just before the war — after much heartsearching — he embarked on an affair with an attractive woman who was active in the LBC. He was very much in love, but his uxoriousness demanded that Ruth approve the affair in advance. Ruth was ambivalent. In some respects it was a relief to her that Victor should find sexual satisfaction elsewhere and she therefore gave the relationship her formal blessing. When she knew it was about to be consummated, she gave him a morocco-bound copy of his favourite poem, Wordsworth's The Excursion, a long philosophical investigation of man, nature and human life. It was inscribed 'for a very special occasion'. At the same time, she was not entirely without jealousy, and took pains to ensure that she would not again meet Victor's mistress. She was unable to do what Victor required of her — to remove from him all guilt at his infidelity.

In many respects Victor's extra-marital relationship was satisfactory. Although the woman was a communist, their affection was undamaged — indeed if anything it was enhanced — by political differences. There was mutual intellectual respect, friendship, love and sexual passion (for Victor was a considerate and tender lover). The woman made no demands on him and allowed him to make the running. Yet on many of the evenings they spent together in London Victor's guilt overwhelmed him. He would spend hours talking about his inner torments — particularly childhood guilts and fears, and his dread of advancing fascism — and these would merge into the immediate experience of sexual guilt. From time to time, especially towards the end in 1943, he would ring and say the affair had to end. She would agree and he would then change his mind after a week or so.

There was no doubt about the sincerity of Victor's guilt. In a letter to Leonora Eyles, author of the highly successful *Commonsense about Sex* he wrote in August 1942, apropos of her plans for a new version:

> . . . perhaps we might meet and talk the matter over before you get too far with the work. It is possible that I might be able to make a suggestion or two. In particular I have in mind:
> 1. The relation of tenderness to sexuality.
> 2. The question of the possibility of a relation of friendship, involving intercourse, outside marriage not damaging the marriage.
>   The other topic to which you don't refer in your letter . . . is the very terrible increase in venereal disease.

Later events were to demonstrate that at this time Victor was almost certainly suffering, at least sub-consciously, a very real guilt-induced fear that VD was the inevitable punishment for his sexual self-indulgence. Certainly the guilt itself was an ever-present backdrop as he drove himself mercilessly to help the war effort and alleviate the sufferings the war created.

CHAPTER FIFTEEN

WAR: EMBRACING TOO MUCH

AFTER CLOSE ON two years of dedicating his best efforts to unmasking the reality behind CP propaganda, Victor was freed, in late June 1941, of an enormous burden. He instantly took up another. He had justly believed himself peculiarly fitted to warn the gullible against the CP; now he felt supremely qualified to persuade the public of the virtues of the Soviet Union while admitting its deficiencies. Anglo-Soviet co- operation could win the war and create a stable and more fair world thereafter, if Victor taught the British to understand the Russians.

His article on Anglo-Soviet relations in the new situation appeared in the July *Left News*. Its theme was the necessity for understanding how the Soviet Union worked and thought, how superior it was to the fascist countries, and how its traditional and often justified suspicions of its new allies could be laid to rest. He also praised its superlative propaganda, which roused the people to heights of self-sacrifice while directing its venom at Nazism and exculpating the ordinary German. The article concluded with a brief discussion of the present state of the CP. Pollitt was back as general secretary, having reverted smartly to his uncompromisingly anti-Nazi line of autumn 1939. Palme Dutt, caught in a theological quagmire, had lost his job. While he advocated support for the Soviet Union against Hitler coupled with struggle against British imperialism and Churchill, Pollitt, a gut-communist, came out unequivocally for maximum Anglo-Soviet co-operation behind Churchill and Stalin. Now that the CP's weight was thrown behind the war effort, said Victor, 'we welcome them wholeheartedly, unless and until there is another turn, as comrades in a common fight . . . And we shall strive to avoid a single further word of controversy with them in this journal, except such — and we hope the occasion will not arise — as may seem to us necessary in the interests of a People's Victory for Peace and Socialism.'

Citing Pollitt's letter of July 8 rallying the CP, he continued:

We beg them . . . not to 'ram the Soviet Union down the throats of' the British public, not to speak and act as if nothing but the Soviet Union mattered, not by implication to depreciate Britain's part and Britain's achievement.

A campaign for closer understanding between Britain and Russia is . . . a most urgent, a literally worldsaving, necessity, second only to the necessity for the closest military collaboration. As the situation develops, powerful forces working, at present underground, to split the new Allies will emerge into the open: already the *Catholic Herald*, while urging military aid for the Soviet Union, says that Sovietism is a 'worse tyranny' than Nazism. Every bit of effort will be required to defeat such forces. To indulge in propaganda of the kind we are deprecating would be not to defeat but to reinforce them. Enthusiasm for the Soviet Union is sweeping like a great wave through the masses in this country: nothing must be done to cause a reaction. The enthusiasm is occasioned by a feeling of relief at the respite which Germany's attack on Russia, and Russia's magnificent resistance, has given us: our job is to convert this emotion . . . into that permanent and solidly based understanding which can come only from a completely honest and realistic approach.

The day he sent his article to press, Victor decided to turn it into a book. Called *Russia and Ourselves*, it was assembled, printed and bound within a fortnight. The *Left News* text was slightly modified for what he termed the 'medium politically instructed public' and amplified by the inclusion of the full text (Shelley and all) of his previous month's trumpet blast of evangelical socialism. The potential for a successful partnership even after the war was summed up thus:

The problem of the modern world is to reconcile an economy centrally planned for the public good, with personal freedom. There in the Soviet Union, for all who will see it, is the planned economy, and there too is the drive, the inspiration, the compelling power that come from a common national purpose. Here in Britain we have a deeply rooted love of personal freedom, and, when all reservations have been made, a great deal of rough and ready experience of how to achieve it. If both Britain and the Soviet Union can throw their best not only into the peace settlement but into the years and decades and perhaps centuries of fruitful co-operation which, if we are wise, will come after it, then the terror and agony through which the world is passing may be but the prelude to the establishment, in however remote a future, of an abidingly peaceful United States of the World, in which no man shall ever be hungry, and no man ever a slave.

Victor was more sanguine than many of his readers. However, the main part of the book was so fair in its treatment of past misunderstandings and Soviet defensiveness, and in its proposals for helping

Russian resistance now (to the ultimate benefit of all victims of fascism), that it was very positive in its effect. He declared a sales target of 10,000 copies: in the event, he sold 35,000 — staggering, outside the LBC, for a book of its kind. All the wartime problems of paper shortage and printing delays had been swept aside to capitalize on the topicality of the issue. Large numbers of advance copies were in the hands of influential people in the last week of July. Artlessly, Victor explained to one of his authors that this had been done 'by printing it in London (at double the normal expense) with magazine printers who are personal friends of mine and took it on as a special favour.' He revealed too that, although he sometimes raised prices deliberately to limit demand, he had kept the price of his own book low to stimulate sales. (It took some time for Victor to realize that some of his authors might see such tactics as rather arrogant.)

Victor had always been a master at securing puffs. Particularly in the case of his own books, once an appreciative letter was received from an advance reader, he had no compunction about persuading the individual concerned that he had a political duty to allow Victor to quote him in advertisements. 'I do not know what to admire more:' wrote Koestler, 'the lucidity of the argument, or its eloquence, or its just balance, or the speed at which author and publisher worked.' Victor grabbed that sentence for publicity purposes, but naturally ignored the following sentence, which for those who knew Koestler would have shown better how highly he regarded the book: 'I had the rare feeling that I couldn't have written it better — this sounds conceited but you doubtless understand what I mean.' 'I wish everybody in England could read it this weekend. It is so just and sober and balanced and true,' said Lettice Cooper. And Captain Basil Liddell Hart spoke of its magnificent commonsense, admirable balance and grasp of the root of the matter. Reviews were on the whole enthusiastic: the *Manchester Guardian* even gave the book an accolade ('invaluable') in a leading article. The book's patent honesty disarmed all but the far Right and the embittered Left, though there was occasional misunderstanding. 'Gollancz wants unity with the British CP', commented the *Reynolds News* reviewer. Victor, drawn out in the open, contradicted him: 'after what the Communists have done during the last two years, I should fight tooth and nail against any idea of so-called "unity" between the CP and the Labour Party.'

The *Daily Worker* was no longer around to give the official line on Victor, but his relationship with the CP remained one of enmity: the scars ran deep. The right were not muzzled, and some of them paid him the compliment of seeing danger in his argument. Victor wrote to protest to Walter Monckton at the Ministry of Information (with whom he was on friendly terms) that a ministry official at a Rotary Lunch had condemned this 'mischievous book which takes advantage of our alliance with Socialist Russia to encourage Communist activities in this country.' Ernest Benn in *Truth*, in an article objecting to the 'Continental' habit adopted by some Jews of writing anonymously, went on apropos of Victor: 'He is perhaps our most energetic disseminator of poisonous political philosophy. But he is also good enough an Englishman to put his name on the label, and we like him all the better for that.'

Had Victor required confirmation that he was on the right lines, he would have received it from his press and post-bag. He had, in fact, never doubted that his kind of propaganda was what was needed. Even before getting his material into book form, he wrote to Cole on 14 July (commissioning what became *Europe, Russia and the Future*, the October Choice):

> Oughtn't we to start up (now is the time, when there is a wave of enthusiasm for the Soviet Union which is quite ill-based and may quite rapidly die away) some sort of really representative Anglo-Soviet committee? I believe we could get a lot of big names to join: and I should be glad to do the donkey work from this office. It would, of course, be absolutely vital that it should not be dominated in the smallest degree, directly or indirectly, by the communists or the Soviet Union . . . The utmost care should be taken, also, to keep communists away from the day by day direction. They, and Soviet representatives (if possible) should co-operate in a 'genuine' capacity. Though on second thoughts I am not sure that there should be any communist representatives — though there should certainly be Soviet ones.

Cole, like many others to whom he trailed the idea, approved, and was one of those attending a meeting on 3 September to discuss the formation of what became known as the Anglo-Soviet Public Relations Association (ASPRA).

In the event, no communists were asked to join. Victor told Harold Nicolson in October, over an Ivy lunch, that he believed they were already taking over meetings under innocent Labour auspices, and would blame Churchill if Russia lost her war with Germany. He had no intention of allowing them the merest foothold in any organization of his. (One experience under which he smarted was that of having omitted to resign the vice-presidency of the National Council for Civil Liberties before its domination at that time by the CP became apparent.)

The extent of Victor's professional, political and personal network was evident from the more familiar names among the 33 people who attended on 3 September, and the others named who had already agreed in principle to join. Friends included Gerald Barry, Norman Bentwich, David Low, Rose Macaulay and Alan Thomas. Authors and political contacts included Acland, Brailsford, Boothby, Violet Bonham Carter, Joad, Laski, Professor John Macmurray, Kingsley Martin, Eleanor Rathbone, Strachey, George Strauss and Leonard Woolf.

Margery Fry and Lord Listowel came from the China Campaign Committee, in which Victor continued to play an active part. The officers elected included the Royal Physician, Lord Horder, as president, and Victor as honorary secretary. A telegram was despatched over their names to the Soviet Embassy: 'MEMBERS OF THE CONSERVATIVE LABOUR AND LIBERAL PARTIES SCIENTISTS SCHOLARS RELIGIOUS LEADERS PUBLICISTS EDITORS WRITERS HAVE TODAY FORMED THEMSELVES INTO AN ANGLO-SOVIET PUBLIC RELATIONS COMMITTEE [later Association] STOP ON BEHALF OF THIS COMMITTEE WE SEND YOU EXPRESSION OF OUR ADMIRATION FOR THE SOVIET UNION'S MAGNIFICENT RESISTANCE AND OUR FIRM HOPE FOR FINAL VICTORY IN OUR COMMON CAUSE STOP'

The aims of ASPRA were ambitious. Seeking to build up 'permanently cordial relations' between the two powers 'on a basis of mutual confidence, toleration and good will', its functions were detailed as:

a. to improve means of intercourse between Great Britain and the USSR and to increase knowledge of each country in the other;
b. to watch the developments of Anglo-Soviet relations and to take any action considered desirable to remove possible misunderstanding;
c. to call the attention of responsible authorities to any special needs or difficulties;
d. to study specific problems, by means of sub-committees, etc., and to prepare and circulate reports;
e. to arrange any public functions, meetings, etc., required to further the general purposes of the Committee.

Two rooms at Henrietta Street were made the headquarters of ASPRA, some temporary secretarial help was hired and Victor hurled himself into his new enthusiasm. 'I am rushed to death at the moment,' he wrote to Negley Farson on 15 September, 'the Hon Secretaryship . . . taking a terrific amount of my already overburdened time — it is one of those things that are just growing like wildfire, as the Left Book Club did in the early days.'

It soon became clear that he had taken on a commitment far more unwieldy than the LBC. Instead of two selectors and a large staff under his direction, he was bound to operate in conjunction with an executive committee of fifteen and a general committee which expanded to over 300 within weeks. By 22 September he was already worried that the organization was failing to keep pace with events, and was pressing for an ASPRA-hosted lunch in honour of Churchill and Maisky, an Albert Hall meeting, a memorial to the Prime Minister and a letter to *The Times*. All his demands were ultimately agreed to, but not without long and irksome discussions of detail that sorely tried Victor's patience. Deputations to Brendan Bracken and Anthony Eden elicited encouraging noises and a letter to *The Times*, signed by the officers, called for future co-operation between the British Commonwealth, the USSR and the USA. ASPRA was on the public map.

Big names like Julian Huxley, Maynard Keynes, Gilbert Murray, H. G. Wells and Sir Henry Wood joined ASPRA as the weeks went on, so Victor's frustrations — at the redrafting sessions, the tedious discussions over sub-committees and his inability to get his own way save by pleading and persuasion — were kept under control. He firmly believed that such an illustrious membership must have a considerable impact on political decision-making. He was dismayed by their failure to get Churchill to the public lunch, but mollified when the second choice, Eden, accepted the invitation — for 21 November. In the early part of November, in addition to carrying out many speaking engagements, he worked devotedly on the plans for the lunch, memorial and late-December Albert Hall meeting. He made free with his own time and that of Sheila Hodges, charged nothing for use and operation of the firm's roneo machine and — from his own pocket — contributed the major part of the funds necessary to keep ASPRA in being. To Victor it seemed only fair that he, the pivot of the organization, should be allowed to run it with the minimum of interference. Not all his distinguished colleagues saw it that way. The chairman, Professor A. V. Hill, MP, (a physicist soon to be a Companion of Honour) took strong exception to Victor's insistence on controlling the choice of speakers for the Albert Hall meeting, and his refusal to consider having an industrialist as a vice-president. Hill circulated a memorandum in advance of the executive committee meeting of 13 November and invited Victor to produce one outlining his objections to its proposals. Victor declined, promising to respond orally. He then cut the ground from under Hill's feet by resigning the secretaryship.

Wishing to keep both distinguished chairman and irreplaceable secretary, Lord Horder found a compromise. On 13 November, he was able to read to the executive and have accepted a statement worked out with the protagonists. The style smacked of Victor.

1. Until after the Lunch and the Albert Hall meeting (with which the Honorary Secretary is preoccupied), the list of Officers and of the Executive shall remain as to-day constituted, and no proposal shall be made for modifying them until after these events.

2. In the opinion of Mr Gollancz, who has had wide experience in arranging meetings, and in particular has arranged and presided at four meetings at the Albert Hall, it will be impossible to make the meeting a success (which in the event is exceedingly difficult in existing circumstances and cannot be guaranteed), unless he is given carte blanche *this week* to go ahead within limits laid down by the Executive — that is to say, unless he is in a position to approach in each category of speakers, No. 1, then No. 2, then No. 3 and so on.
Moreover, Mr Gollancz, who is very busy with the Lunch, cannot find the time for any further meeting this week. It is therefore proposed to proceed at this meeting, and immediately after the Secretary has made a few announcements, to the final drawing up of the lists of speakers for the Albert Hall meeting.

3. Mr Gollancz withdraws his resignation.
I just want to add this: having, of course, been in close touch with Mr Gollancz in these matters, and having had the opportunity of reading the very complete statement which Mr Gollancz had drawn up for submission to this meeting, I ought to make it clear that Mr Gollancz's resignation was prompted by no trivial personal considerations, but by what he felt to be a matter of basic principle seriously affecting our whole character and work.

The lunch went off extremely successfully and received widespread attention in the press. The *News Review* published a piece rightly describing ASPRA as the brainchild of the 'restless and dynamic' Victor. It included a memorable pen-picture: '[He] is burly, dome-browed. Greying curls wreathe his gleaming pate. With a juggler's dexterity he passes his cigar from mouth to fingers . . . as he talks at terrific pace, he criss-crosses the room with long strides.' And reporting the Savoy lunch, it went on:

Foreign Secretary Anthony Eden and Russian Ambassador Ivan Maisky, the guests of honour, sat under a huge hammer-and-sickle flag and the Union Jack. Some 350 guests drank their toasts in Château Lynch Moussas, 1934, at 7s. 6d. a bottle. The Soviet Ambassador reverently bowed his head when the Bishop of Malmesbury said Grace . . .

Gollancz effaced himself during luncheon, sat with the topnotchers but made no speech. His baby had been launched in the best society and he was happy.

His happiness did not last long. Although he had been temporarily fortified by Eden's and Maisky's warmth on the subject of post-war co-operation, he was discouraged when events outside his control led to the scrapping of the Albert Hall meeting. Maisky politely rejected such schemes as the publication in Russia of a British information bulletin along the lines of the London-published 'Soviet War News'. The British government smiled on ASPRA, but paid it little heed. ASPRA's discussions became more mundane, in pace with its ambitions. The dead hand of organizational complexity came down on the euphoria. Victor struggled on gamely, with earnest but ineffectual sub-committees and abortive book-lists, until mid-January 1942, when he again tendered his resignation as secretary. He nobly continued quite frequently to attend committee meetings until, in the early summer, ASPRA virtually wound itself up. With the signing in May of an Anglo-Soviet Treaty, which in Hill's view achieved the principal aim of ASPRA, and with the pragmatic impossibility of any real contact with the USSR, there was nothing left but to go half-heartedly through the motions. Victor made no protest. He had put far more work into ASPRA than had been justified by events: while it had shown good-will towards the Soviet Union and somewhat modified public opinion, the results could not be measured. For Victor himself ASPRA had done two things: it had satisfied his urge to extend the hand of friendship to the Soviet Union, and it had taught him that his talents were wasted in big committees. Perhaps in the hope that in these changed circumstances his old CP friends might not see him as an enemy, he wrote to Sheila Lynd (who had married Peter Wheeler before the war) to congratulate her on the birth of a son. He asked to be forgiven for any wrong he had ever done her. When eventually she replied, in July 1942, she assured him she had got over the insult of being sacked:

> what really severed our friendship was neither personal nor trivial; the transformation of your attitude to the Party and above all to the Soviet Union, and the dirty work you put in on slandering them, when slandering the SU was more fashionable than it is now.
>
> Realities like that can't be wiped out by memories of lovely days in Paris or Venice — however sad the memory of them makes one.

She offered a measure of friendship. Victor's reply acts now as an encapsulation of how he had come to view human relationships.

You have 'got me wrong'. How on earth could I ask *you* to forgive me for wrong political opinions or actions? Only one of two persons could do that — oneself or God (or perhaps history, in the case of more important people), according to one's cosmology. Incidentally, and to avoid misunderstanding, I feel today far more convinced than ever that my political actions from August 1939 were necessary and right. That conviction may, of course, change: for as one turns fifty one realises how infinitesimally little one either knows or understands.

No: I meant, of course, actions to and relations with *you*. I meant, for instance, as an example of what I think *right*, my decision that your connection with the Left Book Club should cease. For such an action as that, I said, I cannot ask to be forgiven and reconciled. But I thought, and think, that I must have done things in my relation to you that were wrong; and for these it is necessary to ask forgiveness, if there is to be reconciliation.

I thought and think it for the following reason. We had had a precious human relationship (that was the point of my reference to 'torrents of spring'): a relationship which, whatever may have happened since, you know as well as I do was a true and real relationship. The essence of such a relationship cannot be altered by the mere fact of a change in development of political opinions in one of the persons or both: if one person *really* loves another (I don't mean sexually), his love cannot be changed merely because the other becomes converted, for instance, from atheism to theism, or vice versa. The essence of such a relationship can be changed only by the entry of something false and bad into the relationship itself. Well, I think that on my side (as well as, frankly, on yours) something false and bad may have entered into it. I feel as deeply about politics as you do — perhaps, simply because I am older, even more deeply: and just as you felt that I had 'betrayed', so did I feel that you, in your capacity as a member of the CP and as still adhering to it, had done so. And so, wrongly and indeed wickedly, I may have allowed an intellectual judgement about your political opinions to produce an element of hostility to your personality (though in the main I never ceased to love you) which meant that I did not retain sufficient respect for your personality. It is proper to ask forgiveness for that, because it may have had its share in destroying a relationship which certainly had value for you as it had for me. You, I think, acted similarly: but I can be responsible only for my own side of the matter. In any case, I was older and should have been wiser.

I said that a relationship cannot be altered by the mere fact of a change in or development of political opinions in one of the persons or both. But there must be a reservation to that. You may have formed the opinion that my views were not genuine: that they were dictated, for instance, by motives of fear or gain. In that event, you may have judged that my personality was different from what you had believed: that you had never really known me: and that our relationship had, therefore, never been real and true. In such an event, the mere fact of political change or development might alter a relationship.

But I cannot believe that you really made that judgement. for it would involve the ultimate blasphemy: the arrogation to yourself of the right and ability to look into and judge of another person's heart and soul, and a person's to whom you were bound by close and longstanding ties.

Well, there it all is. I repeat that I am truly sorry for anything that I did wrong; and I shall always be grateful for the friendship you gave me, of which I have a thousand very precious memories.

He did not send the letter. Presumably he saw no point.

Victor's dwindling enthusiasm for the Anglo-Soviet issue left a vacuum: his nature abhorred it. Since 1940 he had been appalled by a series of broadcasts by Sir Robert Vansittart, chief diplomatic adviser to the government, who contended that the Germans were peculiarly warlike and that Nazism was but a logical development from their whole history. Victor never missed an opportunity to state that the war was being fought as much for the benefit of the ordinary German — oppressed by a ghastly tyranny — as for the persecuted Jews or conquered peoples of Europe. As early as January 1941 Laski had written for *Left News*, as a formal expression of editorial policy, an attack on the Vansittart doctrine, urging readers to remember the Burke aphorism that 'I do not know how to draw up an indictment against a whole people', and to argue against a Carthaginian peace. When Vansittart's broadcasts were published as a hugely successful pamphlet — *Black Record* — Victor began to write a refutation, but abandoned it for a time when he became dissatisfied with the extent of his own grasp of German history. Embarking on a reading programme to alleviate his ignorance, he contented himself with a brief attack on Vansittart in the March *Left News* and the issuing of Laski's article as a penny leaflet.

Preoccupied elsewhere, for several months Victor confined himself to occasional warnings against unthinking hatred of the enemy. While the need to win the war was uppermost in his mind, worries about the nature of the peace were only incidental. The *Left News* section, International Socialist Forum, was steadily hammering home the message that fascist countries included in their communities good socialists who could be relied upon to bring about humane régimes when the war ended. In August 1941 Victor was greatly reassured by the Roosevelt/Churchill Atlantic Charter, enshrining the desire for a peace without territorial aggrandizement, bringing freedom and decent living standards to all people.

For a time, Victor's main political concern was global, as he pushed for the recognition of the USSR as an equal partner in war and peace;

he was utterly convinced by Russian propaganda that she would be a powerful anti-punitive force in any post-war settlement. The ASPRA honeymoon over, he narrowed his aims to a local British matter where he knew he could be personally effective: the countering of Vansittartism. At the end of November 1941 he delivered a 10,000-word Fabian Society lecture explaining the underlying reasons for German militarism and nationalism. It was imperialism as the essential factor in international relations that had made it possible for Germany, with her historical problems of disunity and delayed industrialization, to develop into a society dominated by junkers, industrialists and militarists. Germany had never been fertile ground for a democratic social revolution, so it would be necessary after the war to encourage the German people, the majority of whom were anti-Nazi, to revolt against their own oppressors. The lecture concluded with a brief peroration on the evil and futility of hatred.

Victor's personal beliefs were by now so individualistic that even propaganda with which he agreed often struck him as deficient, either in emphasis or in scope. During November and December he had a correspondence with the author of a manuscript called *Guilty Germans?* in which his position was spelled out in detail. A. E. Douglas-Smith had sent Victor in July a synopsis and specimen chapters of an historical investigation countering the *Black Record*. Victor was delighted, and announced it in the September *Left News* as the November Choice. The full manuscript turned up in good time, but publication was somewhat delayed by libel queries. When Victor finally got around to reading the book as a whole he had second thoughts, and he took the increasingly rare step of asking for advice from Laski and Strachey. On the one hand, he told them, it was full of excellent material which should be made available now that 'the most vital need of the day is to counter the Vansittart stuff (which, according to my information, is carrying increasing weight, and not least in the Labour movement). On the other hand, I dislike the book intensely: although I believe the man is not either an open or a secret member of the CP, it is "CPish". And, while he clearly is violently anti-Nazi and expresses this several times, nevertheless, the whole book, and in spite of these passages, makes a slightly pro-Nazi impression on me (probably wrongly).'

Strachey's reply is not on record. Laski was no help:

1. The work of Mr Douglas-Smith cannot be described as having a Nazi undertone.
2. It is damn dull.
3. It is trivial.

4. It is totally uninteresting in his personal impression.
5. He [Laski] therefore concludes that if you publish it as a Left Book Club book, nobody will be deeply interested, but nobody ought to be profoundly offended. Q.E.D.

So Victor tried alone to bend the book — which meant influencing its author — to a shape he found acceptable. On 9 December he dictated a letter just short of 5,000 words, agreeing broadly with the analysis, but criticizing the tone of the book as (a) faintly 'CPish', (b) redolent of a suppressed hatred of England, (c) unpleasantly sneering about liberalism and (d) liable to alienate rather than win over the middle ground. Douglas-Smith was overwhelmed by the numerous suggestions for minor and major alterations to be made by the 18th, and the range of overall criticisms. He began in his turn (on 11 December, the day the US declared war on Germany and Italy) a lengthy self-defence. In one telling paragraph, Douglas-Smith spoke of Victor's remark about 'a sort of suppressed hatred of England'. That remark

(which immediately followed a reference, slightly obscure, to Marxism, which again followed the Communist accusation immediately) filled me with a sort of blaze of anger which I am determined if possible to keep out of this letter, though as it is very late and I am tired and have found your letter a very considerable blow, I may not altogether succeed. I read on, and my anger evaporated when I noticed your qualifying clauses, though it took me some time to try and sort out what you meant before I came to the conclusion that you hadn't the slightest idea yourself.

In a long appended note tackling the 'CPish' accusation, Douglas-Smith described frankly his own political development and linked it embarrassingly with Victor's own record. High points included the revelation that Victor had turned down a synopsis of his in the mid-1930s because it was too anti-communist. Then, through reading LBC books (particularly by Strachey), hearing a highly effective speech of Victor's and being impressed by Victor's association with communists, he slowly moved towards Marxism.

What amazes me is that in your present fury against the Communists you forget your own part in influencing thousands of Englishmen to similar conclusions. If you publish such books as Hewlett Johnson's and Seema Rynan Allen's [*Comrades and Citizens*, Choice, November 1938], let alone Pat Sloan's [*Soviet Democracy*, Choice, May 1937], what do you expect? The odd thing about your own obsession (you will pardon me if I can find no other phrase) is that it appears to become retrospective, and I gather from your notes that you object to your writers praising Stalin's policy even *before* Sept. 1939; you also appear to condemn all continental communist activity, before as well as after the war of 1939.

He had recognized the inner consistency of the CP after the Pact, disapproving of many aspects of its behaviour while disinclined to join in 'execution'. He was now strongly in favour of Anglo-Soviet-US co-operation. Going laboriously through Victor's textual criticisms one by one, Douglas-Smith's patience gave out:

> I have endeavoured to answer more of your notes, but it is no good. They simply make me so annoyed that I shall be rude. So far as I can see, you make the following demands from your writers
>
> (1) That all references to Russia should be critically adverse if not hostile
> (2) That any reference to Communists in any country in Europe, either before or after Sept. 1939 must be accompanied by denunciations, however irrelevant.
> (3) That nothing must be said to expose the Pétainist danger from the British Right . . .
>
> It seems to me that your object is to get me to cancel the contract. If so, you are going to too much trouble . . . We can scrap the book . . .

Victor's frantic telegram of denial was followed by another of his 5,000-word letters of confutation and amplification. His only purpose, he explained, had been to increase the conversion potential of the book, best done, he had thought, by describing freely and frankly just how he had himself reacted.

> As I finished, for a split second the thought passed through my mind: 'Will he misunderstand this?' And I asked my secretary, one of whose jobs it is to prevent me from sending foolish letters, whether she thought you would react badly. She said: 'Certainly not: it is so obviously useful that you should say with complete freedom and frankness what you feel.' Nevertheless, a slight feeling of uneasiness remained, and that is why I added the sentence: 'I hope you won't hate me too much for all this'.

(Any secretary would have known that Victor's apparent invitation to criticize on such occasions was in fact a demand for approbation. Most employees placed in such a quandary — to tell him he was going over the top or to reassure him that he was only being reasonable — had to balance against the satisfactions of honesty the rewards of a continuing association. If they wanted to enjoy his confidence, they had to keep telling him he was right, and put up with it when he cited them in corroboration. Only those who knew him very well were able to develop subtle methods of influencing his decisions.) Whatever the recipient learned from such outpourings, they are a vital record of Victor's inner workings. He was coming to know himself better.

Douglas-Smith had admitted that he tended to be provocative about the English, having heard at the age of six his father's contention that they were the finest race in the world. Victor produced a burst of fellow-feeling: his own father had been similarly responsible for making him detest Jewish 'chosen racism'. Likewise, and for the same Freudian reasons, the left-wing tendency to appear 'anti-English' was a reaction against chauvinism. He admitted that in pre-Pact days he had been weak in giving in to CP pressure to make his books 'conform to a certain type'. A 'great deal of incidental harm' had thus been done, but it was far outweighed by the good. And he stoutly denied that after the split he had ever failed to admit the virtues of his communist opponents.

That being said, there was no point in accusing him of an inconsistency in his attitude to communists. He was well aware of it. But while co-operation with communists on the Continent was desirable, in England it was impossible. '*Quite rightly from their starting point*, Communists have no respect for truth as such . . . This does seem to me to render co-operation quite out of the question . . . (Which isn't in the least to say that, in a great number of qualities . . . the Communists are not in the main, apart from a certain number of hate-ridden paranoiacs, greatly superior to all but a few in the other Left parties.)'

A compromise was worked out in amity, but some of Douglas-Smith's criticisms, fully though Victor had answered them, continued to rankle. In another letter he exaggerated his contribution to Anglo-Soviet *rapport*: 'I was entirely responsible, after two months' intensive work, for producing a speech by Mr Eden at the Savoy Hotel reversing all previous Government speeches which suggested Anglo-American domination of Europe, and stating in explicit terms the necessity for the closest co-operation with the Soviet Union in the post-war world.' (It would have been more accurate to say that he had given Eden an excellent opportunity for making public a diplomatic policy that he, Eden, had at last persuaded his colleagues to accept.)

'I am greatly interested by your Left Book Club Peccavi, which is news to me and explains a good deal,' wrote Douglas-Smith. 'I did not know that your Retreat from Moscow, if I may call it so, had gone so far — behind pre-war frontiers, so to speak. It is not for me to judge, though I confess I find the repentance more distressing than the sin.' Like many others who had never been as close to the communists as Victor, he felt the scale of Victor's reaction to be disproportionate. But then only a tiny number were sufficiently intimate with Victor to know the personal cost to him of admitting real sin. Writing in *My*

Dear Timothy of his childish fear of deprivation — his spiritual greed
— he elaborated:

> . . . it has persisted during the greater part of my adult life. It has taken
> many forms: fear that I might do wrong, fear of having already done it,
> fear of a guilty conscience: fear, in general and above all, of not being good.
> It has been dormant from time to time for long periods, and I have been
> wholly unaware of it: and then suddenly, as something happened that gave
> it its opportunity, it would come leaping out and almost physically choke
> me.

From the time of Munich that fear had intermittently played a major
part in Victor's life. In his controversy with the CP there was a large
element of making reparation, and now Vansittart had provided the
best opportunity to date to compensate for the sins of his past: Victor
could stand for absolute goodness and the purity of the doctrine of
'Love your enemies'. Margaret Cole and Douglas-Smith, among
others, took issue with his public injunction (in the Fabian lecture) that
one should not hate Hitler. So he went further: one must *love* Hitler.
He was eventually prevailed upon to excise that idea from *Shall Our
Children Live or Die? A Reply to Lord Vansittart on the German Problem*,
which he put together over December 1941 and January 1942. At the
time he accepted that it would be a counter-productive provocation.
Later he regretted his pusillanimity.

His first thought had been simply to publish in a pamphlet a
somewhat enlarged version of the lecture, but lengthy correspondence with critics on the left gave him the impetus to widen the
spectrum of issues covered. The general thesis about the cause of the
German problem and its solution was augmented by lengthy reflections on guilt, hatred and punishment. He was still well short of the
morally absolutist position. Although he now considered everyone to
be guilty through omission of allowing the exercise of power by Nazis
and capitalists, he was urging on the German people a revolution
which would inevitably be bloody. 'I would certainly like to see the
German people kill the chief Nazis in the quickest and most merciful
manner,' he told Margaret Cole, 'not because I believe in retribution,
which I don't but because I believe [and here he was quoting her] "that
such sources of a revived aggression as we can get at should be
removed".' Still more important was to dispossess 'Big Business',
which had made possible the Nazis' rise; in his book he went so far as
to say that at the end of the war it might be necessary to kill Hitler and
'quite a number of others' to protect society. He stipulated that the
Germans must do the killing and the Allies stay out of it.

The planned 25,000-word pamphlet swelled over Christmas to 40,000 and ended up in late January as a 70,000-word manuscript (dedicated to Vita and Francesca 'for being so patient and quiet' while he was writing it). It included a long section on the deficiencies of the Atlantic Charter from the socialist point of view. In his foreword he left his readers in no doubts about his bellicosity:

> [This essay] is about winning the peace. I have always held, and hold now if possible more strongly than ever, that winning the war is more important than winning the peace: and that, if either the one or the other had to be sacrificed, it must be, without hesitation, the second rather than the first. If I thought for a moment that Vansittartism of the less unworthy sort, or even the extreme of hatred and revenge against the German people, were necessary for winning the war, then I should keep silent, and fall back on the desperate expedient of helping to undo the evil in the moment of victory. But I am convinced that this propaganda, by compromising with the spirit of the thing it is fighting, impedes victory; for it robs our war-effort of a dynamic as powerful for good as the Nazis' is for evil, as surely as it plays into the hands of Dr Goebbels and so weakens the growing movement of German revolt. And, even if other things were only equal, it cannot be a matter of complete indifference whether victory is to be followed by another war in five, ten, twenty, or 'even' fifty years' time: or whether the whole world is to be infected with the Nazi spirit of hatred . . .

Victor had persuaded Allen Lane to issue *Shall Our Children Live or Die?* as a Penguin, with an initial print of 100,000. In the event he could not bear to let it out of his own hands. Besides, Lane could not guarantee to publish in under a month. (He offered it again to Penguin at the end of the year when the hard-back market seemed sated. In view of Victor's refusal hitherto to let any Gollancz books go to paperback, this was a piece of effrontery. Lane refused with great courtesy.) Victor found a printer to do him a personal favour and the book came out within a fortnight. A low price, superb pre-publication puffs (Acland and Liddell Hart), several warm reviews and lavish expenditure on advertising helped to bring the sales to 50,000 copies. The book did a great deal to dispel the widespread view that the Germans had a double dose of original sin. Even outside socialist circles, its effect was undeniable, and it provoked a 72-page rebuttal entitled *Gollancz in German Wonderland*, written by two German refugees.* Its purpose was to prove that post-war Germany must be

---

*It was an interesting irony that one of the authors, Carl Herz, who had been an international socialist and mayor in pre-Nazi Germany, was married to the sister of Israel Gollancz's widow, with whom the Herzes lived.

unilaterally disarmed and kept under control until she abjured her militaristic philosophy: it would be necessary to purge not just the superstructure, but the permanent administration and the courts.

There were few readers prepared to go all the way with Victor. His utter condemnation of hatred even of the worst Nazis was too much — in the middle of a bitter war — for all but fervent adherents of the Christian-socialist or humanist ethic in its highest form. Nor were there many left-wingers who believed that the Germans, if left to themselves, would organize a socialist revolution. Right-wing opinion, meanwhile, saw him advocating the replacement of one kind of oppression by another. In treating such an idiosyncratic book, even the most sympathetic reviewers found something to quibble with. Victor responded, of course. He complained to the *Sunday Times* that the reviewer had not read him properly and displayed two tendencies common among 'so-called socialists': strong emotional sympathy with Vansittartism and contempt for a 'straight socialist solution'. Rose Macaulay, at his behest, replied to an accusation, in the *Spectator* review, that he was fomenting class-hatred.

The hundreds of letters he received about *Shall Our Children Live or Die?* were a testimony to his ability to provoke, persuade and inspire. He published extracts from 67 of them in the April *Left News*. The correspondence as a whole, he said in his introduction,

> strongly reinforces a conclusion to which I have been coming for very many years. I do not want to say here what that conclusion is: I want rather to ask members to write to me, for publication in a later issue of the 'News', *their* conclusions. I will only say about my own conclusion that it is, on balance, one of hope, and that all mixed up with it is a belief that our appeal should be to reason, to commonsense, and above all to what is best in men and women, and not to what is worst.

His selection of extracts made it clear that Victor's conclusion had to do with the importance of individual effort in the struggle for a just society; many of them spoke of a need to make a personal contribution to the improvement of Britain and the world. The keynote was hope, but there was widespread doubt about the means by which good intentions could be put into practice. The strong message of his correspondents was that they needed leadership: Victor, in April 1942, with the CP, the Soviet Union and now Vansittart substantially off his list of jobs, was in the mood to provide it. He had had some time for reflection immediately after finishing *Shall Our Children Live or Die?*, laid low with what was diagnosed as pseudo-angina, brought on by over-work and too many cigars. With no political work mapped out other than the usual speaking engagements, a little work on the CCC and ASPRA, membership of the 1941 Committee and the Fabian Society's Socialist Propaganda Committee and participation in the furtherance of the anti-Vansittart campaign, he was itching for some truly demanding cause to give urgency to his every waking moment. He thought he had found it amid the confusion of the Left.

Like many socialists, Victor felt the Labour members of the government had been feeble, failing to pursue their advantage by forcing the implementation of socialist policies. Inevitably, he under-rated their gains and overestimated their freedom of action. 'I looked in at the Labour Party Conference on Tuesday,' he wrote to Daphne du Maurier in June 1941, 'and was really horrified by its complete deadness and absolute complacency'. Like Bevan and his colleagues on the editorial board of *Tribune*, he strongly denounced the electoral pact between Labour and Conservative, but had little enthusiasm for Bevan's attempts to make *Tribune* a rallying-point for the disconten-ted Left. Although he remained on the editorial board along with Strauss until early 1942, personality and policy clashes made severance inevitable. Soon after, he also resigned as a director, probably over Bevan's unremitting hostility to Churchill.

During 1941 he had been part of an informal left-wing ginger group, the 1941 Committee, dominated by Richard Acland of Forward March and J. B. Priestley, whose wartime broadcasts rallying the common man had been a huge popular success. The twenty or so regulars included the Bishop of Bradford, Thomas Balogh, Cyril Joad, Kingsley Martin, A. D. Lindsay and Stanley Unwin. That attendance was so regular, Acland put down to the fact that the host, Edward Hulton (publisher of *Picture Post*), provided excellent grey-market food in a virtually bomb-proof cellar in Mayfair. Violet Bonham Carter was one of those who opted out of 'its woolly futility'. The Committee's finest hour was in September 1941, when it organized a conference of 200 people at Bedales School in Hampshire to discuss the Atlantic Charter and ways of bringing about a humane and stable post-war Europe. Then, in February 1942, it achieved some publicity with an open letter to the War Cabinet pressing for the creation of a 'vital democracy', to release the energies of the people in an imaginative way.

Victor's heart was not in it. The 1941 Committee's lack of real unity was exposed by Richard Acland, who had persuaded the group that it should support independents in by-elections. Acland, with Priestley, worked out a 'Nine-Point Declaration', to which independent by-election candidates would have to adhere as the price of the

Committee's support. The key issues were common ownership of property, vital democracy and political morality.

Acland's initiative caused problems for Victor, who was fond of him, agreed with him on almost all the political issues of the day and shared his underlying political and moral philosophy. By April 1942 he had himself scheduled for 30 and 31 May an LBC conference on how to make the progressive forces effective. As far as he was concerned, the issue came down to one of heart versus head. Acland was an inspiring speaker, a tireless organizer and a moral giant (as leader of Common Wealth he was to give away to the nation all but a tiny part of his vast inherited estates). Victor had given him the opportunity to disseminate his views through the *Left News* and from LBC platforms. His *What It Will Be Like in the New Britain* had been the December 1941 Choice. On the other hand, Victor always believed that Acland was irremediably upper-class and thus handicapped in attracting mass support. He doubted that any body other than the Labour Party could ever seriously challenge the Tories.

The Nine-Point Declaration of 2 May put Victor in a very difficult position *vis-à-vis* the LBC, now looking expectantly towards him for a lead. Laski and Strachey, though critical of Labour, were both far more committed members of the party than Victor (for all that he was president of his local constituency), and were convinced that Acland's initiative could only lead to a weakening of the party: it must be discouraged at all costs. Victor believed in using every means possible to spread the socialist message and the compromise he proposed to the Labour members of the 1941 Committee supports Garry McCullough's view that he attempted 'to adapt the political line of the "popular front" period to the circumstances facing the British Left in 1942.' Those circumstances were clear: the electoral truce seemed about to break up. Victor's compromise: in constituencies where a by-election promised a Labour victory, the 1941 Committee should support the party; in constituencies where Labour's chances were poor, a candidate of the 'non-working class movement' should be given Labour support.

Strachey and Kingsley Martin favoured the pragmatic *quid pro quo*. Laski did not. He wanted to push Labour to leave government if certain nationalization demands were not met. Victor took issue with him in a letter of 8 May. With the Labour Party Conference coming up, he was desperate to find a more realistic line. 'The alternative tactic that I want to propose is to press in every sort of way — at the conference, through the press that is friendly to us, through the Labour members of the Left Book Club groups, and so on — for the ending of the electoral truce . . . ' If the truce ended, the 'atomisation process' within the Left (which Laski abhorred) would end, thus strengthening the hands of the Labour leaders. The only purpose of the truce had been to avoid distracting the government in war time. Independents were already providing distraction by their by-election challenges, so the reason for the truce had gone. After recent speeches at Oxford and Bristol, said Victor, he had found unanimous enthusiasm for ending the truce. 'What, therefore, I personally would like to see at the [LBC] conference would be that we should urge those members of Left Book Club groups who are members of the Labour Party to do everything in their power, through their organisations, to get the truce renounced.' He would not oppose Laski if he felt it necessary to have a head-on clash with Acland, but he was against it.

> You can look at Acland in two ways: as a man spreading the idea of socialism, and as a practical politician. The club also has two aspects — it is primarily a body for spreading socialist propaganda, but also we want, through the groups, to take political action.
>
> On the question of Acland as a propagandist for socialism you and I do, of course, differ. You don't like his 'righteousness' approach: I do (in fact, I believe that, in very modern times, I invented it!). I feel quite sure that you underestimate Acland's power, by his freshness and burning sincerity, to reach large numbers of people that could not be reached in any other way. I never overestimate the importance of isolated letters: but the mass of correspondence that is reaching me from every quarter seems to me quite conclusive.

As a propagandist, Acland would be an invaluable ally for the LBC: together they would be much more effective than singly in winning many people over to socialism. The worst result would be hostility between two groups of the Left. A *modus vivendi* must be sought. The dangers of atomization should be pointed out to 'one's own Labour Party people'. In his recent speeches Victor had warned them to stick with the party and

> not go a-whoring after false gods. We should *qua* Labour Party people, try to retain our people in the Party, and try to get them to make more members: but I don't think we help this end by attacking those who are putting forward what is in effect a socialist programme.
>
> None of which means that I don't entirely agree with you that there is infinitely more chance of winning power through the organised working class movement than in any other way: and I have made this view perfectly clear to Acland . . .

Of course, just as you wouldn't take a line at the LBC to which I didn't agree, I need not tell you that I wouldn't dream of taking a line to which you were hostile.

No compromise proved possible. At the end of May the Labour Party Conference approved the electoral truce by a narrow majority. And at the ensuing LBC conference in the Royal Hotel, Laski and Strachey on one side and Acland and Tom Wintringham on the other fought it out to a courteous stalemate. Victor kept his promise and took no sides. He was encouraged by the laudatory speeches about the Club, full of optimism about its future as a propaganda group. In his summing up at the conference he urged individual effort to spread sanity and enlightenment. He had come to believe, he said, that this was another historic moment for the Club. As in 1936, there was an 'awakening of large sections of the population which have never been "political" before; and there is a wonderful opportunity for the Left Book Club so to take and train these people in socialism that they can never be caught by any fascist movement.'

In truth, Victor was only in lukewarm support of the programme he outlined. Had he been free to come in on the Common Wealth Party, born in July with the merger of Forward March and the 1941 Committee, probably he might well have been fired by the scale of the organizational challenge. (Despite their close friendship, he would then, of course, almost certainly have tried to wrest the leadership from Acland.) Slow, patient work to nudge people gently in a socialist direction was not his style, especially when wartime conditions ruled out any dramatic upsurge in membership or great rallies in the Albert Hall. His temporary enthusiasm for the Acland initiative had led him to try to reactivate the groups, but after the LBC conference he decided, for rather unconvincing reasons, not to send them any organizers from the centre. His heart was not in it. To Margaret Cole he wrote in July 1942 that he saw the future of England as an economy run 'by some such combination' as Oliver Lyttelton (Conservative minister, from a business background), Cripps and Keynes, in alliance with the trade unions. 'I believe,' he went on to say, 'the important thing is to recognise in our own minds that this is likely to happen, and the grave danger of it, and to work for giving the arrangement a "leftward" tendency.' It was a dull prospect after six years caught up in highly emotional causes. Its unattractiveness caused him to decide to renounce for ever his ambitions to be an MP. The *Left News* shows that he never even tried to get the members going. After Laski blocked his amended 'popular front' idea, he left the membership to get on with it. The *Left News* was filled with useful articles on socialism in all its various manifestations, and more particularly, the International Socialist Forum, but from mid-1942 Victor's presence in its columns was negligible.

For a time, during the summer of 1942, he read widely for a projected book on the relationships between psychology, economics and politics: it would, he predicted, take him five years. He made relatively few public appearances. Then, as the summer and autumn wore on, he again became involved in a cause. This time the emotional strain was to be too much.

Although Victor had given substantial help to individual Jewish refugees, the first hint that he was making the problem of European Jewry his own came in July 1942, when, along with Brailsford and others, he was recruited to the Jewish Fighting Force Committee — after years of estrangement from the Jewish establishment. To join such an organization was a major step for Victor; his antipathy to British Jewry had never really diminished since the days of his youth.

Through Ruth he had met a network of sophisticated in-laws, deeply concerned about the future of the Jewish people. In the late twenties he had even had some informal contact with Zionist pressure groups. Still he kept Jews *qua* Jews at arm's length, and his relationship with Leonard Stein, a leader among Anglo-Jewish Zionists, had nothing but a negative effect. A change in his attitudes, of course, had come from 1933 onwards, but though he knew that Jews were being persecuted, tortured and killed on the Continent, he had only a glimmer of the ghastly truth. Until 1942, he resisted any suggestion or internal prompting that Jews were anything special to him.

Contact with Jewish sources during that summer made him realize that he had been seriously underestimating (in common with the rest of the world) the horrors to which Nazi policies were leading. By now, evidence from Europe on the extent of the extermination programme, was building up remorselessly. Victor had heard enough by August to realize that anti-semitism could no longer be put on a par with other evils: the Nazis had made it the greatest wickedness of all.

Of the major chapters of his life, this is the least well documented. It seems that he was at first in such a state of confusion and emotional turmoil that he could not trust himself to write about it. There are only a few clues to his state of mind, but they are telling ones. One was the sacking (a rare occurrence) of a member of staff, with salary in lieu of notice, on 21 August 1942. In Sheila Hodges' letter to the dismissed man (Victor got her to do the job), she wrote: 'If you reflect a moment, I think you will see that it is impossible for a firm, whose head is a Jew, to continue the employment of anyone who not merely feels an extreme antipathy towards the Jews (which is, of course, entirely a man's private affair) but is also unable to restrain his expression of these views in the office.'

In the *Left News*, in November, he began the serialization of *Race and Racism* by the anthropologist, Ruth Benedict, for the benefit of members 'who wish to clear their own minds and to help others to see clearly, both about the noxious Nazi doctrine of racism and about the hardly less noxious forms of the same doctrine that are to be found, in a disguised form, among a certain percentage of other populations.' By December, he had met the Polish underground emissary, Jan Karski, and had heard in detail about the extermination of Polish Jews. He was in a state of near-hysteria. As was all too typical of Victor, it was in absurd over-reaction to a harmless criticism that he first wrote on a vital subject.

In a *New Statesman* review of an Ogden Nash collection, the reviewer had attacked the principle of pre-publication puffs: 'on the back cover, under tributes from rival publishers, we find Mr Victor Gollancz exclaiming "I adore Ogden Nash". How nice, how very nice, for Mr Nash, to be the adored of Mr Gollancz! Is it mutual, one wonders, and will Mr Gollancz's next pamphlet on Vansittartism bear a declaration from Mr Nash, "Victor is my honey-bun"?' On 14 December, Victor wrote to John Hadfield of the publisher, J. M. Dent.

> I have just seen the enclosed from the 'New Statesman'.
>
> I do not, I think I feel as honestly as anyone can feel anything, care about the personal aspect: it would, indeed, show a lack of sense of proportion to bother at such a time about a tiny personal pinprick. But am I wrong in thinking that there is another aspect, which is perhaps not so unimportant? The opinions of three publishers are quoted by you: mine is picked out by Stonier [the reviewer], and the other publishers' names are not mentioned. I cannot help thinking that, however, unconsciously (and, as I do not know Mr Stonier, I am quite prepared to believe that it is indeed unconscious), I am picked out in this way because I am a Jew. If this is not so, why Gollancz rather than, let us say, Faber, who is certainly as well known?
>
> The whole implication is, of course: 'What a self-advertiser the man is', and the more stupid and thoughtless type of reader will say: 'How self-advertising the Jews are'. This is not altogether without importance at the present time, when, while four million Jews are being murdered in the most horrible circumstances in Europe, anti-semitism is increasing so rapidly in this country that it is by no means uncommon to hear people saying (even in the midst of the European Pogroms): 'There is one good

thing at least that Hitler has done, and that is the way he has dealt with the Jews.'

Hadfield might therefore like to tell Stonier that Victor had merely given the puff as a friendly gesture to another publisher. 'I hope you do not think I am being unduly sensitive: if you think I am, you will excuse me with the thought that it is perhaps not unnatural for a Jew to be over-sensitive at the present moment.'

'It isn't for me to say,' answered Hadfield,

> 'whether you're over sensitive or not. Heaven knows, there is enough justification for every Jew in Europe to be over-sensitive just now. For my part, however, I didn't care for Stonier's reference to you, but it never remotely occurred to me that any anti-Jewish element entered into it. I took it as a wisecrack at the expense of — or merely prompted by — your undoubted eminence in the public view. You may say Faber is quite as well known, but his fame is of a more placid and uncontroversial kind. Victor Gollancz, whether he wishes it or not, hits the headlines with a bigger bang than any other publisher, and is consequently fair game for the commentator or humorist. It would require Mass Observation to assess the extent to which this is due to (a) a dynamic personality, (b) anti-Vansittartism, (c) the Left Book Club, (d) your publishing scoops, and (e) the fact that you are a Jew. I'd be inclined to give about 5 per cent to the last component, not more.
>
> However, as I say, I didn't like Stonier's comment, chiefly because it seemed petty and beside the point. Now you mention it, I can see that a certain type of reader may react to it anti-semitically, and for that reason I'm sending your letter to Stonier . . .
>
> I'm sorry this has happened. It is an unpleasant return for your friendly gesture towards the book.

At last, in December 1942, many realized that, without drastic action, millions more Jews would be wiped out. Their horror was compounded by the impossibility of persuading those in powerful positions that anything could be done to arrest the holocaust. Through the work of Jewish organizations and a number of sympathetic politicians the message had at last got through to the government that the cumulative evidence of the reports was not to be shrugged off. But in the House of Commons, on 17 December, Eden could promise little more than the exaction of retribution for these crimes once the war was won. Asked what could be done in the meantime to save Jewish lives, he replied that 'we shall do all we can to alleviate these horrors, though I fear that what we can do at this stage must inevitably be slight.'

Every day of inaction meant more death, yet at domestic and international level there continued political justifications for entry-quota restrictions. Victor, lacking direct political power, could throw behind the cause only his weight as writer, publicist, committee worker and speaker. He did so unstintingly for the first half of 1943. His first major contribution was the 16,000-word pamphlet, *Let My People Go*, which he wrote at Christmas at Brimpton. Its powerful content and simple style made it the most moving of all his publications. He had no need to exaggerate his case: the facts spoke for themselves. And his appeal for action had about it nothing Utopian or ideological. He wrote directly for anyone — conservative or socialist — who cared about the preservation of human life. The issue was straightforward. Of the six million Jews in pre-war Europe, one to two million had already been deliberately murdered in circumstances of unspeakable brutality.

> This policy, which has been pursued since the outbreak of the war, has been greatly speeded up during the last few months. It is now reaching its climax. *Unless something effective is done*, within a very few months these six million Jews will all be dead, except the fifty thousand or so in the countries at present neutral, and perhaps a few tens of thousands whom Hitler may find it convenient to work to the last ounce of their strength in his own war factories.

The policy of promising retribution was not only wrong; it would save not a single life.

His proposals were straightforward: the Allies should work out a rescue plan and approach Germany and other Axis governments to let the Jews out to countries of refuge; Jews should be exchanged where possible for enemy nationals; sympathetic countries (with Britain giving the lead in generous spirit) should undertake vastly to increase their intake of refugees (these plans he worked out in some detail); and many more Jewish immigrants should be allowed into Palestine. 'No Zionist with any sense of responsibility would use the present desperate situation for political, that is to say for Zionist, purposes. But equally no one, whether Zionist or not, could leave Palestine out of the picture as a means of dealing with the immediate crisis, just because Palestine is a centre of political difficulties.' The refusal of people to make exceptions to meet this desperate need was, he rightly concluded, a failure of imagination. Introducing a section on the nature and scope of the atrocities, he begged his readers to do something 'which is as painful as it is necessary'.

> You will read that ten thousand Jews are being sent every day from Warsaw to the slaughter camps further east: you will read that one hundred and fifty

men, women and children are being packed into a sealed coach just big enough to hold forty, so that when they arrive the living, the dying, and the dead fall out together, and the peasants fly from the stench. Forget 'ten thousand': forget 'one hundred and fifty': or rather, remember them only for purposes of multiplication, and in order to grasp the magnitude of the horror. For a few brief moments, *be* just one of those human beings, whose body, with its nerves that can suffer so, and whose mind and soul, with all their resources of terror and despair, are concealed by the cold abstractions of 'one hundred and fifty' and 'ten thousand' and 'six million.' And then be another, and another. Be the mother flinging her baby from a sixth-storey window: be a girl of nine, torn from her parents and standing in the dark of a moving truck with two corpses pressed close against her: be an old Jew at the door of the electrocution chamber. And only then, when you have been each of these for a few short moments, do the multiplication.

That done, each reader should go on to bring maximum influence to bear wherever possible on government, press, MPs, political parties, church or trade unions. 'Dare you refuse to do everything you humanly can? Dare you take upon yourself the responsibility of murder? For that is what it comes to. "A country," writes Mrs Blanche Dugdale in the *Spectator*, "that does not open its doors to those who are hunted by murderers participates in the crime"; and *you* are the country.'

The advance copies of *Let My People Go* were out within days: within three months it had sold 250,000 copies. It was translated into many languages and had a widespread circulation abroad, having a particularly deep effect in Palestine. Its success took Victor unawares. On 13 January he was telling someone that he kept his Saturdays and Sundays sacrosanct for reading for the major book he was planning. Only two weeks later he was crying off his annual lunch in London with his adored Daphne du Maurier:

> I am just off to Oxford for four days, speaking there on the Jewish business: I must be here [Brimpton] on Monday to clear up what will be frightful arrears: then I go to London from Tuesday morning till Thursday night, and literally have not only every meal but every second of the day taken up with interviews, etc., on this Jewish business: the work arising out of the pamphlet has been tremendous. I would cancel one of the meals in any other connection: but in this particular connection I dare not do so.

Among the venues at Oxford was the Union, where he had the greatest oratorical success of his life. He had a great deal going in his favour. The LBC years had turned him into a first-class public speaker; as those who worked with him could testify, he had the lungs and diaphragm of an opera singer, and when his rich voice throbbed with emotion, his listeners were held stationary. In Acland's view Victor was by now one of the country's dozen best speakers, capable on occasion of matching Churchill, or J. B. Priestley at the top of his form. If his listeners were out of sympathy with the content of his speech, the effect of his emotionalism could be negative, but when there was no such barrier, he swept them along with him.

At the Oxford Union he supported the motion 'That this House urges that a more energetic and practical policy be pursued by the Government towards the rescue of Jews in Europe'. He was not addressing natural followers, but in attacking the government he had an excellent case and he gave it all he had. At the end of the debate, the Opposer of the motion and all but a dozen of his followers got up and crossed the floor. It was an unparalleled triumph in that most cynical of chambers.

The speech tours went on, hand in hand with fund-raising, and to cope with his correspondence he had to open a special office. Meanwhile, there were innumerable meetings with those concerned with the broad issues, individual visa applications, or both. On 16 March 1943, when his article on progress to date appeared in the *Left News*, there was pitifully little to report. The government's main unilateral initiative had been to give permission for the Palestine immigrant quota actually to operate at the level agreed before the war. International solutions were being considered with painful slowness.

In the battle to get movement on the issue, Eleanor Rathbone was foremost among the many disaffected MPs. It was she who created the National Committee for Rescue from Nazi Terror, with the Marquess of Crewe as president and numerous religious leaders, MPs and other dignitaries among its vice-presidents. She took the unglamorous title of vice-chairman. Victor was a vice-president and member of the executive committee. Together, they were the organization's driving force. (Berl Locker of the Jewish Agency paid public tribute to Victor's tireless work many years later when he was under attack in Israel.) The committee worked to mobilize public opinion and MPs, but its 12-point programme of action (very similar to that in *Let My People Go*) bore little fruit. The committee and the executive committee each met weekly, and Victor took on (without the title) the work of honorary secretary. Although he was under no illusions that much could be achieved, he felt any amount of effort justified if it saved even one life. In March 1943 he anticipated devoting himself to it for many months, 'perhaps even for many years' and refused to take on any new commitments.

The appalling evidence that came before the committee haunted Rathbone for the rest of her life. On Victor, it had a devastating effect in the short term. Fearing that his speeches might become stale, he took too literally for comfort the advice he had given in *Let My People Go*, and began a practice of arriving at the speaking venue half an hour early. He would spend that time 'feeling myself, with all the wholeness I could manage, into the situation of people at Dachau or Buchenwald. One night I was being gassed in a gas-chamber: the next, I was helping others dig our own mass grave, and then waiting for the splutter of a machine-gun.'

Towards the end of June, his régime brought about a very serious nervous breakdown.

CHAPTER SIXTEEN

WAR: BREAKDOWN AND RECOVERY

VICTOR WAS SUCH a hypochondriac that his accounts of his own illnesses are always suspect, but on the gravity of his nervous breakdown, family evidence bears out his own autobiographical accounts. However, in attributing it directly to his identification with the Nazis' victims, he was simplifying matters. Certainly the crisis was precipitated by the horrors he subjected himself to, but there were other factors.

First, there was the background of overwork. He could maintain punishing schedules on very little sleep, but until 1936, there had been frequent and luxurious holidays, a marvellously varied social life and regular attendance at concert halls. Thereafter the holidays grew shorter and music and other diversions were sacrificed to the LBC and the Popular Front. From 1939 he took no holidays at all, virtually abandoned music (except for the gramophone) and his social life was mainly restricted to talking seriously with friends who came to Brimpton. He was drawing deeply on the reserves of his vitality and on his nervous energy. In the background too was the emotional upheaval of the Pact, with its consequences for several important relationships, and the necessity of admitting that he had sinned against moral standards he knew to be absolute.

Despite all this, right up to 1943, he appeared to be thriving. The year 1942 he recalled later as the happiest of his life since 1917 — his second year of wonder, joy and inner peace. In a passage in his memoirs that was less than frank by Victor's standards, he explained:

> On both occasions . . . certain human relationships were no doubt the immediate cause of the experience; and on both occasions it may have had, again in an immediate sense, a physical and perhaps even narrowly sexual basis. But it was essentially religious none the less, by which I mean that it was an experience of greater access to reality: an experience that foreshadowed what release from division and reunion with reality — . . . 'the restoration of all things' — might be like: and an experience of the fact that this reality, which came to meet a man and encompass him, while he

was himself yet already included in it, could not be less of a Person than he knew himself to be but on the contrary must be immeasurably more of one.

It expressed itself notably in a heightened perception of those things of which he was always unusually conscious: 'the greenness, the freshness, the slenderness, the littleness, the gentleness, the strength, the taperingness, the sun-acceptingness, the daisy-and-buttercup-enclosingness, of the benign and far-stretching grass.' It was unaffected by the simultaneous consciousness of horror going on all around him: he seemed able to experience the ecstasy on one plane while suffering agony on another.

The 1917 year of wonder had not been followed by a nervous collapse, but more than a quarter-century on, Victor was physically, mentally and emotionally exhausted, as well as trying and failing to come to terms with sexual guilt. In an oblique reference (for Victor —in deference to Ruth — displayed some seemly inhibition about publishing details of his infidelity) in *My Dear Timothy*, he implies that suppressed guilt was an element in the 1943 episode, although he relates it rather to guilt suppressed as a child. Its importance as a contributory cause was to be made manifest in some of the symptoms of his nervous breakdown.

According to a letter he wrote in June 1961 to Berl Locker (furnishing details omitted from his autobiography) the first symptoms appeared after a month or so of going through the pre-speech imaginings: 'A rather terrible thing happened: I began to get what Christians call "stigmata". My body began to burn intolerably, and my skin became so sensitive that I could feel gravel through my boots, and a walk of even two or three minutes produced huge blisters. This gradually developed into an appalling hyperaesthesia generally that developed into total insomnia.' There were outward signs in the red spots that spread over his body, in his inability to sleep and in the prolonged and desperate explosions of temper which he unleashed on Ruth, different in violence and duration from those to which she was accustomed. They horrified Vita and terrified Francesca, who wept at their severity and the strain under which they were putting her mother. Afterwards, there were violent fits of crying in which he begged to be forgiven.

Inwardly, he said in *More For Timothy*, 'a dirty sort of pain, low, vague and indiscriminate, possessed the whole of my body, and made me abominable to my consciousness.' Along with this went a sense of social degradation, utter dereliction and a perpetual fear that promised to last forever. For the first and only period in his life, he wished for oblivion and death. More particularly there developed a terrifying symptom that occurred several times daily:

> the instant I sat down, whether to eat or read or talk or rest or attempt a sort of stupefied doze, my member would disappear: I would feel it retiring into my body, and would know myself, with a catch of the breath and a stab at the stomach, as not only unmanned but dehumanised. The reason for this phenomenon is obvious: just as the *membrum erectum* gives a confident greeting to the life in another, and would be one with it, so if a man is in terror of life . . . his member has the impulse . . . to shrivel and vanish; and the movement of muscles that sitting involves gives this impulse its chance.

There is another and more obvious inference to be drawn as to why his worst symptom afflicted his sexual organ.

Lord Horder diagnosed his condition as hyperaesthesia — extreme sensitivity of nerve endings — and prescribed sleeping pills which for a long time had no effect.

It was in June that the seriousness of his condition first became apparent. On 7 June, he was working at high speed on translating Edmond Fleg's *Why I Am a Jew* and was planning to finish it within a fortnight. This slight but moving memoir, written in 1927, concerned Fleg's youthful rejection of Judaism and all its practices, his rediscovery of a feeling of solidarity with Jews after the Dreyfus affair, and his ultimate arrival at a joyous understanding of the spiritual beauties of the religion, pride in his people's tenacious tradition of a familiar relationship with God, and an absolute commitment to Zionism. If, as the timing suggests, it was the emotional effect of the book, heightened by fear for his old friends the Flegs — caught in occupied France — that finally tipped Victor over the edge, then identification with his people had indeed come with a vengeance. He abandoned the translation as his insomnia took a terrifying grip, and Ruth took him to Scotland in the hope that rest would cure him. For some days, there were no signs of improvement. In hotels at Craigelachie and Nethy Bridge he continued to suffer the hopeless misery of an outcast. He met in Scotland the biologist, Sir D'Arcy Thompson, who talked to him of wild flowers, and William Walton, who played the piano for him, but his intercourse with them 'was like the gaiety of a man who goes about on his lawful occasions after committing a murder, and the music and small flowers were but reminders of a paradise lost. The subjectivity of my pariahdom, and the absence of all basis for my terror that decent people would outlaw me, cannot affect my understanding of what, in the heart of a pariah, pariahdom must mean.'

Horder had warned him that he might never sleep without an anaesthetic, a desperate measure Victor was afraid to try.

One forenoon, when my terror and despair seemed to be at their height . . . I set out for a walk with my wife. We went very slowly, my arm resting on hers: for my body was weak after a total insomnia that had lasted for twenty-two days, and every muscle and nerve in it ached . . . About half an hour later we turned, sharply left, into a dark and open space — a sort of water-meadow, with herds grazing, and a high inland cliff just in front of us. There was dappled sunlight everywhere, and a slight breeze. I felt suddenly very still: and then I heard the inland cliff, and the grass and water and sky, say very distinctly to me 'A humble and contrite heart He will not despise'. When I say I heard them say it I mean, quite literally, that I *heard* them say it: a voice came from them: but they were also themselves the voice, and the voice was also within me . . . I said to my wife 'The trouble is over': and that night I slept a little. The trouble, in one sense, was not over, for a year or two were to pass before it was more or less completely behind me: I was nevertheless right, because thenceforth, even at the worst moments, there was always a glimmer of light, however minute, at the end of the tunnel . . . And now it is only by the greatest effort of will, if even so, that I can realise in recollection that terror and that despair, which have long appeared nothing to me; and when I live again in those days, as I often do, I live in the love that faithfully cared for me and saw me through to safety.

'The love that faithfully cared for me' — certainly, the debt that Victor owed to Ruth was never so obvious as during 1943. For years she had put up with demands of a kind that few would have found tolerable: Victor's need to know her whereabouts precisely, his terror if she was delayed, his childish tempers, his selfishness and egocentricity, his daily need for praise and reassurance, and his requirement that whatever he did, however he drove himself and whatever path he trod, Ruth would be beside him giving practical help and telling him he was right. In 1943 he was in despair, and though in his reminiscences he makes it seem a solitary affliction, in truth he communicated the condition violently to Ruth. 'Ruth just loved me' was how he put it later, yet she did so through travails that few could have endured without collapse. Many of their common acquaintances found her rather impersonal and reserved: that is not surprising. She subjugated her own spontaneity and kept almost all the warmth she had for her insatiable husband. From June to October of 1943 she was with him almost every moment, night and day, assuring him of steadfast love. She played for him endlessly on the gramophone the 78 rpm records that needed changing every few minutes. Francesca remembers her playing an entire opera as he slept, lest he might wake if it stopped. In future years he was frequently to treat her as badly as he had ever done, but he never forgot his debt, nor failed to take opportunities to acknowledge it to her and proclaim it to others.

After Scotland, the Gollanczes returned to Brimpton, but for some months Victor took little part in the affairs of the firm. Gradually, over the next year or so, he worked himself back into running it in the old way. There was one hangover from the breakdown which continued for a time even after the war. Back in Henrietta Street, some of his colleagues discovered that though his affair had ended, he was suffering from what can only be described as hysterical venereal disease. True to form, Victor's desperate period of spiritual and mental agony gave rise, at the end, to an episode of total absurdity. Experiencing what he thought to be the symptoms of VD, he felt the need for regular inspection of his penis. Frequently, alone in his office, he would betake himself to the frosted window, open his trousers and check anxiously for tell-tale signs. This practice came to an end when he received a letter from the staff of the theatre across the road, pointing out in a charming way that the window panes were more transparent than he had thought.

By the winter of 1943, he had regained a certain peace of mind. He had finished and published the Fleg translation, offering his work 'to the memory of my father, a man of simple honour whom I failed to understand; and also to a Jewish woman, one of those of whom it was written "Blessed are the pure in heart, for they shall see God"'. Additionally, he had read a great deal in the literature of darkness of soul and recovery therefrom. Poetry, fiction, biography, and spiritual writings that dwelt on the ascent from the depths of spiritual bleakness through serenity to joy had nourished his glimmer of light. (This reading was the basis for his two anthologies, *A Year of Grace* and *From Darkness to Light*, published in 1950 and 1955 respectively.) He had learned too that the best way of defeating insomnia was not to care whether you did or did not sleep. A sleeping pill helped, as did the gramophone music. (This was only a temporary phase: Victor disapproved of recorded or broadcast music for a great deal of his life, because it encouraged familiarity and robbed music of the vital element of communion with other listeners.)

Victor was later to feel deep gratitude for his breakdown, as a lesson in the meaning of suffering and acceptance. It had a considerable effect on his development as a writer and preacher; it was also to make him a patient and sensitive comforter to many undergoing mental suffering. But learning to be in charity with himself did not make him any more patient or reasonable in his dealings with ordinary people who affronted or threatened him. He was hardly back part-time at the office when he became embroiled in a dispute that cost him a valued author and further soured his relationship with an agent. It is an illuminating insight into Victor's behaviour as a wartime publisher.

Throughout the war, it was the exigencies of paper rationing that dominated the trade, placing a strain on author/publisher relationships. From 60 per cent of 1939 usage, the quota had fallen in 1942 to $37\frac{1}{2}$ per cent, whence it climbed painfully slowly to $42\frac{1}{2}$ per cent in October 1944. Where many publishers agonized together in the Publishers Association (PA) over how their quotas should be eked out, Victor continued to operate as the fancy took him. His needs were in any case exceptional. He liked to keep himself free to satisfy at short notice the market's demand for any manuscript he thought worthy. When it came to books of no political importance, he liked to keep matters simple and print 100,000 copies of Cronin or du Maurier, rather than tinker with small re-printings of books by ten or twenty less well-known authors. That suited Cronin, but du Maurier jibbed a little. 'I hate', she wrote once, 'to think that you might have to turn down four other novels, for my awful bloated book. Would it not be possible for you to print say 70,000 copies of "The King's General", and not 100,000? Thus saving the extra paper for the other people?' Victor graciously agreed, but maintained his strategy. He was in any case well ahead of his competitors in instituting economies with thin paper and unusually small typefaces.

At the end of 1941 the Ministry of Supply had offered to make available for book publishers another 250 tons, equivalent to an extra 2 per cent, provided the PA could prove it was being used properly. Most members were delighted to apply for the bonus specifically for the production of 'essential' books. They were taken aback in the spring of 1942 by the opposition of a small group of publishers, led, in a beautiful irony, by two champions of freedom of speech — Victor Gollancz and Douglas Jerrold. Victor denied any committee the right to decide between the relative merits of Karl Marx and the New Testament: Jerrold was totally opposed to anything that smacked of government interference.

The Gollancz-Jerrold cabal was defeated (by chicanery, Victor thought) in the row over what became known as the 'Moberly Pool'. The row had the happy result of bringing the two of them back to friendship: forced at the beginning of March 1942 into a stiff collusion, by mid-March they were back on 'My dear Douglas', 'My dear Victor' terms, and Jerrold was happily writing to Victor of the next PA meeting: 'I shall be there to wave my little red flag and trust that you will be there with your little Union Jack'. Victor rediscovered the joy of Jerrold's sardonic wit and Jerrold the exhilaration of Victor's company. From then until Jerrold's death they were to lunch together for the sheer pleasure of each other's company, continuing political differences in no way affecting their mutual affection.

To the trade at large, however, Victor was once more a disagreeable renegade. The PA had put a great deal of work into improving the general conditions of the publishing trade, and he was queering the pitch. (It was an organization with which he dealt solely when he needed it.) That October, he was locked in a violent controversy with Fredric Warburg, who had suggested a post-war planning committee to improve publishing. Suggested measures included preventing the distribution of anti-social or blatantly pornographic books. Allen Lane had given the idea a measure of support, and Victor intervened. 'The present war', he concluded his letter to *The Times Literary Supplement*,

> is a vast episode in a battle of far wider breadth and depth — the battle for the freedom and development of human personality. That freedom is the end; everything else is mere means and machinery, about which there can and must be innumerable differences of opinion. But about the end there can be no compromise; you are either for it or against it; and if you are against it, you sin against the Holy Ghost. Writers, and in a humbler way publishers, are by their very vocation called to lead the army of emancipation; and for even a single publisher to be on the enemy's side is a blasphemy.

Though sorely tried later, Victor never reneged on his commitment to complete freedom of speech. Meanwhile his stand against any kind of planning mechanism in publishing, even for such matters as improved wages, somewhat perplexed those who knew him mainly as a publisher of socialist tracts. In fact, that stand made sense when taken in conjunction with his allegations that various PA agreements were, effectively, restrictive trade practices. Yet he usually signed the agreements under protest. (An important exception was the new Net Book Agreement in 1957. 'Net' prices were fixed retail prices which could not be discounted. Gollancz was the only publishing house to refuse to sign this, on the grounds that it was a restriction on freedom — but Victor was glad to shelter behind it, and kept strictly to its terms.) Only casuistry could explain his attempt in autumn 1943 to persuade the PA to combine against agents and authors.

Again A. D. Peters was the offending agent. The previous spring he had threatened to claim back from publishers the rights to books by those clients of his whose entire output remained out of print. Victor had partially circumvented him by appealing over his head to Lettice Cooper, Negley Farson, Phyllis Bentley and L. A. G. Strong. Farson had complained that Victor's political work made him inaccessible, and Strong was smarting from accusations of bad behaviour, but they all backed Victor against Peters. Nevertheless, a modest reprint of at least one book by each of them was undertaken. Victor had given ground, and it niggled him.

During his absence the firm had been run efficiently by Hodges, Horsman and Dunk. Sheila Hodges, in effect managing director, had risen with great adaptability to the challenge, and everything had run smoothly during the summer. When Victor returned to the office he had been horrified to discover that a one-book contract had been signed with Strong, at his request (Hodges, of course, being in no position to initiate disputes with agents or authors). Victor had some reasonable cause for complaint: even before his illness, Strong's desire for a one-off contract had been known but, through a tangle of communications failures, the issue had not been raised with him. They had a meeting, after which Strong wrote to re-affirm his unwillingness to sign up for three books. 'Your proposal', he wrote,

> is that I should either go elsewhere — which you say you do not want — or that I should sign a three-book contract, and afterwards make such representations as I may wish, in reply to which you promise nothing but that they shall be heard in a friendly spirit. In other words, I must put myself in your hands absolutely.
>
> Before deciding to do this, I feel obliged to consider one or two other things which you said. The first was that, if your choice lay between reprinting a work of fiction and publishing a new book of political or social importance, you would not hesitate to give the paper to the latter . . . there is no guarantee that your ethical zeal might not go further, to discriminate against a new work of fiction. . . .
>
> Before you reply that this is a distortion of what you said, remember that you have in effect asked for an absolute vote of confidence. You have asked for the abdication on my side of all bargaining rights. You say, you will not negotiate at the pistol's point. Might it not be fairer to say that, on your own showing, you will not negotiate at all? . . .
>
> You said, in reply to a remark of mine, that it would be only reasonable if I had considerations to raise about the reprinting of some of my books after the war. Later on, you said that you would of course remember to

their credit those authors who had behaved well, and their books would have the first call. The good boys would be rewarded. That left me to reflect that, as Peters and I had not been good boys, — ?

He had, he said, taken advice from three objective sources. All had concluded that Victor's demand was less than reasonable. 'In fact, two of the three used the adjective "dictatorial".' He ended with expressions of regret that he had become a bone of contention between 'two old and valued friends'.

It is rare to find any correspondence in which Victor's recollection of a verbal confrontation accorded with that of his opponent. This was no exception. Strong, he averred, had not only distorted his words, but was aware that he had done so. Victor had merely been talking about using a small typeface for novels in order to save paper for books on politics and sociology. He had a 'call' to publish progressive political literature, but was no less a 'keen' fiction publisher than anyone else. Surely Strong knew him well enough to know he would do the best for any book he published, and that his 'call' could not be fulfilled unless the general list flourished? He had taken 'hardly' an earlier threat of Strong's to reclaim the rights to his out-of-print cheap editions. Then had come his request for a one-book contract. Rebuking him for imagining Victor capable of nourishing resentment against ill-behaved authors, Victor denied being dictatorial: Strong was in no way in his power and was absolutely free to do as he wished.

He offered three options: sticking to the one-book contract for the already set book, cancelling the agreement (Gollancz to bear the cost of composition), or signing a three-book contract. There could be no preliminary parley, but after signing he would be happy to discuss with Strong any points he wished to raise. He ended by making it clear that it was option three that he favoured.

Strong responded, holding to his recollection of Victor's words on reprinting priorities and grateful authors. And he was unrepentant about the cheap editions: Victor had reprinted none until the 'threat'. 'To be consistent, ought you not to have refused out of hand?' Common sense made it impossible for him to sign a contract of the kind proposed. Though he knew that Victor would be generous, it was wrong in principle that one party to a contract should have to trust to the other's magnanimity. 'Such an arrangement may be good for your *amour propre*, but it's bad for mine. It's not equitable and I won't do it.' With 'real unhappiness' at a breach after fourteen harmonious years, he parted company with Victor. And as if to prove the truth of Strong's trust in his generosity, Victor, denying to the last that he had said the things attributed to him, annulled the one-book contract (thus losing the cost of setting the manuscript), and simultaneously waived all his rights in Strong's books, including *The Garden*, which was ready for reprinting. Such gestures always made him feel good, but they cost the firm money — as did his disapproval of certain authors' political lines. (A striking example was the rejection of *Animal Farm* in April 1944. 'I am highly critical of many aspects of internal and external Soviet policy: but I could not possibly publish . . . a general attack of this nature,' wrote Victor to Orwell's agent. Although Cape and Faber also turned it down, Gollancz suffered more, since Orwell was, to his relief, now at last free to take his fiction to a non-interfering publisher. Gollancz lost to Warburg not only *Animal Farm*, but *Nineteen Eighty-Four*, a book which was in tune with Victor's thinking when it was published in 1949. He later described Orwell as 'enormously overrated'.)

None of Victor's colleagues objected to the grand gestures that wrote off relatively paltry sums. Nor did they dispute his right to publish what he liked. Harder to bear was the occasional breach with a profitable or reputable author occasioned by Victor's whims or intransigence. In the short term there were plenty of fish in the sea, but in the long term it became increasingly damaging. It was another of Victor's internal contradictions that as he grew older, more accepting, wiser, and more spiritual, his sense of his own dignity increased and made him less inclined to accept the inevitable indignities of business. As a young publisher making his way he had frequently swallowed his pride; now his reputation was made, he could rarely bring himself to do so.

If it was incongruous that a man with a passion for liberty should try to force Strong to sign a three-book contract without negotiations; it seemed positively perverse that despite his deep-rooted objections to the PA he should ask it to gang up against Peters when the agent tried to force publishers to write approximate print numbers into contracts. The point emerging from such episodes was that Victor's preoccupation with liberty was directed at maximizing his own. Whereas other publishers might oppose new contractual rights for authors on business grounds, Victor fought against any potential shackle on his freedom of action.

Plausible justifications for arbitrary decisions had long ceased to surprise his colleagues, and most outsiders saw only a few of the twists and turns he made in the pursuit of absolute liberty for Victor Gollancz. His correspondence with Kingsford of the Cambridge University Press (about Peters' demand for estimates of print runs) was a classic of self-deception. 'I am most violently against anything which savours of a trade combination against the public: and for that reason, since I joined the Publishers' Association I have always scrutinised most carefully the various undertakings which from time to time one has been asked to sign, and have signed a minimum.' Examples followed.

> But the suggested form of undertaking, in this matter of demands for printing numbers, is by no means in the nature of conspiracy: on the contrary, it is an attempt to *defeat* a conspiracy . . . I regard this as a conspiracy by agents, not merely against the publishers, but, in the long run, against the authors too . . . agents are middlemen, and nothing whatever more.
>
> My own feeling is that once this business becomes general we are going to slide into the position that the only nexus between author and publisher is a cash one. More and more, in a growingly commercial age, this is happening: and I believe it to be disastrous — as I say, every bit as much in the interests of authors as in the interests of publishers. Efficient publishing, in my view, cannot possibly be done except on terms of trust between publisher and author: and how can there be that trust, if books are going to be auctioned according to the amount of paper that the publisher may have available at some particular moment?

The PA were unable to deliver him from this new conspiracy: some publishers had already agreed to the modification of contracts. Peters was not the only agent to press for it. On the whole the agents were reasonable men, but many were sick of Victor's whims and wished to tie him down.

Against the background of these rows he was easing himself back into a little public as well as publishing work. For a year after coming back to the office, though he undertook a number of speaking engagements or meetings he thought particularly important, he stayed well within the limits of his endurance. Ruth had found that the building up of their small pottery collection was an excellent and diverting hobby for him. Since the early twenties, starting with Leeds teapots, they had collected English pottery in a haphazard way, but it was not until he began convalescing from his breakdown that it became a passion. She was able to tempt him away from work to visit shops where another treasure might be found. Victor had a remarkable eye for fine specimens and he built up a collection that was widely envied. When he insured it in 1945, he estimated its worth at over £1,100 (junior clerks were then on £4 per week) and most of it had been acquired recently. He could have afforded much more, and he coveted a great deal more than he bought. Meanwhile, he continued as always to give away money — £200, £100 to causes (largely Jewish relief now); or £50, £20, £10 to individuals. His emotional commitment to the Jewish problem had not lessened. On 11 November 1943 he wrote to Norman Bentwich that he was reading

> for a little book of my own (probably not more than 30,000 to 40,000 words) to be called The Necessity for Zionism, which will deal with the matter from my own particular angle. I decided to do this the other day, as the result of an interview with one of the bigwigs of the movement: I was a good deal horrified by his general attitude, which seemed to have almost nothing in common with my own. Between ourselves, I have been made a rather important offer in connection with the movement: but I don't think I shall accept it, as I doubt whether I could 'work in'. In any case, I couldn't accept it before first going to Palestine — this might be a reason for going.
> Thanks, I am sleeping much better, but otherwise am pretty mouldy! The fact is, I suppose, that the present world-orgy of hatred and obliteration doesn't suit my condition.

What the job was is not documented, and events were to confirm that he could not 'work in', though for a time all was harmony with the Jewish community. He had been elected in June 1943 as a United Hebrew Congregation representative on the Jewish Board of Deputies — a considerable honour. Later he was appointed to their Defence and Publications sub-committees and on the latter in particular he proved to be a tremendously useful acquisition. After a few weeks' illness early in 1944 (physical, this time, though no doubt connected to his fraught state of mind), he gradually stepped up his work both for Jewish rescue and Zionism. He embarked on a programme of Judaic publications, and although none of them had the success of Why I Am a Jew, which sold over 26,000 copies, a steady stream of books and pamphlets emerged from Gollancz describing the persecution of the Jews, combating anti-semitism, exalting the successes of the Jews in Palestine and arguing in favour of Zionism.

He explained in May 1944 his conversion to Zionism in an address on 'The Jewish Problem in the Post-War World', given before a youth rally under the auspices of the Association of Jewish Refugees in Great Britain. The Jewish Chronicle covered it.

> Up to eighteen months ago, he had taken no active interest in Jewish affairs. He spoke that day from the standpoint of a Socialist and an internationalist, by which he meant one who wanted every nation in the world to be really free and really happy. The roots of the Jewish problem, in his opinion, lay in two incontrovertible facts: the Jews throughout the ages had refused to die and the non-Jewish world had persecuted them most horribly. He confessed that in the past he had been under the

impression that anti-semitism was of a sporadic nature but now he knew that there had been really one almost continuous wave of persecution lasting for 2,000 years. The results of these centuries of evil were mirrored in the distortion of character in a large number of Jews. They had been deprived of natural expression in statecraft, of access to the land, and of proper connection with working-class productive, mechanical, non-sedentary life.

Believing that the Jewish problem would be even graver after the war, and assimilation impossible, he was now convinced that some form of Zionism was the only solution. Palestine was the natural as well as national home of the Jewish people and there they should be totally self-governing. He was about to publish a book★ proving that Palestine could absorb 'many millions of people': it could be, should be and would be a model for the whole world. 'If I were a Jewish young man or woman who, like so many in the audience to-day, had been uprooted from the land I had called my own, I would look to-day to Palestine with a glorious, joyous singing in my heart.'

He was an important and valued recruit to the hard-pressed British Jewish lobby: further accolades included his appointment as a Governor of the Hebrew University of Jerusalem (for which he made out a covenant for £100 annually — a big gesture, as Victor loathed the commitment involved in signing a covenant). There was no doubt about the depth of his newly developed sense of Jewishness. His sensitivity about anti-semitism continued to make itself felt. In August 1944 it came out in his reaction to a manuscript by Eleanor Rathbone. His criticisms of *Falsehood and Facts about the Jews* ran to 2,500 words and were overall very damning:

> You will forgive me for saying that *if I had not known you* I should have said 'Here is a terrifically humanitarian woman who loathes any form of persecution and has an extremely strong sense of decency and justice: but it's perfectly clear that in her heart of hearts she really dislikes the Jews, and finds them objectionable. Of course I can't say whether I should have felt that because I was a Jew — that is to say, from over-sensitiveness: I can only say that I don't believe that to be the case. I came, as a matter of fact, myself to pro-Jewishness not at all as a Jew but as a universalist and hater of oppression. And if it makes that impression on *me*, surely it will make it a hundred times more on active or latent anti-Semites? And the moment that impression is produced, all logic goes by the board.

What had upset him was Rathbone's saying — to a gentile audience — that ostentation, flashiness, clannishness and other characteristics of

★W. C. Lowdermilk, *Palestine, Land of Promise.*

some Jews aroused dislike which was wrongly applied to all Jews. 'I would put it to you: apart from what you have *heard*, how many Jews have you actually *come across* to whom any of these things apply? It is the same with the legend of the "noisiness" and "loudness" of Jews. Whenever, in point of fact, I get a Jewish refugee working in my office, I am always struck by his extraordinary and indeed almost indecent quietness!' If there was anything in what Rathbone said, it was attributable to 'continental', not Jewish, origins. 'The trouble, as a matter of fact, with the majority of *well-established* Jews in England is that they tend to reproduce somewhat to excess the British reserve.'

While there was much sense in all this — and Rathbone accepted it — Victor's letter was of interest not just because of its passionate defence of his people against criticism, but also because it shows again how unaware he was that he, more than most — in his public and private character — perpetuated an outdated Jewish stereotype. Without Jewish family loyalty (or 'clannishness'), he would never have got the capital to start his firm. He was ostentatious, not in personal expenditure, but in his extravagant parties and his constant demand to be the centre of attention. His cheese-paring in business attracted the epithet 'Jewish'. And above all, he was deeply emotional and was usually the noisiest person in any group.

At every stage of Victor's life, whether at daggers drawn or at peace with the Jewish community, he was described by fascinated gentile observers as 'intensely Jewish'. The pillars of the Jewish and Zionist organizations in Britain looked at him from their English perspective and found him embarrassingly extrovert. But it was Victor, not they, who held centre-stage in gentile society and politics. Jews knew him for the unique bundle of talents, contradictions and neuroses that he was. Gentiles tended to explain away his eccentricities with a laugh or a sigh as typical of a people about whom they knew little. Interesting too were Victor's suggestions to Rathbone for additions to her list of great Jews. His newly discovered pride in Jewish history was becoming apparent, and prejudice had provoked him to abandon his old belief that a man's nationality, race or religion was irrelevant.

> I can't understand why you omit Jesus of Nazareth from your list of great Jews. It can't be for theological reasons, because the best Catholic (and indeed Church of England) doctrine is that Christ was perfect *man* as well as *God*, so that I don't see how you offend any susceptibilities by saying that the greatest religious teacher that the world has ever seen, and the greatest of all the influences in our Western civilisation, was a Jew. It seems to me also desirable that people should be reminded of this: and personally

I find it more valuable in combating anti-semitism with religious people than anything else.

Then there is the question of Marx and Freud. I know why you leave them out: because you think that Marx will frighten people, and that Freud was a dirty old man. But, forgive me, these are idiosyncratic opinions of yours, and it does seem to me quite grotesque, in any book dealing with the Jewish contribution, to omit them. The plain fact is that the modern way of thinking has been made by five people — Darwin, Fraser, Einstein, Marx and Freud: and of these five three are Jews. For my own part, I also believe that, while the doctrine of Marx wants a great deal of correction and the doctrine of Freud has led to many extravagances, the hard core of these two doctrines are two of the greatest keys to sanity and happiness for mankind in the future.

As early as the middle of 1944 he began to show signs of restiveness in his role as a part of the respectable Jewish establishment. In August he pleaded overwork and tried to resign from the Board of Deputies' sub-committees. He agreed to stay on for a while, but scaled down his involvement to that of consultant. The Judaic publishing programme shifted its emphasis: for fear of stirring up hatred, Victor chose to avoid books about the oppression of the Jews, concentrating instead on such positive issues as the future of Palestine. His gradual disengagement can be attributed to a number of things: he was unhappy that his work might be seen as predictable since he was a Jew himself; try as he might, he still disliked the Jewish tendency to see their first loyalty as to their own people (his sympathy towards Arabs met no echo in militant Zionists); he disliked being identified with a group viewpoint; he could not take over any of the organizations involved and run them the way he wanted; and coming over the horizon were two issues on which he felt he had a particular and individual contribution to make — the forthcoming general election and the future of Germany after the war.

He did not completely sever his connection with Jewish refugee work, but his last major contribution was to write not the promised book, but a pamphlet in May 1945 (after the German surrender), entitled *"Nowhere to Lay Their Heads": the Jewish tragedy in Europe and its solution.* It was a plea for the opening up of Palestine to Jewish immigration on a large scale. He made it very clear in the foreword that he was speaking as an individual. 'I am not a member of any Zionist organization, nor should it be assumed that the views I express on this question, or on any part of it, are necessarily identical with those held by the majority of Zionists.' He kept his account of what the Jews had suffered to the bare minimum necessary to get the reality across to his readers; for his purpose, as he made clear throughout, was to help the survivors rather than stir up hatred for the murderers of the dead. As with all Victor's political pamphlets, it was meticulously researched with the most expert help available, and its catalogue of numbers and locations of the refugees was precise. There was a cool but telling description of their ghastly conditions and bleak prospects. He found frightening indications of growing anti-semitism in Europe. His case for Zionism was, in essence: that without a homeland the Jews would inevitably face widespread persecution again; that there was nowhere else for them to go; that Palestine was historically and spiritually Jewish; that it had been promised to them by the Balfour Declaration; that its prosperity could only be greatly enhanced by a large influx of immigrants; that existing settlers had already proved their ability to transform a barren waste into productive land; that there was plenty of land to share out between Arabs and Jews; and that, in the long run, it would be to the benefit of the Arabs to have a Jewish Palestine.

Large-scale free distribution and brilliant publicity made this another hugely successful publication, generating an enormous correspondence, most of which was ecstatic and grateful. He found the time to dictate long and usually patient letters to members of the public who questioned aspects of his argument, and he was still important enough in Jewish circles to be called in to advise Chaim Weizmann about political tactics in the autumn of 1945, but *Nowhere to Lay Their Heads* had effectively been his swan-song. A half-hearted promise to visit Palestine in 1946 went unfulfilled, and henceforward, matters concerning the Jews were generally pushed aside for concerns he thought more urgent.

The prospect of a general election captured his interest during the spring and early summer of 1945. Even at the worst points of the war he had always been determined to flood the market with socialist books when the time seemed ripe, and indeed had maintained the flow of Victory books throughout. Immediately after he returned to work in 1943, Gollancz launched the most successful polemic since *Guilty Men*, this time with Michael Foot as the sole author. *The Trial of Mussolini*, which demonstrated that his guilt was shared by the appeasers, sold almost 150,000 copies and again had many Tories foaming at the mouth. It was just one more in a long line of what became known as 'Yellow Perils' issuing from Gollancz right up to the 1945 election. There was no other polemicist quite in Foot's class, but the series as a whole kept up a high standard of political partiality and invective. Tory MPs and candidates all over the country came to

hate the name of Victor Gollancz. *Your M.P.* by Tom Wintringham
dug the dirt on the voting record and business interests of pre-war
appeasers; Nye Bevan's *Why Not Trust the Tories?*, written at Victor's
suggestion, savaged the Tories' performance after World War I; and
John Lawson, unsolicited, submitted in February 1945 what was to be
the highly successful *Vote Labour? Why?*. Like the other election
books, it was published under a Latin pseudonym, and the postal
discussion of which name would be suitable produced an erudite
telegram from Victor:

> DISLIKE APPIUS CLAUDIUS STOP THE FIRST ONE WAS A BLACKGUARD AND WILL
> GIVE EASY PLAY FOR ATTACK ON BOOK STOP THE SECOND WAS NOT WHAT
> WOULD HAVE CORRESPONDED TO ANYTHING LIKE A SOCIALIST IN THOSE TIMES
> BUT WAS MORE OF A LIBERAL WHO OPPOSED CONSULSHIP FOR PLEBS STOP
> LICINIUS A VERY REAL SOCIALIST IN CONDITIONS OF THAT TIME AND MOREOVER
> UNITED ALL ELEMENTS OF PLEBS AGAINST PATRICIANS STOP PROPOSE PUTTING
> LICINIUS UNLESS WIRE RECEIVED FROM YOU TO THE CONTRARY BY 9.30
> TOMORROW FRIDAY MORNING WHEN WE HAVE TO START MACHINING

To those under attack it must have seemed as if Victor was
malevolently working night and day on pre-election propaganda.
Especially upsetting for the victims was the impossibility of catching
the books out as libellous. Victor enjoined his authors to check and
double-check all their accusations and Harold Rubinstein combed the
manuscripts with special care. There were furious condemnations in
the press and from election platforms: Victor was even described as an
immigrant peddling foreign dirt, lacking decent gratitude for his
country of refuge. But of all the individuals attacked, only one could
show that he had been libelled. Given his own horror of being
misrepresented, Victor was always warmly sympathetic to those he
felt had been unfairly treated in any of his publications. Accordingly,
his apology to this Tory MP, Commander Bower, was so generous
that they ended up having dinner together and exchanging compliments in private and public.

There was no clue in the hugely successful Yellow Perils to Victor's
increasing ambivalence about the Labour Party. His resolution to
abandon parliamentary ambitions seems to have faltered in 1942. At
some time during the war he had toyed with the offer of a Labour
candidature for his Berkshire constituency but had cried off — not
because it was unwinnable but because he had come to the conclusion
that he was not a party man. He had consulted Douglas Jerrold among
others about his quandary and been advised to stand for Oxford
University constituency as an independent. Jerrold, Victor reported
to Cole in February 1945, believed 'that, with the general swing to the

Left, proportional representation and (between ourselves) general disgust with Herbert's buffooneries [A. P. Herbert, the delightfully idiosyncratic Oxford MP], there might be a chance of slipping in. The more I think of this the more I like it. It seems to me that there's just a bare chance of getting in, and nothing lost even in the event of a disastrous defeat.'

The idea proved to be a non-starter, as Cole was himself standing for Oxford for Labour. (He was defeated by Herbert.) Eleanor Rathbone's suggestion that Victor should stand for Cambridge, generally thought to be 'more Left than Oxford', came to nothing either, and Victor contented himself with a supporting role in the election. That was easy enough for him when it came to publishing things written by others. He stood foursquare behind his front line polemicists. One of his more splendidly offensive letters defended Michael Foot, author of yet another tract, *Brendan and Beverley*, an attack on Bracken and Baxter. One indignant reader wrote that having bought it, he considered himself to have been robbed and wanted his money back. His letter ended: 'With regards to the boys in the sedition section'. 'My dear Sir,' Victor wrote back,

> I enclose a postal order for 2/7 — 2/6 of it being the cost of *Brendan and Beverley*, and the other 1d for the loss of your no doubt valuable time in writing to us.
>
> I should be glad, if you would like me to do so, to send you the titles of a few books which might start you on the road to educated and responsible citizenship. The 2/7 might go towards the cost of them.
>
> Michael Foot, the author of *Brendan and Beverley*, would be interested to find himself described as 'seditious'. So would his father, old Isaac Foot. So would Lord Beaverbrook, who employed Michael, until very recently, as editor of the 'Evening Standard'. So would the electors of Devonport, who, if they have the wit to understand the real meaning of British honour and British interests, will in a few weeks' time be returning Michael to Parliament.
>
> *What* an ass you are!
>
> Yours in all (and quite genuine) friendliness — I think I could convert you to sanity if we could meet —
>
> Victor Gollancz

Enthusing about Foot and his kind was one thing. What was difficult for Victor was personally to come out in strong support of a party led by Attlee, Morrison and his other old opponents. He loathed the Labour Party *en masse* at the best of times. 'Are you going to bloody Blackpool?' he asked Zilliacus (author of *Can the Tories Win the Peace?*) in May 1945: 'Gawd! It used to be said that the worst possible seller in fiction would be a novel about a mixed marriage between a Jew and an Irishman, with the setting in Cape Cod. I'm not sure which is my idea of the lowest hell — a Labour Party conference or Blackpool. The two together. . . !'

He had not changed his view of the relative merits of Acland versus Labour Party socialism since 1942, but the history of Common Wealth in the intervening three years had confirmed his belief that only Labour could defeat the Tories. 'I believe, of course, in the spirit of Common Wealth far more than in that of the Labour Party,' he wrote to an acquaintance before the results of the general election were announced in July 1945. 'On the other hand it seems to me perfectly obvious that Common Wealth can never attain power. That is why I want to see the Labour Party strengthened and permeated, if possible, with the Common Wealth spirit while, at the same time, I want to see Common Wealth kept going as a small ginger group inside the House with a big movement supporting it outside.' His honourable compromise had been to speak for the individuals he wanted in the House. In May he had spoken for the successful Common Wealth candidate in a by-election at Chelmsford, and for many Labour Party candidates during the general election campaign. He also supported in person Tom Wintringham of Common Wealth against a Tory in Aldershot, and Richard Acland against a Labour candidate in Putney, and sent a message in support of Kitty Wintringham against a Labour candidate at Midlothian.

After the landslide Labour victory in July, Common Wealth was left with only one MP, and many of its supporters joined the Labour Party. It was a sad blow to Victor's hopes for a strong pressure group keeping the Labour Party up to the mark on socialist and moral principles. Nevertheless, his post-bag was gratifyingly full of letters congratulating him on his part in bringing Labour to power. 'The victory of the Socialist Party at the General Election', said a disgruntled Conservative in 1946, 'was undoubtedly due to their active and subtle propaganda during the war years through such bodies as the Fabian Society, the Gollancz Press, and Transport House. The Left Book Club had published over six million books between 1936 and 1946, and the Fabian Society claimed to have 229 members in the new Government.' (He might have included Allen Lane's influential Penguin Specials, which were mainly left-of-centre.)

There were many other factors, of course, including the general feeling that Churchill was a man for war but not peace, the desire for change, Labour's superior campaign and the good impression made by its leaders in the National government, which made the party a credible opposition. Otherwise, that Tory was not far wrong. All the propaganda had been on the Left, and the right had failed miserably to counteract it. What had been achieved, as Stuart Samuels puts it apropos of the LBC, was the popularizing of a new political vocabulary, 'especially such terms as full employment, socialized medicine, town planning and social equality. Almost imperceptibly this new verbal consciousness helped to prepare Englishmen for the economic and social changes after the war.' What had been unknown or alien concepts in the mid-1930s had become matters for common discussion during the war. Tories had been taken aback by the enthusiasm which greeted the Beveridge Report in 1942, for it spelled the end of state control as a bogey to frighten the majority.

Any attempt to measure Victor Gollancz's contribution to all this must begin with the impact of the LBC, which in later years was dismissed by many a disillusioned socialist as a flash in the pan. The evidence of Victor's own archives and the recollections of old LBC members (at home and abroad) are enough to discredit this simple view. For Victor's main aim for the club had been achieved. He had turned many of its members into missionaries, and whether they had seceded from the club or not, they used their wartime opportunities to the full to instruct their fellows in the ideas and vocabulary of socialism. A Captain Smith who wrote to Victor in August 1945 was not even aware whether the LBC was still in existence, but he commented: 'The Labour Party's magnificent victory at the polls is due in very much greater degree than has been recognised to the work of ex-LBC members in both forces and factories. We have good reason to be proud of our contribution.'

It was not only the ex-teachers (who wielded so much influence in the Education Corps and the Army Bureau of Current Affairs) who corroborated Captain Smith's view. Two old LBCers put the case in a 1979 television programme. The first was Norman Wiseman: 'I think I was made most aware of the influence of the Left Book Club in my later days in the army, when I became what was called an Education Sergeant, largely on the strength of my earlier well-educated political speeches made to soldiers in the unit. And I found then when we were discussing different matters with different groups, whatever the nature of the group . . . always the most articulate . . . had been Left Book Club readers.' The second, Philip Jackson: 'I worked in two engineering factories also during the war, and . . . there was some tremendous discussion went on in the canteens . . . when these discussions used to commence, actually more than one card game [would] close up, so that people could come across from the card game to be participants in the discussion.'

All the evidence suggests that their experiences were typical. After all, at its peak the LBC had had groups in almost every town in the British Isles, and every active LBC member felt it a duty to spread the message in the workplace as well as in social gatherings. There was no other comparable organization, for the LBC did not only furnish reading material: through the groups it taught people how to debate. Armed with facts and figures about the failings of capitalism, and with formidable articulacy, they went forth in their thousands to make converts to the left. Nor did this knowledge or ability fade when their membership lapsed. Its penetration into the workplace, the trade unions and finally the forces was the LBC's real exhibition of strength. Victor was proud that eight LBC authors — Lord Addison, Attlee, Bevan, Cripps, Philip Noel-Baker, Shinwell, Strachey and Wilkinson — were in the new government, and that six more — Maurice Edelman, Michael Foot, Elwyn Jones, J. P. W. Mallalieu, Stephen Swingler and Konni Zilliacus — were MPs. He had even more to be proud of in the large number of Labour MPs, who, without LBC rank-and-file effort to change the working class's perspective, might not have been in the House of Commons at all.

For that conversion a great deal of credit goes to the pedagogic gifts of John Strachey, the most influential writer in the Club. Yet without Victor he would have had only a tiny audience, and without Victor's organizational brilliance and impassioned messianism, Club members would not have gone forth to multiply.

That the Fabian Society made a considerable impact cannot be denied, but its influence was primarily on the intellectuals. And even there, Victor came into the picture as the enthusiastic publisher of numerous Fabian Society books and pamphlets. More, he had personally made a major contribution to the Fabians during the war years, in the Socialist Propaganda committee and as a speaker at a succession of summer schools. His style was more vital than the academic Fabians, and Cyril Joad was among those who thanked him for rekindling his faith in socialism.

Exceptionally important too were the Yellow Perils, most of them forgotten in later years. In the Liberal *News Chronicle* in 1947, A. J. Cummings harked back to 'the famous Gollancz yellow-books [which] demonstrating in vivid language how near Baldwinism had brought us to the edge of the abyss, did so much to influence the General Election in favour of a Labour Government and a new approach to the spirit of the age.'

For an individual without official position, Victor's colossal influence on a vital election remains unmatched in twentieth-century
political history. In his consciously modest moments he underplayed
his contribution. In his resentful moments, bitter that the Labour
Party had ignored what he had done, he would claim the primary
credit for the 1945 result. For once he was probably right when he
was cross. Socialism would have been a far more frightening
prospect, the Tory party would not have been so widely vilified, and
Labour's victory might have been a good deal less dramatic, if Victor
Gollancz had not expended his energies as he did for a decade before.

Victor never undertook any public work in the hope of winning
medals. He was incapable of espousing any cause unless he was
excited by it. Still, the meanness of the Labour Party towards their
obstreperous benefactor went beyond decency. Admirers felt he
deserved a peerage, and Victor thought so too. Attlee, understandably, was leery of having Victor Gollancz as a thorn in his flesh in the
House of Lords, but it was strange that he could not find it in his
heart to give him any consolation prize. No one would have been
made as happy by recognition as Victor, but his innate sincerity had
ruled it out of court. Although he had helped the Labour Party
immeasurably, he had been an unreliable supporter; and by speaking
for Common Wealth he had compounded Labour distrust. Four
years later, writing to one of his authors about plans for pre-election
books and the failure of the party to help in any way, he remarked
that he sometimes thought the leadership was jealous of his efforts to
help.

> In the case of the last one, it was several months before Herbert Morrison
> wrote me a couple of sentences: and then only, I understand, after George
> Strauss had asked me whether I had been thanked, and had expressed
> great indignation when I told him I had not. It is not that I want thanks —
> it is the last thing in the world I care about: it is only the light such goings
> on throw on the whole business.

It was distrust, not jealousy. And Victor was deluding himself
when he claimed not to mind, for he disliked ingratitude above all,
and his intimates knew him to be shocked and disappointed. That
made it all the more creditable that he continued to give support to
the party. But resentment was probably a contributory cause to his
becoming the severest critic among their friends, all the while
admiring Churchill in the depth of his being and regarding Attlee as
an unimaginative poor fish, who, to add insult to injury, had lost
him money on his books.

When the election results came in, Victor had a spasm of excitement about the role the LBC might play during the Labour term of office. For the *Left News* of August 1945 he wrote the first in what was to be a series called 'The Left Book Club and the Labour Victory: Retrospect and Prospect'. The article was about the pre-war history of the Club, and he dwelt on its most celebrated triumphs. 'For the moment I will leave it at that,' he concluded. 'Next month I shall say something of the war-time history of the Club, and of the supreme opportunity — and obligation — which now awaits us.' Next month came and went with a note from Victor saying he had been too busy yet to write the promised sequel. It was not referred to again in the columns of the *Left News*, for Victor had taken the plunge again. This time, the cause was the salvation of the German people.

CHAPTER SEVENTEEN

POST-WAR: THE EMERGING PHILANTHROPIST

VICTOR'S WORK FOR defeated Germany was rooted in his particular passion for the moral underdog, not forgetting his sheer enjoyment of the drama and excitement of being seen to take up an unpopular cause. He always showed sincere concern for those suffering from poverty, torture or oppression of any kind, but he had a special place in his heart for those reviled by others. In the case of the Jews, it was the anti-semitism directed at them on top of all their suffering that catalysed his involvement in their cause. Later, he was to champion murderers against society's condemnation. Now the Germans were at the mercy of a world long trained to hate and despise them, it was quite consistent that he should move in their defence.

He had never ceased to push the anti-Vansittart message by every means at his disposal, even during the period when his attention was mainly directed elsewhere. One valuable piece of counter-propaganda had been *Above All Nations*, a compilation of reports from many nations in many theatres of war, relating acts of kindness between enemies. It was conceived by Vera Brittain and her husband, George Catlin, but Victor had found its execution wanting — too long, not specific enough, and pacifist-inclined. Sheila Hodges had been brought in as a collaborator. It was published early in 1945, with a foreword by Victor himself. Nazi policy was uniquely barbaric, he said, but 'nevertheless, Germans — and Englishmen and Frenchmen and Russians, and the rest — can show themselves to be men and not brutes precisely at the moments when, were it not for the aweful [*sic*] compulsion of the good instinct, brutality would be so much easier.' Valuable though such publications were, they made little headway against the tide of public loathing of the whole German nation, as the foul truth about the concentration camps came fully home to the public.

The liberation of Buchenwald by Allied troops in the spring of 1945 provided the press with pictures which made graphic an intensity of suffering beyond the compass of most imaginations. The starving and tormented survivors, as Victor pointed out in the pamphlet — *What Buchenwald Really Means* — he wrote in April, included a significant number of gentile Germans. Yet a large section of the outraged press and public had found their proof that the Germans must be collectively punished. Victor's pamphlet was directed to spelling out in precise detail how Buchenwald proved the opposite: all the Germans had not been guilty; there was ample evidence that hundreds of thousands of heroic gentiles had been persecuted for resisting the Nazis; and, to the objective mind, it was clear that millions of Germans, loathing the régime, had been terrorized into silent acquiescence. Victor castigated all those English people who, living in a free democracy, had made no attempt to save the Jews even when it was known that they were being exterminated: 'Your case is morally worse than that of the "ordinary" Germans'. He concluded with a brief analysis of the theory of 'collective guilt', which he berated as a Hegelian throw-back to pre-Christian barbarism. He quoted Abraham's plea to the Lord to save Sodom and Gomorrah as the first protest against collective guilt, with Ezekiel ('the son shall not bear the iniquity of the father') as a mark of Old Testament progress, brought to perfection by Christ in his pronouncements on the sanctity of individual personality. This Whiggish interpretation of Judeo-Christianity was the first salvo in the war Victor was to conduct with Jews for the rest of his life, for few devout Jews, many of whom spent their lives in charitable work at the injunction of their prophets, took kindly to being told that Christ's was the voice of moral progress.

The pamphlet provoked a predictable range of reactions. 'What you say is exactly what I would like to have said,' wrote the star of the Brains Trust, Cyril Joad, 'had I had the chance and the wit to say it and I don't really see how it could have been said better.' His praise was echoed in many other letters. A smaller number were stridently critical. This example is not untypical of the hate-mail Victor attracted. It caused him little distress because, as was often the case, its logic was flawed by an inadequate grasp of salient facts:

> Frome,
> Somerset
> 9 June 1945

You Lousy Foreign Rat!

I have just been reading your ill-timed and disgraceful attempt to fasten on the shoulders of the British nation the blame for the horrors perpetrated by the Germans in their prison camps. Having already obtained some idea of your queer political views from previous literary efforts, and from the

fact that you are the publisher of those scurrilous yellow-backed publications which have for some time past been defiling our newspaper stalls
and book shops, one is not altogether surprised at your latest Anglophobe
effort. What is surprising to a Briton, however, is the fact that our
governing authorities are as indulgent towards such as you as they are.
Why in the name of good fortune you should elect to remain in a country
which, according to you and your friends with the Roman pennames, and
others whose names are as un-British as your own, can do nothing right, is
to the ordinary home-loving Briton, one of the major mysteries. Here, at
any rate, is one Briton to whom it would give the greatest pleasure to
bundle you and all your fellow Jewish European scum — Poles, Czechs,
Slovaks, and whatnot — neck and crop out of our country, and back to
where you had your misbegotten origins, and a thousand pities it is that
you can't be sent to one of those camps in Germany, the blame for which
you so unreasonably and unfairly wish to cast upon a people who have
done least of all peoples to deserve it.

'Briton'
(and no Tory either!)

'Briton' had a point. Victor, publisher of vitriolic and unpitying
condemnations of the Tories, asked a lot when he called for sublime
Christian ethics in the treatment of the defeated enemy. He was
himself honestly bewildered by charges of inconsistency. Had Neville
Chamberlain been set on by a howling mob, none would have come
more quickly to his aid than Victor. But so long as the Tories
remained confident and prosperous they were fair game: it was his
duty to lay them low in the name of socialist righteousness.

Victor was in an unassailable position: no one could accuse *him* of
failing to work for the defeat of fascism or for the salvation of the
European Jews. However, the overall tone of self-righteousness in the
pamphlet somewhat limited its appeal. Nevertheless, the central case
was so strong that it stirred many consciences and his fan-mail was by
no means restricted to socialists. Certainly, there were letters from
Jews who had lost all their loved ones in concentration camps and
could feel only hatred of the Germans and bewilderment at Victor's
message, but other survivors of the holocaust exhibited great nobility
of spirit and cited evidence in Victor's support. 'Shall I ever forget,'
wrote one refugee,

my friends [German gentiles] who taught their little girl to pray for
'Uncle Mayer' when I was at Dachau? Shall I forget the old general who
postponed his Christmas visit to his daughter because he did not want my
wife to be alone during my internment? Shall I ever forget my colleague
who took over some of my clients, and who sent me a considerable sum

because he refused to 'get fat by robbing a colleague', or the old judge who resigned his office, and who, when he met me in the street, told me that he wanted to make it clear that he had no wish to betray the ideals of a lifetime? . . . Nobody will ever persuade me that all these men and women (and every refugee knows dozens of those cases) are hopelessly wicked and deserve to be punished.

Victor called on this correspondent and others to support him in a *Spectator* controversy about *What Buchenwald Really Means*. The pamphlet had been distributed free to many influential people, but it also had considerable sales and ran to numerous foreign editions. Dwight Macdonald wrote from America to congratulate Victor on his 'swell pamphlet', offering to sell or give it to the readers of his *Politics*. 'In your cable it stated you had "already distributed here 160,000 copies" of your pamphlet. Is that a misprint for 16,000? If not, it's absolutely phenomenal — how in the world do you do it? Over here even the CIO [Congress of Industrial Organizations] considers 50,000 a big edition for a pamphlet.' 'MANY THANKS YOUR LETTER JULY 25 STOP', came the reply. 'AM GLADLY SENDING YOU 1500 FOR FREE DISTRIBUTION STOP 160000 WAS CORRECT FIGURE NOW 180000'.

Victor was of course disinclined to let the matter rest there. Fresh anti-German propaganda by old enemies fuelled his fervour. In May 1945, Vansittart wrote an article denying there had been an effective German resistance movement, despite the propaganda of 'optimists like Mr Gollancz . . . publishing books like "100,000 Allies If We Choose".' He went on chillingly:

> To the immediate future Field-Marshal Montgomery has already made an invaluable contribution. His order against fraternisation is a model. Forgiving and forgetting are always construed as weakness by that twisted German mind we have got to straighten out. This time it is essential to bring home to the nation as a whole the horror and loathing that its manifold cruelties have inspired in Europe as a whole. The indispensable moral lesson may then be learned in measurable time — otherwise never.

The non-fraternization policy, Victor wrote to the *Manchester Guardian* on 28 June, was the worst of all:

> Why on earth doesn't somebody say quite plainly that . . . non-fraternisation, which means, I understand, 'not treating a man as a brother,' is just simply wicked? 'We are a Christian people,' said Montgomery, when 'explaining' this policy to the Germans. But what he really meant, as the context shows, was this: 'Sometime or other we shall behave like Christians, when and if, but only when and if, you show us that you have given up your un-Christian Nazism.' That seems to me, as a Jew who

believes in Christian ethics, a somewhat heretical application of Christ's teaching: and fifty bishops will not make me, who can read the New Testament as well as they, think otherwise.

That passage was part of a letter primarily concerned to protest against the expulsion from Czechoslovakia of the Sudeten Germans. *Inter alia* he raised the alarm about the conduct of Russian towards German in the territories under Soviet control (Kingsley Martin refused to print the letter uncut in the *New Statesman*). The gloating press coverage of executions, and the inhuman attitude of so-called liberal, socialist and religious factions in Britain led Victor to suggest that the war had been morally lost.

He published that letter, with two others to the *Guardian* and one to the *News Chronicle*, in yet another pamphlet, *The New Morality*, in September 1945. Christ and Blake were cited in support of his protests against the expulsion and neglect of Czech and Polish homeless, the self-interest dominating international affairs, and, above all, the use of the atomic bomb to win the war with Japan. For all his wartime bellicosity, Victor had always opposed the indiscriminate bombing of civilians. He was appalled in August that the *Guardian*, which he greatly admired, should defend the use of the atom bomb, stating that it was 'illogical to judge the morality of bombing by the size of the bomb used'. It was a matter of quality, not quantity, Victor averred.

> In the devilish business of war, there is only one aim on either side, and that is to win. If therefore in a just, defensive war your best or quickest chance of winning were to submit to agonising torture all the children of the enemy, such a method of warfare would no doubt be as 'logical' as the bows of Agincourt. But would it be decent, or wise, or, to use a word now almost out of currency, right? No: poised on the brink of that unspeakable wickedness, men, or all but the basest of them, would realise that they had come to a point at which formal logic was no longer valid, but must give way to spiritual reality . . .
>
> I say that by using the atomic bomb we have committed just this further debasement of the human currency. . . . The atomic bomb is not merely two thousand times more powerful than the biggest and best of the previous bombs: by very reason of that power it is something new in kind — a threat, and for the first time, to the very existence of humanity. By our blasphemous presumption in using it we have taken another step to the abyss: by renouncing its use we might have staggered back to moral sanity.

Journalists and politicians were morally wrong to justify feeding the vanquished on grounds of self-interest alone. He concluded:

> All this is, to put it bluntly, sin: and the wages of sin is death, however

cunning and however powerful may be the ramparts we build against it. Why, then, in this awful crisis of human faith, are the leaders of Church and Mosque and Synagogue, except the Pope, so strangely silent? Why do they not proclaim and proclaim again to every man and woman in the world, irrespective of nation or creed, that our only hope is to conquer the evil in our own hearts — and to conquer it in its innermost citadel by listening at last to the ancient words of sanity and salvation, and applying them to every act of international policy:

'But I say unto you, Love your enemies, bless them that curse you, do good to them that hate you, and pray for them which despitefully use you, and persecute you;

'That ye may be the children of your Father which is in heaven: for he maketh his sun to rise on the evil and on the good, and sendeth rain on the just and on the unjust.'

That powerful letter, reaching a far wider readership than even Victor could usually command, confirmed his status as a religious prophet. It went down particularly well with the Catholic press, which over the years had altered its traditional view of him as a proponent of secular socialism and had begun to quote him approvingly in editorials as a leading defender of Catholic values. Although the Church of England press was also broadly in support, no newspaper matched the *Catholic Herald* in its enthusiasm for his next long letter, a deeply-felt appeal in the *News Chronicle* of 27 August (also printed in his pamphlet) that the nation be saved by 'an act of genuine repentance: a determination here and now to turn our backs on the whole evil tradition of self- interest and self-righteousness in international affairs — a determination, for instance, to feed Europe this winter not because if we don't we ourselves may suffer, but simply because it is right to feed our starving neighbours.'

It was becoming clear that Europe was facing a winter of famine. Victor's condemnation of the 'new morality' which saw mercy and pity as otiose qualities, aroused an enormous response. He received some excellent advice from a genius:

> as from Trinity College
> Cambridge,
> September 4th, 1945

Dear Mr Gollancz,

I have read your article 'In Germany Now' in the 'News Chronicle' of August 27th and was glad to see that someone, publicly and in a conspicuous place, called a devilry a devilry. A friend, when I praised your article to him, gave me your pamphlet on Buchenwald.

I am deeply in sympathy with your severe criticism (and it cannot be too severe) of the cruelty, meanness and vulgarity of the daily press and of the

BBC. (Our cinema news reels are, if possible, more poisonous still.) It is because I strongly sympathise with your attitude to these evils that I think I ought to make what seems to me a serious criticism of your polemic against them. I shall try in this letter to put the main line of my criticism in a sketchy way; but I should like to have the opportunity some day of making what I mean clearer by word of mouth. I shall, in what follows, be blunt in order to be clear.

There are two ways of diluting and weakening an accusation or criticism. One is to couch it in half-hearted and ambiguous terms. This is not what you have done. But there is another way, which is to embellish a point which you have expressed forcefully by half a dozen subsidiary points which, even if they are not weak and dubious, draw away the reader's attention from the main issue, and make the polemic ineffectual. I know it is often difficult to refrain from raising these side-issues. One does not wish to suppress them, sometimes out of vanity, sometimes because one doesn't want to make the article too purely aggressive and offensive. Yet, considering the terrible impotence of even the most forcefully written article, if it is to be heard above the shouting of the daily press and the radio, these sacrifices must be made.

If you want to point out a foul scandal and to tell people, 'Remove it, it stinks!', then, for Heaven's sake, don't add remarks about the lovely smell of roses. Such remarks, even if they are true, immediately put your writing on a wrong plane, on the plane of talk and inaction.

If you really want people to remove the dirt, don't talk to them about the philosophical issues of the value of life and happiness. This, if it does anything, will start academic chat.

In writing about the wrong attitude of people towards the Buchenwald horrors, e.g., did you wish to convince only those who agree with you about the Old and New Testament? Even if they do, your lengthy quotations serve to sidetrack their attention from the one main point. If they don't — and an enormous number who might be seriously shaken by your argument do not — they will feel that all this rigmarole makes the whole article smell slightly fishy. All the more as they will not gladly give up their former views.

I will stop now. — If you ask me why, instead of criticising you, I don't write articles myself, I should answer that I lack the knowledge, the facility of expression and the time necessary for any decent and effective journalism. In fact, writing this letter of criticism to a man of your views and of your ability is the nearest approach to what is denied me, i.e., to writing a good article myself.

If this letter sounds impolite, this is not because it was my intention to be offensive, but because I have such difficulties in writing at all clearly that the additional task of expressing myself politely would have made it impossible for me to write at all.

Yours truly,
L. Wittgenstein

Wittgenstein had put his finger on Victor's deficiency as a rouser of the public conscience: he could not leave well enough alone. In his determination to put his own gloss on every straightforward argument, he irritated or distanced many readers who might otherwise have agreed with him. Since early LBC days, he had stopped his ears to any criticism of his writings unless it dealt with factual minutiae. Wittgenstein was given short shrift. Victor was not well up on modern philosophy, and presumably failed to realize that he was not dealing with some obscure don:

11th Sept. 1945

L. Wiltgenstein [sic], Esq.,
at Trinity College
Cambridge
Dear Sir,
  Thank you for your letter, which I am sure was very well meant.
Yours truly,
Victor Gollancz

Victor was poised to stride on to the international stage, and earn adulation far beyond anything he had so far experienced. In many respects he was exceptionally well qualified to extend the hand of friendship to the German people: he was a Jew, he was sincere and he had *mana*; his practical experience and ever-growing network of contacts equipped him splendidly to mount a campaign of private individuals; at fifty-two, his physical energy was unimpaired and the envy of his contemporaries; and in his firm he had an excellent deputy in Sheila Hodges. On the debit side, his vanity was straining against the bonds in which he had hitherto contained it. The breakdown had taught him much of value, including the way to cope with his guilt, but it had dented his self-esteem and so exacerbated his need for constant approbation. He had always been arrogant, and now more and more people were calling him a saint. Even before he set about saving the starving people of Europe, he was demonstrating all too often a voracious appetite for praise that few had yet sated. Maurice Browne, the impresario who had first launched *Journey's End*, was one of those who genuinely admired Victor without qualification and lost no opportunity to tell him so. On 9 July, writing to commend three of his pamphlets, he said: 'I don't want to be effusive, but may I say just these two things. Your prose at its best seems to me worthy to stand beside the prose of any of the great English masters of prose. That's one thing. The other is this. To be your fellow-citizen makes me very proud of being an Englishman. God bless you — and more power to your elbow!'

Victor had long ago rid his circle of intimates of anyone who might have scoffed openly at such hyperbole: there was no corrective available. 'My dear Maurice,' he replied,

> It was extraordinarily kind of you to write and, do you know, you've at last said something that I always wanted someone to say! I know very well (however much you may think to the contrary) that I never really succeed in getting across what I want to say: I am always horribly dissatisfied. But for years, when I have re-read my things, I have thought the prose really *was* very good: and I have always been rather irritated that no one ever said so!

His prose was very good, but it did not rival that of the great English masters. In its lucidity and purity of style, it was testimony to the thoroughness of his classical training and his love for the language. He struggled hard to make it perfect: good though the first drafts were, he revised interminably up to and including the galley proof stage. Yet his was the felicitous prose of a master craftsman, rather than that of an artist.

For the moment, Victor's need to prove himself as a writer was put aside in favour of more pressing concerns. Rightly convinced that the new government lacked the will to increase the supply of food to Europe at the expense of tightening rations at home, he determined to whip up public support for domestic self-sacrifice, and so force the government's hand. The situation was frightful. The British Zone in Germany could not feed itself, and every day absorbed more refugees expelled — usually in cattle trucks — from the Russian area of control. Under the terms of the Potsdam agreement the defeated enemy was entitled to average living standards 'not exceeding the average standards of living of European countries'. There was no lower limit set. Since Potsdam also recommended de-industrialization (to keep the lid on Germany's war potential), it was clearly impossible to sustain the existing population without massive shipments of food.

Neither Attlee nor most of his colleagues had any urgent sympathy for the Germans. They had no wish to see them starve, but were disinclined to augment their standard of nutrition beyond barest subsistence while the British people remained on short commons. Indeed, as Victor pointed out, government spokesmen even seemed half-ashamed of their humanitarian actions, and they and the BBC kept stressing that Germans had to be fed so they could work, and that attention to the Germans' health was necessary because any epidemic might spread to the occupying forces.

Spurred on by his fan-mail, Victor spent much of August selecting and canvassing his supporters. Early in September, he sent the following appeal to the *Daily Herald*, the *Manchester Guardian* and the *News Chronicle*. His signature was supported by those of Congregationalist Ministers (Dr Sidney Berry and the Rev. Henry Carter), George Bell (Bishop of Chichester), A. D. Lindsay (Master of Balliol), Gilbert Murray (now an OM), Eleanor Rathbone and Bertrand Russell.

Correspondents in Berlin have been sending to their newspapers a description of conditions in that city which must have been read by many with grave disquiet. Expelled from their homes in the Sudetenland, East Prussia, and the whole vast region of Germany taken over by the Poles, sometimes at thirty minutes' notice and without the provision of food or transport, a horde of Germans is struggling daily into Berlin — and being turned away, because there is no food for them. The majority are old men, women and children.

Some of these persons, too weak to wander further, have been seen under the bomb-wrecked roof of the Stettiner railway station, dead or dying. 'One woman,' writes the reporter of a leading London newspaper, 'emaciated, with dark rings under her eyes and sores breaking out all over her face, could only mutter self-condemnation because she was unable to feed her two whimpering babies. I watched her trying desperately to force milk from her milkless breasts — a pitiful effort that only left her crying at her failure.' The correspondent of another responsible London paper writes that 'at a conservative estimate — given me by Dr Karl Baier, anti-Nazi, now installed as head of Berlin's Social Welfare Committee — there are 8,000,000 homeless nomads milling about the areas of the provinces around Berlin. If you take in the Sudeten Germans expelled from Czechoslovakia and those on the move from elsewhere, the figure of those for whom no food can be provided rises to 13,000,000 at least. This proportion of Germany's population must die before winter if nothing is done.'

If we call attention to this vast tragedy, it is certainly not because we fail to realise how grievously our allies are suffering, nor because we would wish any preference to be given to ex-enemy nationals. Nothing is more urgent than the speediest relief of Europe as a whole. 'I believe,' said Sir Arthur Salter recently in the House of Commons, 'that if the lorries that we and the American Army have near the spot where they are required were used quickly, the transport problem of Europe could be solved. I believe that if the reserves of meat and clothing which the Armies have were freed and quickly used, a great deal could be done to meet the other necessities of Europe.' We wholeheartedly endorse this plea. But we are profoundly troubled by even the bare possibility that mass starvation cannot be prevented without some cut in our own rations, and that the authorities may hesitate to ask us, after six years of war, to make this sacrifice: and also by the fear that, amidst so much misery, the actual death by hunger of German nationals may be disregarded.

We do not think that the Government need feel such hesitation. It is not in accordance with the traditions of this country to allow children — even the children of ex-enemies — to starve. But we have reason to believe that in any case numbers of our fellow-countrymen would be willing to make some voluntary sacrifice in this cause. We ask, therefore, all who read this letter, and who share our concern, immediately to send a postcard (not a letter) to 'Save Europe Now', 144, Southampton Row, London, WC1, giving their name and address and saying that they will gladly have their rations cut, if thereby alone men, women and children of whatever nationality may be saved from intolerable suffering.

The postcards arrived: 30,000 within the month, 60,000 by early 1946 and 100,000 come the spring. The volunteers in the tiny office at the National Peace Council worked gamely to acknowledge them, but it was soon clear that a proper organization had to be set up. (Victor had Peggy Duff to do it — the perfect organizer. She had begun her remarkable career in 1944, with Common Wealth, and when Acland announced in September 1945 that he was joining the Labour Party, she was out of a job. She immediately became Victor's personal political secretary, and in due course secretary of Save Europe Now.)

Victor had decided on a two-pronged attack. He published another pamphlet, mainly composed of articles by others emphasizing the seriousness of the problem (*Europe & Germany: Today and Tomorrow*), and mainly for distribution to MPs. He also set about organizing a large public meeting, designed to put pressure on the government, who must secure international action against further expulsions and for the prevention of starvation. Invitations in huge numbers were sent out to MPs, religious leaders, trade unionists, the press and representatives of science and the professions. The venue was the Conway Hall on Monday, 8 October. Bertrand Russell was first choice to take the chair, but Victor became alarmed at the vehemence of his attacks on the Russians. When he was shown a letter from Russell destined for the *New Statesman*, Victor felt impelled to write to him, enclosing, in some trepidation, a redraft. The correspondence throws light on his private view of the Soviet Union.

Everyone knows the horrible dilemma we are in. Apart from the vital principles involved, if we fail to protest against Soviet goings-on a situation will arise when somebody or other will eventually say 'It must stop' and then God help us. On the other hand, given the Russian mentality, protesting may create a war atmosphere.

I am with you all the way in the view that, faced with this dilemma, we *must* speak firmly and mustn't appease. But I do think — forgive me — that your letter gives an appearance of bellicosity. And, if the letter appears on Friday, then it and your chairmanship on Monday will inevitably be linked together and the meeting may be given something of the character of an 'anti-Bolshevik crusade' in the bad sense. I am told that already, as a result of the things they have seen, a lot of soldiers in Berlin are saying 'Goebbels was right': we don't want *that* sort of development. . . .

I believe this 'Save Europe Now' movement is so important, not only for what it may directly do but as a step towards stopping the descent into every kind of immorality, that I am desperately anxious that we shouldn't get the kind of controversy round it which might wreck it.

His letter had crossed one of Patricia Russell's questioning whether her husband was in fact the right man to take the chair. 'As you have asked me so frankly,' replied Victor

I do think that, in the circumstances it would probably be better for your husband not to take the chair. As this is the first meeting to be held on the subject, there is a certain symbolism about the chairmanship: and as I think I know that your husband will inevitably be moved to write a good deal about Russia during the coming weeks or months it is perhaps important that people shouldn't be able to say in the lying way they do that this is nothing but an anti-Russian stunt, and that the choice of chairman for the original meeting proves it.

He hoped, however, he would still attend.

Quite apart from all this I do wish he would find the time to reconsider the phrasing of the *New Statesman* letter. I well know the passionate mood of indignation against ruthlessness in which it was written: I am constantly in that mood myself and was indeed banned for ever from the Soviet Embassy four years ago because, in what I thought to be a balanced speech, I said that the Soviet Union had undoubtedly committed not merely some blunders, but some crimes.

Plain speaking was vital, but criticism, however severe, 'should give the impression of being considered rather than explosive.'

Please ask your husband to forgive me for all this. I feel like what the Jews call Amhoerez (a man of the soil, an ignorant man) talking to a great Melammed (sage) for, as I think I wrote some months ago, when he wrote to me about my little Buchenwald pamphlet, his writings (or such of them as I can understand!) have expressed for me more of the essential truth than any other in our time.

Russell agreed to amend and hold over his *New Statesman* letter until after the meeting. But, said his wife,

> He cannot of course publish your amended version, since it does not read like him, and does contain statements that are the opposite of what he thinks — e. g. that friendship without hypocrisy is at present possible with Russia. This he does not think, as the Russian system and pretensions appear to him to be based on hypocrisy. But where friendship is impossible he believes that the only sane policy is to make clear what we will stand and what we will not. This he will attempt to do without 'bellicosity' . . . The difficulty is that long suppressed feelings when at last freed are apt to be volcanic, and my husband has been forced for lack of agreement to suppress his feelings about Russia since 1920. But the substance of the letter is simply what he thinks, and though he refrains from publishing it, he wants you to know that those are his views: that there is not a pin to choose between Germany and Russia, and that Russia wants peace only in the sense that Hitler wanted it — at its own price. He won't mind at all if you would rather someone else took the chair — in fact he would be relieved, as he hates taking chairs — just as you like.

She assured him in another letter (3 October) that Russell was unoffended and would continue to support Save Europe Now (SEN★) and come to its meetings. 'I hope', she went on, 'you saw his second *Forward* article, which was reprinted in yesterday's Manchester Guardian, and was much more moderate in tone. I think myself that it is a very useful article, but even so, best kept away from your chair.'

Victor was delighted by the article, 'I think this wanted saying badly, and wants to be repeated often. In point of fact your husband is a little more "pro-Russian" in one or two points than I would be. For instance, I very much doubt whether "what is evil in the Soviet system is very largely the outcome of fear generated by Western hostile intervention after the last war". That may have been a starting point: but I am afraid I have come to the conclusion that the whole Leninist ideology . . . is what is really mainly responsible.'

He did not agree with Russell that there was nothing to choose between Russia and Germany — Stalin was quite as much a fanatic as Hitler, but while Hitler preferred to get what he wanted through war, Stalin would rather get it by peaceful means. Friendship with the Soviet Union, remote though the possibility was, should be sought.

★The organization was always spoken of as Save Europe Now, but the initials SEN were occasionally used, as here, to save space in documents.

There is another point in the article which worries me and has worried me for a long time. He writes 'We should concede a free hand to Russia in Eastern Europe on the ground that in that region we cannot effectively intervene'. But does that mean that we are just to keep silent if Russia or her puppets commit the most horrible atrocities in those countries? Supposing, for instance (and I am not sure that this is not even now the case), that we knew on irrefutable evidence that large-scale massacres of political opponents were taking place in those countries: we are not to protest? And if we don't, then don't we make nonsense of our protests against Hitler's atrocities before the war? Suppose for argument that there were large-scale anti-Jewish pogroms, deliberately fostered by Russia, in Eastern Europe — although it is unlikely: how could we just say nothing about it, when we spent half our time protesting against Hitler's anti-Jewish atrocities in Germany? I haven't the faintest idea what the answer to this question is: but for my own part I just can't help protesting against cruelty and injustice wherever it may occur.

I'd immensely like to talk all this over with your husband some time soon. It seems to me awfully important that we should get some clear line of action, as the situation is unquestionably going to get worse and worse during the coming months.

Victor was trammelled again. He was receiving letters from MPs (including Lyall Wilkes and Zilliacus) warning him of the dangers of contamination with anti-Soviet agitation, which would be counter-productive in terms of world peace and do nothing to help the refugees. To avoid the enmity of left-wing socialists he had to tread warily, while to keep SEN's conservatives and liberals happy he had to denounce Soviet barbarities. He was to show great self-restraint in avoiding arguments with the CP, who were now strongly in favour of a vengeful policy towards Germany, and whom he had given up as a bad job. Victor realized that all his war-time hopes that the Soviet Union would favour a humane peace had been proved grotesquely ill-founded at Potsdam and after. He had already decided that, though LBC members could be useful in SEN, he would not encourage them to form groups, which he feared would inevitably come under CP, and therefore Moscow's, control.

Victor took the chair at the Conway Hall in place of Russell. The event was successful beyond even his expectations, and at the last minute an overflow meeting had to be arranged at the Holborn Hall with Eleanor Rathbone in the chair. Even there, people were turned away. More had accepted his invitation than he had expected, and a remarkable cross-section of distinguished figures graced the attendance lists. As well as three bishops and sundry MPs, names like Sir William Beveridge, Cyril Connolly, T. S. Eliot, Cyril Joad, Sir

Walter Layton, Harold Nicolson, George Orwell and Sybil Thorndike strike the eye. The speakers were Richard Crossman, Barbara
Ward of the *Economist*, Violet Bonham Carter, Gerald Gardiner and
the Bishop of Chichester, and the audience was moved to support
with enthusiasm the resolutions proposed, urging the government:

1. To negotiate with the Russian, Polish and Czechoslovak Governments
   with a view to stopping the expulsion of Germans from their homes in
   Eastern Europe forthwith and throughout the winter, and to develop
   an agreed inter-allied policy on this subject before the spring;
2. To concert with the American and French authorities an immediate
   common policy for the reception into their respective zones of such
   numbers of those already expelled as can be housed and fed in view of
   the existing commitments of the Western Powers to their own peoples
   and to the liberated countries;
3. In view of the crucial importance of the Ruhr coal mines for the
   economy of the whole of Western Europe, to concert plans with the
   French, Dutch and Belgian Governments for increasing production by
   all possible means, including the provision of adequate rations for the
   miners and their families, the production of railway rolling stock,
   track, etc., and, for the purpose of stimulating production, the
   allotment of a proportion of the output for German household needs;
4. To mobilise all available motor vehicles, whether British, American or
   German, to break the transport bottleneck;
5. To use the civilian and military reserves of food and other resources
   which can now be released owing to the termination of hostilities
   (together with the necessary cargo shipping and in conjunction with the
   United States of America) for the urgent needs of the various
   populations;
6. To press forward with the establishment of a Supreme Economic
   Council for the co-ordination of the assistance to be given to and by the
   different countries concerned, and for the longer-term reconstruction
   of all needy and devastated areas.

The Prime Minister was asked to receive a deputation, and the
government as a whole called upon to sponsor a practicable scheme
enabling individuals voluntarily to forgo part of their rations.

Attlee received a deputation on 26 October, and its proposals
(which now included a scheme for bringing German children to
stay in the homes of welcoming individuals who would share their
rations with them) were put into the melting-pot of government
for consideration. Members of the deputation included Beveridge,
Gardiner, Countess Russell, Rathbone, Brailsford, Crossman,
Boothby, two bishops, and Quintin Hogg — the man who had
defeated Lindsay on the Munich ticket at the 1938 Oxford by-election.

Lord Templewood, one of Victor's most loathed Chamberlainites when he had been plain Samuel Hoare, sent a telegram in support. (Victor was beginning to learn that there were Tories other than Churchill and Boothby who did not have horns. He had been surprised at the quality and quantity of support for his Buchenwald pamphlet from right-wingers concerned about Christian values. It was an important part of his political education: he was never again quite so whole-hearted in his anti-Tory propaganda.)

On 6 November another deputation went to the Ministry of Food to see Sir Ben Smith, an ex-docker and anti-German who eroded further Victor's faith in the decency of the Labour Party. SEN proposed a number of methods of making voluntary contributions, all of which were met with an unenthusiastic response, although the minister agreed to have them looked at by his department. Three days later Victor was writing (in answer to a member of the public who wanted him to help set up a new Fabian Society committed to supranational socialism):

> I couldn't possibly be more in agreement with you. Not only is what you say true of other countries, but it is true of our own. Minister after minister here is giving expression to views, in private as well as in public, which are quite definitely National Socialist. This applies particularly to one of the most *important* of the *Catholic* ministers. And National Socialism is not superior to liberal capitalism: it is appallingly inferior to it.
>
> I am spending every second of my time in campaigning on behalf of the ideas you put forward, both directly, and indirectly through such movements as 'Save Europe Now' and so on. Whether we can go further and actually form some society I will consider most carefully. Please keep in touch with me.

Like so many of the ideas proposed to Victor and promised his consideration, this one came to nothing. He really was too busy, keeping up remorseless pressure on the government. Before he had had a formal answer from Smith, he was horrified at his announcement that rations would be increased in Britain at Christmas. Victor rushed out a booklet of photographs of starving German children (*Is It Nothing to You?*), with a foreword that trenchantly reminded his readers of the real meaning of Christmas.

> I hate the argument that because, for instance, America is giving little from her superfluity, we should now 'look after ourselves'. I hate the shoddy lies by which our selfishness is rationalised: if we are in such danger of epidemics from malnutrition, why does the Chief Medical Officer of the Ministry of Health tell us this very week that 'there is no evidence

whatever of any weakening of the physical health of the people of this country'? But most of all I hate the excuse that, because few can be saved by some extra effort, it is not worth saving any. 'Are not two sparrows sold for a farthing? and one of them shall not fall on the ground without the Father.'

Choose any one of these children who look so unlike your children and mine — choose at random — and ask yourself whether, if you can do even a little to assuage the suffering of even only that one, you dare refuse to do it . . .

The photographs in *Is It Nothing to You?* were indeed harrowing, but they touched mainly the converted — those who wanted to help but were stymied by government foot-dragging. Smith turned down all but one proposal for getting food to the Continent: the sending of parcels to individuals abroad, for instance, was rejected because of black market considerations; the proposed withdrawal of the adult confectionery ration and the point-coupon rationing of main meals in restaurants were seen as compulsory cuts that could not be entertained. Smith's only concession was that money could be raised for the Council of British Relief Societies Abroad (COBRSA).

Depressed but undaunted, Victor organized a mass meeting at the Albert Hall on 26 November under the chairmanship of the Archbishop of York. The speakers were two Labour MPs — Foot and Stokes; two independents — Rathbone and Sir Arthur Salter (later to become a Conservative); Clement Davies, Leader of the Liberal Party; Bob Boothby; Air Vice-Marshal Hugh de Crespigny, a regional commissioner in the British Zone; and Victor himself. His speech left his audience in no doubt that they were participating in a moral crusade. He began with a passionate attack on the unreasonably high level of food reserves and the government's determination

in the supposed interest of our precious health, that no one should voluntarily give up anything. This is intolerable. We are free citizens of a free country and even if all this talk about health were not frankly nonsense, how we balance our obligation to ourselves against our obligation to our neighbours is a matter for our own conscience, something between us and God. Sir Ben Smith is not the keeper of our consciences, but the temporary Minister of Food in a temporary British Government.

He dealt forcefully with Smith's rejection of various proposals and went on:

Well, this campaign of ours is by no means over: but, even if it were, it would certainly not have been in vain . . .

I am alluding to the fact that our campaign has given an opportunity for the common man and woman to express their concern — by postcards, by resolutions in organisations great and small, and by meetings which are being held in ever increasing numbers all over the country. That, my friends, is democracy — and I glory in it.

I glory too in the revelation, if revelation were needed, of the amount of sheer decency which still survives in this country, and which, if only given an opportunity, may yet mend a broken world . . .

I know moral indignation is thought nowadays to be sterile, and that any protest against accomplished facts is useless. Well, I can't help it: there is something in me which compels me to protest from this platform, and to protest, I believe, in your name, against extra rations not for our health — there is no pretence of that — but for our jollification, when children to whom they might have been given are — as you see them in that booklet on your seats.

Briefly he touched on international relations, the fraternal links with the United States and the sympathy felt for the suffering of the Soviet Union

so infinitely greater than our own, that she has endured with such heroism during these years of war, and which is the explanation, though not, I think, the justification, for those of her policies which we deplore. And now I come to my final point, which is by far the nearest to my heart.

This is not a meeting about feeding Europe, or rather, that is only part of what this meeting is about.

Call it if you like a meeting about future world peace, or about the control of the atomic bomb, or, most truly of all, about whether the human race is to sink into total bestiality, or to rise to heights, as it can rise, of unimaginable splendour.

We all know the condition of the world today, and I refer not exclusively or even mainly to the physical condition, but to the moral condition. We all know the brutality, the bestiality, the suspicion, the hatred, the narrow nationalism, the racial intolerance — all the things that we sum up in the word Antichrist.

We also know that, if another war comes, it will mean the end of decent living perhaps for generations, perhaps for ever.

And what is the cause of every war? I say every war — not merely the war that is just ended, but the war of 1914–1918, or the Boer war, or the Franco-Prussian war, or the wars of Louis XIV, and so on to the dawn of recorded history. The cause of every war is the same — greed and selfishness in their various forms.

The last and only hope was immediately to substitute selflessness for greed and co-operation for exclusiveness.

I would go further, and say that only the common people can do it. Our great Foreign Secretary, Mr Ernest Bevin, said two or three days ago that the common people everywhere would have prevented every war if the facts had been put calmly before them, but that they were kept separated. I believe this to be profoundly true, and I believe it to be true also that the common people everywhere would desire to heal the wounds of the world, if only their best instincts were appealed to.

That is why I believe this meeting to be one of the most important ever held in the city of London: and I dare to hope that it may be the starting point of a great international movement of the common people every-where.

For we, the ordinary men and women of Britain, are calling from this hall tonight to the ordinary men and women of the whole world; and we are asking them to join with us in carrying into effect here and now the real message of Christmas; which is *not*, Your Grace, more sugar or fats for our own bellies while our neighbours starve, but practical charity, mercy in the hour when mercy is most needed, and so at last, God willing, that goal on which we fix our saddened but still not wholly despairing gaze, the brotherhood of man.

The meeting and its overflow were a huge success, but Victor had to give the supporters of SEN something practical to do to demonstrate their moral lead. On the very day of the meeting he had appealed in writing to Attlee over Smith's head, and got a reply indicating that the Prime Minister was unmoved by the 'two sparrows' argument. 'It is my belief,' Attlee said in the course of his answer, 'supported by the best advice that I can obtain, that voluntary schemes such as those which you sponsor could not make an effective contribution to the solution of this problem in Europe, even though they might satisfy the consciences of particular individuals.' His assurance that the govern-ment were doing their utmost and sending extra supplies to Europe did not mollify Victor.

The only scope for immediate action was in fund-raising: the Ministry of Food had offered to sell COBRSA £100,000-worth of surplus, and a Food Relief Fund was opened in December. This gave Victor a rationale for constituting SEN formally as a Council rather than an informal pressure group. He showed that he had learned well the lessions of ASPRA. The sponsors — Berry, Bell of Chichester, Lindsay of Balliol, Murray and Russell — gave SEN status but were active only in an advisory capacity. The executive committee was made up of people he could rely on to back him: Brailsford, Henry Carter (treasurer), Peggy Duff (secretary), John Collins (Dean of Oriel and already a good friend), Michael Foot, R. R. Stokes, and the two well-known humanitarians, Eva Hubback and Roy Walker.

Victor was chairman, Rathbone vice-chairman. SEN and its Food Relief Fund were formally launched early in January; by April the £100,000 target had been reached and fund-raising suspended.

It was a considerable blow to Victor when Eleanor Rathbone, his right hand on the executive, died suddenly on 2 January, just after finishing a draft circular she had promised. He had greatly admired her as a doughty and patient worker for the unfortunate and though they were never friends, they had worked together well and shared the same values. She was not replaced as vice-chairman: Victor and Peggy Duff ran SEN between them and their activities went far beyond laborious fund raising. Already, by 3 January, 2,000 public figures had signed a Memorial to the Prime Minister. Headed by the Archbishop of Canterbury (Victor's Repton headmaster), Geoffrey Fisher, they begged that 'without prejudice to the claims of special categories, such as children, nursing and expectant mothers, and heavy workers, general rations in this country should not be raised so long as there is famine on the Continent of Europe.' The crucial part of Attlee's response to Victor (25 January 1946) was as follows:

2. His Majesty's Government are not prepared to give so wide an undertaking, which indeed could only properly be given to Parliament, nor do they think that it would be right to do so. It would not be possible for any Government to make the standard of life of its people dependent on conditions, however brought about, in countries over which they have no control.

3. On the basis of what is practicable, however, there is little prospect of any substantial increase in the level of home consumption while world supplies are as short as they are now. This does not mean, however, that the government are ready to undertake that in no circumstances will there be any general increase of rations. It may be shown to be necessary to provide some variation of the present monotonous and unexciting diet in order to secure increased production at home and thereby build up the export trade on which our future depends.

He ended with an uncharacteristically long justification of government policy, insisting that any further increase in supplies for European relief must come from the food-exporting countries, whom the British government were urging to help.

Victor was not to be thus fobbed off, and he embarked on a series of letters to the press and speech tours around the country, growing ever more eloquent and vehement. The clash between him and Attlee was described by a commentator of the 1950s as the cleavage between Utopia and original sin: Victor believed there was no limit to man's capacity for goodness: Attlee thought it so unlikely that his countrymen would respond to a call for self-sacrifice that any such an appeal would be folly. Even if Victor was being unrealistic in asking Attlee to appeal to the altruism of the British people, there was nothing unreasonable about asking for permission to make moral gestures possible. Among those who backed Victor's campaign was a supporter he could have done without — Evelyn Waugh. In May Waugh wrote to the *New Statesman* deploring 'the policy of starving the Germans' and the banning of food parcels, but went on:

> surely the prohibition lies at the heart of Socialism? Conscience has been nationalised. Private charity, like private thrift, has no place in the world Mr Gollancz has striven so conspicuously to create. The law which forbids selfishness, forbids with equal justice unselfishness. Our food is not our own property by right of purchase to dispose of as we think fit; it is a ration allowed us by the State in order, as has been made clear in the Parliamentary replies quoted in Mr Gollancz's recent pamphlet, to keep us strong to work for the State. In this, as in all matters, the State is the sole judge of what is best for us.
>
> There are many of us who deeply resent this principle, but it is hard to see what right Mr Gollancz has to complain. He has probably done more than any living man to secure its popular acceptance.

In his frustration, Victor was driven to sit down and write his best polemical book: *Our Threatened Values*. His urgency was so great that before finishing it he issued a modified chapter as a pamphlet — *Leaving Them to Their Fate: The Ethics of Starvation*. Quotes from Clement Attlee and Marcus Aurelius made strange bed-fellows on one of the preliminary pages. Victor had lifted the 'standard of life' sentence from Attlee's letter of 25 January; from Marcus Aurelius he quoted: 'There is someone who says Dear City of Cecrops! Will [someone] say *O dear City of Zeus?*' The pamphlet was dedicated to 'my friends Renée and Léonce Bernheim, of Paris, who suffered and presumably died under the Nazi terror, but would have wished that, when the war was over, all suffering should cease.' (They were sister-in-law and brother to Edmond Fleg's wife, Madeleine. Both died in a concentration camp.)

The pamphlet specifically concerned itself with the recent treatment of Germans in the British Zone, where the food shortage was worsening as the spring went on. He recommended the adoption of a seven-point programme (similar to that adopted by the executive of SEN) which was 'immediately practicable, and falls, indeed, far short of what I personally think possible and right.' It included the sending to Europe of a proportion of reserve stocks, bread rationing, the surrender of a one-point coupon after a restaurant meal and the lifting of the ban on sending food parcels abroad. In a postscript written on 11 April he was delighted to report some positive movements on the international front and the imminence of bread rationing in Britain.

Leaving Them to Their Fate was widely distributed in Britain, and extracts sent to individuals on the Continent who might find it encouraging. Fleg, who had escaped the Nazis but lost both sons during the war, approved broadly, with the slight reservation that Victor had ignored the problem of Jewish refugees. It was clear from Victor's response that he believed Jewish refugees to be marginally better off already than others, and that he felt he had already done his special pleading in *Nowhere to Lay Their Heads*. Martin Niemöller, the famous German pastor and theologian who had suffered years in a concentration camp for his unrelenting opposition to Hitler, wrote of the pamphlet glowingly, but feared it was already too late to prevent mass starvation.

> I myself doubt that any help could be arranged in proper time even if the wish to do so were general which certainly it is not — I know that we have no right of complaining, and I don't. But tired as we are unto death, we feel a real gratitude that all over the world human beings are suffering by heart with those who can't be saved, as it appears by now, and we look upon this fact as upon a hope, and the only hope for those who may survive after all . . .

That of course was the vitally important aspect of Victor's work for post-war Germany: the moral and spiritual effect of giving large numbers of disparate people the opportunity to show that they cared.

About 75,000 copies of *Leaving Them to Their Fate* were distributed free. About as many again had been sold, when it was usurped by the book, *Our Threatened Values*, which reached the bookshops early in June. The central value of Western civilization was in it described as 'respect for personality', — the uniqueness of every individual, and the *essential* spiritual equality of all human beings. The curbing of self-assertion and development of co-operation was demanded 'by respect not only of others but also of ourselves'. The ideal society 'is one of fully developed personalities, freely co-operating, but each one of them with an inner core of unassailable loneliness.' The Nazis had turned these values upside-down; communism now posed the greatest threat. Yet only through 'a liberal and humanistic socialism' could Western values, now being weakened by economic chauvinism, be realized: not through partial materialist socialism as practised by the Labour government, but through true international socialism. On the

Continent, civilization was being turned backwards by the normaliz-
ation of unfortunate traits developed during the resistance period, by
the intensification of nationalism and by a reversion to a more barbaric
concept of justice, as exemplified by the Nuremberg trials. What was
crucial was the fostering of these precious values through example: the
treatment of Germany would be the test case.

Victor's argument was brilliantly developed and sustained, and
although parts of the book are necessarily very topical, some of the
chapters have a strength and universality that give them immediacy
almost forty years later. Particularly impressive is his defence of the
principle of free speech against pressure groups on the left and in the
Jewish community — backed by the National Council for Civil
Liberties — who were trying to outlaw the expression of fascist and
anti-semitic opinions. The whole book was a magnificent expression
of his faith and his denunciations were couched with deadly effectiveness. Perhaps because he wrote it in a hurry and had to keep it short, it
showed less than usual of the self-indulgence that Wittgenstein had
condemned, and hence attracted a wider constituency. There were
new names among the fan-letters. Randolph Churchill's was one: 'I
trust you will not think it impertinent for a stranger to write and tell
you how deeply moved he has been by "Our Threatened Values". It is
a brave and good book, and I hope it will have the influence which it
deserves.' Churchill pressed it on his father, who referred to it in the
House of Commons as 'a remarkable book'. Lord Winterton, a
minister under Chamberlain, wrote that he had read it with 'real moral
and intellectual profit'. Victor's response mentioned the letters from
Conservatives as having confirmed his view that 'however passionately we may differ in the practical application of fundamental
principles, the overwhelming majority of people brought up in the
British tradition are basically liberal in outlook.'

He went further in a letter to an admirer who deplored the
government's failings but sought to explain them: 'The Labour
leaders are a mixed lot. My experience is that to a few of them your
apologia may apply: but very many — it is terrible to have to say it —
are even cruder in their general xenophobia (which always comes into
the open when an ex-enemy is concerned) even than the Tories.'
(Victor, of course, had a wide definition of xenophobia. Nothing less
than total love and forgiveness for the enemy was enough. He did not
like the attitude expressed by people like Laski — who endorsed *Our
Threatened Values* warmly but added 'My one criticism would be that
it would be far more persuasive if you put in a special section,
addressed to the Germans, on the urgency of repentance.')

T. S. Eliot was one of the *litterati* who responded warmly, writing of his deep interest and warm agreement 'on the immediately relevant issues'. He was later to refer to the book in his *Notes on the Definition of Culture*, as a confirmation from a very different standpoint of his contention that culture was in decay.

Of all the lavish praise heaped on the book, the most welcome to Victor seems to have been a comment by a Christian of Jewish extraction, then a refugee in Nairobi. 'I was particularly pleased', he wrote in answer, 'by the fact that you called the book Voltairian. So it is: I am actually much more of a Voltairian than anything else: but most people don't seem to understand that, because of the religious phraseology.' (It was not a fair guessing-game Victor was expecting his readers to play; according to time, mood, or interlocutor he was of Aristotelian, Jewish, Christian, Anarchist, Marxist or any one of a number of other persuasions — or a mixture of any or all of them.)

Two letters were redolent of past associations. One was from an old pupil, Alan Ayling, who had been prompted to write by the discovery of an unanswered letter from Victor dated March 1919. '"As for my future" you write "God knows. It definitely *must* be something either political or educational; how on earth, unless one has the joy (and I dare say misery) of being an artist, can one do anything else. For after all the post-war situation is far worse than the war situation was: such an exhibition of greed and hate and stupidity on every side . . . "' That letter and *Our Threatened Values* 'brought Gollancz before me, not as the name on the back of the wrapper, the stimulant or irritant, but as Victor, stalking about in haste as he orates, thumping the floor with a stick, the young man who helped to provide me with my Golden Journey; the kind; the lover of Shaw and Shelley, someone with a little-that-might-become-a-lot of Prometheus and Socrates in him; with just the right mixture of Mild and Bitter under the iridescent froth . . .'

'I am very glad that you are happy', wrote Victor. 'I am nowadays a rather tortured sort of person whom you would hardly recognise from Repton — intensely happy in my home life, horrified about the world, hating the business side of publishing, wanting to cultivate my garden, study and write, but prevented from giving up publishing because there are things I can do through it that I couldn't do in any other way. And I'm getting to the age now when so many of one's friends are dead or dying . . .'

The other old friend was Harold Rubinstein, whose family and business connection with Victor had kept them in close and friendly contact over the years — Victor the leader, Rubinstein, when his conscience allowed him, the disciple.

24 June 1946

My dear Victor,

Reading your new — and finest — book has taken me back to the early days of our friendship when, as a juvenile Shavian, I liked to consider myself a thorough-going Socialist, and you, as a complete Liberal, persuaded me (though I may not have admitted it) that socialism was a cart that could only be usefully employed so long as it functioned *behind* the Liberal horse. What I always specially admired was your capacity for keeping first principles consistently in mind while arguing anywhere on the lower levels. In fact, the lower levels didn't really attract me, and when later on your passion for getting things done took you into party politics under the socialist banner, it was a constant regret to me that, finding myself hopelessly bewildered in that atmosphere, I dared not follow you into the arena. And now, by a turn of the spiral along which all true progress lies, you appear suddenly, as it were, poised above the arena, arrayed in your old Liberal garments, only transfigured (kind of) by the pure Christianity which, in the intervening years, I have been imbibing surreptitiously . . . or trying to imbibe.

This is all very clumsily rhetorical, but it may give you some idea of the emotions 'Our Threatened Values' has stirred in me — pleasurable emotions, on the whole, in spite of your grim theme, and your relentlessly honest treatment of it. I was also reminded of the Shavian Preface of the best period, in which, however much one might squirm at the painful implications, one was forced to recognise the voice of one speaking with authority.

I have been shocked to find that copies of the book are not easily obtainable at ordinary bookshops. Is somebody trying to organize a boycott? If so, I trust and believe you'll find a way of circumventing the conspiracy. The gist of the book *must* somehow be absorbed into public opinion. But perhaps God will see to that.

With thanks and love
Harold

Other letters also complained of bookshops not stocking the work, and Victor was convinced that there was indeed some kind of 'half-boycott'. He attributed it to his violent attack on the press. The truth was probably more mundane, as Victor would have been the first to point out to any author in similar distress: there was a slump in the market for political books. However, for a book of its kind, *Our Threatened Values*, well reviewed and publicized in a masterly fashion, sold spectacularly well. Though exact figures are not available, a fair estimate is that it sold about 50,000 in the first edition, and more in the cheaper version that followed. Additionally, it was the LBC Choice for July 1946 (membership was down near the 10,000 mark) and, as usual, distributed free to a large number of influential people in Britain and elsewhere. An ex-professor of Greek, Thomas Callader, sent Victor £50 to pay for copies to be sent to heads of universities and colleges in North America. It had a considerable international sale, for Gollancz was a successful exporter, the yellow covers a familiar sight throughout the British Empire and Commonwealth. Victor even sent a copy to Gandhi on the recommendation of two mutual friends: 'Both of them have also said that one could possibly find peace of mind by coming to see you. Perhaps one day I shall ask to be allowed to do so.' He received a letter from a secretary saying Gandhi was reading it. He did not leave it to God to handle the circulation. His sales manager, Jane Savager, sent a letter, along with extracts of reviews to all booksellers in late July, once more calling special attention to *Our Threatened Values*. 'As Mr Gollancz is anxious', she concluded, 'that the ideas expressed in the book, which he believes to be shared by very many, should reach a wide public, he has asked me to say that we will be willing to supply any number of copies on a "see safe" [sale, or return for credit] basis, provided that the books are well shown . . . ' One of the Gollancz travellers received a severe wigging for failing to persuade Selfridges to stock the book. Victor also kept an eagle eye on press coverage. Violet Bonham Carter was enjoined to use her influence to get it reviewed in the *News Chronicle*; Rose Macaulay was called on to protest against cuts made in her review in the *Spectator*; John Collins was asked to object to the *Church of Ireland Gazette* about 'the damned impudence' of 'the fellow' who referred to Victor as a 'secular socialist'.

When Victor came across a word of adverse criticism in a review it cut him to the quick, however ecstatic the general coverage. Equipped as he was with excellent quotes from representatives of the Conservatives (Churchill), Labour (Foot), Liberals, I.L.P., 'Left Socialist' and Common Wealth, and from Catholic, Church of England, Jewish, Methodist, Congregational, Baptist, Unitarian and Quaker sources not to mention a full-page rave from Joad in the *New Statesman* and expressions of deep approval in the *Economist*, a less sensitive writer might overlook the occasional thrust from an obscure source, but that was never the case with Victor. Ethel Mannin was castigated for saying in *Values* that he should logically be a pacifist; and the clergyman who had so wounded him in the *Church of Ireland Gazette* was reminded in the letters column that the real sin against the Holy Ghost was spiritual pride. That elicited a letter so full of uncomfortable home-truths that it should have taught Victor (but of course did not) that reviewers are best left alone.

May I say briefly, in reply to Mr Gollancz, that my use of the word 'secular' was not 'loosely' meant to convey the ideas either of atheism or agnosticism. By a 'secular socialist' I simply mean a man whose socialism is the expression of the belief that humanity is capable of fulfilling its destiny in this world and to whom, therefore, the world beyond death is secondary. I have never said or implied that Mr Gollancz is an atheist or agnostic. If he wants to know my grounds for calling him 'a secular socialist', I shall be pleased to oblige. But I shall be still more pleased to hear Mr Gollancz's denial of my description of him as 'a secular socialist'.

It was certainly my impression that Mr Gollancz had undergone some change in his religious views, but it seems I am 'totally in error'. All I can say is that I heard Mr Gollancz many and many a time in Left Book Club meetings and conferences, when I never heard him mention religion at all, either one way or the other, except once. It was in a conference in a hotel in Southampton Row, London, when in answer to a question he jocularly denied that his socialism had anything to do with Christianity *and still less with Judaism*. That's the point. Mr Gollancz then was purely humanist. He talks and writes much more now about religion than he ever did in the heyday of his Left Book Club. From that I inferred — surely not unreasonably — that his views had undergone some change. Such change may be a matter of emphasis as well as substance or content. Does Mr Gollancz deny any change in emphasis?

Mr Gollancz need ask me for no forgiveness when he reminds me of the peril of spiritual pride. I thank him for it; for I know how easy it is to be guilty of it. Not even Mr Gollancz is immune. Is it spiritual pride to be honestly mistaken about Mr Gollancz's spiritual progress? Incidentally, Mr Gollancz is in error when he says that the real sin against the Holy Ghost is spiritual pride. If he will look up St Matthew xii.24–32, he will find there that Christ states that the sin against the Holy Ghost is the perverse attribution of God's good works to the devil, which is the final fruit of pride.

Yours, etc.,

D. R. Davies

Charges of inconsistency maddened Victor, and they came frequently from columnists and leader writers who had not studied in depth his self-analytical and self-justificatory accounts of the logical progression of his ideas. 'Having done more than any other single man to put a Socialist Government in power,' commented the *Birmingham Mail* in a typical gibe, 'Mr Gollancz is climbing back on the bandwagon of Liberal humanism.'

There was some compensation in the adulation he was beginning to attract as a spiritual leader. 'I have only one comment to make,' wrote an Indian journalist.

You who are responsible for the book are really a Mahatma (a great soul) and the England in which you live is a great nation if not for anything else at least for the fact that there are people like you living in this country.

If all the politicians who have been crowding Paris for the last few weeks care to read a few pages of 'Our Threatened Values' every day before they go to the Conference Room, I feel sure, they will be able to make it a real 'Peace Conference'.

His old friend Eric Strauss, the psychiatrist, finding that the book 'seems to say all the things that I have been saying for years' went on with tongue slightly in cheek. 'You know of course that from the beginning of time mankind has slain its Prophets. That does not matter all that much to the Prophet, however.'

Victor drew the line at 'Mahatma', but was quite happy to be called a prophet — he had been heading that way all his life. With *Our Threatened Values* he had taken his message on to a high spiritual plane, and many had heard it. He discussed the prophetic role in a letter to Acland, who was worried in his own life as a propagandist about the conflict between absolutism and expediency, arrogance and humility, in fighting the communists.

In theological language, we are merely God's instruments: we must therefore be quite absolute about the message in so far as we comprehend it, but humble to the last degree in recognising the feebleness with which we understand and convey it.

Surely this is the key to the mixture of utter humility and extreme 'arrogance' which has troubled a lot of people in the life of Christ? He, a raw and, by academic standards, ignorant young man of thirty, drove the money changers out of the temple without the smallest hesitation, because he *knew* that to make his Father's house a place of traffic was *wrong*: but that he should have thought himself personally superior to even the worst of those money changers seems to me quite unthinkable. And Christ was not really peculiar in this respect: He simply had both qualities — the personal humility and the arrogance about absolutes — in a higher degree than, so far as we know, anyone else has had: but the same mixture is to be found in every Prophet whom I have read — and indeed in a very great number of ordinary monks and nuns, or in such men as Father — I can't remember his name, but the Dominican of Hampstead who died about three years ago of cancer of the throat. I used to go and talk to him up in his church. I never met a man more utterly convinced of the truth of his doctrine: but his personal humility was so great that he wouldn't even ride in a bus — he walked everywhere — because he thought that he was the least worthy of men, and should therefore have fewer conveniences than others.

. . . One day perhaps I shall try and write a real quarter of a million word book about it all, instead of a glorified pamphlet.

Victor possessed the arrogance of the prophet; there was often the necessary power; he always had the necessary sincerity. What continued to bedevil him was the humility. In private—and increasingly in public — he was beginning to dwell on his consciousness of his own inferiority to even the worst sadists or murderers — a line of approach that often caused even the well-disposed some bewilderment, especially if they had experienced Victor's normal absence of humility in his treatment of those around him. Only a few came to realize that it was Victor's bad conscience that drove him to make an issue of the reverence he owed the personality of Adolf Hitler. He was temperamentally incapable of taking the path of the admired Dominican priest, sacrificing his own comfort and convenience to his beliefs. Nor could he follow the example of Richard Acland, and give up all but a tiny fraction of his worldly possessions. Yet in his heart he believed them to have done the right thing, and tried to compensate for his own shortcomings by ever greater exaggerations of his own unworthiness. His guilt about his own style of life was only slightly assuaged by his generosity to causes and individuals, since he never gave away more than he could easily afford. If he went on holiday, he and his secretaries would often refer to it as 'a tiny holiday', or 'the first holiday he has had for many years'. Any refusal to provide a handout was couched in such terms as to suggest that he did not know where his next square meal was coming from. His extreme vulnerability in this area was almost certainly the cause of a breach with an intimate of the 1930s, Dr Stella Churchill, with whom the Gollanczes had shared some happy times in Europe. She was more a friend of Ruth's than Victor's, which perhaps explains her tactlessness:

15 June 1946

Dear Victor,

It was a great treat to read your book, although you do harp so much on the Christian starving! Revenge is not such a vile motive if it is done with justice? Anyhow it is surely dangerous to ignore the role it must play in the ravaged people's minds?

And why only the Germans? Hungarians are starving. Likewise Yugoslavs and Greeks. Charity begins at home. And—forgive me being personal — do *you* know what it is to live on your rations?

I wish we could meet — properly — (or not) on my return from Switzerland.

Love to both
Stella

Victor does not appear to have answered this letter — an omission that usually meant he was deeply hurt. Stella Churchill appears no more in his archives, but turns up in *Reminiscences of Affection* as 'our Jungian friend whom I greatly loved and who greatly loved me, until she quarrelled with me years later because she thought me wrong for not hating the Germans'. She had had the bad taste to state openly what was his greatest disadvantage in pressing the government for ration reductions: he had indeed not the faintest idea of what it was to live on his. Ruth and the sole gardener remaining cultivated an excellent vegetable garden at Brimpton, where she kept chickens. Victor ate his lunch and frequently his dinner in restaurants like the Ivy which never produced unpalatable food. He was not being a hypocrite: he pressed as enthusiastically for restaurant meals to count against rations as he did for any of his other proposed measures, but his condemnation of greed rang hollow in the ears of many housewives who were striving vainly to introduce variety into their families' dreary diet. But while Victor could imagine himself as a starving German, he had neither the will nor the ability to put himself less dramatically in the shoes of the majority of his countrymen — physically healthy but sick to death of spam fritters.

Nor had he suffered from the loss in war of loved ones. There had been occasional fatalities among ex-colleagues or acquaintances, but neither family nor close friends had been killed. And lacking the international family network of many Jews, he had lost no one he really loved in a concentration camp. The handful of victims he had known, including the Bernheims, had been no closer to him than a few hundred other acquaintances for whom he felt rushes of warmth after a pleasant meeting. He was always prepared to admit his good fortune in this respect, even admitting that real grief might have made forgiveness difficult, and he did at least show some humility in preaching against revenge to people who had lost their nearest and dearest. For the most part, however, he could put such reservations behind him when demanding that the British people and their leaders love their enemies. Some of those who came in for his more vitriolic and contemptuous attacks must have wondered wistfully why he didn't try loving his friends more and his enemies less. It was an excellent thing for those who badly needed his help that his sense of righteousness was untroubled. Any softening could only have reduced his effectiveness.

He had had a wonderful stroke of luck in the appointment in May of John Strachey as Minister of Food in succession to Ben Smith, whose economic illiteracy and pugnacity of manner had led to his replacement. Victor started in on Strachey straight away, and at a dinner with him early in June got his agreement in principle to the sending of food parcels. However, Victor was less than pleased with Strachey's attitude to his job. As he explained to Acland:

> It is, of course, the hypocritical self-righteousness which is the worst part of our whole situation. *Between ourselves*, John Strachey, though of course in a totally different class to Ben Smith, and though he will improve matters materially, may even worsen matters spiritually. He is, thank God, going to give us our food parcels and, almost certainly, our voluntary surrender of 'points': but he will certainly not do the really important thing — deliberately and appreciably lower the general standards while famine exists abroad: and, just because he speaks with a far more internationalist and humanitarian accent than Ben Smith, he will persuade a great number of people, who want to be so persuaded, that we really have done and are doing everything possible — whereas Ben Smith outraged them into the realisation that we haven't and aren't. I have already found some weakening among our supporters as a result of his broadcast on Sunday evening.

In late July, while Strachey was labouring to steer the lifting of the ban on food parcels through his ministry's committees, Victor set off on a voyage to the Canary Islands on a banana boat. He wrote twenty years later of his disappointment:

> It was not a conveyance we should have chosen in ordinary circumstances. There was nothing to sit on outside except blazing bits of deck, which seemed made not of wood but of iron: a yard or two from our cabin . . . the diesel panted and throbbed day and night, as well as smelling: and dinner was served at five-thirty, and consisted, as often as not, of rather fierce fish and chips. I was a bit nervous, too: I had been conspicuously, even ostentatiously, anti-Franco, and feared that, on arrival at Tenerife, I should be grilled and perhaps tortured, and end up in some villainous jail. I saw the captain, and begged him to get our consul on board as soon as we berthed: he said he would do his best, and when the sub-consul's secretary eventually turned up (the rest were busy), he assured me that I had nothing to fear. No one in these islands had ever heard of me, he felt quite certain: he had never heard of me himself . . .

Victor had gone on holiday with a large pile of books (lent by Dr James Parkes, a leading writer on Judeo-Christian history and theology) concerned with the period of separation between Christianity and Judaism. He hoped they would give him the background to write his own contribution to the debate while on his travels. In his three weeks away he failed to produce a manuscript: theology always tended to act as an inhibitor on him as a writer. He returned refreshed, but his project had to be shelved.

Strachey, over-ruled by the cabinet, had still failed to deliver on the food parcels, and although the government — both as a result of international pressure, and because they genuinely wanted to avert European famine — had quietly given way on many of SEN's proposals, the food parcels were symbolically vital. Victor was determined to keep up the momentum. He started another round of speech-making on the theme of Western values and the wickedness of the press, and launched the Save Europe Now European Relief Fund, in aid of several British relief societies. (By December 1948 it had collected just under £128,500.) With the announcement of another minor concession allowing clothes parcels to be sent to individuals in the British Zone, SEN had plenty of work on its hands: there was as yet no parcel post to Germany, and SEN took charge of the shipping of parcels to Hamburg, where they were put in the internal post by the *Evangelisches Hilfswerk*, the German Protestant Relief Organization.

Recognizing that second-hand reports were a handicap, Victor applied early in September 1946 for a permit to visit the British, French and American Zones, and fired off innumerable letters demanding facts, figures and names of people he should meet. He was determined to spend longer there than any previous observer. Lord Beveridge, who had done trojan work in the press and on the BBC reporting the frightful misery he had seen on his August visit, had stayed for only a fortnight. Victor decided to stay for at least six weeks. In one significant respect this was a real effort, for he had to go without Ruth, who almost always accompanied him on his travels. Apart from the occasional overnight separation if he travelled alone to make a speech, Ruth had been with him virtually every time he left home since their marriage. The only exceptions had been business trips in the early days when she was tied down by pregnancy or babies. To leave her voluntarily for six weeks was an heroic sacrifice made possible only by the strength of his determination to gather the truth, for revelation to the people at home. He set off on his mission on 2 October.

CHAPTER EIGHTEEN

CAUSES

VICTOR WAS TO compile on his return a book called *In Darkest Germany: The Record of a Visit*. Baulked by the weakness of others he was unable to spend more than eighteen hours a day gathering information, but every one of those hours was utilized to the full. One of the Control Commission of Germany (CCG) personnel who wrote to him in later years summed up his visit:

> You may not remember me but as a member of Public Relations Branch I ran around with you on some of your trips at Zonal Headquarters, and there about.
>
> I well remember the tremendous effort needed to keep up with your requirements — charts, diagrams, statistics. And the fanatical enthusiasm and drive you put in to the job — which resulted in your book being produced in an almost incredibly brief time.

Most of the CCG staff, were on Victor's side; a very high proportion of them were desperately doing their humane best, foiled by their London masters' blindness to the serious problems they faced. (Henry Hynd, the minister responsible, had spent a total of only four weeks in Germany in the previous year.) Victor was given an interpreter and a chauffeur-driven car and showered with invitations. CCG staff welcomed him warmly and did everything in their power to furnish ammunition for use on his return. Had they read parts of his first letter to Ruth, they might have scaled down the hospitality; Victor was as alert to British over-indulgence as he was to German suffering.

> On the Nord Express
> 7.30 pm
>
> My worshipped darling —
> All the lights in the train having failed, I'm writing this by the light of three candles which the already very resourceful X— [his female interpreter] has fixed me up with. The journey has been pleasant, but extraordinarily leisurely. It took us $2\frac{1}{2}$ hours to get to Dover — we meandered there via Canterbury and all sorts of impossible places — and 2

hours from Dover to Calais on a perfect sea. So far, what has impressed me most has been the abundant food. On the Naafi carriage from London to Dover we had 2 enormous tongue sandwiches each, 2 cakes and 2 bars of chocolate each for 2/10 the lot. Dinner on this train consisted of an excellent soup full of vegetables, a large cutlet, pommes rissolés and peas, sweet, cheese, white bread and coffee. No charge — included presumably in the price of the train — but a bottle of very ordinaire vin blanc cost 7/6.

You know what I thought of while crossing. But, though I was melancholy, I was not unhappy — but *already* looking forward to coming home to you: and dreaming of all sorts of trips abroad, d.v. in the future — to Paris, to Florence, to Venice . . .

Long interval here. A very pleasant Brigadier Treadwell (Director-General of Public Relations), came and introduced himself, gave me brandy, and talked for a couple of hours. Wants me to stay at his mess — so I shall now have to choose between him, the CIC, and General Fanshawe. Also asked me to a party tomorrow night!!!

What I was going to say was that as we got to Calais it was already getting a little dark, and the whole thing had the peculiar French melancholy. The big building and clock tower at the quay is of course destroyed — temporary concrete being in its place. The destruction at Calais itself, insofar as one could see it from the train, not as bad as one expected.

Moses is here — as well as with you. The President [God] (who, apparently, takes a special interest in you and me) has made special arrangements for the duplication of his personality — . This is the first time such a thing has ever been done.

Good-night, my own darling
from
your
tiny B

Love to children and Tiny [Hodges] and all

The pace was hotting up within a couple of days.

LEMGO
5.30 am Saturday
5 Oct.

My darling —

As you see, I'm writing this in bed in the early hours — in a bed in a vast room at 'Schloss Nuremberg', the headquarters of General Fanshawe, Unrra [United Nations Relief and Rehabilitation Administration] Chief in the British zone. It is the highest room in the highest house I've ever seen — grotesquely like a very rich mid-Victorian English house — exactly the same sort of furniture — huge corner sofas with bric-a-brac woodwork behind them — room with a little sort of enclosed corner for the chateleine's escritoire — even the swivel shaving mirror on a wooden stand of the kind that my grandfather Michaelson used.

I'm writing so early partly because one has to be up betimes in order to make a few notes of the previous day — as one is on the go either working or socially from 8 til midnight — and partly because X— has developed a frightful cough, which comes at me through a wooden door on the scale of everything else here and has kept me awake all night. Why do women cough so much? I shall try to persuade her to stay in bed today. My own cold and cough are still bad, but no temperature.

Its no good my trying to give you any real impressions yet. These 2 or 3 days are preliminary — in a country district, and contacts so far only with 'big' Englishmen—or mainly so. General attitude—varies from decent and even very warm-hearted to disgusting — the latter a small minority — but even at its best horribly the attitude of the superior conqueror to the inferior conquered. As for me, even after hearing the most awful stories of horrors perfoliated by Göring & Co which were revealed at Nuremberg and didn't get into the press, which make one really almost physically sick, I find myself loving the Germans in general just because they're despised and rejected. I've no doubt I shall find a great deal of self-pity and insensitiveness to the horrors committed by 'Germany', but I don't believe that will make any difference to my feeling, which however isn't at all affecting my judgement.

I got on *extraordinarily* well with the big shots, and particularly the military. Dined last night with the C in C in a stolen chateau (of course all the HQs etc are stolen) and had a fascinatingly interesting time. He made me promise to go back to his HQ at the end of the trip and give my impressions. Said he agreed with 85% of OTV [*Our Threatened Values*] — but I have the idea that he would have told Vansittart he agreed 85% — or perhaps only 80% — with him. The quiet luxury of the food at all these places — the 'No 1 Mess' at Bunde, at the C in C's, here at Gen. Fanshawe's — is spiritually nauseating and physically delightful. One had forgotten such meals were possible. Its not — the food, I mean — disgustingly lavish; but just the right amount of the *right* things properly cooked with the necessary adjuncts.

I am made a fuss of and treated almost as a VIPI (very important person indeed).

I expect to leave for Kiel and De Crespigny tomorrow, and then for Hamburg — where I shall get into touch for the first time with *Germans*, both official and common and garden. That will be the real job. But these first 2 days with the big noises will prove to have been worth while.

I must write a few notes now. All my humble and kneeling love, beloved. Pl. also give my love to Mrs B [Mrs Baker, the Gollancz family housekeeper], Sophie [a German refugee then living with them], the children (6) [the sixth was the Modigliani portrait], Lee [a dog], my own little Dods [another dog], *your* Moses (mine is behaving nicely), my sweet Tiny, and all my special favourites at the office. Don't forget to send these letters, or any of them that you think interesting to Tiny to type and show to Duffy [Peggy Duff], Poo [Livia] etc. I wish I could write more fully, but the idea of writing really full accounts is quite impossible.

LEMGO
Sunday 6 Oct

Darlingest Mummy

Got your heavenly letter yesterday. Only time for a v. hurried line, as we're just off to motor up to Kiel. Very strenuous here — working in all about 18 hours a day. Cold bad, but otherwise well. All v. confusing, and I feel I am not getting much grasp yet. Pl. send enclosed to Tiny — And go on writing every day, please. My Moses sends love to your Moses, and I send my overflowing love to you.

Monday 7 Oct.
Before Breakfast

My most beloved darling —

I can only manage a hurried note this morning. Yesterday we motored from Herford to Kiel via Celle (a lovely little $\frac{1}{2}$ medieavil [*sic*] place, untouched but v. sad) and Hamburg — which is horribly damaged — totally different to anything we know in England. Here at Kiel De C [De Crespigny] lives in an incredible palace of a place which belonged to the Renutlows — I have a sort of flat of my own — 3 incredibly luxurious rooms. Breakfast in 2 or 3 minutes — was talking to De C till 2 last night, and up writing my notes at 6. I'm *beginning* to get some sort of picture of the situation.

My general mental state quite different, so far, to what expected. Interest submerges most other emotions — in fact, I doubt whether I've ever been so much interested. Apart from my longing for Mummy, I haven't any sort of desire to hurry away.

X— turns out to be quite efficient but very trying — she exclaims and moralises too much. But I'm not getting irritable. Whenever I'm with another woman for a few hours, I realise afresh how peerless Ruthie is. And *my* Moses doesn't let me forget it.

Your adoring
Tiny B
&

Wednesday
9 Oct.

My own darling darling darling —

I'm writing this in bed at 7 in the Atlantic Hotel Hamburg, whither we came last night. It's a filthy place, and I'm transferring today to Harry Walston's Mess (food and agriculture). It was absolutely lovely to find waiting for me your letter of Friday (which is only the second I've had from you). Your first took 2 days; the second nearly five days to Herford, and then a day here.

Continue to write to the same address as before — ADPR etc HERFORD — right up to the end of my trip.

I'm in a state of complete mental confusion, as everybody contradicts the last person, and its frightfully difficult to understand the highly complicated structure of Government. I've got a very poor brain for grasping that kind of thing.

Much the worst thing I've seen is the condition of the 'expellees' from Polish-occupied Germany, of which there are 1,300,000 in Schleswig Holstein. It is beyond any possibility to describe their misery. This is something of quite a different quality to the devastation or even the living conditions of the ordinary Germans, which are more or less as one visualised them. But the expellees are something different. We visited a ship in Kiel harbour on which about a couple of hundred have been living for six months: it is the only time since I got here that I was quite unable to prevent myself from crying the whole time.

X— is really rather a myth — incidentally, her German is rather poor, and she is therefore a bad interpreter. She has a C2 brain, and very often misses the point. Often with my non-existent German, I spot that she has misunderstood what a German has said, and that means that I have to go on and on pegging away to clear up the point. But don't think I'm being irritable — I'm concealing my feelings — as adequately as I can!

I'm rather tired, as I'm working literally about 20 hours a day — quite continuous except for about 3–4 hours sleep. I sleep v. well *when* I sleep, and am well, except for my cold, which won't go.

Forgive this shortish note, but I've got to lay out my ideas of what I want to do in Hamburg; it's now 7.15, and the Public Relations man is coming at 9. I can't tell you how much love I send you: and please give some of it to the darling children and to Tiny — and to your Moses . . .

Of his other letters to Ruth, other than brief notes and one, much longer, written for publication, few survive. Those that do — and especially if they were written when he was tired — provide an interesting stylistic sidelight on his more studied mature prose.

History does not record whether Victor's patience finally gave way under the stress of an inadequate interpreter. By now he was into his stride, gobbling information insatiably, interviewing British and Germans at every available opportunity, and demanding escorted visits to every scene of deprivation within reach.

Harry Walston, the director of agriculture, greatly took to Victor and afterwards became a close friend. He confirms the evidence of Victor's correspondence from members of the CCG. Most were captivated by his warmth, interest and exuberance and deeply grateful for his timely expenditure of energy. (They had only a handful of dedicated publicists on the Home Front: Beveridge, the Bishop of Chichester and Dick Stokes MP were the leading lights apart from Victor.) All, of course, was not harmony. The CCG was not denied the experience of Victor's egocentricity. There was a famous occasion at Walston's mess. Victor had explained — to the interest of those at the dinner table — the insidiousness of taboos. Despite his intellectual rejection of the Jewish dietary laws, what he always referred to as his 'ancestral stomach' revolted at the prospect of pork or shellfish. He had not mentioned that he coped cheerfully with crispy bacon, which was served next morning at breakfast. Victor came down early and devoured the modest ration intended for the whole mess.

John Midgley, then *Manchester Guardian* correspondent in Germany, recalls another such occasion. Sympathizing with Victor in his desire for humane treatment of the Germans, he drove from the Ruhr to Hamburg to brief Victor at length (in Walston's mess) on conditions in the industrial heartland.

> A lot of this talking took place at dinner, which was, by the standards prevailing in Germany at the time, rather a decent dinner. I don't want to sound ill-natured, but it obviously wasn't costing Victor anything. When we'd finished dinner and I had talked to him some more, and he'd got out of me as much as he'd wanted, he courteously escorted me to the door. I looked out into the courtyard and said, 'My car's gone'. And Victor said, 'Oh, has it? Well, goodnight.' It was left to Harry Walston to take pity on my plight, and to see that I was provided with transport back into Hamburg. Victor's unconcern about the fact that my long journey, and my long hours devoted to helping him, had ended in my having my car stolen was really quite striking in a man who had devoted himself heart and soul to the welfare of mankind. I appreciated it. I appreciate it to this day. You can't not: it was quite rich.

But then, as Midgley pointed out, echoing many others down the decades, 'his philanthropy was perfectly genuine but it didn't include consideration for individuals'. (Midgley had no way of knowing that Victor — especially when his compassion was aroused — could on occasion show enormous consideration for others.)

Despite such absurd incidents, the CCG could only be awed by the speed with which Victor began to use the data he had garnered. He wisely restricted himself to the British Zone, spending most of his time in Hamburg, Düsseldorf and the Ruhr, and mastered the detail of the CCG's problems in record time. By the end of October (he stayed in Germany until 15 November) he had started his press campaign with a letter to *The Times*. Substantially, it was a graphic account of the effects of malnutrition in Düsseldorf, where 100,000 people were said to be suffering from hunger oedema or the equivalent. He led into his account by describing 'the almost unbearable sense of shame' he had felt on reading press reports of a speech by Strachey, who claimed that the food position in England was in many respects better than before the war. Challenged over his figures, Victor fought back with a letter which ended:

> The most horrible of my experiences has been a visit to the camp at Belsen, where I saw the tattoo marks on the arms of the Jewish survivors. I am never likely to forget the unspeakable wickedness of which the Nazis were guilty. But when I see the swollen bodies and living skeletons in hospitals here and elsewhere; when I look at the miserable 'shoes' of boys and girls in the schools, and find that they have come to their lessons without even a dry piece of bread for breakfast; when I go down into a one-roomed cellar where a mother is struggling, and struggling very bravely, to do her best for a husband and four or five children — then I think, not of Germans, but of men and women. I am sure I should have the same feelings if I were in Greece or Poland. But I happen to be in Germany, and write of what I see here.

Back in Britain, Strachey had lain himself open to further attack along with the unfortunate Frank Pakenham, newly appointed to be the government spokesman on Germany in the House of Lords. Pakenham had been an occasional LBC chairman in the Popular Front days, was a great admirer of Victor and knew him quite well. He was greatly in sympathy with his crusade, but was immediately catapulted into defending the government's conduct in a Lords debate. He ended by wringing his hands over what he called 'a tragic mess, but a mess of her [Germany's] own making.' That was widely reported without his codicil: 'God forgive me, if to say that is to speak unfairly of a people who are suffering as they are suffering now.'

From Germany, where Victor kept in touch by having his conducting officer steal newspapers for him from various messes, came

a denunciation of the government, not excepting his two friends
Strachey and Pakenham. The *News Chronicle* carried his letter:

> The shamelessness of the Government becomes intolerable. Turkeys and
> poultry specially imported, extra meat, sweets and sugar — these are
> among the luxuries which Mr Strachey announces for Christmas. I don't
> know what sort of part my friend Strachey has played in making this
> monstrous decision; if any part at all, he is not the Strachey I worked with
> for so many years.
>
> Have these Christian statesmen of ours the slightest idea of what is going
> on in Germany? Apparently not, for if they had they would not make the
> idiotic statements that cause such consternation among intelligent mem-
> bers of the Control Commission. Let me tell them, then, something about
> life here in this ruined city of Düsseldorf.

Facts and figures followed, culminating in the assertion that

> that portion of the Düsseldorf population that cannot, or will not,
> supplement the ration by a few hundred extra calories from the black
> market or other sources — the old, the feeble, the lonely, the very poor,
> the hardest working and the over-conscientious — have been living these
> last days on anything from 400 to 1,000 calories. Four hundred — and I
> have been in many homes where this has been the daily ration — is half the
> Belsen rate.
>
> I wish Mr Attlee, Lord Pakenham — whose speech in the Lords was a
> model of feebleness and futility — and Mr Strachey could have been with
> me a couple of days ago in the big hospital here, when I spent a ghastly
> morning photographing cases of hunger oedema and emaciation. I cannot
> believe that they would not have been as sickened as I was.
>
> Our prestige here is pretty near the nadir. The youth is being poisoned
> and renazified. We have all but lost the peace — and I fear that this is an
> understatement.

Strachey made a dignified response in the *News Chronicle*, claiming
that everything possible was being done, that turkeys were a lower
priority than more essential commodities (which Britain did not have
the resources to provide) and that the solution must be internationally
based. Victor countered with a letter demanding permission for
voluntary food parcels. Why had the scheme worked out in tedious
detail with the ministry not been implemented?

> Because bread rationing was introduced, and the Government, alarmed by
> an outcry which was very largely as bogus and engineered as it was in any
> event disgraceful, simply refused to face the hypothetical charge that 'in so
> grave a domestic crisis' it was allowing food to go out of the country . . .

I challenge both Attlee and Strachey to deny that this is a true statement of the facts; and I say that this is just one example of indifference — or, if you like, comparative indifference — to elementary human needs in the British zone . . .

As for John Strachey, he is so intelligent, and his reply so feeble, that I must assume that he has got himself mixed up with a policy of which he disapproves, and is making the best of it.

. . . He misses the point that to give us extra Christmas rations, over and above the high general standard of living of which he talked with so much pride recently, is morally degrading to ourselves and must add still further to the growing cynicism with which the Germans regard 'Western democracy' . . .

The mountain of letters that reached the *News Chronicle* split two-to-one in Victor's favour. The paper printed a selection of them under photographs of the combatants. The high-minded were all on Victor's side; lined up on Strachey's were many whose opinions must have made him shudder. Meanwhile, Victor enjoyed the support of the 100,000 who actively supported SEN.

For months they had been bombarding the Ministry of Food with letters of protest about the parcel ban. All were now encouraged to write instead to the Prime Minister in the same week. The Cabinet capitulated and on 25 November the ban was lifted. Vicky's cartoon in the *News Chronicle* a couple of days later showed a tiny Victor, clad as Santa Claus, sitting on a reindeer. He grinned happily up at Strachey, a solemn giant similarly attired, who held the reins of a sleigh, loaded with a massive sack labelled 'Food Gifts from the people of Britain'. The caption read: 'Who said there is no Santa Claus?'

For SEN this was a moment of glory — the triumph of imagination over bureaucracy, of generosity over caution — but the work had hardly started. The parcel post to Germany was not to reopen until six weeks later, and meanwhile the charitably-inclined had to get a four shilling label from SEN and a permit from the food office before the parcels could be shipped to Germany by private carrier. SEN issued leaflets explaining the scheme, and undertook the distribution of parcels not addressed to individuals. Thousands of parcels poured into Henrietta Street, destined for the three zones to which the scheme applied (the Russian was excluded). Victor claimed later that the very first person to arrive for a label was a page acting for Queen Mary. Peggy Duff, in her account of the venture, confined herself to organizational details — as well she might, for she bore their brunt (in 1971, she said she still had nightmares about parcels):

For six weeks we acted as the one and only post office for Germany. It was a tremendous strain on a small organisation. Temporary offices were opened all over London and temporary depots set up all over the Provinces. Voluntary helpers flocked in to help, including at least a dozen workers lent by the Friends Ambulance Unit. Across the North Sea, in Hamburg the Evangelisches Hilfswerk coped with the tens of thousands of parcels arriving in thousands of bales and crates, and their difficulties were even greater than those in London . . .

Yet, in spite of all this, only a few hundred of the 50,000 prisoner-of-war parcels [POWs were now allowed to send food to their families] and the 60,000 food and clothing parcels failed to reach their destinations, although most of them were at least three months in transit . . .

Recollected in tranquillity this period of our existence seems like a nightmare, but it was memorable for the extraordinary patience of ordinary people trying to cope with a new and complicated process, for the great kindness and generosity of those who came to help and of all those who sent their gifts, for the assistance we received from organisations such as the Friends Ambulance Unit and Government departments such as the Air Ministry, which gave us in March, 1947, 1,000 lb a day air transport for three weeks, and the Control Office for Germany through whom we shipped. At the same time we were, of course, collecting and shipping many thousands of parcels for general relief to nine European countries.

This was probably Victor's finest hour. The food parcels themselves were, as he had been ceaselessly reminded, a tiny drop in the ocean, but they were of great symbolic significance to both the givers and receivers. The worst aspect of the suffering in Germany was the general feeling prevalent among its people that they were outcasts. Their gratitude for acts of kindness was pathetic; the acts themselves of enormous benefit to the raising of morale. The parcels decision got wide publicity, and many Germans were awestruck that it had been engineered by a Jew.

Victor did not rest on his laurels. There was near-panic in Henrietta Street: the firm looked like disappearing under the weight of parcels, and long queues formed of people demanding labels. A more considerate but less effective man might have hung around sympathizing. Victor left his staff to it and stayed ensconced at Brimpton writing, pausing from his labours only for one long and predictably fruitless encounter with Attlee, and a meeting with Commons sympathizers. 'I have tried to make contact with you for several days,' wrote his author Tom Harrisson on 22 November, 'but you are surrounded by Guardians of the Grail, and are about as difficult to contact as Stalin.'

From Brimpton he despatched letters and articles to the *Daily Herald*, the *Manchester Guardian*, the *New Statesman*, *The Times* and *The Times Literary Supplement*. They covered shortcomings in the provision of food, clothing and consumer goods, the appalling housing situation, the problems of health care, the counter-productiveness of the denazification programme, the inadequacy of educational resources, the viciousness, illogicality and arbitrariness of the deindustrialization policy (which involved blowing up factories capable of manufacturing the peacetime goods so desperately needed), and the *Herrenvolk* mentality that resulted in daily humiliation for Germans pushed to the end of queues or kept at arm's length by the occupier. He described graphically the difference in the standards of living of conquered and conquerors, and printed a number of menus brought home from officers' messes.

Within a fortnight of his return, eighteen of his letters and articles had appeared in the press, and these Victor reshaped for his book, supplementing them with extra information sent to him by well-wishers in the CCG. He added 144 photographs, most of which had been taken in his presence in Germany. 'I must beg pardon for the intrusion into some of them of my body, hand or even face. I thought that my visible presence would add verisimilitude, and obviate the charge, for instance, that these were really agency photographs taken in China in the year 1932.' It was a wise decision. The incongruity of Victor's worried face, atop his plump body, gazing down at undernourished and ill-clad children, jammed with them into over-crowded shelters, lent a bizarre immediacy to the illustrations. The book was published in January 1947.

Did he exaggerate? Yes, of course, but, as Peggy Duff put it:

> He could not help it but his extravagance rose from the quality of his concern, not from deliberate, cold-blooded distortions . . . I met in Germany one of the men he interviewed and quoted in the book. He complained that he had been misquoted but added that, since so many were minimizing conditions in Germany, Victor felt justified, no doubt, in exaggerating them. I told him that I thought he was wrong about this. V.G. had not deliberately distorted. He had convinced himself that what he wrote was the truth and this he always did. His exaggerations were emotional, not political.

Walston was one of those who wrote both to congratulate him on *In Darkest Germany* and to defend the CCG.

> There I do think you have not only been unfair, but also very misleading. In spite of some of the kind things you have to say about some of the

officers, the impression that is left upon the reader is that the Control Commission is, on the whole, full of people who are living in the greatest luxury themselves and paying no attention to the sufferings that go on around them. There are, of course, a few like this, but I am quite sure it is not anything like the number you believe it to be . . . you certainly saw nothing like a random sample of the people, any more than you lived in a fair sample of the Messes. As an important visitor you stayed at the best places, but you must remember that the majority of the people out here live in conditions which, on the whole, are perfectly comfortable, but which are certainly not luxurious . . .

In other words, while life in the Control Commission is infinitely more comfortable than it is for the average German, it is on the average no more comfortable than it would be for the same people in England . . .

Taking it as a whole, life out here has some material advantages over life in England (tho' not nearly so many as one would gather from reading your book). But these advantages are small recompense for the isolation from home and from normal living and friends that everyone out here has to endure. However, more important than these points is the one you raise about the lack of feeling of the English personnel out here for the Germans. This I strongly dispute. It would be impossible for anybody living here to allow himself to feel the whole time the appalling conditions that many Germans have to put up with in exactly the same way that it is impossible for a doctor in a hospital to allow himself to think continuously of his dying patients. But because he seems to have a rather callous approach to disease, it does not mean to say that he is a hard-hearted man . . .

But it is unfair of me to spend so much space criticising what is only a very minor part of your book. I only hope that it will reach a very large number of the unconverted, and if it does I am quite sure that it will have the effect that you want it to . . .

Robert Birley, who had spent November in the British Zone sorting out educational arrangements, also took issue with Victor on the *Herrenvolk* sections, feeling that he had got a distorted picture from Hamburg.

I do not want to give the impression that I dispute your general picture. But I feel that it is essential to give credit where it is due, or those in the Control Commission who are trying to do better than the rest will feel even more isolated and misunderstood . . .

My other comment goes deeper. From Germany I went to Czecho-slovakia and the experience was intensely interesting, though in many ways depressing. I found an almost universal belief that we were being ridiculously sentimental about the Germans. They were wrong, of course, and I tried to show them why I felt they were wrong. But their attitude, after all they have been through, was indeed understandable.

But what really matters is that we cannot hope to solve the German problem alone. Part of our task is to build up, patiently, the right relationships between Germany and her neighbours. This, I feel, will need extraordinary tact. I know your own record in this matter in the days when too many Englishmen were ready to turn a blind eye on Nazi atrocities, and I hope you will not mind my telling you that I often spoke of it to Czechs. But in your writings nowadays about Germany I feel that, in spite of your references to Auschwitz and Belsen, you give the *impression* that you do not know what the occupied countries went through. Auschwitz and Belsen do not mean as much to them as what they themselves suffered in their own countries. Revenge is silly. There is no point in saying that it is right for German university students to be hungry, because Czech students were shot — quite apart from the fact that it is wicked to say it. But I believe that, when writing of sufferings in Germany now, to refer to comparable sufferings in the occupied countries, though it may weaken the effect, is really wise . . .

And I feel too that it is very important that we should do this from the point of view of the Germans themselves. The senseless suffering which they are now experiencing is having the effect of making them forget what they have done themselves. They ought not to forget it. They ought to be made to realise, I feel, that for them to say, 'We were not responsible' is itself a confession of ignominy. Englishmen ought to say these things to them, but their position must be very secure before they have the moral right to do so or will effect anything by it. Your own position is secure and you could do it . . .

I hope you will forgive my writing this. It is only because I agree with you that what is happening in Germany now is really tragic — and not only tragic in the sense of physical suffering — that I do so . . .

Victor listened to those gently expressed criticisms more than he did to most. References in his speeches to CCG personnel became marginally kinder, and occasionally he took an opportunity to indicate to non-Nazi Germans that they might bear some responsibility for the acts committed in their name. But as for the government, he had no desire to weaken his case by adulterating the ferocity of his attacks. Emotionally he was committed to the view that English democrats were more at fault than indoctrinated Germans, so he had to direct his fire at his own countrymen.

He could not secure for *In Darkest Germany* the sales he had achieved for *Our Threatened Values*: all those photographs made it more expensive, even though the price was set at an uncommercial level. He also claimed to be hampered by a new constraint. 'I wish', he wrote to an admirer, 'I could advertise the book "more widely", but as I am both author and publisher it is rather awkward. One's other authors get so annoyed!' Still, he was again lavish with free copies. About

1,500 were sent to leaders of public opinion, including every MP. The least rewarding of many letters that came back was from a predictable source.

My dear Gollancz,
    Thank you very much for sending me your book.
                                                    Yours sincerely,
                                                    C. R. Attlee

Others were as complimentary as even Victor could have wished. 'I think the work you are doing is magnificent,' wrote Seebohm Rowntree, 'and not only the German people, but people of goodwill everywhere are greatly indebted to you for your unselfish service.' The Bishop of Chichester was 'filled anew with admiration for your courage and forthrightness and energy'. Edmund Blunden gave 'deep thanks for the humanity which you defend and show'. 'It is a great work you have been doing,' commented the architect, Sir Charles Reilly. 'First with your Left Book Club you did more than anyone to put this Government in and now you are keeping them up to the mark in human duties.' Two old friends — both clergymen — wrote in strikingly similar terms. 'I am proud of the work you are doing,' said Spencer Lees. 'It is in the spirit of the Prophets, from whom you draw your ancestry.' And Nathaniel Micklem was 'immeasurably thankful that you have been raised up like a Hebrew prophet to testify before the world'.

Victor drew great comfort from the admiration. As he explained to Lady Pethick-Lawrence, who regularly applauded his work: 'As I am fundamentally an extremely self-distrustful person, your letters help me a great deal.' He did not, however, answer a letter which, had he but known it, was probably the greatest compliment of all.

Dear Mr Gollancz,
    Thank you very much for sending me a copy of your book on Germany. It has made me regret a letter which I wrote to the 'New Statesman' some months ago. I am sure that, if you troubled to read it, you were far too busy doing your good work to give it another thought. But I should like you to know that I am sorry I involved your name and your admirable organization's in making an unimportant political debating point.
                                                    Yours sincerely,
                                                    Evelyn Waugh

Again, there was acrimony when the reviews appeared. The editor of *The Times Literary Supplement* responded coolly to Victor's letter of complaint:

3 February 1947

My dear Gollancz,

I must take time to consider your letter; but on the instant of glancing at the first paragraph let me say that it surprises me that you do not see that your cause, and your personal connection with it, are not recommended by the sort of 'reply' you send.

You describe the review as 'very kind', some sentences as 'bristling with bad ethics, bad science and bad history, not to mention the usual easy self-righteousness'; and you proceed, in the length of four pages, to lay down a thesis regarding our national 'self-righteousness' which is bound to create in the reader a suspicion of the personal and individual 'self-righteousness' of the writer. I recommend the avoidance of any talk about self-righteousness.

Yours,
Stanley Morison

5 February 1947

My dear Morison,

'I couldn't agree with you less', as they say nowadays. What you are saying in effect is that one shouldn't attack self-righteousness because either one is, or may be suspected of being, self-righteous oneself. By the same token, presumably one should never attack sin, for clearly we are all sinners. I can imagine nothing more cowardly.

I think what you really object to is not self-righteousness but dogmatism. You dislike 'bad ethics, bad science and bad history'. But I believe in calling a spade a spade. Obviously when anybody speaks of bad ethics, he implies the qualification 'in my opinion': but could anything be more tedious than to insert a qualification which any rational reader takes for granted? It would also of course be very easy to 'wrap up the whole thing' — to say something like: 'Your reviewer's reading of history is surely open to question'. But that would be mock modesty, which I personally detest.

Nor do I see why you object to my describing the review as 'very kind'. I thought it *was* very kind! — in the sense that it was extremely sympathetic. I simply happened to differ from your reviewer on three general points on which his views seemed to me (seem to me) untenable. Indeed, the suggestion about 'humility and self-criticism' during the heydays of Britain and France strikes me as one of the most grotesque that I have ever read — and incidentally has so struck several of my friends.

However, wash it out. I had thought that you would print it this week, and it seemed to me necessary to reply. But by the following week no one will remember the review, and I have no desire to start a controversy on the question.

Yours,
Victor Gollancz

The research and writing up of the material for *In Darkest Germany* had occupied Victor to the exclusion of everything else for over two months. For another eighteen, Germany remained his main interest. He was established as the pre-eminent campaigner for Germany in Britain, and in Germany he was the most famous British humanitarian. His voice was heard above the Bishop of Chichester, Beveridge, Stokes and all the others in chorus. Victor was a master at manipulating the media; he cajoled or bullied friends to give him space or coverage; his sources were superb; he collated, shaped and issued new topical information that editors could not ignore; and he attracted attention in local newspapers all over England (excursions to Wales or Scotland were rare) by making provocative speeches in their area. Very occasionally he was co-signatory, but between 1945 and 1948 he had at least 22 letters relating to Germany in the *Manchester Guardian*, 17 in *The Times* and countless others in any newspaper or periodical prepared to give him space. Not all his letters saw print: *The Times* in particular frustrated him by rejecting some letters and insisting he cut others. (Cutting Victor's letters without consulting him was a perilous procedure: Wilson Harris of the *Spectator* cut one of Victor's long epistles by 226 words, and was saved only by the 'Not sent' convention from the knowledge that his action typified 'the growing contempt for other people's rights'.) Virtually all the letters were expressions of outrage — backed up with facts and figures — at some new lunacy, wickedness or omission on the part of the authorities concerning rations, dismantling, the totalitarianism implicit in the denazification programme, or the evils of the trials of war criminals.

In August 1947 Victor made a further visit of two weeks to Germany with his friend Dick Stokes. On his return he contributed articles to the Quaker *Friend*, the *Guardian* and the *Observer*, published the following month, with additions, as a pamphlet called *Germany Revisited*. Victor could not deny some improvement in conditions, nor the heartening signs that German democratic politicians were getting organized. Nevertheless, the poverty and distress were still widespread and morale was at a low ebb. The job was not finished, and Victor's lamentations were as anguished, his rhetoric as fiery, as ever. Like most observers, he failed to perceive the underlying grim determination of the German people to get their country back on its feet: the economic miracle did not begin to manifest itself unmistakably until late in 1948.

Yet there were optimistic signs at the British end. In April 1947, Frank Pakenham had been made Minister for the British Zones of both Germany and Austria, and no one could doubt that he brought to his job enormous sympathy and sincerity. By the time of his appointment he had fallen completely under Victor's spell. 'I leave out of comparison the clergy, my relatives, and my teachers,' he wrote in 1963. 'I can then say that there is no individual in this country who has influenced my thought as much as Victor.' Pakenham had a tender conscience, and such people were vulnerable to Victor. He reacted as did hundreds of Victor's acquaintances and thousands of Victor's readers — in a way well expressed by a total stranger (writing about *Our Threatened Values*): 'I admire your courage and persistence and above all your magnanimity. I confess I'm generally humbled when I read you and that you've a way of making me feel guilty of the laziness and cowardice you speak of in your recent book. Well, thank you for your challenge and inspiration.'

Pakenham consulted Victor. Was it possible to reconcile an occupation policy 'with a care for the natural feelings and just demands of the Germans'? 'I believe you can do it,' said Victor, 'if you stick to the principle of partnership.' No one could have thrown himself more enthusiastically into that role of reconciler than did Pakenham. In his fourteen months in the job he found himself in constant trouble with his master, Ernest Bevin, who had once summed up his own quandary in the arresting sentence: 'I try to be fair to the Germans, but I 'ates them really.' Pakenham's empathy with their suffering was appreciated by the Germans, but was an irritant to his own government, and the need to defend distasteful policies such as dismantling often made his new role a torture for him. When he was kicked upstairs to the House of Lords in June 1948, his disappointment was tempered by relief.

He did not, of course fully satisfy Victor. As Pakenham said — again in 1963 — if Victor had ever been a minister or had held high office 'he might recognize the element of dilemma which haunts me continually when we try to give political effect to abstract values.' Victor could never have borne life with that dilemma, and conspicuously avoided the danger of having to face it. In public, he was not very fierce with Pakenham, whom he came in time to view as 'one of the best and most compassionate of men, as well as the untidiest.' Though (as with all his male friends) he denigrated him sometimes in private, he was fond of him, and recognized that he was doing his best in difficult circumstances to act according to the Christian ethic.

Through Pakenham and a number of other politicians under his sway, and through his speeches and public meetings, Victor continued to wield effective influence on both politicians and the public at home in pushing the climate of opinion towards more generous treatment of the Germans. That was his primary task as Chairman of

SEN. The fund-raising and parcel distribution went smoothly under Duff's direction, and she and Victor worked jointly on one other important area of SEN's activities: the campaign to get the German prisoners of war (POWs) sent home from Britain and the Middle East.

In 1946, after a Save Europe Now conference, it had been decided to press the government on this issue. Stokes kept up a steady stream of questions in the House of Commons, and Victor drafted a memorial to the Prime Minister, sent to him in August 1946 with 2,000 distinguished signatures. Attlee was begged to draw up and announce to POWs a definite scheme for their release at the earliest possible dates.

Press coverage helped to bring concessions. A scheme of gradual repatriation was announced, and POWs were given more freedom. Early in 1947, the four control powers agreed that full repatriation would be achieved by the end of 1948. Victor considered this wholly unacceptable, and Attlee received yet another, even better supported memorial in August: with a rate of repatriation of 15,000 a month plus 'compassionate' cases, a significant number of the POWs (282,431 in Britain and 81,988 in the Middle East on 31 May 1947) would still be in custody over three years after the end of the war. The memorial described the POWs as essentially 'slave labour', whose absence from home caused appalling suffering to their families. If British values were not to be betrayed, it was vital that repatriation be speeded up.

Attlee's reply included the contention that POW labour was one of the few means by which Germany could make any practical reparation — a statement that led Victor to rail against the climate of national and political selfishness 'that corrupts a man even as good as he'. He was filled with dismay that the language of national self-interest and economic particularism should dominate in a country run by the heirs of Keir Hardie and Morris. (This article was incorporated in full into *Germany Revisited.*) In the event, Attlee soon announced a number of improvements in POW conditions, and promised to speed up the rate of repatriation so as to have all POWs home by July 1948. He kept that promise. For that achievement Victor could claim a great deal of credit, but his had not been the only petition. One similar had already been set up by Christian Action, an organization with which he was closely associated. According to Pakenham, both petitions were instrumental in tempering the Cabinet's stance.

Christian Action had come into existence in December 1946. Initially doing much of its work in parallel with SEN, it was to overtake and outlive both it and its own inspiration and founder: the inspiration was Victor; the founder John Collins.

By the time Collins came up with the idea which sparked off Christian Action, he had been growing ever closer to Victor for about eight years. Collins in 1935 was Vice-Principal of the Cambridge theological college, Westcott House, a confirmed Tory, celebrating Baldwin's victory with his favourite student, Mervyn Stockwood. By 1939 he had become, like Stockwood, a convinced socialist, and through his ex-pupil he came into contact with the three men who were to be his best friends and greatest influences: Stafford Cripps, Richard Acland and Victor Gollancz. Of the three, Victor was to become the most potent in shaping Collins's outlook.

The friendship developed during the war, and Collins, a chaplain at Bomber Command, used to visit Victor quite frequently. After the war, their intimacy grew swiftly. Collins and his wife, Diana, felt inhibited at first by Victor's age (he was twelve years Collins's senior), fame, and power of personality. Collins only just avoided developing total hero-worship for Victor. Diana adored him at their first real meeting, over lunch at the Ivy. He was on his best behaviour, utterly charming, and produced for her small son Andrew his full range of monkey faces. The nascent friendship survived the test of the nervous Collinses' first dinner party for the Gollanczes, where, having understood them to be free of Judaic orthodoxy, they served up a series of dishes which revolted their guests' ancestral stomachs. The evening was a success, the honoured guests heaping equal praise on the substitute poached eggs and the excellent Burgundy, specially purchased for the occasion.

From the time he returned from the RAF to Oriel College, Collins had been trying to find some way of boosting the churches' role in moral and spiritual leadership. An attempt by a group under the chairmanship of the Bishop of Chichester, to work out a programme of action, had fallen apart through disagreements over priorities. Collins was eager to find a way for the small Christian Fellowship that gathered around him in Oriel to put their aspirations into practical effect. When he read *Our Threatened Values* he was deeply impressed and wondered if the book could be 'a catalyst to bring prayer and action together into the reality of positive Christian living?' Called away for a few days in April 1946, he asked the group to read the book in his absence and discuss it at their weekly meeting.

> I returned to find the Fellowship transformed. They had accepted the book for the challenge it was, had been inspired by it, had been fired by a fresh vision, released from frustration, and given a positive and realistic sense of direction. They had suddenly become what all the time I had hoped they would become, young men determined to change the world. After further

study and prayer we decided that our first step was to organize a public meeting in Oxford, 'A call for Christian action in public affairs', with the double object, first, of rousing individuals to a sense of their responsibilities as Christians in the public life of the nation, and, secondly, of hoping to impress the leaders of the Churches with the demands of some at least of the rank and file for effective Christian leadership.

They decided to make the meeting non-denominational and inter-party, and to bring it down to earth by giving opportunities to those who wished to put their principles into action. It was fixed for 5 December 1946 in the Town Hall and the Oriel Fellowship, now augmented by recruits from other colleges, threw themselves into organizing it.

A tyro in such matters, Collins was pessimistic about the size of audience it would attract, and at dinner with Diana and the Gollanczes before the meeting the cold rainy weather convinced him that the event would be a failure. As it turned out, even the last-minute borrowing of St Mary's Church for an overflow could not accommodate the queues. In addition to the 1,600 in the Town Hall and the 800 in St Mary's, over 500 had to be turned away. The crowds were attracted both by the spiritual purpose of the occasion and the distinguished line-up on the platform. Bell of Chichester was in the chair, and the speakers were Acland (Church of England), Barbara Ward of the *Economist* (a Roman Catholic and gifted speaker on humanitarian issues), Roger Wilson, a Quaker who for six years from 1940 had been General Secretary of the Friends Relief Service, and Victor. The speakers moved two resolutions, the first exhorting Christians to recruit others to play a full part in national life and the second calling on the leaders of the churches to press for a positive Christian approach to Germany. Victor, who described himself merely as a guest of the meeting since he was not baptized, spoke on the second resolution in the terms of *In Darkest Germany*, which he had just sent to press: 'we simply dare not compromise in our application of the principles of charity and faith in our behaviour towards our neighbours.'

There was only one vote against the first resolution, cast by a Pembroke undergraduate who objected that Acland and Victor were self-confessed Marxists. Collins's report of the objection ran: '"Sir Richard Acland", he said, "is an aristocrat who went to Rugby and Mr Gollancz is a very rich man who went to St Paul's. I cannot see how they reconcile their call to Christian action with the class hatred they preach so consistently . . . " At this point Mr Victor Gollancz, just returned from speaking to the overflow meeting, humorously refuted the charge that he was a Marxist, self-confessed or otherwise.' (Victor's skills in dealing with hecklers had been finely honed. If he could not defeat them by reason or a clever riposte, he could usually drown them out by raising his voice. On one occasion he became so angry that he descended into the audience, confronted the offender and simply bellowed at him: 'You foolish man!' What he never did, however sorely tried, was to have them thrown out.)

The second resolution was passed unanimously and, on an initiative from the floor, the whole meeting pledged itself to support SEN, which was given the balance of the collection. The meeting was well reported and Christian Action was off the ground.

Collins was determined not to lose impetus in discussions about priorities, so he pushed his enthusiasts straight into working for reconciliation with Germany. They did not confine themselves to helping SEN, but developed their own programmes, helping POWs, organizing an international summer school in which old enemies were brought face to face, forging a link with the University of Bonn and bringing over to Britain for a tour the Berlin Philharmonic Orchestra, then restricted to playing light music for American troops. From the start, Collins showed that he intended to be his own man, taking Christian Action in the direction he thought right for it. Over the years there were to be clashes with Victor, as Collins became less of a disciple and more of a leader, but, for the most part, Victor learned to live with it. He accepted that his support would be welcomed when it was asked for, but that his advice might not necessarily be accepted. He was so entranced by Diana that he tried to avoid conflict with John.

There was no friction at all in the early days, and Victor was the star speaker at Christian Action's second great public meeting in November 1947, at which he addressed (on 'Reconciliation') 2,000 people who packed the Sheldonian Theatre in Oxford. His mind was still on Germany, and much of his long speech was addressed to that familiar theme, but there was much discussion of the essence of Christianity and the possibilities it offered for perfect brotherhood if individuals would take seriously Christ's 'quite painfully and terribly explicit imperative, "Be ye therefore perfect" — and the context shows that perfect here and now, perfect in this world, perfect in human relations, is what is meant — "even as your Father which is in heaven is perfect".' Only through the love and service of man could mankind love and serve God. Quintin Hogg, who along with Cripps, Pakenham and Templewood, was one of the leading political supporters of Christian Action, took the chair. Victor was not the only speaker, but he was the star, and without dissent the following resolution was passed:

> We Christians present at this meeting, having heard the challenge made by Victor Gollancz, resolve and call upon all Christians to support us in our resolution to do all in our power to make the principle of reconciliation operative to the maximum degree possible in our national policy towards Germany and all other needy countries.

The press was favourable, but the *Church of England Newspaper* was not the only one to spot the irony that a spiritual lead to Christian Action was being given by one not a member of any Christian church.

> Many must have come to hear Victor Gollancz speak because of the reputation for sincerity he has deservingly won in his approach to the question of Germany: there are many problems on which the large audience would have liked to hear him.
>
> Instead, a new Gollancz emerged and some may well be puzzled in wondering whether a Jew or a Christian was speaking.
>
> It surely seems strange that a preacher, who is commonly regarded as a Jew, should preach a view about man that he presumably does not accept. Victor Gollancz has rendered an immense service to the cause of humanity by his courageous presentation of the German situation, but he should have stated his own position more clearly before attempting to expound what he regards as the right relationship of men and women to one another.
>
> The Christian doctrine of man is essentially a Christian doctrine and not a Jewish or humanist one, and his brief dismissal of Professor Niebuhr★ and those whom he chose to call 'princes of the Church' cannot be allowed to pass unnoticed.
>
> Nevertheless, a great deal of what Mr Gollancz said deserves to be taken to heart by those of us who claim to be Christians, and his plea to us to think in terms of human beings and not in terms of an impersonal government machine was a timely reminder . . .

Victor was not amused. A fortnight later the paper carried his response:

★Reinhold Niebuhr, the great American protestant theologian. Victor's dismissal of him at the Sheldonian was not recorded in print, but early in November he had spoken about him at the Trinity College Dublin College Historical Society in the following terms: 'I violently disagree with the view for instance of Niebuhr that while Christian ethics have an absolute validity *sub specie aeternitatis* they have only a partial and conditioned validity in this our temporal world. That is the dualism which is leading us to disaster.' Niebuhr offended him also by contending that a man could 'be saved by hope and faith'. That, in Victor's view, was irrelevant bribery.

What on earth do you mean by saying that at the Sheldonian Theatre meeting on Christian Action I 'preached a view about man that I presumably do not accept'? No one has the smallest right, whether a Christian or not, to say such a thing about anyone else.

The theme on which I was speaking was 'Thou shalt love thy neighbour as thyself.' Are you unaware of the fact that this was a Jewish doctrine long before it was a Christian doctrine? If so, I suggest that you should read your Bible. But when I say this, I must not be taken to deny that Christian ethics, properly understood, develop the Jewish ethics they took over into something spiritually far deeper and, in the best sense far more uncompromising. On the contrary, I have always made it perfectly clear that this is my view. But I would emphasise the words 'properly understood.' No one can be said properly to understand Christian ethics who deliberately imputes insincerity: and it is imputing insincerity to say that a man preaches a view that he presumably does not accept.

The *Church of England Newspaper* had been foolish in expressing itself so loosely, and wrong in speaking of 'a new Gollancz', for though Victor's emphasis had changed and the Christian absolutism was coming ever more into the forefront the change was simply one of degree. Since the end of the war he had earned a deliciously paradoxical reputation: the Jew who was 'the best Christian in England'. There were many who assumed — and Ruth was not entirely immune to such fears — that he would ultimately be baptized. Yet it was never a possibility. He despised the Archbishop of Canterbury and was frequently impatient with the Pope. The Quakers, with whom he was in many ways most in sympathy, lacked the intellectual bite that he needed, and though he helped and approved of them he did not seek them out. He loved the society of clergymen, of any denomination, with whom he could indulge in theological wrestling matches, but he found their grasp of the essence of Christianity sadly defective. The 'overwhelming majority of Christian theologians and apologists', he told his Trinity College Dublin audience, espoused a version of Christianity that involved 'a species of bribery'. The only pure kinds were two. One was that which 'simply presents itself as a revelation of truth . . . which must be accepted for its own sake and quite irrespective of any ulterior consideration.' The other was that of St Francis or Beethoven, which 'is nothing but the ecstatic or better still the tranquil adoration of God, as revealed in Christ.' Victor, need it be said, aspired to represent both.

There was another major obstacle to baptism for Victor. Even had he been convinced that any single church had got its theology right, he

could never have surrendered his freedom of action to be bound by
any dogma or structure. Remaining outside the Christian church, he
acted as a 'divine gadfly', nagging it for its failure to live up to the
standards of the Sermon on the Mount. There were few things
Victor enjoyed as much as pointing up the unChristianity of a bishop
— especially if he were Geoffrey Fisher.

He published a slightly modified version of his address in a
pamphlet called *On Reconciliation*, sent to press early in December
1947 and dedicated to John Collins. In his foreword he issued a
warning to 'the youthful and unwary that I am neither a philosopher
nor a theologian, but a man in the street. I should not have mentioned anything so self-evident but for the remark of a distinguished
don after my speech at the Sheldonian Theatre: "The typical product
of a man who got a first in Mods, but never read Greats."'

The other speech in the pamphlet was one he had given at the end
of July at the Wilton Park Training Camp to a largely German
audience. He had been drawn into occasional contact with POWs at
Wilton Park largely through the agency of a remarkable German
Jewish refugee, Heinrich Schultzbach, who made a seminal contribution to the re-education of German POWs. Victor occasionally
spoke to them and one or two came to Brimpton.

This speech was extempore, taken down in shorthand. Its fluency
suggests that he had at least been thinking hard about its subject-
matter for some time, for he usually took a great deal of trouble to
prepare non-standard speeches. Although he dwelt on the familiar
themes of human relationships and the brotherhood of man, he was
more sympathetic to the difficulties of the British government and
more blunt about Germany's record than was his wont with English
audiences. That was, of course, entirely in character. He was facing
an audience mainly of POWs, who, though suffering loss of liberty,
were being decently fed and housed. They regarded Victor as a saint
who would understand their distress at being cut off from their loved
ones: he had already proved his commitment to securing their
release. On the other hand, Victor was getting a little alarmed, not
only at the vociferousness of some POWs but at the tone of some of
his mail from Germany. He had spoken there to politicians and
others about the defects of the British government and his consciousness that it was failing in its duty to a conquered people, but in his
heart he expected in return an admission that Germany had much to
be ashamed of. He was caught in the conflict created by one of his
own contradictions: in reaction to majority British opinion he had to
assure the Germans that what had been done was not their fault, but

when they took him at his word he was shocked by their failure to show repentance.

The speech at Wilton Park therefore lurched a little. There was moderate criticism of the Allies, who 'have acted no better, on the whole, than might be expected from average human nature.' There was condemnation of the concept of collective guilt, but this time it was extended to include the English, who were not as a whole to be blamed for deficiencies in the treatment of the Germans. And he upbraided Germans for not putting themselves in the shoes of those who now ruled them:

> They are showing little willingness to make the qualifications they ought to make when condemning conduct which, ideally, they are quite right to condemn. I myself condemn some of this conduct, as you know; but it is one thing to condemn a thing in oneself and quite another to condemn it in somebody else. I do find in the letters that I get from Germany a good deal of self-righteousness. Many letters say: here you are, starving us; what is all this talk of democracy? God forbid that I should reply: have you forgotten what was done in your name, have you forgotten things that were infinitely worse than a diet of 1,000 calories? I would never dream of making such comparisons. But I do say that just as we should try and see ourselves in the position of the Germans from 1919 to 1945, and should above all wish them well, so now the Germans should wish us well, in spite of many things which they rightly object to in our conduct.

He ended on a plea that those in the audience about to go home to Germany should fight against any growth in bitterness or resentment over the lost territories. (He had been deeply worried by the signs of German nationalism which he feared might lead to new international tensions and even war: Konrad Adenauer was the politician who worried him most.) It was up to the German people to accept that loss as irrevocable, and remember that ordinary Russians were not to be blamed for the excesses of the Kremlin.

In publishing this speech in his pamphlet, Victor was making a deliberate effort to demonstrate to his countrymen that he genuinely saw two sides of the question. Yet he did not put the pamphlet on the market with the usual flourish of trumpets. If the absence of letters among his archives is anything to go by, free distribution was cut down, and the Gollancz publicity machine only ticked over. The pamphlet did not have a wide enough circulation to rid the public — and particularly the Jewish — mind of the strong impression that Victor excused everything the Germans had done and nothing the British did.

He continued for a few more months to preach the SEN message, but his interest was beginning to wane. An enormous proportion of his time since 1945 had been taken up with individual cases of hardship that found their way to Henrietta Street, and the success rate in solving them was heartbreakingly low. Many letters asked for practical help that he could not give. He had been generous with financial contributions to relief organizations. What is more, he had kept quiet about them, something he aspired but usually failed wholly to do. He gave in often to the very human temptation to explain that he could not give to Cause B because he had just been open-handed with Cause A, or to tell a pottery dealer that he had to pass up a fine piece because he had just dispensed of his bounty to a worthy cause. But in the case of Germany he made unusually strenuous efforts to curb this tendency. One gift of £1,000 (for footballs for German boys) was never mentioned in any reminiscence or any surviving letter bar one he got from the recipient, and other substantial sums were paid out without any advertisement. Victor was never predictable on such matters, but by and large the guiltier he felt about not giving enough the more he tried to conceal having given anything at all. Steeped as he was in details of German deprivation, and with an avalanche of mail hailing him as a great philanthropist, he felt embarrassed by the knowledge that he was still living very comfortably.

He had been careful not to publish in Germany anything likely to stir up anti-British sentiments. (*Our Threatened Values* was translated for a Swiss edition with a preface carefully written for a non-British public, and *On Reconciliation* was also published on the Continent.) But the German media made up for the lack of his writings by their adulatory press, and equally adulatory letters from German citizens piled up.

Extracts from a few of the translations made for him will give the flavour of what Victor was reading about himself. In March 1947, a Stuttgart periodical initiated a series called 'Good Deeds!' Referring to *In Darkest Germany* it regretted the absence of a German edition of 'this ardent appeal to the conscience of the world', but 'a few quotations suffice to give an impression of the firm and resolute personality, uniting in itself kindness, courage and wisdom, whose achievements we, therefore, give the first place in our series *The Good Deeds*.' A brief survey of his 1946 trip followed. This 'incorruptible observer' realized 'that his personal fears were widely surpassed by the facts'. The British people did not 'feign deafness' when he appealed, 'for the truth of the facts which he gave and the integrity of this first pleading for the guilt-laden German people were vouched for by the name with which they were signed: Victor Gollancz.'

> Who is this man, of whom his conscience demanded that he should meet with neighbourly love the enemies of yesterday, and whom an English bishop [George Bell of Chichester] has called the 'first Christian of England'? — Victor Gollancz is a theologically learned Jew, a kind paterfamilias of five daughters, a born Englishman, and for thirty years a member of the Labour Party. His true humanist sentiment sees no essential difference between Jewish and Christian ethics and the ideals of Socialism . . .

A brief account of his political publishing career and his work for SEN followed.

> So, it is due to the initiative of this man that in favour of the starving Germans bread-rationing has been re-introduced in Britain, that German prisoners of war in Britain have been allowed to send to their families in the British zone parcels up to the value of 200 marks . . . and that to-day every Englishman can send to Germany food, for which he pinches himself out of his own rations. All this is, perhaps, only a first, modest success as compared with all the warnings and programmes which Victor Gollancz brought home from Germany. Its moral importance, however, cannot be valued too highly; for in this period of moral confusion this success is the first decisive step on the way towards a humanly dignified solidarity of the nations of Europe, and for this step we have to thank one man alone, Victor Gollancz, — for an intrepid Englishman's, good European's and good man's *Good Deed* . . .

In May a profile came from a Munich paper:

> 'You'll find me all right . . . ', he called to a couple of his friends in London, when they wanted to know in 1943 what he was going to do after the war would be over. 'I don't yet know where my biggest task will lie, but I shall tackle it . . . ' Meanwhile the war is over, Gollancz has 'tackled it' — and Europe is talking of him . . .
>
> [He] wrote of the Germans in a letter he sent from Jülich to his wife in London: 'One must love them for their suffering and their valour.' Thus wrote the same Gollancz who in the days of the Austrian Anschluss had caused demonstrations in front of the windows of the German Embassy in London, who had warned of the growing Fascism and condemned the Munich agreement in his sensational pamphlet, *Guilty Men*. To-day, he bears with equanimity the reproach of 'sentimental obstinacy' and of anti-Russian sentiment. He suffers it as a few years ago he had suffered the accusation of being an 'agitator' and 'communist' — or as he had suffered those bombs which upset his office and drove away his employees but

were unable to keep him from squatting down before his fire-place and lighting the fire.

A brief biography of the years to 1928 follows. 'Since those days, this enterprising, compact and heavy man, whose lined features and always slightly ruffled hair remind so much more of a kindly family doctor than of a tenacious and not easily diverted publicist, plays an established role in the political and cultural life of Britain . . . ' There was more about publishing, and the essential role that observers attributed to the LBC in bringing about the Labour victory in 1945. 'Victor Gollancz thereby experienced the realisation of his second major aim: — he became a truly popular figure. But what is popularity? The sound of praising phrases, the knowledge of being the trusted friend of the mighty suits Gollancz just as little as a ponderous office building which he has resisted up to the present day. (By the way: — All his employees are partners in his firm[!]) He staked his popularity at once . . . '

Given the pathetic state of the German press, these mixtures of fact and fantasy tended to get passed on, ever more embellished, from paper to paper, and to inspire more people to write to him, school-children to compose essays about him as an example of goodness and even amateur writers to try their hands at stories, poems and the occasional play about him. For many poor, desperate Germans the 'Jüdisch Philantrop' was a symbol of love and hope in a sea of indifference. In their gratitude they invested him with a range of qualities no one person could be expected to possess, and credited him with having single-handedly roused public opinion in Britain and brought about a change of attitude.

All this made good copy, and Victor's name attracted international recognition. Journalists from far beyond Europe — especially those of German descent — were intrigued by the story of the 'Jewish Apostle' and wrote of him almost as unrealistically as did the German press. Those who came to interview him were overcome by his mighty personality and retired to write confused paeans to his goodness. The following paragraph (in translation) from a German weekly in New York in November 1947 was not untypical:

His room in which he received me is simple, like the man himself. But this simplicity is anything but the simplicity of Spartan austerity, which to me has always been suspect. The office of the man who was in no need of becoming 'the good uncle of the new Germany', because he is also one of the world's greatest publishers and one of the most influential politicians of the Commonwealth — his office is as simple as a room in Montmartre, or a student's digs in the Quartier Latin. You feel a kind of self-assured joyousness in the room. I soon found out then that Gollancz is more like a Frenchman of the 19th century than an Englishman of today. His kindness has nothing in common with the oily condescension of the professional 'do-gooder'. Rather it is the sort of human kindness you find in Heine.

This was a distinction that Victor himself never failed to point out. As he explained at Wilton Park:

I happen to feel by instinct a complete equality with every human being with whom I come into contact, or of whom I read or hear. For instance, I occasionally go and lecture to prisoners. About a month ago I lectured to the old lags at Wandsworth Prison — some were confirmed criminals, and one of them had been in and out of prison for forty years; but it would never have occurred to me for a single second that there was the smallest inequality between myself and any of those prisoners to whom I was talking. This is an attitude, as I say, that some people possess as a matter of instinct: but you can train yourself to it also; you can acquire it by the proper spiritual approach.

(There was some truth and a great deal of nonsense in this. It was true that when he was confronted by someone like an SS man or a convicted murderer, towards whom most people would feel some sense of moral superiority, Victor made huge efforts to imagine himself being so conditioned as to end up in their predicament. To that extent he regarded them as equals. Yet his family, colleagues and social acquaintances were certainly not his equals when there was conflict of needs, priorities or egos. It had been so since his childhood, and Victor thought it normal. He could prove that he viewed men as equals because his packers called him 'VG'. He could prove too that he was no respecter of rank: he would lose his temper quite as violently with a member of his board as with the lowest of his staff. But often, in anger, he forgot such principles completely; he was not averse to name-dropping when dealing with bureaucrats who offended him. One was the Chairman of the Newbury Rural District Council, whose staff had been inefficient in negotiating over the sale of the now redundant hut in the Brimpton meadow: 'I cannot help wondering', wrote Victor, 'what my friend [and neighbour] Mr Aneurin Bevan, the Minister of Health, would think about them [these proceedings].' Even better was his response when the British Museum Reading Room asked him for a reference before they would issue him a ticket: Victor suggested the Prime Minister might be suitable.)

Not all the foreign press was favourable. The memory of Victor's work for the Jews was swamped in the wave of outrage from certain quarters at the logic of his expressed position, which was that a member of the British Jewish community could be more guilty of the death of a relative than was Streicher. Jews who applauded the execution of leading Nazis did not take kindly to Victor's rebukes, delivered on the basis that they were falling short of a superior Christian ethic. Victor was under attack from 1946 in the Jewish press at home and abroad. And he had achieved a new distinction: he was being vilified in the Soviet Union, in terms reminiscent of those that Dr Goebbels had once used to explain his activities.

A BBC monitor sent him a translation from a 'Moscow in Yiddish' broadcast in March 1947.

> Victor Gollancz has become the hero of the day in the pro-fascist Press of Britain and the USA. Gollancz is a Jew from Hungary who was clever enough to flee to England from the Hitlerite danger. He is a journalist, a publisher and, on top of all that, a business man; with the help of his corrupt pen, he has managed to accumulate a nice fortune in London.
>
> Recently, he made a trip to Germany and published his impressions in the British Press on his return. He shed bitter tears over Germany's fate and conducted an organised campaign to persuade the world to forgive her sins. He is devoted to Germany and demands that the Allies should not let her disappear from this earth or pay any reparations at all. Gollancz certainly knows how to forgive.
>
> However, he is not satisfied with that. He demands Germany's industry should be returned to her. What Germany possessed in the days of Hitler should be returned to her, so that the Germans may concentrate on revenge. It is said that in the Western zones he has seen many Jewish victims, an endless number of hungry and dead. Thus he had an opportunity of seeing what Hitler had done to these people in camps. Nevertheless, he does not say a word about that in his impressions. His pity applies exclusively to the inventors of the Majdanek death trap vans. What is the origin of Victor Gollancz's pity for Germany? Why has he become such an enthusiastic defender of those who oppressed countries and nations and killed 6,000,000 Jews? The Jewish Press abroad explains this by pointing out that a campaign as conducted by Victor Gollancz is bound to be popular with certain people in Britain and the USA. And this means money and a career.

It was the second time Victor had achieved temporary international fame. (It would happen once more during the 1960s. Always it came about in a controversial manner.) In the LBC days he had been famous more for his organization than for himself. In the controversy over Germany, he caught the bouquets and brickbats for himself. It was hard on the other campaigners who had worked along with him or in parallel. Men like Bell, Beveridge and Stokes did not attract the recognition they deserved; in time even Victor largely forgot their contribution and believed his had been the sole voice crying in the wilderness. His head was swollen by the volume and intensity of the praise, and his dislike of criticism increased yet further. Though he enjoyed adulation, his passion for the German issue diminished as the supply to the Germans of life's essentials grew. SEN was beginning to get involved with specific projects like educational reconstruction, but it had no particular niche that others were not prepared to fill. Its last major undertaking was the sponsoring of an International Conference at Fredeburg in the British Zone in September 1948, to consider the problems of vagrant, wayward and endangered children and youth in Germany. The conference made a number of recommendations to the Military Governors of the British, French and US Zones. Victor did not attend, but he did broadcast in December on North-West German Radio, appealing for funds for welfare work. A Munich paper reported it as part of a short story — 'A Light for German Youth! — A Christmas Tale round Victor Gollancz.' It ended thus:

Christmas of 1948 was approaching. The misery among homeless youth was terrible in German lands . . . In the bitter cold of the winter, boys and girls went freezing and hungry, without hope and helping love, without kindness and protection, from one cellar-hole to another . . . begging from door to door.

But suddenly, like a Christmas miracle, a call rang through the ether: 'Rescue the German youth! For God's sake, save them! They are not guilty!' It was the kind voice of the Friend, sounding across the sea from his island, and magically appealing to the conscience of men: 'Rescue this youth! — Save them now!' And the Friend spoke over the radio of the sacred force of active love and charity taking possession of the hearts of men at Christmas time, and moving even the poor to give presents and help to the poorest.

Radio transmitters and newspapers, churches and governments, took up the Helper's call and spread it throughout the land. Those who had much, gave much. The poor did their best, each according to his conscience, which was in many cases stronger than his means. Every one sacrificed some comfort for this youth, and contributed to the good work, to give material proof of his active love.

So the light of hope was kindled in the dark world of forsaken young people. It was Christmas time. The love of God had come to the hearts of men.

The appeal resulted in the setting up of the *Victor Gollancz Stiftung* [Foundation], which awarded scholarships for students to train as social workers. Victor's broadcast had raised enough money to get it going and, although he had almost nothing to do with it afterwards, the magic of his name continued to help its fund-raising. This was the first practical way the German people had of showing their gratitude to him. Other honours were to follow over the years, and until his death he received grateful letters. The winding up of SEN caused little resentment. Helped by Marshall Aid, German reconstruction was under way.

SEN closed down its activities during the last six months of 1948; Peggy Duff (who had had early warning of Victor's waning enthusiasm) moved on in December to work for *Tribune*, and the organization formally went out of existence in March 1949. Duff wrote:

> By that time, VG was more than a little bored with Save Europe Now. He was never a one for long campaigns. He liked to finish them off before they started to languish. 'There is nothing so depressing', he told me once in a taxi, 'as a movement which has attained its aims.' Many of his early campaigns had eluded his efforts to close them, but with Save Europe Now he was luckier. Towards the end of 1948 we started shutting up shop. The hundred thousand postcards were packed into boxes and stored in the Henrietta Street basement.

As Save Europe Now began its decline, Victor was already well advanced with the next of his cycle of causes — spreading the gospel of Christian ethics among the Jews.

CHAPTER NINETEEN

MORE CAUSES

ALTHOUGH VICTOR HAD failed to write down his thoughts on Judeo/Christian relations during his 1946 Canaries holiday, he had not finally abandoned his projected tract. Jewish hostility towards his SEN propaganda kept him alert to the topic, and in December 1946 he specified his writing plans, when he took exception to a *Humanitas* review of *Our Threatened Values* by a research student in English Literature, J. W. Lever.

Lever was both sympathetic to and deeply critical of the book. His review was so brilliantly perceptive about Victor that it was bound to lead to trouble. 'Mr Gollancz has a marked capacity for making his readers uneasy,' it began.

> It is not because of anything novel or provocative in his view-point: if it were so, his books would be widely acclaimed. It is not that his manner of expression gives offence: no one could be more patient and conciliatory. But he will persist in urging causes upon their official sponsors. For years he has expounded Christianity to Christians, liberalism to Liberals, and socialism to Socialists. He is so insistently on the side of the angels that his approach makes every cherub wriggle in his seat. And those of the devil's party fare no better. Mr Gollancz forgives them their devilishness, and refuses to believe them when they say they chose their leader because they liked him.

After summarizing the argument of the book, the review lamented its failure to consider the causes underlying the decay of fundamental values. 'Why, one asks, should it be necessary to "remind" men of principles instilled into them since childhood? The fact is, not that they have forgotten, but that they have chosen not to remember. The psychological foundations of totalitarianism may be sought in that active resentment which sprang up against both religious ethics and their humanistic variants during the nineteenth century.' That resentment led to a series of attacks from men like Marx and Nietzsche, who ultimately provided the climate for totalitarianism. 'Mr Gollancz hopes to repel the attack by an appeal to whatever principles the old creeds have in common. For this purpose he is ready to confound Christianity with liberalism, and liberalism with social democracy' —an attempted syncretism that could not succeed. 'One cannot set up popular fronts of the spirit.' In the last resort, Victor was neither Christian, liberal nor socialist, but sought from them 'some vague but congenial ethos which might satisfy his hankering for community without encroaching upon his innate spiritual dissent.'

Lever was absolutely right about Victor's obsessive syncretism. 'He was always trying to reconcile everything,' said Longford once in conversation: 'Marx, Jesus, Seneca, Kafka.' And to that list could be added dozens more, from Marcus Aurelius to Teilhard de Chardin. Victor had reached the threshold of the final philosophical stage of his life. Henceforward, as he read voraciously on matters spiritual, he sought to weave a synthesis that satisfied him, and each time he believed he had got the synthesis right, he had to go out and preach it, so that others could share his wisdom and spiritual fervour. Christ was to be revered above all other men, but he had only pointed the way. Victor was improving on his message and bringing it up to date with the help of the best thinkers of the intervening two millennia. Lever was right when he went on to say that 'the reiteration of familiar precepts' was insufficient without 'a reasoned and systematic doctrine' to provide agnostics with a guide to future action, or to make a unity of incompatibles. Yet he under-rated Victor through not knowing him: he did not understand the force of his personality, which could leave those who read or listened to him sympathetically marked by his message, however familiar the precepts might be.

> These objections are raised in no carping spirit: such is the state of the world that any mockery of men like Mr Gollancz would at once fetch echoes from the infernal vaults. Rather it is hoped that Mr Gollancz will, by careful self-searching, come to a realisation of his true position and consequent responsibilities. For he is, in his deepest self, a Jew, and the core of his message is Jewish. First taught by the prophets, those troublers in Israel, it has been sustained by a people which has never since ceased to trouble the world. From that people's obstinate rejection of universal creeds, its clinging to its own integrity through successive epochs of Christianity, humanism and now demonism, its consciousness that its destiny is only half-fulfilled, Mr Gollancz may draw comfort and guidance. As the years pass he has come increasingly to inquire into the Jewish view of life: perhaps the time will arrive when he will be in a position to restate that view in terms that will give positive direction to those who live in this cataclysmic age.

Lever was remarkably shrewd here. Victor was indeed in his deepest sensibilities a Jew, who might turn his back on the old religion, but never walk away from it. He just went on reacting to it as he had to his father. When his people were in torment, he put his whole soul into trying to help them, then began to resent their attempts to embrace him as one of them. After the war, Jews were to feel again and again that he was deliberately trying to goad them. As he had persecuted Alex with liberalism, so he persecuted the Jews with Christianity on and off for twenty years. Lever's review brought a letter more ominous than angry. Victor wanted the editor of *Humanitas* to tell him if Lever were Jewish.

In their ensuing correspondence, Lever, who was a Jew, defended himself courteously but uncompromisingly. When informed that Victor intended to take part of what he had written as 'the quite perfect text for the pamphlet that he proposed to write over Christmas, to be called "A letter to the Jews"', Lever assured him that he was looking forward to it 'eagerly'.

Lever was unlike almost all Victor's Jewish critics in his breadth, the cutting edge of his intellect and his refusal to conduct the debate on an emotional level. For, as Victor in his publisher's hat frequently complained, the Jewish community in Britain was musical and artistic rather than literary, and few of them were able or willing to take him on calmly on his own ground, wielding the weapons of the intellectual. Meanwhile, most gentiles were uninterested in Jewish internal strife and merely assumed — if they were sympathetic to Victor — that he was being opposed by a lot of old fuddy-duddy traditionalists.

The pamphlet was not written over Christmas, perhaps because Victor was more uneasy about it than he admitted, perhaps because he was inundated with SEN work. A letter Edmond Fleg sent him at the end of January may have given him pause. Fleg had flicked through the photographs in *In Darkest Germany*, and found himself 'hardly moved. I have in my eyes and heart images of Auschwitz, a hundred thousand times more dreadful, and I have in my ears and my soul the charges laid the other day at Nuremberg against the criminal doctors of Germany. Do you feel that they, too, should have escaped judgement, and that, when all is said and done, there is not a sort of collective responsibility in a country which produces such monsters — and which is alone in producing them?'

He had finished *Our Threatened Values*, but

the more I read your pages, the less — for all that the great liberalism and efforts at objectivity natural to me helped at first — the less easily could I follow you. It is hard anyway to understand how you could suppress, by such an effort at abstraction, your Jewish sensitivities. The cruel past, so recent, no longer lives in your memory; a word or two barely recall it; a silence falls over it. And you fail to take into account that your idealist dream will serve a form of politics that you abhor. For those great personages who seem to share your pity for the Germans now are thinking of anything but pity and justice, for they are the very ones who, in Palestine, are breaking their promises and making mock of those famous unwritten laws Antigone speaks of, which are engraved on every human heart. . . .

Victor explained to Julius Braunthal that Fleg's hostility was a result of his being French. Yet he must have recognized that if a Jew of Fleg's liberalism could reject the argument even of *Our Threatened Values*, it was unlikely that the proposed pamphlet would make many converts. In any case, he was horrified at the anti-Zionism of Attlee and Bevin, and it was clearly not the time to weigh in with criticism of the Jews. The project was shelved, though Victor still brooded on ways of getting his syncretic message through.

The Palestine situation was in a fearful mess during 1947, with the Labour government so frightened of alienating Arab opinion and having Britain's access to oil threatened, that they had Jewish opinion ranged against them. Terrorism was rife in Palestine, along with illegal immigration, on which the British government was taking a very tough line. President Truman was at loggerheads with Attlee and pressing for the admission of 100,000 refugees, and, as positions hardened, neither Jews nor Arabs wished to negotiate. In the view of his biographer, Kenneth Harris, Attlee's failure to come up with a solution to the Palestine problems 'is the worst entry on his record'. He effectively passed them over to the United Nations with the announcement that Britain would pull out of Palestine when its Mandate ended in May 1948. While the UN deliberated, terrorism mounted, and Victor was left wringing his hands over the activities of the Irgun and the Stern Gang, and the refusal of the government to make any concessions that might lower the temperature. Of course, he was not unsympathetic to the Arab side, and while he continued to publish Zionist propaganda, he made efforts to tone down accounts of Arab atrocities. His major initiative during this period was to write to Attlee in March 1947, imploring him to understand the reasons for Jewish terrorism — caused by people being driven crazy with grief at the holocaust — and to make some effort to appease Jewish opinion. He prefaced the letter by giving his credentials:

I think I can see the situation as objectively as most. Only a Jew can really understand the Jewish aspect of the matter from the inside, and I am not one of those British Jews who think it incumbent on them to prove themselves more gentile than the Gentiles. On the other hand, though a partitionist for many years I am in no way connected with any Zionist group. Finally, my habit of mind has always been such that I cannot be blind to the Arab case . . .

(There was a great deal of good sense in the letter, but Attlee's mind was already made up. Besides, he was unlikely ever to respond to an emotional appeal from any private individual, and he had little time for Victor. For his part, Victor, who secured his best results by mobilizing public opinion, could never understand that a persuasive letter from him alone might not move mountains or an obdurate Cabinet. That fruitless letter apart, Victor was, for some time, vocal on the Palestine issue only in a protest to the *Daily Herald* at the forcible return to Germany of a contingent of illegal immigrants.)

Victor's connection with Christian Action was banking up resentment in large sections of the Jewish community, where it was felt that he was acting strangely for a delegate to the Board of Deputies. Indeed, in September 1947, his loyal relative, friend and admirer Norman Bentwich persuaded him that he must do something to counteract the bad press he was getting from European Jews as a result of his SEN activities. Victor reluctantly wrote a piece for a Jewish paper in Germany outlining his record as a worker for the Jews and stressing that, when in Germany the previous year, he had visited Belsen and also met a number of Jews in every city he visited.

I believe that the real ground for the misunderstanding and indeed misrepresentation to which I have referred is dislike for my attitude to the German people. I am sorry that my attitude should be disliked, but cannot help it: I must do what my conscience tells me to. A week or so ago an article of mine was published in *The Observer*, in which the appalling growth of tuberculosis in Germany was referred to (and lest I should be attacked for this, I hasten to add that I am a Vice-President of the Anti-Tuberculosis League of Palestine). I got an anonymous postcard from a Jew (it wasn't a fake, because some of the words were written in a beautiful Hebrew script) saying that he would pray on Rosh Hoshanah that every German, man, woman and child would die of tuberculosis. God forbid that I should pharisaically attack him for this: for all I know, his relatives may have been gassed at Auschwitz, and anything, if that is so, may be forgiven him. But I cannot, for all that, regard his postcard as an expression of good Judaism: and I may perhaps put my whole attitude in a nutshell by saying that in my attitude to the gentile world, and in particular to the German people, I am endeavouring to be a good Jew, as I understand the teaching of our prophets.

It was hardly surprising that Jews found Victor perplexing, irritating and inconsistent: there were few who could see how being a good Jew was compatible with preaching Christianity. The *Jewish Chronicle* was editorially rather tolerant of Victor, at least for a time, but as it remarked (in a comment on the *Church of England Newspaper*'s reaction to his Christian Action speech): 'The wonderment [as to whether he was a Jew or a Christian], I fear, is not confined to Christians! It reminds me, however, that it was a Christian critic of Mr Gollancz the other day who referred to his expressed view in the Christian Action campaign as "the faith of an extramural Christian"!'

The *Chronicle* was moderate in its attitude to Germany and hence to Victor, but in March 1948 it expressed its reservations. It was deeply alarmed by evidence that anti-semitism was again developing in Germany, something that those mobilizing public opinion on behalf of the Germans 'are bound to gloss over'. 'Some do it in good faith, and, for example, no one, even though he disagree bitterly with Mr Victor Gollancz, and think him quite misguided, will impugn the high principles which move him.' Others, it feared, wanted a restoration of German nationalism.

If Victor had confined himself to preaching Christianity outside the Jewish community, his waywardness might have been overlooked, but that was the last thing he wanted to do. He was determined to confront the Jews with Christ and effect a reconciliation. In April 1948 he stirred up a great furore by accepting an invitation to address the Federation of Liberal and Progressive Jewish Youth Groups on the future of Judaism. The Beth Din banned Dr Feldman, Warden of the Great Synagogue, from taking the chair, ostensibly because they disapproved of a representative of orthodox Judaism participating in such an ecumenical gathering, but clearly because they objected to Victor's presence. The content of his address made things worse: in rejecting Christianity, the Jews had thrown away 'the culmination of their own philosophy'.

> He wanted the Jews to go back to the point 2,000 years ago and to accept universalism. The Jews had been reaching towards the idea of the life of charity, and this idea culminated in the teaching of Jesus.
>
> In the future, Mr Gollancz said, he would like to see the Jews becoming a sort of great Jewish Society of Friends. The ultimate aim should be that Judaism, Christianity, and all other religions should vanish, and should give place to one great ethical world religion, the brotherhood of man.

It was in its way a good ecumenical speech for, as the *Chronicle* pointed out, it must have 'offended Liberal no less than Orthodox Jewish sentiment'. The letters of protest included one decrying his 'appalling statements which are tantamount to apostasy'. He was accused of total ignorance about Jewish ethics. One correspondent recalled being told by Dr Albert Löwy (Ruth's grandfather) 'that the ethics of Jesus were and could be only Jewish. For Jesus the Jew knew nothing of Pauline Christianity.' Victor was 'a false prophet' when he spoke of universalism, which must come about from a Jewish aspect. One of the most devastating letters was printed in shortened form.

> It is amazing that Mr Gollancz is so far behind the times as to rehash a long-since exploded fallacy: the superiority of the Christian over the Jewish ethic; and to dish it out for the consumption of Jewish youth groups — of all people. His thesis lies at the foundation of the Higher anti-Semitism; and I can only attribute Mr Gollancz's appalling blunder to ignorance of Jewish ethical teaching, and to an attitude of self-contempt that such ignorance induces.

It was poor consolation to outraged Jews that Victor published a long letter on Palestine in *The Times* a couple of days later, describing himself as a Jew, 'as loyal to Israel as to Britain'. Speaking for like-minded Jews, he urged the Jewish Agency to parley with the Arabs. He was immediately attacked by both the Arab Office and the Jewish Board of Deputies.

The Jews were rapidly tiring of their turbulent prophet. In May there was a titillating item in the *Jewish Chronicle* headed 'Mr Gollancz's Position', and covering the annual meeting of the United Hebrew Congregation: 'Mr Basil Sandelson, giving a report of the congregation's representatives at the Board of Deputies, stated that, with the exception of Mr Victor Gollancz, they had carried out the mandate of the congregation. . . . ' By June the *Chronicle* had become hostile: it condemned Victor's 'perverted counsel' to Jewish youth 'to despise the ethical teachings of the Synagogue'.

Victor had cause to feel misunderstood and misrepresented. It was manifestly unjust to accuse him of ignorance about Judaism. By now, for a layman, he was exceptionally well-informed on both Judaic and Christian history, dogma and practice. Veering between a passionate desire to see a Zionist state in Palestine and alarm at growing Jewish militarism, he was caught up with the future of his people. His SEN activities had given him the excuse for pushing Jewish concerns aside for a couple of years; now they were his pre-occupation, fanned by discussions early in 1948 with liberal Jewish intellectuals — including rabbis — about the danger that the essential spiritual qualities of Judaism would be wholly submerged by materialism and pro-Israeli nationalism. In November 1947 the UN approved the partition of Palestine, and in May 1948, the State of Israel — covering more than half the territory of Palestine — was proclaimed. Unco-ordinated troops from five Arab states entered the country and were humiliatingly defeated. Almost one million Palestinian Arabs were to leave Israel during 1948 and 1949, and for many of them the consequent hardship and suffering was intense. Victor was torn between his Zionism, his horror at terrorist outrages, his dismay at the heartless treatment of refugees and his fury at the resultant upsurge in Britain of anti-semitism. It was probably the latter that precipitated his temporary but consuming concern with matters Jewish.

At last he had come to accept the truth of Lever's contention that he was, 'in his deepest self, a Jew.' An unpublished article he wrote in the autumn sought, *inter alia*, to clarify the nature of his Jewishness. The balance of the dual Israeli–British loyalty he had so recently evinced had shifted.

I adore England: I adore her sun, her fog, her heat, her cold, her grass, her autumns, her London, her Oxford, her Bath, her gardens, her people, her institutions. Whatever my other ancestry, England is my mother; and while I have long followed the more idealistic aspects of Zionism, and particularly the way of life in the Kibbutzim, with passionate interest and sympathy, I can no more imagine myself deserting England and adhering to the State of Israel than I can imagine myself becoming a German or a Czech. I am, first and foremost, a citizen of the world: but after that I am an Englishman.

And I am also very Jewish. What is Jewish? Heaven forbid that I should try to answer that all but unanswerable question. It may be that scraps of what I learned and felt and did as a boy in a moderately orthodox Jewish household still cling to me, and that nothing more than this is involved in my 'Jewishness'; it may be so, but I do not think it is. To begin with, some of the things I feel and do which seem to me distinctively 'Jewish' belong to a climate totally different from that of my childhood, a climate into which I have gradually moved as the years, and particularly these latter years, have spun themselves out. When the day, for instance, is specially fine and the countryside is specially beautiful, not only do I spontaneously rejoice as everyone else rejoices, but I consciously feel a sort of added happiness in that an opportunity has been given to me to say a Br'cha. I doubt whether my father felt anything of the kind. I love to recite Shehahionu; and as for mitzvoth — I mean, of course, human mitzvoth, not fasting on Yom Kippur or blowing the Shofar — I feel the same kind of happiness when they come my way as the very orthodox used to feel (or so one reads), and may still feel for all I know, in submitting to the yoke of the Law. All this and much else I call 'Jewish'. Behind it, I suppose, is a certain quality of spiritual joy in, and gratitude for, *this* world. I would not suggest anything so grotesque as that only Jews feel like this; but it is true, I think, to say that historically there is something rather specially Jewish about this way of feeling — a way of feeling that tends to degenerate into the gross materialism which, though really its opposite, so often, alas!, disfigures us.

He had come to realize that his eloquence as a Christian evangelist was making enemies rather than converts among the Jews; a new approach was needed. Lever had suggested eighteen months previously that Victor might yet restate the Jewish ethic in a positive way for his contemporaries. Events in Palestine were his inspiration to gird his loins for one of his most ambitious missions yet — 'a spiritual regeneration of Jewry' through example. If he could not persuade Jews to accept the theory of Christianity, he must induce them to practise it under another banner. In mid-1948, with hundreds of thousands of Arabs already homeless and every Israeli gain adding to their number, the opportunity was there to show that Jews could love their enemies. That could be achieved only through an organization impeccably Jewish in its membership and drawing on the spirituality and humanitarianism of the greatest pre-Christian prophets. To this desirable end, Victor was prepared to play down his idiosyncratic Christianity.

His own reputation with most of the Jewish community was in tatters, so Victor turned for help to his liberal friends. All were attracted by his idea of forming a society, along Quaker lines, to give human service to those in distress, and they were happy to begin by helping Arabs — a charitable endeavour they saw as entirely in keeping with their religion. Their aim was to see a secure Israel, at peace with her neighbours and operating by the highest Jewish ethical standards. Some, such as Norman Bentwich, saw Victor's proposal as potentially important for Arab-Israeli reconciliation. Others, such as Rabbi Leo Baeck and Michael Rubinstein, saw the proposed society as an opportunity to demonstrate the innate spirituality of their religion. (Michael's father, Harold Rubinstein, like Victor, was near to being a Christian fellow-traveller.) This variation in emphasis was the seed of a division of opinion.

A large majority believed that in Palestine help should be offered to distressed Jews as well as to Arabs. Victor, his imagination aflame with the vision of Jewish relief workers suffering and even dying alongside the Arabs they were succouring, was out of sympathy with the idea of helping anyone except the enemy. Unable to go it virtually alone, he was obliged to compromise in order to enrol the supporters he needed. The as yet unnamed group became publicly active in August 1948, with the despatch to the press of a letter signed by Bentwich, Baeck and Victor. Bentwich's name carried great weight within the Anglo-Jewish establishment and Baeck's credentials were beyond reproach: the spiritual leader of German Jews during the 1930s, he had settled in England after his release in 1945 from a concentration camp. Appealing for £1,500, the letter set out the group's objectives succinctly:

> A group of Jews, concerned to give expression to the universalist ethic of Judaism, has decided to sponsor the sending to Palestine of a few social workers who desire to relieve the suffering of Jews and Arabs indifferently. Volunteers have come forward, and, while the project is admittedly a venture of faith, we believe, after enquiry in Palestine, that there is reasonable hope that women going out in that spirit will be permitted to achieve the desired purpose. But whether they succeed or not, we are convinced that the attempt will itself have value as an act of reconciliation.

The letter brought in about £1,000, and the group foundered immediately on the problems of Arab-directed relief. Bentwich's investigations abroad had revealed that no Arab territory would accept Jewish help of any kind, under any auspices. A member of the group, Jane Leverson, despatched to Israel to reconnoitre, returned with a series of workable proposals that only incidentally benefited Arabs. Victor and the Rubinsteins were deeply disappointed, but the majority of the group felt it better to go ahead immediately with practical relief projects, rather than flail around in search of good works which might never materialize; several weeks had been spent taking soundings abroad and squabbling at home. Victor bowed to the inevitable and agreed to the Leverson report in the hope that its implementation might provide a springboard for expansion into Arab territories. He bent his energies to getting the group properly off the ground. In October it constituted itself formally and belatedly as the Jewish Society for Human Service (JSHS) — a name thought drab by some of the more evangelical members, who had come up with suggestions like 'Seekers and Helpers' and 'Wings of God'. Baeck became President, Bentwich Chairman, Victor Vice-Chairman, Harold Rubinstein Treasurer and Michael Rubinstein Hon. Secretary.

Victor was put in charge of a £10,000 fund-raising drive. Even as he made the preparations, he was unhappy at the position he found himself in: trying to galvanize an organization whose stated aims and immediate objectives differed from his own. As early as 18 October he was writing dispiritedly to Harold Rubinstein:

> I cannot escape the conviction that we have been 'jockeyed' (I don't use the word offensively) into a position — for which I must take my full share of responsibility, as I fear I ought to have been stronger — where, while we set out to relieve the appalling distress of the Arab refugees, we have ended by primarily helping Jewish immigrants, with a little distribution of clothing to Arabs in Jewish Palestine. The more I think of it, the more topsy turvy it seems.

And to John Collins he described his sufferings: 'I am hideously thick in the launching of my Jewish Committee for Aid to the Arab refugees. All sorts of hideous difficulties and constant committee meetings and consultations — including sandwich lunches here! Horrors! . . . '

It must have been clear to all his intimates that Victor's perception of the JSHS was very different from that of the majority. Certainly, even as he drafted leaflets and letters appealing for money for Jews and Arabs, he was making his own individual position clear in articles designed to awaken Jewish consciences. The first lengthy piece (which included the passage on his Jewishness quoted above), destined for the American journal *Commentary* but not published, preached the 'Love your enemy' doctrine by means of a highly individualistic extrapolation from an Old Testament prophet. His argument developed what was for him a new doctrine — indeed, an apparent turn-about: the idea of collective responsibility. The frightful misery of the Arabs was a consequence of the foundation of Israel, and therefore, though the UN, the British and the Arabs also bore responsibility for the Arab-Israeli war, the Jews were 'in a special sense morally involved and obliged to do what little we could to lessen its gravity'.

He was writing his article only a few weeks after publishing in *The Times* a letter defending Zionists against the allegation that they bore collective guilt for the Stern gang's murder in September 1948 of the UN mediator in Palestine, Count Bernadotte. (Credited with having saved 20,000 Jews during the war, Bernadotte had been killed because of his proposals for allowing Arab refugees to return to their homes in Israel.) The distinction was absolutely clear to Victor. From Ezekiel — 'The son shall not bear the iniquity of the father' — he argued convincingly in his article the case against collective guilt and

condemned the many Jews who had imputed guilt to every German.
He continued:

> . . . there is a sense in which collective responsibility is an inescapable
> religious fact. If my father has sinned — if, to pursue the Ezekiel quotation,
> he has oppressed the poor and needy — then as my father's son I have a
> special obligation to succour where he has oppressed: as the other member
> of a fellowship — the family fellowship, for our present purpose, of two —
> I am not only specially called upon to do right *because* my father has done
> wrong, I am specially called upon to do right just *where* my father has done
> wrong. It is a question of restoring the balance not in any formalistic or
> juridical sense, but in a spiritual sense. We are all no doubt called upon,
> simply as human beings, to do as much good as possible to 'make up for'
> the evil of ourselves and others; but when evil has been done by members
> of our own fellowship, then the restoring of the balance requires extra
> action from *us*, and not only so but action *at the very point* of the evil. This, I
> repeat, is an inescapable fact, rooted not in logic but in spiritual reality . . .
>
> Those, then, who like myself . . . feel themselves to be of the Jewish
> fellowship are for that very reason imperatively called upon to succour the
> Arabs . . .
>
> In love, and in the acts that spring from love, is the only salvation. The
> religion of love, which has at least done something to leaven the lump of
> human wickedness, is Jewish, so far as the West is concerned, in its
> ultimate inspiration. Shall we be false to that inspiration now? . . .

(The Freudian overtones come as no surprise, for Victor's relationship
with his father was as important to him emotionally during his fifties
as it had been during his adolescence. The twists and turns in his
relationship with British Jewry during the 1940s mirrored the
retrospective attempts to understand his father which reached their
apogee when he wrote *My Dear Timothy* in 1951.)

Trepidation about extending fund-raising activities to America
made Victor decide against publishing this article. It would almost
certainly have proved counter-productive. The implication in the last
paragraph that the great achievement of the Jewish religion had been
to prepare the ground for Christianity would have antagonized many
opinion-formers. Whenever he expressed himself at length, he
brought Christianity into it, and every compromise he made within
the JSHS made it more difficult for him to compromise outside it.
What he saw as honesty, others saw as perversity. In a row with the
Jewish Monthly in November and December 1948, the impossibility of
Victor's ever harmonizing with Jewish sensibilities became clear.

The *Jewish Monthly* welcomed contributions from Christian and
Jewish literary figures: its young editor, Harold Soref, though

politically poles apart from Victor, offered to carry an article by him entitled 'Why Jews Should Help Arab Refugees'. Victor provided a compressed and slightly amended version of his unpublished *Commentary* piece. Soref was impressed, and declared his intention of publishing it in the December issue, as it was of 'immediate interest and importance'. He had one serious reservation, concerning a sentence that Victor had added specifically for the *Jewish Monthly*: 'I . . . feel myself to be a member of the Christian fellowship.' Although Soref could not understand this, he was certain it would be anathema within the Jewish community and would undo the good achieved by the rest of the article: he wanted to erase or amend it.

Victor was still feeling bad about the pusillanimity of an appeal leaflet he had recently produced, and Soref's request was the last straw. He wrote back, refusing to make any changes, 'I may add that this kind of obscurantism is what has long been killing British Jewry. It seems to me outrageous that in what I am given to understand is supposed to be a serious organ of Jewish opinion my views, however heretic they may be, should not be allowed to find free expression.' Soref reiterated his view that the sentence would harm the JSHS; he denied being an obscurantist, and asked Victor either to modify or amplify the term 'Christian fellowship'.

He was quite well aware, wrote Victor, that the sentence would 'create opposition in some quarters, and that the response would be greater without it. But there are matters in which the truth must nevertheless be told: and if I omitted that sentence I should be lying by omission — and that I must not do.' He offered to change 'Christian fellowship' to 'Christendom'.

Soref consulted, among others, Victor's ex-partner, Leonard Stein, now president of the Anglo-Jewish Association, the publishers of the *Jewish Monthly*. He reported to Victor that he had unanimous backing. 'I have rarely', responded Victor,

> read a letter which seemed to me so intellectually and spiritually shameful. You are supposed to be a forum for the expression of opinion by Jews. I am a Jew and recognised, I hope I may say, even by those who most strongly differ from me, as not irresponsible. Yet, because you object, or think your readers would object, to my statement about Christendom, you deny me access to your columns. . . . If the prophets were living now (not that I am comparing myself to them for a moment) you would have denied them access to your columns. The episode is indeed a most striking illumination of the thesis I hold about the appalling results of the Jewish attitude to Christendom — and I shall make good use of it in the book I propose to write on the so-called Jewish question . . . can't you see what a horrible

blasphemy you are committing? I suppose the most fundamental of all the elements in Judaism is the belief that every man, as the mouthpiece of God, must say what God tells him to say. This theme recurs again and again in the prophets. Yet you, Harold Soref, and your advisers, arrogate to yourselves the right to prescribe 'this he shall not say'. In other words, you arrogate to yourself a privilege of God, and break the seventh commandment.

Soref found this 'preposterous'. The *Jewish Monthly* was a platform for all expressions of Jewish opinion, but 'one can be either a Jew or a Christian and I do not see how you can be both at the same time.' He had mentioned, at a meeting of the Anglo-Jewish Association, Victor's intention of publicizing the dispute.

'I never suggested that I was a Christian,' Victor wrote back.

I said I felt myself to be a member of Christendom. Gilbert Murray is a passionate atheist; but not only does he feel himself to be a member of Christendom, but he has written to this effect in *The Times*. Moreover, even on the narrower religious ground it is of course within your knowledge that for many decades, before the final split between the church and the synagogue, people were both Christians and Jews — that is to say, people who proclaimed themselves Christian were considered by the Jewish authorities a sect of Jewry.

There followed a long elaboration of this argument, leading to the contention that any British Jew not feeling himself part of Christendom had only one course of action open to him: emigration to Israel.

I have the highest respect and admiration for people who do that: none whatever for the people who want to make the best (which always means the worst) of both worlds.

As to the question of the book I propose to write (though God knows when) on the Jewish question, I think you misunderstand me. I do not propose (if indeed I ever write the book) to refer to your paper. What I propose to do is to say that I was unable to get publicity in Jewish quarters for the statement that I felt myself to be a member of Christendom: and to quote this as an example of a pathological taboo from which Jews have suffered for centuries and which they must get out of their system . . .

This epistolary defiance ensured that an important group of liberally-minded Anglo-Jews would henceforward regard Victor as a trouble-maker best avoided. His appeal for money to help Arabs had already infuriated his traditional enemies, some of whom raised their voices in loud protest in the columns of the *Jewish Chronicle*. Edward Atiyah, the Secretary of the Arab Office in London, had written to the

Daily Telegraph to describe the appeal as 'an act of doubtful taste', since it came from Zionists. And although the Christian — and particularly the Catholic — press was warmly in support, the heavily stressed Jewishness of the JSHS considerably limited its attractiveness for philanthropic gentiles.

These setbacks left Victor less inclined to take a conciliatory line within the JSHS itself. By November he bitterly regretted his initial pragmatism, and had set himself to drag the society back into line with his original vision of its purpose. He had secured agreement for an appeal for clothing solely for Arabs, and applied himself to obstructing any relief work on behalf of Jews. His views were gaining ground within the society, mainly because its wider membership (upwards of 50) met only monthly. For the most part, decisions were taken by the executive committee, on almost half of whom Victor could normally rely for support. Indeed, he often had an absolute majority, for his staunchest supporters — the Rubinsteins, Albert Hyamson and Hugh Schonfield — were faithful attenders, while those less in accord with his views — such as Rabbi Baeck, the Ellenbogens and Victor's cousin, Hugh Harris — were often unable to get to meetings, which were held in Henrietta Street, and had a way of being scheduled for times that suited his supporters.

Norman Bentwich, appointed chairman for political reasons, was Victor's biggest problem. Bentwich was no cipher. He was a highly intelligent lawyer and a formidable liberal influence within Zionism and the Anglo-Jewish community. A man of total integrity, he was not about to yield to what he considered a distortion of agreed policies. Level-headed, pragmatic and prosaic in character and style, he was in almost perfect counterpoint to Victor. In the power struggle that developed between them, Bentwich had experience, prestige and common sense on his side. Victor, in addition to a much stronger personality and an inspirational style, had many practical advantages. The JSHS was located at Henrietta Street; until early in 1949 Peggy Duff was its part-time organizer; the Rubinsteins were fully in sympathy with their vice-chairman; he was the society's greatest benefactor (he contributed £1,000 towards it in the spring of 1949); and his prowess as an organizer and fund-raiser made him invaluable. Moreover, as is the way of prophets, he knew himself to be right.

His religious position was at last absolutely clear — at least to himself. After years of turmoil he had reached a synthesis that he held to in all essentials for the rest of his life. It enabled him to reconcile his whole-hearted acceptance of Christian ethics with a spiritual yearning for many of the beliefs and practices of Judaism. He drew on those elements of both religions that most appealed to him. Thus, one of his Judaic inspirations was contained in the esoteric mysticism of *Kabbala*, on which Victor frequently drew to chastise dogmatic Christianity for failing to have at its centre 'the establishment of the kingdom of God on earth': 'It is said, with that quaint mixture of childishness and profound wisdom which the Cabala so often displays, that God destroyed his own unity by splitting Himself up and putting a tiny bit of Himself in innumerable human beings: and that only when those human beings have come together in perfect love, brotherhood and peace, will the unity of the Godhead be restored.'

Victor identified himself with Saint James, 'the Lord's brother' and head of Christianity's mother church in Jerusalem. Saint James had believed that Jewish converts to Christianity should, like him, adhere to Jewish observances. Victor, 1,900 years later, found in James a pretext for staying free of either Jewish or Christian institutional authority, 'worshipping' Christ while acting, when the mood took him, like a free-thinking rabbi or prophet.

His syncretism also gave him a justification for what had long been a habit — bringing religion into politics without apology. Possibly his best explanation of the right to do so was to come in a letter to the *Guardian* in September 1949, when he defended John Collins (now a canon of St Paul's) against Vansittart, who had proclaimed that to invoke Christ in an argument about the dismantling of German industry was 'a presumption which modesty and a sense of proportion might alike forbid'. Victor's defence of Collins also showed a new-found defence against accusations that he personally lacked humility.

> The Canon is behaving, thank God, just as great religious leaders behaved in the days before religion fell into decay. When the Hebrew prophets castigated the political and social wickedness of their day — not in vague generalities but in precise detail — they cried, quite categorically, 'Thus saith the Lord': indeed, on occasion they went still further and spoke as if they themselves were God, and not mere intermediaries. And while I must of course approach a later period with extreme caution, I should have said that the Canon, in the question at issue, was endeavouring to follow the example of Christ Himself, as his Christian duty required. . . .
>
> Humility is quite another matter. The humble are not those who are inhibited by considerations of human fallibility from proclaiming the will of God as they see it: the humble are those who fearlessly proclaim it out of the very 'fear and trembling' by which their inner life, their relation to God, is ceaselessly governed.

Victor felt much more comfortable with Christ the most revered of all Hebrew prophets than with Christ as God. (Indeed there is strong evidence to suggest that he came to reject the idea that Christ *was* God.) That way, he was free to act as a self-proclaimed prophet in the Hebrew tradition, while drawing on those utterances of Christ and others that seemed to fit the occasion. He had achieved a brilliant integration of the intellectual and the emotional, finding a religion to live by and to preach without sacrificing one iota of his personal liberty. For himself he had certainly made the best of both worlds; those who thought he had made the worst always either amazed or infuriated him. It was a fine example of Victor at his most contradictory that, as a prophet, he wished to make converts, while choosing a message so Victor-specific as to be indigestible to almost anybody else. Jews persisted in thinking him an apostate and Christians found him perverse in his refusal to be baptized. Even his disciples in the JSHS could not accept lock, stock and barrel Victor's individual brand of Judeo-Christianity. They valued his inspirational qualities and prophetic zeal, and kept their reservations to themselves.

Bentwich was not immune to Victor's eloquence, and had already agreed in November that Jews should receive no more help from the JSHS than Arabs. He set off in mid-November on one of his regular trips to Israel, committed to seeking alternatives to those Leverson proposals that most upset Victor. Before he left he sent to the executive committee members a letter which greatly annoyed Victor, acting chairman in his place. He answered it on 1 December with a *cri de coeur* more than ten pages long, taking issue among other things with Bentwich's phraseology.

> Let me start with what is the heart of the matter — such phrases as 'to help both peoples, and particularly the Arabs who are in Israeli territory', and 'I hope that nothing will be said or done to cause any rift about our aims, which must be genuinely to help both Arabs and Jews.' As I have pointed out many times in conversation — and as I thought, when the circumstances were recalled to you, that you agreed — our essential aims have been nothing whatever of this kind. What has happened has been that our aims have been gradually distorted: from time to time we have made strenuous efforts to recover the original inspiration: but in spite of that there is a hangover of distortion.

After a long rehearsal of the origins and history of the JSHS he went on to state his demands: if possible, a team should be sent to Arab rather than Israeli territory; otherwise, the team should work in Israel for Arab relief, but only on work that could not be done by the government. He was unhappy about a JSHS decision to give money for the Arab inmates of a home for crippled children in Jerusalem: that would be relieving the Israeli government of its responsibilities.

Objections to other consensus decisions followed. He then took up Bentwich's proposal that Leonard Cohen, head of the Jewish Committee for Relief Abroad should be asked to join the executive committee. It would be 'undemocratic' to bring him in to strengthen the point of view of the 'very small minority' who approved the Leverson proposals for work in Israel, as it would be wrong to 'appease' Jane Leverson: since she had not carried her point, there was 'nothing whatever' to be said for going part of the way to meet it. Tolerance was invariably a virtue, but compromise could be 'the devil'. The essence of the JSHS was 'no compromise': it had to act '*prophetically*'. Money was now rolling in from Jews and gentiles alike, because the society had unequivocally asked for aid for '*Arabs in distress*': Although not a resigner, 'I could not remain actively associated with a body the aims of which were becoming quite other than those I had conceived.' If he was not supported on fundamental questions, he would have to resign and start a new organization. 'Harold and Michael Rubinstein, and Peggy Duff, who have read this letter, ask me to say that they entirely agree with it . . . '

Bentwich's patient reply was optimistic about finding ways of helping Arabs. He answered Victor's points in a down-to-earth and economical way, stressing the importance of practical work: 'We decided early on that we would help Arabs and Jews in the present crisis. That was in the first published letter, which you composed and in the leaflet which you largely composed; in all our declarations and our approaches for support.' Arabs were now in direst need and should be helped forthwith, but 'We should not be acting in the spirit of our declaration if we neglect the Jewish need at this time or overlook the problems of the Israel Government, particularly their Arab problems.' He wanted Leonard Cohen to join the executive because he was more experienced than any other Jew in the organization and work of relief teams 'and also because he shares our fundamental standpoint. Admittedly our present Committee is weak in persons with practical knowledge. You are a master of appeal and of putting the thing across but you would not claim to be an expert in relief . . . '

Victor was in far too headstrong a mood for such pedestrian advice. As Bentwich laboured over negotiations with Israeli political and military authorities, with relief organizations and with other interested parties, Victor was busy transforming the JSHS spiritually. By mid-December he was writing happily to Bentwich that the society was in an excellent state. He had convinced everyone that Arab needs were paramount and that 'there was nothing to be said for persisting in error because we had sent out a prospectus we regretted'. A full meeting had been informed of the decision to change direction, had approved it unanimously, and had authorized a letter to subscribers explaining the new position. There had followed a discussion on the aims and work of the JSHS, conducted 'on a remarkably high level: we all spoke completely frankly, and my "Christendom" references aroused no hostility whatever (except a little from Hugh Harris!).' The only fly in the ointment was shortage of funds, which seemed stuck at rather less than £3,000 — quite insufficient for the project on which Bentwich was concentrating: the provision of a fully staffed ambulance to work (mainly for Arabs) in Israeli territory.

There was no hope that Bentwich and Victor would see eye to eye. Although he was no slavish admirer of the Israeli government, Bentwich was disposed to give it credit for relatively high standards of humanitarianism during wartime. Being on the spot, he could see that there were Jews as well as Arabs living in miserable conditions. Knowing and trusting a number of Israeli administrators and soldiers, he was grateful for any help they offered. It was with some pride that he informed the executive that he had solved their financial problems. The Israeli government had offered co-operation with an ambulance team, and assistance in feeding and housing a JSHS team in occupied Galilee. This Victor saw as a total sell-out. With Israeli military superiority becoming more apparent week by week, and the state's survival no longer in doubt, he was on the lookout for any manifestation of inhumanity or ruthlessness. He wanted no co-operation with the Israeli authorities. Newspaper reports of the misery of hundreds of thousands of refugees filled him with horror and vicarious suffering. Ideally, he would have liked the JSHS to scrap all plans for work in Israel and send the money it collected to relief organizations working in Arab-controlled territory. He had already unilaterally discouraged Leonard Cohen from joining the executive, and stymied his offer to co-sponsor a JSHS appeal (to the Jewish community in the Manchester area) by refusing to sign a letter which suggested that Jews would be helped other than incidentally.

He set to work to block the ambulance project. Grudgingly, he agreed that the two relief workers already hired should go as planned to Haifa in January to work with the Quakers. In compensation, he got the executive to agree to the suspension of all other activities in Israel, and to a substantial contribution to the Save the Children Fund in Damascus to buy transport. This news was communicated to

Bentwich by cable, and that temperate man wrote strongly to express his resentment that his advice had been disregarded.

> I have been made to look a fool and a busybody and compromised my position. The greater part of the last two months that I have given to our work is wasted and I have still no reason given me for this complete change of plan made against my advice.
>
> I am resigning the Chairmanship, as you and the Committee clearly wish me to do; but I shall continue to direct the work here to the best of my ability.

On the day that he wrote, 2 February 1949, his chief adversary was himself suffering a serious setback. Having heard that the ambulance could be run for a mere £225 a month, the executive decided to fund it if it operated under the auspices of civil authorities. Victor wrote to Harold Rubinstein the next day that he had decided to resign from the JSHS when Bentwich returned. Bentwich, and probably Rabbi Baeck, would be with those who had pushed through the ambulance project; Cohen would be brought in.

> Even so, the Society may well do very valuable work of a sort. But it is not my sort. What I wanted was a body of Jews who would act not merely as decent Jews, but as *men* (which I think is the only hope of human salvation now). But there is a group determined to act, not as men, but as Jews, albeit decent Jews: and either they will have their way (which is unlikely) or, by what they say and do, they will spoil what one can only call the prophetic zest of the whole affair. I am sure a point will eventually be reached at which either I went or they went: and it is clearly less disruptive that I should go, and try to do what I can in other ways.

When the absent chairman's angry letter arrived a few days later, Victor realized that a pre-emptive resignation by Bentwich would ruin things. He wrote to mollify him, and the next executive meeting passed a motion pleading with Bentwich not to resign. They had their way: Bentwich agreed to hold his hand until he came home at the end of February.

He got back to find Victor, as he put it, 'straining on the leash to get going on a big appeal' for Arab relief outside Israel. Bentwich's argument that priority should be given to provision of personal service — possible only in Israel — was swept aside. 'Other things being equal,' Victor wrote to him, 'personal service is preferable to the giving of money: but it seems to me the height of egoism to prefer personal service to the giving of money, when by giving money you can be more effective in alleviating distress.' In any case, he assured Bentwich, 'it would be wholly impossible to raise more money, at any rate on any scale, for the ambulance project as such. The Zionists are not interested: the non-Zionists and anti-Zionists regard the matter as one for the Israeli Government. The Gentile public would not even consider such an appeal.' The matter of Arab relief 'is quite as much a matter of conscience with me as the other point of view is with you. I feel that this Arab question is the biggest challenge to us as Jews that has happened in our lifetime; and I personally feel quite unable not to do what I can in the matter. To use a hack phrase, Jewish honour is desperately at stake.' Even if it were not, Victor, as an Englishman, would still want to help Arabs, and it was absurd that his JSHS membership should prevent him doing so. 'It would indeed be a paradox if that was what had resulted, so far as I am concerned, from my idea of founding this body.' He would resign if necessary because he was determined to launch an appeal soon. If he did it under JSHS auspices, he would specify that a small part of the proceeds go to the upkeep of the ambulance.

Bentwich was trapped: Victor was by far the better fund-raiser, and everybody knew it. He decided against resigning but refused to sign a letter to *The Times*, which was printed over Victor's personal signature, and bore all his hallmarks:

Sir, Thrice in a decade there have been expulsions or flights of a kind that makes a man ashamed of his humanity. First and most horrible — and this should be remembered whenever present events are discussed — millions of Jews were packed up and dispatched, not to a less convenient address, but to the terror and shame of the incinerators. Then, in conditions of unspeakable misery, millions of Germans were sent trekking from their homes. And now there are the Arabs. Are we to be as careless of them as we were of the Germans and Jews? To sidetrack immediate help by arguments about responsibility is sickening. Responsibility lies, not with Zionist nationalism or Arab irresponsibility or British intransigence or American opportunism, but with the wickedness in all of us and the history in which we are all involved.

He called on the Israelis to co-operate wholeheartedly in planned resettlement outside their country. Of the British public he demanded money for drugs and transport. He described the JSHS's 'trifling contribution' to date and appealed for a few hundred pounds for the ambulance project and very many thousands to assist relief work in Arab territory.

The letter received acclaim from a remarkable source. Sir John Glubb, known throughout the world as the legendary 'Glubb Pasha', was at this time commander of the Arab Legion. He wrote to Victor from Amman on 9 April.

I hope you will allow me to say how much comfort I derived from reading your letter of 19th March in the Times, which I have only just seen.

Fifty years ago, the Jews were known throughout the Western World as idealists, intellectuals, musicians, and the most patient of workers for international peace and understanding. In Palestine during the past year, I have been working on the other side and so I may be prejudiced. There is doubtless much idealism inside Israel, but it is not extended to Gentiles.

What we can see of Israel looks like an exact copy of Hitler's Germany. The same ruthlessness, the same indifference to human suffering, the same unscrupulous breach of pledges given, and the same lying and blaring propaganda. Of course I realise these things are not essentially Jewish. They are Nazi and Soviet methods learned in Eastern Europe. But they form a sad contrast to the old liberalism, humanity and love of peace which, in happier days, we associated with the Jews.

It was for this reason that your letter gave me so much pleasure.

I am writing this to you personally, instead of to the Times, so that you may believe that it is dictated by real feeling and that I am not trying to score a propaganda point . . .

Glubb was not alone in being moved by Victor's letter. The response to it was markedly better than to earlier appeals. Operating alone in his old swashbuckling style, Victor saw his efforts rewarded by the substantial sums of money that began to arrive in Henrietta Street. His *Times* letter was amplified and sent out to the thousands of SEN subscribers, who were told of SEN's demise and urged to support its descendant. The terms of his letter had deterred Jewish subscribers, and the particularism of the JSHS's title limited its appeal for gentiles, yet within three weeks he had received over £4,000, which grew to £17,000 within five months.

Victor could not follow up the appeal, as he departed for the United States on publishing business in late April, but he left behind him strict instructions for the allocation of all funds as they arrived. The bulk was to go immediately to the International and the British Red Cross. He insisted that no more than a few hundreds — as specified in his letter — could in propriety be given to the ambulance. Bentwich, recognizing that he had been outmanoeuvred, wrote sadly to him on 2 May that he was 'confirmed in my conviction that you and Harold want me to resign the chairmanship, unless I am prepared to accept your views without any qualification. I will fall in with that wish when you return. What restrains me from doing it now is the desire not to prejudice either the appeal or the work of our little unit . . . ' He felt the ambulance was doing good work in the spirit of the JSHS, even though the Arabs it was saving were not, according to Rubinstein, technically refugees. Victor's appeal had 'cut away the ground' from under him and ensured that sufficient funds could not now be raised for it. He was uneasy about Victor's and Rubinstein's 'indignation' about any clothing being used for needy Jews.

Bentwich, having failed to raise much for the ambulance, hung on for a few months, watching wistfully as many thousands of pounds went to the Red Cross. By the early summer, Victor had begun to feel that his work for the Arabs was done. The JSHS was starting to discuss its future direction. One member favoured fighting colour discrimination in South Africa, while Victor pressed the case for helping refugees in Germany. Clearly, he was determined that the society should always concentrate its efforts on those regarded as enemies by the average Jew. In July, urging the cessation of the ambulance project and the sacking of the relief worker, he made his case unanswerable: the JSHS had given away virtually all its money . . .

> I am even more pessimistic than I was at the last Executive about the possibility in present circumstances of raising any further sum: nor could I myself undertake to help in doing so (first, I am exceptionally busy, and secondly, my specialists have warned me that to go a bit slower in the immediate future may literally be a matter of life or death). I think I also ought to make it clear that it would be impossible for me personally to subscribe another penny. I have already given far beyond my means.

'I recognise the immense contribution you have made to our work,' responded Bentwich, 'both personally and by your power of moving the Public Conscience. We cannot fairly ask you for more.' It would be up to the rest of the executive to raise money, should it prove possible to provide the ambulance to help the Quakers outside Israel. He was about to leave for Israel, and asked Victor to make his views known at the next meeting.

On 9 August, the executive ordered the winding up of the ambulance project. As a small sop to the absent chairman, maintenance for the relief worker for three months was agreed. A Red Cross representative pleaded for £10,000 for Arabs in the Old City of Jerusalem, where many thousands were in a state of absolute destitution.

> The Vice-chairman [Victor] expressed his willingness to launch an appeal for the £10,000: but laid down, as absolute conditions for his doing so, (a) that it should be for this specific object — i.e., for the non-refugee Arabs in the Old City — and for nothing else whatsoever; and (b) that the question

of using any part of the money, however small, for any other purpose, however good, should, from the beginning, be considered out of order . . .

The Committee gave Mr Gollancz full support, accepted his conditions, and asked him to proceed.

Knowing that the public was weary of appeals, Victor was pessimistic, and the £6,000 subscribed bore him out. Nonetheless, it was a considerable achievement, and he had the added gratification of a warm letter of thanks from the Chargé d'Affaires at the Jordanian legation. Bentwich objected to the exclusivity of the appeal and wrote from Israel to complain. Victor decided that the time had come for a final confrontation. With the JSHS ending its connection with Israel, and dependent on gentile rather than Jewish money, Bentwich had become superfluous. Victor forced the issue by distributing a letter on 19 September announcing that 'for personal reasons' he would resign from the vice-chairmanship and the executive when the Old City campaign was finished. It was a shrewd move, which bore fruit at the executive meeting three weeks later, when Bentwich resigned as chairman in Victor's favour. Betraying no resentment, Bentwich became vice-chairman and wrote to the usurper very cordially that he would clear up the ambulance project 'and I expect I shall have some troublesome suggestion or other to make.' With Victor presiding over an obedient executive, the way seemed open to make the society more vital and effective. Instead, it began to peter out: for all his intriguing, Victor's interest in the JSHS was on the wane.

In the winter of 1949 his best energies were devoted to his anthology, *A Year of Grace*, published in 1950 — by which date other concerns, including publishing, seemed more immediate. A visit to the Middle East might have excited his compassion for the Arabs, but he did not find the time. A couple of small-scale appeals in 1950 raised some money, but did little to justify the continuance of the JSHS.

There were four real options open to the society. The first was to become a significant fund-raiser for particular crises, channelling money through relief organizations like the Red Cross. The second was to take the Bentwich line, and concentrate on small projects of benefit to Arabs and Jews alike, making modest and uncontroversial financial appeals to well-disposed Jews. The third option was to turn the society into a small study group for the discussion of religion and ethics. And the fourth was to launch a full-scale attack on Jewish nationalism, bringing about, through righteous eloquence, some mass movement for spiritual regeneration.

Victor was fed up with fund-raising, so the first option was a non-starter. His attention span was short at the best of times, and after fourteen years of campaigning on various fronts, he wanted more time for other fulfilling occupations: publishing, reading, writing, conversation, travel, music and so on. Anyway, the best the JSHS could hope for was to be a feeble supplement to bigger, more popular charities: it was too narrowly based. Exclusively Jewish in its membership, it had appealed only briefly to gentiles by the novelty of its fraternal attitude to the Arabs, and Victor's cold-shouldering of Zionism had alienated most Jews. There was little attraction for Victor in a long charitable grind for paltry results.

The second option was the most practical of the four, but Victor was still firmly against it and Bentwich was now quite powerless to bring the executive round to his point of view. The third had been tried in a small way with occasional papers and discussions, but other than the Rubinsteins and Hugh Schonfield, few of the tiny member-ship were of the abstract turn of mind to enjoy more than an occasional rarefied theological debate. As Victor frequently reminded his colleagues, the society had been set up to put into practice the Old Testament ethos: 'In the beginning was the deed'.

In the spring of 1950, Victor decided to pursue the fourth and prophetic option. An appeal was sent out to members for a small subscription to cover the costs of keeping the JSHS going and oft-discussed plans for a public meeting were dusted off. The practical objective was to win new members and set up a 'Personal Service Bureau' for those who wanted to give personal help to the distressed. The Conway Hall, which holds 500, was booked for 28 June.

During Victor's absence in America the executive did its best to advertise the meeting. Handbills headed 'Call to Serve' invited the public to attend. Victor was back in time to make the decisions about the order, content and length of the speeches. Bentwich took the chair, Victor was the main speaker and in his support were Baeck and Magnus Wechsler (an executive member and a London county councillor). As if to verify the narrowness of the JSHS's appeal, the turnout of gentiles and Jews alike was poor.

Victor was in uncompromising form. He 'confessed, as a Jew, to a feeling of shame that the people who had inherited the teachings of the Jewish Prophets and had given to the world "the sister religion which had become the greatest and, in many ways, the most noble religion of the world" were by no means conspicuous in carrying out those fundamental ideals of human service.' This was intensified by the discovery that the best and strongest emotions of Jews were going into nationalism, which fostered exclusiveness and a hostility to other people.

'Yes,' wrote one of his supporters, 'last night's meeting would appear from its immediate results to have been a failure and the audience was flat and unresponsive but something tells me that you did not waste your time and somehow I feel that you really *did* something last night I am absolutely sure of it though you yourself may never know.'

'Thanks awfully,' responded Victor.

> I would like to have a talk with you very soon about helping me with this 'Personal Service' Bureau! Things didn't end so badly, after all. The new enrolments came up to 25, and I had one or two extremely touching letters. We now have about 80 members and my idea is:
> (a) to write a little brochure explaining the aims of the Society, and,
> (b) to call together our 80 members very soon, in pleasant surroundings, and, very informally, to go into the whole matter and to try to get everyone present to pledge themselves to enrol two new members. If they succeeded in doing so that would put us on a secure basis.

He followed up his Conway Hall speech with an address to a Jewish Society in Ilford, where he attacked nationalism and the universal growth of selfishness. He attracted censure in a column of the *Jewish Chronicle* and wrote furiously to the editor, complaining of misrepresentation. But it truly mattered little whether Victor was fairly or maliciously reported: his message made no impact whatsoever on more than a tiny minority of Jews and he lost heart. Financial strictures made it necessary to dispense with the JSHS's only paid official, and various schemes for practical activities came to nothing. Victor never wrote his brochure, nor did he launch the promised membership drive. Within a few months of its only public meeting, Victor let the JSHS slide into limbo, whence it emerged occasionally to raise funds *ad hoc*. As an instrument for the spiritual regeneration of all Jews, it was defunct. That crusade was not entirely abandoned, but Victor would further it by other means from now on.

From 1945 onwards, first SEN work and then the spreading of the Judeo-Christian message gave ample opportunity to lambaste the Labour government: from the moment they took office, Attlee and his colleagues rarely measured up to Victor's standards. As regards their domestic initiatives, he was critical of style rather than substance, but their foreign policy gave him constant offence, through sins of omission and commission alike. He was publicly mute, on the whole, when they did right by his standards (as with India), but he was pitiless when they failed him — most notably over Germany, Palestine, and the movement for European unity.

It goes without saying that Victor's loathing of nationalism made him a natural proponent of world government, and a government of a democratic, socialist and humanitarian hue at that. He was thus automatically sympathetic to any movement of the most limited scope that might contribute to a shift in that direction. In 1945 he became a vice-president of Federal Union, a society which sought European federation as the first step on the road to a united world. His enthusiasm for federalism grew in proportion to his despair at the inhumanity of Stalinism. Writing in April 1946 to the Federal Union organizer about a speech he proposed to make on their behalf, he explained that one of his main points would be that 'while I am a more passionate socialist than I ever was, the real battle today is not between capitalism and more socialism as such, but between the liberal or Western ethic and the totalitarianism of which the Soviet Union is now the major exponent.'

The Federal Union, however, was too lightweight for Victor: there was little chance it would make a public mark, so he responded enthusiastically to an invitation in November 1946 to throw in his lot with a non-party group, led by Winston Churchill, to promote the idea of a United States of Europe. He was invited, it seems, at the behest of Bob Boothby, Victor's closest friend within the Conservative party. Within a few days he was having second thoughts, as the Labour Party's distaste for the initiative became evident. He wrote to Duncan Sandys, the originator and driving force, that he was withdrawing, regretfully, from the meeting of the Handling Group.

> If it had turned out, as it seemed at first it would be likely to turn out, to be an all-party affair, the situation would have been entirely different: but I am sure you will understand that in a predominantly Conservative set-up even my attendance at the preliminary discussion would do more harm than good. As you are perhaps aware, I am busily engaged at the moment in somewhat vigorous polemics with my party on the question of Germany: and I am most anxious that any effect I may have may not be diminished by unfair accusations. I feel certain that, for the moment, the best contribution I can make to the cause of European unity is to keep myself 'uncompromised', so to speak, in my relations with the party.

For the Conservatives, the Labour Party's stand-offishness made it vital that well-known independent socialists be recruited to the group.

Boothby was set to persuading Victor of his duty, and convinced
him that enough Labour dissidents would be found to make their
presence felt along with the Liberals. He kept the pressure up. On 17
December he wrote a short encouraging note: 'This is just to let you
know that King (Labour MP), Gibson (TUC), Berry (Free
Churches), Gilbert Murray, and Walter Layton, are coming to this
meeting in Winston's room at the House of Commons at 5 o'clock
to-morrow. So, if you can possibly manage it, you will not find
yourself in disreputable company.' Victor suppressed his misgivings,
went along and made his contribution to the discussion about
suitable members and goals for the proposed organization. A stirring
statement of aims was approved that Victor thought 'could hardly be
bettered'. Boothby wrote again:

> Winston told me last night that he was greatly impressed by your
> performance at the meeting, and by your grasp of essentials.
>   He added that he was depending a good deal on you and me to make
> the thing go; and that his services were at our disposal. I have written
> to Duncan Sandys urging the inclusion of Russell, Lindsay and
> Trevelyan . . .

Victor could not fail to be flattered by praise from the great man,
who, moreover, had only recently lauded *Our Threatened Values* in
the Commons. In a letter to Churchill a few days after the meeting
Victor thanked him for his remarks about the book: 'I felt extremely
proud about this: for while, as you know, we differ so profoundly on
many questions, I do not forget, as some appear to do, the supreme
debt owed to you by every one of us — a debt we can never repay.'
The same letter begged Churchill to include Bertrand Russell in the
group.

> There is no living man with a more truly religious spirit, in the broader
> sense: and I know of no one who has this cause more passionately at
> heart.
>   Forgive me, also, if I say (though this is comparatively of no import-
> ance) that his inclusion, and that of Lindsay, would make my own
> position much easier. They are both, as you know, members of the
> Labour Party: and without them I should feel in some difficulty, as the
> Labour side is very weak, the two MP's being light-weights . . .

Churchill's answer was typical of the great courtesy with which he
treated Victor. He approved of the idea of recruiting Russell, remarked that he had read *Our Threatened Values* with 'the greatest
interest' and hoped that they would be able to discuss it one day.

Lindsay and Russell joined and the Labour Party took fright. On 23 January 1947 Victor was sent a letter by the party Secretary, Morgan Phillips, spelling out the decision by its National Executive Committee (NEC)

> that while it is desirable to encourage the maximum co-operation between the nations of Europe, it should be clear that an organisation led by Mr Churchill is not likely to stimulate such co-operation at the present time.
>
> The Labour Party is firmly committed to the belief that the future of Europe depends on the success of the United Nations, and on the strengthening of friendly collaboration between Russia, America and Britain. Mr Churchill's committee explicitly excludes Russia from Europe, and in view of his personal record and his known opinions, it is likely to be interpreted, rightly or wrongly, as aiming essentially at the elimination of Russian influence in Europe.

Party members were therefore advised to withhold their support from the United Europe Movement (UEM) committee and concentrate 'such of their energy as is not absorbed in direct work for the Party on organisations such as the United Nations Association, whose aims and inspiration are above suspicion.'

This letter added to Victor's unease. Refusing an invitation to publish a statement (in the *Common Wealth Review*) as to why he had signed the European Unity manifesto, he explained in confidence

> the reasons that led me and such people as Bertie Russell, etc., to join the Committee. We do so only just on balance, and as a result of a great number of conflicting arguments. Briefly, it was a question of certain very important (from the Left point of view) European politicians who would probably come in if we joined, and not if we didn't. There was also the question of certain dangers if we didn't join, as the thing was going to go on anyhow . . . I think it is better, in view of all the various moves that are going on all over the place at present, to say nothing for the moment. The right time will come . . .

Victor was temporarily, and unhappily, in a state of indecision. He had no wish to be out on a limb defying the Labour Party, and thus lose any influence over the German question. Yet he was greatly in sympathy with the leading Tories in the movement. Sandys, for instance, wrote to him in late January about *In Darkest Germany*: 'It is by far the biggest thing that has been done by anyone to compel people to take notice of the tragedy and folly of events in Germany. If I can be of any help to your Save Europe Now campaign, you only have to let me know.'

After correspondence and meetings with fellow left-wing committee members, Victor at one point decided to resign, hoping to bring the others out with him. His great fear now was that, as the committee expanded, Labour Party disapproval would render it indistinguishable from a purely Tory body. He was troubled too by the headlong speed at which the organization was developing, leaving no time for the Left to develop a coherent cabal in committee. Resignation proved to be unnecessary. Largely at his urging, the UEM Labour members wrote to Churchill asking not to be pushed into giving opinions on policy before they had time to agree on a joint position. And Attlee wrote to one of the MPs in question, Evelyn King, that he personally was neither for nor against Labour Party members joining the committee. 'In view of this,' wrote Victor to Russell, 'I think the Labour Party Executive campaign against the committee is pretty shabby.'

Thus reassured, Victor was content to ignore the NEC. For some months, he simply attended UEM meetings and monthly lunches when his other activities permitted: his Labour colleagues worked to widen the membership from the left. In May however, he came publicly into the firing line. He was invited to speak at the first UEM public meeting in the Albert Hall on 14 May 1947. It was a difficult assignment, as he explained to Churchill when he sent him the advance text: 'This is what I propose to say on the 14th. It has been an abominable experience! I usually speak for an hour or so, with perhaps half an hour's preparation and a half-sheet of notepaper, but this ten minutes' affair has taken me about fourteen hours! . . . ' Churchill's telegram was worthy of Victor himself: 'I THINK IT IS SPLENDID STOP ONLY QUERY COULISSES MAY NOT BE UNDERSTOOD IN ENGLAND WINSTON CHURCHILL'.

The line-up on the platform, politically ecumenical, was promising. In addition to Churchill and Victor, speakers included Lady Violet Bonham Carter for the Liberals, George Gibson, an ex-chairman of the TUC, Oliver Stanley, the Conservative MP, the Moderator of the Free Church Council and, in the chair, Archbishop Geoffrey Fisher. Victor's opening was striking.

> I speak as a passionately convinced Socialist. I see the hope of a sick world not only in a free, democratic Socialist Britain, but above all in a free, democratic Socialist Europe. In view of a great deal of misunderstanding I think I should explain why precisely, as Socialists, some of us accepted the invitation, which with the largeness characteristic of him, the great enemy of our party extended to us when forming the United Europe Committee.

Socialism was about freedom from poverty which, in turn, led to spiritual freedom. The threat to freedom was still there; fascism was not dead, and there was the threat from another totalitarianism on the left.

> It is true that the totalitarians of what is called the Left, or at least the best of them, regiment and oppress for the sake, as they religiously believe, of a larger freedom in the days to come. But to ruin even a single human soul so that other, and even millions of others, might benefit is a blasphemy. . . . Means always become ends and once totalitarianism is riveted on a society its own inherent logic precludes emancipation.

When he read of the horrors now being inflicted on masses of human beings, 'I look around me for a bastion to defend — I am speaking of spiritual, not, God forbid, of military defence — the values of which I believe.' One great bastion would be a united Europe, which must become 'not only the guardian and evangelist of Western civilisation, but by the very reason of her unity a foremost preserver of the world's peace.' It would have the mission of liberalizing by example. It was not important that his vision of a united Europe differed from that of other speakers. 'To conquer Europe for the idea of unity is the immediate task, and Mr Churchill, by bringing it from the lurking wings to the very centre of the stage, has added something to the overwhelming debt which civilisation owes him already, and which, if a political enemy can be allowed to say it, can never adequately be repaid.' Hatred was the ultimate bondage.

> Most of all I long to see mutual hatred vanish from the Germany I pity and the France I adore. For too long Europe has been disfigured by their secular strife. There was the Germany of Bismarck and Kaiser Wilhelm and Hitler. There was the France of Richelieu and Louis XIV and Napoleon and Poincaré.
> There was, however, another France and another Germany. There was the France and Germany of Christendom, the France of Voltaire and the Germany of Enlightenment. Let that France and that Germany be remembered. Remembering them, let Frenchmen and Germans at last hold out to one another, in a great act of world saving and world uniting reconciliation, the hand of human brotherhood.

A 'simply magnificent declaration' wrote the Labour MP and UEM member, Gordon Lang, and the *Sunday Times* thought it probably 'the most moving' speech at the Albert Hall. But Victor, whatever he felt about the effect of his own speech, was deeply unhappy about the meeting as a whole. As he and Russell wrote to the other Labour members of the executive committee in June, they had both 'disliked the atmosphere of that meeting, for it was far more a pro-Churchill demonstration than a demonstration in support of European unity, or at any rate of European unity envisaged for the reasons for which we envisage it.'

After the Albert Hall had come the Labour Party Conference at Margate, where hostility to Labour participation had been expressed. Both Victor and Russell had decided in principle to resign, but were prepared to listen to advice. They were granted an audience with Attlee, which proved 'extremely inconclusive'. Boothby bombarded Victor with letters assuring him that the movement was poised on the brink of success and needed his name if not his active participation. His anxiety to keep Victor associated with the UEM was well found-ed, since Victor was at the time very well regarded in European socialist circles.

It was the prospect of a Soviet incursion into free Europe that finally persuaded Victor and Russell to postpone their resignations inde-finitely. Both President Truman and Ernest Bevin were making promises to curtail Russian encroachment into Central Europe, and Boothby intimated to Victor that Bevin was now sympathetic to the idea of Western unity. Victor stopped worrying about the Labour Party. His personal position *vis-à-vis* the government was made easier by word from Attlee that he would favour his joining a UEM delegation to Paris in July. (In fact, he was too engrossed with SEN to undertake anything so demanding for UEM.) 'I believe passionately in this project', he told an audience in Kensington in October. The USSR would encroach little by little unless Western Europe united, and then war would be inevitable. Europe was divided already and it was 'nonsense to make out that "that wicked Mr Churchill and his friends" are driving a wedge down the middle of a happy family.'

In January 1948 his passionate belief was put to the test when the Labour Party NEC passed a resolution declaring it inadvisable for party members to be associated with the UEM campaign. Victor was furious, and met the challenge head-on at a UEM meeting in Birmingham Town Hall on 6 February, where he shared the platform with his Oxford Union contemporary, Harold Macmillan. He sent out the text in advance to colleagues and press. He spoke as a socialist, who would regard anything but a Labour government as 'a disaster of the first order.' As a result of the NEC resolution, socialist leaders on the Continent might be deterred from going to the great European Conference at The Hague in May. This he deplored, and he would himself have ignored the resolution had he been free to go to the Conference. He went on to defend the UEM against Labour Party criticisms. Its aim was not 'the sterile one of military containment of the Soviet Union, whereas the Labour Party wants Western Union for its own sake.' He found that a sloppy hypocritical argument. Bevin was in fact a recent convert to the idea of Western Union specifically because of the need to contain the Soviet Union. The next objection — that the UEM was headed by an anti-socialist — was schizophrenic. The urgent priority was 'to lay the foundations of a Western Union based on democratic freedom and Christian values', and that brooked no delay. 'The aim of our movement is to popularise the idea of a free, democratic, and I would add forgiving and merciful, united West: and in this work of popularisation every one of us, whether socialist, liberal or conservative, can work *for the time being* side by side, provided always and only that he is untainted by any sort of totalitarian ideology . . . '

This spirited demand for a Popular Front delighted Churchill: 'THANK YOU SO MUCH FOR YOUR ADMIRABLE AND COURAGEOUS SPEECH', he telegraphed. The wind in his sails, Victor published an expanded version in *Everybody's* in March, which Sandys (with whom he was now on 'My dear Duncan' terms) thought would do a lot of good. Victor was also one of the UEM broadcasters in a series on Radio Luxembourg that month. None of his efforts diminished the NEC's hostility to the UEM, but a fair number of party members ignored its remonstrations. Indeed, in May the *Daily Worker* featured an article by Palme Dutt which indicated that the movement was causing serious concern in communist circles by virtue of its all-party strength.

> A WARMONGERS congress opened at the Hague yesterday under the presiding leadership of the Grand Chief Preacher of the Holy War Crusade, Winston Churchill.
>
> Twenty-seven Labour MPs, 25 Tory MPs and seven Liberal and National Liberal MPs together with a galaxy of lords and ladies, literary gentlemen and Mr Gollancz, will comprise the 'British delegation' meeting in happy coalition under the presidency of the Leader of the Tory Party . . .

Among the inaccuracies was the statement that Victor would be in attendance. In fact he was in America at the time. He had gone on publishing business, but he bore a letter of introduction from Churchill to General Marshall. 'Mr Victor Gollancz is a well-known publisher of Left-Wing literature and of books against the Conservative Party. He is also a prominent Socialist who has been working cordially with me in our All-Party Organization of the United Europe Movement, of which he is a Vice President, and he has vigorously championed its cause. He puts these questions far above our serious Party differences. In this, as in the treatment of Germany, he has the root of the matter in him.'

Victor did not see Marshall, but he treasured Churchill's letter. For the rest of the year he gave active help to the UEM. (He was to become, along with Leo Amery and Violet Bonham Carter, one of the three vice-chairmen of the council of the movement and a vice-president of what was later the British Council for European Union.) In November, he proposed a vote of thanks to Churchill when he opened a United Europe Exhibition in London, and deprecated the Labour Party's negative stance, while describing himself, with what one paper called 'ceremonious Chinese modesty' as 'the most miserable creature in the Labour ranks'. However, his contribution was sporadic, and tailed off steadily. Quite apart from his other distracting responsibilities, the European movement was not really Victor's style. A plethora of groupings, both national and international, a solemn procession of ponderous conferences (so unwieldy they made ASPRA seem like a one-man show) and political complexities at every turn — these were not the conditions under which Victor flourished. He turned down invitation after invitation as time went on — always for convincing reasons — and left others to flounder at European conferences and in domestic committees. By 1950 he stopped bothering with excuses. Invited to a UEM meeting in the Albert Hall, he left his secretary to reply that he was always out of town on Friday nights.

He was wise to extricate himself: the movement failed to realize its promise when its leader again became Prime Minister in 1951. But at least Victor had stood up and been counted at the critical moment: he could not have forgiven himself otherwise. There was a price to pay for his self-respect: a further souring of his relations with the Labour Party. Reading and listening to the imprecations Victor directed at Labour from 1945 onwards, many found it perplexing that he still proclaimed his loyalty to the party. Sir Andrew McFadyean, a prominent Liberal, expressed this mystification when he wrote to Victor (apropos of SEN) that 'every time I think of your humanitarian work I wonder how you manage to remain a member of your soulless party. Why not come on into Macedonia & help us?' Others pointed to Victor's love for traditional liberal causes — such as freedom of speech — as evidence that he was in the wrong party. They were ignoring the sincerity of Victor's commitment to socialism, and his recognition that only the Labour Party could bring it about. The idiosyncratic factor was his constant distress at the party's limited horizons, and his consequent struggle to convert it to the path of moral righteousness. Far from being its enemy, he saw himself as its best friend, offering unpalatable but worthwhile counsel. When the advice was rejected, he raised his voice to the point where an uninformed observer could easily misapprehend the nature of the relationship.

For the party itself it would have been a convenience and a relief to ignore Victor completely, but that was impossible. He was stirring up disaffection from public platforms, but he was still valuable to them as a publisher. As Victor stumped up and down the country vilifying the Attlee government, the Secretary of the Labour Party Research Department, Michael Young, was reflecting on his potential usefulness. In June 1946, he wrote to Harold Laski, who had recently completed a year as chairman of the party, to ask if he saw any possibility that the LBC might provide solid educational material for party members.

Laski thought the idea admirable, especially since it would greatly increase the influence of the LBC, now down to fewer than 10,000 members. Young met Victor during the summer and they reached a measure of agreement. The note Young prepared for the party's Policy Committee made an overwhelming case for co-operation with an outside publisher.

> The obvious answer is Gollancz. Gollancz rendered outstanding service at the General Election, is highly enterprising, has a first-class publicity and sales organisation and is associated with many of the best socialist authors . . .
>
> Gollancz is not of course willing to hand over the choice of all Left Books to the Labour Party since he may wish to publish some Books which would not receive official Party approval. But he is quite ready for the Party to select some of the Books.

The compromise proposal was that the party select every second monthly book, and that the Labour Party Choice be distributed to special Labour Party members. If the committee felt they wanted an official representative, Victor should be asked to add one to the LBC's three-man selection committee.

The Policy Committee was keen, but Victor procrastinated. He was weary of the LBC and impatient with members who wrote to bewail its shortcomings. In July 1946 one such, less than satisfied with the internationalist bias of the Choices, wrote a seven-page letter with a plea: 'What we are in dire need of now is books on such issues as Nationalization of the Basic Industries, and the advantages of Controlling the Bank of England, and the Pros. and Cons. of the

National Health Service.' He received a two-paragraph reply, the key sentence of which offered little hope: 'My feeling is that it is most important of all to concentrate on international politics, because (a) international politics are much the most important thing in the world today, and (b) the weakness of the Labour Party at the moment seems to be precisely their concentration on national issues.' Another member wrote in September to complain about the *Left News*, which Victor by now left entirely to Julius Braunthal and internationalism.

> This originally was devoted to information of forthcoming choices, reviews of books which were to be published, Political theory and so on. Today if it weren't for the fact that I have been a continuous member you couldn't tell that the Left News had anything to do with the Left Book Club . . .
>
>   I am concerned as to what is happening to the Club. Incidentally I don't even know who the selection Committee is now, nor how the Club is progressing or otherwise. If the whole scheme is not enlivened I can see its early demise because the success of the Club in its early stages was because of its vitality.

Victor's secretary wrote back that he was too 'over-rushed' with preparations for a trip abroad to reply personally.

If Victor could offer these and other worried LBCers scant comfort, he had even less to offer the party which was proposing a publishing partnership. In January 1947, widening his criticism about the treatment of Germany, he had an article in *Tribune* called 'We Could Have Done Better'. Speaking of the aims of the LBC and *Tribune* on their foundation — the triumph of Labour and the defeat of fascism — he elaborated:

> We saw Labour not as a class with selfish economic interests in rivalry with those of the capitalist class, but as the standard bearer of Socialism; and we saw Socialism as something far more than a particular method of industrial organisation — we saw it as a way of life which would so strengthen the altruistic elements in human nature that, slowly perhaps but very surely, grab and greed would be superseded. We saw it, finally, not as national but as international Socialism: any other conception of it would have seemed a childish and indeed shameful contradiction in terms.

Fascism had been militarily defeated and Labour was in power. 'Have our hopes been fulfilled? I do not think so.' He conceded that the state of the world would have been 'infinitely' worse had Hitler, and 'immensely' worse had the Tories, won, but

> for all that, we have failed, and failed disastrously. The plain fact is that, while our Government has many fine, and one or two magnificent

achievements to its credit, it has shown an almost complete absence of the one thing which above all was wanted in the most desperate crisis that humanity has ever faced — I am talking about the post-war, not the war, crisis — namely, moral leadership.

It may be said that I am mixing up politics with religion, and that it is the job of the churches to provide the moral leadership of which I am speaking. Such an idea is based on a false dichotomy: it embodies a misconception springing from that fatal dualism which has cursed Christendom almost since its establishment, and which is almost the only intellectual sin of which the ancient Jews were not guilty. There can be no salvation for the world until we recognise that politics are religion and religion politics, and until we act in the light of that recognition. Moreover, in modern conditions it is the voice of the statesman and not of the prelate that has the power to set the whole tone of national life.

If Mr Attlee and Mr Morrison and (he must forgive me) Stafford Cripps had said the right things these last eighteen months in the right way, the influence of any one of them would have been immeasurably greater than that of a whole constellation of Popes and Bishops. I shall, no doubt, bring down on my head the fury of the 'anti-Ernieites' when I say that the only really prominent member of the Government who has on occasion found the right accent has been Ernie Bevin.

He produced an example of the appalling state of national morality. A train-load of Germans expelled from Polish-occupied Germany had arrived in the British Zone in December: some were frozen to death, some had to have limbs amputated. ' . . . How many people in England cared a damn? How many bothered to remember that, as Potsdam signatories, we as a nation were jointly responsible for this horror? How many tried to imagine in their own persons what it must feel like to be old, sick, robbed, expelled, starved, and finally frozen into unconsciousness and death?' Why were the local Labour parties, who had in the 1930s protested vehemently over 'beastly things' being done to Spanish Republicans, now silent when 'equally beastly things' were done to old Germans?

The really horrible aspect of all this is that such humane and international spirit as there is would appear to be largely concentrated outside the Labour Movement rather than within it. The 'Save Europe Now' movement has had, from the beginning, much readier support from unattached people of liberal mind than from professed Socialists, and it is only very slowly indeed, and more than eighteen months after the end of the war, that powerful elements in the Party are beginning to shed that nauseating anti-internationalism with which they betrayed its ideals while the conflict was on. We must all be happy to notice the first indications of a change; but it is a change that must become far more rapid and far more

complete if we are not to discover that the hopes so many of us had when
Tribune was founded were foolishly based on a false diagnosis.

(Obvious truths, such as that the Spanish Republicans had been
regarded as heroes and the Germans as enemies, or that supporters of a
political party tend to avoid criticizing it in government, cut no ice
with Victor: he would have seen them as based on immoral
assumptions about human nature.)

Despite this philippic, negotiations continued towards a Labour–
LBC partnership. Victor wrote peevishly to Michael Young in
March, complaining about the party's failure to help stimulate
demand for Young's *Labour's Plan for Plenty*. 'Once the new scheme of
co-operation with the Left Book Club gets going, we shall not have
this problem,' responded Young. 'The new scheme won't meet the
point altogether,' said Victor, 'it will only cover those actually chosen.
My point is that there's simply no sale at present for democratic
socialist literature at all . . . we are back in the old situation which
made me start the Left Book Club. But what is wanted, it seems to
me, is some effort by which, not merely a few selected books, but the
quite considerable output of this literature can get a decent show.'

The truth was that Victor did not want the co-operative venture. By
March 1947 he was sick rather than just tired of the LBC. With fascism
defeated and a Labour government in power, the aims for which it had
been set up were now irrelevant. He had come to loathe party politics,
so co-operation with the party had no appeal. Besides, the publishing
climate of the 1940s would have made any resuscitation of the Club
impossibly expensive. 'I have grown to detest book societies (including the Left Book Club!)', he wrote to Rubinstein. That same month
he announced the demise of the *Left News* on economic grounds. The
Club had become a serious financial liability: Choices were still only
2s. 6d. and print runs were low. Unwilling to reorganize and revitalize
the Club for Labour's benefit, Victor abandoned the idea of co-
operation and, in October 1948, the LBC — down to 7,000 members
— went out of existence with hardly a whimper.

Victor could never have worked in harness with the party. Even
after SEN ceased to interest him, certain government policies
concerning Germany aroused him. He wrote thousands of words in
the press condemning dismantling in general and in detail, and
blaming on the government indications that Nazism was resurgent.
'Why is it', he enquired of the *News Chronicle* in August 1949, 'that
when men go into politics they become either spiritually or intellectually infantile, or both?' That letter, like many he wrote about

Germany, polarized the readership. One anti-German correspondent put the case against Victor violently but rather well.

> . . . According to Mr Gollancz (and to the Germans themselves), if the Germans are defeated and become aggressive, it is the fault of their conquerors. If, however, the Germans are victorious and commit unheard-of cruelties, it is the fault of the Europeans who did not defend themselves against German aggression. If the Germans are permitted to rearm then German militarism is the child of European leniency.
>
> If, however, the German factories are dismantled, Streicher has to reappear. If the Germans are rich then it is the fault of other poorer countries that Germany becomes imperialistic; and if Germany is hungry, it is our fault that they are pro-Nazi.
>
> How good it is to be a German! . . .

This writer, and those who shared his exasperation at Victor's ubiquitous sermons, were usually outmatched in print by his small army of supporters. Nonetheless, Victor's inflammatory language and the savagery of his attacks kept that army small. With the possible exception of Vansittart, no Tory seemed to have the power to upset him as much as individuals and groups on the left who spurned his guidance. And when he was upset he took little account of the feelings of those who had earned a rebuke. His treatment in September 1948 of G. D. H. Cole, the most prolific of all LBC authors, and of Harold Laski, still nominally a co-selector, was harsh and unfair.

The issue arose over the case of three German Field Marshals who were returned from a British POW hospital in August, first to Nuremberg and then to the British Zone. They were held in a military hospital awaiting a decision on whether to try them as war-criminals. Liddell Hart wrote in protest to *The Times*, quoting a long letter from one of them — von Manstein — detailing harsh treatment. He was backed up by T. S. Eliot, Gilbert Murray and Osbert Sitwell among others. Victor set out to organize a supporting letter from luminaries of the Left, to record 'our shame that so grave an affront to the national traditions should be committed by a Labour Government.' Two answers from those canvassed infuriated him. G. D. H. Cole wrote, 'German generals are not my pigeon. If one keeps signing letters one only destroys any value one's signature has; and one has to save up for those that have some special appeal. Sorry; but I am unmoved by their sufferings.' Harold Laski, in a very friendly letter, reserved judgement until he had heard further evidence, and observed that reference in von Manstein's letter 'to the Negro guard suggests that, despite the Field Marshal's disavowal, he puts Negroes in a lower category than white people.'

Victor sent a copy of the letter 'from little Laski' to Dick Stokes, the MP most closely involved, along with a copy of his reply, which he then expanded into an article for *Tribune* headed 'Those German Generals'. He explained the circumstances of his request, and how he had received refusals from two 'exceptionally influential intellectuals . . .'

> Both have given far better service to the Labour Movement than I, and I recognise that I am on weak personal ground in criticising them; but the terms of their refusal impel me to do so, for they indicate a cancer which, unless it can be rooted out, must make Social Democracy useless as that alternative to capitalism, on the one hand, and Communism, on the other, for which we have all been seeking.
>
> One replied briefly to the effect that German generals were 'not his pigeon' and that he was 'unmoved by their sufferings.' The other was rather more considered.

He went on to quote most of Laski's letter. The Negro reference had to do with a single phrase in von Manstein's long letter: '"But we were strictly isolated from everyone, always a guard — a Negro — in the room of each of us. Although I have never been an adherent of the silly theory of the *Herrenrasse*, this method of putting a Negro as guard at one's bedside seems to me a perverseness of taste."' Victor rehearsed the details of the Field Marshal's grievances, which amounted to 'mental and spiritual torture'. The delay in charging them was particularly unjust: 'can any Allied national, who, as living in a democracy, must shoulder his own share of responsibility for all this, feel anything but shame? . . . There are apparently some who can. Not Gilbert Murray, who is a liberal; not T. S. Eliot, who is a man of religion; and not Liddell Hart, who, whatever his politics may be, has a noble respect for the fundamental and eternal decencies. No: it is left to a distinguished Labour intellectual to be "unmoved by their sufferings", since, with a meticulous selectiveness, he does not regard German generals as his pigeon. In God's name, what sort of Socialism is this?'

Laski, whom he also did not identify, had written an even more 'deplorable' letter. He

> picks on a trait characteristic of reactionaries everywhere and finds in it an excuse for the ill-treatment of men who happen to be Germans and ex-enemies . . .
>
> People who would do to a German what they would not do to an Englishman, or to a General what they would not do to a miner, or to an enemy what they would not do to a friend, or to a racemonger what they

would not do to an internationalist — they may call themselves Socialists till they are blue in the face: but what they are, in fact, doing is to apply in a new way precisely that discrimination against persons, that failure to understand what it means to be a neighbour, which Socialism, like Christianity, came into the world to replace.

Three of the four relevant letters in the next issue of *Tribune* were critical. (One picked Victor up for forgiving von Manstein but not the 'Labour intellectual'.) Cole's was the exception: he wrote to identify himself as one of those attacked, endorse Victor's case for the generals, and point out his reasons for not signing letters of protest indiscriminately. Victor published a letter thanking Cole for his generosity but ramming home the point 'that when people are antipathetic to us it is surely the more, not the less, necessary to protest against injustices to them.'

Victor's insensitivity was such that he would have been honestly bewildered if Cole or Laski (who could easily be identified through the grapevine) had remonstrated personally with him. The irony was that Victor's accelerating tendency to attack his friends was a reflection of his increasing spiritual desire to be a good man. Privately, he was working with some success to control his rages. Although he was still very prone to explosions, his intimates noticed that he gave way to anger rather less frequently and less violently than before. In public, he pursued goodness by preaching the ethics of Christ, and with an altruistic vehemence. More and more of those who found themselves publicly attacked — friends or not — chose to keep their distance. Others found his quirkiness and resolute refusal to temper his absolutism an embarrassment when the times called for pragmatism. Even the morally fearless Richard Acland had felt it proper to keep Victor at arm's length when he stood for Labour at the Gravesend by-election in November 1947. Although, by prevailing standards, Acland was fighting an almost dangerously honourable campaign, Victor's offer to come and speak for him had him writing unhappily, 'I do hope you won't misunderstand me, — I'm sure you won't, — but what I'm really afraid of is that you'll think I'm a rat, — and I'm still more afraid of the possibility that you might be right! However that may be, I am almost sure that the whole mood of the campaign we're waging here would not fit in with the mood of the things you have been working at for these many years past.' Although Acland constantly reminded audiences of their international responsibilities, the election was perforce being fought on domestic 'bread and butter' issues. 'All this, I know, may be deeply wrong. But yet it seemed to me that there wasn't really any decent hope for any decent cause whatever, unless, as a foundation for all of them, it could be shown at by-election level that this bloody Churchillian policy of a return to "Everyone-out-for-his-own-self-interest" could be smashed at the polls.' He felt the campaign was gaining ground, but feared the effect of the Dalton resignation.★ 'I don't think you would want to come and make a speech which would either have to be out of key with all the rest that you've been doing, or would be out of key with our limited, — and perhaps immorally limited, — campaign.'

It was a masterly brush-off and Victor, while recognizing its finality, was only slightly wounded. For the record, though, he had to point out to Acland that his position had been misunderstood.

> . . . you are in error in thinking that I should have made the speech you seem to think I should have made! One does not come to a by-election in support of a candidate, and spend one's time in attacking that candidate's party! I should have begun by confessing freely to certain mistakes on the part of the Government (my dear Richard, what is the use of denying them: one just makes a fool of oneself with educated public opinion. I was dining with John Strachey about a fortnight ago: you should have heard the terms in which he spoke of Dalton and what Dalton had done! Unless one begins by confessing all this, one just cuts the ground from under one's feet).

He would then have gone on to attack Tory statements 'to show that not only were the Tories attacking the Government because the latter were not making their mistakes in an extreme enough form (if you understand what I mean) but they were also attacking them for not making a quite different order of mistakes, and a very much worse one. I should then have done the sort of stuff which you have, leading up to a peroration on the lines of a speech I recently made at Trinity College, Dublin (attached) . . . '

(If he read the Trinity speech, Acland must have been doubly relieved at having shed Victor as a supporter: high-minded though he was, he wanted to win a seat. Victor's peroration, which explained that the Labour Party was still the hope of the world, regretted its 'colossal blunders', 'inefficiency' and 'quite respectable share of original sin'. Uttered from a Labour platform, it would have been a gift to the Tory press, and that part of the speech that dwelt on the mistakes of the government would have frightened off most electors. Victor perceived the government's worst mistake clearly: they had encouraged the export drive with a view to improving the standard of

★Hugh Dalton, Chancellor of the Exchequer, had recently had to resign because of an injudicious leak to a journalist immediately before his Budget speech.

living. He was of course against letting any section of the population sink into material wretchedness

> but you go fatally wrong when you regard material conditions as the most important thing in life: and your error is increased when you talk of high standards of living in the terms in which it is appropriate for men to talk about their religion . . . curiously enough I find this odd philosophy most insistently expressed by, I think, the only member of the Government who constantly proclaims his Christianity, I mean my friend Sir Stafford Cripps. Sir Stafford will speak with the utmost eloquence about the necessity of self-sacrifice on the part of each one of us and about the great and high conflict to which we are called. But when it comes to it, why are we to sacrifice ourselves? In order that we may have more to eat and more clothes to wear later on. And what is the high struggle? Precisely the struggle to win back our standard of living.

The accent should instead be on global rather than British prosperity.)

Victor again claimed to have tested his thesis on (unnamed) associates before writing to Acland, taking advice 'as to whether this sort of speech would do you more good than harm. The unanimous opinion was "nothing but good".' He went on to express his fear that Acland might be in danger of hoodwinking himself 'about the issues on which you have stood so magnificently firm'. The 'bloody Churchillian policy' was also that of the government and Cripps. And the government was equally Churchillian in trying to secure a favoured position in the administration of the Marshall plan. He was still committed to the Labour Party, but, though he

> would not dream of saying it at a by-election, and although I believe their policies to be thoroughly wrong headed, I find the morality of many of the younger Tories, and of a great number of Liberals, immensely superior to that of a great number of our own supporters — who simply have the capitalistic mentality in reverse.
>
> I do not know why I am writing all this: I suppose with the hope — in my incorrigibly priggish and school-masterish way — that when you get in, as I pray you will, you will fight for the real things as you always fought — and will not 'catch' even a microscopic germ of the disease I have seen developing in our ranks during the last couple of years.

With a last piece of helpful advice to brush aside the Dalton affair 'and tell these people not to make beasts of themselves by being so censorious', Victor brought his letter to a close. He was genuinely delighted when Acland won the election.

Victor's synthesis of socialism, liberalism and Christianity was ready for public exposure in March 1949. At the invitation of Gilbert Murray, he spoke for an hour and a quarter to a Liberal audience on

'Personal Freedom'. The speech is worth examination for its close parallels with his version of Judeo-Christianity. Like his religion, his politics (and they were of course intermingled) appeared to him to be dictated by revealed truth, and were, in fact, inspired by the same unconscious need to reconcile his own idiosyncrasies of intellect and emotion so as to remain free to conduct his life as he wished.

The speech opened with a declaration breathtaking in its self-delusion.

> I am not a philosopher, nor a metaphysician, nor a theologian, nor a political scientist, nor even a politician . . . I am what is called a plain man, and it is precisely as a plain man, I suspect, that I have been asked to speak tonight: you want me to express, I mean, some of the feelings and thoughts about liberty that the plain man feels and thinks. So you will doubtless put up with my plainness. But I am something worse than a plain man — I am a socialist . . .

He cared so much about personal freedom that he might even put it above peace. It was 'essentially an inner thing; something inside a man.' Its opposite was 'inner slavery', which was 'preoccupation with the self in all its forms . . . we are all, to a certain extent, enslaved, because no one of us is completely free from those selfish motives, from that selfish preoccupation which imprisons us in ourselves.' This came in different degrees and kinds — the 'morbid, the neurotic, the psychotic form', or 'common-or-garden selfishness and greed, absence of public spirit, the habit of thinking in terms of one's own comfort and one's own future security.' Everyone was more or less prone to such selfishness, but what appalled Victor was its enormous growth over the past few decades: 'people, on the average, are nowadays far more selfish, far more preoccupied with their own interests, far less interested in other people's concerns, than they ever were when I was a boy.' He contrasted nineteenth-century concern for Dreyfus with the failure of the British public now to give generously for Arab refugees.

The other form of enslavement was 'the state of being hagridden: of being, in particular, the prey to guilt and fear in their various forms.' This too was an epidemic, mainly because of international developments:

> . . . that is a serious augury for the future sanity of our race. It is doubtless unnecessary for me to emphasise the point that guilt and fear are forms, essentially, of preoccupation with the self, and therefore of enslavement. A man feels guilty not so much because something has been done, as because *he* has done it; a man feels fear, diffused, undifferentiated fear . . . not

because something may happen, but because something may happen to
him. The reference is always personal . . . and that is personal enslavement.

(In this passage the reference was personal in another sense: Victor was
describing the condition in which he had found himself in 1943, and
from which he felt himself to have fully recovered.)

In Victor's definition, personal enslavement, 'preoccupation with
self, reaches its climax, of course, in hatred.' The supreme expression
of inner freedom 'is as obviously love'. But in all this the self should
not be denied: 'Our duty . . . is to let "our" self grow, to preserve it
from constraint or outrage, and to submit it only to the purposes of the
greater, Total Self — which is not indeed submission at all, but perfect
inner freedom.' He went on to build on the legend from *Kabbala* about
the splitting up of God: the essence of a man's duty to God was to
preserve one fragment inviolate and, by loving his enemy, demonstrate his freedom and 'increase life'.

He spoke of himself more directly: as a colleague, husband and
father he had found that 'like elicits like' and that if you met a person
with love you freed him. This was clear also from his correspondence
with Germans: 'I must ask you to believe that what I am going to say
contains no iota of exaggeration, and is wholly devoid of, in the
prejorative sense, "idealism" or "sentimentality" — I am, in fact, a
very hard-headed person.' In dealing with individuals inured to
Nazism in its most poisonous form, he had observed them 'freed', by
meeting gentleness. (There were indeed a number of former Nazis
who wrote to Victor to announce their repentance — a declaration on
which he always gave them the benefit of the doubt. He was less than
'hard-headed' concerning those whose cases he took up — like Field
Marshal von Manstein or Ernst von Weizsaecker, the German
diplomat imprisoned by a US War Crimes Tribunal. Once his
emotions were engaged, and he had assumed the innocence of the
accused, he stopped his ears to contrary evidence. The only German to
whom he was less than entirely kind in public statements at this period
was Rommel, whose cult he deplored as a glorification of militarism.)

Inner freedom or enslavement depended on individual contacts, the
co-operative or profit-inspired nature of the social order, and infant
experience as explained by Freud. The ideal society was 'a kind of
Christian anarchy', for 'that society is best in which there is the
minimum of outward restraints — the minimum of restraints on a
man's freedom to do what he likes. (An odd statement, you will think,
from a socialist: but that is because you fail to understand what

socialism essentially means — and so do the majority of socialists.)'
Christian anarchy was at present unattainable; it was not appropriate to
struggle against a large measure of centralized planning in economic
life, which would bring with it certain restraints on freedom. Such
restraints, operating socially, must be limited to those that interfered
only minimally with inner freedom, and those that actually increased it.
At all costs, no restraint on freedom of expression could be tolerated,
for that was 'the inner citadel, the holy of holies'; in the unlikely event of
any socialist government trying to interfere with it, Victor would fight
'in the last liberal ditch'.

Only slightly less objectionable was restraint on freedom of movement. Many could

> be spiritually maimed by being shut off from the world. That is why the
> present restrictions on foreign travel★ are so outrageous. The economic
> arguments cut no ice with me at all: it is a question of priorities, and if we can
> consider priorities in times of war then we can consider them in times of
> peace. To prevent people from getting about in this heavenly world, from
> enjoying its sights and sounds and smells, and from mixing with Parisians
> and Venetians and South Africans (I mean Negro South Africans) and
> Chinese, is to put a padlock on God's open door. I feel bitterly ashamed that a
> Labour Government should have countenanced such wickedness — I really
> do think that wickedness is the word: particularly since, as everyone knows,
> the rich are allowed, for the most part, to evade these restrictions with
> impunity.

Industrial conscription or direction of labour was also wrong, and
though nationalization as currently experienced involved no loss in the
sense of freedom, he had a warning:

> A lot of people get great fun, get a sense of the glorious freedom that stems
> from self-expression, out of running shops or little businesses 'off their own
> bats', and there is no possibility, with such enterprises, of their exploiting
> others. It is crucial, therefore, that we should combine with nationalisation
> of the basic resources the widest possible area of free enterprise, but limiting
> ourselves, in this respect, to units of a certain size. A man must have the
> feeling that he can always start up something of his own if he wants to;
> and if I were Prime Minister of a socialist State . . . I should encourage little
> men to start up their own little businesses and little shops by State loans and
> credits, if they hadn't sufficient resources of their own.

Next, Victor addressed himself to positive restraints which would
enhance inner freedom through increasing love and the sense of co-

★The strict limits to the amount of currency that could be taken out of the United
Kingdom.

operation. Success depended on making the right kind of appeal, which the government had disastrously failed to do. The National Health Service, for instance, was an immense boon, and given proper handling, the majority of doctors would respond to the 'enhancement of inner freedom by a growing sense of public service'. In conclusion, he regretted that he could not sing the Chorus from *Fidelio*, and recited instead Shelley's paean in praise of freedom.

There was no one close to Victor who was also free to point out the more glaring inconsistencies and weaknesses in his speech: for instance, that he ran his firm along autocratic rather than Christian-anarchist lines; that small businesses and the despised profit motive went hand in hand; and that most of the negative restraints to which he had objected were so obviously contrary to his own self-interest that they virtually destroyed his case. Anyway, the sincerity with which he held his carefully-wrought views would have rendered him immune to any such criticism.

It says much for the tolerance of sections of the Labour Party that Victor was invited the following month to stand at the next general election as Labour candidate for Newbury. He declined, saying he was too busy, but, as a safe Tory seat, Newbury was not a tempting prospect anyway. Although he privately complained that all the Labour government had done was make capitalism 'not work', there was no doubt about his anxiety to see his party win the election, and he was eager, despite the Labour-LBC *débâcle*, to keep his self-assumed mantle of party propagandist. In June 1948 he wrote to Foot asking for ideas for election literature. Despite a request to the party, he complained, he 'had not had a *single* suggestion. And yet here I am willing to publish anything useful that does not positively outrage my conscience!' It had been a noble gesture, for the only socialist books Victor really enjoyed publishing at this time were those (like his friend R. W. Mackay's *Britain in Wonderland*) that represented the dissident viewpoint. Foot, also in the penumbra of the party, was another favourite who continued to publish with Gollancz. But he could do little to stimulate more orthodox colleagues to come up with exciting books.

The Gollancz publications for the 1950 general election were unimpressive compared to the old Victory series, and gave Victor little pleasure. The slump in the market for political books spelt poor sales figures, and the Labour Party, despite Victor's imprecations, was indifferent. *Steel is Power*, by Richard Evely and Wilfred Fienburgh of the Research Department, was the book that most soured relations between Victor and the party. He agreed to rush it out in October 1948 as a contribution to the case for nationalization. He enumerated his grievances that same month to the Minister of Health, his neighbour Aneurin Bevan. Not only had he been 'shabbily treated', but he felt that, from the point of view of party propaganda, the whole matter had been 'shockingly handled'. He had agreed to get it out in record time and had priced it uneconomically. Although he had explained to Michael Young that it was vital to have an introduction by an important member of the party — and preferably of the government — if the book was to have a chance with the booksellers, Herbert Morrison had refused, and so had the party chairman, Jim Griffith. 'Eventually I had to fall back on Morgan Phillips.'

He had been promised that the party would push the book in every way possible, and buy in bulk for local parties. He had been thinking in terms of 5,000 instead of which 500 had been suggested — a figure he thought unacceptable. In the event 25 had been ordered. The final insult was that the party was bringing out a pamphlet on the same subject at a very low price, and he had heard of this only by accident.

> Well, there's the whole story. I feel very sick and sore about it, both from the personal and from the Party point of view. As you know, I threw everything I had into the last general election: I have already arranged for six 'yellow books' for the forthcoming election: but my experience with *Steel is Power*, though it cannot affect my desire to see the Party returned and my determination to do everything I can to help in this respect, does produce in me a feeling quite the opposite of the buoyancy and enthusiasm necessary to achieve success . . .

Through Bevan's intercession, the order was increased to 500, but Victor's troubles were not at an end: he received a writ alleging plagiarism. Rubinstein settled it to his satisfaction, but the Labour Party was reluctant to insert the agreed apology slip in their copies. They gave in when Victor threatened to see Attlee about it.

His troubles with the book made him all the more determined to make it a success, and his tactics showed that he had lost none of his flair. Having offered it to booksellers on a 'See Safe' basis, he received only 244 orders. He immediately announced this in an advertising column in *Tribune*, asking if the booksellers were correct in assuming that the public were political illiterates. To prove they were not, *Tribune* readers should buy the book. Within a few weeks Victor was writing smugly to the *Observer* that their political correspondent was out of date in reporting low sales for *Steel is Power*: the booksellers had already ordered 6,000 copies.

That coup only blurred the truth about the political slump, so 'frightful', Victor assured Foot, who with Donald Bruce was the author of *Who are the Patriots?*, that he would put in hand a first printing of only 5,000 — and could therefore offer only a very small advance. Although the book — published in the autumn of 1949 — did better than Victor had prophesied, its sales were small by the standards of 1945. At the time Victor blamed neither the market nor the Tory booksellers, but the party's failure to give the book proper coverage in its newspaper, the *Daily Herald*.

To augment his slender stock of election literature, he launched a competition in the *Daily Herald* offering a prize of £250 plus a 10 per cent royalty to the best election-winning manuscript submitted. 'I shall be the sole judge, and shall make no award if I consider no manuscript good enough. Some qualities I shall look for: accuracy, logic, power to inspire readers with firmly-based and lasting enthusiasm. No appeal from my decision — not even to Herbert Morrison.'

Jon Evans thought two entries good enough to publish, but they did not match Victor's exacting criteria: no award was made. The election book for which he had had highest hopes, an account of the Tanganyika ground-nuts scheme espoused by Strachey, was dropped when the book proved critical of what was turning out to be a disaster*. In addition, Attlee refused to up-date his *Labour Party in Perspective*, and re-publication of the original was a failure.

If Victor could not contribute much as a publisher, he sought, as the election came up, to give good advice to his disappointing party. That advice erred on the negative side. John Strachey, like Pakenham, one of the two ministers still friendly with Victor, received from him a jeremiad in late October 1949, following Attlee's announcement of cuts in public expenditure. The letter took a novel line, explaining why the election had been 'placed in final jeopardy, and perhaps lost, yesterday.' Since Attlee's speech about the cuts, Victor had found the government 'a laughing stock — I am not exaggerating — among the middle classes formerly friendly to the party — and on their attitude the result will turn . . . ' It had worked up 'a terrific scare' about the economy, and then announced cuts so small that there was 'not a single individual in this country who will feel the smallest extra pinch because of these "cuts".' It was the 'old "wolf wolf" business.'

Another thing. I can imagine nothing more insane than announcing the extra Christmas holiday — at the very moment when everybody is being

*As Minister of Food, Strachey was in charge of a massive and impracticable scheme to increase supplies of natural oil by growing ground-nuts in Tanganyika. His career was to suffer from the £30,000,000 fiasco that ensued.

urged to work harder, with the alternative of bankruptcy and starvation. Members of my own staff were shocked by what they consider this extraordinary piece of levity. 'Of course it is very nice to have the extra holiday,' one of them said, 'but it seems rather odd if things are as bad as the Government say. I suppose they are bluffing.' . . .

And a final point. The schizophrenia of several members of the Government, and in particular of Stafford Cripps, about the 'private enterprise sector' is disastrous. I am not talking about things like taxation of profits: for my part I do not care a tuppenny damn whether there is a tax on distributed profits of 30% or 50%. What I am objecting to is the psychological approach. In the *same speech* business men are begged to cut costs to increase production etc. etc. in the public interest — i.e. they are talked to as public servants: and *in that same speech* these same men, in their aspect as 'profit makers' — Winston was quite right on this point, profit makers, not profiteers — are sneered at and talked about as if they were criminals. It just won't do. All profit making may be wrong, and indeed, as you know, I think it is wrong — I think so far more uncompromisingly than Stafford Cripps ever did or ever will: but the private enterprise sector cannot possibly continue unless at any rate some profits are made: and to blackguard men whom you are appealing to in fact as public servants, merely because, so long as the private enterprise sector remains, they *must* make profits as the very condition of their existence — this is contemptible.

Sorry about all this. But I feel wretchedly disillusioned this morning: and I know that a great number of people, who are only too anxious to feel enthusiastic about the party, are in the same mood . . .

PS Of course when I say that not a single individual will be a penny the worse off, I do not mean this literally — I am talking of the psychological effect. For instance, people in the lowest income groups for whom medicine is really necessary will in fact be a trifle worse off. But the thing will not *hit* them in that way at all. Who on earth is really going to feel 'How terribly grave things are! What sacrifices I have got to make! Next time I am ill I shall have to pay a shilling for my bottle of medicine!'

That letter showed the extent to which Victor was out of touch with wider public opinion. It must have irritated Strachey that its special pleading for businessmen was overlaid with the moral superiority of Victor's stance on private profits. (Victor was genuinely untroubled by the level of taxation on distributed profits. He drew about £11,000 from the firm at this time, waiving his right to a great deal more, on which he would have had to pay 95 per cent in personal taxation. It was preferable to have the cash go into reserves.) But then Strachey knew his Victor. He always, said Arthur Koestler, seemed both affectionate towards and repelled by him. The friendship had survived the scarifying attacks Victor made on

Strachey as Minister of Food, and Victor had not denounced him publicly since he left that job.

Strachey was an exception. Typical of the breaches that Victor did not understand was that with Elwyn Jones. To Jones's wife, Pearl Binder, Victor wrote in March 1950 that he had a nagging half-memory from a party where they had met that

> you said something about hoping that, though I had quarrelled with Elwyn, I had not quarrelled with you.
>
> Most emphatically I have neither quarrelled with you, nor conceivably could. But equally emphatically I have never quarrelled with Elwyn. I detest his views on punishing Germans, or indeed on punishing anybody, and I am sure he detests mine: but that does not in the least affect my personal feeling. So don't have any such idea, please.

Elwyn Jones, who as a Nuremberg prosecutor had experienced Victor's scorn, had of course not been privy to Victor's views on human relationships as explained in the 'Not Sent' letter to Sheila Lynd years earlier. Among the others who had failed to realize that it was the sin that Victor hated and not the sinner was the chief butt of his admonitions — Stafford Cripps. At a time when Cripps, that rock of austerity and integrity, was wrecking his frail constitution as Chancellor of Exchequer, his wife wrote from 11 Downing Street.

> 19 December 1949
>
> My dear Victor,
>
> Christmas is here, & one's mind dwells on times one has lived thro' linked with 'old friends'.
>
> I have given thought before writing, but something urges me to make contact with you & ask you one question. 'Why are you so bitter against Stafford?'
>
> There is sadness in this for people who in their individual ways seem out for the same kind of things.
>
> Bitterness corrodes the Spirit.
>
> Could we meet one day — you & I — & talk quietly — unless you would rather not.
>
> Yours
> Isobel

> 20 December 1949
>
> My dear Isobel,
>
> I am very glad you wrote.
>
> I had heard for some time that you thought I felt personally bitter towards Stafford; and I have, several times, begged John Collins, who told me this, to endeavour to remove the impression. It is, in fact, quite untrue.

He was opposed to the government's economic policy, first, because of its emphasis on British interests.

> To this is to be attributed a whole range of phenomena — from the attitude towards German starvation, to the attitude towards European Union. The old internationalism is completely gone, and the present frame of mind is almost symbolised by the British attitude towards Michael Scott* at UNO and Listowel's† speech in the Lords about trusteeship. Did you read Brailsford's article in last week's *New Statesman*, 'Were We Utopian?' That represented my point of view completely. . . . [Then there was the Government's materialism.] That is why we are getting more and more of an insistence on piece rates, payment by results, and so on — things which Socialists regarded with horror when I was a boy.
>
> Similarly, what has been the *essential* plea when people have been asked both to work harder, and for the time being, to 'go without'? Not 'Do these things so that the world as a whole may benefit' but 'Do these things so that you yourselves may be better off in the years to come.'
>
> I am not such a fool, I hope, as to underestimate the appalling difficulties of the situation: and I daresay that, if I had been in politics, I should have succumbed to the same temptation. But that doesn't prevent me from feeling that all this is utterly wrong . . .

The only hope of salvation lay in internationalism and an appeal to the spiritual element in people's nature. And although he was appreciative of such domestic achievements as the National Health Service, he believed that, in the world setting, 'the economic "tone" and the economic policies of the Government are both disastrous.'

> Now Stafford is, of course, infinitely the strongest personality mixed up with this policy: and so symbolically one sometimes uses his name in connection with it. But that doesn't in the least argue *personal* hostility to Stafford himself. . . .
>
> I hope you will not feel, from what I have written, that I do not want to see the Labour Party returned to power. I do: for I think that, by reason of its very origin, it must in time recover its old ideals, provided that dissenters are prepared to say what they feel. And, incidentally, for what it is worth, I would far rather see Stafford Prime Minister than any other statesman or politician in any party, and have said so on several occasions.
>
> So much for the question of personal hostility. While, however, I have

*The Reverend Michael Scott was the spokesman for two tribes in South West Africa, mandated by the League of Nations after the First World War under the care of South Africa. Scott presented their case at the UN, scant interest being shown by the British authorities. Victor had introduced him to Collins late in 1949 and he was taken under the wing of Christian Action.

†Lord Listowel, Victor's old friend and CCC colleague, was now Minister of State for Colonial Affairs.

certainly not felt this, I have from time to time, felt some irritation. This has arisen because Stafford is one of the very few people in the Government who really care about ethical religion, and one of the only two who constantly and publicly (and very rightly) declare that they care about it. Now when I say that the Government's policy has been materialistic and anti-internationalist, that is another way of saying that, in my view, it has been anti-Christian: and accordingly I have found it difficult on occasion not to feel irritation when the man most symbolically associated with what I feel to be an anti-Christian policy has publicly proclaimed Christian ethics. This doesn't mean for a single second (if I may be excused for even suggesting such a thing) that I doubt Stafford's complete sincerity: it has simply seemed to me a case of the partial blindness that descends on even the best men when they are absorbed in the daily necessities of politics. No doubt, if I were so immersed, I should be even blinder.

I thought it well to set out the above quite fully. But, of course, I should always be happy — indeed — to talk things over with you, or Stafford, or both. It has not, honestly, been my fault that I have not done so before; in so many years you and Stafford have never given me the opportunity! . . .

22 December 1949

My dear Victor,

Thank you very much for your careful & clear exposition. I think we must meet & not thrash it out on paper. It seems so clear in the written word! & to a good deal of it I subscribe myself. The whole situation is something on which one can but try & increase one's understanding.

I join issue with you on one point, because I have more opportunity of assessing its truth than you have.

Even here, I will not argue. *If you will apply the same question to yourself with the relevant approach* 'it has simply seemed to me a case of the partial blindness that descends on even the best men when they are absorbed in the daily necessities of politics'. This has a partial truth in the sense of 'necessity' because of human limitations — not otherwise.

But — let us meet, you say it has not been your fault we have not met.

I don't look upon things as 'faults' in this way so much as force of life's circumstances . . .

I suggest it is a little unfortunate to use an individual's name to express views on a whole Government, when that person is not at its head! except on points in which he is known to be directly responsible . . .

There are no more recorded attacks by Victor on Cripps during the ten months Cripps remained in office. Whether that was because Victor took Isobel Cripps's words to heart or because of other reasons is not clear. (When ill-health drove Cripps out of office in October 1950, Victor wrote him a very warm letter of sympathy, which —

while admitting he had not always agreed with his government's policies — went on to say

> but if, decades or even perhaps hundreds of years hence, it is understood in this country that political and economic policies are valuable only insofar as they are expressions of moral and religious principle, you will have done more than any other man of our time, if I may say so, to give that understanding.
>
> I do not know whether you are spiritually as well as physically tired. If so, believe me — *experto crede* — that it passes completely and leaves only a deeper faith and a greater inner wealth . . .)

When the general election was called for February 1950, Victor's loyalty reasserted itself and he campaigned hard for Labour. He made much more in speeches of the government's virtues than he did of its deficiencies. Yet his speaking engagements were far fewer than his oratorical skills might have warranted. Invitations came from those who admired him personally, like Elizabeth Pakenham, a candidate, or Peggy Duff, a worker for Kenneth Robinson.

In five years, through a combination of his own temperament and circumstances beyond his control, Victor had fallen from a position of vital importance to one of virtual insignificance within the Labour Party. The combination of the closure of the LBC, the poor state of the book market, and his fussiness about what he published greatly reduced his value as a political publisher. The publicity he generated left him with only a few left-wing friends to balance those who thought him a nuisance or an irrelevance. If he made any contribution to Labour's hair's-breadth return to power in 1950, it was probably a negative one.

Victor did not mind his unpopularity or lack of influence. His conscience was clear and his freedom untrammelled. And if he was insufficiently appreciated at home, he had thousands of letters and a huge pile of press clippings to attest that the prophet was held in honour outside his own country.

CHAPTER TWENTY

MEANWHILE . . .

HAD VICTOR DELEGATED power as well as responsibility to his staff, and let the outside world know he had done so, they would have found it easier to preserve Gollancz's reputation while the managing director was busy with his public life. As it was, except for a few months in 1946, Victor held on to the reins of policy, strategy and, for the most part, tactics. His staff were permitted to do the day-to-day work, but decisions of any importance were held over until Victor had time to address himself to them.

Immediately after the war, the key figures in the firm were still Hodges, Horsman and Dunk, who were all efficient, accustomed to hard work and used to Victor's vagaries. They were helped to keep things running smoothly by whoever was Victor's secretary of the moment. Unless those secretaries were intelligent, highly literate, tolerant and sensitive, they did not last in the job more than a few days. (That they be attractive was a prerequisite for recruitment.) From 1947 to 1949, for instance, the incumbent was Anna Clarke, who later went on to become a distinguished writer of detective stories. Edgar Dunk was petrified by Victor, but he worked at the other end of the building and saw little of him. Dorothy Horsman enjoyed doing extremely well the job she had fallen into accidentally, and though her relationship with Victor was often stormy and he bullied her unmercifully, she showed no inclination to leave. For Sheila Hodges and the secretaries, the horror of working for Victor was bound up with the joy; there was no way of predicting his moods. Any working day might be a day for champagne at the Savoy, the unveiling of Victor's brilliant new idea for doing down the opposition, a temper tantrum over a misfiled letter, or the beginning of one of Victor's protracted sulks, all too obviously aimed at some hapless and mystified transgressor — a viper in his bosom who had no idea how he or she had offended, and was afraid to ask. As his deputy, Hodges experienced Victor at his perverse and unreasonable worst, but that was offset by the exhilaration of being his trusted confidante, bound up in the excitement that imbued his every idea and decision. As a woman, she did not incur his jealousy, and she was too tactful and too loyal ever to make him feel threatened by her competence. But his deficiencies as a delegator caused her problems, exemplified by a correspondence in May 1946, when Victor was engrossed with SEN.

Daphne du Maurier's books were much in demand, and the paper shortage was losing her a lot of money. Her agent, Spencer Curtis Brown, had suggested to Gollancz that some of the Australian rights be released for a period of two years: there was plenty of paper in Australia. With Victor too busy to consider the issue, Hodges had no choice but to stall for some weeks. Using the only lever he had, Curtis Brown formally reclaimed all the rights in four of du Maurier's out-of-print titles if they were not re-issued within six months. 'I am sending you this letter only because I can get no answer from any previous requests for information.' Victor read the letter and rolled his sleeves up.

> So far as I understand, there had been no previous question of reversion of right: there had been a conversation a month ago about cheap editions in Australia. We had been looking into this, as certain very important questions are involved.
>
> We now get your letter of May 14th dealing with the general question of reversion of rights.
>
> I am on the friendliest possible terms with Daphne du Maurier, and I am perfectly certain that she wouldn't for a single moment countenance a letter of this type: nor, if I may say so, would your father have been capable of writing it. Entirely apart from the question of our friendship and the confidence between us, I imagine that Daphne du Maurier is sensible of what I have done for the novel of hers which we have just published, and of which a reprint is in hand. I doubt whether any other single novel has had such a printing this year.
>
> I don't know whether you care, first, to withdraw your letter, and secondly to apologise for it. If not, I shall send it on to Daphne and ask her what she thinks about it. . . .
>
> We certainly haven't the faintest intention of allowing any of these rights to revert. As the paper situation becomes easier, we shall get all the Daphne du Maurier titles back into print.

'Your letter was full of gusto, but it does not really answer my point', commented Curtis Brown. The delay had been excessive. 'I have now broken down the iron curtain of silence, but I have not yet got an answer to my question.' The proposal was reasonable, and du Maurier knew all about it; Victor was welcome to send the correspondence to her.

Victor saw the matter 'quite otherwise. I am aware that there was a delay — a delay of about a month, up to the time at which you sent me your last letter. The reason was that it was a point that had to be referred to me personally, and I happened to be working during that period quite literally twenty hours a day on European relief work, which I am afraid I regard as of more importance even than Daphne's Australian editions.'

With a pistol at his head, Victor would not negotiate. He sent the correspondence to du Maurier, who regretted the argument, admitted she had approved the idea of Australian editions since Gollancz's paper allocation could not meet export demand, and assured him she had no wish to prejudice his rights. Curtis Brown explained that he had gone through Hodges precisely because Victor was otherwise engaged, and unwittingly landed her in trouble by reporting her as saying 'that it would be almost certainly impossible for you to export any cheap edition of Daphne's old books to Australia for two years or more. . . . As to the flourishing of pistols, I think we have both done a little of that and I suggest that we both put the weapons back in our holsters.' He had no wish to take away the rights; he just wanted a decision. 'If my letter has had the effect intended of getting you to consider this Australian business quickly then I will gladly withdraw the notice. I shall in return expect to have your decision very soon and if there are any points you would like to talk over with me I will walk down the road to you at any time . . .'

'Sheila Hodges', wrote Victor, 'tells me that there must have been a serious confusion, for she certainly never said, and never intended to convey, that there would be no possibility for two years of exporting any of these books to Australia. What she did say, she tells me, was that, if we gave these Australian rights, a two years' termination clause would be advisable. She thinks, as I say, that there must have been some confusion between these two ideas.' He made a handsome concession of the rights to *Gerald* and *The Du Mauriers*, her non-fiction and least popular books. More, when he learned the terms on offer he also gave the rights — terminable after eighteen months — for two novels. While paper was short, this deal was highly advantageous to Gollancz, who stood to gain 50 per cent of the proceeds. However, on 2 July there was a burst of generosity: Curtis Brown was sent the last letter of the rally, telling him that Victor had decided to waive the firm's share of royalties on the Australian edition.

Despite such occasional bonuses, agents sometimes tried, quite understandably, to place their authors with more predictable publishers. Curtis Brown made such an attempt with Elizabeth Jenkins, whose three-book contract was almost up. Collins wanted her badly, and were prepared to offer better terms, including doubling the £150 advance she had been offered for a new contract with Gollancz. She admired and loved Victor but had to make a living. Curtis Brown, presumably eager to present Victor with a *fait accompli* and so avoid a prolonged argument, contravened publishing ethics and urged her to sign with Collins without more ado. In August 1946, Elizabeth Jenkins, with a sensitivity and tactfulness that rivalled Richard Acland's, sent a long letter to Victor explaining the situation.

> I did not think that you would be likely to suggest as much as they do, first, because their offer (which includes an advance of £300) is obviously in excess of my commercial worth and only made by them because they want to buy in an educated author, and secondly because you have taken up with such a very important kind of work as regards publishing, one cannot expect that your fiction list shall be your first earthly concern . . .
>
> On the other hand I should be absolutely heartbroken if my leaving you were to cause any anger or ill feeling to you. It is perhaps absurdly conceited of me to suppose for a moment that it would but I will at least be candid if not sensible and I have been miserable for the past few weeks at the idea of the possibility of a break in our friendship which is so real although we meet but seldom. I cannot bear the painful idea of quarrelling with one of the few truly good men in the world.

Curtis Brown was keen on the move, she thought, because Collins's vast sales organization would secure greater income for him. He was afraid Victor might match Collins's offer. (He had warned Elizabeth Jenkins that even to name Collins's offer would be unethical.) 'I myself do not think this in the least probable and I know you will not misunderstand my motive for telling you or imagine I am doing it to hold a pistol to your head . . . ' She was drawn to Collins because she thought they would re-issue her Jane Austen biography, Gollancz permitting — 'a project I have set my heart on.' She begged Victor not to tell Curtis Brown about the letter. 'I have worked myself into such a preposterous state about the matter I have to keep on reminding myself that I haven't actually committed a crime.'

'You are not to be worried or unhappy', responded Victor,

> In fact, it is rather wicked of you to be worried about such an affair in such a world! And in any event *you* have neither done nor are going to do anything wrong! I am bound to say that I find Master Curtis Brown's proceedings a little off-colour. . . .
>
> But what really astounds me is that young Curtis Brown, after suggesting that you should sign a contract with another publisher before letting your own publisher know anything about it, should go on to

suggest that it would be 'unethical' to disclose Collins' terms. This is topsy-turvy morality: what is unethical, as I see it, is precisely for an author to face his existing publisher with a *fait accompli*. If in fact you had done that, I should have been horribly hurt: but I am not in the very least hurt by anything in your letter, which seems to me to combine morality with common sense.

It was the imminent slump that had kept the proposed advance as low as £150. Victor described in detail the mechanism by which it had been reached. 'I mention all this, so that you may understand that, when I offer you (as I am going to offer) a considerably higher figure, that does not mean that the original figure was not a proper one — indeed, we wanted to propose, and thought we had proposed, something rather generous.'

He was very anxious to retain her because 'I read very few novels with real pleasure. I dislike equally low-brow stuff, middle-brow stuff and coterie-high-brow stuff: what I enjoy is stuff with some beauty and of real intelligence: and that's why, quite apart from my feelings of affection, I should hate to lose you.'

He knew that — as during the three pre-war years — there was 'a sort of atmosphere growing up' that because of his political activities the firm was no longer interested in fiction.

This impression is partly an honest one (so to speak), arising out of the circumstances: but it is also, to my knowledge, quite deliberately put about by publishers (and agents acting on their behalf) who want to get hold of my authors. It is perfectly true, and it would be dishonest of me to deny, that I regard the use of my publishing business for certain political and humane objectives as my main job: but that is far from meaning that we don't attach the utmost importance to our fiction and general list. It means, in fact, the precise opposite: the more I indulge, through the business, my personal political whims, the more incumbent is it on me, as chairman and managing director of Victor Gollancz Limited, to safeguard the foundations of what may be called the 'ordinary' publishing side of the business. To have a long list of established novelists, etc., happy and remaining permanently with the firm, and 'pushed' to the limits of our ability, is not less, but more, important for us than for such a firm as Collins.

Collins's sales organization was probably less good than his. Not wanting to bid just 'a little bit above Collins', he would offer a £500 advance. 'Now, you are not to think (as you probably will) that I have been "jumped" into making an uneconomic offer. It *is* uneconomic in one sense — in the sense that it's not, in my view, justified by a consideration of probable sales in the difficult times ahead: but on a larger view it is economic — on the all-over consideration of "keeping one's list" (and keeping on it an author whose "flavour" and quality we particularly like).' He suggested he should write to Curtis Brown, doing 'a little bit of plain and quite "ethical" lying', to say he had heard another publisher had offered better terms and that Gollancz would revise their proper business offer to keep her on their list. 'If you will let me know that this is OK, I'll write to the little man . . . ' Inevitably, Elizabeth Jenkins behaved like a gentleman and insisted he reduce his £500 offer to match Collins's.

By no means all of Victor's authors accepted so cheerfully that his public work took precedence. His reputation as the most exciting publisher in London aroused expectations that were bound to be disappointed when his attention was elsewhere. Complaining about the treatment given his book, *Children of Vienna*, Robert Neumann wrote to Hodges in March 1947 to say that he felt his agreement with the firm had been violated in spirit and possibly in law.

> If yours were not VG's firm, with you as a director, I should know how to act. As it is, I am at a loss — all the more as VG on receiving the manuscript promised to read the book at the following weekend and to regard our venture not as a publishing deal but as a matter of personal trust. It was on that assurance that I gave him the book in preference to other publishers and that . . . I felt I could waive the advance which you were prepared to offer. In fact, VG never so much as read the book, and he never moved a finger personally to promote it — with the consequences you would expect in a concern so highly individualistic and un-commercial as yours . . .

He was particularly peeved that the book had not been offered to the Book Society, unaware, apparently, that Victor had developed a temporary aversion to that organization and at this time never offered them books.

Neumann had no case in law, and Victor wrote screeds of self-justification. The matter was settled fairly amicably, but whatever the rights and wrongs of it, it was bad for the firm's image. Even Victor's friends among his authors were getting upset. James Parkes suffered precisely because of Victor's interest in his *Judaism and Christianity*. He sent in the manuscript at the beginning of August 1947, just after Victor had left for three weeks in Germany. By the middle of September Victor had still not had time to read it and took it away with him on holiday. 'I'm not complaining or trying to jump the queue,' wrote Parkes to Hodges, 'but it was VG's own suggestion [that Gollancz rather than another firm should publish it]. I'm not underestimating how important his work is for Europe, but I wouldn't have agreed if I had known of the delay which would occur.'

That same month and, with less reason, Bob Boothby became upset about the lack of attention given to his manuscript of *I Fight to Live*.

> I doubt if any non-professional author can ever have had less assistance, guidance, or encouragement from his publisher.
>
> I was warned about this by John Strachey. 'Remember', he said, 'that VG is no longer a publisher. He is a politician. He takes no interest in his books; and you will get no help from him. But I advise you to go to him because of the name and the organization he built up when he *was* a publisher.'
>
> I did not believe him, because this particular book occupies a field in which you have made yourself a Master. I thought, therefore, that you were bound to take an interest in it. But, so far as I am concerned, there is no reason to suppose that you have even glanced at the proof.
>
> I still think it is a good book — perhaps an important one. But I know it could have been a better book if you had given it quite a small piece of your time, and of your mind. That is why I feel a bit sore . . .

In fact, Victor had given a good deal of time to the book — a fact Boothby acknowledged the following day when he excused his hasty letter on the grounds of 'nervous exhaustion'.

> I now bite the dust.
>
> In particular, I would ask you not to judge John harshly. Remember, he is my oldest and closest friend. He simply told me that you had yourself revised all his books; and that, now you had become a public man, I must not expect this. The remark about your having once been a publisher was purely jocular.
>
> In fact he urged me — passionately — to get you to publish the book, if you would . . .

Retracted or not, Boothby's worried letter indicates how Victor's change of emphasis was affecting the firm. His brilliance and hard work as an editor and salesman in earlier days had established a standard too high to sustain while he was so heavily involved with his causes. The personality cult, which he encouraged, made an author feel cheated if he dealt with any subordinate, however talented. Successful promotions of certain books showed that he had lost none of his flair, but was exercising it on only some of his titles. And jocular remarks like Strachey's fed the gossip and made authors disinclined to stay with, let alone join, the Gollancz list.

The press began to make disturbing remarks in 1947. A profile in the *Leader* in February ended:

The day will come, of course, when Germany will again be feeding itself, and Gollancz will have to look for new worlds.

Some of his admirers even hopefully prophesy that fiction will one day regain its place at the top of his publishing lists, instead of being tucked away at the bottom as something not quite worthy of the times in which Victor Gollancz has to battle for the Rights of Man.

And a hagiographical article on Victor as crusader took the same story to Canada in August.

The cynics among his opponents maintain that he is a man in search of a cause. 'When Germans are well-fed,' they say, 'he will have to find something new to turn his energies to . . . Is it possible that it may be the publishing of books?'

Gollancz, who has a sense of humor, laughs at that kind of talk. He has long since come to accept the chastisement which is the lot of any man who sets himself up as 'the conscience of a nation'.

Victor's sense of humour did not embrace this kind of publicity. On the one hand, he protested at any suggestion that he was doing less than he should; on the other, publishing gave him little fulfilment. The firm depended largely on fiction for prosperity, yet Victor had no real interest in the general run of novels. To Harold Rubinstein he wrote in August 1946 asking if particular passages in a book were 'likely to cause any trouble? The difficulty is that, as I hardly ever read a novel, I just don't know what is and what isn't common form nowadays.'

To Graham Greene he wrote in 1948 that he thought his *The Heart of the Matter* superb — 'the first time for very many years that I have read a new novel with real interest.' He was probably exaggerating for effect, and therefore compounding the damage involved in such an indiscretion to a rival publisher — Greene was then a director of Eyre & Spottiswoode.

His boredom with contemporary fiction was aggravated by the harsh market realities facing those books that now really interested him — politics, philosophy, theology and the rest: they usually lost money and could be published only in small numbers. He cut costs as much as he could and exhorted his staff to ever harder work and better time-keeping. He explained to one of his staff, who had appealed to him against dismissal, the facts of life:

I gather that, among other things, you have been far too ready to leave your work and go and chat with the men in the main office and round about the trade counter. This is very human, and I don't want to make a great deal of fuss about it: but you know the kind of economic state in which the country is at present, and the plain fact is that if the country is to pull through there is simply no time for this kind of pleasant dalliance . . .

I am very sorry that it has come to this, as dismissal is extremely rare in our firm and I am quite certain that you have done the very best you can according to your lights. The trouble is that you entered working life under the strain of the war, when all sorts of things could be overlooked that can no longer be overlooked: and you haven't managed to adapt yourself to the new conditions. But don't be downhearted about it: you will have no difficulty, I hope, in finding a job and you will do well to make a completely new start and determine really to put your back into your work every moment of the day, as I feel perfectly certain you can if you make up your mind to do so.

(It was true that dismissal, like resignation, was rare at Gollancz, though Victor on a few occasions had a junior executive unfairly sacked because he had failed to live up to unreasonable expectations. For the most part, his *mana* operated even on the most junior staff, who were caught up in his permanent sense of urgency about the most menial tasks. Although they reeled when he erupted over a trivial inefficiency, there was a sense of pride in the crucial part they played in the firm. He treated them as individuals, teased them like children, and showed them compassion and generosity when they most needed it.)

Worrying about staff costs and overheads was a tedious business, especially when there were no publishing adventures to compensate. By April 1947 Victor had decided that long-term fulfilment lay outside the firm. With his contract coming up for renewal, he made a decision about his future. To Cyril Nathan, who handled this aspect of the firm's legal work, he wrote:

The more I think of it, the more disagreeable I find the prospect of continuing as Managing Director here for another six years, as there is other work that I am most anxious to do. I know very well that most people who reach my time of life feel the same, but have to put up with it: but that doesn't make it any easier!

I calculate . . . that $2\frac{1}{2}$ years should enable me to complete a thorough and satisfactory reorganization of the business . . .

'In fact', he explained to his co-director, Frank Strawson, 'I shouldn't be surprised if things were even more prosperous in the future than in the past. This will be assisted by certain new blood that I am bringing into the business, which I will tell you about subsequently. As a matter of fact, a considerable renaissance, so far as the business is concerned, is taking place at the present time.'

The deal he proposed would set him up for retirement at the end of 1949 — or any time thereafter on six months' notice — on a pension of £2,000 a year. (Victor was certainly not contemplating an austere old age. That pension was almost six times his secretary's annual salary, and would be supplemented by dividends from the firm and the few other investments Ruth had made. In 1947, of course, inflation was not a factor he took into account.) 'No one has any right to oppose it [your decision]', said Strawson; Victor's path to freedom was clear. There was only the matter of the new blood.

It had been Victor's intention after the departure of Norman Collins that the firm would ultimately be taken over by Harold Rubinstein's son, John, thought to be even more able than his brothers Michael and Hilary. The plan was cruelly scotched when John died in 1943 on active service with the RAF. Within a few years Sheila Hodges had proved her ability and was heiress-apparent. Victor's first major step in strengthening the team that would replace him was to hire John Bush (Sheila's husband) as assistant company secretary, putting him in charge of exports. No more important appointments were made before the end of the decade, for once Victor had organized his escape route, liberty began to lose its appeal.

The other work of which he had spoken to Strawson of course included SEN, but Victor also had it in mind to write a book called *Present Priorities in Human Affairs*. He discussed it with the literary agent, David Higham, in hopes of finding a publisher other than Gollancz, and Hodder announced its interest. Victor changed his mind, and reverted to his earlier plan of writing a book about the Jews, but made little progress. Disappointment on that front, loss of interest in SEN, and disillusionment with the JSHS all militated against his early departure from Gollancz. More important, he had an experience in 1948 that rekindled his interest in publishing — his first trip to the United States.

It was the example of his competitors that precipitated Victor's book-buying trip to America. Since the early days of his firm he had enjoyed good relations through business correspondence with a number of important publishers there, and had frequently announced his intention of going in person. His inability to delegate effectively had been the first barrier, followed by the LBC and its demands (although he had toyed with an invitation from American socialists to make a swift tour to get an American equivalent going). The war and then SEN had ruled the visit completely out of court until 1948, at which time a shortage of saleable manuscripts from

British sources, and the appearance, on the lists of rivals, of exciting American books, drove Victor to take the plunge.

He set sail with Ruth in April and was away for almost two months. American publishers knew of him by repute as a great publisher of the 1930s and now a well-known British do-gooder. They were unprepared for the bombshell that burst on them in the guise of an elderly man (Victor always looked older than he was) who resembled, in Philip Jordan's description, 'a benevolent elder son of Father Christmas'. Where other British publishers normally stayed about three weeks and did their business at a sedate pace, Victor devised for himself a schedule which, between business, socializing and reading manuscripts (on which he took snap decisions) allowed him to sleep between 2 and 5 a.m. 'His scouting practices', recalled Cass Canfield of Harper and Brothers, 'were as original as everything else about him. . . . He would devote a day to each American publisher whose list he admired, ferreting out every editor he could lay his hands on. In this way he'd acquire the English rights to the most promising books.'

Ruth acted as his organizer, escort and support and together they conquered all before them. Away from the normal distractions, Victor was free to concentrate on impressing a vast new range of acquaintances with his energy, flair and *joie de vivre*. Authors, publishers and agents were captivated by him at his merry, funny, enthusiastic, well-informed and opinionated best. And after the serious life he had been leading for thirteen years, Victor found the American literary scene wonderfully fresh and invigorating. For him it was the ideal way of doing business. Instead of fighting the tide of English opinion that considered him *passé*, he could acquire manuscripts of excellent potential by a quick skim and an immediate oral agreement. There was the bonus that American books could be reproduced photo-lithographically and thus much more cheaply than by type-setting. (Victor pulled off one of his cleverest business *coups* by insisting that it would be far more gentlemanly and straightforward if neither Gollancz nor its opposite numbers in America charged for reproduction rights. Victor's justification lay in his strongly held principle that typography should be in the public domain, but the arrangement was to the financial detriment of American firms, all of whom sold more books to Victor than they bought from him.)

When Victor returned from the United States he was anxious to place his gratitude for the experience on record. He wrote to the New York *Publishers Weekly* to pay tribute to the 'extraordinary kindness and most generous hospitality' of publishers and agents alike. 'My heart has been warmed by it, not only as a publisher and as an

Englishman, but as a citizen of the world; for surely nothing is more important at the present time than Anglo-American friendship. Again a thousand thanks.' It was a clever move, but no less genuine for that. The confidence and affection he had generated among his new friends was evident in the easy warmth of letters from America and the generosity of Christmas gifts. One publisher, William Sloane, summed up the practical effect the trip had had. 'You will be amused to know that I had a very stately Sunday with Jonathan Cape, who spoke warmly of you and observed, in a kindly way, that he felt that during the war years the Gollancz list had suffered a considerable diminution. I said, "In that case he is certainly going about the problem in the right way", and he inquired what I meant. I said, "He is taking on our books one after another, and there is no faster way to build up your list." To this remark there was no rejoinder . . .'

'As to Jonathan,' replied Victor, 'perhaps he is right. I cannot feel any deep sense of shame in having allowed only a part of my mind to be occupied with publishing during a war for the survival of civilisation. But I think it might be amusing to take our two great book reviewing media—the Sunday Times and the Observer—from January 1st of this year, and make a little statistical analysis of the relative number of various publishers' books reviewed. I think I shall do it!' (He did, and it seemed to prove his point, but the analysis did not make nonsense of Cape's remark, for books reviewed are not necessarily saleable books and the Gollancz back-list was at that time unimpressive.)

A New York trip quickly replenished a depleted list: by 1951 American books accounted for half the publications of the firm. Victor and Ruth were to make a long visit to the United States every year from 1948, bar two, as much for pleasure as for business. Victor loved the change of scene and people, and found the voyages enormously enjoyable. America takes the credit both for bringing Victor back to active publishing and for reintroducing him to pleasures he had been missing for several years. One of them was what he called 'honeymoons' with Ruth: 'The world, at such times, was no longer with us: we were with one another in the world.' He waxed rhapsodic in *My Dear Timothy* about the symbolic part played in their American honeymoons by the 'love-feasts' she prepared in the kitchen of their suite and which they ate 'at a little glass-topped table sitting side by side on a sofa: breakfast in particular, quiet and slow, with its sense of a recurrent expectancy and a recurrent fulfilment.'

Had an American publisher, a London agent, a member of the Anglo-Jewish Association, a Labour minister or intellectual, a German field marshal and a spiritually-minded newspaper reader assembled in the late 1940s to discuss Victor Gollancz frankly and at length, the meeting would have broken up in confusion. Unanimity would have been made even more remote if his five daughters had been asked to contribute.

In 1947, Victor explained to the German POWs at Wilton Park his experience of fatherhood.

> I have five daughters, the youngest seventeen, the eldest twenty-seven, so I know quite a lot about the upbringing of children. It invariably happens that if you have a child who is 'behaving badly' and you feel even a passing hostility, then the hostility communicates itself to the child and the child becomes worse. Whereas if you can overcome your hostility, if you can put out an effort of sympathy and understanding, then the barrier comes down and you can see the result, a change for the better, immediately.

As usual, Victor's difficulty was to put his excellent theories into practice in his personal life. He made sporadic efforts to be a loving and helpful father, but had a rather limited vision of what that entailed. He was happy, for instance, to visit daughters at Badminton and deliver a highly successful lecture to their schoolmates; he liked advising them on their reading and giving them books; he enjoyed practising Socratic dialogues with Vita in advance of her interviews for a university place; he, like Ruth, welcomed to Brimpton friends of their children. But he had neither the time, the patience nor the disposition to foster intimate and mutually rewarding relationships with each of his five complex and highly individual girls. And he felt rejected if, in his terms, they became difficult or failed to show him affection. By the late forties, relations with some of them had deteriorated further. He was no closer to Livia, who was still a successful professional musician. His gesture of dedicating to her *Our Threatened Values* was not sufficient to compensate for many rows over the years. She lived a very independent life.

Diana had caused consternation to her parents by marrying, in 1947, Leopold Prince zu Loewenstein-Wertheim-Freudenberg (known to intimates as 'Poldi'). This marriage, which was to be a perpetual source of irritation to Victor, was the direct result of his own generosity and liking for good company. In 1944 he ran into Poldi (whom he knew only slightly) and invited him to Brimpton for a few days to get away from the flying bombs. There Poldi met Diana, eighteen years his junior and, by his own account, immediately fell in love. His high birth and intellectual gifts were no compensation in the eyes of Ruth and Victor for his being still legally married, well-nigh broke, and such a snob that few occupations were open to him. It was a matter of grief to Ruth that he was a Catholic (she would have preferred the girls to marry Jews and she had a particular antipathy to Catholics); after his divorce came through the marriage had to be held in a register office. Victor spent a great deal of effort over the ensuing years trying to find a job which his son-in-law might regard as worthy, but always Poldi set his sights too high (diplomat or civil servant) for one of his limited experience, or else the positions he was fixed up with (travel agent or literary agent) folded mysteriously. And while Diana's paintings and drawings showed talent, her cast of mind was amateur and her freelance work in commercial art was not financially very successful. She often had to take relatively menial jobs, and she and Poldi, who liked to be surrounded by beautiful things, had to be satisfied with seeing them in the houses of the rich, whom they visited at every opportunity. They were a popular couple and Diana's fastidious charm and sweet nature won her many close friends.

No one ever doubted that Poldi adored Diana as extravagantly as Victor adored Ruth. He thought her the most beautiful woman he had ever known and wrote later of her 'dark, luminous eyes, sensitive, aristocratic features, a delicately sensuous and perfectly shaped mouth', hair the colour of 'dark burnished amber' and a 'grave little face' that 'shone in the light of heaven when she smiled.' Yet it was also clear that he had looked to her father to keep them in reasonable style, either through direct subsidy or by providing suitable employment from his network of contacts. Alas, Victor was less rich than Poldi had apprehended, and unable to swing a job fit for a prince. Diana, like her sisters, was given a sum of money to set her up in life, and except for occasional presents and cheques (in response to appeals) her parents quite reasonably felt they had done their duty. Before the marriage, they had been getting on less well with Diana, although Victor always had a very soft spot for her; afterwards there was increasing ill-feeling. Her parents felt that Poldi had remade Diana in his own image and turned her against them. Poldi's partisan version, written after Diana's tragically early death, in *A Time to Love — A Time to Die*, was that Victor's harshness, egocentricity and tormenting of Diana had soured their relationship long before he, Poldi, had come on the scene. He also wrote at length (and while she was still alive) of Ruth as a cold and 'strangely impersonal' woman with whom it was impossible to form a relationship.

No one ever knew whether Diana had in fact nurtured real resentment about her parents before her marriage, or whether Poldi was making retroactive the attitudes she developed later. Certainly,

Poldi's lengthy description of dreadful mealtimes at Victor's in 1944, when the ogre chided, ridiculed and terrified all his children, was totally out of perspective. An Austrian aristocrat was ill equipped to understand the Gollancz family's vocabulary. Diana, for instance, was known as 'goose' and 'idiot', but in better days she regarded these happily as terms of endearment. And whereas Poldi reported Victor making 'indelicate jokes' at his daughters' expense, the girls would, at worst, have found them merely tiresome. Victor, in his turn, was happy to be addressed in his baldness as Francesca's 'impertinent, exquisite, smelly, Egg.' He could be annoying; he was always egocentric; he was often overbearing, acerbic and over-critical; but it was only in his tempers that he inspired fear, and they were usually quickly over.

Julia's engagement in 1946 to Harold Simons did not improve matters with her parents. Harold was a scientist, and Victor viewed science as 'an unutterable blasphemy'. For his part, knowing how Julia had suffered, Harold was not disposed to like her parents. Yet Victor took a well-meant if tactless leading part at their wedding. A synagogue ceremony was out: Harold's father was a Jew but his mother was not. At the reception after the register office 'I became a temporary Rabbi myself, for I had the temerity to marry them all over again before the assembled company, in accordance with the beautiful old ritual: blessings (in Hebrew, with English translations for the *goyim*) and canopy and wine-glass-breaking and all.' His enthusiastic performance went down better with most of the audience than it did with the happy couple, who thereafter maintained a polite but formal relationship with her parents.

Vita, the most successful of all the girls academically, won a scholarship to Cambridge, and through a chapter of accidents got a disappointing result in her degree, which gave Victor scope for more tactless teasing. (She worked first as an MP's secretary; some time later as assistant to the architect, Sir Hugh Casson.) As an adult, she got on less well with Victor than before. Her shyness inhibited her and he treated her sometimes kindly, sometimes rudely and was often strained and tense, finding it difficult to express fatherly affection.

Francesca always enjoyed a happy co-existence with Ruth and Victor, with a naturally outgoing and affectionate disposition that found a ready response in them. In the late 1940s she began training as an architect. Like Livia, Vita and Julia and Harold, she lived for some years in the Ladbroke Grove house. Victor stayed there during the week being looked after by a housekeeper, and Ruth, based at Brimpton, came up midweek. The family home was still at Brimpton:

the other operated more like a hostel, its denizens leading separate existences. It was there, in 1949, that an event occurred of overwhelming importance to Victor: Julia brought home his grandson. Victor was overjoyed, and climbed the stairs every morning to address Timothy in Latin. By the time the Simonses had left Ladbroke Grove, the baby had given Victor the inspiration for his autobiography.

CHAPTER TWENTY-ONE

1950: A YEAR IN THE LIFE

THROUGHOUT THE TWENTIES and early thirties, Victor had subordinated all else to making a success of publishing; once his crusading urges were unleashed in 1936, they took precedence over all else until 1948. Thereafter, he proved less capable — except for short periods — of holding any one objective consistently at the top of his priorities. Indeed, his effort was dissipated across an ever-widening range of activities. As a publisher, a public campaigner, an organizer and a friend he had aroused expectations not even he could fulfil entirely; inevitably, he let some people down.

Publishing never ceased to be a troubled area. With SEN out of the way and Victor brandishing an exciting list full of American bestsellers, he was expected by many to act once again as a full-time enthusiastic publisher, but the revival of his interest was patchy. If he wished to take time off for a trip abroad, to work on a book of his own, or in the name of some short-lived crusade, he did it, and authors grew tetchy when they found themselves pushed into second place. His staff (Hodges was now referred to as his 'partner'; Bush was sales director; and from 1950, Hilary Rubinstein was an up-and-coming editor) were still on a tight rein, and Victor's post-war elevation to the rank of prophet was beginning to have a deleterious effect on his character. Far too accustomed to being compared with Gandhi, Schweitzer, Ezekiel and Jesus Christ, Victor had come to regard criticism as *lèse-majesté*, and his rows with authors and agents were the stuff of gossip and legend. His associates did business in a friendly and effective way, but their solid work in building up good relationships could be set to nought by one blast of ill temper from their boss, though those who had worked for him for a long time could forgive him much in appreciation of the partial but very real progress he had made in his heroic struggle to control that dreadful temper.

As a public figure, he was besieged with invitations to join or lead campaigning bodies, to speak at venues all over the country, to bring injustices to the public eye or to champion individuals in trouble. He accepted when the mood took him, but often failed to follow through. Typical were his dealings with two Jewish organizations. Victor was an executive committee member of the Anglo-Israeli Association, but rarely attended its meetings or functions — although he gave helpful advice behind the scenes to its secretary, Nancy Mackinnon, because he liked her. His behaviour as a governor of the Hebrew University of Jerusalem was even more cavalier. Three things were expected of a governor: to attend gatherings in London; to attend a meeting in Jerusalem annually; and to contribute generously to the university's funds. Victor hardly ever turned up; almost every year he made a faithful promise to the chairman, Bentwich, that he would come to Jerusalem next time, and always excused himself, often at the last minute; and, once his covenant ran out, he refused to renew it. In response to pleas, he sent the occasional cheque for £5, explaining that other causes took precedence. Nonetheless, he enjoyed the status brought by this and many other honorary posts, and relished the feeling that he had a finger in many pies.

A considered division of his time between publishing and philanthropy would have been well within his range, but he had three other lives to live. The political Victor would not lie down, and came out to do battle over a succession of domestic and international issues. Victor the author was coming into his own: he had been reading for years towards his anthology, *A Year of Grace*, and was working hard on the final compilation — a process he found so rewarding that from now on he always had a major writing project on hand. Finally, he was now allowing himself the leisure others took for granted, stealing time from everything else to visit pottery dealers or send them haggling letters; he was going again to concerts and opera; contract bridge, which he had played during the 1920s and 1930s, had recaptured his attention; and, within the constraints of the hated foreign currency restrictions, from the early 1950s he took regular holidays.

He complained frequently of overwork, but revelled in it, for he held the initiative. In any one year he could decide, say, to launch some new publishing venture, write a pamphlet against Israeli militarism, study metaphysics intensively and take a trip to the Middle East, and nobody could stop him. He was perfectly free — and not least in his conscience — to scrap any or all of the projects as and when another caught his eye. It mattered not at all that the secretary and travel agent who had laboured over the details of a trip might feel irritated at its sudden cancellation. (Poldi, in a brief incarnation as a high-class travel agent, once arranged an excursion to India for Victor and Ruth. No sooner were arrangements complete than Victor changed his mind.)

Friends, too, were chagrined when detailed advice on itineraries and letters of introduction were jettisoned without warning; but Victor, at the hub of his own universe, believed himself to hold a similar place in that of others. With Edith Sitwell writing of him as 'one of the very few great men alive', he was unperturbed about the inconvenience he caused busy people.

It was Victor's volatility and arrogance that upset his authors most. His friends and colleagues had learned to respond with resignation or amusement. The Collinses, along with a few others, took the latter course, appreciating the richness, warmth and excitement that Victor brought into their lives, loving him for the life-enhancer he was, and seeing the funny side of each fresh Victor outrage. For those who found humour in incongruity, the frequent contrast between Victor's public utterances and his private conduct was a delight to be savoured as long as they were not themselves the target of his rages or the victim of his arbitrariness. Most people were privileged to see only one aspect of his essentially contradictory nature, and were left perplexed by sudden reversals. To some he was the soul of kindness, always patient and generous. As he would empty his pocket for a tramp, lend hundreds of pounds to a mere acquaintance facing fraud charges, or undertake the support of a family of refugees, so he would comfort a minion in trouble, award a bounteous pension to a retiring packer, or correspond at length with an ex-employee in the throes of a nervous breakdown. Equally, as he would pour scorn on a misguided minister, upbraid violently an innocent author who suggested that Gollancz had served him poorly, or savage an impertinent member of the public, so he would seize unjustly on some minor and even imaginary misconduct by a member of his staff, accuse the unfortunate of every crime in the book and go so far as to call on a colleague to arrange a discharge. There are people therefore who worked briefly for Gollancz and view their ex-boss as a man of bottomless goodness: there are others who consider him a monster of vindictiveness.

Victor could be both, and to those within his inner circle the sincerity of his passion to be good compensated for the natural egocentricity which had flourished in the environment he had created. He was master at home and at work and a completely free agent as a campaigner and writer. His friends accepted the impossibility of an equal relationship and went along with his moods. Those who became most intimate realized the truth that kept his secretaries deeply attached to him despite his appalling demands: that he was blessed with remarkable gifts of intellect and personality; that he had a rare appreciation of most that was good in life; and that he was cursed with the emotional immaturity of an insecure child. He was simply incapable of functioning without constant attention and approbation. When he got it, it swelled his vanity. When it was lacking, he railed and stamped with anger. And he was consumed with envy if those he saw as competitors seemed to be enjoying what was properly his.

For those who achieved success in fields that were not his, he found it easy to show admiration. His avowed esteem for Churchill as a war leader was one example, the reverence he expressed for George Bernard Shaw another. And there were a small number of great men whom he saluted as 'Cher Maître', signing off his letters with the valediction 'With homage'. They included an educationalist (A. S. Neill), a composer (Stravinsky*), a cellist (Casals) and a novelist (Ignazio Silone, who once described himself as a 'socialist without a party, a Christian without a Church'). Victor's homage was not offered unconditionally: it was withdrawn if he felt himself treated discourteously. Albert Schweitzer he venerated above all others until in the early 1950s he considered the great man had snubbed him.

In his own areas of endeavour — publishing, politics, spiritual leadership and British-based philanthropy — he could tolerate no peers. In publishing, Leonard Stein and Norman Collins had already fallen foul of his jealousy, and the list would grow during the 1950s and 1960s; in politics he had done his worst, for the thirteen years of Tory rule from 1951 would remove the spur to attack the Labour Party; in spiritual leadership he kept up his war with bishops and rabbis to the end. Even the saintly Bishop of Chichester, with whom Victor agreed on most things, suffered. As Minister for Germany, Pakenham had observed with fascination a heated argument between the Bishop and the man whom he had tagged 'the best Christian in England'. In his memoirs, Victor failed to give Bishop Bell his deserts. In philanthropy even John Collins was to become a target when he had the temerity to become famous.

When a competitor fell from power, failed or died, no one could be more generous than Victor. Cripps was deeply touched by the encomium he received when he ceased to be Chancellor, and after his death in 1952 his widow received a letter from Victor which included: 'As you know, there were certain things which, with my no doubt over-polemicism, I criticized. But I have never had the slightest doubt that Stafford was one of the best men — and one of the few real

---

*In the 1930s, on hearing from Victor that he and Ruth had plighted their troth during *Firebird*, Stravinsky wrote out for them a few bars of the Wedding March with the inscription 'Pour Monsieur et Madame Gollancz de la part d'Igor Stravinsky, qui était en quelque sorte témoin de leur union matrimoniale.'

socialists — of our time, and that he will rank with Schweitzer as one of the two greatest Christians-in-action that the last half century has produced.' Laski died in 1950 — he was only 56 — and his widow was told that though they had not 'seen much of each other of recent years . . . we at one time worked so closely and harmoniously that, when I read the news, it was like something tremendously alive being withdrawn, and a horrible gap left.'

Victor's sympathy for great men fallen on hard times came out very clearly in the episode of Cyril Joad. As Professor Joad of the Brains Trust he was nationally famous for the clarity and forcefulness of his expositions on matters philosophical, and for his prowess as a pundit. Victor was Joad's publisher, and they occasionally exchanged expressions of mutual esteem, but their relationship was distant. Then, in April 1948, Joad was found guilty of travelling on a train without a ticket. As a public figure he was ruined, and Victor became an ally and defender. He read and commented glowingly on Joad's manuscripts, and advertised enthusiastically books whose sales potential had been seriously diminished by the appalling publicity. Complaining to the editor of the *News Review* in mid-1949 about a back-biting review, he wrote:

> Personally I consider this baiting of Joad as damnably bad taste, in view of the unfortunate railway ticket episode . . .
> I personally know Joad only quite slightly: my first interest in him was aroused when I heard him on the Brains Trust during the war. He invariably stood up for the sane, decent and humane line about almost everything, at a time when it required great moral courage to do so. Personally, I think that sort of thing infinitely outweighs the miserable bit of dishonesty on the railways; and I often wonder whether the people who are so ready to judge have not on occasion behaved at least as badly as this.

And to Joad's agent he wrote that 'I think that the reaction — and in particular the sacking from the BBC and the Reform Club — was disgustingly pharisaical. I had a row with the Reform Club about it only the other night . . . ' For the rest of Joad's life Victor wrote to him warmly, met him socially and described him (albeit anonymously, for reasons of taste) in *More for Timothy* as 'an old Oxford friend' whom he had visited while he was dying of cancer.

A reasonably detailed and chronological description of one year, 1950, will suggest the spread of Victor's activities and interests in the later period of his life. The documentary record is, by its nature, silent on most of his leisure pursuits and private conversations, and almost indigestibly cluttered with the thousands of letters he received that year in his capacities as publisher and public man. The account that follows is compressed and highly selective.

When the year began, Victor was losing interest in the JSHS, of which he had recently become chairman. He had spent all his free time for months, including Christmas 1949, finishing *A Year of Grace*, a 576-page compilation of 'passages chosen & arranged to express a mood about God and man'. It was dedicated to Ruth, Timothy and Peter Victor Collins — Victor's much-loved godson, to whom he was unfailingly kind and considerate, and, at times, extravagantly generous. Subsections were dedicated to four others: 'Acceptance' to 'Tiny' (Sheila Hodges); 'Integrity' in memory of Eleanor Rathbone; 'Humility' to 'Bone' (Francesca); and 'Freedom' in memory of Bernard Strauss. (Until it went to press in the summer of 1950, Victor was hard at work checking the typescript, applying for permission to quote — a massive job — and checking the proofs.) The India trip was off, and he had cancelled a lecture he was to give in Geneva in January, under the auspices of the International Red Cross, but he was excited about a visit to Germany planned for early February and organized by Karl Anders of the publisher Nest Verlag. The occasion for the visit was to be that firm's publication of extracts from Victor's writings, *Stimme aus dem Chaos*, edited by Julius Braunthal, ex-editor of the International Socialist Forum. A year before, Victor had planned to go to Germany to study 'to what extent nationalism is growing, and the reasons', only to abandon the idea when publishing work caught up with him. Since that disappointment, a flood of tributes from Germany had made him determined to pay a visit there as soon as possible. In July 1949 he had been offered an honorary doctorate in law by the University of Frankfurt, to coincide with the bi-centenary of the birth of Goethe. The awarding body, in selecting Victor, wished 'to honour a man who, irrespective of political trends and popular opinion, has fearlessly taken up the cause for the principles of justice and humanity . . . ' Victor was thrilled. Years of selfless effort had so far yielded him only two honours, one serious and one a joke, both awarded in 1947. (The first was the Glorious Star of China and the second a Grand-Duchy of Nera Rocca, awarded him by the self-styled King Juan I of Redonda, the poet John Gawsworth.) He was unable to receive the degree in person but sent a delighted telegram which was read at the ceremony in August:

I WISH TO EXPRESS TO YOU AND SHOULD BE GRATEFUL IF YOU WOULD CONVEY TO ALL PRESENT MY HEARTFELT GRATITUDE FOR THE HONOUR YOU ARE DOING ME IN MAKING ME A DOCTOR OF LAWS OF YOUR GREAT UNIVERSITY STOP THE WORLD IS CRYING OUT FOR GOETHES LOVING HUMANISM AND SPIRITUAL JOY

AND I AM HUMBLY PROUD TO BE SO HONOURED BY A UNIVERSITY THAT BEARS HIS NAME STOP MY AFFECTIONATE GREETINGS VICTOR GOLLANCZ

The Lord Mayor of Frankfurt had offered Victor the 'Goethe Medal for Distinguished Service in the Cultural Field', awarded that year to seven other 'internationally recognized writers, artists and scientists', including André Gide. Victor's telegram for this occasion ran:

PLEASE CONVEY TO ALL PRESENT ON SUNDAY MY GREAT PRIDE IN RECEIVING A GOETHE MEDAL WHICH WILL BE A SOURCE OF THE DEEPEST HAPPINESS TO ME FOR THE REST OF MY LIFE STOP PLEASE ALSO CONVEY MY AFFECTIONATE SOLIDARITY WITH MY GERMAN BROTHERS AND SISTERS ON THE OCCASION OF THE BI-CENTENARY OF A SUPREME HUMANIST STOP IT IS MY STRONGEST HOPE THAT THERE MAY SHORTLY BE A COMPLETE RECONCILIATION OF ALL PEOPLES RACES AND CREEDS AND THAT THIS RECONCILIATION MAY SEND THROUGH THE WHOLE WORLD THE SPIRIT OF JOY WHICH GOETHE SO NOBLY EXPRESSED AND FOR WHICH HE LIVED STOP ONCE AGAIN I THANK YOU FROM MY HEART FOR THE HONOUR YOU HAVE DONE ME VICTOR GOLLANCZ

(His enthusiasm for Goethe was genuine: he was quoted seven times in *A Year of Grace*.)

Victor was proud of his certificate and the enormous plaque from Frankfurt. Germans recognized the importance of the honours. The Goethe Prize, said Erich Hirsch (Secretary of German Educational Reconstruction, a British charity to which Victor gave help and support),

is one of the greatest honours which Germany can confer on anyone today, and one of which you may really be proud. I am sure that it was given to you in appreciation of the idea of the human approach to all, including political, problems, for which you and your friends stand, and of which you are the most eloquent spokesman; and to my mind it is a very timely token of appreciation, of your ideals rather than of your fights against the foolish policies of the British or other people, in this case in the interest of Germany.

There was little congratulation from insular British sources; Gilbert Murray was one of the few to express pleasure about the awards. Victor was appreciative, and wrote to say so: 'Any tiny thing I may have been able to do (I find it rather comic being coupled with Gide!) is due very largely indeed to your influence in those pre-1914 days, to which one looks back with such affectionate gratitude.'

The encomia from Germany continued apace. In December, the Federal State's first president, Theodore Heuss, spoke publicly of his shame about the holocaust and closed with the words: 'It would be wrong, at such a solemn hour, to omit to mention one name, the name of Victor Gollancz. I have not made his acquaintance, but I know his works. When I first heard of him, he appeared to me to be a sign. A sign which I should like to call "Courage of love". Hatred follows the indolence of heart, it is cheap and easy. Love is always a risk, but those who take risks win.' Then came a suggestion in a Munich newspaper that Victor should be awarded the Nobel Peace Prize, and there were many letters in support. Victor would have loved the Nobel Prize even more than a seat in the Lords. Good cases for both could have been made at particular times, but both honours proved elusive.

The year 1950 opened agreeably with a New Year's greeting organized by a welfare worker in a children's home in the American Zone, who wrote to express gratitude for a message Victor had sent the previous October. The translated version began: 'On the first day of the holy year 1950 I should like to send you, Mr Gollancz, the helping father of many poor German children, my sincerest wishes coming from a grateful heart. May God, who is Love, bestow upon your great soul, also in the future, those mercies by which you made listen a whole civilized world, when you appealed to mankind, in unmistakable terms, to remember the first laws of a living and just God, whose children we all are.' A photograph of the children was appended, with their message: 'We children wish father Gollancz and his highly esteemed family a healthy, blessed holy Year 1950.' Victor was very touched, and had the missive forwarded to Ruth at Brimpton.

He was also pleased at an approach from a British admirer and friend, Sir Robert Mayer, a campaigner for Anglo-German friend- ship as well as music. He wondered if Victor would like to join a dining club, the Whitefriars, which was recruiting 'men like your- self, with varying interests, who love talk and unostentatious and cheery gatherings of this kind.' Victor was 'delighted' to agree and was duly elected.

Less delightful was Gilbert Murray's hesitation over yet another joint letter about the Weizsaecker affair, on the grounds that their names were no longer of much value. Elwyn Jones wrote to *The Times* that Victor and Murray had in fact been misinformed in their attack on the American court's sentencing of Weizsaecker. Victor wrote immediately to Roger Baldwin of the American Civil Liberties Union, asking for a suitable draft reply to Jones's allega- tions. (The campaign fizzled out in Britain because of the difficulty of conducting an argument with American justice.) It was also in January that Victor wrote to the press to deplore the cult of Rommel.

Making his plans for 1950, he announced to Elmer Rice that he would be in America in April, and to Max Wolf of the Red Cross that his lecture should be possible in the autumn. (It never materialized.) Anders kept him in touch with plans for his German visit, which would involve his being fêted by Heuss and other senior politicians. However, in mid-January a general election was announced and Victor cabled that his visit would have to be postponed: his place was at home, supporting the Labour Party.

He spent a little time that month on the JSHS. An executive meeting discussed the discouraging news that some Arab institutions had turned down money from this Jewish source, and there was disagreement over whether money should be donated anonymously, or racial prejudice of this kind be fought head-on. A small appeal was launched for a non-sectarian anti-TB league. Victor took the lead in proposing a handsome *ex gratia* payment to the relief worker in Israel whose premature return to England he had insisted upon.

January also brought him a difficult moral quandary, when he was invited to sign a letter to the press asserting that the use of the atomic bomb could never be justified. Victor's abhorrence of the Stalin régime had modified the view he had held at the time of Hiroshima, and his response was very honest:

> Your letter puts me in a dilemma. I need not say that every instinct prompts me to sign: but I am not sure that I am morally entitled to do so. I cannot be sure that if the Communist world were winning a war against the rest of the world by the use of the atom bomb, and the only hope of survival were to use it in our turn — I cannot be sure that I would not agree to its use.
>
> I think that the atom bomb is so much more horrible than other weapons that there is a clear case for saying that in no circumstances would one agree to its *first* use in a war — as we used it first in the last war. But once it has been used, I do not see the issue so clearly. I doubt, indeed, whether, in religion or logic, one can draw the line at particular weapons. I am inclined to think that one must make up one's mind between material force (of whatever nature) and active pacifist non-resistance. I am more and more believing that one must go one hundred per cent for the latter, but have not fully made up my mind . . .

Nor did the year start without problems on the publishing front. One author made an accusation that offended Victor deeply. Victor's rejoinder included the passage: 'I have been a publisher for twenty-two years, and it may interest you to know that this is the first occasion on which I have ever been accused of breaking an agreement. Of course, on the basis of the written documents alone, I have technically broken the agreement, but I have not broken it even technically in view of what verbally passed between us, and I have not broken it morally at all.'

Then there was the case of his admirer, Maurice Browne, who wanted to break the Gollancz rule on advances. Victor let him have £150 on signature of the contract as he was short of money, but made his offer subject to Browne's agreement to changes in the manuscript if sexual references made it unacceptable to the circulating libraries.

Victor was also being pestered by an American *Saturday Evening Post* journalist, who wanted to pick his brains about Hewlett Johnson. 'I understand your reluctance to discuss the Dean of Canterbury', wrote the journalist:

> in my talk with the Dean, however, I've come to think of you as one of the formative influences in his life, and intended to devote a passage to this relationship in our forthcoming article. Because of our wide and critical reading public, I would have welcomed a brief talk with you to straighten out a few things in my own mind before putting them down. I would, of course, not quote you or even mention the fact that I had seen you. In view of the importance of this article, won't you change your mind and give me a few minutes of your time?

Fear that his own history, conduct or views might be misrepresented occasionally outweighed Victor's usual lack of interest in biographical research into his contemporaries, and so it was on this occasion. There was simultaneously a heavy weight of lecture preparation, travel arrangements, evaluation of invitations and general correspondence connected with the German trip. One German woman wrote reminding him of an earlier meeting in London, and asking to see him in Frankfurt. 'Ask Anna whether I really like this girl,' Victor pencilled on her letter, 'I can't remember!' His secretary found out: 'Anna says she was Junoesque, blond, charming & you loved her.' Victor's response to the lady began, 'How could I forget you?', before going on to indicate that it was unlikely they could meet.

Towards the end of the month he received news from Karl Anders that perturbed him greatly and occasioned a letter to a minister at the Foreign Office, Hector McNeil.

> My dear Hector,
> My wife and I are going to Germany for ten or twelve days on February 24th by German invitation. Among other things I shall be lecturing at the universities of Frankfurt and Hamburg: I understand that we are being officially entertained in the various cities: and for the four days we shall be spending at Bonn we shall be the guests of the Bundespräsident Dr Heuss.

Our hosts write: 'A Foreign Office stamp in your passport: "Facilities authorized US/British zones" is very necessary. Anybody can now get a visitor's visa without facilities. Make sure that you get the "facilities authorized" stamp, otherwise you have to sit on horrible wooden benches in German trains and you are not allowed to use comfortable military trains or sleepers. This is quite vital.'

His secretary had learned from the Foreign Office that stamps could not be affixed for private visits. 'But as my hosts make such a point of it, cannot it be done?' Since he and Ruth were to stay with Heuss, 'it would be very awkward, and lead to disagreeable misunderstandings if the facilities requested were not given.'

McNeil explained that the policy was to 'normalize' conditions in the new republic by having private visitors use German accommodation and transport, which were anyway much better than Victor had been led to believe, but agreed to make an exception. Victor was very grateful. 'Good luck to you in the election,' he wrote in his letter of thanks, 'I hope I shall be in the position of badgering you as Foreign Secretary one of these days!'

(Victor's antipathy to discomfort had grown markedly during the 1940s. During his LBC days he sometimes tolerated poor food and inadequate facilities during his travels. During the war, he made sacrifices fairly cheerfully for the sake of the communal objective. The war over, his low threshold for sub-standard food, accommodation or travelling conditions made much work for his secretaries. He always sought the best cabins, the best rooms and the best tables. He felt some shame: secretaries were often required to fix his queue-jumping for him, and when he personally presented himself as a special case, the justifications he concocted were ingenious and tortuous.)

February was largely taken up with Germany, although there were election speeches to be made and many publishing decisions proper only to Victor. He proposed lunch with the Municheer Lord Templewood to discuss Templewood's proposed book against capital punishment, which Victor described to Spencer Curtis Brown as being 'a greater horror to me than anything else — even, I think, than war.' There was a problem with a valued American author, Darwin Teilhet, about Gollancz's rejection of his wife's latest book. Victor smoothed things over:

My only excuse is (and it is a poor one even though true) that our decision came at the end of a whole afternoon's discussion of the matter — at the end of which, after appalling indecision, I said with great annoyance 'Oh well, we had better let it go' — and forgot to remember that I must write to you personally. . . . Do forgive me.

Now as to the reason, or rather the two reasons. Neither of the reasons alone would, I think, have made us come to an adverse decision: it was the two together that made us do that.

The reader's report had pointed out that the book turned on 'the Communist plot business'. Although Victor and his colleagues were all 'violent anti-Communists', and published 'serious expositions of the Communist menace', they were unhappy about making a tragedy the subject matter of a thriller. The second problem was that sales of Hildegarde Teilhet's previous book had been poor. He then made an offer for the book, because of the quality of the work of both Teilhets, and because 'if you will allow me to say so, we have a personal affection for you both.'

Practised Gollancz authors knew that Victor paid little heed to his colleagues' opinions of political significance attached to any given book. 'There is really no editorial "policy" in this firm,' he wrote in a burst of honesty in 1954. 'I publish what I like from time to time: at one time I may like one thing, and at another another.' In that of course he was not unique among publishers, but the rapidity with which his moods and interests changed made things bewildering for authors dealing with controversial subjects.

The day he despatched the comforting letter to Teilhet, he had a delicate mission to perform — the distribution to his travellers of a private letter about the forthcoming *A Year of Grace*.

> This is a book on which I have been engaged, in a desultory sort of way, for about eight years, and intensively for about a year. As you will see from the Foreword . . . it is not the ordinary sort of anthology: it is intended to be read through, in the first instance, from beginning to end — and used after that as a bedside book. It is really an attempt to express, in other people's words, my own attitude to life. As you can deduce from the list of authors, it is a book of a type very rare nowadays — both religious and humanistic. It is mystical rather than dogmatic, and is optimistic, in the sense that (in spite of the hydrogen bomb) it expresses faith in men.

It was full of overwhelmingly beautiful material, 90 per cent of which would be unknown to most people. 'As this is my own book I find it naturally difficult to say freely what I think of it from the point of view either of quality or of sales possibilities: but, as Chairman of the firm which is publishing it, I should say at least something about both.' Being only a compiler of the writings of others, he could without shame say that it was 'a book of quite exceptional beauty'.

As to sales, I believe that there are altogether exceptional possibilities, and I should not be surprised if they surpass the sales of 'The Bedside Book' [a best-selling Gollancz anthology by Arthur Megaw]. And for the following reason: I say in the Foreword that the mood the book expresses is an unfashionable mood. By that I mean that it is unfashionable among what are called 'highbrows': for 'highbrows' nowadays are either anti-religious, or, when they are religious, they are extremely dogmatic — that is to say they are neo-Calvinists, or something of that kind. But while, from that point of view, the mood expressed in the book is unfashionable, I believe it expresses perhaps the most prevalent of all moods among ordinary people at the present time, and one which a particularly large number have been longing to see expressed. for there is in the general public a very widespread religious feeling, coupled with a repudiation of dogma. And there is also an intense desire to turn away from cynical pessimism and nihilism to an optimistic belief in the destiny and possibilities of mankind.

Moreover, his name and his personal following would help sales. 'I think, therefore, that I am safe in recommending you to go "all out" and to try and make this one of the biggest bestsellers in the history of the firm. We are definitely publishing in the first week of September — as we believe that the possibilities of this as a Christmas present are very great indeed.'

He went into considerable detail about the 'lovingly' planned production and the book's attractiveness to music lovers, and concluded 'I know I can rely on you to make an exceptional effort with this book . . .'

George Orwell was in the news following his death at the end of January and Victor was unhappy with the publicity about his rejection of *Animal Farm*. He wrote a 'Not Sent' letter to the *Bookseller*:

My firm was the first to be offered 'Animal Farm'. I read it with the greatest delight and agreed with every word of it. But the manuscript came to me at one of the most critical periods of the war — I believe during Stalingrad, though my memory may be at fault here — and I felt immediately that to publish so savage an attack on Russia at a time when we were fighting for our existence side by side with her could not be justified. I made it clear that this was the reason for refusing the book. To my knowledge, at least one other greatly respected house took the same view.

He had released Orwell from his contract, he explained, because of his courteous understanding of Victor's attitude. (His memory was slightly at fault in that he saw the manuscript after the German defeat at Stalingrad, but in any case the Russians were still fighting desperately. It was a justifiable source of irritation to Victor that his rejection of *Animal Farm* prolonged his out-of-date reputation as a communist stooge. And it was true that except initially — when he sought to keep Orwell under contract on a technicality — he behaved generously towards him and bore him no resentment. When Orwell was ill in 1947, Victor wrote to him very kindly, offering to send books.)

The visit of Victor and Ruth to Germany from 25 February to 9 March was a happy one. Their hosts were so passionately anxious to demonstrate the gratitude of a free and prospering people that they treated their guests almost like visiting royalty. German newspapers announced the visit in advance and covered its public moments lavishly. Bouquets were thrust on Ruth, and there were photographers waiting to capture all the highlights of the trip — particularly Victor's meetings with prominent German politicians.

One such event was a celebrity-packed gathering at the Opera House in Nuremberg, where the city's Oberbürgermeister welcomed him officially.

> Although the Bundespräsident awaits you in Bonn, although you actually 'belong' to the British Zone, and although the name of our city must carry with it particularly painful memories for you — in spite of all this, you have come first to Nuremberg. But if anyone is astonished by this fact, he certainly has not read your speeches or your books, he does not know the views you upheld before, during and after the war, and — he does not know *you*.

He hailed the tolerance that had led Victor to raise his voice,

> even during the war, for conciliation, and in the German people — forsaken at that time by all the powers of goodness — you steadily refused to see the incarnation of evil, either in each and every one or even only in the majority.
>
> In your profound sympathy for the people of Europe, you founded soon after the end of the war the organisation 'Save Europe Now!', which proved so extremely beneficial to Germany. A modern Nathan the Wise, you never preached hatred and revenge against the German people, although you know only too well the nameless atrocities committed by a loathsome minority of our people.

There was plenty more in that vein before Victor took the stage. Sixteen years later he recalled his reactions in *Reminiscences of Affection*:

> Despite my ambivalence about Wagner, I had never ceased to cherish Die Meistersinger — Die Meistersinger von Nürnberg: and when I found

myself on the stage to start my address, and looked at the audience that crammed every corner, I could not speak for several minutes. Standing there, a Jew and but recently an enemy, I somehow felt myself all mixed up with, even a participant in, one of the greatest works of art that the world had ever known, and a very German one at that; and I felt that there was nothing, at that moment, to divide me from the people I was looking at. The barriers, that even a year before I had occasionally remembered but tried to forget (after all, any one of these people might personally have murdered Renée Bernheim), were now wholly down.

(This was not entirely true. Victor suffered the rest of his life from a curious ambivalence about Germany also. He never ceased to be a friend to its people, but for years he declared himself incapable of going there on holiday. He also refused to handle books by ex-Nazis that other English publishers were happy to take on.)

Victor delivered his lecture on 'Religion and Humanism' in English.

. . . a good deal of comedy ensued. They wanted a sentence-by-sentence translation, and a distinguished-looking man in our box . . . volunteered for the job. Now my stuff was no doubt a bit difficult: it was all about the coincidence in *Fidelio* of Leonore's pistol with God's trumpet-call, which, as anyone who has read any of my books will remember, is one of my favourite themes. Anyhow, the translator was flummoxed, and Karl Anders came down to assist him. But Anders was flummoxed too. I would say something, and they would confer: but when they gave voice to what they imagined I had said, I had to interrupt them, for I knew just enough German to realise that they were putting their own words into my mouth. Chaos threatened, so I took it upon myself to announce that further translation would be dispensed with: anyone who didn't understand English should leave. No one did: to judge from the murmur of applause, everyone seemed not only satisfied but relieved: and there was such a storm of clapping and stamping when I finished that I felt, perhaps erroneously, that they really had understood me and sympathised with what I had said.

His lecture notes survive and suggest very clearly the difficulties faced by the interpreters: the vocabulary was philosophical and theological and, as with all that Victor said on such themes, *nuances* of meaning were of great importance. As one journalist remarked, he preached rather than lectured. There was a long attack on anti-religious humanism which, by regarding mankind as self-sufficient, ultimately justifies an individual's rejection of any allegiance save to himself. This progression had reached a climax in Nazism. Anti-humanistic religion was the second of two modes of thought largely responsible for the human tragedy. It gave a view of man as a 'wretched, powerless, worthless sinner, miserable slave of a God conceived of as capricious and omnipotent tyrant' — the result of the disastrous victory of St Augustine over Pelagius. It deterred men from seeking to establish the Kingdom of God on earth, and condemned such a quest as a product of man's sinful pride. Experience and intuition operated against it. 'Everyone knows — by intuitive perception beyond logic — that he is most *real* not when he feels worthless and powerless, but when he is creating freely. It is then he feels he is most fully expressing himself, his own essence, and it is when we express ourselves most completely that we feel most in communion with reality.' Salvation for the world lay in religious humanism alone. Humanism meant a belief in man's potentialities — in Victor's view a belief that man himself partakes of the Godhead. Religious spirit could be felt even by an atheist, for it is simply, in Rudolf Otto's interpretation, the 'sense of reverence or awe in presence of something better, greater and more perfect than ourselves, with which we are nevertheless in communion.' Religious humanism was the conception of 'man as fellow-worker with God, and living our lives devotedly in light of this conception.' His lecture notes continue with a revealing description of his Judeo-Christian perception of what that meant.

> In conception I am describing, man puts his creative faculties, as a free being, at service of God.
>
> In this conception, man not God's slave: man *freely helps* God: *freely helps* (both words important): and by this very act of *free help* he is obeying God's will.
>
> Freely helps in what? In completing the work of creation.
>
> *Freedom* is the keynote here — the giving of one's essence, one's potentialities, one's gifts in this service.
>
> Thus poet, musician, philosopher, statesman, all helping to complete creative design.
>
> Even one act of human charity is eternal, and enrichment of reality.
>
> Note that when we freely help God we are at once intensely proud and intensely humble . . .
>
> Perfect synthesis of pride and humility shown in man who, before composing a piece of music or writing a poem, or planning a constitution, or even making a speech, humbly prays that he may not be utterly unworthy to be God's instrument — and then proceeds to the work with greatest joy and pride.

The lecture ended with a discussion of *Fidelio* and the reading of supportive extracts from Nicholas Berdyaev, Jacques Maritain and

Rilke — all of whom were quoted many times in *A Year of Grace*, the implicit theme of which was also that of the lecture. Victor repeated it in the crowded University Hall in Frankfurt, where the Dean of the Faculty of Law delivered the encomium, which was further remarkable testimony to what Victor had achieved in Germany, and interesting for its unusual frankness.

The University had bestowed the degree, said the Dean, because

we have wished to acknowledge a man who, in a time full of inhumanity, nay, even full of danger to the idea of humanity itself, has given a brilliant example of humanity. An example: for the values are old ones, these threatened values he teaches us; but he has made himself their embodiment with a purity, and defended them against all his time with a bravery, which have not their equal. You have thereby done no less than that for which youthful peoples revere their saints: you have given back to us our faith, the faith in Man.

They had also wished to testify to the central value of his work — respect for personality.

'That we recognise in every human being' — those are your words — 'something special, particular, concrete, individual, unique' . . . And you have added the redeeming word: 'I also am a personality that I must respect; there is indeed nothing self-abasing in respect for personality.' We do not wish to be misunderstood: it is not the fact that you have applied this teaching to men who have committed crimes in the name of our people, which has made us profess this. That has rather made it more difficult for us to profess this; for you have thereby made us feel deeply ashamed. That is the very reason why our avowal has a special meaning beyond that. And now I say something which we have refused and still refuse to say to the Pharisees and the self-righteous (many of whom would only take it for an excuse to do new injustice): yes, we have — all of us — committed and omitted things of which we are ashamed. That you make it possible for us to say this to you without having to abase ourselves, that is the reason why we are thankful to you . . .

The Gollanczes went from Frankfurt to Bonn, where they visited the Bundeshaus and dined with President Heuss. It was at that dinner, Victor said later, that he told again for the first time since 1933 the Jewish stories that had been a speciality when he was a young publisher attending literary parties. (There is ample evidence that this dramatic claim was nonsense, and that he told his delightful stories many times in the late 1930s and afterwards.) He told them superbly, in Jewish accents, with a gusto and enjoyment that left his audience hysterical. (He recalls in one of his memoirs that he and Humbert Wolfe 'pleased' Max Beerbohm with this Jewish dialogue:

> What sort of composer was Mozart?
>   Mozart? *Mozart?* Rotten! Why, he wrote Faust.
>   No, he didn't.
>   What, he didn't *even* write Faust? Didn't I say he was a rotten composer?)

He and Heuss swapped Jewish stories that evening to their mutual delight, even though they had to tell them through an interpreter 'who made an unspeakable mess of them'. (Victor was to acquire in America a considerable reputation as a teller of such stories, and he and the writer Leo Rosten added to each other's store of them.) Victor and Ruth visited Beethoven's birthplace next day and Victor's *Journey Towards Music* includes a touching tale of what occurred there. He believed that the staff had been tipped off to pay special attention to them and

> as we were about to leave, the custodian asked me whether there was anything else he could do for us. Now one of the things he had made a special fuss of was a piano by Graf, a bit smaller than the modern sort, inside a heavy glass case: it was one of the pianos, he told us, on which Beethoven had composed. So I said rather hopelessly 'Unlock that case and let me touch the keyboard'. He shook his head decisively and said 'No'. Then he smiled, said 'Wait a minute' and went off. He was gone for half an hour: returned with a huge bunch of keys: unlocked the case: and said 'Bitte'. So I touched a single note, without pressing it down; and that was that. I asked him afterwards why he had changed his mind: 'I got special permission', he answered, with a certain pride in his voice, 'from the President.' I suppose he meant that he had telephoned the President's office.

After Bonn, Victor delivered his lecture once more at the University of Hamburg and the Gollanczes returned home. Victor had somehow found time for brief visits to Cologne, Düsseldorf, Kiel and Lübeck. He had met officials, expellees, social workers, academics, students and politicians, and had renewed contacts with old acquaintances, including Princess Margaret of Hesse. He came home laden with documents and correspondence. The trip had been highly successful, though not without at least one stormy moment. One Kiel academic wrote to apologize 'for having used this special occasion to tell you our worries about the present situation, instead of stressing the really most important thought uniting us all, whenever your name is mentioned: our most hearty gratefulness for what you have done for Europe and humanity . . . '

Victor apologized in his turn: 'I am afraid I was a bit snappy: to begin with, I had been horribly distressed by what I had seen in the Lübeck camps; and, secondly, because I have appreciated the German point of view, when England is attacked in my presence I inevitably re-act by becoming a sort of bulldog Churchill . . . '

Once home he was full of fervour to draw on his experiences for the benefit of unfortunates. He wrote an article for the *Guardian* on 'Nationalism in Germany' reporting how heartened he was to find little trace of what he had feared: aggressive nationalism threatening war over the lost territories.

> Now all this seems to me pretty remarkable. Think of recent German history: vile Nazi indoctrination for twelve years; a disastrous defeat; an entire nation proclaimed pariah; vast territories lost; the country divided; at least nine million expellees and refugees; the starvation after 1945; the utterly ruined cities; blastings and blowings-up, not just after victory, but five years later. Was there ever more fertile ground for aggressiveness and bellicosity, and isn't it rather extraordinary that one finds so little of it?

The Social Democrats, a few hundred of whom he had addressed in Nuremberg, were 'far more internationalist in outlook . . . than the Social Democrats of many other countries, including our own.' He made one caveat, and issued one warning. He was worried at the emergence of two nations, one living in luxury and the other whose condition 'varies, in the main, from hypercrippsian austerity to utter destitution.' Conditions at the Lübeck expellee camp had moved both Gollanczes to tears. The warning was that further dismantling would cause resentment and so play into the hands of communists and neo-Nazis.

Letters against dismantling were sent to *The Times* and the *Guardian* and Victor also had to deal with a huge work-load arising out of his trip. In addition to letters from people he had met in Germany, thank-you letters and the like, there was voluminous fan-mail and a terrifying number of pleas for help from people who had read the press reports of the trip. He made heroic efforts to give advice, offer consolation and use influence where he could to solve individual problems. As ever, though, most were intractable: families behind the Iron Curtain, hopeless applications for visas, Jews being denied restitution of their property, Germans claiming unfair treatment at the hands of the Custodian of Enemy Property, and so on. Victor had one or two minor successes at home, and occasionally he tried to get a matter taken up in Germany, but he could apply himself seriously to only a tiny fraction of the miseries he was presented with. He answered most of the letters he received (except for the occasional abusive ones), but he took up fewer and fewer cases as time went on. He had neither the resources nor the power to help individuals fight bureaucracies. For much of March and April he was feeling overwhelmed by the ever-growing pile of demanding correspondence.

He had also stored up trouble for himself by making promises he could not keep to speak in the future in various locations in Germany. And he announced that he was to work up his thrice-delivered lecture into a 30,000-word essay 'as the first of a volume of essays in which I am engaged'—another undertaking that came to nothing. Nor, in March, could he confine himself politically to matters German. Christian Action had moved fast into African affairs since the meeting at which Victor had introduced Collins to Michael Scott. Victor was on the periphery of the controversy over Seretse Khama,* composing with Collins an unpublished letter to *The Times*.

He was also upset by an allegation in Parliament by the Conservative MP, John Boyd-Carpenter, that Strachey had 'personally informed the publishers' that publication of the ground-nut book 'would be stopped'. Strachey 'did nothing of the kind,' Victor wrote to *The Times*,

> or anything remotely resembling it. There is fortunately no censorship in this country: not even Mr Attlee could 'stop' a book I was determined to publish.
>
> It is a fact that I regretfully decided not to publish the book — in certain respects a very valuable one — as the result of certain observations made about it in a letter written to me by Mr Strachey after reading the proofs: a letter in which, I should add, he made no suggestion that he contemplated proceedings for libel. The contents of this letter greatly surprised me. It was my duty to assess Mr Strachey's observations in the light of the book's previous history and of such knowledge as I might have of the personalities involved; to consider the public interest; to weigh up certain personal considerations which the whole character of the book inevitably presented to me: and then to decide, in perfect freedom, what course I ought to take. I decided that I could not publish . . .

(He was telling the truth, but the whole affair was nonetheless an embarrassment to one who was always protesting his independence of his party.)

*Khama was Chief of the Bamangwato tribe in Bechuanaland, a British Protectorate. As a result of both African and British racial prejudice, he and his white wife were banished. Collins was involved in an unsuccessful attempt to mediate among all parties.

The JSHS was also active in March, with an executive meeting at which Victor drew attention to conditions in German expellee camps and launched a small appeal. The committee also decided to hold the public meeting after his return from America.

He got involved in a correspondence with Melvin Lasky, whom he liked. Lasky was organizing a 'Berlin Congress for Cultural Freedom' in June, and wanted support from Victor along with others such as Gide, Koestler, Russell and Silone. Victor agreed to be a sponsor, but explained he would be unable to attend the Congress. Lasky then asked for a message to be read out at a plenary session and received a letter from Victor's secretary saying he was too over-burdened with work to give the matter the thoughtful attention it required.

On a personal level, there were advances: he resolved the coolness with Pearl Binder and paid his tribute to the late Harold Laski. But one episode in March caused him considerable irritation. He was normally loath to grant interviews to the British press, for he always felt himself traduced or short-changed in whatever appeared afterwards. He was much happier with the German press, who often mangled facts but could almost always be relied on to paint him in saintly colours. However, the previous November he had rashly agreed to co-operate with a sympathetic journalist, Claud Morris, on a 3,000-word profile for the *Leader*. He took the precaution of extracting a promise that nothing would appear without his *imprimatur*. The unfortunate Morris produced a highly perceptive and essentially very favourable profile. His subject read it with horror, and what followed goes a long way to explain why friends normally avoided writing about Victor, and why such pieces as did appear were either fulsome or sanitized. Morris had presumably been convinced by Victor's oft-repeated assertion that he never minded what was said about him if it was factually accurate. He failed to understand that 'facts' held a special place in Victor's vocabulary, at least where his own doings were concerned.

16 March 1950

My dear Morris,

With real friendliness, I must say that I just can't consider the 'piece' appearing in anything like its present form. I assure you that it is *wildly* inaccurate, not once or twice, but many times on a page — indeed, several of the statements are the *opposite* of the facts. There is really hardly a sentence that could stand, and apart from misstatements of a most serious kind (not only about myself or about others) there is a great deal in it which I am afraid I should be bound to regard as highly libellous to me personally, and most damaging to my firm — though I know that this was far from your intention.

The only possibility would be for me completely to re-write the thing in your general framework. This would be a very awkward and indeed unsavoury job (!) but I would make the attempt if you really so wished. It is simply out of the question, however, for me to attempt it now. I am going to America in a month, and shall be terribly over-pressed until I go — I really have not got a moment of time. If you so wish I will attempt the re-writing on my return: but I would far sooner that the whole project were dropped. The thing that is really essential, however, is that in no circumstances must it appear in its present form, or anything like it . . .

Morris, a freelance, very much wanted to have the article published: he had clearly done a great deal of homework to produce a piece so accurate. He showed some steel in dealing with Victor.

17 March 1950

My dear Mr Gollancz,

As you may imagine, and with equal friendliness, I want to say that the last thing I intended was to have anything upset you. I have a very real respect for all you have done in this country . . .

The Editor of the Leader, of course, has the article and was waiting today for a go-ahead. My suggestion is that we meet some time at your convenience next week and go through the article so that you may have the opportunity of deleting any inaccuracies or statements opposite to the facts. This will also give you an opportunity of deleting anything which you consider to be libellous to you personally, or damaging to your firm . . .

Victor wrote to the editor, enclosing copies of the correspondence.

I am, of course, willing to see him, but I do not know what can be done. It is not a question of the correction of a few misstatements, or the cutting out of one or two passages which are libellous to me or damaging to my firm: I repeat that the thing is *honeycombed* with inaccuracies, misstatements, and statements directly contrary to the facts, and that there are many passages which, being contrary to the facts, also gravely libel me personally and would be seriously detrimental to the interests of the business of which I am Chairman.

No article on the subject, written by Morris, should be printed without Victor's approval. The editor, who thought the piece very favourable to Victor and his firm alike, nonetheless agreed to suspend publication.

Victor found time to rewrite the article the following week. The changes were many and comprehensive. A few choice comparisons between the Morris and Gollancz versions must serve:

Morris: Mr Victor Gollancz, whose publishing business was founded 21 years ago this week, can be found any morning in his Henrietta Street office, delivering triumphant monologues at his editorial conferences, approaching with a glorious flourish one of his more successful authors — 'My dear Daphne' — or welcoming with an affectionate gesture some visitor who is down on his luck and wants to claim the Gollancz sympathy or championship.

Gollancz: Mr Victor Gollancz, whose publishing business was founded twenty-two years ago, can be found most mornings in his Henrietta Street office, presiding over editorial conferences, preparing to take an author out to lunch, or welcoming with an affectionate gesture some visitor who is down on his luck and wants to claim the Gollancz sympathy or championship.

Morris: His may not be the largest, by any means, of the publishing houses, but it is still the noisiest.

Gollancz: His may not be the largest, by any means, of the publishing houses, but it is still the most prominent.

Morris: He has always been cautious with his advances, too, though never ungenerous.

Gollancz: In the matter of advances against royalties, Gollancz steers a steady course between extravagance and niggardliness.

Morris: Spending so little time in bed he gets rather bored at times. 'How can I find enough to do?' — you can almost see the question circulating in his large head.

Gollancz: Spending so little time in bed, when other people are there, can get rather boring at times.

Morris: He is to some a strange mixture. But he is, in fact, a happy conjunction of an immense Jewish commercial ability with a kind heart. With his money, and his pen, and his business acumen, he is a fighter for better things.

Gollancz: He is to some a strange mixture. But he is in fact a happy conjunction of commercial ability with a kind heart. With his pen and his business acumen, he is a fighter for better things.

There was still enough of Claud Morris left for him to accept the Victor version, but, he informed Victor, the editor of the *Leader* thought otherwise.

He asked me to run an 'amendment' of the first piece, with extra material.
So in accordance to my promise to you, and after discussing with him

what he wanted, I had to disagree with his view. I have also, in accordance with our discussion, told him to kill both pieces. No article will therefore appear unless he obtains one eventually from some other source.

This is a great pity and I am the loser by it, but as I explained to him, I had talked the matter over with you and could not break my word in this matter.

I hope that you yourself understand . . .

My dear Claud Morris,

Very many thanks for your letter. I greatly appreciate your attitude and shall not forget it.

I am a little disturbed at two possibilities. The first is that although you have given instructions that the first piece is to be killed, it perhaps still remains in existence. Would it be possible for you to have it destroyed? The second is the possibility that the Editor may get someone else to write up a piece, perhaps on the basis of your first piece. As you know, I did regard quite a number of the statements as seriously libellous (but not with any such intention on your part — this was clear to me from the first and still clearer, if possible, after our dinner) and I really should be compelled to take action if any of them crept in.

Morris had already retrieved the article and assured Victor it had been destroyed. This was not the only time Victor instructed others to destroy material by or about him and failed so to instruct his own secretary.

April saw a spate of press ruminations on the achievements and heritage of Harold Laski, and inevitably Victor's political record was under the microscope. The *Statist* looked back sadly to a period when capitalism failed through complacency to defend itself against its intellectual opponents. That had happened first in the London School of Economics and later with the 'infamous' Left Book Club publications when 'the forces of free enterprise were content to see the minds of the new generation in politics "pirated" by the Left Wing without any adequate effort to ensure that this educational process was countered by an equivalent setting forth of the opposing case.' *Truth* lamented that moderate Labourites 'still do not realise how they are led by the nose by Left Book Club types, who consider the Yellow Book period, when Socialists and Communists marched shoulder to shoulder, defying Hitler and Mussolini, as the most glorious era in British Socialist history.' And the *Economist* smiled on a book on culture in England by Randolph Churchill in which he 'skilfully debunks the Gollancz – Lehmann [of the *London Magazine, New Writing*, and the Hogarth Press] – Strachey groups of public-school revolutionaries.'

It was hard on Victor that within two months the deaths of Orwell and Laski should have provided the press with opportunities to throw

The family at the time of Victor & Ruth's silver wedding, 1944

Victor at a Left Book Club rally

Victor at Dartington Hall, 1941

Norman Collins   Sheila Bush, née Hodges

In Germany, 1945

Above: Diana and John
Collins

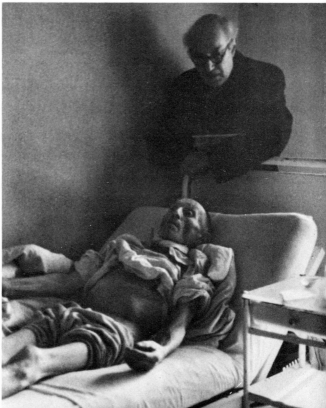

In Germany, 1945

Victor & Ruth at Brimpton

Gerald Gardiner

Arthur Koestler

Elinor ('Tessa') Murphy

Victor in 1945 after his breakdown

Hilary Rubinstein (*c.* 1950)

John Bush (*c.* 1970)

Livia Gollancz (*c.* 1975)

James MacGibbon (*c.* 1965)

Ruth & Victor leaving Frankfurt, 1960

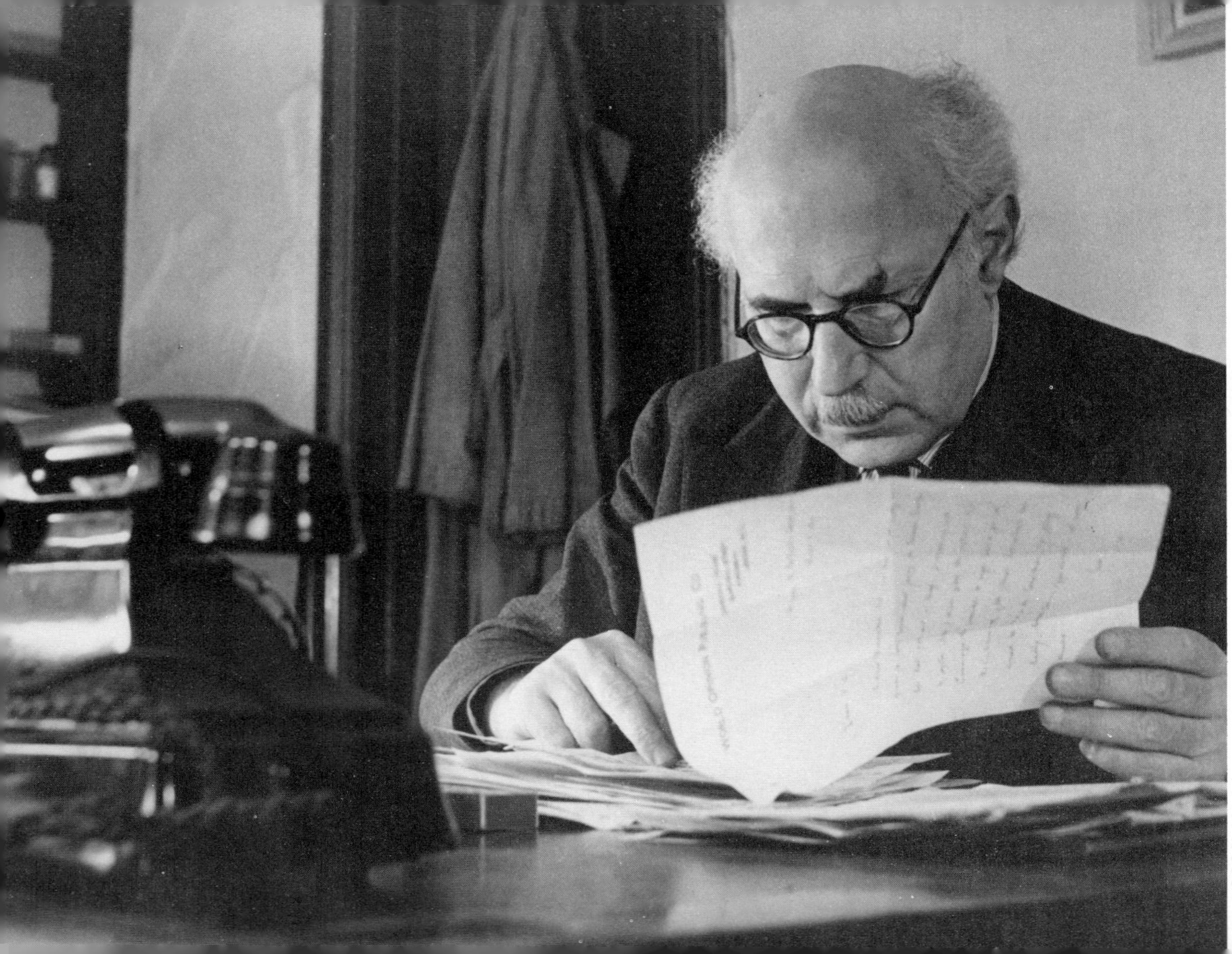

VG working at his desk

his past in his face. He avoided controversy. In April he concentrated his political efforts on Germany (briefing Dick Stokes to make a fuss about expellees), the JSHS (plans about increasing membership and for the public meeting) and Africa. On the 17th he spoke at a Central Hall meeting, organized by Collins, to give Scott a platform to explain his UN crusade. That meeting led to a gradual opening of doors to Scott and took Christian Action even faster along its destined path — combating racialism. Victor's interest in Africa had been sporadic, but at this stage he became very keen. According to one reporter, the meeting was serious, but 'with scarcely any manifestation of emotion — at least until Victor Gollancz took the platform.' Scott was the star, but Victor spoke pungently. He was

> appalled by the attitude of 'cold contemptuous superiority' shown by so many white people towards those of another colour, and he urged that 'no principle of colour, race, or class prejudice in our own midst should go unchallenged or unopposed.' Referring to economic conditions in South Africa, he said that if necessary we in Britain should be prepared to accept a lower standard of living, if by so doing we could raise that of Africa. 'I am sick', he said, 'of getting a little more here and a little more there and getting a more comfortable life, while fellow-humans are living in such utter misery.'

He received one letter of support that meant a great deal to him.

Dear Mr Gollancz,

As a close friend, — of more than 30 years standing, — of Albert Schweitzer, I would like to thank you for your inspiring message at the Central Hall, yesterday evening.

As always, listening to you is a treat and your speech, as well as your publications quickly command attention.

Your reference to Albert Schweitzer heartened me, as indeed he is a prophet and man of action alike.

When next time he visits England I will invite you to lunch, or tea at my Restaurant where many of his friends gather.

During the war when working in my spare time at the Central YMCA I regularly posted literature to Albert Schweitzer in Africa, among them also your book 'In Darkest Germany' which Schweitzer appreciated and read with great interest.

Thank you for allowing me to offer you enclosed photo of him and also an autograph letter by him of which I possess scores of them. You may care to add it to your collection as the Doctor refers in it to your book 'In Darkest Germany' . . .

With kind regards,
Yours sincerely,
Emil Mettler

Dear Mr Mettler,

Very many thanks for your letter. It was most kind and gracious of you to let me have the letter and photograph of Schweitzer both of which I shall greatly treasure. I have long regarded Schweitzer as the greatest living human being.

It will be an immense pleasure to me if you will invite me to meet him when he is next in England . . .

Victor was in generous vein that month, sending an unsolicited £100 to International Help for Children and offering a regular £2 per week to an ex-employee — one of the many people who had always relied on him for a handout in time of need.

He left England on 25 April. The staff, who always sent flowers to the ship, were too late with one of their typical telegrams. 'VICTOR GOLLANCZ CARONIA SOUTHAMPTON DOCKS ADORED CHIEF OFFICE FURNITURE FLOATS IN ROOMS AWASH WITH TEARS OF YOUR DESOLATE DARLINGS WHO WISH YOU AND MRS VG GODSPEED BRILLIANT TINY OBSCENITY JENKINS THE BEAUT DISTINGUISHED CORNY HOMELY GANY- MEDE AND ALFIE' (Victor's penchant for devising esoteric nicknames for his staff did not diminish with age).

His bookhunting in America was again immensely fruitful. He threw caution to the winds with a £1,000 advance on demand for a book he particularly wanted. To Hodges he wrote (in one of dozens of letters from New York) that she must not see this as a relaxation of the no-advance-before-publication rule. 'The point is I'm afraid that the very salutary rule may go by the board once we start weakening — but on the other hand, we must be careful not to let good books go when we *absolutely can't get them* without breaking our rule.' As if to nip in the bud Victor's experiment with flexibility, the author in question died suddenly in October with the book unfinished.

All was not sunny in America: Edmund Wilson (the literary critic) was 'very difficult and rather nasty'. But overall the trip had its usual reviving effect and when he returned in mid-June he tackled the mountain of work awaiting him with no signs of strain. He found one item in his mail that gave him great pleasure — the manuscript of a 'Hymn to Freedom' for a mixed choir, dedicated by the composer, Professor Rudolf Niedermayer, to 'Victor Gollancz, the fighter for freedom and human rights'.

He faced reversals in business stoically. News came from Spencer Curtis Brown that Gollancz's first bestselling author, R. C. Sherriff, was dissatisfied with the handling of his two most recent plays and wanted to change publishers. Victor agreed 'in all friendliness' to cancel the contract; he had long ceased to be a play publisher except in special cases — Rubinstein, for instance — and therefore felt no pain at the loss of Sherriff. (Later, Sherriff returned to Gollancz with his autobiography, which Victor published with great pleasure.) There were apparently no fireworks about a libel action which was being handled efficiently by Arnold Goodman, a partner at Rubinstein, Nash & Co. Writing to Professor John Macmurray to request a foreword for the Rev. N. H. G. Robinson's *The Claim of Morality*, Victor was depressed rather than angered by the state of the book-trade. 'We are most anxious to go on publishing books of this type, but the loss they normally involve in the present state of the market is appalling. The booksellers are becoming more and more Americanised — concentrating on a few popular best-sellers: — and the reviewers, though they have not yet reached that stage, rarely touch anything unless they see a fair general market for the book.' (Victor allowed himself to take on a varying number of losers annually, and guarded jealously his right to do so. In one of his letters from America — seeking information about Viennese music — he demanded instant action, for 'if I'm not to have this I shall take another loser.')

June's good works included taking Bertrand Russell's discarded and desperate wife, Patricia (Peter), to lunch, and pleading with Gerald Barry to find her a job. 'You are a dear,' she wrote. 'So few people really bother about anyone else's problems, and I know how busy you are.' He also succeeded, at the request of Sheridan Russell, in getting a permit extension from the Home Office for a Polish war widow. Karl Anders wrote asking for help for a German goldsmith now starving in England and Victor sent the JSHS secretary to see him, subsequently giving money for the man's support and buying some of his work.

On a wider front, he was confronted with a petition to him personally — to be forwarded to the government — from the islanders of Heligoland asking permission to return home. (The island was returned to West Germany in 1952 and repopulated.) As a vice-president of the National Peace Council (NPC), Victor co-signed a letter to *The Times* appealing for funds to establish a permanent peace centre in London for NPC work. That newspaper carried a review of a book by David Somervell, reiterating Somervell's view that Churchill and Victor shared the credit for Labour's victory in 1945. A large 'X' in the margin of Victor's copy of a *Tribune* article by T. R. Fyvel draws attention to the remark: 'quite a few "Left Book Club" books were shockingly bad, and Mr Gollancz has since apologised for them.' Although Victor was prepared to admit that some LBC publications were flawed, it seems unlikely that he had singled out Fyvel's observation because he liked it.

June was also the month of great activity on the JSHS front, with two meetings of the executive and the disappointing Conway Hall 'Call to Serve' event. Victor's plans for a Personal Service Bureau, though abortive, had affected his own thinking. A few days before the meeting he wrote to the Chairman of the Prison Commission, Lionel Fox, that he wanted from the autumn to devote a day a week to prison visiting at Wormwood Scrubs. Fox proved enthusiastic, and after a meeting with Victor organized matters at the Scrubs. Victor ultimately fixed on 20 October for his first weekly visit. He also considered taking some classes there.

In July, Victor was contemplating changes in his living arrangements. He was still happy at Brimpton, and often commuted from there, though he found the train journey trying; the London house was much less to his liking. 'My dear Jack,' he wrote to the Earl of Huntingdon, a Labour parliamentary secretary, 'We have been talking over that idea of coming to The Albany and are really extremely keen. We just *long* to get away from our ruined and mouldering barracks at Ladbroke Grove. If you *could* fix up that meeting with the Manager, we should be immensely grateful.' The idea came to nothing.

In Henrietta Street, July was notable for the retirement of Edgar Dunk. There was press coverage, and Victor proved very understanding. Enclosing a clipping from *Cavalcade*, he wrote to Dunk: 'I imagine it must be unpleasant for you', and appended a letter he proposed to send as a correction.

> Dear Sir,
>   Your note *Dynamic Bookman*, referring to Mr Edgar Dunk, who has just retired from the Secretaryship of this Company after serving with it from its formation, appears to be based on a misunderstanding. Mr Dunk, as Secretary of the Company, had to do with its finances, not with its policy: it is only in this sense that he can be said to have had 'much to do' with the Left Book Club which (as you no doubt rightly remark) did much to bring Mr Attlee to power. I am sure Mr Dunk would wish me to point out that he had been a life-long Conservative.
>   Moreover, he was not in publishing 'on his own' before he joined our firm. He was Secretary of Messrs Williams and Norgate, and it was in that capacity that he had to do, in the days of the first World War, with Litvinov, who, as an exile, was a clerk in Williams and Norgate's counting-house . . .

Victor sometimes suffered vicariously over press comment on others more than the subjects themselves. That same week he wrote to an American author, John Franklin Bardin, enclosing three reviews of his *The Burning Glass*, and begging him not to be distressed by them:

'George Malcolm Thomson is a man who just loves guying and tearing to pieces anything he spots as what he would call "highbrow". Francis Wyndham is a callow young man from Oxford, miles too big for his boots. Pamela Hansford Johnson is a typical low-to-middle-brow, with no real insight at all.' Bardin was delighted by Victor's kindness, though he considered the reviews quite favourable, and intelligent by American standards. 'I wish', he added, 'I could in some way better express the feeling I have that you are what I always thought a publisher should be — and a damn nice guy to boot.' (Victor promptly underlined 'damn nice guy' and sent the letter on to Hodges for appreciation of the compliment. It was the sure knowledge of how happy he was made by words of love and praise that led his close female colleagues and friends to write to him like lovers. No one could accuse him of keeping his needs secret. When du Maurier eventually reciprocated the 'Darling Daphne' opening with a 'Darling Victor', Hodges wrote to her to report that he was cockahoop over it. And when Peggy Duff thoughtlessly wrote to him as 'Dear VG', he sent the letter back with a demand that she change the 'Dear' to 'Darling'. She went one better, and signed the amended version 'Yours passionately'.)

Victor was beginning to move in religious circles that were novel to him, and there were indications of it that summer. Through the ecumenical contacts of Christian Action, through Roman Catholic friends such as Dick Stokes, the Pakenhams, and Harry Walston's wife Catherine, and also in response to the veneration shown him by the Catholic press, he was becoming a figure on that social scene. Early in July he was writing to Jerrold (also a Catholic) to protest at an indiscretion. Jerrold had told a mutual acquaintance that Victor disliked Barbara Ward. 'Not only did I say nothing of the kind, but it is totally inconceivable that I could have said, or could ever say, anything of the kind. . . . I regard her as that very exceptional thing, a woman who is (a) beautiful, (b) clever, and (c) good: and I am rather specially fond of her. Apart from that I always find her conversation unusually fascinating.'

In late July he went, without Ruth, to a dinner in honour of the retiring Jesuit provincial superior, Father Martin D'Arcy, along with the Jerrolds, the Pakenhams, Graham Greene and Evelyn Waugh. There were many others present, but, it appears, no other Jews. It may have been reports of that event that led one of his female admirers to write an (undated) letter which began

Dear VG, . . . I just *cannot* bear seeing Moses in the R.C. Church. Do

> persuade him not to do it. . . ! He is one of the few individualists left in this
> world who are not afraid to think for themselves. He must not become one
> of many!! If he suffers from cosmic loneliness at present — it will pass
> again, but if he commits himself now . . . he might when in a better mood
> bitterly regret this step, when confronted with much pettiness and gross
> intolerance of the R.C. Church . . .

(If only the Claud Morris profile had appeared, she would have been
cheered at Victor's description of himself as 'a liberal, humanistic
Judaeo-Christian, with heretical tendencies to Pantheism, Pelagian-
ism, and Abelardianism.') It was also in July that Victor attracted
criticism in the *Jewish Chronicle* by his speech at Ilford about Judaism.

A major political issue raised itself in June — the organization of a
civil liberties society. There had been a couple of attempts since the
war to set up a non-communist rival to the National Council for Civil
Liberties (NCCL). The first was the Freedom Defence Committee
(FDC) — chairman: the writer Herbert Read, vice-chairman:
George Orwell, and treasurer and driving force: George Woodcock.
It was a reconstitution of the Freedom Press Defence Committee of
which Victor had been a sponsor, but he had declined in 1945 to lend
his name to the FDC because it condemned military conscription. In
1946 he co-operated over an individual case and co-signed a protest
letter to the Home Secretary, but refused Woodcock office space at
Henrietta Street. In the same year, Koestler was prominent in a move
to establish a 'League for the Dignity and Rights of Man', which
would have much wider concerns than the FDC. Koestler involved
Orwell, Bertrand Russell and Victor in discussions on the aims of the
proposed organization. He and Russell then sought Victor's help with
a petition to the British government, proposing steps in psychological
disarmament to reduce tensions between Russia and the Western
Powers. They wanted Victor's advice on the politics of the plan and its
practical execution. Embroiled though he was in SEN work, he was
gripped by Koestler's ideas.

> . . . I am tremendously in favour of your new League for the Rights of
> Man, and think this should be pressed on with immediately. . . . The only
> other point is how far the new league would cut across the Freedom
> Defence Committee . . . [which] has always struck me as very much a
> hole-and-corner and *coterie* affair: and is rather closely identified, I think,
> with philosophic anarchism.
> 2. The intellectual disarmament memo requires much more careful
> thought, and I'll write to you again in a week or so. I think it's extremely
> important to get the idea across, mainly for the purpose of illuminating the
> actual situation (I don't think it will have any other result): but there are

things in the draft that I don't like — for instance the suggestion, if I have understood it aright, that some point of principle in international affairs might be sacrificed in return for raising the iron curtain . . .

Koestler was delighted. Neither he nor Orwell was placed to run the League, the first step for which

> would be to set up an organising committee, an office, etc. I know how much you have on your hands and how over-burdened your apparatus is. But I know nobody else with your drive and experience who could take the initial steps. I am convinced that once the thing has been set rolling it will roll on by itself. I know a number of people in France, Italy and the States who are only waiting for the initial spark to come in whole-heartedly.
>
> . . . I believe that the time is ripe for such an initiative and that the league would quickly have a considerable international echo.

Victor did not immediately reject the leading role Koestler had offered: in September 1946 he told a French correspondent that he was working on it. But with his German trip, and the increase in SEN activities, he let the matter drop. Koestler lost heart, and his initiative came to little, although it was later to bear fruit in the Congress for Cultural Freedom.

A third approach to Victor was made in 1950 — a better time. Roger Baldwin had resigned the chairmanship of the American Civil Liberties Union to work whole-time on behalf of the International League for the Rights of Man, and sought a British organization that would affiliate with it. Although the NCCL had put its house in order in 1949 (leading to the dissolution of the FDC), Baldwin did not feel it met the bill, and Victor believed it still to be communist-controlled. Baldwin asked Victor to set up a meeting for him in London, with people interested in civil liberties at home and internationally.

Victor organized a meeting of thirty at the St Ermin's Hotel on 13 July. Those attending included Acland, Violet Bonham Carter, Fenner Brockway, Frank Byers, Diana and John Collins, Dingle and Michael Foot, Benn Levy, the Pakenhams, Michael Scott, Dick Stokes, Harry Walston, Rebecca West and both Gollanczes. To Victor's disappointment, neither of the invited Tories, Boothby and Hogg, was able to attend.

Baldwin's address stimulated the enthusiasm of a nucleus, and Victor got to work to organize a follow-up meeting, where the foundations of an association would be laid. Even in the absence of Tories, there were enough problems between Liberals and Labour to wreak havoc. Ensuing correspondence between Bonham Carter and Victor shows the width of the gap.

26 July 1950

My dear Victor —

Last night's discussion was an interesting and enlightening experience. It revealed a deeper cleavage than I had guessed at between the Liberal and the Socialist conception of essential liberties. On two of the three disputed points — i.e., Closed Shop and Direction of Labour — I know that you are with us. On the right to possess something of one's own you are against us . . .

I am . . . puzzled by the fact that if all Socialists think 'property' an evil thing they should personally indulge in it on such a lavish scale.

I can understand and reverence the pure 'Christian' attitude: 'Sell all thou hast and give it to the poor'. But unless and until I am good enough to do this myself I could not say that others ought to do so, or rather, that they have not an inherent right, as I have, *not* to do so.

Moreover the value and the beauty of the 'Christian' attitude seem to me to lie in its *voluntary* impulse . . .

As to brass tacks: I was intensely amused by your arbitrary dissolution by a coup de main of the Drafting Committee which had just been set up by the assembled company! no less than by your brushing aside of the strongly supported suggestion that it should go ahead on the Constitution and finance without attempting any detailed statement of aims. I think this last suggestion clearly represented the 'sense of the meeting' and if put to the vote would have been carried . . .

But do remember one thing — i.e., Dingle Foot's statement at our first meeting that the old Civil Liberties Association, in its palmiest days, *long* before it was captured by the Communists, was always unwilling to face up to threats to liberty if and when they came from the (so-called) 'Left' — i.e., Trades Unions etc., though absolutely fearless and uncompromising in meeting them when they came from the (so-called) 'Right' — i.e., the Government or the police etc.

If the new body we are trying to create is to have real integrity of spirit — *and this is what I am concerned with* — it must face both ways and fight both ways . . .

Victor wrote to her on the same day:

My dear Violet,

I am rather disturbed about last night's affair, and thought I would try to clarify the issue. I do myself think it would be a thousand pities if we had to abandon the enterprise . . .

I believe that in practice the group of people so far gathered together would find itself in agreement over the overwhelming majority of cases that came its way . . . I think it would be quite wrong to allow theoretical considerations, however precious they may be to us, to prevent us from giving succour to people who may be in the gravest distress and even peril.

On the question of the property clause, though of course I entirely respect (and also completely understand) your point of view, the opposite point of view is quite as much a matter of conscience with me. To put in a clause stating the right of every human being to individual property *implies* (though it does not state) that individual property is *essentially* a good thing. I do not think it to be essentially a good thing: I think it to be essentially a bad thing. If you will read the passages in St Matthew about the lilies and Solomon in all his glory, about taking no thought for the morrow, etc., etc., you will perhaps understand why.

The matter is, of course, of no practical importance whatever. The ideal of human life which Christ presented cannot conceivably be lived at present except by a minute number of people (if by them). But I am quite certain that it is the ideal of the *good* life. I have not the smallest pretensions to being good personally: nor have I the capacity of so being: but that does not affect the fact that I could not, with any decency, associate myself with a statement which denied, in my view, the goodness of the good . . .

I hope you did not misunderstand — as I fear you perhaps did, from your good-natured parting shot— my suggestion that we should wash out for the time being, that drafting committee.

He had made the suggestion because the committee members proposed were certain to clash, and wreck the group. He was more pessimistic after he read her letter of 26 July, which had crossed his: 'You are,' he replied, 'in my opinion, and if you will forgive me for saying so, so horribly one-sided.' Liberal socialists, he explained, attacked right-wing liberals for wavering in their support of civil liberty when property rights seemed threatened and capitalism ('which I prefer to call the economic system which is based on the operation of human greed') undermined. Surely Bonham Carter could not really believe that a starving man was truly free. The Left believed deprivation to be inevitable while private capitalism 'continues in the great industries'. But it would be 'utterly fantastic' for the Left to put such beliefs into an all-party document. Bonham Carter, therefore, should refrain from inserting ideas unpalatable to them.

As to the question of an inconsistency in Socialist beliefs and Socialist performance, your jibe, if you will forgive my saying so, is a little unworthy. All but quite the most exceptional of human beings are incapable of living up to their beliefs. But because (a) I believe that property of any kind is a hindrance, and not an aid, to the truest freedom and (b) I am morally too feeble to divest myself of all my possessions — that is no reason why I should add to my sins by proclaiming that the possession of property is an aid to the truest freedom. If I did so, I should be merely adding blasphemy to an already existing weakness. Of course, each man solves the obvious dilemma between belief and performance as best he can. I do it in my own way — which I do not reveal — and I have no doubt you do it in yours.

He had handled the meeting as he believed the majority wished. Everyone present thought the question now was whether the group could go on at all, so there was no point in a drafting committee. Had he put the matter to the vote, he would have had a majority.

PS It seems to me that the necessity of a Civil Liberties body concentrating on that range of questions which are *ordinarily* called Civil Liberties is made quite obvious from my own position. As you know, I do not myself follow any 'party line' in this matter. I think, for instance, the Labour party attitude to personal petition as disastrous as your attitude to property. I strongly object to direction of Labour as a normal basis for civilised life, though I would support it in special circumstances, when not to do so would mean a lessening of freedom generally. I am ambivalent about conscription — loathing it morally, but unable to see how it can be logically opposed. Finally, in many matters I am an extreme anarchist, and go far beyond the Liberal position. To give you one example, I am violently opposed to punishment by the State (because I am violently opposed to punishment) in any shape or form. In other words, as you will see, I am in this matter of liberty neither a good Liberal nor a good Labour Party man, but a little mad! I believe in these various things passionately: but wouldn't it be the height of idiocy to attempt to write my beliefs into the basic aims of a Civil Liberties group?

He had no real hopes that his eloquence would move her. To R. S. W. Pollard (a lawyer), he wrote a few days later that he doubted whether the group could work together.

Too much stupid militancy on the part of Violet Bonham Carter on the one hand and some of the Labour people on the other. I have had a really intolerably didactic, contentious, self-righteous and one-sided letter from Violet Bonham Carter. It is a thousand pities that people cannot see that there are a hundred-and-one things on which everyone can unite — and that all they have to do is to leave the hundred-and-second alone! . . .

Her next letter made him no happier. She believed the majority had been in favour of going on with the drafting committee; the group should now proceed empirically, by trial and error, as it would never agree on basic principles; there would be problems about the closed shop; she could not accept his argument about property: 'Let us avoid definitions, which can only crystallize divisions, and go ahead on building the Association in the hope and faith that *in practice* we shall react alike to the tragic human situations of suffering and injustice, which it is our common aim to deal with.'

Victor saw little point in this approach, and during the next few months he confined himself to talking around the impasse with sympathetic people. Otherwise, he was more or less absent from the political scene, apart from a few epistolary arguments. He took issue with one commentator, who suggested in the *New Statesman* that Victor over-rated 'the stability of relationships between nations on a moral or ethical plane'.

> How can I overrate it when I rate it as nil? For God knows how many years, in books, pamphlets and letters to the Press, I have begged people to remember that, as all history shows, what they so passionately feel today about the inhabitants of another country is not in the least what they will feel tomorrow. But they never learn . . .
>
> It seems to me desirable . . . to remind people, while there is still only at worst a pre-war situation, that the common or garden citizens of the State they may one day (God forbid) be fighting are just as decent as anyone else. If such a task were undertaken by great and powerful organisations, religious or otherwise, instead of by some wretched little private publisher, it is conceivable that, if and when the worst happened, a few men and women might remember . . .

(When Victor was being especially arrogant — and here he was implying, after all, that he was the only campaigner against nationalist hatred — he often took cover behind an exaggerated humility.)

He was even more hurt by a circular letter from Professor Ulrich Noack, a German academic, who quoted him as saying (personally, in London in 1949) that 'the Russian danger has taught me that we need again a German army'.

> I said nothing whatever of the kind, and I should be obliged if you would refrain from making this statement, which, I am told, you have made on other occasions.
>
> I said something entirely different. I said that I believed in the perfect equality of Germany with all other nations: and that therefore, if and when there was a European army, for whatever purpose, Germany ought to have as much right to have a contingent in that army as any other nation . . .

Noack submitted a detailed account of their conversation, and an assurance that he always stipulated that Victor was speaking in the context of a European army. Noack himself disagreed, being convinced that the remilitarization of Germany would lead to war with East Germany. When he condemned to audiences the view Victor shared with Churchill, he preferred to mention Victor's name because of his credentials as 'an honest friend of our people'. Victor's wounded response claimed (a) that his views had been completely misrepresented and (b) that Noack was gullible about the Soviet Union.

This was a difficult period for Victor, torn as he was between total pacifism and the need for powerful resistance to communism. His fears for Europe had been exacerbated by the communist incursion into South Korea. No one was ever likely to sum up his position in a way that pleased him. While he would describe himself as 'violently anti-Communist', in private he could describe Rebecca West, whom he greatly liked, as a 'crazy Communist witch-hunter'. While these contradictions were susceptible to lengthy explanation when the occasion arose, they could be extremely confusing for everyone other than Victor himself.

As a publisher, he was getting particularly excited about books on Africa and anything to do with racial oppression. He was about to put out a 'startling' book on the Malan regime called *White Man Boss*, and was very interested in Fenner Brockway's projected *African Journey*. In August he published with great success *Scottsboro Boy*, a black fugitive's exposé of prison conditions in the American South, and was furious with Denis Brogan over his *Spectator* review. Brogan deemed hysterical the blurb's description of the fugitive's treatment as 'one of the world's greatest crimes against humanity', and so revealed himself, Victor adduced, as a victim of the arithmetical fallacy. If the description was hysterical, 'then a little more "hysteria" — as well as a little more "sentimentality", that other grossly misused word — is just what the deadened conscience of 1950 requires.'

A review of a book on Italian genius also prompted an angry letter, as it criticized a quote on the jacket. 'For a long time', concluded Victor's complaint to *John O'London's Weekly*, 'a tendency has been growing for reviewers to criticise, not the book, but the jacket. It is time this silliness should cease.' He was coming close to publication day with *A Year of Grace*, and was finding new material 'practically every day'. If the book was a success, he wrote to James Parkes, '(which I doubt) I may bring out, in a year or two's time, an enlarged edition, making it, perhaps, up to 800 pages!' He was consulted by André Deutsch, who was planning to set up his own firm, and offered 'good advice and a sympathetic hearing'.

By Victor's standards, it was a relaxed month. He hated missing any of the summer glories of Brimpton and wrote apologetically but warmly to a Jewish refugee (now naturalized) that he could not see him in August as he went home almost every night. (This young man's life had been changed by Victor's generosity in the late 1930s. He was employed in the firm for a time and was given or lent money when he needed it; he rewarded Victor by standing on his own feet as soon as he was able, repaying the borrowed money, and showing simple gratitude and affection for the kindnesses of the Gollanczes.) Victor took pleasure in seeing his grandson, Timothy, who stayed for a while. Anguished by the proposal to make neighbouring Alder-maston a nuclear weapon base, he wrote to Dick Stokes that it was 'the most unsuitable site in the world': Salisbury Plain was the right kind of place for 'this horrible business'.

As though in payment for the easy tempo of the preceding few weeks, Victor drew a controversy upon himself early in September. Its occasion was a letter to *The Times* giving his thoughts on the world crisis. He wrote as a non-pacifist who believed that the non-Soviet world would inevitably feel compelled to fight the Soviet strategy for world domination. That being so, to resist Soviet offensives now in Korea and Europe made a third world war less probable. While he stressed his respect for pacifists, he could not follow them because of his horror at what would be the physical and spiritual consequences of a world war. 'The real objection to pacifism is that in a world largely totalitarian, where ordinary people are so difficult to reach, it makes war more probable.' Surely it was possible to resist while yet striving for peace? The developing war psychology must be countered by a new ministry — a Peace Office — charged with getting through to Russia and her satellites the message that 'we wish them well'. Attlee and President Truman should hold an immediate conference with Stalin, where they should show unreserved goodwill, but no weak-ness or gullibility.

Of the letters that arrived in consequence of this at Victor's office, two elicited memorable replies. One woman wanted chapter-and-verse proof that communism aimed at world domination, and was given more than she bargained for: 'you have to have a complete knowledge of Communist theory and practice — starting with Marx's Capital and Communist Manifesto. In addition to Marx, you would have to read Lenin's collected works which run into at least a dozen large volumes!' A pacifist who took issue with the essence of Victor's argument committed the folly of telling him that it was the result of a common failing of the age, 'i.e. what Albert Schweitzer calls "A lack of ethical theory".'

'You must forgive me', responded Victor,

if I say that your letter seems to me to show that spiritual and intellectual arrogance which distresses me so in so many (but not all) pacifists. I find it odd that you should imagine that the considerations you put forward have not occurred to me and been endlessly brooded on — for a period, indeed, of nearly 50 years.

I am very familiar indeed with Albert Schweitzer, and the only photograph on my desk is a very beautiful one of him, caressing fawns. I do not think that he would accuse me of 'a lack of ethical theory'. In my Anthology 'A Year of Grace', which is being published in a fortnight's time, more space is devoted to him than to any other of the 250 odd authors.

The man wrote a mollifying letter back, dwelling on the agony of mind experienced by pacifists. Victor replied civilly, stressing his sympathy with humble pacifists and ending: 'Comparisons as to the relative painfulness of various positions are rather futile: but if the genuine pacifist suffers as much as the sensitive soldier (and sometimes, but by no means always, he does) I doubt whether the distress of either of them is greater than that of a man who shares the whole basic philosophy of the pacifist, and yet feels that he had to resist Hitler and will have to resist Stalin, if it comes to that.'

An admirer praised Victor's 'energy, drive, idealism, enthusiasm and — foresight', listed some of his recent good works, and ended with a rather tall order: 'I wish you would now concentrate on the last item, and strive for a meeting of the Big Three.' Certainly Victor continued to operate in the spirit of his *Times* letter. He refused an invitation from the National Peace Council (of which he was a vice-president) for fear of compromising 'any small usefulness I might have at the moment' by appearing on a platform with pacifists, and he tried to secure space in the *News Chronicle* to develop his idea of a 'Peace Office', which had been a damp squib in *The Times*. He was courteously turned down, but if he was disappointed it was not because he could think of nothing else to do.

On the very day he wrote to the *News Chronicle*, he applied also to Michael Foot, the editor of *Tribune*, for *carte blanche* to write for the paper a pamphlet on the wrongness of the Labour Party's appeal to self-interest: they were in effect guilty of national socialism, which was as morally objectionable as the old capitalist imperialism. He thought he would call it 'Socialist Morality'. Foot agreed and Victor was temporarily excited by the idea. He was rehearsing his arguments when he spoke for the Labour candidate in Newbury a week later. Having explained as usual that the Labour Party was the hope of the world, he added a word of caution against inverted capitalism. 'I find there is a tendency on the part, particularly of the working class and more particularly certain elements of the working class, to say now that we are in power we will squeeze the last atom out of everybody else.'

There was personal satisfaction in a farewell letter of true gratitude from a Spanish refugee and long-standing Gollancz beneficiary, now emigrating to Mexico, and a deal of unpleasantness from another, similar quarter. A virtual stranger had taken advantage of Victor's impulsive generosity and borrowed £600, repaying only £200 of it. Legal proceedings were threatened, and Victor tried thereafter to make gifts rather than extend loans.

All this activity was peripheral to Victor's main preoccupation of the autumn: the launching of his anthology on 2 October. It was bad luck that its appearance coincided with the beginning of a limited strike by printers, which made it impossible to have advertisements set for some journals. (Victor got round that with *The Times Literary Supplement* by providing a stereo of a Gollancz advertisement in his own hand-writing.) The strike spread quickly and stopped publication of many of the weekly journals in which Victor might have expected reviews: these misfortunes put him on his mettle.

There was nothing novel in Victor's promotional methods, but the scale of the operation was bigger than usual, and his sense of shame less. Two things should be borne in mind. The first is mundane: he stood to make not a penny out of the book, having assigned all the royalties to his daughters. The second is an important point in his defence: Victor was passionately anxious to reach a wide readership because he believed the book to be a real power for good. It truly was a superb anthology, not only diverse and profound, but bound together by its joyous expression of religious humanism. His eclecticism might irritate the narrow-minded or pedantic, but to those less trammelled by orthodoxy, *A Year of Grace* offered wisdom and comfort of a high order from a range of sources to which few had access. Moreover, its highly personal nature provided, for those inclined to read between the lines, a quite revealing autobiographical insight. As Victor explained in his foreword, the book was full of surface contradictions, but the mood was consistent and his own. It was

> the mood that has dominantly been mine ever since, as a very small boy, I sniffed the air and sang for joy amid the late autumn leaves in a narrow London garden. Now, when I am fifty-seven, 'the dust and stones of the street' are still 'orient and immortal wheat'; and 'what my heart first awaking whispered the world was', that and nothing other my heart whispers still. But I would not care to suggest that the mood, though dominant, has been invariable. There have been hours and days (as there will

be hours and days again) when, appalled by the evil in myself and others, I could no longer feel that love, with pity and mercy as its chief attributes, was the only reality, and that I, being real, was in communion with it. There was even one whole year, following the year of grace to which my title refers, when I lived second by second in the hell of terror and despair. It is not irrelevant to my theme to mention that only by the greatest effort of will, if even so, can I realise in recollection that terror and that despair, which now appear nothing to me; and that when I live again in those days, as I often do, I live in the love that faithfully cared for me and saw me through to safety.

The distinguished theologian, Canon Alex Vidler, in a long and enthusiastic review, described the work's merits perfectly. The review concluded:

> . . . if *A Year of Grace* springs from faith in a living God, it flows out into a resolute and entirely unsentimental concern for close and compassionate human relations. Especially searching and challenging in this connexion are passages from Jewish sources, Rabbinic and Hasidic; for example, this from the Talmud:
>> An aged man, whom Abraham invited to his tent, refused to join in prayer to the one spiritual God. Learning that he was a fire-worshipper, Abraham drove him from his door. That night God appeared to Abraham in a vision and said: 'I have borne with that ignorant man for seventy years; could you not have patiently suffered him one night?'
>> *A Year of Grace* will not necessarily lead its readers to make Mr Gollancz's faith their own, though there is no book that will serve as a better introduction to the grounds and scope of Hebrew-Christian belief. What it will do, however, is to give concrete and vivid substance to all the abstract commonplaces about the importance of 'spiritual values.' Its readers may still decide that the faith in the reality of God and in the potentialities of human existence, which this volume brings to life, is too good to be true; they will not in that case be able to lay it down without a sense of consternation at what they have lost or at what they have not yet been able to find.

Vidler was amazed that the book was selling at 10s. 6d. (55 pence); it would have normally been priced at twice that. Victor's contract allowed him 100 presentation copies, which he inscribed and sent to friends — a category which of course overlapped with the much greater number of influential people who received advance copies.

As the thank-you letters came in Victor was poised to underscore comments suitable for use in advertising, and his secretaries were geared up to take dictation of letters of gratitude, explanation, or rebuke. Victor soon had a bumper crop of puffs. 'It's a wonderful book', wrote the Bishop of Chichester, '— so generous in its wisdom, so rich in its comfort, so catholic in its choice. It is a real spiritual experience to read it.' 'I am sure', said Lettice Cooper, 'that no book could be published which would have more value at the present time.' The forgiving Cripps, at this time still Chancellor, had been 'reading it avidly & enjoying it greatly and we shall both treasure it.' Daniel George, the literary critic, was so ecstatic that Victor underlined nine-tenths of his letter. A sample: 'it appeals to the active but thoughtful of all ages in a workaday world.' Dean Inge pronounced it 'excellent', and Storm Jameson 'noble'. Du Maurier, who had not yet read it, said 'I feel it is going to be the bed-side book of all time'. Victor asked if he could use the quote, but she went one better: 'I felt it was going to be the bedside book of all time, and it was!' Rose Macaulay disappointed him by failing to produce anything quotable, and even admitted she had been dipping into it — an approach that undermined her criticism of certain inclusions (Blake in particular). Victor sent her Daniel George's letter and a long one of his own.

> My dear Rose,
>   . . . Alas, alas! You have disregarded the introduction! Perhaps I didn't emphasise there sufficiently that the reader will go all wrong if he considers a single item in isolation. Somebody to whom I sent an advance copy has said that it reminds him of a Beethoven symphony. Not being a fool, he wasn't comparing me to Beethoven at the millionth remove: he was showing me that he understood exactly the method of the thing. Nobody could 'agree' with any particular phrase or melody in the Ninth Symphony — or even with any complete movement: but you can agree with the whole thing . . .

Macaulay continued to raise questions about Blake. The quote 'Sooner murder an infant in its cradle than nurse unacted desires' worried her. Victor defended his old hero's belief that the suppression of life and energy was invariably bad. 'To reach the stage (which a very few rare men have reached) in which the central fire never has to be damped down, but comes through as selfless love, is to be what is called a Saint.'

Many of the thank-you letters were unusable for puffs, either because their writers were obscure, because — like L. P. Hartley's — they were phrased unsuitably for use in advertisements, or because — like Jung's and Arnold Toynbee's — they were carefully moderate. Of the thoughtfully selected potential reviewers, Harold Nicolson came closest to damning the book with faint praise: 'It is much more austere than any anthology I should write myself and explains your high idealism and your Messianic moments. I cannot promise to review it, but I can promise to keep it with great pleasure and to read it frequently.'

Most of the respondents, however, were so appreciative that Victor was ill prepared for the disaster that befell him less than two weeks before publication. On 22 September he wrote to his London traveller, Reg Dignum, about W. H. Smith's 'unbelievable' order for only 100 copies of *A Year of Grace*. Anyone with any sense of 'bookmanship . . . must know that this is the biggest chance we have had for years for a sale on the biggest scale — both immediately and for many years — and, in particular, for Christmas presents this year. Our view of this is confirmed by the more than one hundred letters received from the recipients of advance copies — literary critics, litterateurs, religious leaders, philosophers, and ordinary members of the public.' Though that was 'a very serious blow indeed', what really horrified Victor was Smith's treatment of him personally, after a business association of almost 25 years. 'I don't quite know how to describe my feeling about this: words like "lack of courtesy" or, to borrow from the title of the book, "lack of grace" don't quite describe what I mean. I suppose what comes nearest to it would be a certain, and really rather appalling, lack of spiritual sensitiveness.' Had they wanted to show generosity, they would have taken 5,000; if caution had tempered their goodwill, 2,500 would have been appropriate; and even had they had no faith in the book and had not wished to show any special generosity, 1,000 would have been the minimum order necessary to avoid 'in a spiritual sense . . . flinging the thing back in [our] faces.' To take, as they had, only 100 copies, was more of an insult than taking none.

Nevertheless, despite this reverse, Gollancz had no doubts about the book's saleability. 'But that is not the question. Business judgment on such matters must always differ. What is so profoundly shocking — and it is part of the whole collapse of civilisation, which is leading us all into final disaster — is that a firm with the great past of Messrs W. H. Smith should regard the *only* criterion in a case of this kind, with all the special circumstances involved, as the criterion of profit and loss.' He wrote to Smith's, who stoutly denied they had acted from a non-business motive. The reason was more prosaic: the bookbuyers had been 'disappointed and puzzled with the book'.

The reviewers were better endowed with spiritual grace, and the anthology received a small but appreciative press. Victor had to put only a few of them straight. He wrote to John Hadfield to thank him for a 'kind note', but asked him to correct the impression given that the book's message was predominantly Jewish. Herbert Read, in the *New Statesman*, completely missed the point, suggesting that Victor must be disillusioned with politics. Victor pointed out trenchantly to Read's editor that his purpose was rather to demonstrate that politics was an essential activity for every man. 'The whole business about Read is really very tragic', Victor confided to an acquaintance, ' — several people have written and spoken to me about him. Something appears to have happened to him.' Still richer vituperation followed when the *Oxford Mail*'s anonymous reviewer, while broadly approving, referred to Victor as a 'disconcerting' person and described the book as having been compiled by Ruth from the passages marked by her husband. Victor's indignant repudiation secured a less than satisfactory apology, which had him protesting again to the editor about 'this extraordinary person', and asking Collins for clues to the identity of this 'horrible, offensive man'. When the reviewer wrote personally to Victor at the behest of the editor, he did so hamfistedly and made matters worse by failing to admit he had been wrong about Ruth's involvement. This, Victor explained to him, was a 'sordid and dishonourable' accusation which showed what spiritually bad shape he was in.

That anybody should think it was not all his own work was a specific mortification. Victor had other, wider-ranging troubles. 'It is a tragedy for me, as well as for the rest of my authors,' he wrote to a friend, 'that the London printers' strike has closed down the overwhelming majority of serious papers that review a book of this kind. Over a hundred such papers — religious weeklies, as well as secular weeklies — did not appear last week, and may not appear for weeks to come.' Casting about for alternative reviewing media, he leaned on John Collins to engineer a special mention in the Dean of St Paul's weekly *Telegraph* column. (He was already in Collins's debt, for it was through him that the book reached Alex Vidler's attention.) Victor intensified his advertising campaign, careless of the possible reactions of his authors. One helpful correspondent suggested in September that he should advertise in the anthroposophical* annual, the *Golden Blade*, and he had happily replied:

It is a fact that we don't normally advertise in 'specialist' magazines, but I am perfectly prepared to break the rule in my own case! I think I had better take a page while I am about it as I never believe in small spaces. But one thing rather worries me. I don't think a mere description of the book

* Anthroposophists aspire to the development of a faculty for spiritual perception that is independent of the senses.

would make it clear to anthroposophists that they would be interested by it: and certainly a mere statement to that effect by me would be quite useless. I wonder, therefore, whether an anthroposophist would write a short sentence, simply stating that the book is of interest to anthroposophists. I don't know whether you have looked at it sufficiently to be able to say this yourself . . .

By the end of October, the anthology had sold almost 9,000 copies and looked set fair to be a big Christmas success. Perhaps ingenuously, more likely with tongue daringly in cheek, Victor's co-director Frank Strawson had said to him in September that 'but for your natural diffidence in pushing it, I think it should prove a best seller.'

Of course, other Gollancz books were not ignored. Feeling somewhat aggrieved with booksellers at the beginning of October, Victor had advised one of his authors that to do more than hint at incest, in his book,

> would be a great mistake. The booksellers and circulating libraries spend 90 per cent of their time in thinking up reasons for not stocking books: and they would regard a suggestion of incest as a very useful alternative to 'book too thin', 'binding too light in colour—will soil easily', 'public not interested in religion', 'public only interested in religion', 'too early to buy for Christmas' (on October 31st), 'too late to buy for Christmas' (on November 1st), and so on . . .

He had reason and found time to complain about a *TLS* review of a Gollancz book, and some authors too were getting on his nerves. One wrote an innocent and friendly letter that implied criticism of the Gollancz sales department. Such complaints are the bane of any publisher's life and this one caught Victor on a bad day:

> Every publisher gets letters like that regularly: I imagine that the rubbish in every publisher's wastepaper basket consists largely of them. But how *on earth* can an intelligent man, who presumably knows his way about the world, write such stuff? Do you imagine I could have built up a successful publishing business by failing to subscribe my books to the Times Book Club, and by failing to execute orders from country booksellers? Wouldn't a moment's thought have told you that the one thing in the world a publisher wants to do is to sell his books, and that he gets up to every kind of shift to do so: and that, therefore, when anomalies of the kind you mention come to light the explanation is, not that the publisher suicidally refuses to supply his wares, but that the booksellers in question, or their assistants, are either ignorant or lying?

After proving conclusively that Gollancz was in the right, he concluded: 'This letter no doubt sounds angry. Well, I am a bit angry for a passing moment. When unintelligent people write to a publisher like that, the publisher smiles tolerantly and puts the letter in a suitable place: but that a man of your intelligence should do it. . . . '

His most enthusiastic author's encomium that month harked back to old glories. Gwyn Thomas was delighted to have been placed by his agent with

> so large and exalted a publisher. Quite apart from the pleasure it has given me personally, this will cause the stocks of my literary standing to shoot like a rocket among my valley comrades because Victor Gollancz is one of the few publishers to have carved his name deep into the consciousness of these folk here. For years membership of the LBC was a synonym of literacy and social awareness and courtships were often smashed to atoms on the grounds of one partner having failed to get his or her teeth into the latest choice.

Then there was the matter of the sexologist Victor had approached for advice. He wanted to know why a Gollancz book called *Human Growth* was not selling: was it the price or the jacket? She concluded that people were either too poor to buy books or did not consider them priorities; that they did not want to know about things, having had too much government propaganda; and that they were afraid of anything serious. 'I know', she said, 'we are in a transition period. I know that if another war came our people would be heroic. But for the first time in my life (at 61), I am feeling despondent about my fellow creatures.' Victor was depressed: 'with horrible reluctance', he wrote, 'I agree with what you say. The situation is terribly tragic.'

Many of Victor's reactions to changes in society were those of a man older than his years. He had started early to talk about the superiority of people in general 'when I was a boy' — language more to be expected from a conservative than a socialist. Yet splenetic nostalgia was to some extent typical of his generation, who had lived through two great wars, and even more characteristic of idealists disappointed that the sufferings of World War II and the triumph of the Labour government had failed to bring about a much better world.

A not-untypical pessimism permeated a letter Victor wrote to André Deutsch, whose plans for starting up his own business had now become a reality: all he needed was a little capital. 'I hate to say no,' wrote Victor on 3 October,

> I have carefully considered overnight your letter of 2nd October and our talk about this.

But I really do feel that I oughtn't to help financially. As you know, I think the capital on which you propose to start gravely insufficient. A lucky hit or two, achieved early enough, would of course provide you with some, or all, of the extra working capital necessary: but I do not think it is sound to gamble on the chance of this, though I well understand that, in your position, you may feel you've simply got to.

I hope you will not think that I am attaching undue importance to the possibility that I might lose any small sum I might put up. I am thinking mainly of a certain uneasiness I should feel at helping, in however tiny a way, to finance a business which might (with complete honesty and the best will in the world on your part) 'let in' various people if things went wrong.

Possibly I am too much obsessed by the frightful difficulties which I am sure the publishing business is going to face during the next few years. Possibly, also, I have lost the adventurous spirit of my youth. But even when I started, 22 years ago, I really would not have started with anything like so small a sum.

Anyway you have my very best wishes: please believe that . . .

André Deutsch went on to make his reputation and Victor continued to look about him gloomily. He was deeply upset that an agitation whipped up by the *Daily Herald* had led the BBC to cancel a repeat of a television play which showed a Labour politician in a bad light. He wrote an unusually brief letter in support of a *News Chronicle* leading article deploring the BBC's action: 'Allow me, as a member of the Labour Party, to support your leading article on "Party Manners". A genuine libertarian will avoid like the plague not only the smallest interference with liberty of expression, but anything that might conceivably look like it.'

He spent a few weekends trying to write the *Tribune* pamphlet, and reiterated its proposed theme in speeches in Cambridgeshire on behalf of Harry Walston, in Oxford on behalf of the city candidate, and at a meeting of the Oxford University Labour Club, of whose chairman, Shirley Catlin (later Williams), he was very fond. That month, he was also permitted to preach from a real pulpit: he addressed a crowded Anglican congregation in Bristol on religious humanism.

Spiritually, he was bowled over by a book by Erich Fromm.

I sent you a wire immediately after finishing 'Psychoanalysis and Religion'. But I feel I cannot trust impersonal electricity to convey what I feel.

Honestly, I never remember a book which gave me so comforting and heartening a sense of *recognition* (you will know what I mean). Every now and again I couldn't help jumping from my chair and saying 'that is exactly right', 'if *only* they would see it', and so on.

I am awfully proud to be publishing it . . .

(He must have failed to pass on to Harold Rubinstein his admiration for Fromm's book, otherwise the lawyer's letter clearing the book for libel would scarcely have contained the paragraph: 'I have heard it suggested that Fromm is the American "opposite number" of VG. If I ever see this stated in print, I shall advise VG to sue for libel! The author of this book appears to be a crypto-atheistic Humanist, completely and complacently blind to the possibility that there may be more things in the Great Commandment and the Beatitudes (with which *A Year of Grace* commences) than are dreamt of in his neo-Freudian philosophy . . . ' But then Rubinstein did not share Victor's enthusiasm for Freud: nor was he thinking, as Victor was, of writing an autobiography to explain how his childhood experiences had made him the man he was.)

Victor's personal service as a prison visitor began on Friday 20 October. A couple of days before, he had written to an author of a book about the experience of madness, and the letter says something of the frame of mind in which he was approaching prison work. The book, said Victor, showed

> that there may be just the same kind of value in the experience of a 'lunatic' as there is in the experience of the great religious mystics, etc.; in other words your book has the effect of removing, from at any rate one kind of 'lunacy' the discredit (to use a rather comic word) which normally attaches to it. I do a good deal of lecturing to prisoners, and I invariably have the instinct that the people in front of me have a certain holiness: I felt the same in the other connection in reading your book.

(The dearth of other evidence suggests that 'a good deal of lecturing' was an exaggeration.) His prison visiting commitment required sacrifice: he could not get away from London on Friday afternoon, as was his habit, in time to see the Brimpton garden in daylight.

'What gigantic footprints your personality will leave on the sands of Publishing and Literature!' wrote one *Year of Grace* reader at the beginning of November. Victor was by then buoyant about the excellent sales figures, and was already collecting material for an enlarged edition. There was correspondence with and about reviewers, and Christmas sales prospects were enhanced by a new round of advertising. Booksellers in Wales received the full text of a review in the *Western Mail* by one of Victor's most consistent admirers, A. G. Prys-Jones. (*A Year of Grace* became a Christmas bestseller. Indeed by the following June it had sold about 40,000 copies, staggering for a book of its kind. Victor never admitted that its success owed anything to his efforts as a publisher. To an enthusiastic member of the public he wrote in February 1951 that 'People do seem to like the book — I am so glad, because I really compiled it entirely for myself and didn't think anybody else would care about it. I suppose that is how "best sellers" sometimes happen.')

The book gave him what was probably the happiest moment of his year — a fan letter written on 15 November (translated here from German).

Dear Mr Gollancz,

I thank you from my heart for sending me your beautiful volume of religious sayings. It is a wonderful anthology, in which I found so much that I did not know, and so much that it was a great joy to me to rediscover. I was moved that you gave so much space to the ethic of reverence for life. I knew that it meant something, but did not believe I should ever live to see that it would be recognised. And now it has turned out so.

I am writing to you from Lambaréné, where I am occupying myself with the direction of my hospital after a year's absence in Europe and America. The burden of work is now almost too heavy for me, but I am trying to bear it as well as I can. I want your beautiful book to have many readers, who may carry something from it in their hearts.

Forgive my writing. I suffer from writer's cramp, and can therefore not write to you so clearly as I would wish.

With my best thanks,
Yours sincerely,
Albert Schweitzer

Victor used part of the letter as a puff, had the original framed, and stood it on his desk beside the Schweitzer photograph and the Stravinsky *Firebird* extract. (He remained proud of the letter, but his delight in it was diluted a few years later when his hero came to London and Victor was invited to meet him along with other admirers at Mettler's restaurant. He was affronted by Schweitzer's failure to suggest a private meeting and did not attend the gathering. The hurt showed in a letter of August 1955 to an American publisher about a book he was publishing by Helen Keller: 'I have an immense reverence for Helen Keller (although it is silly to talk of the greatest living human being, I think she has a greater claim to be called that than, for instance, Schweitzer, who is constantly called it) . . . ' And in the anthology, *From Darkness to Light*, that he finished compiling that same year, Schweitzer was remarkable by his absence.)

Victor was in the political news in mid-November, with a letter to the *Guardian* supporting its editorial line against the exclusion by immigration officials of suspected communist delegates to the proposed Sheffield Peace Congress. Victor deplored the government's actions: while the investigators who had grilled the visitors were unlike the Gestapo, 'a faint stench begins to arise . . . from these drains and to pollute our air.' The proposed Congress was, he said, unquestionably 'a war Congress', but that was no justification for using such methods. His letter was cited approvingly by Acland in the Commons debate on the Congress.

At the Cambridge Union he spoke in favour of the motion 'That political orthodoxy is the last refuge of an infirm mind', and, according to a student reporter,

> showed us all up. After his speech one felt that there really was little left to say, and one wrily fingered the notes of an as yet undelivered speech. He spoke to us as if dictating an important article in his office. With thumbs in waistcoat pockets or finger wagging, he brought his searchlight mind to bear on the problems of the motion, now and then slapping the dispatch-box for emphasis. Again, there was little that anyone could disagree with in his sane analysis of the trends in our democracy.

Victor was so impressed by the speech of one of the undergraduates, Douglas Hurd, that he wrote to congratulate him, adding, 'Between ourselves, I found the evening rather depressing: so many carefully prepared epigrams and jokes, not, alas, of first-rate quality. Your speech shone for its seriousness, its grace, its good sense and its excellent delivery.'

With his mind on so many other things, Victor effectively wound up the JSHS organization in November and regretfully fired the secretary, then tried to get the civil liberties group going again. A series of meetings with like-minded people led to a decision to begin again without the troublesome elements, by means of a nucleus composed of three Labour MPs (Frank Bowles, Michael Foot and Sidney Silverman), one Labour ex-MP (Benn Levy) one Liberal (Dingle Foot) and two non-politicians — R. S. W. Pollard, and Victor himself. He put a great deal of work into selecting names for a council, but the whole business proved a failure. Over ensuing months meetings were postponed and in April 1951 he wrote to Pollard that he had abandoned the idea 'for the time being. It seems to me that, with the exception of one or two of us, people have behaved with abominable carelessness in this matter: and it is no good trying to get an organisation going with people who don't care.'

Conflicting priorities led to problems at the end of November. Victor had been spending his weekends 'making a desperate effort to get going on a new book'. (It may have been a project which he had mentioned to du Maurier in October — 'an immense poem about our

modern situation in the metre of Don Juan — beauty and satire and
anger all mixed up together' — or it may have been his autobiography.
Either way, he made only false starts.) His attention had been shifting
to the Korean crisis, amid fears that it might spark a world war. It was
probably activity on that front that led to his cancelling — on the very
day he was expected — an address to a World Congress of Faiths
meeting on Monday the 27th. (Friday and Monday engagements were
always particularly vulnerable to sudden cancellation if Victor was
desperate for a long clear weekend in which to write.) After
consultations with Collins, he sent a long letter to *The Times* over their
joint names (in their capacities as chairmen, respectively, of Christian
Action and the JSHS), explaining the point of view of the Americans,
the Chinese and the Russians and begging that statesmen adopt a
totally new technique of negotiation.

> After all, what are we facing? Not merely the destruction of our own great
> cities, and a life of vagrant misery for the remnant of our population: but
> unspeakable agony, during perhaps an eight years' war, for millions of
> human beings who, whether 'friends' or 'enemies', are our neighbours in
> the Christian sense, and as close to us, under God, as our own families.
> Faced with this, dare we go on with the traditional round of manoeuvring
> for position, 'tactical replies', propagandist denunciations, and the rest? Is
> this some game to be played out by permanent officials according to the
> established rules? Rather let statesmen look upon their rivals as fellow
> human beings involved in a common doom: let them find it in their hearts
> to break through the red tape of the chancelleries, and talk as members of a
> household trying to compose a quarrel. Above all, let us eschew that
> national pride and prestige which prompts so many of these country-
> thrusts. All pride, and national pride pre-eminently, is of the devil.
> Nothing can save us now but humility.
>
>   The opposing statesmen, then, and Nehru, should confer without
> delay. However certain it may be that communism drives steadily to
> world domination, it is no less certainly implicit in our faith that where
> two or three are gathered together, there grace may enter . . .

Even after Victor had cut his letter by 750 words, *The Times* still
found it unsuitable for publication. (It was a matter of distress to
Victor that after Barrington-Ward's retirement as editor in 1948, *The
Times* showed less inclination to publish his letters.) There was
nothing for it but to expand his argument into a pamphlet, which he
set to work on in the weekend of the 9th and 10th. He was so
determined that this pamphlet should make the maximum impact that
he refused to sign a letter against first use of atomic weapons, in case it
rendered some readers less susceptible to his arguments.

That was also a factor in his decision to turn down an invitation from the Oxford Labour Party to stand at the next election, unless '(having already too many more important jobs) you can suggest anyone else who would be willing to stand for the ideals that you put forward whenever we hear you speak? Oxford could be won by a minor prophet but she needs an au dessou de la melée [*sic*] man or woman, who would stress blood, sweat & tears, in fact religion in action rather than party.'

'If anything in the world could have tempted me to stand for Parliament,' answered Victor, 'a request from Oxford would have done so. Indeed I nearly fell. But not quite: I am sure that any little usefulness I could ever have would be greater outside Parliament than in.' The desire to keep his independence also had him writing to the Oxford University Peace Association to say that he would not share a platform in January with Tom Driberg (Labour far-left) 'nor anyone of his political complexion', lest it 'prejudice any work I may try to do'.

The pamphlet, *Christianity and the War Crisis*, was written over two weekends and approved by John Collins, nominally co-author. Victor sent it to press and went away to Paris for a week's holiday on 19 December. He had announced a few days previously at a party for a Catholic journal, the *Month*, that he intended to spend the week reading John Scotus Eriugena in the original. In the event, he spent it re-drafting the pamphlet. Back in London he and Ruth spent the evening of the 26th with the Collinses, correcting the proofs and writing in his amendments until 2.30 am. It was back with the printer on the 27th and the free copies were on their way to politicians and other key figures on 3 January. It led to a large correspondence, a meeting with interested Labour MPs and others, and a row over misrepresentation by the *Church Times*.

At the beginning of 1951 Victor was intent on giving every spare moment to this new cause. Sheila Hodges was sent to the United States in place of the Gollanczes, for Victor was not prepared to leave the country during the international crisis, lest 'at any moment the Heavenly President may require me to use my infinitesimally tiny oar'. He was taking on speaking engagements and considering writing a pamphlet every month, 'hammering away not only at this war question but also at the fundamental moral situation out of which the international situation ultimately arises'. His priorities were absolutely clear. On 20 January 1951 everything changed. Victor at last found an approach to autobiography which would not exclude his reflections on the present. In his Brimpton library on that day he wrote the first few pages of *My Dear Timothy*.

CHAPTER TWENTY-TWO

APOGEE

———————

THE AUTOBIOGRAPHICAL URGE did not sit happily with Victor's need constantly to comment on the present and give guidance on the future: the charmless constraints of a chronological account of his life would rapidly have snapped his patience. He resolved the conflict brilliantly when he conceived the autobiographical letter to his grandson — *My Dear Timothy* — in which he admitted: 'one of my pleasures in writing this letter is that I can say anything I like on any topic I like in any order I like.'

He set out to write a short book in his free time, but soon became engrossed. 'I am so thrilled with it that I cannot bear not to devote every possible moment to it', he wrote to an acquaintance in March. By July, other concerns were largely set aside, and he had written so much that even he was getting worried. 'The trouble is', he told Noel Brailsford,

> the enormous length of the thing. It has a sort of circular motion starting in my library in the January of this year, going back to 1942 and then doing half of my experiences at Repton during the first war, then (to explain the other half) going right back to my early childhood and so forward through Oxford to Repton again. I have not yet finished Oxford, and have already written about 140,000 words! I now have to go forward to Repton — and then the whole business from the end of the first war right on to 1943. It looks to me as if the very minimum that I can do it satisfactorily in will be something between a quarter and a half million words!

Before long he was describing it as an 'informal spiritual and political autobiography', likely to run to half a million words. He decided that if he published it at all, it would be in three volumes at intervals of a month. By November he had reached 1914, the manuscript was 180,000* words long and 'not a word too much', and the whole work was set fair to reach three quarters of a million words. The first volume should be published quickly, he felt, 'owing to the present war and economic crisis'.

*As a point of comparison, the length of an average detective story is 65,000 words.

As Victor himself admitted, *My Dear Timothy* was written in a 'very peculiar' form. The main narrative was frequently broken up by italicized notes that varied between a couple of lines and several pages and consisted largely of contemporary political or social commentaries, interspersed with bursts of joyful appreciation of some unfolding beauties in the Brimpton garden. Here and there the reminiscences were interrupted by lengthy philosophical essays. Indeed, Victor's moral excursuses took up so much room that he could cover properly only his first 23 years. His discussion of socialism, for instance, occupied more than a third of the book and included a 10,000-word eulogy of the Arapesh culture, culled directly from Margaret Mead's study of New Guinea tribes. Almost 30,000 words were given over to reflections on Jewish orthodoxy. It was finely written and attracted readers of a spiritual cast of mind, but irritated those who just wanted the story of Victor's life and provoked those who found his ubiquitous sermons intrusive. Even within the former category, there were few who did not feel that *Tim I*, as it came to be called, would greatly benefit from severe cutting. Victor gave the proofs to some of his intimates in March 1952 and assured them that all criticism was welcome. Canon Charles Raven, with whom he had become very friendly, made some suggestions (largely ignored) for excisions, but was so fulsome about the religious parts as to cause no offence. John Strachey was consulted on the long disquisition on socialism (he appears in the book in the guise of the materialist socialist, Stephen Appleby-Smythe, who argues against Victor's religio-humanistic socialism) but seems to have made no unacceptable stylistic criticism. Rubinstein and Hodges liked and applauded the volume as a whole. The Collinses, however, were disappointed in it and made a serious error of judgement: unaware of Victor's hypersensitivity, they took him at his word and criticized the book frankly, recommending substantial cuts and alterations. He was desperately wounded. As his dearest friends among married couples, and highly religious people to boot, they were expected to *understand* the book, but had failed to grasp — among its other merits — what Victor now firmly believed to be the symphonic construction of the *opus*.

The Collinses persevered in the climb back to Victor's favour and were forgiven after a few months: Victor needed them as much if not more than they needed him. In any case, once reactions to the advance copies started to arrive in August, Victor could afford to be magnanimous to his misguided friends. Edith Sitwell's was one of the first, and expressed her deep gratitude to him for 'this great record of one of the only great living spirits'. No one else quite attained her heights of ecstasy, but there were plenty of enthusiastic letters that yielded excellent quotes for publicity purposes. Unfortunately the main body of reviews bore out the truth of the Collinses' criticisms. Some critics were delighted, but for the most part, the book was judged absorbing — even compelling — in parts, while undisciplined and self-indulgent overall. Nor were many entirely enamoured of the man who emerged from the book, for what Victor had achieved was a vivid if limited portrait of himself at fifty-nine.

The review most full of insights was that of Leslie Paul, who had been unsparing in his praise of *A Year of Grace*. His long broadcast on the BBC European Service demonstrated the impact Victor could make on a reader who knew of him mainly by repute and had to form a personal judgement on the basis of *Tim I*. Paul described him to his listeners as 'the man upon whom rests much of the responsibility for bringing the middle classes over to the Labour side' before 1945, and went on to give an account of Victor's childhood and the atavistic horrors that remained with him still.

> They explain I think the violence of his temperament, about which he is so unsparingly candid. He is pulled from the old orthodoxy to new doctrines with the fanaticism of a man who fears they may be torn from him and wishes to make that impossible. . . . He is a man whose home is nowhere and in this is a symbol of his age: pulled towards the Christian church, he overwhelms it with criticisms and reproaches; intractable in his socialism, he regards the Party he is going to put into power with lukewarmness and distaste; hating capitalism he becomes a successful capitalist of the kind who spends his leisure time easing his bad conscience by denouncing the profit-making motive. In fact, contradiction is the essence of his life, and his compromises become as ritualistic as the tabus he has broken with . . .

Paul regretted the paucity of pictures of other people and the 'long harangues on Jewish orthodoxy, vegetarianism, psycho-analysis, and socialism.' He saw it as a letter to God, in which Victor revealed himself as a man of wrath in the style of an Old Testament prophet. Victor's doctrine of human goodness, Paul believed, relied on 'philosophical commonplaces' of pre-war Oxford, and he rejected his passionate Utopianism.

> Of course, the extravagance is the man. Victor Gollancz reacts to everything with the same passion which carried him night after night to the opera as a boy. What he feels he must do, he will do. But his strong emotions wing him into realms where reason comes panting a long while after. Let me give a typical example. A year or so ago a man was charged with the murder of two little girls. At the end of the proceedings after his

arrest, the crowd booed him . . . But what made Victor Gollancz angry
was the booing, and in this book he includes a long, even frenzied section
in which he rails at the crowd which booed a man he describes as 'sick unto
death'. The act of booing suddenly becomes worse than the whole
criminal calendar, an act of 'unimaginable lack of charity — the greatest
vileness of them all.' Now I will not, out of charity, enter into an analysis
of the emotional folly involved in this topsy-turvy defence of a child
murderer against his booers. But I will say this — all his life Victor
Gollancz has been a booer. Not of criminals outside courts of justice, of
course, but of all those in authority in the world whenever, and it was
often, they transgressed his sense of justice or good sense. Or of the rest of
us when we sat idly by when evil was being done.

One of Victor's most generous acts had been the SEN campaign,
which 'was one long organised boo at the British government.' So
much on the side of the underdog, Victor had little charity left over for
the rest of mankind. Paul found it disarming that Victor frequently
admitted this, but saw in that too a rather frightening irresponsibility.

(There was one aspect of the book on which Paul might profitably
have brought his insight to bear: Victor had made an enormous effort
to understand, defend and make his peace with his father, who was
mainly responsible for making him into a lifelong booer at authority.
If that effort was cathartic, it refreshed rather than diminished the zeal
with which Victor lambasted figures or symbols of authority still
extant; by discharging his debt to his father, he had cleared his own
conscience, and the 'man of wrath' could return to his task untrammelled by guilt.)

It is a tribute to Victor's power and range of self-projection that his
reviewers reacted with such vehemence, while producing a great
variety of compliments and insults. However bored many of them
were with the discursive pages, almost all were fascinated by the
personality revealed. The exuberant affirmation of his individuality
was perhaps best caught by the anonymous critic in the *Listener*:

> . . . he remarks with characteristic simplicity in what may be called one of
> the many cadenzas in this enormous concerto for Universe and Solo
> Grandfather, 'Is it that I have grown so accustomed to expressing myself
> that I must express myself now about everything?' The incredulous reader
> will say that the answer is in the affirmative, and will skip much of the
> more garrulous material in the book. He will not be able to escape however
> from the final impression that here is a true and humble-minded effort to
> show how the author's personal life-story represents something which
> cannot be destroyed by the combined forces of heredity, social orthodoxy,
> public opinion, economic pressure, and the tyranny of the state. That

something is the conscious self who once having been summoned to stand before the burning bush must always conduct himself in obedience to the words that came from the heart of that mysterious fire.

Victor had expected to be attacked for his sexual frankness, though most reviewers either ignored or came out enthusiastically in favour of his candour. The only reader to focus specifically on that aspect of the book was Alfred Kinsey of the Indiana Institute for Sex Research, to whom Victor's American publisher, Max Schuster, sent a copy. 'The book, is of course, outstanding,' said Kinsey.

> It gives a fine portrayal of an obviously kind man who shows considerable wisdom in regard to many human affairs.
> It is, on the other hand, one of the best demonstrations I know of the impossibility of an individual breaking away from his Orthodoxy on matters of sex even though he intellectually decides that his Orthodox training was wrong, and believes that he has actually broken with it. His ambivalent attitude toward things like masturbation and the homosexual, provide an intelligent and penetrating insight into the impossibility of abandoning Orthodoxy after one has once been immersed in it.

Victor considered Kinsey 25 per cent right, presumably admitting the kindness, wisdom and ambivalence while disputing the contention that he remained trapped by his training. (Whatever the reasons, his attitudes on many sexual matters were perplexing. Homosexuality was his area of greatest confusion: in his writings he worried about whether it was the purest form of love or an unspiritual waste of seed; in public he happily became a member of the executive of the Homosexual Law Reform Society; privately, he usually avoided the company of known homosexuals, and confided to a friend that in thinking about their activities he was repelled by images of faeces. He published with enthusiasm Fritz Peters' *Finistère*, which he considered to be the first really good homosexual novel, but he was deeply suspicious of anything that smacked of a homosexual literary coterie.)

The Jewish press, not surprisingly, was generally hostile. Victor's confessed debt to the spiritual inspiration of Judaism was little compensation for his long animadversions on the hidebound atmosphere in which he grew up. His father was no advertisement for orthodox Judaism, yet the most telling sections of *Tim I* use him as an Aunt Sally, and Victor's dwelling on the absurdities and illogicalities of the faith was made more offensive by his long paeans to Christ. To a gentile reader, Victor's had been a struggle towards freedom and away from pointless and anachronistic practices. To a Jewish reader, his had been a blind and egotistical reaction against an atypical environment, ignorantly rejecting most of the virtues of the religion in which he had been brought up. He had failed on his mission for syncretism, but stopped his ears against anyone who reminded him of that. One young Jewish refugee, orphaned by the Nazis, wrote to offer some constructive criticisms and thus provoked a blisteringly offensive reply.

One of the kindest reviews in a Jewish organ — the South African *Zionist Record* — reflected sadly on Victor's indoctrination at school and university, and on the lateness of his introduction to the saintly Chassidim,★ who could have satisfied his spiritual needs. (It was a perceptive comment. Having discovered Chassidic writers while compiling *A Year of Grace*, Victor had announced to an audience of schoolboys that Chassidism was the nearest thing to an ideal religion.) Chief Rabbi Rabinowitz considered the book 'an indictment, not so much of the treachery to Judaism on the part of Victor Gollancz, but of the failure of our Jewish educational system to provide for the spiritual needs of its youth.'

Victor was deeply dissatisfied with the reviews both in Britain and America. The vicious ones did not render more palatable imperfections in the others. A deeply appreciative Church of England cleric, Jakob Jocz, wrote a long defence of the book entitled 'The Great Quest', and spoke of its author as 'an Israelite in whom there is no guile and who is nearer the kingdom of God than many who say, "Lord, Lord," but do not do the will of His Father.' He sent it to Victor with a note expressing his personal admiration and begging forgiveness if he had failed to do him justice. Victor thanked him for his generosity and understanding, but took issue on two incidental remarks: 'One of them is that I am not a great writer. Well, I don't know about great, but I am certain that I write exceptionally well — reading over my second volume this weekend I have been filled with admiration for myself. The other is about not having great political influence. Why, most people in the know . . . regard me as having had a very great deal to do with bringing the Labour party to power: and I agree with them!'

All criticism stung, but two examples hit him particularly hard. In *Tim II*, which he began to write as soon as *Tim I* went to press, he included an 'Interlude about Critics' which took issue with all those

---

★Chassidism, or Hasidism, in the eighteenth century, injected into the Jewish religion a new emphasis on the importance of piety and joyful communion with God in every human activity. The Hasidim survived the condemnation of orthodox rabbis, who objected to their pantheistic tendencies and their espousal of Kabbalistic teaching. Few Hasidic communities survived the Second World War.

who had failed to understand, and referred to two notices 'clearly intended, for some reason or other, to be offensive.' The reviewers in question were George Malcolm Thomson (to whom Victor gave the pseudonym 'Papageno') and Malcolm Muggeridge (whom he called 'X'). Thomson's hostility had occasioned another salvo of letters asking friends for quotable quotes, and indeed the review he wrote was of unmitigated harshness: ' . . . He [Victor] is earnest, greedy, voluble; has a fine gift for indignation; is unjust — and with a passion for justice. He can hardly admire a flower without seeming to patronize Nature. He is arrogant; never more so than when he is being meek. His breast-beating, his acute sense of sin, have an excessive quality. Prayers for forgiveness are thundered at Heaven.'

According to his mood in his letters, Victor was by turns entertained, indifferent and grieved when he read the Thomson piece. He had secured all his quotes by the time the review by 'X' came out in the *Daily Telegraph*, so the references in the manuscript of *Tim II* are the only evidence of how much Muggeridge had hurt him. The notice is vintage Muggeridge — uncharitable, cruel and funny. (The author's later trudge along the spiritual path adds a pleasing irony.) Headed, 'Henrietta Street Mahatma', its mockeries concluded:

> For those who have strong enough stomachs to get it down and keep it down, a perusal of *My Dear Timothy* will be rewarding. It is a compendium of all contemporary follies — as rapt as Tagore, as sincere as 'Mein Kampf' and as cultivated as the Third Programme. As a moral strip-tease artist Mr Gollancz is in the first rank; when he puts on his crown of thorns he is less impressive. Few, for instance, will partake of his anguish at the conversation he has to endure in first-class carriages. He could, after all, travel third.

Negley Farson, similarly afflicted by Muggeridge a few years earlier, had dismissed him in a letter to Victor as a 'horse's ass'. Victor tried to be more understanding. In a passage omitted from the final version of *Tim II* he wrote that 'Mr Muggeridge, who was formerly, or so I'm told, a left-winger and idealist, spits on my liberalisms, and calls them follies, because contemporary wickedness, in its impact on his passion for the good, has made him a cynic; and spits on me as a person because he cannot separate me as a person from the folly he sees in me.'

'Moral strip-tease' was the hardest to take. The published version of *Tim II* included:

> Does he really think I revelled in exposing some of the things I felt bound

to expose? Does he really think, for instance, that I found it agreeable to dilate on my boyhood sexualities? He would no doubt reply that this is just what he does think: that, in his opinion, I get a kick out of self-revelation, and that it's the very pith and marrow of my egoism. I believe him to be wrong, for I tried desperately hard to wriggle out of that particular bit of self-revelation, until I knew that I mustn't and couldn't. But suppose — for self-deception is always possible, even at times of unusual groping for integrity — suppose he's right: isn't it valuable, then, to expose a delight in self-exposure . . .

Simple conclusions about Victor seldom serve, and that passage illuminates the difficulty. He did get a kick out of self-revelation. There seemed to be no subject that so enthralled him as his own feelings, though it apparently cost him dearly to re-examine the misery that went along with masturbation. Yet, once he had written his account, he was unperturbed, even delighted, to have it read by numerous people quite unknown to him. The same goes for his groping for integrity, frequently self-deceptive as it was — and the *Tim* books contain a considerable amount of self-delusion. All that said, there was nonetheless a passionate desire throughout to be honest. Yet it was difficult for readers to care very much in the end where his apparently endless self-analysis might lead.

He dealt in similar fashion with accusations of arrogance, prolixity, indiscipline, self-indulgence and the rest. (He ignored the trivial complaint that the book lacked an index. Victor, for reasons of economy, did not approve of indexes; and in the case of his own book this dislike was compounded by his reluctance to have people dipping into it and thus destroying the symphonic construction. The wildly unchronological *Tims* put up almost impenetrable barriers to use as works of reference.) Selective as always, Victor focussed on letters from members of the public who had greatly enjoyed and taken comfort from *Tim I* when he decided against any change in format or approach for the continuation of his autobiography. *Tim II* came out just 20,000 words shorter. There were *ad hoc* digressions about later events, but as narrative the book took Victor's life story only up to 1919. He had originally intended to call it *And Also Much Cattle★*, but for selling purposes had decided on *More For Timothy*. Despite

★A quotation from the Book of Jonah. 'Then said the Lord, Thou hast had pity on the gourd, for that which thou hast not laboured, neither madest it grow; which came up in a night, and perished in a night: and should not I spare Nineveh, that great city, wherein are more than sixteen thousand persons that cannot discern between their right hand and their left hand; and also much cattle?'

anxieties and occasional writer's block, the proofs were with friends in May 1953. This time John Collins made no mistakes: 'VICTOR GOLLANCZ THE BEVERLEY NEWYORK TREMENDOUSLY EXCITED BY WHOLE BOOK CONSCIENCE SECTION MAGNIFICENT EXPRESSION CHRISTIAN GOSPEL I NOW KNOW MORE CLEARLY THAN EVER BEFORE WHAT HAPPENED LAST YEAR JOHN' and Rubinstein cabled 'TIM TWO BETTER THAN EVER AND HOW MAGNIFICENTLY ALIVE CHARITABLE HEARTENING AND COMPELLING'.

John Strachey took issue with his explanation of his current position on two closely related matters: having finished *Tim I*, in which he had justified not being a pacifist, Victor found that he had argued himself into becoming one; he also now espoused Christian communism, but was unable to live by it. Thousands of people for the rest of Victor's life were to point out that he was having the best of both worlds: Strachey put their case in a long letter in June 1953. What troubled him most was Victor's inconsistency in preaching two absolutist creeds but living by only one of them. 'In fine, oughtn't you either to be a *participant* in the worldly struggle, preaching the ideal of course, but frankly recognising the necessity of relativist sin, such as exploitation and armed resistance to sufficiently evil (mistaken!) regimes; and recognising the necessity of such sin *for yourself*, as you do now, in practice, in the case of exploitation and profit making, but do not in the case of armed resistance.' The alternative was to '"go into the wilderness"' and become 'a prophet, fakir or Rabbi' who acted out both creeds and provided a pattern of conduct which the world might strive to emulate.

Victor found the letter incomprehensible. His position was clear: 'I am already able, with the *whole* of me, to be a pacifist, but am not yet able, with the *whole* of me, to live like a Christian Communist.' He freely acknowledged the falsity of the position but knew that 'just as I wasn't a pacifist until I sufficiently *wanted* to be a pacifist, so I mustn't live like a Christian Communist until I sufficiently *want* to do so: the corollary being that, as the best part of me wants to do so, the important thing is to go on increasing one's want — and then . . . I think the thing will happen.' It was a question of defeating the weakness of the flesh in stages. He was already a pacifist, had that day become a vegetarian and hoped that Christian communism would follow. He linked his approach to the concept of 'waiting on God' (discussed in a long disquisition on Simone Weil in *Tim II*) and convinced Strachey of the religious power of his argument. They could not reach agreement on Strachey's objection to Victor acting in effect as a selective and part-time 'fakir'.

Victor edited this correspondence, presumably intending to incorporate it into *Tim III*, but *Tim II* was published without amendment. Victor struggled on as best he could with his vegetarianism and the conflict Strachey had pinpointed. (The vegetarianism lasted for some months until the food — 'watery, inflationary, pasty, regurgitatory, sawdusty stuff' — became unendurable.) The presentation copies went out in September, and though many recipients responded enthusiastically, there was this time a distinct shortage of quotable puffs. The Bishop of Chichester for instance, could say nothing publicly because of the portrayal of Geoffrey Fisher in the Repton chapters. Gilbert Murray was noticeably general in his remarks. Richard Acland had been persuaded to release his encomium of *Tim I* for publicity purposes and took care to avoid it this time — and many more of Victor's famous friends also hid behind careful phrasing. The novelty of the first volume had worn off. The Repton chapters were gripping, the tracts indigestible, and the topical commentary intrusive and often annoying. One of Victor's authors, Morchard Bishop, greatly daring, ventured some good advice. He feared that the ideas in the *Tims* were in danger of being 'strangled' by the manner in which they were presented, and cited as an example Victor's assertion that 'It's life that I'm after, not art.' Did that mean anything? 'Do you think that Beethoven would have made such an observation? Art, as far as I can see, is nothing but the presentation of what one has to say in the best manner possible. Life is what we live, and a book can no more be 'life' than it can be an elephant. And again, it is begging the whole question to say as you do in the next paragraph — that your book is really like a concerto: for books are one thing, concertos another.' Could Victor not siphon off into pamphlet or article form those topical comments designed to have immediate influence? 'A book with as much thought in it as yours ought to be readable by posterity.'

Victor disagreed courteously:

Far be it from me even to whisper the sacred name of Beethoven side by side with my own, even when alone in the most remote corner of my own house. But as *you* have mentioned it, I would remind you that Beethoven's last quartets were considered, in his day, so completely to break every rule of musical form that it was decades before they began to be understood, or even seriously considered, by the mass of 'musical' people — who said 'All very wonderful, perhaps, but not music.' And didn't *Ulysses* break every literary rule? Liddell Hart, as a matter of fact, has described my book 'as a sort of *Ulysses* written in good English'!!

He particularly defended his digressions on Craig and Bentley★ during the Repton chapters, which had been found 'poignant and spiritually effective' by 'quite "ordinary" people'. Uninterested in literary fame or posterity, he cared only about '"doing something about it" in a world plunging into disaster'. The high sales for both *Tims* had come about because 'I have managed to get something *living* across to people'.

Bishop had been tactful. Another author — the Irish poet Monk Gibbon, whom Victor liked, whose work he admired, and who had been wildly enthusiastic about *Tim I* — was more blunt. Knowing Victor only slightly, he wrote frankly that while the book had many virtues, it was 'cruelly, almost outrageously discursive.' Their immensely long correspondence centred round Victor's determination to prove that Gibbon was attacking him because of some personal grievance while Gibbon begged him to 'take a further step towards sanctity and kill out your own hypersensitiveness.' Victor explained that on the contrary, he was 'rather unusually insensitive' to criticism. Rejecting every one of Gibbon's detailed points, Victor announced his conviction that Gibbon was motivated by 'a subconscious reaction to my failure to write to you about the books you were so good enough to send me.' For that lapse he apologized — it came from overwork. Gibbon ended the correspondence rather dazed, but with his dignity intact and Victor's wrath defused.

Although his actions were instinctive rather than strategic, Victor succeeded in picking off his private critics one by one and ensuring that they would never again offend. He blasted them into silence, invoked intelligent and honourable intimates to undermine their confidence in their own judgement, and played on their guilt at having hurt a man they so admired. Those who loved him dared not criticize at all profoundly; those that did so criticize were enemies. The anonymous (and Victor loathed anonymity in reviewing) *Times Literary Supplement* critic was adjudged anti-semitic because he found Victor unEnglish in his lack of reticence; the *Observer* critic, Christopher Sykes, could be disregarded because he was 'an extremely dogmatic Roman Catholic'; the vast majority were a product of their cynical times and Victor had erected a shield against anything they

★In 1953 Christopher Craig shot a policeman when in the company of Derek Bentley on a house-breaking expedition. Craig was sixteen, Bentley nineteen. Bentley was hanged. Many pages in *Tim II* are given over to Victor's horrified response to the way in which the judicial process operated. In the course of his savaging of Lord Goddard (the Lord Chief Justice and a judge noted for his harshness) Victor was only slightly put off his stroke by Sheila Hodges' reminder that Goddard too was a product of his environment.

might say. As he had explained to a novelist in July, reviewing was mainly 'in the hands either of boys in their early twenties, with little or no experience of life — or, for that matter, of literature — or of homosexuals; and often of people who are both. The result is that anything of sanity and solid intellectual power tends to be over-looked or even sneered at, in favour of nasty little cynical work.' *Tim I* had sold well 'in spite of the fact that the young, so-called intellectuals either ignored it or sneered at it (the balance was restored by enthusiasm from the old, and real intellectuals, but unfortunately they never review novels) . . . '

Unable to bring the hydra to heel, he had to content himself with lopping off the occasional reviewer's head when the opportunity presented itself. No target was too obscure. A Karachi paper was ticked off for reprinting a knocking review of *Tim II* from the *Evening Standard* — 'an obviously, and even excessively, pagan newspaper.'

Hypersensitive or not to what was said about him, Victor troubled himself little about others' feelings when he had a point to illustrate, and real characters, living and dead, frequently appear in an unkind light in the *Tims*. Most chose to ignore the comments, but he met occasional remonstrances. Canon Prestige of St Paul's demurred at an attack on him (anonymous, but as one of only four canons, easily identifiable) in *Tim I*. Victor assured him that he had merely quoted what Prestige's colleague, John Collins, had passed on to him. Margaret Cole disputed his statement in *Tim II* that Amyas Ross had died of self-neglect, when he had in fact died of sudden pneumonia. Victor, who had seen almost nothing of Ross for years, stoutly defended his interpretation against her, Ross's close friend. The acquaintance who wrote in defence of the Red Dean, cruelly and very cleverly lampooned in one of Victor's more amusing digres-sions, was dismissed. The Dean himself (who after all had been a protégé of Victor's initially and who had maintained his charity to his mentor along with his loyalty to the CP) made no protest, although he must surely have been hurt. Geoffrey Fisher could not answer back. Worst of all was the report of a conversation with David Low, a friend of over twenty years' standing; it concerned General Templer's reprisals in Malaya, and Low, said Victor, had played 'Hitler's ace, Stalin's ace, the Devil's ace. Namely: means, however appalling, may possibly — he didn't go further than that, but may possibly — be justified by the end, if the end is important enough.' It was all placed in the context of Low's great virtues, but the man himself was less than enchanted.

17 September 1953

Dear Victor,

Very many thanks for the advance copy. It seems to be a good job, many illuminating pieces, much enjoyment and reflection. I am sure it will have great success.

I am honoured to be mirrored in your gallery. I have taken people apart in picture so often myself, that I am puzzled to find how provocative your slight analysis of me can be. How is it that I, who am never moved to answer back to openly hostile thrusts, must now find time to point out two crumpled roseleaves in the bed of fragrant adjectives you have set me in? But you do me wrong. This is a time for candour between friends.

First: I am not so compromising as all that. If I seem to be so to you, it is because I am moved to be so in your company, my dear fellow, and to find good in the other chap's case, because you have become terribly downright and sweeping in your judgements of late years (despite your protestations otherwise).

Second: I remember very well that dinner. There was a lot of cross-talk and sometimes it was difficult to get out more than a sentence. I was making the point that we should not condemn Templer on the strength of 'hot' words, but wait for the facts. I said that whatever Templer had done it seemed to have been effective against the so-called 'bandits'. A pertinent and permissible remark, however much one might deplore the means. Upon this, you turned away while I was still speaking and began your conversation with Mrs Collins. Now either the tentative exchanges of the dinner table should not be taken as declarations of positive belief, or one should howl down one's host and insist on completing one's remarks, clearing up all the implications. In this case I might have concluded by saying that I was not in favour of frying villagers, even if it meant the saving of Civilization, but I thought everybody knew that.

I saw you jumping to your wrong conclusion and when we parted I said to Madeline: 'Victor should not have cut me off like that. I didn't make sense . . . ' Now in your book you send me down to Posterity, in the nicest way, but decorated with revolting words like Lidice★ as a weak-kneed waverer, in the company of Hitler, Mussolini, Stalin etc. . . . Well, it's all experience.

Yours ever,
David

PS This is friendly, of course.

21 September 1953

My dear old David,

I am terribly, terribly sorry that you have been a wee bit hurt, though you tell me so as gently and friendlily as anybody could.

When I wrote the thing, it didn't occur to me for a single second that it

★The Czechoslovakian village liquidated in reprisal for the assassination of the Nazi Heydrich in 1942.

might hurt you. The thought *did* occur to me when the proofs arrived: so I showed it to four people who know you very well, and they all thought that there was nothing at all in my scruple. One of them was Ruth, who is exceedingly sensitive to this sort of thing. She said you could not possibly be hurt by a little bit of friendly ragging, in the course of which I ragged myself far more than I ragged you! After all, I called myself a fanatic.

I am exceedingly sorry if I actually misunderstood what you said: but, although we can never recognise ourselves in other people's pictures of us (I certainly never recognise myself in other people's pictures of me), I had thought that, by and large, I had got you not too inaccurately.

However, I shall take the opportunity in Tim III of a) correcting my view of your views 'for the record'; and, b) of applying a little balm in the process.

Do please forgive me.

> Yours affectionately,
> Victor

PS One thought appals me. I don't feel a bit critical really about you, but I feel immensely critical about Rebecca [West, whose *The Meaning of Treason* he had criticized]: and if you feel a little hurt with me, God knows what she will feel.

Incidentally: if I make amends in *Tim III* for my misreading of your views, you ought to make amends, some time or other, for your misreading of my physiognomy, some time back in 1936!!! To say nothing of the little devil you portrayed on the title page of that book you did with Kingsley about Russia. (I hasten to add — I didn't mind a bit: but I don't think it was like me!)

> 24 September 1953

My dear Victor,

OK — We will regard it as quits for the drawing I did of you. But I wasn't 'hurt'. I was just *telling* you — putting you right, since you were an old friend. It isn't a public matter to me so you don't need to put anything about it in the next volume, unless you feel it would be good for the book.

> Yours ever,   Love to Ruth,
> David.

That Victor could not see the difference between drawing an affectionate cartoon of a friend and traducing his views on morality was perhaps not a surprise to Low. Like so many others, he found it easier to let the matter drop. (Victor made handsome amends at Low's memorial service in 1963: his moving description of his friend included an accurate account of his argument at the dinner party.)

Victor could not long maintain his optimism about the public reaction to *Tim II*. Despite his efforts, it sold half as many as *Tim I* and it did not appear in America. Indeed Victor's activities as an author were something of an embarrassment in the relationship between Gollancz and certain American publishers. *A Year of Grace* had been published by Houghton Mifflin under the title *Man and God*. Victor had helped as much as he could by sending over a stream of puffs and reviews, and was delighted when the book was made a Book of the Month Club Choice, with 195,000 copies taken up. He was much less happy that Houghton Mifflin could sell only about 5,000. He wrote to complain of inadequate advertising and was told that they had already spent double their normal allocation. Putting the failure down to poor publishing methods, he switched to Simon & Schuster for *Tim I*. To the great embarrassment of Max Schuster, who was truly fond of Victor and admiring of his book, even an immense advertising campaign (based on a quote from an English review that *Tim I* was 'a confession as reckless as Rousseau's') sold only 1,412 copies in the seven months after its publication in January 1953. American reviews were poor, and Victor had neither a mighty reputation nor strings to pull on the far side of the Atlantic.

Simon & Schuster were under contract to publish *Tim II*, but Victor felt that his pacifist objections to American conduct in Korea (it was the use of napalm that finally converted him) would infuriate American opinion, among reading public and critics alike. On balance, he concluded, the book should not be published in America 'at any rate for the time being'. One of these days, he might 'write something specially slanted on America!'

DEAR VICTOR YOUR LETTER NOVEMBER TWENTY-FOURTH NOT RECEIVED UNTIL FIFTEEN DAYS LATER STOP WE HONESTLY MOST AFFECTIONATELY AND DEVOTEDLY BELIEVE IT WOULD BE TO YOUR BEST INTERESTS AS WELL AS OURS TO CHANGE FROM TIMOTHY SCHEDULE TO SOMETHING ESPECIALLY SLANTED ON AMERICA AS YOU YOURSELF SUGGEST STOP THEREFORE WRITING YOU ABOUT PROPOSED BOOK ON JOYS OF CREATIVE LISTENING TO GREAT MUSIC OR TRAVEL IMPRESSIONS OF AMERICA ESPECIALLY NEW YORK STOP LOVE SEMPRE MAX.

16 December 1953

My dear Max,

TIMOTHY

Many thanks for your cable, with its sigh of relief! But you misunderstood me about a possible book 'especially slanted on America'. I haven't the faintest intention of writing a book on the joys of creative listening to great music or on travel impressions of America — nor indeed of writing anything unless and until I feel compelled to do so. What I meant was, when I have finished Timothy for British consumption I may, if I feel moved, deal, in a manner specially slanted for consumption in America, with some of the topics covered in Tim II and forthcoming Tims — pacifism, capital punishment, etc., etc. The point is that I have something that I regard it as exceedingly important to say, and I seem to be able to say it in a way that a big British public, but a minute American one, understands. So I must try, one of these days — but very much one of these days — to say it in a manner that a decent sized American public will understand.

Yours ever,
Victor

Simon & Schuster had failed with *Tim I*, of course, precisely because of the disquisitions. Like the majority of Victor's public at home, Americans were potentially interested in Victor's reminiscences about politics and publishing rather than his abstract opinions on topical issues. Perversely, of course, he was less and less inclined to give people what they wanted. Already he was envisaging that *Last Words for Timothy* (*Tim III*) would be followed by *Postscript*. (It was Sheila Lynd, whose fate — as 'Mary Joyce' — he had regretted in *Tim II*, who suggested to Betty Reid — now Lewis — that there should be a volume entitled *Are You Still Listening, Timothy?*)

Livia was later to salvage for the posthumous *Reminiscences of Affection* the few thousand publishable words of *Tim III*. In them, he described his and Ruth's courtship and marriage. Determined to be as frank about married life and the sexual relationship as he had been about everything else, he concluded this section by stating that

> The argument must turn on monogamy.
> Do I 'believe in' it?
> Yes, after my own fashion.

Adultery was a difficult area. He called on theologians of all persuasions to rule on their churches' views, and Christ's in particular. The answers came out confused, inconclusive or unacceptable. Neither his advisers, his theological reading nor his close study of the gospels could furnish the confirmation he needed to condone extra-marital sexual adventure. He spent many thousands of words on inner argument, lurching more than somewhat as he sought a justification for two periods of infidelity to Ruth. The first was the love affair before his nervous breakdown. The second was current. From the mid-1940s, and sporadically until his stroke years later, he had a sexual relationship with a woman he loved and admired. Ruth, though privately hurt, had again given her permission; but no more than with the earlier affair could Victor avoid guilt. The first affair he managed initially to justify and he made the case in the manuscript of *Tim III* by putting words into the mouth of an imaginary interlocutor. (He had just proved to his own dismay that perfection in God's eyes lay in the exclusive unity of one man and one woman.)

'Take', you may say, 'an extreme combination of circumstances. Imagine A and B happily married, intensely happily married; imagine their love unimpaired, even constantly increasing: imagine B, for a period, as no longer desiring physical intercourse: imagine the period, in both their opinions, as likely to be permanent: imagine A physically vital, and wanting, for spiritual as well as physical reasons, to give himself sexually — let us say to C, who reciprocates and will be, not at all damaged, but much enriched, by the experience: imagine him certain, and correctly certain, that his marriage with B will nohow be thereby impaired: imagine him fearing, on the other hand, that abstinence will fret his nerves and run the risk of impairing it: imagine B as equally certain and equally anxious: imagine her as devoid of all sexual jealousy: imagine her, even as gaining a new happiness because she is adding to A's and imagine A as loving her the more because she is doing so — are you telling me that A ought to refrain?

Even with this version of events, Victor failed to persuade himself that his first affair was vindicated: this boded ill for his second, for by the early 1950s Ruth was beyond the menopause and no longer had to restrict intercourse. He was going on with the second affair because he enjoyed it, not because he needed physical release.

In the *Tim III* manuscript, Victor strove erratically to legitimize his own conduct, trying to read between Christ's lines, regretting that man was not equipped, like some variant on a Hindu god, to have simultaneous physical union with two or more women and so promote an even higher form of unity. He could not escape the conviction that the relationship with 'B' suffered if 'A's' congress with another woman perforce excluded her. Equally worrying was his fear that, should he manage to find a way of exonerating himself, he might have a corrupting effect — especially on the young. Finally, the book foundered on an historical investigation of the nature of the marriage contract. Embroiled in an analysis of the Married Women's Property Act of 1882, he copied out many pages of a book on finance. *Tim III* ground to a halt.

Victor's virtues and vices in synthesis brought his autobiography to a premature end: he blamed the *impasse* of sex and marriage for the non-appearance of the book, but he could never have successfully written what the reading public wanted. In describing his early years he could eschew documentation and rely on memory. For the Repton episode he had enormous help (inadequately acknowledged) from David Somervell's unpublished account. Had he once embarked on publishing and politics, he would have found it hard to avoid research among his own papers at least, and that would have forced him to face unpalatable truths about a past he had sanitized. The carefully-preserved balance of his self-image was, if anything, more threatened by his own past writings than by contemporary commentators. For years he claimed (and probably convinced himself) that there were no papers in his files that had any bearing on the Left Book Club period: his blanket assertion that everything had been destroyed sent many an historian away desolate. He was unhelpful even to researchers who wanted to look at straightforward publishing files, assuring them that there was no relevant material in them. Primarily, this was because he did not want staff time wasted and hated the idea that papers might get messed up. But there was also in him a general nervousness that somewhere, some omission or commission might come to light. He denied a friend of his beloved Rupert Hart-Davis access to papers on the Frank Harris biography of Shaw on the grounds that they were 'hideously confidential' — years after the deaths of both protagonists; he can only have been loth to have his own past scrutinized by others. Of course, he could have laundered the documents, but he would probably have thought that as wrong as it was difficult. He would never have taken on the drudgery of going through his papers himself, and it was hardly a job he could delegate. He did not worry about what might happen after his death. As he had explained to Morchard Bishop, he cared little about posterity's view of him; and he was much too busy with living life to the full. 'I wish I could have been alive from the beginning of time, and could live for ever!' he wrote in *Tim I*.

> Only once, for some months in 1943, have I had any sympathy with Wandering Jews and Flying Dutchmen and suchlike, and their stupid peripateticism in search of a pure woman's love that might save them from the burden of living. I should like to have been an aristocrat at the time of the French Revolution, and also a revolutionary leader: I should like to have been Max or Anatol in Schnitzler's Vienna: I should like to have been Gandhi: I should like to be Schweitzer: I should like, most of all, to be the man who will come at the end of the long human story, even if the second law of thermo-dynamics is applicable to the spiritual as well as to the physical world, as I do not believe, and even if there will be a last man, with nothing but a featureless waste to follow him!

Most of what he read from choice — except detective stories and some fiction by old favourites — interested him only for its bearing on the present. History was studied for its lessons; philosophy, metaphysics and theology as aids in determining how men should live to make the world a better place. When he spoke of the future, it included him. He had decided to live to well over a hundred and had no fears of satiation. He was anxious to do all he could to ensure that there would be a posterity, but was unhappy at the idea of a future without himself in it.

Having failed with *Tim III*, Victor had to find some other means of spreading his word. (He had a few years earlier tinkered with an *Everyman's Prayer Book*, but the *Tims* had pushed the project aside.) *Tim III*, started in April 1953, was shelved the next winter, and Victor had to face the fact that it would never work as a vehicle for what he now felt to be the most pressing of the autobiographical issues — the 1943 breakdown and the manner of his recovery from it, touched on only briefly in *Tim II*. He felt deep compassion for anyone who had suffered a hell akin to his own, and was eager to offer hope.

His solution was to compile *From Darkness to Light: a Confession of Faith in the Form of an Anthology*. That intention was clearly in his mind in June 1954 when Megaw asked him to commission *The New Bedside Book*. Megaw, now an octogenarian, had been begging Victor for some years to reissue his *Bedside Book* in its complete form, and had been assured that economics would fix the price impracticably at a guinea. He was advised to try Eyre & Spottiswoode for a commission for its successor. 'As you know, even the best anthologies (except apparently mine!) have long since been a drug on the market: but, I suppose about every five years or so, one suddenly comes along which, by reason of its particular character, and probably of all sorts of adventitious circumstances, captures the imagination of the critics and public. This happened in my own case.'

A Year of Grace had been published in 1950 and Victor set out to produce *From Darkness to Light* at high speed. The extracts came from almost 400 authors, some of them old favourites, some recommended to Victor in letters discussing *lacunae* in *A Year of Grace*, and some discovered through his normal reading programme, which encompassed an ever-widening spectrum of writers about the spirit. 'I am enjoying the reading for it quite enormously,' he wrote to du Maurier in December. 'Apart from ordinary times for reading, I read every morning, in the quiet, from 4 a.m. till about 6.30.' Early morning reading, he told Diana Collins, was 'an ecstasy of joy and praise'.

The new anthology was a compilation even more personal than its predecessor; though it addressed itself to those suffering any kind of darkness of soul, it concentrated particularly on the kind of despair he had experienced. Blake and Coleridge were the best represented, run a close third by Victor himself. There were prayers, too. Quite apart from the labour of selection, the mechanics of typing and securing copyright clearance made Victor's determination to go to press in July

1955 a nightmare for those around him. He met his self-imposed deadline by his usual obsessive methods. He even excused himself at the last moment from attending the wedding of his nephew Michael Rubinstein — that tower of strength in the early days of the JSHS — by pleading the urgency of work on the anthology.

The four and a half years between commencement of *Tim I* and completion of this second anthology had been emotionally dominated by the demands of authorship, crammed by the pressure of publishing work into the very early mornings and the weekends. It was a tough time for a publisher, especially one with Victor's resistance to change. At one time or another he complained bitterly in conversation, letters or even speeches, about aspects of his trade that distressed him. These included inflationary price rises, long production delays, greedy and illiberal trade unions, paperbacks, stupid and insensitive reviewers, the vulgar public taste, occasional disloyal and incompetent members of staff, uncultured booksellers, the heavy editing popularized in America by Maxwell Perkins, the impudence of agents and the idiocy of authors who expected to live by writing instead of combining it with full-time jobs. All these annoyances he saw as manifestations of the intellectual and irreligious spirit of the times, against which he battled with his own books and the unprofitable sections of Gollancz's list.

Consideration of all those resentments, and of the counterproductive squabbles with authors, agents and American publishers caused by Victor's arrogance, obstinacy, inconsistency and hypersensitivity, might easily suggest that early retirement would have benefited firm and chairman both. In fact the irritations barely tarnished the joys that publishing offered him, and only very disgruntled staff and authors would have wished him gone. He remained the most interesting figure on the publishing scene, and could still launch bestsellers better than anyone else when he so chose. Under Victor's guiding hand the house of Gollancz showed, in the early 1950s, the form of twenty years earlier in a long run of successes — from British and American sources — that included Edna Ferber's *Giant*, Guareschi's Don Camillo stories (which Victor adored) and Amis's *Lucky Jim* (which he admired). The list was long and filled with young talent; even Victor's gloomy prognostications could not disguise the fact of the firm's prosperity. The financial results announced in April 1954 were so impressive that Victor, on a whim, awarded extra bonuses among his staff. His lamentations about the desperate state of the publishing trade were often useful, persuading authors to take smaller advances or reduced royalties. Not everyone was convinced, though few were brave enough to argue with him. His old adversary A. J. Cronin maddened Victor year after year by ridiculing his pessimism and standing firm on financial matters, even to the point of insisting on a continuation of the very high royalties he had received in the era before production costs made them crippling for all publishers. Given ammunition by a visit to the new Gollancz flat in Eaton Place, Cronin wrote in June 1955:

> Dear Victor,
>   I have your letter of 27th May with its pathetic enclosures, which make my heart bleed for the book trade in Britain and for all those poor publishers who have Modiglianis in their West End apartments and are forced to sustain life at the Caprice and the Mirabelle. Are things really so bad with you, my good friend? It seems that every other month I have a communication from you which virtually implores me to accept a reduced royalty on one or other of my books . . . Should the breadline threaten, don't forget that I want to buy the Modigliani . . .

Victor responded tartly: it was not 'a question of whether I possess a Modigliani — no more than there is a question, when I am discussing royalties with you, of your possessing oil wells!'

> My dear VG,
> Pax vobiscum.
> Ever,
> AJ
> PS I will swap an oilwell for the Modigliani.

> MY DEAR AJ EYE WOULD INFINITELY PREFER MANUSCRIPT TO OILWELL BUT FEAR COULD NOT TRADE MODIGLIANI EVEN FOR THAT LOVE VICTOR

The good old easy days were over: Victor could no longer rely on having a small string of authors certain to deliver a bestseller every year. Du Maurier and Cronin were still money-spinners, but reader-loyalty counted for less, and Victor had no one in his stable whose sales could be guaranteed far into the future. More and more, best-sellers had to be created. He had responded correctly by massively widening his list and hedging his bets, but it was a time-consuming and stress-inducing process. A three-week trip to the States in the autumn of 1951 wore him out and he judged it intolerable. The next year he was away for six weeks and returned complaining of exhaustion and a long attack of pseudo-angina. In 1954 he fell ill there and came home with shingles. Such warning signs never persuaded Victor to slow down. He raced from one obsession to another, complaining loudly all the way of overwork and myriad painful or debilitating — but always very brief — illnesses. One of the few people prepared to point out to him that his troubles were of his own making was Edna Ferber. From New York she wrote in June 1953 to Ruth, that it was 'more baffling than I can convey to you to have failed to see you and Victor before you sailed . . . I wish that your visit here had not been quite so feverish. One hears quite a lot about the mad pace of the American business and professional man. But I know no one here who carries on in the fashion of Victor Gollancz in New York.' She regretted that Victor had 'not seen fit to read her autobiography: I tell you frankly that I resent, as writer to publisher, the reason for his not having had time to read it. Your letter says "Victor is very busy at work on his own proofs." The first duty of a publisher is toward his writers, not toward the proofs of his own writing.'

Neglect was felt most keenly by Victor's contemporaries. Younger authors were more inclined to take him on his own terms. They were curious to meet the famous man and flattered by his attentions. For many, lunch with him was a memorable experience, and they were perfectly happy otherwise to deal with one of his subordinates. They can have had little idea of the complicated relationships behind the scenes. The problem, as ever, concerned the senior staff. The women fared better than the men. Though Dorothy Horsman refused to flatter him, and they often fought, Victor respected her competence and she posed no threat. Sheila Hodges and the succession of superior secretaries knew how to prop up his ego, defuse his anger and mother or flirt with him as required. (One secretary boldly insisted on an explanation of a days-long sulky silence: he had been cut to the quick by her failure to replenish the stock of Fry's Chocolate Cream Bars she kept, by unspoken agreement, in her desk drawer, and which he raided from time to time in her absence. Profuse apologies resolved the crisis.)

While Hodges was unchallenged as No. 2, the senior men were protected to a considerable extent from Victor's jealousy. However, in 1953, the strain of seventeen years of overwork and emotional demands convinced her that she had to get out. Her pregnancy in the summer offered an excellent pretext, but she suffered an early miscarriage. After recuperating in Switzerland she returned healthy but resolved to leave. To Victor, who had been telling authors she was his 'alter ego', her intention spelled nothing less than treachery. Paroxysms of rage proved ineffectual, so he froze her out of his life.

She abandoned ship formally in January 1954. Victor, either unwilling to accept the permanence of the departure or determined that no one should know about it, maintained in public that she had gone on indefinite sick-leave. She soon became pregnant again, and the matter was settled. For months Victor would have nothing to do with her, but ultimately his need for her editing skills overcame his petulance and she began to do part-time work for the firm. By 1955 she was again a friend, forgiven her grievous disloyalty, and in time she was restored to the pantheon of those he loved. He was affectionate and generous to her daughter, Clarissa, as he was to many of the children of his friends.

For her husband, the sales director and company secretary, John Bush, it was a difficult period, for he was guilty by association. He survived it because, like his wife, he deeply admired Victor's virtues, and because his temperament was equal to the challenge. Besides, his job kept him free from the worst kind of interference: Victor rarely saw non-editorial people as possible successors, so Bush was spared at least some humiliation.

For Hilary Rubinstein, a director since 1952 and now Victor's deputy, Hodges' departure might have been good news in career terms. Victor was intending to retire in 1958, when he was 65, and Rubinstein seemed a natural successor. When he had joined the firm in 1950, straight from university, his relations with his uncle had been good. Victor had been well-disposed towards all the Rubinstein children throughout their childhood and when Hilary was at Oxford he and Victor occasionally used to meet, correspond and swap books on philosophy. In his first three years with the firm he benefited to an extent he could not have realized from Hodges' presence. He enjoyed publishing — particularly contact with authors — and never having worked anywhere else, he was more accepting of the peculiarities of Henrietta Street than those with outside experience proved to be.

Once Hodges had left, Rubinstein became the focus of Victor's jealousy. His first move was secretly to invite a friend of long standing, Jim Rose (ex-literary editor of the *Observer* and now Director of the International Press Institute in Zurich) to join the firm as his deputy. For a time Rose, beset with internal political troubles, played with the idea, but in May 1954 he turned it down. In the same month Livia joined Bush, Horsman, Rubinstein, Strawson and her parents on the board. She had started work in the firm the previous year, having given up music mainly because her teeth had suffered from constant playing. At a critical moment in 1953, as she was despairing of seeing through an ambition to study medicine, she ran into her father and he offered her a job. Her first task was to type labels for parcels of review copies, but she quickly graduated to designing jackets and advertisements and displayed a flair for typography. Still, she was much too junior to be a contender for Rubinstein's position, and he was temporarily secure.

From then on there were long periods when Rubinstein could do almost nothing right. If he made errors he was a contemptible fool; if, through his excellent contacts, he brought valuable acquisitions to the list, he posed a threat to Victor's supremacy and had to be cut down to size. It was Rubinstein who wrote to his acquaintance Kingsley Amis to suggest he send Gollancz his first novel. Victor went to town on the promotion of *Lucky Jim* and greatly appreciated the money and prestige that accrued from this brilliant new discovery, but he could not forgive his nephew for deserving the primary credit. He took over dealings with Amis, just as he muscled in on any author of Rubinstein's who brought lustre to the firm. Nadine Gordimer was a particularly sore point. As a close friend of Rubinstein's she preferred to deal with him, and the Gordimer files are full of episodes arising from Victor's interference between them.

Many authors were unaware of the less healthy aspects of Victor's interest in them, and were flattered by his attentions: Amis was one who became fond of him and was amused by his patronizing references to 'you new young chaps', and he was not even bothered by the realization that Victor did not really like his books. Those who were exposed to ugly manifestations of Victor's envy of Rubinstein reacted with hostility. Godfrey Smith had perhaps the worst experience. An Oxford friend of Rubinstein's, he published his first novel with Gollancz and they were both taken out to lunch by Victor. Humiliation was the order of the day: Rubinstein was refused the food he wanted — steak, kidney and oyster pie — and Victor at the end of the meal bought cigars only for Smith and himself, possibly to punish, like a surrogate father, his nephew's temerity in flouting the prejudices of his uncle's ancestral stomach. So ended Smith's association with the firm.

Rubinstein would never have laid claim to Victor's dazzling gifts as a publisher, but he had many talents — not least the ability to get on well with authors — that equipped him to be an invaluable deputy. Victor saw things differently. In April 1955 he hired a bright young man, John Rosenberg, as an editor, and the appointment was to be the overture to a power-struggle in Gollancz that continued for twelve years.

One of the most distressing aspects of Victor's frequently tyrannical behaviour as head of the firm was that the people he persecuted or exploited were all admirers of his ability, his achievements and the values for which he stood. If they could not accompany him all the way along the path to Christian communism or pacifism, they had no difficulty in agreeing with the line he had taken on the Germans or the Arabs, or his stance against capital punishment and other social evils. Recognizing that they were unlikely ever to meet a greater man, and certain that in public life he was a force for good, they steeled themselves against the excesses of his egotism. All cultured and intelligent people, they would remind themselves of the personal deficiencies of Churchill, Picasso and Tolstoy, and that Victor was typical of his kind in making his intimates suffer while he did good work for the masses. They swallowed their pride and their anger and soldiered on in Victor's service. If his demands became too much, they could always leave.

As with his colleagues, so with his friends. Of course, none of them was exposed to the treatment meted out to employees, but as Victor's vanity grew, they were constantly having to decide where to yield and where to assert their independence. Harold Rubinstein had long ago settled for acolyte status: Rose Macaulay played it the other way. She would not compromise her literary judgement by uncritical adulation of his published work, and must have greatly offended in 1955 when she refused on principle to allow him to quote her for publicity purposes on *From Darkness to Light*. She died in 1958, their friendship but a shadow of what it had been in the 1930s and '40s. The people who stayed or became close friends with Victor from the early 1950s onwards had a great deal in common. All people of high integrity, they yet accepted the necessity of minor concessions to truth and dignity. It was no great hardship to have to overpraise his books when they approved of a large part of their message. They wriggled with embarrassment sometimes at the blatant demands for puffs or the fixing of reviews, as Acland had over the *Tims*. John Collins abandoned all scruples about such a relatively unimportant matter. He stoutly maintained his independence as Chairman of Christian Action and frequently ignored Victor's advice: in return he lent his name when it was required. (One story that caused hilarity among Victor's subordinates arose from his demand for a Collins quote in praise of *Don Camillo*. Collins, who liked the book, was agreeable. Victor instructed him orally to approve 'Millions will love it'. Mishearing him, Collins said in some desperation: 'I'll say anything you like, Victor. But why Indians?')

Victor's close friends shared two other important characteristics: humility and a sense of humour. Acland, for instance, truly believed Victor to be a far better man than he was himself — and indeed, with his instinct for good, to be the only saint he knew. Yet he could take huge delight from an exchange like this:

Acland: Of course, some people want only fame and popularity.
Victor: Really? Is that so? I am just the opposite.

Some were to wonder later if they were partially responsible for the deterioration in aspects of Victor's character during the 1950s and '60s — had they fanned his arrogance with their praise and encouraged self-delusion by letting obtrusive inconsistencies pass unremarked? On balance, though, they concluded that challenges would have made no worthwhile impression, merely ruptured friendships. Still others blamed Ruth for letting Victor get into despotic habits, and were appalled by Victor's behaviour towards her. There was the matter of the tea that she brought to him every morning at 5.30 because, although he had to have it, he was incapable of making it for himself. (Her life changed greatly for the better with the advent of an automatic teamaker — then he would take her a cup.) There was his refusal to leave dinner parties while he was enjoying himself even though Ruth had to face a long drive home and an early awakening. There was his insistence that she accompany him to America when her father was ill in England. There was his appalling rudeness to her when they played bridge: in the eyes of their friends, Ruth and Victor were on a par as bridge players, yet rubbers lost through error were always her fault, and his reproachful howls of 'Ruthie! Ruthie!' punctuated the play. Nor were they quite comfortable with her apparent acceptance of Victor's avowal in print that he had been unfaithful.

Yet though Ruth pandered eternally to Victor's whims, she stood up to him in her way. She could quietly rebuke him in public for exaggeration, and she occasionally permitted herself a sour comment on his self-delusion. One friend, informed by Victor that he could never bring himself to kill a wasp, was electrified by Ruth's interpolation that he always got her to do it for him. By the early 1950s she had made some strides in securing independence. Until 1953, when the Ladbroke Grove house was exchanged for an attractive flat in Belgravia ('the slummy part of the Eatons', Victor defensively described it), she stayed at Brimpton for much of the week, working hard to maintain the garden's glories; she continued, as she had always done, to paint a little, particularly on holiday; and on a couple of occasions she went abroad without Victor. By such means she preserved a measure of inner privacy and detachment. There were many things in Victor's autobiographical writings that Ruth could have corrected, but either she did not read them, or she shrugged off the distortions. She seemed untouched by Victor's public exposure of himself and their relationship. All in all, she was ideally suited for marriage to such a man, and must have drawn strength from the knowledge that in the 1930s and '40s he had realized his potential in causes of which her liberal soul approved. Most important, for all his faults, Victor's ability to express his love and dependence never waned. He kept up his lover-like attentions: the long telegrams from Moses on her birthdays; the flowers and presents; the little notes of appreciation; the public boasting about her beauty and virtue. She resented his two affairs but can never have doubted the truth of Victor's asseverations that she was superior in his eyes to all other women. In 1948, after twenty-nine years of marriage, in the thick of campaigning he could write in a sudden access of inspiration a poem that meant a great deal to her:

> For RG
> Do you remember the Italian hours
> When in the greenness of the silent close
> We sat encalmed, and knew its nature ours,
> And robbed it of its Botticelli rose?
>
> And do you remember — on the Elysian way
> 'Our spirits grew as we went side by side',
> And in the sunshine of that Christmas May
> 'The hour became your lover and my bride'?
>
> Forgive me, dear, if my mortality
> Could seem to rob us of immortal things
>   And doom us to the common human fate;
> Yet all remains, its essence unimpaired:
> The loyalty, the rapture and the grace,
>   The Union of mate with perfect mate.

Even more affecting perhaps was a more mundane little note he wrote to her from the office around the same time.

My dear beloved Ruth —
    Please let the hurt be healed. All through lunch I've been pretending to talk to Bernard Newman but I've really been thinking about your unhappiness, & longing to make you happy again. I'm sorry a thousand times if I've been discourteous & wounding. But please remember, not the unrealities but the realities of our life — the mornings in Florence cloisters, & the Paris walk on the winter afternoon, & how you looked after me in Scotland, & when we were happy & very close drinking cocktails in the Savoy. I love you very very dearly & in eternity, & I feel immeasurably tender towards you: everything else is superficial. Please, dearest dearest

Ruth, remember that when next — for I know that there's almost bound to be a next — I offend.

Your

V

For Ruth, the move to Eaton Place was a marked improvement. With all her children grown up, she felt a need to find work in areas where she was needed. She became a governor of an art school and joined an education committee of the London County Council.

For Victor, the move was wholly delightful. He could now have Ruth with him full-time and to himself unless he chose otherwise, and enjoy London during the week as much as he enjoyed Brimpton at the weekend. He was free of any family ties. The girls were leading their own lives and by 1954 he was entirely rid of the family responsibilities that had irked him since childhood. His parents were dead, he had purged his guilt about his father in *Tim I* and his responsibilities to his siblings had ended earlier than he had expected. May had been an annoyance; all her pathetic letters praising his goodness and bewailing her poor state of health had never warmed his heart, for she had a claim on him. Though he supplemented his father's legacy he often resented doing so, especially because he suspected he was subsidizing the friend who lived with her. Ruth was always kind to May and kept in touch, but Victor rarely wrote more than a line in reply. He had been particularly irritated in January 1952 when May's friend wrote to report that May was very ill and dreaded going into hospital. She wondered if Victor could pay ten guineas a week for her to go to a nursing home. Victor's answer expressed sorrow at the news and asked that May be given his love but advised strongly against nursing homes: hospitals gave much better treatment.

I cannot understand why May should 'dread' being at a hospital. I think she must be thinking in terms of half a century ago. Everybody goes into hospitals nowadays — that, among other things, is the meaning of the Health Service, which has revolutionised the country. I can call to mind, off hand, the following people, who, to my knowledge, have been in-patients at hospitals during the last few years:

Eleanor Rathbone, who was a wealthy woman; my former secretary, Anna Clarke, the daughter of Sir Fred Clarke; Miss Nancy MacKinnon, who is a relative of the Queen; and Julia, who has had both her children at a hospital in a ward . . .

I shall of course write to May myself, but, meanwhile, please give her this message and tell her not to be in the least distressed.

Of course I should like you to let me know how she is from time to time, if she is unable to write herself (she wrote to us last week). Surely she is able to do so — any little activity of that kind relieves the tedium of illness . . .

May herself wrote two months later to report internal bleeding, severe anaemia and a possible growth. She was about to go into hospital and feared death. 'I wonder Dr Calwell was so positive there was nothing wrong but nerves . . .'

My dear May,
Pull yourself together! A little internal bleeding might come from anything, such as a pile. I understand from Calwell that, though it is not entirely inconceivable, it is *most* improbable that what you call a 'growth' would not show in an X-ray — and nothing of the kind showed in yours. Even a stomach ulcer, which is a comparatively common thing (Mrs Baker [their housekeeper] has just had one), would almost certainly show on an X-ray.

Yours,
Victor

Victor's absence of sympathy for what he took to be other people's imaginary illnesses contrasted with his own hypochondria, which used to send him off regularly to the Queen's Physician. History does not record whether May's death from cancer at the end of April 1952 as he was sailing back from America caused him any guilt or regret. The absence of any reference to her ever again suggests that he put her out of his mind. He certainly had no difficulty in doing the same with Winifred, whom he had subsidized but otherwise quite reasonably ignored for twenty years, when she died in the November of 1954. His complete lack of interest in either sister showed clearly in *Tim I*.

Alone with Ruth in a flat without a spare bedroom, he could see his daughters as much or as little as he chose. Despite occasional rows, he was now on better terms with Livia than he had been since her childhood, and was happy to have lunch with her and Ruth (whose attachment to Livia was considerable) every Thursday after editorial conferences. Livia was hardworking and competent in the office, and though she was no more able than anyone else to meet his standards consistently, he was disposed to see her succeed.

Diana and Poldi might infuriate him, but he was happy to invite them to the occasional party and show off her beauty and his cultivation. He was financially generous on occasion to Julia and Harold, who were properly grateful, and he enjoyed seeing Timothy, though he too proved to be a bone of contention. His parents (and he himself when he grew up) were embarrassed about the taking of his name for the *Tim* books. Julia and Harold had never been asked for permission. They were also resentful that Victor was selective in his approach to his grandchildren (they had four boys). 'Which one's mine?' he asked, when introduced to their twin sons, and only in Robert Victor did he show the faintest interest. He wanted to pay for Timothy to go to public school, and when he was ill wished to bring in expensive private consultants. Harold refused both offers. Victor, he told him, had a simple choice: either he subsidize all the children the Simonses might have or none of them. Victor chose the latter course.

Vita, with an active social life, a busy job, and a strong interest in art (later she became a professional painter) was not much involved with her parents. She occasionally attended parties at Eaton Place and went to Brimpton sometimes at weekends, but there were often strains in her relationship with Ruth and Victor, the one rather remote, the other volatile.

Francesca, who became a qualified architect in 1952, could do no wrong in Victor's eyes. He and Ruth took to Stuart Jeffryes, whom she married in 1956, and both bride and groom hugely enjoyed Victor's rabbinical performance afterwards. Stuart, like Francesca, was of equable temperament, enjoyed her parents' company, and was untroubled by Victor's foibles. They were both to find them kind grandparents to their two sons, even though visits were necessarily brief, as Victor easily got bored with small children.

Only with Livia, and then largely because of her job, was Victor or Ruth closely involved. In Ruth's case, the hesitancy was to some extent a feature of her objection to possessiveness; also, of course, she still had little emotional energy left after soothing her husband's tortured psyche. In Victor's case, there was a principled disapproval of giving one's own children priority, quite apart from a practical inability to absorb grown-up children and young grandchildren into the centre of his life. With friends he had a social life tailored to his own needs. He could choose the people he wanted and lavish hospitality on them, and his generosity continued unbounded. The emphasis from 1953 was on town rather than country hospitality. With a smart flat and some domestic help, the Gollanczes were able to give frequent dinners and small parties and have bridge evenings, as well as hosting lunches and occasional dinners in restaurants.

Victor had switched allegiance from the Ivy ('because I suddenly found . . . [the proprietor's] habit of coming and sitting at the table and talking unintelligible drivel to me intolerable') and now favoured the Savoy, to which he remained faithful henceforward. He rapidly became an institution there and was treated with a friendly deference that passed for equality. The waiters came quickly to recognize his particular needs: the table he liked normally as against the table he liked when the sun shone; his desire for simple food rapidly served when he was alone; his objection to having a wine list offered unless he asked for one. (This little discipline left him free to be parsimonious without embarrassment. He could buy champagne and Château d'Yquem for an unprofitable but beautiful author and the next day order the cheapest dish on the menu for Kingsley Amis and offer him a glass of beer.)

Eaton Place also had another great advantage: it was well placed for London's musical centres. Within a short time of moving in, Victor and Ruth had regularized their attendance at concerts and operas. Victor was a fixture on the musical scene within months; no one could ignore him. In dinner jacket or red shirt, he drew attention to himself by the exuberance of his applause, his sobbing during music that particularly moved him (*Fidelio* almost always reduced him to tears), and his opinionated but well-informed comments during the intervals and at supper parties afterwards. He began to socialize with Livia's musician friends and even became a benefactor. As early as July 1954 Colin Davis was writing:

> I would like to thank you on behalf of us all for your most generous cheque which has sounded, even as the trumpet call in what I believe is your favourite opera, the release of the Chelsea Opera Group from extinction. It is immensely gratifying that you should consider our efforts so worth-while & now that through your help we are able to continue we shall take all steps to prevent the recurrence of catastrophe so that your generosity will not be brought to nought.

CHAPTER TWENTY-THREE

AND MORE CAUSES

BETWEEN HIS OWN books and his publishing (on which he often claimed to be working a 15-hour day since Hodges' departure), Victor's schedule in the first half of the 1950s was a punishing one, yet he could not bear to stay completely out of politics. Nor did the disbursal of large sums of his own money wholly slake his thirst for philanthropy. Political enlightenment and the welfare of souls were both served, he knew, by the dissemination through his own and other books of messages to save mankind, but his taste for action frequently led him into bursts of direct activity. There were months in which he refused all speaking engagements, but then he would dash to Cambridge, Oxford or other venues to give vent to his emotions on the wickedness of the times. More time-consuming were a number of activities into which he was drawn through his own impetuosity, the dictates of his conscience or the pleas of his friends.

The first and most important of these arose from the dissatisfaction he felt, in 1951, at the reaction to his pamphlet, *Christianity and the War Crisis*, and his fear of world war over Korea. Pakenham — then Minister for Civil Aviation — had read it, considered some of its arguments interesting, and suggested a meeting. Among those attending was Strachey, Secretary of State for War. No records survive from this informal gathering except an exchange of letters between Pakenham and Victor which makes it clear that it foundered on the question of Russian harassment over Berlin which, with Korea, had led to the government's adoption of a major armaments programme. Although Victor had not yet become a pacifist, his ambivalence included hostility to anything he viewed as warmongering, and he was preoccupied with the need to wage a world-wide spiritual campaign to reduce tensions. He was repelled by the pragmatism of the politicians present and more particularly by the vociferous anti-Soviet utterances of Pakenham. The offender wrote to ask forgiveness if, as he feared, he had hurt Victor's feelings, 'not, I should earnestly hope, through my personal discourtesy, but perhaps by speaking crudely or just flippantly on things sacred to you'. Although his religious reading made him deeply respectful of the Christian pacifist position, 'I can't help hoping that you will ponder long before deciding to become one.'

A less humble man might have pointed out — like David Low — that Victor's manner of argument had the effect of driving into the opposite corner those who could not go all the way with him. The profuse apology was met with graciousness. Victor had been upset not 'with' Pakenham, but 'about' him, for he was 'a bit horrified' by his attitude to the Soviet Union. He had been totally bewildered by Elizabeth Pakenham's statement that she believed in resisting evil, since Christ had said 'resist not evil'. 'Honestly, I understand Christians less and less.' He was not implying that there was no case for Pakenham's proposed rearmament programme, or the limited version Strachey advocated. Still undecided about absolute pacifism, Victor might support rearmament if it seemed in the interests of peace. However, he was utterly convinced of several propositions: that there should be no desire for a holy war against Russia concealed behind a defence programme, and that overwhelming reliance must be placed on spiritual weapons in our own hearts.

> It is so easy to be deceived about oneself; for all I know I am deceiving myself in the very act of writing this. This is what Christ meant when He taught final integrity, utterly beyond self-deception. He knew that the only test of love was the love of the *enemy*: He knew that the only test of purity was, not whether you slept illicitly with a woman, but whether you *looked* at her to lust after her: He knew that the only true morality was to be perfect as our Father in Heaven is perfect. I write all this with reluctance and indeed shame, because I am only too conscious of the fact, as I suppose we all are, that I am the worst of sinners. Nevertheless it does seem to me that we must *try*, however feebly, and with whatever ill results, to carry out the morality that Christ revealed to us precisely at the only point that matters — the point where we don't *want* to carry it out. I have the kind of blood that boils very easily; but I struggle and struggle to cool it . . .

The politicians having failed to follow his lead, Victor went to the people. At the end of January he spoke to the Oxford University Society for Liberal Religions on the need for concessions in negotiating, and announced that an organization would shortly be set up to bring about a betterment of conditions world-wide.

The letter in the *Guardian* of 12 February 1951 in which he publicized this idea made two points: the door should be kept open in all circumstances for negotiation 'not in the mood of war but in the mood of peace'; and a great international fund should be established 'for improving the conditions of our starving fellow creatures throughout the world'. By making a large contribution, 'we should challenge the world to a new kind of rivalry, a rivalry in the works of peace'. Anyone approving these two points was invited to write 'Yes' on a postcard and send it to Henrietta Street.

The reaction staggered even him. Within weeks he had received over 5,000 postcards, and a follow-up letter to all the press doubled that figure. An office was opened in Southampton Row and a secretary appointed. 'All this takes up an enormous amount of time,' Victor wrote to Acland on 21 February, 'and on top of it I have to think at every stage what the next move must be.'

Acland had no doubt about the next move. Full of enthusiasm, he and Leslie Hale — a like-minded Labour backbencher — begged Victor to marshal the postcard writers into local branches. 'We could have started a splendid organisation,' Acland wrote in his memoirs,

> had Victor worked at it as he had once worked at the Left Book Club. Leslie Hale and I would have been more than willing to work under his vigorous leadship as had John Strachey and Harold Laski in the earlier period. . . . But Victor was afraid that any mass movement would be infiltrated by the Communists. . . . We missed a great opportunity. Like the eminent who had met in Edward Hulton's basement ten years earlier, we wrote and published pamphlets without any organisation to ensure their wide distribution . . .

Victor was not being honest with Acland: probably at the time he was not being honest with himself. He faced the truth on 21 May when he wrote an interlude in *Tim I* wishing he could bring himself to abandon his voluminous letter, which was fundamentally wrong. 'I am writing about the good life instead of living it . . . I feel that a single unknown act of charity is worth more than all the hundreds of thousands of words that this letter will eventually run to, and that somehow all this brooding and writing and elaborating prevents me from performing it.' He recounted the story of his *Guardian* letter.

> The response was remarkable, and an Association for World Peace resulted. We have done a few things during the two or three months that have elapsed since its foundation, and I have had spurts of energy about it; but my heart isn't in it as my heart was in 'Save Europe Now', not for months but for years; and you make a success of a thing when your heart is in it and not when it isn't . . . my heart is in the writing of this letter, not in the Association for World Peace. I tell myself that we are doing as much as we can, that there is really very little that we can do, and that if suddenly a way seemed open of turning our Association into a genuinely effective

instrument for the preservation of peace I should drop everything else, including this letter, and throw myself into the effort. All that is largely true. But it isn't completely true; for I know that if it were not for this letter I should find ways of making the Association as effective as 'Save Europe Now' was. I was passionate about that: I am not passionate about this, although there is really nothing I wouldn't do to prevent another outbreak of war. And it is the writing of this letter, I repeat, that prevents me from having the passion I ought to have.

(The unacceptable reactions of John and Diana Collins to *Tim I* were to some extent conditioned by the feeling that Victor had let down many people, including them, by abandoning the Association for World Peace (AWP) just when it seemed poised to become a really successful peace movement. Victor's justification was that he was writing *the* book that 'might change the course of history' more effectively than 'yet another movement'. *Tim I* did not measure up to that criterion.)

Acland did all he could to rouse Victor to action, for he knew that without his leadership and resources the AWP was doomed to be ineffectual. Although Victor was chairman, Canon Raven vice-chairman and Hale treasurer, it was Acland who provided the impetus. He and Hale rushed out a short pamphlet called *Tanks into Tractors*, and a committee headed by Harold Wilson was set up to work out plans for the implementation of a scheme for global reconstruction, along the lines originally suggested by the American labour leader, Walter Reuther.

By July, Acland was in despair at the futility of the AWP. After a meeting he wrote a brave memorandum of protest:

> We believe that 'Tanks into Tractors' is the only idea which may be big enough to save the world from destruction. We have taken responsibility for making non-party propaganda for this idea. We have collected to ourselves all the most competent people about it. If any other groups attempted to make public propaganda now for this idea they would meet: 'Oh, no, the *Association for World Peace* is running that: we don't need yet *another* organisation!' We, therefore, who have thus taken (or 'usurped') the position of doing something publicly about this idea, owe an obligation to the idea itself. We cannot pick and choose what we should like to do about it. We have moral responsibility to do all the things which the idea itself requires to be done.

A few thousand people had been sent the pamphlet; there were to be some letters to the press, and

> if one or both of two improbable people will come and fill the place with their names, we are going to run an Albert Hall meeting in $4\frac{1}{2}$ months.

Beyond that, nothing. We do nothing to use or bring forth or demon-strate the immense amount of public support behind this idea. We do not even try it experimentally in one area. This is 'dog-in-the-manger'. We take up a position; we prevent others taking the position; and we don't do what the position requires.

It had been argued that SEN had achieved its ends by means of activities like those now agreed. Acland challenged the comparison: 'what it did was to persuade Strachey to persuade the cabinet to change the policy about food parcels; and to persuade people . . . to send food parcels. With great respect this accomplishment, magnificent though it was, was of a different order from what we are now attempting.' The task of the AWP was to win over public opinion in Britain to an acceptance of sacrifice for others' sake. After that, missionaries would have to do the same in other countries. 'It is unrealistic to believe that we can do this without *somehow* calling into activity the little people who agree with us; *and we are lacking in respect for their personalities if we suppose that the whole task can be achieved by a few selected people up at the top writing letters to the press.*' He proposed in detail a local experiment to involve people and suggested ways of keeping the communists out.

Victor was immersed in *Tim* and ignored Acland's pleas. Wilson's committee, which included Acland, Ritchie Calder, Leslie Hale, E. F. Schumacher and Harry Walston, produced what Victor described as a 'dull but devoted' pamphlet, which through an inspiration of Wilson's was called War on Want. For three months, from May to July 1952, Victor gave some time and effort to the AWP, though it was still Acland who took the leading role. With its subsidiary, War on Want, the AWP was set up at Henrietta Street and a new secretary appointed. (Victor had recently sacked the first because he could not work with her.) Victor's main contributions were attendance at committee meetings, promotion of the pamphlet among friends in the press, expedition of published material, and speeches. Acland had been given permission to try to launch War on Want as a national move-ment and Victor was inclined to be helpful. To a critic he wrote in June 1952:

I am also against the proliferation of societies and I have made it a strict rule, when I have been at the head of any, to see that they were closed down (often in face of considerable opposition) as soon as they had done their job . . .
Now nobody, to my knowledge, is campaigning for the abolition of world hunger . . . nobody is basing a campaign entirely around this idea. It is a terribly important idea, but one exceedingly difficult to bring home

to 'ordinary people': and I am sure that nothing but a sustained campaign can do the job . . .

It was the AWP, rather than War on Want, that really interested Victor. When he, Acland and Wilson launched the pamphlet in Manchester, at a public meeting in July, the passages in his speech that drew most attention were his assault on Labour's lack of internationalism and the announcement of his own emergence from the pacifist chrysalis. He told the *Socialist Leader* that he accepted that a conquest of the world by the Soviet Union would be 'a temporal disaster of such magnitude and horror that I hardly dare contemplate it. In spite of all these things, my pacifism stands: or, it might be truer to say, very largely because of them. For I have arrived at the position that I was struggling towards, but had not reached, at the time of the Hitlerite menace: namely, that one can only reply to such evil by absolute good.'

It did not strengthen the AWP's appeal that both its chairman and vice-chairman were now pacifists. Indeed, for practical purposes, its advocacy of open doors in negotiation was rendered suspect. Acland continued to put the emphasis on War on Want, and ran public meetings around the country. As in Manchester, they all attracted modest audiences and tepid media coverage. Acland still believed Victor could turn War on Want into a real force, but Victor was once again disengaged. Moreover, he was cross with Acland for sacking the new secretary of whom Victor approved. From the Labour Party Conference, Acland wrote on 1 October a disarming letter of apology. He got his way and the secretary stayed sacked, but Victor resigned the chairmanship of the AWP. Acland's apology and his name on *Tim* advertisements saved the friendship. More importantly, Victor was happy to shed his commitments to the AWP and its subsidiary. Acland took on the chairmanship and the organization left Henrietta Street. He let the AWP head wither from the War on Want body, whose vitality was confirmed at a public meeting in Glasgow, which resulted in a great deal of local action and thousands of pounds in the kitty. 'But, in War on Want, I lacked what I had always had in Common Wealth: five or six like-minded people giving serious time to the immediate problems that arose every day . . . the work went on neither failing nor really succeeding. Things might have been different had we immediately mobilised the ten thousands.' (At the end of 1954, when an unknown called Frank Harcourt-Munning asked if he could take over the name War on Want, Acland was happy to agree and delighted with its huge subsequent success as a radical international charity. Victor became a patron in 1957. Ironically, many years after most of the campaigns into which he had thrown himself body and soul were forgotten, he was remembered by many as the founder of War on Want. Acland's contribution was overlooked.)

As a campaigner, Victor had become a dilettante. In *Tim I* he had shamefacedly admitted that he was now less than diligent with distress mail from Germany. He did try to help with the more frightful cases, and from time to time he was briefly caught up in German-related issues. One of them was the proposal for an Anglo-German Association. He had been peripherally involved in 1950 in the foundation of an Anglo-German Institute, initiated by G. P. Gooch. He had added his signature to those of George Catlin, Julian Huxley, Desmond MacCarthy, Gilbert Murray and Harold Nicolson below a letter to *The Times Educational Supplement* in August, proposing a body to promote Anglo-German cultural relations. Pakenham had then drawn him, unwilling, into discussions on how to remove the acting director, and he found himself on an executive committee which included Catlin, Nicolson, and Violet Bonham Carter whom he was concurrently pushing out of the proposed civil liberties organization. As the meetings and negotiations dragged on, he and Bonham Carter made common cause against Catlin, whom Victor liked, 'but the trouble is that he is an ineffable ass, and has carried a self-important pomposity to what our American friends call "a new high" . . .'

Victor played a statesmanlike part in the proceedings but finally, his patience drained by the committee's shilly-shallying, he wrote a letter of resignation to Catlin on 12 February, explaining *inter alia* that he was temperamentally opposed to 'all "Anglo-so-and-so" societies', as they offended his internationalism.

It was presumably Pakenham's persistence that made Victor exercise a *volte-face* and sign a December letter to *The Times*, with several other dignitaries, announcing the establishment of an Anglo-German Association. He took part only in its social activities. His German mail dwindled along with his interest, he steadfastly rejected invitations to visit the country, and he kept out of controversy about it. In the spring of 1953, however, the German Ambassador informed him that his government wished to confer on Victor on his 60th birthday the highest honour in its gift: the Order of Merit. It was the first time it had been awarded to a non-German. On the day itself, he received good wishes from President Heuss, the German Vice-Chancellor, the Social Democratic Party, and others both eminent and obscure. In a letter of thanks for the award, Victor told Heuss that, apart from the Nobel Peace Prize it was the only honour 'in the world' he had really wanted.

The British displayed their usual indifference to foreign honours: Victor was told by Buckingham Palace that he could wear his new decoration only in the presence of the German Head of State. There were compensations in the German press coverage, and reminders of the days of glory. Victor's fears that his activities might be futile never lasted long, but still it helped to hear from an interviewer that every German visitor to London shortly after the war told him: 'There are two things I want to see in London — Buckingham Palace and Mr Victor Gollancz.' It must have been as gratifying to know that he was the subject of a schools broadcast and an accompanying brochure for teachers, in a series called 'Great Humanitarians'. He was touched also when, during the next couple of years, three German cities named streets after him. In May 1955 he wrote to *The Times* to announce the arrival from the German Embassy of an oil-painting symbolizing the gratitude of the German nation for the work of SEN.

From time to time he announced his intention of visiting Germany (one trip was cancelled at two weeks' notice), and in 1954 he made a brief effort to learn German, but other activities kept intervening. As the euphoria wore off he was more interested in taking a sabbatical in India 'to meet the sages' — but he went off the idea and, with justification, pleaded overwork. By mid-1955, though his conscience sometimes pricked him about Germany, it had become very much a concern of the past.

On matters Jewish, his utterances were chiefly occasioned by irritation, and provoked similar sentiments in return. In January 1951, for instance, he had a letter in *The Times*, as Chairman of the JSHS, attacking a resolution by the central council of German Jews against clemency for mass murderers who had been under sentence of execution for three years. And in March 1954, in his private capacity, he condemned in the same forum the world Jewish Congress's protest at the re-interment of certain German war criminals' remains in hallowed ground. (Eden cited his letter approvingly in the Commons.) The daggers were never properly sheathed. When Victor's name appeared among those supporting the Anglo-German Society, it brought an immediate reaction. For once he had agreed to do a job for the Hebrew University of Jerusalem and was negotiating dates with a branch for whom he was to give a fund-raising speech. One of its members wrote in January 1952: 'I have been informed today by the Secretary of our Friends branch in Brighton that they held a meeting last night at which it was felt that your visit in February would not meet with financial success owing to the recent news that you are connected with the newly formed Anglo-German Association. I regret, therefore, to have to cancel the arrangements . . . ' Most Jews found confusing the even-handedness manifest in Victor's co-signature of a letter in 1952 appealing for members for the Anglo-Israeli Association. They might have been more impressed had they seen his private letter to a German complaining of German blindness to Jewish suffering and deafness to claims for restitution of property.

Victor seemed determined not to mend his bridges with majority Anglo-Jewish opinion. At the end of November 1951 the *Jewish Chronicle* was planning a profile, and Edwin Samuel, a director, asked for his co-operation. Samuel, heir to the Liberal statesman, Lord Samuel, a distinguished man in his own right and a member of the Labour Party, was anxious to explain Victor to his readers. He was turned down. Victor disliked profiles because 'they seem to me to be part and parcel, on the one hand, of a mania for publicity (on the part of the subject), and on the other, of a mania to establish contact with prominent people (on the part of the reader)'. Additionally, Samuel had written the only adverse review of *A Year of Grace*. It was not, Victor explained, that he objected to hostile reviews — indeed he preferred them to sycophantic ones — it was that Samuel had shown complete misunderstanding of his ideas: as a person 'not of my kidney', he would be bound to produce something wholly misleading.

The correspondence with Samuel was extensive, but much more curt was Victor's response to an innocent request from the Anglo-Jewish Association for a review copy of *Tim I* for their journal. 'Frankly, I don't feel very much like sending a copy of "My Dear Timothy" for review. Almost without exception, the Jewish press has really blackguarded the book. I don't mind a bit, so far as the book is concerned: but I don't like giving the occasion for this sort of intolerance. I think you will understand.'

In the summer of 1952 he put in preliminary work on a JSHS appeal for Korean children, to operate under the patronage of Edwina Mountbatten, but his resources proved insufficient for so complex an undertaking: he had to confine himself to personal gifts of money. And when he was asked to help an Arab boy in distress in 1953 he had to admit that the society was in a state of suspended animation and could contribute only £7, its entire funds. Victor duly supplemented the amount.

While middle-of-the-road Jewish opinion found Victor confusing at best, turncoat at worst, some of his old friends were deferential to the prophet. Bentwich, perhaps in part out of family loyalty, contained all but mild irritation at the slights he suffered. Leonard Cohen, a mere acquaintance, and with good reason to protest his treatment at Victor's hands, showed great humility. He wrote to Victor in September 1952 enclosing a draft letter to Alfred Krupp. Krupp, it was said, was to receive £30 million in compensation for property seized, and Cohen was advising him to put the money into a War Victims' Relief Fund, so as to make amends for his contribution to the Nazi régime and his use of slave labour. The letter was restrained if emotional, offering the industrialist the chance 'to hear the name of Krupp blessed by millions who now curse and revile it'.

Victor approved the idea, but

> at the risk of appearing smug, I can't find it in my conscience to say so much without adding that I could not personally associate myself with the tone of your letter. It 'hits' me as breaking the Third Commandment. However unspeakably dreadful I may, and of course do, consider what the Nazis did, I cannot think it right to address any human being — and particularly those who have done dreadful things — in mingled accents of sermonising and contempt . . .

Cohen accepted his guidance. Such exceptions apart, most Jews kept their distance. Other than those from student societies, there were few invitations to make speeches or attend social events.

If the Jews quietly wrote Victor off, there were plenty of others who wanted more from him than he could give. Pacifists were delighted with their famous recruit and from mid-1952 he was called on regularly to support the cause. They seemed stoically to accept his tongue-lashings of those of their number whom he considered self-righteous. John Collins valued his presence on Christian Action platforms, where he could be relied on to generate newsworthy controversy. On one occasion at least Victor had qualms about his role. He had been booked to open a Christian Action weekend conference in Oxford in April 1951. It was designed to present 'a challenge' to supporters of the movement who were failing to take the properly Christian line, among them Pakenham and others who shared his views on Russia. Some members objected to Victor as opening speaker, and he and Collins spent an evening discussing tactics. Victor's pugnacity, he himself feared, was turning into just the self-righteousness he abominated in others. 'It is all mixed up with this business of my being a "prophet", "a spiritual leader", "one of the best living Christians" and so on. I really cannot bear this sort of business. I have got no false modesty (which I think a damnable vice) but I know perfectly well that I am not any of these things. Indeed, the fact that there should be all this kind of talk is only a proof of the horrible state the world has got into.' All he had ever done was what little he could for causes everyone should stand up for. He was religious only by desire and wanted humbly to do what he thought right. 'I *don't* want to be a sort of prophet and preacher (except in so far as that might be inescapable in certain circumstances) around whom controversy centres. It all leaves an unpleasant taste in my mouth, and makes me feel bad . . . Forgive all this, but I did come away unhappy last night . . . and I feel that I am getting into a spiritually false position from which I ought to extricate myself.'

Such moods were entirely genuine, but generally short-lived. A compromise was struck: Victor spoke but did not open the conference. He stirred up a furore by announcing that socialism was the only political creed compatible with Christianity, and returned to Brimpton with his blood up. Ruth had to hold him back from returning to Oxford on Sunday to exercise his proselytizing fury on the errant capitalists. Instead, he wrote a long account of the conference in *Tim I*, sprinkled with clues to the identities of the chief offenders.

The Collins/Victor partnership suffered few serious hitches at this time, although Collins lagged behind Victor on the pacifism trail; he found too easy the release from doubts that absolutist pacifists enjoyed. He and Victor were so close in their reactions to human suffering that there were few grounds for contention on matters of detail. Trouble arose when Collins began to acquire a new prominence after a visit to South Africa in June and July 1954. He came back determined to use Christian Action on a much bigger scale to support all those who resisted the apartheid laws. Victor was in close support, and when right-wing opinion pooh-poohed Collins's visit as too short to permit sensible judgments, he wrote a powerful letter to *The Times*; but Collins soon began to attract far too much attention for Victor's liking. When he announced a public meeting at Central Hall in October to report on his visit, Victor earnestly assured him that no one would come, then offered himself as chairman and a guarantee of a large audience. The meeting was a well-attended disaster. In his memoirs Collins described the events with the restraint of one who was still a close friend of Victor: 'Question time at the Central Hall, I remember, proved very embarrassing because my chairman, not realising that most of the questioners were mouthpieces of South Africa House, and one, a very persuasive one, was the editor of a pro-segregation paper in London, decided that I had treated them unfairly, and in an attempt, as he thought, to redress the balance, himself weighed in on their side.' *South Africa* gleefully reported it more fully in a splenetic attack on Collins:

> It was left to the Chairman, however, to deliver the *coup de grâce*, to borrow one of Canon Collins's phrases. Mr Gollancz, stepping aside momentarily from the chair like the Lord Chancellor stepping aside from the Woolsack, himself put a question to Canon Collins. It was a devastating question. If there was going to be an explosion in South Africa in six months or two years, what had Canon Collins to propose in the way of positive action by the British people to influence the situation? Plainly they could not dictate to South Africa. What then? If there was nothing they could do, were they not in danger, merely, of blowing off steam?
>
> It was a question which shook Canon Collins and from which he never really recovered. He must have wondered which side Mr Gollancz was on.

As he left the meeting Collins was tapped on the shoulder by Frank Owen, who said 'Stabbed in the back by a friend.' Collins knew all too well that jealousy lay beneath Victor's conduct, but the coolness that ensued was brief. Early the following month Collins went into hospital with tuberculosis and Victor, terrified he might die, was assiduous with visits and gifts. The following summer he and Ruth had the whole Collins family to stay at Brimpton for a delightful three months which restored Collins almost to normal health. It was one of the many 'golden times' that made the Collinses eternally grateful for Victor's presence in their lives. He was generous to them not just with hospitality (he once took them to Italy) but also, as he might have put it himself, spiritually. Through his eyes they gained immeasurably in appreciation of the wonders he found everywhere around him, from an opening flower or the smell of new-mown grass through to a great painting or piece of architecture. He could express his love uninhibit-edly in letters and in person so as to win their hearts, compensating for even major irritations.

Collins never instilled in him any real interest in South Africa, though Victor signed fund-raising letters, sponsored appeals, pub-lished a few radical books on the subject and occasionally salved his conscience with talk of a visit there to see if he could effect a reconciliation between races. While to defenders of South Africa he was always hot in denunciation of the régime, he enjoyed playing devil's advocate with the Collinses, and quoting the opinion of his traveller — 'a very decent kind of man' — who said apartheid was not at all as bad as it was alleged to be. Overall, Victor failed seriously to identify or empathize with persecuted blacks; Collins had got there first. Victor, the Jew, could hardly fight Collins, his friend, for the chairmanship of Christian Action.

Victor did not of course, entirely neglect domestic politics, but his interventions in the early 1950s were so arbitrary as to create considerable confusion among those who followed his career. He was sometimes to be seen in Labour circles in the Commons, attending fringe meetings such as Acland's Socialist Christian Group or the Tuesday dinners of the supporters of World Government, and declared himself for most of the period an unshakeable supporter of Labour, yet he rarely attacked the Conservatives even when they came to power in 1951. Indeed, he enjoyed explaining to socialists that Conservatives were the better internationalists. True, he criticized R. A. Butler in *The Times* in 1952, but it was on an issue that brought socialist wrath down on him — the cutting of the tourist allowance to £25. Victor found this indefensible:

> For a grotesquely small saving, wholly negligible in view of our total and particularly of our armaments expenditure, he ends foreign travel, except for business purposes — at a time when the world is riven by national egoisms and hatreds, and our only hope is for the peoples to get to know one another. Even in the narrowly economic field it is surely obvious that there can be no real solution for ourselves, or for any other country in the long run, except on an international basis; and how shall we ever work towards that if we immure ourselves behind barbed wire? In view of the world's spiritual necessities, Mr Butler's proposal is wholly retrograde.

He was outraged when the correspondence columns were filled with letters proving the possibility of taking perfectly good holidays on £25 and accusing him of élitism. Particularly maddened by a letter from Robert Birley's wife praising the creative parsimony of young travellers, he wrote: 'It is richly comic that I, who am a socialist, a believer in equal incomes, and an advocate of the capital levy, should be presented as fighting for the denizens of luxury hotels (some of whom will wangle their holidays anyhow . . .).'

It was part of a pattern: he would summon his accountant after Budget Day to cross-question him about the new burdens on the firm, then abuse the popular press for encouraging selfishness with articles headed 'What This Budget Means to You'. Victor's life was made miserable for a time by the travel restriction. He would not contemplate breaking the law even in spirit, and fell back on haggling with his favourite first-class hotels and on the hospitality of friends abroad.

Socialists were even more perplexed by his quandary in July 1953, and the furious correspondence about union rights and duties it sparked off. In a heart-rending letter to *The Times* Victor told the story of one of his employees, an ex-member of a union, who had given up his union card when promoted to salesman. Falling into ill-health, he was offered his old job on the trade counter, whereupon the union refused him re-admittance. This was disastrous. 'If, in defiance of the union, we gave him back his old job, all the union members would doubtless "walk out", and we should be unable to replace them by other union members: accordingly, we should have to become a non-union house — a course that would be repugnant to us.' It looked as if the man would be unable to get any job in publishing. Victor would have done better not to send the letter; it emerged in a *Bookseller* article that his facts were hopelessly wrong: non-membership of a trade union was no bar to employment in the trade department of any publishing firm. The editor of the *Bookseller*, Edmond Segrave, felt obliged to write to the injured Victor to beg forgiveness for the tone of the article.

Through all the turmoil, and in spite of much provocation, there was one person Victor never let down, neglected, resented or bullied — his favourite prisoner. (He wrote of him in *Tim II* as Ronnie Jones; for similar reasons that pseudonym serves here.) Victor started his prison visiting in October 1950 with four names on his list. Within a fortnight he was writing to the chaplain that he could never get to the fourth and would like to drop him. The one he took to was Jones, who broke through his initial truculence and won Victor's heart by offering him one of his precious cigarettes. His father apart, Jones emerges more fully rounded than anyone else from the pages of *Tim*; he was so foreign to Victor that an enormous effort at understanding was called for.

He always . . . treated me like a baby, and as if anxious to safeguard my innocence. He told me once that he had blued £520, the proceeds of a robbery, in three weeks. After working it out in my head I expressed myself sceptical. He assured me he wasn't lying. 'Then how did you manage it?' I asked. 'In the West End,' he replied. 'You know what I mean,' he added vaguely — this was what, in the technology of the radio, would be called his signature tune. 'Restaurants and so on.' 'But that's nonsense,' I said. 'I'm much richer than you, and know all about West End restaurants; and I couldn't possibly get rid of the stuff at that rate — it works out at nearly thirty pounds a day.' 'Well of course,' he said, 'I had a different woman every night: special, you know what I mean. I wouldn't like to tell you. . . . ' I tried to make him change his mind, but couldn't: he was clearly determined not to sully me. He was equally concerned for my freedom. 'Peculiar places, these,' he once remarked. 'They wouldn't suit you at all. I don't advise you to get into one.' His attitude to the Scrubs was rather like that of a man who has chosen a second-rate hotel from motives of economy and now regrets it. I sent him a message one day postponing a particular visit. Next time I went I asked him whether he'd had it. 'Message?' he said. 'They don't give messages here. Shockingly run, this place. You'd be amazed.' . . .

Ronnie was a man of great natural delicacy. 'Jew' and 'Jewish' were regarded in his milieu as terms of opprobrium, as in many other milieus; and if he ever had occasion to use them — as when he asked me about the matsos that he had just seen arriving for Passover — he always pulled himself up at the initial 'J' and hurriedly substituted 'you know what I mean.'

Victor was entranced by Ronnie, dutifully conscientious about his other two prisoners. When they were released, he asked to be left only with Ronnie and after his discharge abandoned prison visiting to finish *Tim*. His prison visitor's report in June 1951 was heartfelt. Ronnie

has had a deplorable life, at no time having had any home ties or steady background: and when I began talking to him I found that Christian ethical ideas were quite new to him. But, if only even now he could have a real chance, I am certain that he has in him the makings of a fine human being. He has, in spite of his criminal background, a sort of natural grace and courtesy, which is more of a spiritual matter than one of mere manners. I have been very much struck with his attitude to me, which has always been respectful without the smallest touch of servility.

He is, I am convinced, a gentle person deep down, but I should think he could be capable of considerable violence if in any way provoked (particularly if he had been drinking), and especially if he felt he was being unjustly treated in any way. He has, or had, — I don't know whether I have shaken him at all in this — a sort of Old Testament feeling that it is immoral not to retaliate against someone whom you feel to have wronged you. In other words, his attitude on this question, as an individual, is very much the attitude, at the present time, of so-called civilised states in their corporate capacity . . .

He feared for his future, but saw the best hope in a gardening job in the country: enquiries had so far yielded nothing. Victor interviewed an assistant governor, and fixed Ronnie up with a job at Gollancz and interim accommodation. Ronnie was a hopeless employee, turning up occasionally for very short days and, unsurprisingly, blueing his earnings. Victor, who threatened employees with the sack if they were more than a few minutes late, and wrote letters to the Postmaster

General if the post was delivered after 8.50 a.m., was forgiving and blamed society for Ronnie's shortcomings. After five months Ronnie was accepted for training by the Agricultural Commission and Victor was optimistic for his future, but the blow soon fell: Ronnie was arrested for stealing sides of bacon. Arnold Goodman (later Lord Goodman and the most famous solicitor in Britain) was put on the job.

The case for the prosecution rested on the discovery of Ronnie and friend on a waste lot near a warehouse with sides of bacon, which, the police claimed, the pair had been throwing to each other on the roof. The defence claimed that they were merely relieving themselves. Victor went to Goodman's office and asserted the inevitable innocence of Ronnie: there was much good in him, and his smile was a smile of innocence. Together they set off to the prison and were informed by the surprised authorities that for all their eminence, they could meet Ronnie only in the normal visiting room. The cubicle provided was for a single visitor. Arnold Goodman is a fat man now; then, he says, he was fatter. Victor was not a little overweight. Goodman vividly recalls the two of them, in bulky winter coats, crammed into the tiny space, confronted with a smile from Ronnie that struck Goodman as decidedly criminal. The only glimmer of hope was that Ronnie's record, sullied by numerous criminal convictions, was thus far clean regarding the theft of bacon.

The forces of law were baffled to discover that Ronnie, who usually cheerfully admitted guilt, was this time to be represented by a Queen's Counsel. Victor had accepted that Ronnie and his friend had to be defended jointly, and a battery of experts was called in — including a meteorologist, who proved that the night had been too dark for the police to see what they claimed to have seen, an MP to back him up from personal investigation, and a forensic expert to testify there was no bacon fat on their clothes. Two juries failed to agree, and the defendants were released. Goodman sent in as low a bill as possible — £369. 17s. 5d. (slightly more than a packer's wages for a year) and Victor answered: 'I think your firm's charges are extremely moderate, and though of course the total cost is far more than I expected, very largely because of (a) the double trial and (b) the length each one lasted, I wouldn't have had a penny of it unspent'

Over the next few years, Ronnie moved from job to job and hostel to digs and applied to Victor for money with each fresh crisis. The sums were small and Victor would have willingly given more, but from time to time he hardened his heart and wrote a stern but affectionate note about the merits of standing on one's own feet. He worried endlessly about Ronnie and, in 1954, through a friend, he found him a job that suited him. Ronnie married and settled down, and sent Christmas presents to Victor and Ruth, both of whom he saw from time to time. Victor never lost touch, and frequently sent thoughtful gifts. He loved Ronnie and he was overjoyed that his faith in him had proved well founded. When Ronnie heard of Victor's death, his response was, 'There's my best friend gone west'; an epitaph that would probably have delighted his mentor more than any other.

Victor never again became a Visitor, but his exposure to prison had focussed his attention on the system and his antipathy to it soon became notorious. In 1952 he published *Who Lie in Gaol*, a book by Joan Henry about her experiences in Holloway. The Gollancz chief reader was unimpressed by its 'very well-worn track', but Victor, for whom the wickedness of prison conditions was a fresh horror, found it fascinating. He published it in September with a flourish of trumpets (and a puff from Bertrand Russell) and it got massive press coverage. He himself was entangled in a controversy in the *Guardian* with both the chairman of the Howard League for Penal Reform (who impugned Henry's motives) and with Lionel Fox, the chairman of the Prison Commissioners, who had helped him to become a Prison Visitor. The book ran to five impressions within a few months and was filmed the following year. In his published statements Victor had announced his conviction that 'many features of prison life here in England are abominable, and a disgrace to a *soi-distant* Christian country.' At the beginning of 1953 he was informed without an explanation that there would be no invitation to be a Prison Visitor in that year.

He told the story in *Tim II*, and summed up:

> The only possible inference is this: the Commissioners are unwilling to give the freedom of our prisons to anyone determined to speak his mind. One thing, however, I ought in fairness to add: I had used some expression — I cannot be bothered to look it up, and am quoting from memory — such as 'the utter abomination of our whole prison system.'
>
> A word in conclusion. Given the utter abomination aforesaid, for which the nation, and no particular individual in any particular establishment, must be held responsible, Wormwood Scrubs, so far as I could judge, is humanely administered.

The chain of events had blurred the fact that Victor had gone cool on prison visiting; he made no effort to take it up again until late in 1959. He would have been welcome among the inmates; his fame as a soft touch spread, and ex-convicts became a recurring nuisance to his secretaries. Gollancz operated a charity fund until 1958, when the burden became too great, but the difficult job of separating fact from fiction in the hard-luck stories fell mainly on Gollancz staff. Elinor ('Tessa') Murphy, Victor's secretary from 1953 to 1958, kept extensive files on all the supplicants, herself writing letters and making visits to one prisoner. On Victor's part, there were episodes of great generosity. He employed ex-convicts in the firm (with mixed results), and sent one prisoner a clarinet, but none rivalled Ronnie in his affections.

By spring 1955 Victor was restive: he had almost finished *From Darkness to Light* (which had a long section for prisoners — almost all critical of society, the law and its enforcers). Richard Acland had captured his imagination by resigning his Commons seat in March over Labour support for the hydrogen bomb. From the *Queen Mary*, Victor wirelessed 'Bravo' and in a letter from New York told Acland he had already decided to stand as an Independent at the next general election 'on this issue, as well as capital punishment and all the other villainies.' He offered Acland a supportive quote for the voters:

> I heartily applaud Acland's resignation from the LP, which I can no longer support in any way myself. The LP support of the manufacture by us of hydrogen bombs, and of the implied attempt to solve our crisis — the world's crisis — by means of fear, is plain support of AntiChrist. There is only one way out now — the Christian way: better a million times to be crucified — for our whole nation to be crucified — than to yield to the worst of all temptations. But I do not believe it would come to that: if we tried love for a change — love of our enemies, and I do believe that the Communists are, in the temporal sense, our enemies — I am persuaded that love would 'work': certainly in the long run, and almost certainly in the short run too.
>
> For God's sake (literally) return Acland: we can do with one Christian MP.

By the time Victor came back to London at the end of April, Eden had announced a general election for 26 May. Acland, who had cherished hopes of regaining his seat in a by-election, now had the odds massively against him. It was too late for Victor to mount a campaign for himself and he was eager to help Acland, but there was no space on the candidate's platform for a declared pacifist, who by now held little appeal for the ordinary voter. Acland dealt with Victor very tactfully but his heavy defeat in the Conservative election victory laid him open to future attacks. After a lunch with Victor in June,

Acland defended himself against two serious criticisms. He excused himself from absolute — and therefore politically hopeless — pacifism, and

> on your other point, — I agree that it is a valid criticism that I made it a one-man show. . . . It would have been a very different thing if you had been in the country and had been willing to undertake the detailed lobbying of the big names from outside, — I rang your office in the hope of getting your advice two days *before* making my speech in the House. . . . But by March 21st, Russell had sent a message and refused to come and speak on grounds of health, Soper had refused to come and speak because he agreed with Nye on the subject of remaining in the Party . . . I didn't have the co-operation of anyone who could undertake big-name-lobbying with any prospect of success . . .

He was convinced anyway that the great and the good could never have influenced more than 1 per cent of the electorate. The kind of celebrities who might have had a more telling effect were broadcasters like Wilfred Pickles, Gilbert Harding and Philip Harben. His friend Julia Lang, of 'Listen with Mother' fame, had helped a great deal. 'But from the streets where the solid Labour vote lives, the Bishop of Chichester, if we could have got him, which I doubt, would have influenced hardly a soul.' (Unfortunately, Victor's response to this heresy is not on record. He had only recently been converted to the wireless, and then only for musical diversion, and he hated television, resolutely refusing to keep pace with the changes in public taste. He had proposed quite sincerely in 1952 that an enquiry into the prison system be undertaken by Gilbert Murray (86) and Bertrand Russell (80). He did suggest there might be 'younger equivalents', but it was a small concession: he frequently denied the existence of any such creature.)

'If it is a personal error of mine,' continued Acland,

> — (could I almost say of ours?) — to find it easier to work in a one-man show, it was an error which wasn't easily avoided in the actual situation, — and if it had been avoided, I doubt if it would have made more than a few hundreds of difference to the result.
>
> Despite this, I hope you will allow me to canvass for you when you take on the by-election which I very much hope you will do. Indeed, I think it would do no harm at all if we could find a series of candidates to run in about two or three by-elections per year on such lines as yours or mine . . .

Acland was fighting another losing battle with Victor, who, although he felt very deeply about the H-bomb issue, had found it difficult to forsake the Labour Party. And to put himself to the test in a by-election would have been to risk massive rejection by the electorate. More important, the attractions of Acland's anti-nuclear crusade paled beside those of a debate where his potential effectiveness could not be in doubt: capital punishment.

CHAPTER TWENTY-FOUR

THE ABSOLUTIST CONSCIENCE

IN JULY 1955, the climate of opinion was auspicious for a further onslaught on capital punishment. The post-war Labour government had seen its abolitionist efforts thrown out by the House of Lords and had let the matter drop. Now, under the Conservatives, there was a great deal of cross-party disgust about hanging. The execution in 1953 of the mentally-retarded Derek Bentley for a murder to which he had been mere accomplice had caused widespread protest. Ruth Ellis, mother of a little girl, was hanged for shooting her violent lover. And there was mounting evidence that Timothy Evans's next-door neighbour, Christie, was responsible for the murder for which Evans was executed.

Victor had for some time been contributing to the debate through the publication of abolitionist propaganda, the signing of letters, and personal eloquence. In 1954 he had tried to persuade Collins to commit Christian Action to a campaign, but the membership was split on the issue and Collins had his hands full with South Africa. Early in July 1955, revolted by the impending execution of Ellis, Victor wrote to the *Evening Standard* backing Raymond Chandler's protest and ending with a quote from Thackeray: 'I pray to Almighty God to cause this disgraceful sin to pass from among us, and to cleanse our land of blood.'

It was Arthur Koestler who catalysed the public campaign. Believing Victor to be the only man capable of doing the thing properly, he came to visit him at Brimpton (when the Collinses were in residence) and made his proposal. The timing was just right: with *From Darkness to Light* at the press, Victor was ready for a new cause. Within a few days he was writing to Joan Henry: 'Arthur Koestler, John Collins and I shall be shortly launching a National Campaign for the Prevention of Legal Cruelty (i.e. for the abolition of the death sentence). The methods to be employed would be both conventional and, though always dignified and reverent, highly unconventional.'

Equally passionate in their loathing for judicial killing, Victor and Koestler were from the outset at variance in their views of the best weapon to use against it. Koestler was for pragmatic reason seasoned with emotion; Victor was bent on the absolutist argument. His conception was clearly expressed in a letter to the *Daily Telegraph* written on 18 July:

> . . . Many of the arguments for and against, though they may have some subsidiary relevance, cannot begin to affect the main issue. There is much discussion, for instance, as to whether or not the death penalty tends to be preventative of murder. For my own part, I believe the evidence . . . to point unmistakably to the absence of any such result; even if, however, a water-tight case could be made out to the contrary, the death penalty would still be wholly inadmissible . . .
>
> The case against capital punishment . . . is something absolute, 'in its own right'. Its absoluteness is bound up with another absolute — an absolute more absolute, even, than the sacredness of life. This absolute is summed up in the categorical imperative, 'Thou shalt not commit outrageous cruelty against any single human being' . . .
>
> The plain fact is that, deep down below all rationalization, the death penalty is an act of vengeance. It embodies something spiritually and morally more primitive even than the command given in the Mosaic code to my remote ancestors — 'an eye for an eye and a tooth for a tooth': because, in the circumstances of the time, the *lex talionis* was an advance on indiscriminate vengeance. And it was an advance that paved the way for the total abrogation of all forms of vengeance by One infinitely (I use the word in its exact meaning) greater than Moses . . .

The first meeting of what was later constituted the executive committee was held on 11 August at Henrietta Street. Victor presided over Collins, Gerald Gardiner (Quaker and lawyer), Christopher Hollis (Tory MP and journalist), Koestler, Reginald Paget (Labour MP and lawyer) and Peggy Duff, recently sacked from *Tribune* and so available to act as secretary and treasurer. Differences in approach were smoothed over, and most of the committee accepted with a good grace that Victor would run things his own way. It was only on matters of detail that they prevailed: for instance, the title of the campaign: 'Legal Cruelty' was dropped in favour of 'The National Campaign for the Abolition of Capital Punishment' (NCACP). Shortly afterwards there were two additions to the executive: Frank Owen (Labour ex-MP and ex-editor of the *Daily Mail*) and Ruth Gollancz (who though deeply interested, stayed silent at meetings and voted with Victor).

The progress of a fortnight proved the wisdom of giving Victor his head. From the Henrietta Street headquarters, funds had been raised informally — quite enough to get the campaign rolling — and there were many impressive names on the Committee of Honour. On 24 August, the NCACP went public with a fund-raising appeal which promised publications, public meetings and the whole current gamut of opinion-forming activities: 'We believe that a wholehearted effort will put an end in a very short time to this blot on our national life.' The conviction that the job could be done quickly was Victor's. The strategy was worked out at the next committee meeting: flooding the media with information, sending circulars to all potentially sympathetic organizations and booking the Central Hall for a meeting in November. NCACP MPs were briefed to enlist support within their own parties. Koestler announced that he had finished the first draft of *Reflections on Hanging*.

In his July discussions with Victor, Koestler had promised a pamphlet. Within two months he had come up with a book — a devastating polemic against the retentionists, and the judiciary in particular — supported by exhaustive research and couched in biting and memorable prose. It could not, of course, fully satisfy Victor. On holiday in October in Florence, he began busily papering over what he saw as the philosophical crack in Koestler's argument. A couple of days into the holiday, he went missing in the early morning. Ruth found him sitting on the lavatory writing *Capital Punishment: The Heart of the Matter*. Back in London, he reported happily to Koestler's agent:

> I haven't the smallest doubt that it [*Reflections on Hanging*] is the most exhaustive book yet written on the subject: as such it will be of the greatest value, and I shall publish it with enthusiasm. My criticism was simply that it is not, in my opinion, the sort of book which is *most of all* wanted at the present time: for I believe myself that more people are likely to be affected by the 'religious or moral' appeal than by the argumentation which Koestler has done so brilliantly. Or perhaps the real fact is that two books are equally wanted — Koestler's and another: with a view to this, I dashed off in Florence a six or seven thousand word pamphlet myself, but unfortunately a pamphlet is not a book . . .

Victor's pamphlet was certainly uncompromising. An elaboration of his July letter to the *Telegraph*, it included the italicized sentence: '*If I felt certain that abolition would immediately be followed by a startling increase in the number of murders: I should still say . . . with undiminished conviction, that the most urgent of all the tasks which confront us . . . is the ending of capital punishment.*' The pamphlet was with the newspapers in time to pre-empt the NCACP meeting on 10 November. Victor had not lost his touch: 400 were turned away even from the overflow meeting in the nearby Church House. (Christian Action backed the campaign and Victor asked Diana Collins to chair the overflow meeting — further proof that his feminism was genuine and a vote of confidence that touched her deeply and set her on a new course as a public speaker.) Koestler, convinced that his foreign accent would put people off, had refused to speak. Gardiner and Victor made long speeches, with support from the broadcaster Gilbert Harding, Montgomery Hyde (writer and Unionist MP), Pakenham, J. B. Priestley and others. The abolitionist resolution was passed by acclamation and over £1,000 collected. (Victor — a masterly fund-raiser — always planned such collections down to the finest detail. On this occasion he had planted Elinor Murphy in the body of the hall to declare at the psychological moment that she had in her hand a cheque for £100.)

Although Victor appeared on television the following day, the media coverage was rather disappointing. Nevertheless, December found ten thousand supporters in the ranks and close on £2,000 to hand. A series of provincial meetings was scheduled. Victor controlled the logistics, including widespread distribution of his pamphlet and another called *Capital Punishment: The Facts*. Gardiner, at Victor's behest, was writing a short book scotching the deterrence argument and Koestler was churning out articles for the press. Koestler had also arranged with David Astor, the editor of the *Observer*, that his *Reflections on Hanging* would be serialized early in the New Year, in advance of publication.

When Victor left England for America at the end of the year, all was progressing smoothly. Back in his office in early February, he found things strangely altered. Thus far, the mutual antipathy between him and Koestler had been suppressed in common cause — a taxing suppression, given Koestler's likenesses to Victor in his emotionalism, aggressiveness, and conviction that those who disagreed with him were by definition in error, especially if they constituted a challenge for the limelight. As Peggy Duff once put it, they upstaged each other in showmanship. Victor was piqued that Koestler had pushed himself forward in his absence, achieving pre-eminence in the public eye as spokesman for the abolitionists. Koestler remembered Peggy Duff's delighted report of Victor's question to her: 'Don't they realise I'm much more famous than Arthur Koestler?' Koestler, in his turn, was angry because he believed — wrongly — that Victor was spitefully holding up publication of his book. In fact, it was Victor's usual caution that was causing delay. Koestler had made a number of amendments to his book to meet libel points raised by Gardiner, and had then confronted a series of queries from Harold Rubinstein. He had been losing his temper with Gollancz while Victor was away and wrote to him complaining that 'once you give in to this sort of legal quibbling, you paralyse your writing and cannot wage a campaign.' Victor gave way for once and the book went unsullied to press. Differences were forgotten in the excitement over the Commons debate on capital punishment on 16 February. Gardiner, Koestler and Victor were all there to rejoice in the 293–262 victory. After the vote the Prime Minister, Anthony Eden, was asked if the decision would be implemented and responded opaquely that the government would 'give full weight at once' to the decision.

It was obvious to Koestler that there was still a battle to be fought in the Lords, but Victor saw it differently. Outside the Commons he informed an NCACP organizer there would be no need now for further public gatherings. Koestler disagreed vehemently and insisted on an early meeting of the executive to discuss policy. Victor consented most reluctantly.

Buoyed up by the telegrams and letters of congratulation, Victor happily set about winding up the campaign before the executive had even met. He wrote thank-you letters to a number of MPs, and replied to a recent offer of help: 'We had a sensational victory in the Commons last night, and there is no further need for a campaign in the original sense. We shall, however, keep going as a vigilance group on a small scale, concentrating particularly on the psychiatrical treatment, etc., of people who would have been executed.'

A letter from Acland, warning that 'it will still need every ounce of pressure that you and your colleagues can muster to get it over the remaining hurdles', was ignored. On the 20th he informed the Bishop of Middleton that the Manchester meeting should be cancelled. 'I cannot imagine that many people would want to turn up to hear about a *fait accompli.*' On the 21st he wrote to an author that the 'Campaign offices downstairs carry huge posters: "No more work" and "No more workers wanted"!' At the executive meeting the following day there were stormy scenes, and Frank Owen resigned. Koestler wanted regional meetings, a fund-raising auction and whatever else was necessary for the long-drawn-out campaign he envisaged. Victor opposed any action other than a huge meeting in the Royal Festival Hall. The superiority of Koestler's judgement was demonstrated when Eden announced on the 23rd that all the government proposed was to allow time for a Private Member's Bill. Duff supported regional meetings, Victor accused her of taking sides with Koestler against him, and relations were strained all round. Koestler wrote a letter recapitulating his grievances and Victor used his time-honoured ploy of submitting a written resignation — this time to Gardiner, in whose favour he proposed to abdicate. Gardiner was a born mediator, and wanted to keep Victor as organizer and Koestler as writer for the campaign. He persuaded Victor to withdraw his resignation pending discussion at a meeting on the 25th. Victor's address to the executive that day was a masterpiece of *post hoc* rationalization, admitting only to the incontrovertible. One paragraph ran:

> My own feeling about what happened outside the House of Commons is different from Arthur's. I expressed myself strongly in favour of virtually winding up the campaign, but always with the proviso that Eden's statement would be a satisfactory one: Arthur may remember my phrase 'We are not going to wind up the campaign here and now'. I opposed a hurried meeting of the Executive, because I felt it better to wait for Eden's statement, & meanwhile, on the assumption that this statement would be satisfactory (and I agree I was quite wrong in making the assumption), to make *provisional* plans, for virtually winding up the campaign. But it was never my smallest intention that these plans should be more than provisional.

He gave way gracefully on the auction: others would be permitted to organize it. Above all, Victor concluded, he was prepared 'to go to the limit' to prevent Koestler's resignation, which would damage the campaign, although he considered less than feasible Koestler's insistence that there should be a weekly meeting of a working committee. Before discussing ways and means of waging a successful campaign, he had to know whether the executive 'really & wholeheartedly' wished him to remain as chairman. If not, he would retire with no ill-feeling — sorry only because he cared so much about the campaign. He apologized if anything he had done had distressed Koestler but urged the executive to forget the past and concentrate on its great objective.

Koestler was hopelessly outmanoeuvred; like all other members of the executive he was quite aware that the campaign would collapse without Victor. His capitulation was not graceful, and once Victor was confirmed as chairman the cudgels were taken up again. By early March Victor was feeling sorry for himself. He had been booked since November to speak at a debate at Cardiff Students' Union Society — he was honorary president — on the subject of capital punishment. He pulled out with days to go, pleading heart strain. The following day a telegram was despatched: 'IGNORE MY LETTER WILL MANAGE TO

COME GOLLANCZ'. He spoke on the 16th, his side won and he claimed that he and Ruth 'had never enjoyed an evening more'. (He also insisted on paying all their expenses, as he almost always did with student societies, even though visits to Oxford or Cambridge frequently involved the hire of a chauffeur-driven car from London.)

The strained heart was heard of no more. There was an anonymous and largely gratifying profile in the *Observer* on 11 March: the issue of capital punishment, it said, 'is now recognised to be an urgent one by abolitionists and anti-abolitionists alike, and no single man has been more responsible for creating this sense of urgency than Victor Gollancz. His abolitionist campaign which was launched last year has had a powerful effect both on Parliament and on public opinion.' The profile was in general highly admiring, but with a few reservations:

> In his personal relations Gollancz is sometimes too noisy, too wilful, too insensitive for the absolute comfort of his associates. It is significant that he is a man who is almost defiantly irreticent, and he has little aptitude for the particular delicacies of feeling which more reticent men achieve. He is regarded with much affection, but there is sometimes an element of wryness in this affection. He is widely and justly admired, but this good-hearted capitalist, with his gentle yet predatory face, inspires alarm as well as admiration.

The ringing conclusion more than made amends:

> Victor Gollancz is an exceptionally good man, a clever man, a powerful man. His brains and influence have been used for excellent purposes, and his generous humanity is of particular value at a time when managerial efficiency is becoming the main concern of most politicians. Few Englishmen of our time have pursued the good with so intense a combination of Greek intellectualism, Christian love, and Jewish fervour. He has done a great deal of good, both in public and in private, and his faults of character, shared by many good men before him, have not detracted from his effectiveness. The wilful man, the egotist, the capitalist — these Gollanczes have formed a bodyguard for the protection of Gollancz the would-be saint. It has been a strange formation, and a remarkably effective and beneficent one.

The *Observer* had given Koestler his most important platform; the kindly David Astor probably had a hand in ensuring that Victor received his deserts in its columns. (Not, of course, that Victor approved of all of it. To another profile writer he wrote on 23 March,

> . . . I don't know whether many look upon me as 'egotistical, hard-headed and insensitive'. You got that, I imagine, from the 'Observer' Profile, which was written by a man who has met me only once: that was in 1939,

and the encounter took one minute. I must leave it to those who know me to say whether I am egotistical and insensitive: but as for 'hard-headed' — I do object to the implication of that term. Those interested in prisoners, down-and-outs, and other people in distress, criticise me, on the contrary, for being far too much the opposite of 'hard-headed' in my dealings with them . . .)

No one could stop the rows between Victor and Koestler, who seemed to vie with each other in bad behaviour. After another executive meeting on 13 March Koestler resigned. No one was sorry; the committee was only big enough for one *prima donna*, and the less essential had to go. 'I like Arthur,' wrote Gardiner to Victor, 'and he started the whole idea of the Campaign and has done an enormous amount for it. I have not, however, tried to dissuade him from the position which he has now adopted because it seems to me impossible to continue the Campaign with Executive Committee meetings of the kind which we had the other night . . . '

Koestler was now convinced that Victor had arranged early publication of Gardiner's *Capital Punishment as a Deterrent, and the Alternative* as a pretext for postponing until April *Reflections on Hanging*. More accurate were his concern about the meagre advertising for Gardiner's book and his fear that it presaged similar treatment for his own. He proposed to Victor that all his royalties should be spent on advertising both. Victor was at first outrageously unhelpful, standing on his dignity as the chairman of Gollancz, constitutionally incapable of modifying policy simply because he also happened to be chairman of the NCACP. He was also more than usually naive, as was shown in his seven-page letter to A. D. Peters:

> We have not been in the weeklies for years. As to the provincial papers, we used to go in at Christmas, but cut this out last year, as experience the previous year had not been favourable. The only case I can think of in which we have advertised in the provincial press for a long time is the case of my anthology, 'From Darkness to Light'. In this case, we advertised in some local papers (a) because in these particular places very large quantities indeed had been sold of 'A Year of Grace', and (b) the advertisements in effect cost my firm nothing, for I took only a $7\frac{1}{2}$% royalty on the book . . .
>   . . . I may perhaps add that the whole episode is unique in thirty-two years' publishing experience.

'It is very sad', responded Peters,

> that you and Arthur, having done so much together for the abolition of capital punishment, should now start bickering about advertising . . .

The advertising issue is quite a simple one. Arthur asks you to depart
from your usual rules for this particular book. You admit that you did so
for your anthology, and you justify this action by saying that it cost the
firm nothing, because your royalty was only 7½%. Surely there is at least
equal justification for doing so in the case of a book furthering the joint
cause on which the royalty is 0%. . . . You are probably unaware of the
comments that fly around our little world about your advertising of your
own books — bitter comments from authors on your list, sarcastic ones
from the rest. Those who wish you well would be delighted to find you
bestowing similar favours on a book in which you were keenly interested
for a less personal reason . . .

Koestler's letter, explained Victor in his six-page response, 'must be
seen against the background of "goings on" in our Executive
Committee. I regret the necessity of patting myself on the back: but I
must go so far as to say that I believe everybody present at two stormy
meetings would agree that I behaved with tolerance and patience, and
did everything possible . . . to meet Arthur's point of view.'

Having proved to his own satisfaction at least that he had
underspent on advertising his own book and overspent on Gardiner's,
he went on to accept the inevitable with as many restrictions as he
could decently muster. 'If Arthur', he concluded 'has any notion that I
propose to "crab" the book because of the unfortunate differences of
opinion between us on the Executive, he could not misunderstand me
more. You will perhaps convey to him that, though I think he is a
more than "difficult" member of a Committee, I have nothing but
admiration for what he has done for the Campaign, and nothing but
goodwill towards him.'

For the rest of his life Koestler was convinced that Victor had
deliberately 'crabbed' his book through jealousy and anger. He steered
clear of the NCACP while Victor remained chairman, though he
continued to back its efforts in press articles. He never lost his respect
for Victor's abilities as a campaigner, nor regretted having persuaded
him to take this job on, but he complained about him bitterly behind
his back. Victor was no more forgiving. He wrote in April to du
Maurier that he had had 'rather a dreadful time' over the campaign,
'largely owing to the goings on of a most extraordinary individual,
highly antipathetic to me (in confidence), named Arthur Koestler.'

With Koestler out of the way, Victor made final his plans for a grand
meeting at the Festival Hall on 24 May. Collins was instructed to 'turn
all his guns' on making it a success. 'My idea is that if the National
Campaign tries to sell the hall out, as if Christian Action were not
associated with it, and Christian Action tries to sell the hall out as if the

National Campaign were not associated with it, we really may succeed in getting a crowd of 6,000 or so. So *please* take it very seriously indeed.'

The meeting was a considerable success and featured among the speakers Belgian, Dutch, Norwegian and Swedish experts explaining how their countries managed without capital punishment. More funds were raised and more supporters enlisted, but the focus of the campaign had shifted to the House of Commons: Sydney Silverman, with brilliant patience, was pushing through his abolitionist bill, backed by the active support of dozens of MPs and lawyers. Silverman was almost as antipathetic to Victor as Koestler had been; indeed, Victor's opposition had been largely responsible for his embarrassingly long exclusion from the committee. According to Leo Abse, Silverman was 'the most quarrelsome man in the House' and Victor was only one of many who could not stand him (although he was enormously kind to Silverman's forger brother Ernest, who used to write to him from prison). Gardiner played peacemaker once again.

It was clear to those who knew him that Victor was bored with the campaign. Clinging stubbornly to the belief that the February vote had been the turning-point, he wrote to a local paper in support of the abolitionist candidate in a by-election that 'nothing, now, can possibly prevent capital punishment from being legally abolished in this country in the immediate future.' There was, he told Collins, only a 'remote' chance that the NCACP might have to start again from square one. The realists correctly anticipated the measure's defeat in the Lords on 10 July, which left only the hope that the government might provide time for the bill to go through the Commons again. Within two weeks Victor had relinquished the chairmanship to Gardiner, pleading overwork. He stayed on the executive, still unconvinced by the pragmatists. 'We are winning,' he wrote to a New York friend. 'Nothing can really prevent the Bill from becoming law during the next year. At the moment, we are organising a national petition, which I am certain will show that people of responsibility are overwhelmingly abolitionist.'

The petition took as its model the one Victor and Duff had presented to the Attlee government concerning prisoners of war: the leading lights of every profession in the country were circularized. Duff recalled:

> Day and night we addressed envelopes, folded memorials, filled envelopes and sent them off. Here I must pay a tribute to Gerald Gardiner. Very often, in the evening, he would come into the office with a large suitcase. He would fill it with the memorials and envelopes, take it off home, and

late into the night he and his wife would fold and fill. Early the next morning, on his way to his Chambers, he would call in again and leave the results of his night's work with us. I have had many chairmen over the years, whom I loved, admired, occasionally hated, often argued with, but there never was any other chairman who did that.

Victor contributed to the proceedings as an adviser, and 5 of the 31 publishers' signatures (from a total of 2,500) came from Gollancz: Bush, Livia, Ruth, Horsman and Hilary Rubinstein (Victor appearing among the authors). He could not have any other than abolitionists working close to him. He once considered for a secretarial job the sister of Lettice Cooper. During the interview, it came out that she approved of capital punishment, and he abruptly dismissed her from the building.

The memorial, asking the government 'to give legislative effect to the repeatedly expressed wish of the House of Commons' was delivered to Eden on 22 October 1956. With the Conservative rank-and-file strongly in favour of the rope, it was never likely that their government would take a lead in abolishing it. The Macmillan government produced a compromise, and the Homicide Act of 1957 retained the death penalty for some murders. Unfair and anomalous though the legislation was, as Duff pointed out: 'at least we saved the lives of ten or more people each year'.

Nothing more could be done until there was a new government, so the NCACP went into a sort of suspended animation, with enough funds in the kitty (from the auction that Victor had opposed) to facilitate resuscitation whenever the moment seemed right. Gardiner and Koestler tried to prevent atrophy — impossible in the absence of Victor's energy and resources.

The NCACP had diverted Victor's attentions from another organization, the object of great enthusiasm in the summer of 1955. It was Pakenham's brain-child, designed to offer after-care to prisoners, who at the time were virtually abandoned by the state as soon as they were freed. Victor suggested it be called 'The Bridge' (later amended to 'The New Bridge' to avoid confusion with an existing group) and in November the *Observer* reported that it had been 'not so much founded as pushed into action by the enthusiasm of Lord Pakenham and Victor Gollancz'. Once rolling, it was to have considerable social significance, through the patient work of Pakenham and a few like-minded people, but Victor played virtually no part after 1955. The long-term philanthropic grind was not his style, and in this case he would have had to play second fiddle to one he considered a protégé with a lot to learn.

Occasionally Victor allowed himself to be drawn into other campaigning activities. Collins had him and Ruth on the platform in April 1956 for a meeting at the Festival Hall, where Father Trevor Huddleston made a rousing speech on South Africa under the auspices of Christian Action and the Africa Bureau. Victor had grave reservations about the occasion 'on the spiritual side'. He was, he told Collins, contemplating a memorandum on 'this African business'.

> I have no solution at all to offer: but I am certain that the Huddleston approach (I don't mean, of course, what he did in Africa, but what he is saying now) is certainly no solution at all, and is likely to make matters worse . . .
>
> I suppose what I really feel is that just as it is awfully easy (I know it is in my own case) to feel complete charity for murderers, but none at all for the Lord Chief Justice, so it is awfully easy to feel total compassion for the Africans, but none at all for their Boer tormentors: and that that is bound to make matters worse, because it is bound to harden the tormentors, and make them torment more vilely.
>
> In the case of capital punishment, it doesn't matter very much, because we can actually change the position by legislation: but we can't do that in Africa, where there is not even an opposition on this question: we *have* to act through the tormentors . . .

There was no future in 'a self-righteous blowing off of steam'.

Victor's memorandum did not materialize. Collins no doubt dealt as usual with this most recent of Victor's suggestions about Christian Action's approach to African affairs — with appreciative words and an unchanged course. Victor continued to publish African books, but himself read relatively little on the subject. His ignorance worried him sometimes. In July 1959, for instance, he turned down a request for a speech on South Africa: 'I have never given any real study to the question at all. I just feel, quite simplemindedly, that any kind of racial discrimination is abominable.'

His ignorance was no fault of his friends. Harry Walston, regretting Victor's lack of enthusiasm for African issues, came to the conclusion that he was too old now to embrace so vast a new cause, and was restricted to those he had taken up in his prime. Collins frequently brought Victor into the company of men like Huddleston and Ambrose Reeves, the courageous Bishop of Johannesburg (whose *Shooting at Sharpeville* was published by Gollancz), but congenial though they were, their concerns could not really fire him.

His friendship with Collins often drew him into Christian Action activities. When the organization set up a fund in 1956 to pay defence costs in the South Africa Treason Trials, Victor was a sponsor and contributor, drafted advertisements and co-signed letters to the press. The drive was spectacularly successful: £170,000 of the £200,000 costs was raised; Gardiner's performance at the preliminary hearings as a Christian Action representative did much to discredit the government; and after a four-year trial all 149 defendants were acquitted. Meanwhile, the fund had widened its scope to become Christian Action Defence and Aid, with terms of reference encompassing not only legal costs but the support of the families of political refugees. Victor continued to lend his name and give useful advice, but he was sparing of his time and effort.

From July 1956, when he resigned his chairmanship of the NCACP, he was rather foot-loose for a time. That same month Nasser seized the Suez Canal and Victor was much perturbed by the bellicosity that ensued. He wrote to congratulate Silverman on rallying opposition to the official Labour attitude: 'Good luck to you. Gaitskell seems to me far to the right of the more liberal-minded Tories.' He favoured the internationalizing of all narrow waterways, including Panama and Gibraltar, and naturally abhorred military intervention. He had discussions with Collins, Kingsley Martin and others with a view to mounting yet another campaign, public meeting and all, and briefly attempted a pamphlet of his own. At the height of international tension, late in October — at the beginning of the Suez war — he went off to Paris with Livia and Ruth for a brief holiday which was cut short by the combination of the war and the Soviet invasion of Hungary. On 5 November he wrote to Negley Farson that he found himself 'really quite engulfed by the ghastly international situation — which calls for all sorts of publishing activity.'

Inspiration came from an unlikely source. The psychiatrist Eustace Chesser sent him and a few other leading Jewish philanthropists a copy of his letter of 5 November to the Israeli Ambassador: 'Please forgive my presumption but it did strike me that now would be the time for an appeal to be made to World Jewry for help to be given to the Gaza Strip Arab refugees. I consider such action would make a profound impression and do much to enhance Israel's stature . . .'

'Something of this kind has been in my mind,' answered Victor the following day. 'I am pursuing the matter.' The population of the newly-occupied Gaza Strip included long-term Arab refugees, being fed by the United Nations Relief and Welfare Association (UNRWA). Victor instructed Elinor Murphy to make contact with the Red Cross, the Save the Children Fund, the World Council of Churches, and the United Nations Council for Refugees to find out what was being done in Gaza, fearing that all such organizations had their attention focussed disproportionately on Hungary. Murphy was also briefed to call a meeting of the JSHS for 13 November.

Bent on a straightforward fund-raising exercise, Victor nonetheless took care to pack the committee with his supporters. In addition to Ruth, his majority included Harold, Hilary and Michael Rubinstein, although he did bring in Leonard Cohen and a couple of other Bentwich suggestions. Murphy became secretary and it was decided in principle to launch an appeal.

The mechanics of deciding the nature of the help and the channels through which it should go caused several weeks' delay. A difference of emphasis within the committee was already evident when the Gollanczes set off for America at the end of December. Victor and Harold Rubinstein had a private letter in *The Times* on 1 January 1957, recommending that the Jewish diaspora take a larger view of their responsibilities to Arabs than did Israelis: Bentwich a few days later sent one of his own, and Rubinstein thought it smacked of Zionism. Victor sent instructions from America that a committee meeting should be avoided in his absence.

On his return, two meetings early in March determined policy. Bentwich accordingly drafted an appeal for money and clothing, and asked Victor to add 'flesh and blood' to his prose. Victor's opening paragraph ran: 'There are some who are still capable of feeling, beneath the statistics of mass misery, the sufferings, as if in their own persons, of so many human beings like themselves. It is to all such that we appeal: we beg them to assist, by specific action and at once, in alleviating the dreadful plight of the Arab refugees, and particularly of those in the Gaza strip.'

The NCACP was given immediate notice to quit the rooms it still occupied in Henrietta Street and Ruth took over there as organizer while the search began for a full-time secretary. Victor wrote by hand to forty-two influential friends and acquaintances asking for publicity, support and contributions. On 20 March Hilary Rubinstein, writing to an author in Victor's stead, explained that 'he is really working round the clock at present: on top of his publishing, which takes the usual twelve hours a day, he is in the thick of organising a big campaign to raise money for the Gaza refugees, who are in a desperate plight. This pretty well takes up the remaining twelve hours . . .'

The press letters were reinforced by advertisements, but the results were rather disappointing by comparison with earlier JSHS efforts: £7,000 and a quantity of clothing were collected for UNWRA. The poor response was not so surprising, given that the Israelis had evacuated Gaza and the UN was now in control. The refugees' situation had not deteriorated noticeably for several years, and their plight therefore lacked the novelty value of, for instance, the Hungarians.

Victor was apprised of this distasteful truth by Leonard Cohen, who was annoyed by a rebuke. He had written to the *Guardian*, and Victor felt he had given 'a pro-Israel slant to the whole thing. Speaking certainly for myself and Harold, we have no such slant: we are simply pro-humanity . . . '

Cohen was annoyed, and counter-attacked by complaining of the five-month delay in announcing the appeal, which, he said, had seriously damaged its potential effectiveness. The charge of procrastination was just; Victor had missed the most propitious time for raising money—and partly, at least, out of his dislike of decisive action in his absence. He pushed on with the appeal through April and May, with Ruth working several hours a day dealing with funds as they came in. Reporting to Bentwich, who was in Jerusalem in May, that the appeal had so far made a profit of £6,000, he admitted no disappointment. He was delighted with the letters that had accompanied contributions: 'There is no doubt that, quite apart from the handsome amount raised, the moral effect has been extraordinary.' He tried for a time to keep up the momentum of the campaign, but after he went to Venice on holiday in June the appeal was allowed to die a natural death.

Eight years earlier, Victor would have scrapped his holiday plans to keep the appeal going. Now, at 64, he could work as furiously as ever for short periods, which might even overlap when projects fired his imagination in rapid succession, but age had progressively shortened his attention span. Variety, it seemed, was essential to stimulate the flow of his adrenalin. The JSHS had lost its attraction.

During subsequent years such occasional donations as reached the JSHS were sent straight on to another charity. The only flicker of activity was in 1960, when an application was made for help to buy an orthopaedic appliance for a crippled Arab girl. The JSHS funds and a whip-round among Rubinsteins and Gollanczes raised £90 and Bentwich wrote from Jerusalem to say they had provided more than was required. 'I wish in future you'd ask me about such applications before you send the money. I may know whether they have weight or are justified.' Victor replied gaily: 'You'd better regard any unnecessary balance as a contribution from me, to last for years, to the Friends of the Hebrew University!' No issue ever again inspired Victor to reactivate the society and by 1966 even Rubinstein had lost heart. Victor agreed that subscribers should be advised to send money to other organizations in future.

Victor's concentration on the Gaza question had been further diluted by his initial work on another new book, with the working title *The Sanity of Christ*. Its thesis was that Christians must reject any compromise with Christ's own absolutism. Christian communism was still posing a severe problem, but Victor had in absolutist terms already gone far beyond the majority of pacifists. He wrote reprovingly in April 1957 to a member of the Standing Joint Pacifist Committee that its recent pamphlet (suggesting that unilateral disarmament would make Britain a less tempting target) was misguided: 'Unilateral disarmament can, in my view, only be advocated with complete honesty if the possibility that one's nation may become a martyr nation is fully accepted.' Similarly, he refused to participate in the campaign to stop the testing of nuclear weapons. Only total disarmament would serve, he explained to the organizer, and he would be compelled to say so if he joined the campaign, voicing also the absolutist necessity to risk the enslavement or annihilation of Britain for the sake of such disarmament. This would tend to damage the chances of success with the public.

After some months wrestling with his book, he departed at the end of December for several weeks in America. During his absence, on the initiative of Kingsley Martin and J. B. Priestley, fifty distinguished people came together to set up the Campaign for Nuclear Disarmament (CND). Peggy Duff suggested the Collins home at Amen Court as a meeting place. Martin, although he took the chair, did not want to head the movement and he pushed successfully for the appointment of John Collins — next to Victor the best-known and most successful campaigner in Britain, and the obvious choice. The CND executive included Ritchie Calder, Michael Foot, Kingsley Martin and J. B. Priestley, with Peggy Duff as organizing secretary. Other old associates and friends of Victor — Acland and Benn Levy — were among those co-opted later. By the time Victor returned, a highly successful Central Hall meeting had been held and CND was on its way.

In Christopher Driver's words, it was 'something of a surprise to connoisseurs of British peace movements' that the name of Victor Gollancz was not among the committee members. To Victor, it was a devastating insult: this was the cause he had been looking for and its organizers had left him out of it. He held Collins responsible, and Collins found it impossible to make him believe the truth — that despite his own enormous efforts to get Victor on to the committee, he had been decisively vetoed by a number of the inaugurators, who wanted to avoid antagonizing the Labour Party and feared that Victor would wreck an anti-nuclear movement by pushing it to extreme pacifism. Victor was broken-hearted. His close friend and disciple was stepping into his shoes and rejecting him through jealousy. The wound, thought Diana Collins, who spent hours trying to convince him of her husband's innocence, was one of the deepest of his life. 'I cry about it sometimes', he told her. The Collinses appreciated that it was a measure of his struggle to be good that he worked so hard to forgive John Collins for the offence he had not committed. His near-inability to believe in Collins's innocence probably had its roots in guilt. In the early days of the Association for World Peace, Victor as chairman had yielded to the view of Dick Stokes and others that Collins's involvement was counter-productive because he did not have the necessary force to sustain the reputation he had secured through Christian Action. Even while protesting his disagreement with the critics, Victor had persuaded Collins to withdraw from the AWP. Collins was hurt at the time, but easily forgave Victor and quickly got over the snub. It is all too likely that Victor subsconsciously needed to project his own jealousy on to Collins and believe that he had taken revenge through CND.

Victor made the gesture of accepting the invitation to become a sponsor, and then set himself to trying to force CND on to the right lines — even from outside its centre of power. His first major move was in his address to a meeting in Oxford Town Hall organized by the local CND, where he shared the platform with the writers John Berger, Alex Comfort, Priestley and Philip Toynbee. (He never tired of Oxford, and took every opportunity to visit again and absorb the surroundings and ambience he had so loved. During the war, when petrol rationing permitted, he used to go there to refresh himself, and show various daughters the sights that filled him with nostalgia.) He had reason to be confident of his reception on what was, for him, his home ground as an orator. Over the years he had made many dozens of speeches in Oxford, and his last one, at the Oxford Union in December 1957, had brought him a terrific press. 'With the advance of Mr Victor Gollancz to the dispatch box electric vitality was injected into a tired debate. Buoyant and dominant, his thick, powerful voice grating from subterranean depths, he could get away with anything. . . . Though a cynic might have thought Mr Gollancz's "love thy neighbour" solution to world problems naive, none could deny that he richly deserved one of the greatest ovations the Union has heard in recent years.'

On 4 March 1958 he had a different effect. The 1,000-strong audience voted 9–1 in favour of the moderate anti-nuclear motion but a clue to its reaction to the speakers came in the next day's *News Chronicle*:

> In some ways, looking up at the grey-haired Mr Gollancz on the platform, and sensing the sincere passion with which he pleads for a moral gesture from Britain, one cannot help thinking of Oxford twenty or more years ago.
>
> Let us not take this too far. This nuclear weapons issue has gripped the students as few things have done since the war. They are determined to avoid the label of woolly-minded pacifists, such as was applied to those students who voted in 1933 never to fight for King and country.

John Berger was very moved by Victor's speech, but, according to *Cherwell* a few days later, the sponsors of the rally 'expressed themselves as dismayed by the "moral, sanctimonious tone" of such speakers as Priestley, Gollancz and Philip Toynbee.' The *Observer* reported that in Junior Common Rooms some of the speakers were being dismissed as 'the woollies'. And the *Daily Express* quoted one student's denigration of 'dear old Gollancz and dear old JB! How naive! They just don't go down with the present generation.'

Victor, of course, felt that neither Priestley nor Toynbee had gone far enough. In his own speech he had criticized the resolution and called for total unilateral disarmament. He explained the following day to Pat Arrowsmith why he did not wish to sponsor the Aldermaston March: 'The fact is that, from my experience at Oxford last night, I doubt whether much is going to be achieved by a campaign run on the present lines. I have only been back, it is true, a week from America, and have not yet quite got the hang of things: but in my view the lines on which the thing is being conducted are not nearly fundamental enough . . . '
He spent the following evening criticizing John Collins and then wrote to make up: 'I had the idea that I hurt you last night, as seeming to crab the efforts of the Nuclear Campaign. I am very sorry indeed if this is the case. I know very well, of course, that, in an agonisingly complex situation, you are doing the very best that, as you see it, can be done to prevent disaster. I know it so well that it hardly seems to me worth saying. The trouble, of course, is that when I feel a thing very strongly I say it in an absolutely uninhibited way.' The only hope of salvation lay in converting sufficient numbers of people to the principle of '100%': total pacifism. Otherwise, CND would have no effective argument, and no public appeal, at a time when the major political parties favoured the retention of the bomb. 'But none of this means that I do not honour and respect the effort you are making in, as I said before, an agonisingly complex situation . . . '

The sincerity of Victor's beliefs and the placatory tone of this letter did not disguise from Collins the hostility Victor was trying to suppress. He made it clear that he still blamed Collins for his exclusion and complained of it to others. He was also very jealous of his friend's new prominence. He had been able to live with Collins's immense success as head of Christian Action, but the leadership of a mass movement was a different matter. On the good days, his affection triumphed: he even wrote to *The Times* to take Collins's side in a controversy with Lord Halifax. On the bad days, envy and resentment dominated. He floated to Acland his plans to run an absolutist campaign to change the climate of opinion, excluding all politicians lest they corrupt it. Acland, honourable as ever, wrote a paper to demonstrate that such a plan was both impracticable and immoral —'we have no right to rejoice in the purity of our principles . . . if we mean to unload on to others the sorry struggle between these very principles and the actual decisions which can be taken and sustained . . . in the world as it is today.' He favoured an 'Absolute Campaign' only if its spokesmen admitted that they themselves would in practice have to compromise. Victor abandoned this idea and decided to go back to writing instead. *The Sanity of Christ* continued to be intractable, and, from Italy, where he went on holiday in April and May, he announced to Elinor Murphy his idea for another book: *Groping and the Unconditional*. In his absence she was to collect the raw material — all his own books, pamphlets, leaflets, and *Times* and *Guardian* letters. In the days when copies of library material had to be made by hand, this was a frightful job, on which she spent much labour. Victor had lost interest almost before he returned to London, for he had started to brood about a book on the more immediate nuclear weapon issue. Although his doubts often recurred, he had temporarily managed to exonerate Collins. To two friends he wrote on 3 July that

> I hasten to let you know that I was very unjust to John Collins the other night. The whole thing has come, happily, completely into the open, and I now don't have the slightest doubt that John has made every effort to get me on to the committee from the very beginning, but has been defeated by hostility (and I am aware of the reason for it) in another quarter. The misunderstanding arose because (unwisely, as I think, and as he now thinks too) he kept the facts from me because he thought they would hurt me — and this produced a general atmosphere of evasion, which I wrongly interpreted . . .

Collins appears to have been cleared by Victor's inspiration that the man really to blame was Priestley, who had in fact been only one of many of Victor's opponents on the executive. He had presumably taxed

Collins with the allegation that Priestley had objected to him — something that could not be denied. Victor had a ready-made face-saving explanation for Priestley's enmity: they had had a dispute many years before over Victor's handling of *An English Journey*. Happy now to lay the blame on a man he had begun to dislike anyway (he was jealous because Priestley got on well with Diana Collins) he successfully suppressed for a time his other resentments about Collins. For his part, Collins was thankful to be on good terms again, and responded enthusiastically to the news that Victor was proposing to write a book about the bomb. He urged him to pull out all the stops in the hope of elevating the CND debate. Victor applied himself to *The Devil's Repertoire or Nuclear Bombing and the Life of Man* in July and finished it in six weeks. It was a 40,000-word religious justification for unilateral nuclear disarmament, addressed to all countries, with the emphasis on discussion of spiritual and ethical responsibility and a few details about the effects of radiation thrown in. He sought advice on technical aspects from a wide range of experts, from Julian Huxley to A. J. P. Taylor. In triumph he wrote to Collins on 18 August that he had just finished and expected it to be out in November.

> Heaven knows what people will make of it! After an introductory chapter, there is a long one which tries to establish the existence of spirit, as I say that you cannot give the spiritual case against nuclear warfare without first asking whether there is any such thing as spirit. . . . Then comes an equally long chapter dealing with the ethics that stem from a spiritual conception of the universe: this goes into a lot of detail, including insects, flowers and stones! Then comes what I suppose is the longest chapter, on the bomb itself: and finally an almost equally long thing called 'The Devil's Repertoire', dealing with catchwords such as 'you can't apply Christianity to politics', 'we want reason, not emotionalism', and so on. . . . I have the suspicion that people will be furious at having to wade through the two long chapters on spirit and ethics, before they come to the bomb. But I was determined to do the book in no other way . . .

'It is', he wrote to Edith Sitwell in September, 'the only thing I have done that I attach any real importance to: for I do feel that perhaps I have said what I wanted to say, and I have never before felt that.' Those who had read it in manuscript thought well of it and believed that 'if it could really be got going, it might have a really big sale and possibly even influence opinion in a serious way.' To improve its chances of achieving that result, the price was to be low and a paper-covered edition available. 'Everything depends, of course, on whether or not the book gets the right kind of publicity: if it falls into the hands of some sneering materialist, it will be killed stone dead.' Would she, if she liked the enclosed proofs, ask the *Sunday Times* to let her review it? She agreed even before reading it. Proofs were also despatched to Schweitzer (now sufficiently back in favour to merit 'With homage' but not 'Cher Maître'), begging a quote which did not materialize.

Briefly in sunny mood, Victor presented Collins with a generous cheque towards the campaign. He then spoiled the effect by writing to the *New Statesman* to point out the moral inadequacies of a recent letter to the editor from Ritchie Calder, a member of the CND executive. His letter appeared on 4 October. A week later Calder responded temperately, but A. J. P. Taylor, another member of the CND executive, was devastating: 'Mr Victor Gollancz is no doubt a very clever man; and his letter to you must have given him great intellectual satisfaction. It is difficult to understand how it helps to promote the cause of nuclear disarmament which presumably he has at heart. The Devil has many weapons; and the temptation to score debating points is not the least of them.'

Victor often placed his friends in dilemmas. Collins had more than his share. On this occasion, it was only the intervention of Diana that stopped Victor from explaining to *New Statesman* readers that Collins had warmly approved of his attack on Ritchie Calder.

John Collins, sympathetic though he was to the moral case, was often compelled to agree with Victor for a more mundane reason: he had to disarm as far as possible Victor's incipient, and potentially damaging, enmity towards CND. He frequently found himself conceding Victor's criticisms of steps he had himself taken to keep his followers united, in the hope of deflecting Victor's urge to interfere more directly. It was ironic that Collins was known to the world as a 'man of wrath' — exposer of clerical hypocrisy, scourge of the Archbishop of Canterbury, confidently despotic over his own campaigns, and capable of making enemies. Like Acland, Pakenham and other considerable men — men who, despite their humility, had ambition, drive and a belief in their own rightness — he was often reduced by the power of Victor's personality to expressing admiration that bordered on sycophancy. Acland and Pakenham saw Victor only occasionally. Collins saw him often and though he greatly valued Victor's assistance at times, he was all too frequently embarrassed by his attentions. Collins's secret weapon, of course, through all the vicissitudes was the combined tact, judgement and charm of Diana.

Advance copies of *The Devil's Repertoire* went out in October. (There was hell to pay when Victor attributed to malice a packing error which despatched four complimentary copies in the wrong envelopes.) A worryingly large number of recipients — from Eleanor

Roosevelt and Theodor Heuss to Anthony Wedgwood Benn — sent their thanks before reading it, but there were a number of consolations. Augustus John asked to draw him some time (an offer which Victor gratefully accepted but which never materialized); Trevor Huddleston thought it 'truly splendid'; and several of his authors enthused. Sitwell again gave most satisfaction: 'WHAT A NOBLE WONDERFUL BOOK GRATEFUL THANKS EDITH'. After meeting Victor in London she was inspired to greater effusiveness:

> What a wonderful thing to have that great book in the form it will appear.
> I can never say adequately what I think it means to the world that a man living at this time could have the courage and the pride to write it.
> My gratitude to you is so deep for giving me one of the first copies.
> What you told me yesterday about your sufferings — your Stigmata — moved me so greatly . . .

There was a long letter from Geoffrey Fisher, who had again been attacked in the book. 'After glancing through your book I am inclined to say that you have all the old virtues of your Repton days supported by your immense sensitiveness and ability. On the other hand, to my mind, you still have the same blind spot that you had then . . .' Victor took Fisher's criticisms well, as he did du Maurier's suggestion that he was unrealistic in his hopes for freedom even after a totalitarian take-over. A recent but much-loved author, Lady Flavia Anderson, who accepted the basic premise of the book, argued that the Creator had implanted in animal and human life the instinct to defend its young. Victor's answer was that it was purely an animal instinct:

> What I can't understand about you Christians (if you'll forgive me for putting it like that!) is that you never seem to pay any attention to what Christ said and did! What do you think Christ meant when he refused to talk to his mother and brothers, or, to put it another way, refused to differentiate between them and anyone else? . . . It has always seemed to me a naive piece of spiritual illiteracy to imagine that the starvation, let us say, of one's own child should concern one more than the starvation of somebody else's child.

Victor was correct in his pessimistic estimation of the appeal for reviewers of his absolutist position. That was little comfort when the *Sunday Times* refused to let Sitwell review the book, and when the *Observer* gave it to 'the most hack of hack Labour party foreign-affairs' men — Denis Healey — he was desolate. The fear of what Healey might say was used as a lever to extract quotes from the sympathetic. As he feared, the press (including Healey) was generally poor. It was not that people thought it a bad book — more that most of them felt that Victor had lost touch with reality. Disconsolate at his manifest failure to fire the conscience of the nation (and more particularly CND) Victor was thrilled by a letter from an American author, Brendan Gill, who thought his advance copy 'a marvellous piece of work'. A copy of the letter was sent on to Collins, 'not because it puffs me up (as a matter of fact, it produces in me a mood of abashed humility such as I rarely achieve), but because it does bear on the whole discussion we've been having about tactics. The writer is Brendan Gill, one of the three most important members of the "New Yorker" staff, and, while a perfectly adorable man, an extremely hard-headed one, who is sometimes (though quite erroneously) considered a cynic . . . '

It must have been something of a relief to Collins when Victor again took off for America at the end of 1958. Relations were clearly still somewhat fraught on his return: an author requested Victor's intercession with Collins, only to learn from a secretary that 'for various personal reasons, which he would prefer not to go into, he would rather not put pressure on John Collins.' However, cordial interludes were the rule rather than the exception, and Victor postponed a holiday to speak on 25 May at the Albert Hall, at a peace rally organized by Collins (jointly with the Quakers) in his capacity as Chairman of Christian Action. Victor contrived to be the most radical of those who spoke — taking as his theme that inspired by his researches on *The Sanity of Christ* — 'Father, the gate is open'. It would only take one nation to leap through the gate of deliverance in faith for all others to follow. 'A qualified Christian ethic is a contradiction in terms', he was quoted as saying, but, added the reporter, it was unfortunate that 'he did not make clear in what ways his hearers should, and could, give effect to their convictions. This lack of practical challenge was perhaps the weakest feature of the meeting.' Another commentator saw Victor's performance as a 'truly evangelical appeal'.

The meeting attracted about 6,000 people, but Collins was too taken up with CND to pursue his inter-church peace initiative very earnestly. He was himself caught between the idealism fostered by Victor and the pragmatic approach proper to CND. It was Victor's influence that had Collins delivering an uncompromising sermon in St Paul's on the theme of 'Be ye perfect, as your heavenly Father is perfect.' (Collins was later to conclude that this was an unrealistic demand.) Yet he had to work day-to-day with the non-pacifists and hardheaded men who could keep CND growing.

The ups and downs continued. On 16 July Victor wrote to his nephew, Daniel Lowy, that he could not address his Wolverhampton meeting in CND week in September: 'I of course passionately approve of the object of the CND, but, for reasons into which I will not enter, I am at the moment taking no active part in it.' Yet the following day Victor agreed to speak in that same week, offering six nights provisionally. Peggy Duff, with whom he was now on poor terms, had transmitted a request from Collins, recently departed for Russia. Victor replied:

> I should wish to feel reasonably assured in each case, that the general character of the meeting, and the numbers likely to be present, would be such as to warrant the giving up of the time and the expenditure of energy. This is because I am at present engaged on the preparation of a book on the allied theme (or rather on a larger theme with which this one is bound up) and the allocation of time is important. To be precise, I think approximately an expected audience of five hundred is the minimum I ought to do . . .

Duff fixed him up with thirteen meetings spread over four evenings. They were later cancelled because of the printers' strike, re-booked with its sudden end, and reduced to eleven. Collins booked him also for the Trafalgar Square rally — Sunday's culmination of the week — along with Bertrand Russell and Michael Foot. Victor was irritated by poor attendances and threatened to cancel his Saturday evening meetings unless audiences of 500 were guaranteed. In the event, there was a good domestic reason for him to back out, but he did turn up for Trafalgar Square. That week's engagement spelled the virtual end of Victor's work for CND, bar his very occasional presence at an Oxford meeting or a Trafalgar Square rally. Collins understood his overt disapproval of the CND line and bore with humour the cross of Victor's resentment at his, Collins's fame, but Victor's unreasonableness enabled the erstwhile disciple more quickly to break free of the influence of his old mentor. Without Diana's unceasing efforts to keep the friendship going, it is unlikely that it would have survived. Ruth refused to get involved.

Nuclear disarmament had also affected Victor's attitude to Labour, which was now even more volatile than usual. In 1955 he had abandoned the party over Acland, and in 1956 he had announced that the only issue in deciding how to vote was where individual candidates stood on capital punishment. Yet he had drifted back to his old allegiance and inspired Michael Foot to write *Guilty Men, 1957*, which pointed the finger at those responsible for the Suez *débâcle*: it did not sell out its print run. His dislike of the Labour leadership prevented him publishing mainstream propaganda, yet in late June 1959 he accepted Anthony Wedgwood Benn's invitation to appear in a party political broadcast to explain why, on balance, he would vote Labour. He changed his mind on 7 September and refused, only to change it again on 20 September when he told the Trafalgar Square crowds that

> until yesterday, although I have been a lifelong member of the Labour movement and voted at every election, I had decided not to vote at this election because, frankly, I saw little to choose between the two parties.
>
> But I changed my mind when Mr Gaitskell ended his broadcast last night with a reference to Khrushchev's speech.
>
> Khrushchev's speech was a breath of fresh air, an abandonment of the fee-fi-fo-fum of politics. Mr Gaitskell accepted it in that spirit. It may have been electioneering; I don't know and I don't care. But, repentantly, I go back to the Labour Party — to vote for it.

The election was set for 8 October. Though Victor had postponed his holiday, he seems to have been without invitations to speak for his party. Instead, he spoke for his local Liberal candidate at his eve-of-poll meeting. He captured the headlines on polling-day. '"I'LL VOTE LIBERAL," SAYS GOLLANCZ' wrote the *Daily Mail* correspondent — going on to describe Victor as 'the fluffy-haired, mild-mannered man who ranks among Socialism's arch-intellectuals.' 'MR GOLLANCZ HAS JOINED THE LIBERALS' announced the *Daily Express* — misleadingly, as the *Guardian* report demonstrated:

> Mr Victor Gollancz, who unexpectedly appeared on a Liberal platform at Mr Derek Monsey's eve-of-poll meeting in Westminster, began by emphasising that he had no intention of leaving the Labour party. Neither did he intend joining the Liberal party, but on this occasion he intended to vote Liberal since Mr Monsey, unlike his rival candidates, believed in complete nuclear disarmament . . .
>
> In spite of his insistence that he was not intending to change parties at present, Mr Gollancz was cheered heartily by the large audience. He had been a Liberal, he explained, when he was about 3 or 4, but had departed from them on economic policy. For that matter, he added, he disagreed with Labour's economic policy too . . .

Victor was furious about the *Express* report and tried to get *The Times* to publish a letter of correction. 'My adherence will, in fact, be given to the Labour Party for the rest of my life unless another should at any time arise closer to my own views, which are those of a pacifist, equalitarian, Christian Socialist.'

When the Conservatives won the election with an overall majority of 100, Victor had no doubt as to the cause of Labour's humiliation. In November, he had fresh thoughts about an Absolutist Campaign, and sent to the Collinses and Trevor Huddleston a prospectus for a group to be called 'Humanitas'. Its members would 'persistently and devotedly' present to the people an alternative to the pagan and materialistic approach of the major political parties:

> Not personal greed, but personal service: not national 'interest', but international obligation: no more hanging, no more flogging, no more bombs: the liberalising of education, as against the increasing craze for more technics [sic] and greater 'efficiency'; the abolition of penal vengeance, and its replacement by a humble and compassionate concern for the personality of offenders — this is the kind of thing we should put forward. There is no question of forming a new political party: the aim rather is to create, during the next few years, such a climate of opinion as might transform all parties. . . .
> I believe that, properly launched and unremittingly pursued, such a campaign might sweep the country. The moment is ripe, for sensitive people everywhere are appalled.

Huddleston found the idea enormously appealing, but pointed out that it would be monumentally difficult, once such a group was launched, to maintain the interest and enthusiasm of supporters. He himself was already over-committed and would shrink from getting involved in anything more.

'Humanitas' was still-born. Victor was no doubt spared a great deal of ridicule: an anti-materialist campaign headed by the prosperous Victor Gollancz would have given the right-wing press a field day. He and Ruth had sold Brimpton Lodge the previous month and were currently disposing of surplus paintings, books and furniture at Sotheby's. Such considerations would not have occurred to Victor, who described himself around this time as 'poorish', and worried about his 'slender capital', but his more realistic friends must have been somewhat relieved that 'Humanitas' never took off. Victor spent a few weeks brooding about the presentation of a spiritual case to the young, and foreswore speaking engagements until he had worked out his pitch. He was not notably successful. When he spoke on disarmament in an Oxford Union debate in February 1960, *Isis* reflected the impatience of the new generation: 'Mr Gollancz's morally outraged voice has been heard too often in Oxford: others could have served the Campaign better; he represents too much the institutionalized fervour that has attended its development.' *Cherwell* was no kinder. It spoke well of the first five speakers, singling out Peter Jay for 'his rare ability to combine a tremendous logical depth of thought with a Union manner that always commands the full attention of the House.' But 'Victor Gollancz was a considerable disappointment to those of us who had heard so much about his previous visits. He indicated early on that he wished to avoid the pitfalls of emotionalism, a word which was rather unjustly thrown around on both sides (a decision of this kind can surely be validly affected by emotion), but he nevertheless fell into moving appeals and illogical argument.' The unilateralists lost by 277 to 185. Victor, who always read his press cuttings, must have been wounded even more by the comments than by the vote. He avoided public speaking for a while.

To Victor, early in 1960, it must have seemed that the times were out of joint. Trailing along behind the leaders on the last stage of the April march from Aldermaston to Trafalgar Square, he was, for all his vitality, a powerless 'old woolly' of the breed disparaged by the youthful element of CND. But there were consolations just around the corner.

First, there was the honorary degree of Doctor in Laws conferred on him at the end of June by Trinity College Dublin. The elegant Latin oration stressed his life-long insistence on the application of higher ethical ideals to national and international life, and went on memorably: 'For the ancient Romans "thunder on the left" was a propitious omen; for us in our generation, the words of prophecy, warning, and denunciation, against injustice and inequality among races, nations, classes and citizens, which were published from "the Left" under his auspices, were equally beneficial.'

Even more exciting was the award of the 1960 Peace Prize of the German Book Trade, whose previous recipients had included Martin Buber (the German Jewish religious philosopher whose work on Chassidism had greatly influenced Victor), Hermann Hesse, Theodor Heuss and Schweitzer. The prize was £1,000 — to be presented in an elaborate ceremony in Frankfurt in September. It was a poor second best to the Nobel Prize, but that did not detract from his simple enjoyment of the honour.

Victor wanted Heuss to make the presentation, but the ex-president declined in some embarrassment. He simply could not 'give a well grounded appreciation of Victor Gollancz's literary work and of his position in English intellectual life', for he had read only his translated writings, and 'to say merely a few words about the moral and political attitude of Mr Gollancz — however important this was and remains — is, on such an occasion, beneath his and my dignity.' Victor, who had been a private dinner guest of Heuss's on his recent visit to England, and who referred to him as a friend, cannot have been pleased by Heuss's explanation that, though he had done the job before for personal friends with whose literary and public work he was familiar, 'in the case of Mr Gollancz this does not apply to a comparable extent.'

Any disappointment was short-lived. The new President, Heinrich Lübke, whom Victor had known slightly in the 1940s when he was helping to set up the Christian Democratic Party, had heard of the event and announced that he wished, out of personal admiration, to make the presentation himself. The weeks of preparation for the visit to Germany were as busy as usual. His German hosts were going to tremendous efforts to make the event pleasurable, arranging for his favourite music to be played and his friends to be accommodated at the various functions. Victor, meanwhile, had written a speech which Julius Braunthal translated, and he rehearsed it with a German Gollancz employee. His efforts were in vain. A telegram was despatched to the organizer on 15 September reporting the impossibility of delivering the speech in German and requesting a good interpreter. There were further complications, as explained the following day in another telegram:

AS APPEARS FROM YOUR LETTER MY SPEECH WENT TO PRESIDENT BEFORE TELEPHONED CORRECTIONS MADE PLEASE INFORM PRESIDENTS OFFICE THAT SENTENCE ABOUT HAVING UNDERSTOOD HARDLY A WORD HE HAD SAID HAS BEEN OMITTED STOP IT WAS ENGLISH TYPE OF JOKE NOT UNDERSTOOD ABROAD THREE EXCLAMATION MARKS GOLLANCZ

Lübke's long *laudatio* on 21 September was extremely well-informed about Victor's work and writings, all of which he rightly saw as inspired by his 'strong and uncommonly deep religiosity'.

Victor Gollancz, *the enemy* who came to us as our best friend, *the Briton* who did not demand our subjection, *the Jew* who did not regard us as murderers, but as 'fellow-members in the all-encompassing brotherhood of Man' won a victory over us then which, in terms of humanity, was far more important than a victory of arms. For it was humanity which he won, human beings that he drew together, and thereby prepared the way for peace. . . .

Victor Gollancz has made the world richer with what he has done and with what he has written. He has taught many men to see how things fit together in a different way, and to think through the problems more thoroughly, and has thereby aroused hopes and given new courage to live. . . .

'The gratitude of the German people is the sort that makes a man humble', Victor had once commented. Now he strove hard to stop it going to his head. In his acceptance speech he quoted one of his favourite Chassidic stories:

A certain Rabbi, who had journeyed to a distant town to take up a new appointment there, locked himself up in a room on arrival, instead of immediately presenting himself to the reception committee, which waited for him outside. Someone heard him pacing endlessly to and fro, and saying repeatedly 'What a wonderful man I am!' 'I am probably the most learned man in the whole of Israel!' 'There have been few such saints as I.' When at last the Rabbi emerged, the man who had overheard asked him why he had acted in this extraordinary way. The Rabbi replied: 'It's a very bad thing to feel proud of oneself, particularly when there's no justification for it. Now of course I knew that the reception committee would praise me far beyond my merits, but feared, nevertheless, that when I actually heard what they had to say I should believe them. So I have been saying it myself, over and over again. For no one, you see, can be impressed when he praises himself: and now that I've got used to this nonsense by constant repetition from my own lips, there's no danger of my believing it when I hear it from yours.'

He had remembered that story when he read the script of the *laudatio*, which

really *is* far too much. Quite honestly, I have never understood why so much fuss has been made about, what, from time to time, I have tried to do with my life, and particularly about what I have tried to do for Germany. I have always thought, indeed, that all this fuss indicates a quite dreadful deterioration, during the course of this century, in the state of the world. I have listened, sometimes, but unhappily by no means always, to the promptings of a very ordinary human heart: hating injustice and oppression and cruelty and violence and war, I have tried, in a tiny way, to do what I could towards mitigating these evils. What is so extraordinary about that? and doesn't it point, as I have said, to a terrible state of affairs that it should be *thought* extraordinary?

Hitler, more than anyone, had been Victor's catalyst. His message of hate had crystallized in Victor what he had always '*nearly* known' — that evil should be met by putting out 'every scrap of the opposite that one could discover in one's nature — every scrap of love, every scrap of gentleness, every scrap of forgiveness'. He realized, too, 'that if there had been more gentleness and love in the world, Hitler might not have been Hitler. He was what life and the world had made him. I remembered that, in the words of William Blake, "Every criminal was once an Infant Joy". And so I could not hate Hitler: and so in this Hall, once a Church, I say, from the bottom of my heart, "May his tormented soul rest in peace" . . .'

(Victor was delighted by one fan-letter he received following this: 'Dear Sir, From the bottom of my heart I congratulate you for your outspoken speech in Frankfurt, calling a spate a spate.' He stuck this on his wall amid a little gallery of absurdities culled from his correspondence.)

The few days he and Ruth spent in Frankfurt were an unmitigated delight. This time he was spared fact-finding tours, and could bask in the honours done him, including a meeting with officials and beneficiaries of the Victor Gollancz Stiftung. His writings were exhibited at the Book Fair and there were photographs of him all over the city. Press coverage was extensive and among the articles in his honour was one from the ever-generous and humble Pakenham. 'Victor Gollancz did more than any other single man after the last war to awaken the British conscience with regard to the suffering of the German people, especially of the inhabitants of the British Zone of Occupation. In this connection I am not forgetting such brave Christians as the late Bishop of Chichester, Dr Bell, or Richard Stokes, but Gollancz attained an ardour of prophetic fire, unequalled among the British public in my lifetime.'

Ruefully recalling Victor's 'merciless' attacks on government, Pakenham judged him absolutely right in refusing to give the benefit of the doubt 'to us (including myself) who were doing our best'. At a time when all Germans were suffering 'torments of the soul', Victor demanded on their behalf the application of the highest ideals of Christianity and Judaism. 'It is no exaggeration to say that all our ethical standards were affected by his annihilating criticism, his inspiring calls for assistance and to forgive those who trespass against us, and his practical achievements in the Save Europe Now movement. I hope that men will always see in him the prophet of justice and forgiveness.'

Victor gave £650 from his prize to the Council for Christians and Jews for conciliation work in Germany — an act of generosity which gave him pleasure, as did the numerous congratulatory letters from Germany. Most pleasing of all was a missive from Schweitzer that made up for his previous omissions: 'I follow everything you say and write and share your opinions and admonitions. I always admire your good example . . . With kind remembrance from your faithful follower'. Victor's cup would have run over but for one criticism, offered by a man of uncompromising integrity. Dr Heinrich Grüber had been the first to make Victor's name known in Germany in 1946; he had written to him warmly on many occasions; and in 1959 he had spoken with him at the Christian Action peace rally. When his letter of 14 October arrived, Victor asked for a full translation, as 'Grüber is a very old friend of mine'. The translation came as a blow. Grüber opened well enough, expressing personal delight that Victor had won the prize, but then he cast sceptical doubt on the awarding body, and continued: 'May I today quite openly write to you on the subject of your articles concerning Germany's guilt: The latter are being published under such headlines as: "Victor Gollancz against Collective Guilt", "Victor Gollancz: Not All Are Guilty" etc. . . . ' He greatly admired all Victor's work for Germany and always, like him, stressed that others were guilty too — those countries that had condemned millions to death by their refusal to take enough refugees. There was a risk in Victor's approach nonetheless. ' . . . I cannot help fearing that your well meaning words are being taken up by the very people in Germany who are pleased to wipe away their guilt in this way . . . ' Yet, 'we were guilty of not wanting to recognize the devilry of all that was yet to come; of not considering possible the full extent of the crimes committed. . . . It is a fact, however, that the very people who tried at the time to contradict and resist, are most conscious of the guilt which they loaded upon themselves by their silence and failure . . . ' He himself was still racked by occasions under the Nazi régime when he had remained silent for fear of making things worse. 'I beg you to understand me when I fear that your well-meaning words may open new paths to the very spirit which is still in the grip of old nationalistic thought and which is coming to life again in Western Germany in such a frightening manner. . . . The spirit of revenge and militarism is growing at an alarming rate.' Even the youth were affected by it, 'in my opinion everyone in a responsible position today should follow this precept: Do not take anyone's part without at the same time showing up his mistakes and making clear his duty . . . '

A reasoned response could have been made. Victor had taken pains to be constructive in anything he wrote for the German public, and if he had occasionally been too vehement, overemphasizing the guilt of the democrats of other countries as against the ordinary citizen in Germany, he had done so from an excess of pity. He could hardly be blamed when his words were wrenched out of context many years later. There was besides an excellent argument to be made against Grüber's pessimistic view of contemporary Germany.

Victor made no such case. He simply wrote 'No reply' on the letter. And when, a few days later, he was asked to contribute a tribute for Grüber's forthcoming seventieth birthday, he did the same. Ten years earlier he might have faced the criticism before rejecting it. At the age of sixty-seven, he could not forgive anything that threatened the cocoon he had built around himself.

Though the late 1950s saw a rapid decline in Victor's effectiveness as a public man, as a publisher he continued to ride high. In many crucial respects out of sympathy with changes in the people's taste, he could still spot saleable books, drawing the line only at publishing what he thought actually pernicious. In 1960 Kenneth Allsop was to write, in a profile of Victor, that he had put out the two 'most influential (and financially staggeringly successful) books of the post-war period, both by unknown authors.' The first had been Amis's *Lucky Jim*: the second Colin Wilson's *The Outsider* which, in Allsop's words, 'stirred the muddled intellectual gropings of the '50's like a paddle in a bowl of porridge.'

Victor deserved the primary credit for the acquisition of Wilson, who sent his manuscript to Gollancz in 1955 after reading *A Year of Grace*. (Jon Evans spotted its virtues and suggested calling it *The Outsider* rather than *The Pain Threshold*.) Having read the manuscript, Victor concluded that Wilson had 'immense talent, and possibly genius.' He was delighted to find a young man interested in ideas, and though he and Wilson were poles apart in their attitudes to religion, they had considerable mutual respect. Wilson was very impressed by *My Dear Timothy* and in the early stages of their relationship believed Victor to be 'probably the only literary man in London (except perhaps Eliot) whose work moves in the direction that I would wish to take, who can sympathise fully with what I want to do.' The firm believed *The Outsider* would do well to sell 2,000 copies, but Wilson's potential was so great and his poverty so dramatic that he was advanced enough money to live on. His book was published in June 1956 and the rave reviews made it a sensation overnight. Patrick Forbes, a recent recruit to Gollancz, did a superb public relations job, and Wilson interviews and profiles saturated the press within days. Victor planned the publication strategy and the brilliant advertising, and thought long and hard about how his new protégé should meet the challenge of instant fame.

Wilson was for a time delighted to be a literary lion. After years of poverty he was unable to resist the invitations that were poured on him to write and speak. His impulsiveness in conversation and the storminess of his private life made him a gift to gossip columnists. He also turned out ideas for books and actual manuscripts in great profusion. Quite reasonably, Victor was rattled, and tried to persuade Wilson of the value of slowing down, keeping out of the public eye, immersing himself in reading, and writing only what he felt impelled to write. He knew all too well that unless he handled himself carefully, Wilson was riding for a fall with critics and journalists. He was appalled by his extravagance and impetuosity and tried to cast himself as a wise father figure.

Their correspondence over several years ran to many tens of thousands of words. Sometimes inspiring each other, sometimes loving each other, sometimes hating each other, they wrestled from their different perspectives with the problem of finding the right path for the phenomenon that was Wilson. Perhaps only Richard Acland, Negley Farson and Herbert Kubly (a young American of whom he had grown very fond) received more of Victor's personal editorial attention and time from the mid-1950s onwards, and they were all enormously grateful and took his advice without question. Wilson reacted differently. In the first flush of success and full of youthful egotism, he took it for granted that Victor's time and energy were his for the asking, and made endless demands on his patience with challenges, complaints, demands for money and rejection of good advice: such conduct was usually made bearable by compensatory rushes of warmth, affection, appreciation and admiration.

'I wonder if you realise what you owe to your publisher's extraordinary genius?' wrote Sir Geoffrey Faber to Wilson in 1957, '*The Outsider* is an astonishing book . . . but it was VG's genius, rather than yours, which gave you your amazing getaway. For God's sake, let him manage your presentation of yourself, at least for the next two or three months, perhaps for the next 2 or 3 years. He, I am sure, knows better than you the dangers ahead of you. Don't be indifferent to his advice, and don't undo it by disregarding it . . .'

As his supporters knew, Victor's concern for Wilson was unsullied by self-interest. A lesser publisher might have been inclined to make a quick profit from his fame while it lasted; Victor wanted Wilson to realize his potential. However well-intentioned, the advice he gave was sometimes ill-judged in its dogmatism. He made Wilson furious by recommending he get a full-time job; he was paternalistic in his remonstrations about money; and in his insistence on toning down or omitting many passages of *Ritual in the Dark* — which in its original form he thought 'filthy' — he censored Wilson far more than would most other publishers. For a few years Victor nurtured Wilson, favouring him with long screeds of good advice, reading and advising on his manuscripts, and corresponding behind his back with friends urging them to restrain him from indiscretions. He kept his temper most of the time despite the flood of provocative letters and the manifold problems Wilson generated. They haggled ceaselessly about money, but preserved their affection for each other. Negley Farson was one of Wilson's mentors, and similar conditions had prevailed in his dealings, as a younger man, with Victor, who had forgiven and still forgave youthful wildness, disrespect and unreliability not only in return for warm and generous apologies, but because he respected abundant talent and sincerely wanted to help it along.

Until 1960, then, Victor could reasonably congratulate himself on being the successful publisher of the angriest of the Angry Young Men. It did no harm to his firm's reputation as a go-ahead publisher that it could handle the shocking Colin Wilson as well as the iconoclastic Kingsley Amis (who, however, had proved to be an extraordinarily easy writer to deal with). Yet, impressive though Victor was in his marketing of fashionable authors, far more impressive was his success in persuading the British public to buy a book which did not suit the mood of the times — Alejo Carpentier's *The Lost Steps*.

A long mystical novel by a Cuban writer was hardly the stuff of which British bestsellers were made in the mid-1950s. Victor had no doubt about its virtues: ' . . . my delight in the book is precisely the delight that I get from the really great novels, in contradistinction to almost all the stuff that is turned out nowadays. Indeed, it is no exaggeration to say that I am quite wildly enthusiastic about it . . . '

'I have the uneasy feeling', he wrote to an American publisher in April 1956 'that the book is not for the big public, though I shall certainly try to make the big public believe that it is!' Proof copies went out to a long list of arbiters of taste, including W. H. Auden, Albert Camus, Robert Graves, Graham Greene, André Malraux, Yehudi Menuhin, J. B. Priestley, Edith Sitwell, Stravinsky, Michael Tippett and Laurens Van Der Post. Priestley, Sitwell and Tippett replied with prompt enthusiasm, and Victor tried to engineer the reviewing, to make sure it did not 'get into the hands of (confidentially) those miserable little pip-squeak juveniles who love sneering at anything they are too minute to catch the size of.' His achievement was remarkable. Although the book had the misfortune to be published on the worst day of the Suez crisis — 'Black Monday', as it was known in the trade — it was so well reviewed by pre-publication enthusiasts and so brilliantly publicized by Victor that it sold 20,000 copies, and went on selling for many years. It flopped completely in America.

Victor wished to repeat the Carpentier performance on behalf of the American author, James Purdy, whose *69: Dream Palace* he received in November 1956. Edith Sitwell pronounced Purdy 'a truly great writer', potentially greater than Faulkner. Victor wrote to agree with her high estimate of him but had one worry:

There are several words which one isn't supposed to print in this country

— not only what one might call the 'simple' words, but two combin-
ation-words. And yet I feel that either to cut them out, or to indicate
them by an initial letter, would greatly spoil the flavour. I am thinking of
the very last word in the book ['motherfucker', an epithet quite new to
him]: the very use of it adds, very movingly, to the sense of compassion
that the whole story conveys. Do you think I *dare* keep these words? I
don't want to go to gaol!

'How like you', she responded, 'to realise that those last terrible
words add to the almost unendurable pity one feels, — add to the
compassion of the whole book. I think, personally, it would be
dreadful to have to cut them out, or indicate them with letters.'
Purdy was, in her opinion, 'the most exciting discovery since
Dylan'. Victor needed no more reassurance. He sat down and
composed a personal information sheet about the novella and its
accompanying short stories for his travellers. The stories had most
impressed him by their utter originality: 'All the qualities that
distinguish the short stories are present in the novel, but with an
added intensity: in particular, the irony is keener, the compassion
more grievous. The stories, as I have said, delighted me: but the
novel — and, most of all, the terror and beauty of its last paragraph
— has haunted me continuously, ever since I read it, and that, at the
moment of writing, is a month ago.'
To the American publishers he wrote a few days later, warning
them against any editing, either artistic or on grounds of obscenity.
As far as the latter was concerned:

Normally, we should of course either omit these words, or substitute
others, or idiotically indicate them by an initial letter, and so on . . . But
I felt, with complete conviction, that these words simply *must* be
retained. They are, in a curious and rather indefinable way, essential to
the atmosphere of the novella . . . perhaps I can best describe what I
mean by saying that they enormously enhance the feeling of the tears of
things — *sunt lacrimae rerum*. This is seen at its most remarkable in the
very last word of the novella. Cut it out, and the terrible pity of that
ending is enormously diminished — to saying nothing of the world of
implication in the 'mother' part of 'motherfucking'.

There was not the slightest danger of prosecution. The following
day he sent off to Purdy the text of a publisher's foreword, intended
to forestall 'the smuthounds'. It made the same argument, even more
strongly expressed in parts. One sentence gave his view 'that to
remove the words, or substitute others for them, would be as
damaging as to soften a discord in a piece of music.' And the final

sentence ran: 'Normally, taste rejects these expressions. Here it imperatively demands them.'

Purdy was so delighted that he had to be restrained from dedicating the book to Victor. Sitwell thought the foreword 'noble', bound to 'shame everyone who wishes to cavil, into respect.' Everything in it was '*absolutely* right & as I have told you before, I am very proud to be living at the same time as you, with your spiritual force and truth and shining honesty.'

Then came the bad news: Leonard Russell, the literary editor of the *Sunday Times*, had refused to allow her to include the book in her selection of 'Books of the Year' because of the obscene language. (The *Sunday Express* the previous year had accused the *Sunday Times* of pushing pornographic books when Graham Greene recommended *Lolita*.) 'I presume', Russell had said, 'that Victor Gollancz will clean up page 55 when he publishes the book here, but that doesn't help me in my predicament, as those lying in wait for us will certainly rush to get copies of the American edition.' Sitwell was of course furious, finding comfort in Victor's 'noble defence of the book . . . Osbert and I are both full of admiration of it.' The *Sunday Times* reaction gave Victor cold feet. In the USA he met Purdy and persuaded him to agree to a number of changes and the excision of the foreword. 'My chief reason for this change', he wrote to the American publisher, 'is the following: my foreword would create a tremendous amount of publicity over here, and I believe that, as a result, attention would be diverted from the quality of Purdy's work itself, and concentrated instead on this question of "obscenity".' He omitted to tell Sitwell, who heard about the changes from Purdy and was '*most* upset. She feels it is imperative to retain the last words, and that it would be a disaster not to have it. The other words are not important, she feels.' Purdy left it up to Victor, who wrote to Sitwell on 19 March that he had been convinced by others that the foreword would have attention focussed on it to the detriment of the book. But since the words in question could not be printed without the foreword, they had to be modified. 'This involved only the loathsome business of putting dashes, except in the case of the last word: for the last word, I substituted "little bugger". This, of course, destroys the sad and beautiful implication of the "mother" part of "motherfucker": but the rhythm is as good: and it has to be borne in mind that even the word "bugger" is not normally printed over here. Moreover the "little" in "little bugger" does give, I think, the same impression of heart-breaking love.' Their relationship did not suffer: no doubt Sitwell accepted Victor's justification at face value.

The parallels with Victor's behaviour over *One Way of Love* 25 years earlier were extraordinary. Then, as now, he had initially taken a brave decision to publish unexpurgated a work of real literary merit despite the prevailing puritanical climate. (In the late 1950s, as John Gross — then at Gollancz — once explained to Kingsley Amis, the circulating libraries could cope with 'arse' but not with 'bugger', and Amis's 'a quick in and out' was one of the idioms to fall victim to their primness.) A simultaneous libel action had reversed Victor's decision on *One Way of Love*: this time the pusillanimity of the *Sunday Times* had brought him down to earth. In both cases the truth was the same: Victor, a political publisher, overcoming his natural reserve, was prepared to see himself in the vanguard of liberalism, and risk public obloquy and legal proceedings over a merely literary issue, until second thoughts at the eleventh hour left him more timid than his competitors. Circulating libraries notwithstanding, there were those who would have taken the risk (as the American publishers did) of printing 'motherfucker' and braving the consequences.

Victor had long had a trick of forgetting ignoble episodes, or burying them under mounds of *post hoc* rationalization: it was called into play more and more in his later years. A quarter-century had elapsed since his experience with *One Way of Love*. John Updike's *Rabbit, Run* came just three years after the reprise with Purdy's work, and the threshold of public tolerance shifted in the interim. In 1959 Victor had published *The Poorhouse Fair* and a volume of Updike's poems, and author and publisher admired each other greatly. Victor was particularly impressed by *Rabbit, Run*, and wrote to Harold Rubinstein that Updike 'has a greater chance of becoming one of the really great novelists than anyone now writing in the English language.' Although himself 'pernickety' about 'sexual "frankness"', he had found it '*totally* inoffensive' in *Rabbit, Run*, 'and I don't think it can be modified without artistically spoiling the book. The sexual frankness is totally integral with the theme: and it produces the effect, not of pornography or anything remotely resembling it, but of tragic humanity. The scenes of frank sexual discussion are, in my view, quite vital to the unfolding of the character of Rabbit, who is so superbly drawn.' He had made up his mind quite definitely to publish. Was there a likelihood of prosecution, which he might well decide to risk?

On the same day he conveyed the same thoughts to Updike, adding a query about one passage. 'Does the word "job" mean something specific? What *is* the practice referred to? I am getting on in life, and thought I knew everything, but can't imagine what you are hinting at. Do please enlighten me.'

Updike was greately 'bucked up' by Victor's enthusiasm. As for the 'outspokenness', he suspected 'that a good deal of it might be omitted without compromising my earnestness or the reality of the physical scenes. Unlike D. H. Lawrence, I have no *mystique* of dirty words — it is just that, in attempting to describe carnal relations, the language offers no other words at all.' He suggested that Victor wait to see what changes Knopf made: perhaps they would answer the demands of English censorship. He went on to explain that squeamishness had made him write 'job' rather than 'blow job' — 'American vernacular for the mouth-genital contact scientifically named *fellatio*'.

Updike's answer crossed with another letter from Victor to the effect that, whatever Rubinstein might say, he was 'certainly prepared to publish the book exactly as it stands'. He wanted to set it straight away, so as to make it one of the two or three leading books of the year. He needed no editorial suggestions from Knopf. 'As I think you know, when a novel is a work of art, and not a mere work of commerce, I have a radical objection to the whole editing process. I like to print the book as it comes from the writer's pen.'

Two days later he informed Updike that he was 'at present in a state of exultation, having just written a description of the book for my travellers', and was 'terribly anxious' to go to press. The personal description for travellers was adamant that 'no one but a man of filthy mind could call it pornographic'. He was known to be old-fashioned in such matters, and to refuse potential bestsellers taken by other respectable houses, but he had found not a single word in *Rabbit, Run* objectionable, 'and to tamper with the author's writing would be, in my opinion, an outrage, for the sexual frankness is *essential* to the tragic and compassionate purposes of the author's theme.'

This document was despatched to Updike. The jacket had been designed 'with a very dignified front', bearing the legend 'A tragic novel'. Victor wanted the corrected manuscript as soon as possible, as page proofs were to be sent out to about 500 booksellers — 'a thing I do only once every couple of years or so'.

> As to the 'sexual frankness', you will now be in possession of my lawyer's remarks, and will of course consider the passages to which he refers. Naturally, if you can modify, here and there, with certainty on your own part that you are not compromising your artistic purpose, then so much the better: and I know you won't compromise your artistic purpose. I leave myself, on this head, entirely in your hands.
>
> Thank you for that esoteric piece of information. The slang phrase is, I think, unknown in England. If I didn't tumble to your meaning, it was perhaps because the practice in question . . . has always struck me as

offensive in the absence of passion, but by no means offensive, indeed beautiful, when passion is present.'

'I am absolutely reeling from all the mail I have been getting from you:' wrote Updike, 'your enthusiasm, and your sense of urgency, are so great it would not amaze me if I did not receive tomorrow in the mail a bound copy of "Rabbit, Run", together with a summons from Her Majesty's censor.' Knopf wanted only three words changed, so Victor need 'have no fear'. Updike was now wishing he had never sent the manuscript to Gollancz. 'Had I foreseen the chain of events this would set into motion, I would have kept it. Now it appears there are plans I will "wreck", other books displaced from your Fall list, mimeographs going out to booksellers — my hands tremble on the keys.' Could Victor not wait and photograph the Knopf edition? 'I am rather afraid of your enthusiasm; it is always better, I think, to have modest expectations and be pleased than high hopes that are dashed.' Victor was still pushing matters forward in March, when, without waiting for Updike's changes, he sent the book to the printers, fearful that their reluctance to work overtime might hold up what he considered to be 'the best novel that has come out of America for many years'. He told Updike on the 29th that he would then scan the proofs for 'passages that might conceivably trouble Her Majesty's police, in case I might be able to suggest a modification or two here and there.'

Victor had lost his nerve by May. The printers ('the least likely . . . to make a fuss about this kind of thing') had objected to certain passages. He not only yielded over the changes they insisted on; he expunged or amended every passage they queried. Hilary Rubinstein, against any cuts at all, tried to save some sections, but Victor was now hell-bent on making the book totally unobjectionable. 'I have borne in mind', he wrote to Updike with the revised proofs in May, 'that neither you nor I want the mess of a prosecution (which would be exploited by the gutter-press) befouling this book, which, as you know, I consider to be one of utter integrity and of rare compassionate beauty . . . I believe that the effect of my changes will be to make a prosecution all but out of the question: and also that, while a few beautiful and sensitive phrases have gone, nothing of substance has, in sum, been sacrificed . . . '

Regretfully, Updike disagreed: first, because Knopf had decided to print the book unexpurgated as long as the English publisher did likewise; second, because he himself had concluded that the 'only one honorable and decent thing for me to do' was to insist that the book be published 'as I wrote it or not at all'. He now agreed with 'cogent arguments' Victor himself had made earlier against any expurgation.

Knopf's lawyers ultimately prevailed on Updike to make a few changes, but Victor would not accept even the amended version without two further cuts. 'It seems to me', wrote Updike, 'that, what with the Lady Chatterley decision in England, and the unruffled reception of my book here by responsible readers — reviewers and friends alike . . . — you might dare do this.' Victor, who had by now convinced himself that he objected to the questionable passages on principle, dropped the book altogether.

At the time, Updike was still so grateful for Victor's enthusiasm that he did not complain about his *volte face*, which was subtly different in kind from the one he made over the Purdy novella, and reflected his increasing ambivalence about the treatment of sex in novels. His reactions were not just unpredictable: they varied wildly according to mood. *Lolita* was a case in point. He read it in the American edition in 1958 and described it in a private letter as 'a bad novel but nevertheless a rare masterpiece of spiritual understanding'. A year later he was telling Colin Wilson that

> I have always made my position about that book perfectly clear. It is two-fold; a) I think it both a boring and a thoroughly nasty book, the literary value of which has been grossly over-estimated. I wouldn't dream of publishing it myself (great efforts were made to induce me to do so), and I very greatly regret that anyone in this country should undertake its publication, because I believe it were better unpublished here; b) on the other hand, I am wholly against prosecuting the publisher if it *is* published: and, in the event of a prosecution, I should be wholly against the conviction of a publisher. This is because I regard the admission of any kind of censorship as being, in the long run, far more opposed to the public good than the dissemination even of genuine pornography, not to say of a work like 'Lolita' which, though in my view disgusting, is not, in my view, pornographic.

In November he sent a letter to *The Times* describing *Lolita* as 'written in good faith and not in any technical sense pornographic, and while containing passages of high literary merit, is in total effect disgusting and offensive to good taste, as well as exceedingly boring.' He greatly regretted its publication in Britain but, remembering the cases of Ibsen, D. H. Lawrence and many others, recognized the possibility of error and wholly opposed attempts to suppress the book legally. He changed his mind the same day and withdrew the letter.

His views on *Lolita* had further hardened in 1960, when he was asked to give evidence for Penguin books in their *Lady Chatterley* defence. To Penguin's solicitor, Michael Rubinstein, he wrote on 22 August:

> I read 'Lady Chatterley' over the weekend, with, for the most part, unutterable boredom. Subject to what I am going to say in the next paragraph, it is a pretty bad novel, and a pretty badly written one too, full of Lawrence's abominable trick of repeating words and phrases for emphasis.
>
> But there is an exception to all this: all the love scenes — all the parts, that is to say, for which the book is being prosecuted — are superb, and, in the main, superbly written. To call them either pornographic or obscene would be fantastic. In their modern terms, they don't fall very far short of the Song of Songs: I would go so far as to say that they glorify the creator of human bodies. . . .
>
> I could not imagine a more deplorable piece of topsy-turvydom than that 'Lady Chatterley' should be condemned, and the really vile 'Lolita' get through. Such a contrast must stink in the nostrils of honest people who have any taste whatever.

In 1961 he assured the *Bookman* that *Lolita* was pornographic.

Although it was not always possible to predict how Victor would react to sexual explicitness, his chief readers, Evans and Hodges, knew his mind well and rarely found themselves in conflict with him. Evans thought *Forever Amber* unsuitable for Gollancz, though he predicted it would sell enormously. He also recommended the rejection of John Braine's *Room at the Top*, which he simply disliked. Victor agreed with him retrospectively even when Braine's book went on to be a huge success for another publisher. Sympathizing with Lettice Cooper's agent about the decline in her sales, he explained that 'Her *kind* of novel, — the solid, honest, leisurely novel of the old tradition, with fine characterisation and deep psychological insight — is at a very great discount at the present time. All the rage is for the characteristic 'post-war' novel of the type of Kingsley Amis, John Wain [his *bête noire* among reviewers], Iris Murdoch — and, God forgive the critics and public — John Brain [*sic*].' Yet he was jealous of the large profits being made by Eyre & Spottiswoode, and in a letter to Evans, suggesting he halve his reading and income, he referred to the rejection of Braine as 'a major disaster, as the book must have sold about 40,000 copies, and is already a big "property".' Honesty drove him to admit that he felt 'pretty certain that you were right and that the whole booming of the book was a put-up job by a group of critics'. Common sense prevailed and he did not send the letter: Evans was a quite superb publisher's reader, transcending consistent professionalism to achieve genius in a generally undervalued field. And like Hodges, he was so steeped in the tradition of Gollancz that he was irreplaceable.

Victor was protected by his subordinates from many of the harsh realities of life — from unpleasant personal encounters, from discomfort, from uncongenial manuscripts and from criticism of his own failings. They sometimes resented the ego-massaging that was an unwritten part of their job descriptions, but those who stayed largely took it for granted. Confrontation was pointless, so they wielded influence through various subtle means, for instance by arguing against the course of action they wanted him to follow.

The second half of the 1950s had been dominated in Gollancz by Victor's search for a second editor who might also become alternative successor to Rubinstein. John Rosenberg, the young novelist whom Victor hired because he believed him brilliant, had soon fallen out of favour because his American background was a handicap to his proof-reading. His perfection flawed, he soon found himself a general bane in Victor's eyes, and suffered the indignity of having John Gross appointed straight from Oxford over his head. Rosenberg left in July 1956, so much under a cloud that Victor even tried to get out of publishing a good book by an author Rosenberg had brought to the firm. Gross stayed for two years, was made a director in 1957, and had very few troubles with Victor, precisely because it was clear virtually from the start that he had no intention of staying long — not to mention his outstanding abilities, and the common ground he shared with Victor by virtue of his experience of Jewish orthodoxy. He kept his distance as far as possible, stayed out of emotional scenes and worked solidly upstairs (where for a short time he shared a room with Anne Williams, the future Mrs Michael Heseltine). He left in August 1958, bearing an ecstatic reference. Patrick Forbes was also hired in the mid-50s and was well regarded for his gifts in public relations. He had no ambitions to be a publisher; he was treading water until he found a more suitable PR job. Elinor Murphy, like most of Victor's secretaries, was far too intelligent for the job. (Victor was in love with her — as he was with most of his female colleagues. Indeed, as he got older, he used to insist that the chief credential for any woman with whom he was to work closely was that he should be able to fall in love with her.) He grudgingly permitted Murphy to give up secretarial work in 1958 (her first successor was fired after two days) to become an editor and director. Since she still found herself for many purposes his personal assistant, she ended up doing one-and-a-half jobs and suffering a good deal from overwork. She was never seen as a possible successor, overtly determined as she was to leave publishing in the near future.

Robin Deniston, asked to advise on a children's list, might have been in the running, but he unwittingly annoyed Victor. Rupert Hart-Davis, whom Victor adored, was at one time asked if he would amalgamate his firm with Gollancz. 'I told him that I loved and admired him very much, but I didn't fancy working with him; which he seemed to think sensible.'

What Victor required of a successor, in theory, was flair, energy and commercial ability to equal his own, along with a sensitive respect for the traditions of the house of Gollancz. In practice, anyone who challenged his ego was ruled out. No one could be found to meet all those criteria, and by the late 1950s Victor had announced his intention of staying as chairman until at least 1963, when he would be seventy. Once Gross left, he more or less gave up the idea of coaching any more bright young men and resigned himself to soldiering on with what seemed to be the permanent fixtures — Bush, Livia and Rubinstein. Rubinstein's prospects had been declining steadily year by year; he had long since ceased to be favoured with the title of deputy, and for three years every brilliant young man who joined the staff was compared with him to his detriment. If the honeymoon proved short, Rubinstein's stock would rise until the next time, as Victor accepted once again that he needed his nephew. For most of the period, however, Rubinstein was under heavy fire, wondering if he should make the break, but unwilling thus to damage his father's relationship with Victor.

A long holiday in 1958 forced Victor to nominate a *de facto* deputy chairman (Ruth held the job nominally). Up till then, during all his long absences in America, he had stayed in touch with the firm through the media of letters, cables and phone-calls. During a typical two-month visit, he would despatch upwards of 80 letters homeward. In 1958 he was worried about his health and decided to take a proper break: he was suffering from mild diverticulitis, a harmless complaint that caused intestinal and bowel discomfort. Fearing cancer, he had sought medical advice the preceding September, and the doctor had hedged his bets, saying it could not be ruled out. Within days, Victor had distorted the import of the consultation: he had been formally told he had cancer. An all-clear on his X-rays allayed his frenzy of fear, and he spread the good word in letters to all and sundry, anathematizing the quack who had misdiagnosed him. Then there had been the horror of the car crash in December, on the way back from Oxford. A nervous passenger at the best of times, Victor had suffered greatly from the shock of what he claimed was a plunge through a stone wall at 45 mph. It had not been quite that fast, and it was a hedge, not a wall, but Victor's total escape from injury (the driver was fine too) was a minor detail in the accident's recital. A doctor was willing to insist that he needed a two-month break on health grounds, and Pakenham, now chairman of Victor's bank, was requested and required to arrange exemption from exchange-control restraints.

The holiday was to last from mid-April to mid-June, and Rubinstein's current standing was indicated by the installation of John Bush as acting chairman. Rubinstein and Livia were appointed acting joint managing directors, and the duties of all the senior members of the firm were laid out in a 7-page memorandum. The general advice given was: 'It is better to lose valuable time than to act too quickly. It is better to act too quickly than to lose valuable time.' The arrangement worked perfectly well in fact, for Bush was a highly competent man, and knew that Victor's tap on his shoulder was not just a mark of approval but also a deliberate snub to Rubinstein. Victor did not yet seriously contemplate Bush, who was short of editorial experience, as a successor. Moreover, he underestimated Bush's qualities as sales director, in which position he was held responsible when sales figures failed to meet Victor's standards. Bush enjoyed as much as ever Victor's zest and cleverness at his job, and the long periods when he was Victor's most trusted lieutenant made up for the occasions when Victor lost his temper violently or, worse, from time to time completely ignored him for days, weeks and once for several months, other than through the medium of curt written communications.

Rubinstein's star was in the ascendant as the 1950s came to an end. If his talent and flair were often overlooked, his success in selling Gollancz titles to paperback firms had impressed even Victor. For almost twenty years after the foundation of Penguin Books Victor had stoutly refused to sell any of his list to the hated 'paper-cover affairs': authors could reap the benefits of paperback royalties only by reclaiming their rights when Victor failed to reprint. He had always been sickened by Allen Lane's success, and convinced that the paperback revolution brought in its train a further decline in cultural standards. In 1954, however, his principle of non-co-operation had been breached when he wrote to Lane enclosing a copy of *A Year of Grace*:

> It is said to be the most successful anthology of the kind since Robert Bridges' 'Testament of Man', published during the first World War . . . I have a great desire that there should now be a very cheap edition. I have had an amazing correspondence about it from all over the world — people writing from their deathbeds, others saying that they have been saved from nervous breakdowns, doctors telling me that they recommend it to

patients who are in difficulties, and so on. As it appears to be useful, I should like to enlarge the circle of its usefulness . . .

Penguin obliged, and since Victor had the royalties fixed at only one penny a copy, it was published at 3s. 6d. ($17\frac{1}{2}$ pence). The precedent set, Gollancz titles trickled into paperback, and Victor could not fail to ibe pleased by the profits which accrued (normally, in those days, 50 per cent of royalties). In July 1959 he was referring to Rubinstein in a letter to Curtis Brown as 'most experienced and immensely successful with this paperback business . . . I should have thought that we sold more paperbacks, relatively to the size of our list, than almost any other publisher — I am often amazed at the deals Hilary pulls off!' (That was almost certainly untrue, for Victor hated to sell any books he thought had a permanent life in hardback.) By 1960, although Rubinstein was still intermittently reviled, there had been a palpable softening in Victor's attitude to him. Writing to Colin Wilson to defend Rubinstein against an attack, Victor wrote that

> he is both one of the gentlest and one of the most honourable people I know, and I believe you would find, if you inquired in the right circles, that no young publisher in England is more widely respected, liked, and even loved. It may often be Hilary's duty, as my second in command, to say something that you don't like hearing . . . and I suggest that you are performing the most elementary of psychological operations, namely, feeling a personal dislike of someone who tells you something you don't like to hear.

If Rubinstein saw the letter, whatever comfort he drew from that paragraph must have been dashed by the next: 'However, the question is an academic one, as, death or ill health apart, it is unlikely that I shall retire for 15 years or so. By that time, you also may have changed.'

By now, in fact, Victor had settled on the idea that he would be succeeded by Livia and her cousin jointly. They were sent off together on an American book-hunt in 1960 and became acting joint managing directors during Victor's absences. Livia considered her cousin to be an editor of great talent, and would have been happy for him to take over the firm. But as Victor had decreed they were to be a team, they adjusted accordingly: daughter and nephew were now clearly tipped to run Gollancz on Victor's retirement, but nobody knew who was to be boss.

Naturally, there was gossip within the firm on the big question of future power politics, and it was coloured by Victor's eternally gloomy prognostications that the business would not long survive him. Independents were steadily being swallowed up by bigger enterprises, and he was appalled by the trend. He had himself been offered the chairmanship of a proposed combine of small publishers, but had refused: he would not be able to control the publishing policy of each component part as he controlled that of his own firm. Gollancz was still doing well, but nothing could change Victor's Cassandra-like view that each year's good results were the last. Every manifestation of a cheapening of public taste, from the rise of television to the closing down of the circulating libraries, was another nail in the coffin.

The financial year 1957–8 was typical. In October 1957 he sent a 5-page memorandum to directors beginning

> A very provisional check up on the year's profits has disclosed an exceedingly serious state of affairs. The figures for the current year will be satisfactory, though not anything like as good as they ought to be, in view of our really extraordinary programme for the year. But what has been revealed is this: overheads have risen so enormously that we can hardly hope to make a profit in any year in which there are not a number of exceptional items (for instance, this year, 'The Scapegoat' and the new 'Camillo'), or a number of unexpected best-sellers (as, for instance, the Colin Wilson last year). This current year, we have had two of our biggest best-sellers, two Book Society Choices [he had again changed his mind on the Book Society], and a Book Society Alternative Choice: but, in spite of that, the profit is far less than it ought to be . . .
>
> The plain fact is that while, even in 1954, we could pay a 10 per cent dividend and put a considerable sum to reserve on a turnover of £260,000, with our overheads as they will be next year, such a figure would not allow us to pay any dividend at all, to say nothing of putting anything to reserve. . . . Another complicating factor is that we, like all publishers, have (to my regret and with my resistance) been depending more and more on 'extra revenue'. But it now seems probable that most of the book clubs — which are declining rapidly — will be forced out of business: and it is also considered probable that of the thirty odd paper-back firms, only three or four will survive.
>
> In view of all this, the utmost economy is essential . . .

The economy measures were to include the withholding of unnecessary letters, use of postcards wherever possible, shortening telephone calls and turning out fires if a room was to be left empty for more than 'a very few minutes'. John Bush was additionally required to inform staff that the firm could not afford 'a single minute wasted through people not working a full 8 hours in every day'.

The note to shareholders at the end of the trading period was brief: 'Conditions in the publishing trade as a whole are becoming more and more difficult, and present ever new problems. In spite of this, however, your Directors are pleased to report a further successful year's trading. In recommending a dividend of 10 per cent less tax for the year 1957, they must point out that the profit prospects for the current year are very dubious.'

Victor's dislike of contemporary vulgarity in book-selling practices sometimes damaged the sales potential of books. In 1958 John Boulting wrote to ask him to adopt for a novel the title of the film based on it: *Private Life* should become *I'm All Right, Jack*, not only because the original title lacked 'the colour and vitality of the book itself', but because sales would in any case benefit. The edition was ready to go out, and Victor disagreed anyway. 'There's always a difference of opinion about this question of titles: for my own part, I can't imagine a worse title for a *book* than 'I'm All Right, Jack'. I've queried a dozen people, and they haven't the faintest idea what it means: and I understand that nobody *can* understand what it means unless they have been in the Air Force, or been very close to it in some way . . . '

'Blimey,' responded Boulting, 'you must mix in a pretty rarefied strata if you know a dozen people who are unable to grasp the implication of the phrase 'I'm All Right, Jack'. At any rate, I cannot believe that people who read books are quite as divorced from the facts of life as all that. Certainly our title not only has vitality, but epitomises the book as a whole . . . '

Victor could not bring himself to put a band round the book saying it was to be filmed, 'dragging literature still further into the gutter'. The author was naturally upset, and the compromise read: 'Serialized in *Punch* as *I'm All Right, Jack*'.

If caution, pessimism and conservatism characterized Victor's private and public statements about the book trade, the Gollancz list was exciting. There were overnight sensations like Elaine Dundy's *The Dud Avocado* and Jessica Mitford's *Hons and Rebels*. The American presence on the list was dazzling, with names such as Art Buchwald, John Cheever, Brendan Gill, David Karp, J. F. Powers, Leo Rosten and Peter de Vries bringing *cachet* and profits alike. Victor's reputation attracted many of these authors to his firm: it was frequently his cunning that made them bestsellers. Art Buchwald's essays, *I Chose Caviar*, sold 5,000 copies in America and 30,000 in Britain precisely because Victor thought them hilarious and made the book one of his pets. Cheever he adored, and although he could not contrive huge sales for him, he did a lot to put him on the literary map in Britain. Yet, though the genius was undiminished, Victor's capacity for starting rows, already legendary, was now approaching dangerous levels. 'You consider yourself omnipotent,' wrote Buchwald in November 1958, announcing his intention of taking his books elsewhere. 'I do not consider myself "omnipotent",' answered Victor. 'I consider only God omnipotent. What I do, however, consider is that, just as it is a gross impertinence for a publisher to attempt to interfere with an author's work, so it is — let us say imprudent — for an author to interfere in the publisher's domain. And I think, also, that you misread as "omnipotence" what is nothing more than a decent measure of outspokenness.'

'Your reputation for being a "difficult" person', wrote one American agent in 1957, 'is well established, and I may say after reading your letter of November 25th, I can now confirm that you are also gratuitously rude and insulting.' And a Simon & Schuster editor in 1959 responded to a furious letter by saying that it was only 'the very warm associations we have had that tempers my exasperation and resentment'.

Victor occasionally admitted to having been 'intemperate' and sometimes made a slight concession to keep a valued author, but most of the rows with American publishers, agents, reviewers and authors merely confirmed his prejudices: American publishing houses were sliding downhill as his old friends died; agents were greedy; reviewers were malign; and authors had no respect for genius and experience. When his wilfulness, rigidity or inflexibility lost him authors, he simply pretended it had not happened. 'I think I am right', he told Buchwald in 1958, 'in saying that you are the only author who has voluntarily "left" me since the end of the war.' Buchwald made it up with him for a time, as so many did, for life with Victor in it, infuriating though he might be, was more exciting than life without him. As one American publisher put it, he was 'a pixie rogue elephant', and 'the most ebullient and stimulating character in London literary society'. The same publisher went on to say that 'more than any publisher I have ever met he is an inspired comprehender and explainer of what is inside the distinguished and important books he chooses to publish. He is a wizard — an alert eight o'clock in the morning wizard — at promotion and advertising. He writes his own copy. He rolls his own without any Madison Avenue filter to soften the tang and pungency of his smoke — and of his flame.'

In his mid-sixties, Victor retained the same capacity to grab the attention of the book-buying public as he had demonstrated in his thirties. In 1957, the *Advertisers' Weekly* spoke of him as the exception among publishers in producing exciting ads: He 'makes — and breaks — his own rules (today, as 30 years ago).' And his knack for audacious publicity stunts was similarly undiminished. One trade journal in 1960 sent him a gossip item they proposed printing:

> I've always considered Victor Gollancz the smoothest operator when it comes to *advance* quotes, but something has come up that calls, I think for censure. On the dust-jacket of a novel, *Annalisa*, by Forbes Rydell (GOLLANCZ, 12s. 6d.), VG prints in large type (in crimson): 'SUPERIOR'. Immediately under — (in small type) he prints 'is what we *hope*'. Underneath that line he prints (in large type) MAURICE RICHARDSON. Lower down he prints — ' — to take his great name in vain — ' (in smallish type). Next line runs 'will call it'. Line below *that* runs 'Anyhow, we think it' (smallish type). Final line (large type) is VERY SUPERIOR INDEED.
>
> Now then, any careless customer looking swiftly at this jacket will read: SUPERIOR — MAURICE RICHARDSON — VERY SUPERIOR INDEED. And I for one don't think it all that fair — to the author of the book (for such a jacket will infuriate the critics as a whole), to Maurice Richardson, the retailers, the paying customers.
>
> The book comes out March 7. Time enough for Mr G to withdraw this offending jacket.

'I object most strongly to the passage in question,' was Victor's response. 'During my 40 years' life as a publisher, I have been accused of many things, but never of deliberate dishonesty. In making that insinuation, your contributor is, in the opinion of myself and my advisors, grossly libellous . . . '

He impressed the book trade when he announced in November 1957 that he was to visit Australia and New Zealand the following year. 'I have the feeling', he was quoted as saying, 'that a great deal is coming out of Australia and New Zealand in the next few years'. 'Mr Gollancz', said a *Guardian* correspondent,

> has been impressed by some recent works like the play 'Summer of the Seventeenth Doll' and the novels of Patrick White: he thinks that a school is emerging where until now there grew only a few isolated talents . . .
>
> Mr Gollancz already spends six weeks of every year in the United States. 'I do very much believe in the younger American writers,' he says. He does not expect to go on to Australia more than once every three years. But it looks as though in future, the younger British writers will meet stiffer competition in getting our publishers to believe in them — and a good thing too.

The April to July trip was organized in fine detail. Friends were set to writing letters of introduction; the Australian and New Zealand representatives excitedly organized itineraries; Victor made plans to pack the necessary reading for three long essays to write on the ship:

'The Case of Colin Wilson', 'Beethoven', and 'Jazz' (which he knew of as a phenomenon but never listened to). Elinor Murphy had even got in touch with the P & O line about the tobacco and cigar stocks carried on board. When all the preparations were complete and advance publicity at its height, Victor cancelled the trip. He stored up further disappointments for his representatives by assuring them it was only a postponement, caused by special circumstances. Of course he never went. Like India, Australasia joined the list of those places Victor had wanted to visit, only to lose their appeal once he was free to go. In 1960 the cancelled trip was Egypt, sacrificed to another long holiday in Italy. Over-commitment and the consequences of ageing — exhaustion, fear of discomfort, and a longing for the familiar — restricted Victor for the rest of his life, in his travels as in his enthusiasms, to well-worn tracks.

CHAPTER TWENTY-FIVE

THE GENERATION GAP

FROM 1960, ALTHOUGH Victor frequently expressed himself forcibly on political and religious issues, capital punishment was the only cause that tempted him out of virtual retirement as a campaigner. In May of that year there was an international furore over Adolf Eichmann's kidnapping from Argentina and transportation to Israel for trial. At the time, Victor was on holiday in Italy, getting over 'the fracture of his ankle' (or rather of a small bone in his foot). He came back towards the end of June to find a letter from his old colleague, Norman Collins, with whom he was again on friendly terms.

> The case of Eichmann fills me with a particular horror. It would appear that this disgusting human being may well be hanged. Already the cheaper cartoons are carrying slogans of 'An eye for an eye'. In other words, the viler instincts which lead to anti-semitism and to Capital Punishment are like to find a joint unholy fiesta. Could you find a group of English Jews to declare in a public statement that at least some members of English Jewry would be opposed to the death penalty?

Victor was disinclined to organize a joint protest, but wrote immediately to *The Times*: '"An eye for an eye" was an advance in the days of unmeasured vengeance. A far greater advance was made when we, the Jews, were enjoined to abrogate vengeance altogether, and to substitute mercy. Moreover: the more monstrous the wrong done to us, the more imperative, by law of spiritual compensation, does mercy become. I pray that Eichmann may not be hanged.' 'My dear Victor,' Collins responded when it was published, 'Bless your heart.'

Victor's letter was obviously destined to go down better with Christians than with Jews. The *News Chronicle* carried a letter from a rabbi, to which Victor's reply was scarcely conciliatory.

> Rabbi Gould asks whether a person whose family had been imprisoned and killed by a monster like Eichmann would agree with Mr Gollancz. The answer is in the affirmative. A Jewish lady, unknown to me, came up to me at the opera last night and said, 'Thank you, Mr Gollancz, for your

letter to *The Times*. I agreed with it wholeheartedly. I may add that both
my parents were killed at Auschwitz.' The Rabbi adds, 'Let Mr Gollancz
not be more merciful than God. Did not Samuel hew Agag to pieces before
God in Gilgal?' It is most distressing to find a Jewish rabbi identifying the
vengeful tribal 'God' of the more primitive parts of the Old Testament
with God as conceived by adult humanity.

At the time, he was not disposed to prolong the controversy. When
asked at the end of June to write a short article called 'Don't Hang
Eichmann', he refused: he was 'completely snowed under'. He was
back in action on a case closer to home in October, when he organized
a 31-signature letter to *The Times* pleading for a reprieve for the 18-
year-old Forsyth. His co-signatories included A. J. Ayer, Kingsley
Amis, Hugh Casson, John Freeman and Christmas Humphries. A
Daily Mail reporter investigated.

> Up the uncarpeted stairs amid the old envelopes and sagging armchairs of
> his Covent Garden office sat the power behind the whole operation, Mr
> Victor Gollancz.
> He had circulated this letter, as he has circulated so many others.
> 'I think this kind of thing has an effect,' he told me. 'We pray it will. Not
> a short-term one, perhaps. But a long-term result. When people see all
> those respectable names they gradually have their prejudices eroded
> away.'
> Our conversation was punctuated with guffaws — as any talk with VG
> always is. 'I picked out seasoned campaigners in the cause, and shoved in
> any others I thought might be sympathetic.
> 'We had to work fast. Benjamin Britten was too late with his
> signature. . . .
> 'This is the way we do things — a collection of widely differing
> individualists banded together for a number of motives, quietly nibbling
> away at public opinion.
> 'Not a short-term result, perhaps . . . a long-term one.'
> But there is only one week left . . .

Forsyth was executed, as had been another murderer — Harris —
whom Victor had worked to save. In November he was labouring
hard at the resuscitation of the NCACP, and a full-time secretary was
hired. The first major casualty of this new involvement was the
organizer of the annual Bishop Bell Memorial lectures. Victor's
secretary wrote to say he had to withdraw from his promise to give the
lecture in April. Pitman, the organizer, wrote in anger that plans were
already well in hand, and that Victor might at least have written his
own excuses. This elicited from Victor one of his most pungent
letters, rebuking Pitman for writing before the sun had gone down

upon his wrath. Victor had had to cancel because his work for the NCACP now involved: the enlargement of the executive committee and the Committee of Honour; the preparation of a national memorial of some 30,000–40,000 eminent people; and the holding of a great national meeting at the Albert Hall on 18 April. 'All this has already involved a tremendous amount of work, the writing of many hundreds of letters, and a great number of personal negotiations — one of which resulted this morning in the acceptance by the Earl of Harewood of the Chairmanship of the Committee of Honour.' Much detail followed about Victor's other heavy responsibilities. Then he became heated:

> I cannot remotely agree with you that 'a moral obligation to the April date was as strong as any obligation you may feel about capital punishment'. In fact, I am beginning to lose my temper as I dictate and must say that such a remark is patently absurd. On the one hand, there is the obligation to fulfil a promise, which, if broken, must involve distress and grave inconvenience to those who have organized the event: on the other hand, there is an obligation to save what may be, over the years, hundreds of human lives — for our belief is that, with an unremitting effort, we shall, in fact, get capital punishment abolished. My ancestors said, in a famous passage, that anyone who saved a single human life was as if he had created the whole universe: I can hardly imagine such a remark being made about the keeping of an engagement to lecture, however important.
>
> You wonder what the late Bishop would have thought of me. Frankly, I regard that remark as grossly impertinent. The late Bishop was an intimate friend of mine, and knew me very well, with all my faults and failings. We worked very successfully together on many causes: and I regard it as tasteless in the extreme to have dragged him into this matter. I also think very badly of your use of the word 'excuse'.
>
> I am conscious of the fact that I have started this letter in a moderate tone, but have ended it in an immoderate one. I am also conscious of the fact that, in spite of my advice to you, I do not at the moment feel like letting the sun go down upon my wrath, and am therefore instructing my secretary to post the letter immediately. But I dare say I shall repent by tomorrow morning: in which event, I shall send you a note of apology, which will probably reach you about the same time as yours reaches me.

A PS followed: 'The reason why I asked my secretary to write to you instead of writing personally, was the obvious one: I was engaged every second of the time with work for the campaign.'

It was widely alleged, answered Pitman, that everyone had a streak of violence:

> You have said your reply is a violent one and I can only take this as an acknowledgement of certain guilt feelings about having let us down.

I am not at all unmindful of the difficulties involved in arranging a campaign of the kind you have in mind but I stick to my original contention that it would have been far better if you'd lifted the telephone and had a personal word with me . . . or the Bishop of Chichester . . . explaining your dilemma. We are all of us busy people but the personal contact of the kind I now refer to would have avoided the acrimonious correspondence which has ensued . . .

This crossed with a letter from Victor simply saying 'I apologise', which of course totally disarmed Pitman, who sent Victor thanks for being 'generous and handsome' and wished the campaign good luck. (Victor's impulsiveness often made him a poor manager of his time. In the excitement of the moment he often failed to make the two-minute telephone call that might save him the labour later of immense letters in self-defence. A letter of apology was very rare.)

Victor blocked an attempt by Koestler to stop him becoming Chairman of NCACP and kill off plans for the Albert Hall meeting. He became Gardiner's co-chairman and was virtually given *carte blanche*. By working frantically during December, Victor had achieved his immediate NCACP objectives when he left for America at the end of the month. The Henrietta Street office was back in operation. The Committee of Honour had swollen to 178 distinguished names, including Acland, David Astor, Bonham Carter, Benjamin Britten, C. Day-Lewis, E. M. Forster, John Gielgud, Alec Guinness, Allen Lane, Russell, Sitwell, Graham Sutherland, Arnold Toynbee, Rebecca West and a clutch of bishops and politicians. The executive committee included two Tory MPs (Julian Critchley and Peter Kirk), two Labour (Paget and Silverman) and Jeremy Thorpe from the Liberals. Preparations were well in hand for the Albert Hall event.

Victor returned at the end of February, and eschewed all other public activities until after the meeting. Koestler, still on the executive, but rarely present, was under control. Victor was now unhappy with the treasurer, Lord Altrincham (the writer John Grigg), who wrote to him on 30 March 1961 that

It rather seems, from your failure to communicate with me since you got back from America, and from your unfeigned astonishment that the Campaign's finances were in good order, that I haven't your full confidence as Treasurer. If that is so, I feel it is only fair to you and to the Campaign to make way for somebody else.

This is not a huffy or a stuffy letter. I really should completely understand if you decided to look for a more congenial Treasurer. The Campaign is your show, in a quite special degree: you are giving your life and energies to it, and you are entitled to pick your officers to suit your own needs and temperament.

For my part, I will do all I reasonably can for the cause, whether or not I am on the Committee or Treasurer of the Campaign . . .

In the interests of unity, he was persuaded to remain in his post. Anyway, Victor was using as his chief lieutenants members of the Gollancz staff. The planning and execution of the Albert Hall meeting went less smoothly than at his last, in 1955. He constantly interrupted Elinor Murphy's briefing of stewards to demand that she do jobs for him. During the fund-raising part of the meeting, he alleged from the platform that the silver collection had not been taken and ignored his staff's assurances to the contrary. There was a panic when National Front infiltrators among the 100 stewards seized the microphone from Violet Bonham Carter. Despite these minor hitches, the meeting was an overwhelming success. The line-up of speakers included Kingsley Amis, John Freeman (of the *New Statesman* and 'Face to Face'), Gardiner, Ludovic Kennedy (author of the influential *10, Rillington Place*, which told the Christie/Evans story) and Silverman: they attracted a bigger audience than could be accommodated even with the help of an overflow meeting in Kensington Town Hall. By the time Victor wound up at the Albert Hall, over £2,000 had been collected. He gave the audience guidance on how to apply pressure to government and public opinion, and begged them to act 'as the shock-troops of abolition'. He then went on to add a word on the specific case which had begun to preoccupy him:

> I must not commit my Executive Committee, nor must I speak in the name of this meeting: but as a human being I can say — and please allow me to say it, not from the Chair, but from this platform — I can say to Ben-Gurion, with the deepest sympathy and respect, 'Do not kill Adolf Eichmann'. If six million have been slaughtered, what can it profit to make the number six million and one? Will *this* lighten the awful darkness of cruelty and hatred that Belsen will cast over history unrelieved unless something can be done to relieve it? Only one thing can lighten that darkness, can redeem and restore, however infinitesimally in mere numerical comparison, the human name: I mean a power, in those whose dear ones have suffered so unthinkably, to spare the killer.
> Ladies and Gentlemen, the rally is over.

Within a few days he had begun to write his last pamphlet: *The Case of Adolf Eichmann*. He finished it on 20 May and immediately began writing 'a sort of platonic . . . dialogue on the whole capital punishment business', a project which he dropped within weeks. Perhaps the rumpus over his *Eichmann* distracted his attention.

The pamphlet had been published by early June, when the Eichmann trial was getting into its stride. Only about 15,000 words long, it commenced with a note: 'I have hesitated a long time before deciding to publish this pamphlet. For a British Jew, whose suffering has been merely sympathetic, to criticise the Israelis, and to suggest what they should and should not do, must seem, even to the writer, intolerably presumptuous. And yet I end by feeling that publish I must.' It briefly acknowledged that the Nazi 'final solution' was a sin unparalleled in human experience, but condemned the trial: it wrongly dwelt on past evils; it would increase anti-semitism; it was itself 'a vast illegality'. No one could say if Eichmann had sufficient free will to be truly 'guilty' of the sins he had committed; the British government and hence the ordinary British citizen had been guilty of many sins of omission, as were many other nations, especially the Americans and the French; and even if Eichmann were 'guilty', he should not be executed, for vengeance was wrong. He quoted at length from Blake's commendation of Christ's precept 'Forgive your enemies', including the passage: 'Man must and will have Some Religion; if he has not the Religion of Jesus, he will have the Religion of Satan, and will erect the synagogue of Satan, calling the Prince of this World, God . . . ' Victor went on to conclude that 'It is precisely the ultimate evil in Hitler's "final solution" that calls, by way of reply to it, for an act of ultimate good.' 'It will be asked', read the last paragraph, 'what alternative would I propose to a sentence of death? To answer that is no part of my purpose. I plead for one thing only: that Eichmann's judges may act in the spirit of what is best in the Old Testament as well as in the New — in the spirit of "Forsake evil: do good, and live" and of "Go, and sin no more".'

The pamphlet attracted a bigger press domestically and world-wide than had any of Victor's previous writings. With the eyes of the world on the Eichmann trial, news editors made much of the 'Jew defends Eichmann' angle.

The Christian press was lost in admiration. The *Catholic Herald*, for instance, headed its leading article 'LESSON FROM A JEW' and spoke of Victor as 'a famous Jew who (let us face it) has shown in his public life a deeper understanding of the Christian spirit in public affairs than most of us.' After rehearsing the argument of the pamphlet, it asked: 'Can we not take Mr Gollancz's plea for forgiveness and clemency towards the willing agent of the Nazi sin as a reminder that we, as professed Christians, are called upon to do something for us personally less hard, namely proclaim not only the wrongness, but the utter stupidity, of the international rivalry and suspicion which holds us in the trap of our own making . . . '

The *Baptist Times* columnist remarked that 'I sometimes think that Mr Victor Gollancz, who is a Jew, is one of the most Christian men in Britain in his views on many social questions and in his spirit towards his fellow-men.' To mainstream Jewish opinion, the pamphlet's tone and content — not least the Blake quotation — made it seem a calculated outrage, more damaging given the attendant publicity.

They had suffered a few months earlier from a 'Face to Face' interview, in which Victor had proved himself a superb television performer, with an account of the constrictions of Jewish orthodoxy that held non-Jews spellbound. Now, in the guise of some kind of Jewish spokesman, he was again on television and enjoying headline status even in the popular papers. Ever temperate in its comments, the *Jewish Chronicle* tried to set the record straight in an editorial entitled 'MR GOLLANCZ'S CONSCIENCE':

> Mr Victor Gollancz's denunciations of Eichmann's capture and trial have gained wide publicity, largely because he claims to write as a Jew impelled by the prompting of his conscience. This has misled several critics. The fact is that Mr Gollancz does not speak for any section of British or Diaspora Jewry on this question or on any other. By all the available means of testing public opinion, the overwhelming majority of Jews throughout the free world and their representatives approve of the trial. Furthermore, Mr Gollancz is only very marginally Jewish by any criterion; true, he has not carried his flirtations with Christianity to a final consummation, but he has long since broken with the faith and community into which he was born. To make the play that he does of his residual Jewishness in support of his public activities is, itself, open to objection.

It objected to his inconsistency in denouncing on moral grounds the right of others to make moral judgements.

> The real key to his objections is to be found in the passage of his pamphlet in which Mr Gollancz blames 'Jewish conspicuousness — in suffering, in success, in poverty, in wealth, in religion, and physical appearance' for antisemitism, and suggests that it 'can be combated only by making no effort to combat it.' This is simply a variation on the theme of those who say the Jews should not defend themselves; it will only make the antisemites angrier. This has not only been disproved by centuries of suffering, but is morally untenable. . . . Mr Gollancz would carry more conviction . . . if he himself displayed the virtues of modesty and humility.

The Board of Deputies discussed the problem a few days later, when Harry Samuels referred to the wide publicity arising from Victor's radio and television appearances in which he claimed to speak as a Jew. The Chairman of the Defence Committee considered that 'dealing with Mr Gollancz would be very tricky indeed'. He suggested a private approach pointing out that his views were likely to cause 'misunderstanding and great harm'.

If they tried that approach it did not work for, months later, Victor gave his reaction as a Jew to the death sentence passed on Eichmann. The Jewish community once again could do pathetically little to defend itself against its famous product.

But it was a writer in the secular press who upset him more than any other. In the *Sunday Times*, Hugh Trevor-Roper said that the trial was being conducted fairly, then accused Victor of

> uninformed and presumptuous libel.
>
> Mr Gollancz's attempts to prove Eichmann innocent seem to me high-minded, but perverse. He tells us that the human will is not free, that Nazism was the result either of impersonal forces or of errors in which we all have our share, and that the British Government, which did not throw open the gates of Palestine (which it did not own) and was over-bureaucratic in its admission of refugees to Britain (during a desperate war), was no less guilty than Eichmann who, after all, was the victim of his fate and no doubt animated by 'positive idealism'. In the beginning, he was innocent because he was obeying orders; in the end, if he disobeyed orders and murdered when he was ordered to spare, he was equally innocent because that sort of thing tends to happen.
>
> In other words, there are no degrees of responsibility in the world, and the greater the crime the greater the innocence. This mystical 'trans-valuation of values' will no doubt be regarded as highly creditable to Mr Gollancz by some readers. To me it seems thoroughly pernicious. I do not think it sheds much light on the difficult moral and practical problem of the Eichmann Trial.

Victor despatched copies of this attack to eight people, including Acland, Altrincham, Vera Brittain and the Bishop of Middleton, asking them to write letters in his defence. If any did it was a waste of time: Victor's letter was the only one published. Its insistence that on almost every point his persecutor had falsified his meaning cut no ice with Trevor-Roper, who replied that he found Victor's distinctions too fine to affect the substance of his argument. There was a simultaneous row with a Jew in the *Guardian*, and Victor was also in the *Observer* correspondence columns putting Philip Toynbee straight. The latter controversy provoked a letter to the *Observer* from Naomi Lewis:

Sir, — May one ask what special right has Mr Gollancz to 'forgive' so lavishly for matters which he has neither experienced himself, nor, clearly, has the sensibility to imagine? For such complacent armchair forgiveness, in any case, neither the 'innocent' nor the 'guilty', in Germany or anywhere else, could ever feel anything but contempt. There can be few graver impertinences offered to the voiceless dead of 1939 to 1945 than Mr Gollancz's jolly *bonhomie* about the whole affair.

To anyone who knew Victor's record, this was clearly dreadfully unfair. Yet it was understandable that anyone else reading his pamphlet should doubt if he had ever cared deeply about the holocaust. Victor wrote to David Astor to express his hurt that he could have published a letter saying

that I haven't the sensibility to imagine what those sufferings were. I do not know how old Miss Lewis may be — perhaps she is too young to remember 1939 to 1945. But surely it is within your recollection that, more or less abandoning my business, I spent that entire period in appealing to the British public to realise these sufferings and to prevail on their Government to do something about it? I was one of the founders of the National Committee for Rescue from Nazi Terror . . . Berl Locker, who was then head of the Jewish Agency in London, has just written to the Israeli press, pointing out that with Eleanor Rathbone, I was its leading spirit. You will also remember that I wrote and published 'Let My People Go', which must have sold a million copies or so throughout the world, and a little later, 'Nowhere to Lay Their Heads', which had a similar circulation. Surely a knowledge of this might have been sufficient to suggest that Miss Lewis's letter should not be published, as clearly it is not a letter that I can reply to, and I must therefore allow this very wounding suggestion to pass unchallenged?

I hope you won't mind my writing to you like this, but I think of us as friends and, as I say, was a bit grieved.

Victor's propensity needlessly to gild the lily grew with age: it was never conscious. He undoubtedly believed by now that he had spent all of six years working single-mindedly to save Jews. Astor, of course, was conscience-stricken. When he rang Victor to ask who should be asked to reply, Victor had already left for a holiday, but Hilary Rubinstein suggested Bentwich, whose letter was as generous as the man.

Sir, — I do not agree with all Victor Gollancz's opinions and philosophy set out in his pamphlet . . . But knowing of his work in the past, I feel impelled to remark on Naomi Lewis's letter. It cannot fairly be said that Victor Gollancz is insensitive to the sufferings of the Jews or of any section of humanity. During the Hitler regime, and particularly during the war, he was tireless in speaking and writing for the persecuted, and demanding that the doors of rescue should be opened. His two pamphlets . . . were moving appeals, just because he had the sensibility to imagine the agony; and they stirred public opinion. If he has felt some mercy even for Eichmann, it is because again he has imagined how the horrible Nazi machine of unspeakable inhumanity was worked.

It is arguable that it required more moral courage of Bentwich — a committed Jew and a Zionist — to defend Victor, than Victor ever needed to attack Jews or the Israeli state. Victor saw it otherwise. 'There are some Jews who share my view [on not executing Eichmann],' he wrote to one member of the public, 'but no Jew in this country, I fear, who would dare to proclaim it.' He was indeed fortunate in his small circle of Jewish friends, who brought on themselves much obloquy by their public defence of him. Berl Locker, now living in Israel, was brave to remind the world of Victor's wartime work, for the whole Israeli press was up in arms over the pamphlet. Briefly, Victor thought of pressing on: Murphy, about to leave Gollancz to become a probation officer, was asked to look out all the JSHS papers for him. Whatever philippic he had in mind never materialized; indeed, the papers seem to have lain in the Eaton Place flat untouched. By mid-summer, the Eichmann controversy had died down and Victor was back in the thick of the NCACP campaign, supervising a massive national petition and planning activities for the autumn and winter.

He was soon at loggerheads with Altrincham, who offended by asking — as treasurer — to be consulted about the use of funds. Victor waxed eloquent about this to Gerald Gardiner, pointing out *inter alia* (and correctly) that he had personally contributed very large sums to the campaign, both in cash and kind. Efficiency dictated that he have the freedom to take decisions without interference. Confronted with the urgent necessity to keep both protagonists in their offices, Gardiner lamented, 'It's a pity that you're both such obstinate people. So am I.'

'You don't know me well enough', answered Victor, 'to know that I am, in fact, the least obstinate person in the world. Anyone here would tell you that, if a member of the editorial staff wants to do a book that I am wholly opposed to, he is always allowed to do it (unless my objection is a moral one).' But what with a 70-hour week on office work and other activities,

it is quite impossible for me even to contemplate discussing (for instance) with Altrincham details of a campaign — of what is to be spent on this and what is to be spent on that, of why I think this essential and don't think that essential, etc., etc. It isn't as if he knew anything about it: he knows nothing, while I have run, I suppose, more than 100 meetings. The sheer irritation of having to explain this or that, in immensely precious time, to a man who cannot possibly understand these things would overwhelm me.

He was willing to consult on any item of expenditure over £500 as long as it related to an item of expenditure, not a project. If that was not acceptable to Altrincham, Victor would remain joint chairman but give up any responsibility other than routine supervision of the office. 'I suppose someone would have to be specially appointed to undertake this sort of job, and he or she could work under Altrincham's financial direction. But how we should get such a person, I do not know.' A decision was needed quickly:

> What I said about being willing to consult Altrincham about any single item coming to £500 cannot, I think, apply to the Albert Hall rally, where a certain type of single advertisement does, in fact, cost, if I remember rightly, more than £500. But I don't think that point need be raised at the moment. When we set about organising that meeting, no doubt the Executive, with Altrincham present, will be prepared to give me carte blanche on such matters as this.

Within two weeks, Victor was in hospital with a broken thigh and Altrincham was writing to impress upon him that they must not let 'this slight clash between an indispensable chairman and a thoroughly expendable treasurer cause any anxiety or distress to the former!'

Victor never did return, as Altrincham hoped, 'to full vigour' in NCACP activities. He was out of action for several weeks, and then went away on a long recuperative holiday in the late spring. Plans for mass meetings were dropped, and the campaign confined itself to holding modest 'question and answer'-style meetings at Central Hall and provincial venues, sending weekly information sheets to MPs and finishing preparation of the petition. Even augmented by deputations, this limited pressure could not dent the government's reluctance to initiate fresh legislation. Victor remained joint chairman, but from mid-1962 the NCACP wound down its activities for the rest of the lifetime of the Parliament. In 1964 Gerald Gardiner became Lord Chancellor in a Labour government pledged to abolish capital punishment. Victor helped in some measure to see the abolitionist measure through the House of Lords, bullying Lord Harewood into supporting the government Bill in his maiden speech there.

Victor lived to see the end of executions in Britain. Sporadic, quixotic, obstreperous and dictatorial in his contributions to the long campaign, he played a vital role, unquestioned by any he worked with, in transforming influential opinion about capital punishment. Without him, there would have been no NCACP. Koestler provided the devastating polemic, Astor the platform and Gardiner the patient argument, but it was Victor who forced the famous to stand up and be counted and provided the unknowns with the means to make their voices heard. Without his efforts and skills, abolition might well have seemed too risky and unpopular to be taken on as a commitment by any government. Certainly, had MPs of all persuasions not been remorselessly bombarded with the facts of the abolitionist argument, it would have had very much less chance of success.

It was perhaps an advantage for the NCACP that Victor had his accident when he did, for he was then in the process of preparing a paper on punishment which would have brought to the campaign counter-productive publicity. The official NCACP alternative to the death sentence was life imprisonment, and it says much for Victor's commitment to the campaign that he did not resign rather than accept this policy. He had come strenuously to reject the concept of punishment of any kind, and was set to make an attack on it at an annual conference of the Student Christian Movement — cancelled because of his immobility. His correspondence over the Eichmann pamphlet had shown that he was no longer interested in meeting pragmatic objections to his arguments against retribution, being wholly opposed to any suggestions that Eichmann should be sentenced to life imprisonment. He shrugged off the objections of those who pointed out that unless incarcerated, Eichmann would be torn to pieces by the relatives of his victims. By the time of his accident, he had already read more than twenty books on punishment, and was preparing himself, *inter alia*, to deliver a critique of the views of that champion of prisoners, Frank Pakenham.

The circumstances in which Victor fractured his thigh were fittingly bizarre. On Sunday 17 September 1961 he was irresistibly drawn to Trafalgar Square, where the respectable CND was being challenged by the Committee of 100 who, under Bertrand Russell, were pledged to breaking the law by obstruction in public places. Victor had been asked the previous year to join Russell's Committee and had given John Collins advance warning of its formation. He and Collins were back in harmony. Victor was being helpful behind the scenes with internal wrangling over the use of the Defence and Aid Fund, and the previous Sunday had joined Collins, Diana, James

Cameron, Kingsley Martin and others to address a CND audience on 'No War Over Berlin'. The Sunday of the 17th was destined to be a very much more troublesome affair. Russell was leading a sit-in, with 2,000 followers bent on civil disobedience. Collins had led a march to the square with thousands of supporters determined to resist Russell's challenge to their peaceful and law-abiding movement. The police made their contribution to the demonstration's notoriety by arresting both Russell and the entirely innocent Collins. The judiciary then assisted in making it world-famous by sending Britain's most distinguished philosopher to jail at the age of 89.

In the brouhaha that ensued, the fact that Victor Gollancz, a mere spectator, had tripped and injured himself secured no headlines. He was relegated to the gossip columns. The *New Statesman* reported:

> For a long time you mill around at a demo of this kind without seeing anyone you know. Then, suddenly, it turns, dream-like, into a party. Almost, indeed, a publisher's cocktail party. In Northumberland Avenue, under a dilapidated sign which reads 'Safari Club', Victor Gollancz is holding court. St John's Ambulance men offer to carry him away but he prefers to sit on his chair. He hails one of his authors: 'I am advertising you next Sunday'. His assured benevolence attracts quite a crowd. (Afterwards I discovered that he had injured himself badly and must have been in great pain.)

By one of those freaks of such an accident, Victor was not at first in great pain. Ruth drove him home, the doctor was summoned and concluded that there was no fracture, and left him without pain-killers. As Victor remembered it, he spent the whole night screaming in agony, yet the following morning, before the fracture was diagnosed, he dictated a letter to John Freeman at the *New Statesman* calling for the Allies to go naked into the conference chamber with Khrushchev and thus avoid atomic war. (He had written a letter in similar terms to the *Guardian* the previous week.) That same day he was transferred to the private wing of University College Hospital where a pin was inserted in his thigh. Once the pain was relieved, he enjoyed himself. The *New Statesman* reported on 6 October:

> Victor Gollancz, I am glad to say, is making a characteristically zestful recovery from the fractured femur which he got from his fall at the Trafalgar Square anti-nuclear demonstration. His room in University College Hospital is like a cross between a publisher's office and a bridge club. Gollancz, in plum-coloured pyjamas, was sitting up reading other firms' detective stories out of one eye and his own firm's manuscripts with the other. I have never encountered a more boisterous invalid. Inside 20

minutes he: passed various jacket proofs; sampled suitable sick-bed delicacies from Fortnum and Mason's, proffered by Mrs Gollancz to supplement the hospital diet, and quoted extensively from the Taoist mystics on the art of falling. He was, he told me, irked because he had failed to observe the precept of the Sage who remarked that if a drunken man could fall off a cart without hurting himself, how much more easily should a sober man be able to fall provided he was in touch with the infinite. He also managed to animadvert sharply on various inaccuracies, ideological and otherwise, in the writings of both Koestler and Orwell, and to congratulate the authors of *The Strategic Air Offensive Against Germany* on having exposed the inefficient brutality of saturation bombing. He assured me that he had personal knowledge that Churchill had been amazed to learn — only when the war was over — that his own orders countermanding saturation bombing well before Dresden had not been carried out.

Victor had a wonderful time in hospital — 'really a gala', he wrote to an American friend, 'with friends, flowers, cigars, smoked salmon and caviar and paté from Fortnums — not to mention books — pouring in. And lots and lots of pretty nurses . . . ' Ruth had a tougher time, for the pretty nurses quickly got fed up with Victor's incessant demands for attention, and she had to do much of the nursing herself. Insomnia troubled him, but he had three volumes of Beethoven's letters to take him through the long nights. During the days he ran Gollancz, continued the controversy in the *Guardian* over Berlin and revelled in the attentions of friends. 'When you are not in action,' wrote Michael Foot, 'the world's pulse seems to beat a little slower. So get better soon.' He was only one of the many dozens who were distressed at the thought of Victor inactive. The letters and gifts that poured in from Britain and America kept him cheerful. In addition, he had the pleasure of hearing from those who had just received advance copies of his *A New Year of Grace*. (*From Darkness to Light* had not sold as well as the first anthology. *A New Year of Grace*, designed for a younger audience, consisted of passages from both books, this time with a linking commentary. At one point Victor ruminated on Christ as 'a unique revelation of goodness', but worried about the troublesome passages which suggested he might have been less than perfect in terms of the '100 per cent' approach.)

He was out of hospital and on crutches within weeks, dealing from home, and occasionally the office, with the substantial correspondence from *Guardian* readers, inspired by his latest epistle.

Sir, — If anyone attempts, in plain straightforward language, to urge that nothing can now save humanity but an uncompromising self-surrender to, and self-fulfilment in, the religion of Jesus and William Blake, he faces an inevitable accusation: namely, that he is ready to preach easy platitudes in a complicated world. And yet I cannot see how, on the day that Russia has exploded her 50- or 60-megaton bomb . . . those who feel as I do can decently remain silent.

For my own part, I have recently made two specific appeals: I have begged Mr Macmillan to negotiate, 'naked' and unconditionally, with Mr Khrushchev, and I have begged my fellow Jews to forgive Adolf Eichmann. These, however, in point of humanity's need, are mere particulars of a universal: and it is the universal which, without hedging or shamefacedness, now cries out to be stated. I could have wished that the Pope or the Archbishop of Canterbury or the Chief Rabbi would have stated it: but as no one of these great leaders has done so, a mere private individual must.

'Man must and will have Some Religion,' wrote William Blake. 'If he has not the Religion of Jesus, he will have the Religion of Satan.' It can be seen now, in 1961, that his vision was piercingly clear. All the Powers and Principalities of the world . . . have either spat upon the religion of Jesus (as in the case of the Communist sector) or have patronised it and 'interpreted' it away (as in the case of the West). Adopting instead the religion of Satan, they are inevitably headed for total destruction.

What is the religion of Satan? It is striving to be first: seeking material prosperity: retaliating: punishing. It is self-righteousness: it is 'justice'. And what is the religion of Jesus? It is accepting to be last: seeking spiritual riches: returning good for evil: forgiving. It is scrutiny of self: it is love. And it is these . . . not more or less but in their totalities. Oil and water cannot mix: the religion of Jesus is the religion of 100 per cent.

The satanism of Russia's bomb and her attitude to Berlin could not be defeated by self-righteous denunciation from nations tainted with similar guilt. In claiming like Niebuhr 'that what is good for moral man may be evil for immoral society', the great theologians had been wrong. 'I shall be asked by what right I make bold to pronounce on the Gospel of Jesus. I reply: the right of anyone who can read English, and believes that there are some men, the greatest of all being among them, who say what they mean and mean what they say.'

One of the dozens of admiring responses came from a Baptist minister who said, 'perhaps I scarcely distinguish you from Moses — whose wisdom as God's appointed leader of the Hebrew people is reflected in your letter to *The Guardian* of Friday last, but addressed to Gentiles.' Some asked Victor to follow through, but apart from letter-writing, he did nothing to develop his 100 per cent argument into a campaign. At the back of his mind was his unfinished *The Sanity of Christ*, which had been blocked by his perplexity at Christ's occasional lapses. Victor found it difficult to decide whether utter-ances such as 'I bring not peace but the sword' or episodes like the driving of the money changers from the Temple were imperfections in Christ or interpolations by his disciples.

He was briefly motivated towards action by a *Times* letter from Bentwich in December, calling for mercy for Eichmann in the light of the teachings of Judaism 'about the Angel of Mercy and the sacredness of human life'. Eichmann he believed to be simply a hard bureaucrat. Execution

> could serve no purpose except to satisfy a feeling of revenge which, however natural and inevitable, is un-Jewish.
>
> Ben-Gurion and other spokesmen of Israel have stressed that the purpose of the trial was not the punishment of an individual but the making of the record of the most infamous crime of history. That purpose it has served . . .
>
> I realise the desperate difficulty of guarding Eichmann in Israel, and so I suggest a short term of imprisonment and deportation rather than life detention. Let Germany take care of him, and let Eichmann be left to his own thoughts and memories.

Victor cabled him requesting the names of about a dozen prominent British Jews who might sign a letter in support, and approached a few directly. He came up against a shortage of personages prepared to sign. Koestler wanted the NCACP informally to organize a petition signed by Jews and gentiles, but after discussions, Victor had to cry off. He was just back at the office, still on crutches, and was very busy, given the absence of Livia and Rubinstein in America; his surgeon had warned him against over-exertion; and he felt that rabbis would not sign the petition for fear of antagonizing their congregations, while gentiles would be wary of being seen to interfere in Israeli affairs. The project died. Victor's zeal was much diminished. He had trailed to Acland the idea of a mass movement for human regeneration, but immediately made it impossible by embarking on a new book, a collection of prayers called *God of a Hundred Names*, compiled in collaboration with Barbara Greene. Immediately his work on that was over, he started to compose another abortive poem, this time in the style of Eliot. Other than routine work for the NCACP, he had little appetite left for more than the occasional letter or broadcast. In August 1962 he was in the news as co-signatory with Pakenham (now Lord Longford) of a letter protesting against a physical attack on Oswald Mosley. The following month he complained in *The Times* and on television about the deportation to the United States of Dr Soblen, a sick man who faced capital treason charges there, but dropped plans to write a book about the case. In December it was again the Jews who attracted his attention. This time, the issue was ritual slaughter.

Apropos of yesterday's debate in the Lords, the idea that 'ritual slaughter' is of the remotest religious import to a modern Jew is quite nonsensical. The thing derives from the biblical injunction 'but the blood thou shalt not eat, for the blood is the life' (or words to that effect), the idea being that 'ritual slaughter', combined with subsequent salting, gets rid of the animal's blood and makes the flesh ritually 'clean' for human consumption. The injunction itself is, of course, a primitive tribal taboo, perhaps magical in origin, perhaps fumbling after reverence for life: if the latter, its present-day equivalent is vegetarianism.

True religion, Jewish or otherwise, in relation to one's fellow-creatures consists, among other things, in causing them the minimum of suffering. As Lord Silkin proposed, there should be a scientific inquiry: and if the result were to show that 'ritual slaughter' is more painful, even by the merest fraction, than 'humane killing', it should be abolished. . . .

If he had set out with the sole purpose of outraging orthodox Jews, Victor could hardly have phrased his letter more provocatively. (In fact it represented a departure from the position he had held for years, when almost every letter he received from gentiles asking him to condemn ritual slaughter met with the response that they were at least unconsciously anti-semitic.) One correspondent wrote 'with great indignation':

What right have you to write of the attitude of the 'modern Jew' to 'ritual slaughter'. If you mean by modern Jew a Jew who has forsaken the religion of his father, you obviously regard men such as myself who are about thirty years younger than you as 'ancient Jews'. It has perhaps escaped your attention that there are to-day many thousands of practising Jews in this country who are quite up to date in their general outlook.

What can have moved you to write this most unwise and mischievous letter is quite beyond me. Perhaps it is only on all fours with your former letters of sympathy with the convicted murderers of the German Concentration Camps . . .

'My dear Sir,' wrote Victor. 'Pull yourself together: abuse is no substitute for argument.' He justified his position, queried his correspondent's knowledge of the Old Testament, and congratulated him on his luck in gravely libelling a man who objected on moral grounds to legal proceedings.

Letters were sent out to various authorities demanding immediate information for a pamphlet Victor intended to write on the subject, but once again he quickly lost interest. There was silence on the matter until, in September 1963, he received a letter from the Chairman of the Shechita (ritual slaughter) Committee of the Board of Deputies, who was distressed to receive from the Council of Justice to Animals its annual report in which Victor's letter to *The Times* had been quoted in full — prefaced by:

> 'In view of the claim by the Jewish authorities that the Jewish method of slaying animals for food is prescribed by the Divine Law the following letter from Mr Victor Gollancz . . . will be of interest. . . . '
>
> I am sure that you will understand when I say that it is most unfortunate that the opinion of one particular Jew — no matter how eminent in other fields — should be quoted against that of the Jewish authorities . . .
>
> I should therefore even at this stage urge upon you the necessity of considering your attitude to this question and if you would do me the courtesy of meeting me, I should be happy to discuss the whole position with you.

Discussion would be useless, responded Victor: he had gone into the matter with the greatest care and now knew ritual slaughter to be indefensible and 'wholly irrelevant to a modern Jew'.

It was the last artillery duel in Victor's war of attrition with the Jews. The story could have ended more neatly just seven months earlier, when there was a brief exchange of letters with a member of the *Jewish Chronicle* staff, Chaim Bermant. A little more than 50 years after writing his first letter to the paper (about the resurgence of Judaism among Oxford undergraduates), Victor wrote his last:

21 February 1963

My dear Sir,

I have a note from my secretary to say that you would like to interview me on the occasion of my 70th birthday.

I am greatly surprised by this request. To judge from your editorial comments about me from time to time, I should have thought that your readers, far from being interested in anything I might have to say, could only wish that I had died earlier.

Yours truly,
Victor Gollancz

'Dear Mr Gollancz,' replied Bermant. 'What you say is true, but the fact is you are alive, and at the very least, our readers would be interested to see your excuse.'

If Victor no longer had the sustained commitment to make more than a peripheral contribution to any cause he favoured, he had for a brief period the power to damage one which he viewed with ambivalence. At the end of 1962 there was a ferocious row about an inaccurate advertisement put out over the signatures of 38 prominent supporters of the Defence and Aid Fund of Christian Action. The High Commissioner for the Federation of Rhodesia and Nyasaland, Sir Albert Robinson, was able to prove that the advertisement contained a number of serious errors. All of the 38 signatories — including Victor — were embarrassed by the very public discovery that John Collins, carried away by emotion, had been careless in checking his facts. A few ignored Robinson's protest; three claimed never to have seen the advertisement; 22, including George Brown, Gerald Gardiner and Harold Wilson, signed a letter of apology with Collins; and six, including Violet Bonham Carter, Jo Grimond and Longford, signed a letter drafted by Victor which apologized more fully, and disassociated itself with certain parts of Collins's letter.

The damage to the Fund was already considerable. The public breach between Collins and his critics — led by Victor — was a very serious matter. Spurred on by Bonham Carter, Victor had composed and signed the alternative letter because he was honestly shocked — as always — by public misrepresentation of facts, and Collins had proved unexpectedly obstinate in refusing to make the concessions demanded of him.

As the leader of the disaffected, it was up to Victor to widen or heal the schism. His dilemma was simple. On the one hand, he could further erode the credibility of the Fund and Christian Action by making public his doubts about Collins's conduct as chairman, and he considered it important to do so in the interests of integrity in public life. On the other hand, he knew full well that he might destroy forever his relationship with two dear friends, who would be bound to feel that he was putting his own reputation before the interests of the Fund. His first test came when *The Times* requested, and received, a full statement of his reasons for refusing to sign Collins's letter. At the eleventh hour he got Ruth to ring Diana, who had begged him to withdraw the statement, to say he had done so. Both Collinses wrote him grateful and loving letters, and he drafted an eight-page reply to Diana on 29 November summarizing his view of the whole affair. 'I know', he explained, 'that John's motives are of the highest: I know that his passionate aim is to stop suffering, racial discrimination, injustice and war. But I am convinced, for my own part, that what he feels to be the necessities of the struggle (not to mention the famous "corruption of power") have landed him in the position of taking the easy way out, of giving the glib but inaccurate answer, even of committing the *suggestionem falsi* when difficulties arise.' He was in danger of believing that the end justified the means. He begged

Collins 'to look squarely at himself', lest he 'land himself in real disaster'.

Collins never got the chance to defend his actions, for Victor did not send the warning. He substituted instead a brief letter simply asking Collins 'to look at everything not as the self looks at it, but as a severe critic might.' He kept his distance from the Collinses for a short time, as he wrestled with a moral problem being posed by Bonham Carter: as the two most principled people among the signatories, they must resign as sponsors of the Fund. She saw Collins as a 'holy crook'.

In view of the fact that one as scrupulous as Gardiner had elected to sign Collins's rather than Victor's retraction; that Collins never believed or acted as if the end justified the means; that he had never had the opportunity of explaining his actions to Victor; that in most people's view, the affair was over and done with; that Collins had on this occasion been taken in by an African 'crook'; that this was the only blot on his record; and that he had promised absolute meticulousness in the future, Victor might have let the matter lie had it not been for the importunate Bonham Carter. Emphasizing his superior moral uprightness, she got his agreement to their joint resignation as sponsors of the Fund. Victor geared himself up to take the necessary action. He wrote an immensely long letter to the Collinses explaining why he must resign, much though he loved them and approved of Christian Action. But he now believed that John had unwittingly fallen victim to the doctrine that the end justified the means. He rehearsed again the post-advertisement actions of Collins that gave him concern.

All this, I fear, must seem terribly self-righteous. Really no: on the contrary: it is my own painful weakness in this very matter on several occasions (particularly in connection with the Left Book Club) that has long made me feel as I do.

So what the matter comes to is this. I support the aims of the Defence and Aid Fund with my whole heart and soul. But you are the Defence and Aid Fund: and I have to face the fact that, in any given circumstance, you may run it, consciously or unconsciously, in the spirit of 'The end justifies the means'. That being so, then if I remain a sponsor I am saying, so to speak, OK; and this I *must* refrain from saying, not out of care for my own wretched little name, but because I believe that a principle is at stake far more important, ultimately, even than the rescue of suffering Africans, which my heart cries out for.

I fear I have hurt you. If so, I do beg you to forgive me.

Yours always affectionately,
Victor

Yet again, he could not face sending the letter. He kept stalling Bonham Carter. 'I am awfully sorry,' he wrote to her in April,

> but I really can't resign until I get back from America (for which I leave just after my birthday party). The point is that they have only been back from America a very short time, and I didn't want to confront them with this as soon as they returned. Further, they have arranged a dinner party for me for next Monday to discuss the Bishop of Woolwich's book with him and with other theologians: and then on Tuesday night they are coming to my birthday dinner. In view of all this, I really should feel quite horrible resigning at this moment. So I feel I *must* defer this until my return from America at the end of May . . .

Ultimately, he had to admit to her that friendship had taken precedence over scruples and he would never resign. Victor had lost too many friends over the years to sacrifice on a point of dubious principle those on whom he most relied for love and intellectual companionship. Besides, Collins was in decline as the object of his jealousy: CND was falling apart, and Victor's own loss of interest in contemporary causes made it easy to live with his friend's more limited fame as chairman of Christian Action.

For the first few years of the 1960s, there was no diminution in Victor's interest in publishing, but he displayed, if anything, a growing propensity to fall out with those he dealt with. In 1960, for instance, his relationship with Colin Wilson well-nigh collapsed. After long arguments about changes Victor had made to *Ritual in the Dark*, to meet what Wilson thought to be unjustified libel allegations, came his horror at Wilson's planned *Encyclopaedia of Murder*. He failed to persuade him not to write it; Wilson sold it to Weidenfeld and then tried to reassure Victor that this would not mar their relationship. There were bound to be disagreements between them, he explained, because he thought of Victor as he did of his grandfather,

> who was also a a man of powerful personality and of great integrity. I was fond of him, but even as a child I was always involved in minor rows with him because his belief in his own rightness was a little too absolute. I think, in retrospect, that he was almost invariably right, but that is beside the point. My ability as a writer (such as it is) is tied up with intense subjectivity and a consequent need for total self-trust, and this has always been so. Authority irritates and offends me when I'm its object. . . . And when I come to see you, I never entirely lose a feeling of being in the presence of a peremptory CO who is liable to interrupt me at any moment or dismiss everything I've said with a brief wave of the hand and get down to the next piece of business in hand. . . . There is a very considerable

difference in the way you regard me and the way I regard myself, even
though I know how much kindliness and consideration there is in your
attitude to me . . .

When Negley tells me of how his relations with you in the past have
been characterised by a mixture of affection and exasperation, I recognise
the same attitudes in myself, and know that this is inevitable.

Wilson was bewildered when Victor failed to reply to his letter.
Writing to him a few weeks later with a question about sales, he got
back a curt letter in which 'Dear Colin' and 'Yours' replaced the
usual 'My Dear Colin' and 'Yours ever'. Wilson asked David Bolt to
investigate. 'He replied that he thought a letter I [Wilson] had written
you [Victor] had rather upset you, but you weren't still annoyed.
This makes me wonder just how far I can go in frankness with you; if
a relatively honest and friendly letter like the one he had in mind
could upset you, I shall begin to feel that nothing can be said with
complete frankness to you . . .'

'I didn't in the least mind', responded Victor, 'what you said about
my effect on you (whatever I may have thought about it), but I
minded very much indeed (not for my own sake, but for Negley's)
that you should have repeated what Negley said about me (and, I am
quite certain, given me an erroneous impression of what he said, as
one can easily do, doubtless unintentionally, by isolating a particular
sentence).'

Wilson was upset, but it was not malice that actuated the twisting
of the knife when he quoted his Cornish neighbour Daphne du
Maurier as saying, '"I'm surprised Victor's stopped advertising your
book in his column".' There *was* anger when he accused Victor of
'playing the despot' and having now 'purely unfriendly' feelings
towards him. This time, although he found the du Maurier reference
'extremely distasteful', Victor made an enormous effort to keep his
temper.

. . . To suggest that my feelings for you are 'purely unfriendly' is
fantastic. I think, as I have always thought, that you are on the one hand,
wildly self-centred, as often as not, extremely wrong-headed, and often
wholly incapable of entering into other people's feelings: but also generous, affectionate, and, in ultimates if not in immediates, of great intellectual and spiritual integrity. I think your capacities both for gratitude and
ingratitude are extraordinary, and that you combine an astonishingly
blind conceit with, in some respects, great humility. I have never
wavered in the view that you are an author of the greatest promise, and I
retain for you feelings, not 'purely unfriendly', but of friendship and
indeed affection.

The truce was blown apart on the question of advertising for *Ritual in the Dark* — 'this habit', wrote Wilson, 'of dropping a book like a hot potato once it fails to shoot to 50,000 in the first week'. Of all the accusations so frequently made against him as a publisher, that one stung Victor worst. Relations deteriorated further, with Victor holding on to his option on the next book and refusing to answer Wilson's increasingly intemperate communications. Wilson complained loudly in public about Victor's high-handedness and was then disarmed by a spontaneously generous act of Victor's that left him better off by £1,000. Further vicissitudes followed and in 1963 Victor had had enough. He wrote a coolly uncompromising letter to Wilson telling him he wished to publish nothing further by him. His six main reasons were: he found Wilson's constant demands for money worrying; he was increasingly unwilling to meet his demands for personal attention; Wilson was unappreciative of the editing work done by Gollancz; Victor was made 'sick at heart' by the suggestion that he was interested in Wilson's work only from the financial point of view; it was impossible efficiently to publish an author with his rate of output; and finally, 'I feel I cannot go on publishing an author who at any moment might produce, through another publisher, such a book as "The Origins of the Sexual Impulse".'

To Wilson's regret, Victor proved obdurate. It was a breach that injured Wilson more than Gollancz: he went through a bad patch for several years afterwards. But troublesome though Wilson had been, he had often been driven to explosions of anger because he felt himself ignored or patronized: the younger Victor had always been able to defuse Negley Farson's rages by taking him to lunch or writing a deeply affectionate and understanding letter. Latterly, with Wilson, he had avoided or rebuked him, and his dismissal as 'filthy' of books like *The Origins of the Sexual Impulse* was deeply upsetting to a serious writer.

The distaste Victor felt for the galloping trend towards sexual explicitness was unsurprising in a man of his age, who, indeed, publicly made much of being 'old-fashioned', while also liking to think of himself as *avant-garde*. It ruled Gollancz out as a possible publisher for certain kinds of books. What was more worrying and must have damaged the firm seriously in publishing circles was that his distaste had become retrospective. Thus, having lost Updike's book by insisting on changes he had initially opposed, he appeared to have forgotten his original attitude to the work. When André Deutsch published *Rabbit, Run* in 1961, Victor explained to *Reynolds*

News that he had turned it down because though it was 'a really magnificent novel', he had

> thought two sentences, however, not only gross but inessential to the author's purpose: he disagreed with me on both heads, and refused, as a matter of artistic integrity, to remove them: so we decided to part company for the time being.
>
> He was as grieved, I think, as I was. We remain excellent friends, and I hope and believe that one of these days we shall come together again as publisher and author . . .

A few months later, he explained to a contributor to the *Bookman* that the sentences he objected to were 'those describing *gustum in ore feminae post fellationem consummatam.*'

Deutsch, perhaps unaware that Victor had made a *volte face* on the passages in question, was grateful that he had gone out of his way to comment favourably on the book and that he insisted publicly that — unlike *Lolita* — it was not pornographic. Trouble arose when Victor reissued Updike's *The Poorhouse Fair* in 1964, with a sentence in the blurb which read: 'We subsequently "lost" him, owing to a friendly difference of opinion: there was a passage in his second novel, *Rabbit, Run*, which we did not wish to print and which he, quite rightly from his point of view, refused to alter.' Updike's restraint was remarkable. Like everyone else he forebore to remind Victor that he had at first wanted to publish the passage in question. Yet, affectionate though he was, he voiced a mild protest about the intrusion into the blurb of a private transaction. He feared it might 'make people feel there is something fishy about that book. Perhaps Deutsch will start getting requests for tearsheets of the "passage" you declined to print.' Alfred Knopf reacted violently.

> I have just seen the wrapper you have written for your reissue of John Updike's 'The Poorhouse Fair'. Never in my life have I seen such a *malicious breach of confidence*, for surely the relationship of publisher to author is generally regarded — and observed — as a professional and privileged one. You apparently intend your copy to call the attention of the censor . . . to 'Rabbit, Run'. I can only hope that you will not be successful! If I have anything to do with Updike's future in England, you will not have to print the word 'lost' in quotes.

Victor was baffled by such reactions. As he saw it, he was raising a point 'of the greatest possible public interest'. It was his duty to stand firm, and visible, in the battle against the erosion of moral standards. Late in 1963 he had been entangled in a widely publicized *Times Literary Supplement* controversy over the work of William Burroughs.

A review of several of Burroughs' books had been headed 'Ugh . . . ', and had contended that the publication of his work would seriously damage 'the cause of literary freedom and innovation'. The publisher, John Calder, had entered a vigorous defence, and then Sitwell and Victor had weighed in on the side of the reviewer. The better sort of pornography, wrote Victor, was to some degree life-enhancing:

> But the bogus-highbrow filth you attack — and its publication has proliferated horribly — is life-denying; spiritually as well as physically disgusting, and tasteless to an almost incredible degree, it offends against value of any kind . . . every bit as much as against public decency. And you are right in suggesting that the current orgy may imperil the freedom of literature by provoking the kind of 'authority' that prosecuted *Lady Chatterley's Lover*. This would be a disaster: better an infinity of open drains than a pinpoint of censorship.

'The real objection by persons of Dame Edith's and Mr Gollancz's generation', wrote Calder in a long letter, 'is an emotional one. They are not interested in examining the very real literary and intellectual values that exist in the work of those schools of writing that have developed since the war, because they are too far removed from the movements that they pioneered in their youth. They also do not like to admit how out of date their attitudes are and therefore abuse takes the place of rational analysis.'

Victor avoided the issue of the generation gap. His next letter answered other points in Calder's letter:

> Mr Calder, in the pride of his shining youth, must not accuse even a palsied old man of commenting on what he hasn't read. I choked down *The Naked Lunch* in America last spring, in spite of almost intolerable nausea.
>
> The rest of his letter is not worth answering. He refers to *Coriolanus, Macbeth* and *The Duchess of Malfi*. A man who cannot distinguish between poetry, tragedy, the treatment of sin and conscience, etcetera, on the one hand, and filth on the other, rules himself out of court.

Although the correspondence continued for another couple of weeks, it ended inconclusively. Victor was not prepared to face Calder's central argument about the attitudes of different generations. Greatly to Victor's credit, while he continued denouncing the 'flood of literary ordure' and stood four-square with the reactionaries on the subject of obscenity, he refused to join a putative cabal of like-minded publishers to initiate a private prosecution (in 1966) against the publication of *Last Exit to Brooklyn*. Still, he only just held back from sending a letter to *The Times* implying that contemporary literary depravity played a part in inspiring the Moors murders. His public pronouncements furnished ammunition to those who wanted censorship, while he declared himself to be against it. In his last television broadcast, in September 1966, he made the plea that publishers should refrain from publishing life-denying filth, and deprecated recent major changes in the publishing scene. It was an interview with an old man, who merely confused things by assuring the interviewer, 'I suppose I'm the most radical person almost in the world.'

The generation gap between Victor and most of his new authors was even more obvious in the 1960s. Nicolas Freeling wrote to him in January 1964, after a Savoy lunch, of the difficulties of meeting a man 'surrounded by a sort of halo of legendary exploit'. He was too young, knew too little, 'and you are too old and much too distinguished. One just feels small, and it is difficult to find things in common. A feeling again of being an undergraduate.' He had felt 'squashed' by Victor, and cross about it afterwards.

Victor was bewildered. 'It is clear that I upset you badly at lunch. Honestly, I can't think why. But I do know myself fairly well, and the idea that I should treat a younger man *de haut en bas* is about as impossible as anything I can think of. It just isn't me, as anyone who knows me would tell you. And, on top of that, I couldn't even do that with a younger man I didn't take to: and that was not at all the case with you . . .'

Freeling, who thought Victor's reply 'gallant', did not leave, but that same year John Le Carré did, citing Victor's 'paternalism' as a major cause. Victor had reason to feel badly treated. Gollancz had published Le Carré's first two modestly successful books and had exploited magnificently *The Spy Who Came in from the Cold*. Graham Greene's advance puff— 'The best spy story I have ever read' — set things rolling, and sales reached 90,000 within a year, bolstered by a superb advertising and publicity campaign. Le Carré had got on well with a newcomer to Gollancz, James MacGibbon, but Victor had grown jealous and tried to take him over. What appears to have annoyed Le Carré particularly was Victor's advice to him to stay in full-time employment, but it is possible too that Victor failed adequately to conceal his astonishment at the critical acclaim given *The Spy*. Wounded though he was, Victor was magnanimous: legal proceedings were obviated, Gollancz relinquished its contractual rights to Le Carré's next two books, and all ended fairly amicably.

All publishing houses lose authors, but at this period, Gollancz lost more than its share, and many other authors were alienated. Cronin departed because he said he was fed up with Victor's elevation of money wrangles to points of principle (he returned several years later);

Edgar Snow complained that his *Red Star Over China* had helped to pay for Victor's picture collection, and was enraged by his refusal to allow him to go into paperback; Elizabeth Spencer, a novelist to whom both Gollanczes had become deeply attached, turned very cold when Victor wrote an insulting letter to her agent, who was a close friend; and Lionel Davidson, author of the bestselling *The Rose of Tibet*, had been annoyed by Victor's heavy-handed attempts to engineer changes in the text, and finally quit because he and his agent found Victor's excessive caution over advances insupportable. Even the devoted Daphne du Maurier was upset by Victor's refusal to let her books go to Penguin, and Spencer Curtis Brown became almost hysterical over what he termed first Victor's 'dog-in-the-manger' attitude and then his 'avarice'. On this occasion Victor gave way, but only because du Maurier appealed to him with a face-saving formula for his climbdown.

These, and many other such episodes, made Victor a liability to his colleagues in his later years. The flashes of brilliance were becoming too infrequent to compensate financially for losses incurred by some pet books on religion and philosophy, and his refusal to come to terms with modern marketing methods. He started up projects and then lost interest. Hilary and Livia for instance, having made a success of Gollancz's first tentative incursion into children's books, were not given the funds necessary to expand the list properly. Victor exhorted his editors to be creative, and then, more often than not, rejected their ideas. His stock had fallen in America, and many agents preferred to offer Gollancz only unprofitable books, unplaceable elsewhere, which Victor might like.

Victor blamed his colleagues for the drying up of books from literary agencies, and Rubinstein bore the brunt. In truth, agents were daunted by the prospect of absurd rows. Victor had only two real friends among agents after 1961 — Herbert Van Thal, who was sweet-natured, yielding and rather unsuccessful, and Graham Watson of Curtis Brown. Watson was a tough agent, and he and Victor had many long disputes, but their relationship survived. Watson never forgot that Victor was a great publisher and he and his wife enjoyed the many bridge sessions: like most of the Gollanczes' bridge companions, they were covertly amused by Victor's blatant cheating — peeking at cards and trying to augment his and Ruth's bidding conventions by the adoption of special tones of voice. Dorothy Watson suspected Victor's fondness for her to be proportional to her prettiness. The relationship between the two couples was much dominated by Moses, who was ever-present during bridge, and even called into business transactions on occasion. Watson's sense of humour appealed to Victor and the nature of the relationship they enjoyed for many years is best illustrated by a famous exchange of telegrams in 1955:

> VICTOR GOLLANCZ ESQ 14 HENRIETTA STREET WC2 DEEPLY DISTRESSED AT OUTBREAK OF OUTSIDE REPAINTING STOP CONSIDER THIS LAMENTABLE CON-CESSION TO NEO-AMERICANISM STOP IF NOT SPEEDILY CHECKED SUSPECT HABIT MAY ULTIMATELY RESULT IN PROVISION OF A CHAIR IN YOUR WAITING ROOM GRAHAM

> DEEPLY APPRECIATE YOUR SYMPATHY STOP TROUBLE IS YOUNGER GENERATION INFECTED NEO-AMERICANISM AND ADVISABLE OCCASIONALLY MAKE GESTURE HOWEVER PAINFUL STOP ASSURE YOU NO CAUSE FOR ANXIETY ABOUT PROVISION OF CHAIR IN WAITING ROOM TO WHICH I WOULD NEVER CONSENT BUT MUST ADD MY SURPRISE AT REFERENCE TO SAID WAITING ROOM OF WHICH I DID NOT KNOW EXISTENCE STOP MUST LOOK INTO THAT SIGNED LORD BRIMPTON AND COVENT GARDEN

(That signature was a concession to Post Office staff. Victor's avowed intention was that, if awarded a peerage, he would take the title 'Lord Balls of Covent Garden', so as to have the pleasure of signing his letters to *The Times* 'Balls'.)

In January 1962, when Livia and Hilary were in America and Victor — still convalescing after his accident — was struggling in the office, he hit on a seemingly brilliant idea to recover the fortunes of Gollancz: he offered a senior editorial job to James MacGibbon of Curtis Brown, a close friend and a reliable supplier of good manuscripts. MacGibbon's credentials seemed perfect. Not only was he a successful agent, but he had been a founding partner in a publishing firm, MacGibbon and Kee, for years until they had to sell out. Victor had enormous affection for MacGibbon, whom he found charming both as a conversationalist and as a bridge companion. For his part MacGibbon was devoted to Victor, revelling in his Jewish stories and his general *lebenslust*. Graham Watson warned him against the move, but MacGibbon could see no flaw in the idea. Ruth had told MacGibbon's wife, Jean, who had ambivalent feelings about Victor, that James was the only man who could work with Victor. His first question on being offered the job was 'What about Hilary and Livia?' and Victor assured him that they were in favour.

Rubinstein learned in America of a report in the *Standard* gossip column that MacGibbon was to join Gollancz 'as senior director of the firm'. It was the first he had heard of the appointment, and there was but small comfort to be found in Victor's corrective telegram:

COMMUNICATE FOLLOWING VERY URGENTLY TO PUBLISHERS WEEKLY STOP IF
THEY PUT ANYTHING ABOUT JAMES JOINING US FOLLOWING NOTE IN TODAYS
EVENING STANDARD THEY SHOULD TAKE COGNIZANCE OF THE FOLLOWING
STATEMENT JUST ISSUED JOINTLY BY GOLLANCZ AND MACGIBBON BEGINS
STANDARD STATES MACGIBBON WILL BE JOINING FIRM AS SENIOR DIRECTOR
STOP THIS NOT SO STOP MACGIBBON WILL BE JOINING IN A REPEAT A BRACKET
INDEFINITE ARTICLE CLOSE BRACKET SENIOR DIRECTORIAL CAPACITY STOP
MACGIBBON MADE IT CONDITION OF JOINING THAT GOLLANCZ WOULD REMAIN
FULL TIME ACTIVE HEAD OF THE BUSINESS FOR AT LEAST TWENTY YEARS COMMA
AND GOLLANCZS CLOSEST ASSOCIATES COMMA HIS NEPHEW RUBINSTEIN AND
HIS DAUGHTER LIVIA COMMA WILL OF COURSE RETAIN THEIR PRESENT
POSITIONS STATEMENT ENDS

This subtle distinction was lost on the book trade. The 'Whitefriar'
column in *Smith's Trade News* several days later carried an item which
began:

That clever publisher Victor Gollancz has made a shrewd move in the
management talent game. Not even Mr G can go on being the benevolent
autocrat-at-the-top-of-the-firm for ever. One day he must think of
retiring and leaving a younger man in charge of his self-made business.
  Mr G is 68. Jimmy MacGibbon . . . is 49. He is a forceful publishing
personality with much experience, and it can be assumed that with other
firms looking avidly for talent of his calibre, Victor Gollancz's move is a
very wise one indeed. The GOLLANCZ list would be in good hands with
MacGibbon in charge on VG's retirement, at some future date . . .

'My dear Hilary,' wrote Victor to America two days later,

A chance remark dropped here the other day suggests that you might think
that the accession of James should not have been put through in your
absence. I do not believe that you think anything of the kind: but to clear
up any possible misunderstanding, I must tell you how the thing
happened.
  I asked James to come round about a fortnight ago, mainly to discuss
why we were not getting more English books from agents (you remember
that I had made up my mind, during your absence, to see as many agents as
possible and ask them about this). In the course of our conversation, I said
'There is no doubt at all that we want to strengthen our editorial
department: we want someone older than Hilary and Livia and younger
than me.' James replied: 'If I were ten years younger, I should apply for the
job myself.' I said nothing at the moment, but talked it over with Ruth:
and next day I wrote to James and said: 'If you were serious about that hint,
would you like to come and talk it over?'. He came across immediately,
said there was nothing in the world he would like more and asked for the
week-end (this was a Friday) to think it over. On the Saturday he rang up,

asked if he could come to Eaton Place, and said he would passionately like the job. We fixed it on the spot.

In the way the negotiations went, it would have been impossible to say 'OK, but I must consult Hilary and Livia first.' Nor did it occur to me for a moment that you would have the slightest objection. After all, it has always been clear — I am sure as clear to you as to me — that if circumstances compelled my virtual disappearance (and I am now quite determined not to retire until I am 80), for John, you and Livia to bear the whole burden would be impossible.

It is, of course, a great pity that such a garbled version appeared in the *Evening Standard* (and there has also been a garbled version in *Smith's Trade News*): but that was put right immediately.

The future position is perfectly clear. Apart from John with especial function as Sales Director and Secretary, and myself as Governing Director, there will be no titles: you and James and Livia will work together — and I am sure with extreme happiness — under my supreme direction. How, over a period of years, things will develop from that point, I have honestly no preconceptions: they will develop naturally as they will naturally develop.

MacGibbon actually took up his title-free new job in April, on a higher salary than any of his younger colleagues and all too obviously Victor's blue-eyed boy. He was uneasily aware by then that both he and Rubinstein had been placed in mutually invidious positions, and grateful that Rubinstein behaved well. Even Livia, who had never wavered in her belief that Rubinstein must in the end succeed her father, accepted that MacGibbon's arrival posed a serious threat. In fact, MacGibbon's star rapidly passed its apogee. He had recently returned to his wife after a year's separation and (as he had warned Victor well before joining him) was undergoing psychoanalysis. Victor was fascinated by this at first and very sympathetic. Then it became manifest that MacGibbon's performance was being adversely affected by his emotional problems, and Victor turned against him. Cut off, now he was no longer an agent, from the pick of the manuscripts, he rapidly became the focus of vocal abuse and pointed silences. Within six months of arriving in the firm, he had resigned. A note was composed for the *Bookseller*: 'We are asked by Mr Gollancz and Mr James MacGibbon to announce that, with the greatest regret on both sides and with unimpaired affection, Mr MacGibbon is relinquishing his appointment with Victor Gollancz, Ltd.'

It was then decided not to make the decision public until MacGibbon had worked out his notice in mid-December 1962. Spencer Curtis Brown, who was mischievous by nature and who loathed Victor as much as Victor loathed him, had offered a job to Rubinstein, but

MacGibbon's impending departure rendered the offer less attractive, and Rubinstein let it go. He went off to America in December with Livia, and in his absence Victor's attitude changed again. MacGibbon had recovered and was working well, and he spotted the potential of Alexander Solzhenitsyn's *One Day in the Life of Ivan Denisovich*, which he brought to the firm. Victor was ecstatic: the book combined spirituality, literary genius and huge commercial possibilities. Happy as a sand-boy, he embarked on dozens of hours of labour polishing up the translation with MacGibbon's assistance. MacGibbon was persuaded to withdraw his resignation but, a few days later, Victor recalled his nephew's strange resentment at the appointment of his new colleague in the first place. Having promised MacGibbon that he would become Livia's right-hand man in a future reorganization of the firm, he wrote to offer yet more second thoughts: his resignation should stand until his colleagues had given their approval. 'Nor do we think it right that cut-and-dried decisions about the more remote future should be made at this stage. This would be as unfair to L as to H. Things must be allowed to develop, after this particular crisis is over, as they will.'

A memorandum was despatched to Rubinstein explaining that 'the whole James situation has radically changed'. His recent achievements were detailed. It would be immensely to the firm's advantage if he could be kept on.

> I want to say something, too, about the business in general. For the first time for several years, I have a feeling of real, buoyant optimism. The November turnover has been very impressive. The acquisition of 'One Day' and — if I can see a way out of the libel situation — of Caroline Glyn's [she was a gifted fifteen-year-old Victor had taken under his wing, and believed to have a great future] novel (which is as much to your credit as 'One Day' is to James's) completes a fiction list for the first five months of next year unique in my forty years' experience. I have indeed the feeling (even something approaching the certainty) that, if we can only reduce our excessive overheads, we are going to weather the publishing storm without falling, not merely for Arthur Barker rubbish, but for Collins and Cassell rubbish too: and without yielding to crippling demands by literary agents. And hardly a day passes without evidence that, whatever these agents may think, we stand immensely high in public estimation.
>
> What I am hoping, therefore, is that you, Livia, John and James will surge ahead with me as a united team in a great new effort, with all past differences totally forgotten. I shall be happy if you can say, with genuine wholeheartedness and without reservation, 'I am with you'.
>
> I ought to add that, given the necessary health, I see myself as a very active controller of the firm, in the fullest possible sense, for a decade or more to come. I feel I ought to make this quite clear.

The covering note explained that the enclosed 'means just what it says — neither less nor (*emphatically*) more. The fact cannot be blinked that confidence has been shaken — doubtless on your side as much as on mine; and my feeling is that we must be sure that we can be sure of one another. I cannot face the thought of living on the edge of a volcano, and having perhaps another upheaval.' Rubinstein responded generously: 'I am of course delighted at what you say about James and nothing would please me more than that he should change his mind and stay on.'

In the spring of 1963, therefore, there were four possible successors working together, for John Bush could not be ruled out. Victor made no effort to clarify their relative status other than by raising Bush's and Rubinstein's salaries to the same level as MacGibbon's. (Livia's was lower as she had no dependents.) Other than announcing cheerily to the *Standard* in February that he intended to retire when he was 100, he ignored the problems of succession. While Victor was in America in May Rubinstein accepted a job with the *Observer* as special features editor and Victor came home from the trip (which had been badly marred by illness) to be confronted with a letter of resignation, which was taken very hard. After an initial explosion, the situation was eased by Rubinstein's disappearance on holiday. Before he returned to work out his notice, Victor wrote to him:

> My dear Hilary,
>
> I think it would really be better if you didn't come in any more (as I am sure you would prefer) . . . Everything has settled down very nicely: there is splendid co-operation all round, and a general sense of happy optimism: and I cannot help feeling that, as in the nature of the case you cannot share our hopes, aspirations and problems, your presence would be embarrassing — every bit as much to you as to us . . .
>
> Though I cannot masquerade and pretend that I have felt other than sore with you (a feeling I am gradually getting over), I nevertheless genuinely wish you the best of luck.

In practice, Victor's resentment was less well concealed; he could not forgive Rubinstein. On one occasion, he found Harold and Hilary sitting behind him at a concert and cut them dead. In time he repaired the breach with the father, but he scarcely saw the son again.

Perhaps the departure of Rubinstein crystallized Victor's long-suspended decision about the pecking order within Gollancz. Over the years he had made many half-promises to others, but neither he nor Ruth really contemplated handing over the reins to anyone other than Livia: by 1965 she had ample production and editorial experience.

He was not (though Ruth may have been) thinking about the succession. Indeed, during his last years, it became common for observers of the rows and the idiosyncratic list to speak of his death wish for the firm. But in late 1965, committed to a long writing programme, he wanted more free time. He announced to the press, with great ceremony, that Livia was now Governing Director and joint Managing Director with John Bush who was also appointed Chairman. MacGibbon, whose time as Victor's pet had proved to be brief, remained, with Horsman's successor, Mary Brash, a director. Ruth was to stay as Deputy Chairman and Victor would become President and Literary Adviser. This slap in the face was too much for MacGibbon, and Victor hastily explained to the press that he was Assistant Managing Director and would act 'as the third member of a triumvirate responsible for the daily conduct of the business' under Victor's active presidency.

The underlying principle was that Victor would henceforward give most of his time to 'writing and public affairs'. He would attend the office only occasionally, and Livia would take over his famous room. In the event, and spurred on by reports that he was retiring, he arrived at the usual time on the day of the announcement, occupied his room, and carried on as normal. The reshuffle had achieved only one thing, but it was of consummate importance. It was clear that when Victor became incapable, Livia would step straight into his shoes.

Victor's brief flirtation with semi-retirement had probably been stimulated by his knighthood in June 1965. For a man who had hoped in earlier days for a peerage and the Nobel Prize, it might have seemed a poor substitute, but now that Victor was out of the limelight, the honour gave him enormous and unalloyed pleasure. Some of his friends were surprised that a professed Christian communist should accept — let alone revel in — a knighthood, but they were innocent of the fact of Victor's twenty-year hunger for a British decoration. Attlee had ignored his contribution to the Labour Party; Conservative Prime Ministers had ignored his achievements as a publisher. Allen Lane had been knighted in 1952, but all the state recognition Victor had ever had was one invitation to a Buckingham Palace garden party.

At last on a par with his two exalted uncles, Victor reacted to his new status like a child who has waited too long for Christmas. New stationery bearing his title was instantly ordered and many happy hours were spent reading and replying to the hundreds of congratulatory messages that arrived from friends and admirers in Britain, Europe and America. Any irritations with the old Victor were suspended as his contemporaries took pleasure in recalling his remarkable career. Of the Gollancz relations, Phyllis Simon, Hermann's granddaughter, was the most perceptive, writing of how pleased Alex would have been. 'My dear Phyllis . . . I thought the same about my Father . . . '. The Attorney-General of India, C. K. Daphtary, wrote to recall their schooldays. Spencer Hurst reminded Victor felicitously of their Oxford discussions: 'I feel that you have carried out most faithfully the ideals you had then. I'm sure Ralph Rooper would have agreed. The only thing I regret is that the Rasher didn't actually succeed in getting you into the Christian Church!' Harold Abrahams, the Olympic Gold Medallist, remembered that 'Nearly 50 years ago you taught me Latin Verses! and other things.' One of the other Reptonians, Brian Bradnack, referred to himself as 'Your one-time much stimulated pupil, & even your follower.'

There were those who remembered his early days in publishing, including the period when Victor was trying to decide to make the break from Benn. Staff and authors, past and present, sent innumerable fond messages. Allen Lane wrote the most generous of all the publishers' congratulations:

> My dear Victor,
>   I was delighted to see your name in the Honours List on Saturday. I'm only surprised that it has not been there before.
>   There is no question that you were the greatest force in the social & political education of our generation & that that is acknowledged as it is now is a cause for general satisfaction.

'What a number of people all over the world', wrote Alec Waugh, 'have been made happy on Saturday morning by the knowledge that public recognition had been accorded to all that you have done for literature — and for the maintenance of honourable standards.'

There were supporters from Left Book Club days, who recalled, in the words of one, how 'your Left Book Club affected my life as it did so many thousands of others'. Elwyn Jones and Pearl Binder were 'delighted that you have joined the Ks and added lustre to the Order!' Intimate associates from his fellow-travelling days were less well represented. With some the breach had never really occurred — Betty Reid, for instance. With some, changing circumstances had permitted a reconciliation: after the Soviet invasion of Hungary, Sheila Lynd had left the CP and she and Victor occasionally had amicable lunches. Nonetheless, the politics of people like Lynd and Reid did not permit them to approve of knighthoods.

Victor's contribution to the Jewish cause during the war had been occluded by his Eichmann pamphlet. However, the Israeli Ambassador did send formal congratulations, as, of course, did his German equivalent, who expressed his gratitude 'for all you have done to strengthen the bond of friendship between our two countries'. As each tide of his enthusiasm and missions had rolled out, grateful admirers had been left on the shore; it was a heartwarming reassurance to Victor that hundreds of them sought to augment his happiness with their tributes.

There were two letters that gave him a special thrill. One was from Isaiah Berlin:

12 June 1965

Dear Victor,

And about time too! and not sufficiently generous — not only in terms of your personal & human claims — to which public honours are in any case inappropriate — but even to your public position and achievements & fame and what I can only describe as historic and symbolic significance in this country and the world. To pay sincere and uninhibited tributes to men one admires is, to me, and I expect to lots of people, a great pleasure: & I should like to go on and on: but this wd bore you & I stop. Let me just say that I hope that if it gives you the faintest pleasure, the greater recognition will be given to your unique courage, goodness and independence: that I shall duly write you again when & if — but I hope when — this occurs: & that then, as now, I shall beg you *not* to acknowledge this: & that I send my fondest love to Ruth. You *have* been lucky! (to be married to her, I mean; & she too) . . .

'My dear Isaiah,' wrote Victor. 'Your letter moved me very much. There is more *hin* [*chayn* — charm, understanding] in it than any letter I've ever received. Thank you.'

A few days later came a spirited encomium from the writer, John Gloag:

My dear Gollancz,

I read the Honours List with enormous pleasure: the pleasure, I may say, being derived entirely from the announcement of your knighthood . . . This recognition is long overdue. I don't suppose you have any conception of the impact you have made on the social life and history of this country: the Left Book Club, a magnificent conception, was largely instrumental in swinging Labour into power after the Second War, though the blind, ungrateful bastards ignored you then. But apart from all that political activity, what you have done for publishing, and for adventure and enterprise in the publishing field generally, and what you have also done to encourage young and new talent in literature, is immeasurable. A good man, it is said, lives twenty years or so after his death in the personal memories of his friends and relatives: a great man lives on for at least a hundred years. You, my dear Gollancz, are booked for the century all right.

I count it as one of the privileges life has given me, to have known you, and once, over forty years ago, to have been a colleague of yours (albeit in a very junior capacity). I have learnt a great deal from you, and although I am a Tory-Anarchist so far as I have any politics . . . I have an unreserved admiration for you, your career, and the charm and rich humour that are built-in characteristics of a very wise man . . .

My dear John (if you will allow me),

That was an absolutely lovely letter! How could anyone resist a feeling of delight at hearing himself praised in such a variety of ways? Thank you and thank you!

Incidentally, I'm really an Anarchist too — though not a Tory one.

The one sour note was sounded by E. P. Thompson, and Victor brought it on himself. Having decided in the week following the announcement of his knighthood to begin work on another book about socialism, religion and sex, he wrote to Thompson for advice on what recent '"retreat from socialism"' books he should read. Thompson was helpful, but his letter ended: 'I cannot congratulate you on your recent honour since I am an old-fashioned socialist fundamentalist who disapproves of handle-bar honours. However, if I wasn't a fundamentalist I would!' Thompson, of course, had no idea of how Victor could be hurt by the suggestion that anyone could be more deeply socialist than himself. He was driven into momentary self-delusion of a patently ridiculous kind: 'I entirely agree with you,' he told Thompson. 'I accepted it for reasons connected with the present state of publishing.'

One of the most pleasing telegrams was the simplest: 'SINCERE CONGRATULATIONS TO YOU BOTH CHRISTOPHER AND ANN'. The senders were Christopher Craig and his fiancée.

CHAPTER TWENTY-SIX

ODES TO JOY

IN DECEMBER 1952, in *Tim II*, after expatiating on the wickedness of Lord Goddard and lamenting the social environment that had stopped Craig from realizing his potential as a human being, Victor had ended with a promise: 'There is one human being, at least, who loves the boy: there is one human being, at least, who would do anything in the world to help Christopher Craig become Christopher Craig.' In the ten years Craig spent in prison, Victor had no contact with him, but when he was discharged in 1963, the old promise was kept. He got in touch with Craig through Longford, who had visited him a few times in prison and was helping him through The New Bridge. After negotiation, Victor decided to collaborate with Craig on writing his life-story. Craig was to be paid £1,000 in twelve monthly instalments against his half-share of royalties, the other half to go to a trust fund for incapacitated policemen, the families of policemen killed 'in pursuit of their duties . . . or in the interest of the prevention of crime and/or in the interest of the rationalisation of punishment.' The press were intrigued and the *Observer* and *Sunday Express* showed a keen interest in serialization rights. By March 1964 Victor was ready to begin work, and he and Craig embarked on a series of evening conversations with a tape recorder running.

Victor clearly began the project labouring under a number of misconceptions about Craig that he had developed during the trial. In 1953 he had written thus to Monk Gibbon in defence of the boy: 'If a child is beaten, tormented, and hated from the cradle until he is ten or so, do you really mean to tell me that you regard it as a "semi-scientific heresy" to say that there is a grave "moral responsibility" on those who treated him like that, if he turns out in the way in which he undoubtedly will turn out?' (His belief that Craig was mentally 'sub-normal' had already proved inaccurate; otherwise he could not have embarked on his biography.) Victor's intentions were clear: Craig was to be shown as a victim of society, and so help condemn, on a telling human scale, the iniquities of the prison system and contemporary notions of punishment.

The 474 pages of transcript are fascinating reading. Both made heroic efforts to overcome the enormous gulf between their generations, experience, cultural attitudes and philosophies of life. Victor tried hard to curb his own propensity to dominate conversations and only half-listen to what was said to him. Nor had he ever really tried (other than retrospectively with his father) so seriously to understand the mind of another.

It is greatly to Victor's credit that he struggled so hard to delve into the mind of Christopher Craig, whose development into a murderer proved uncommonly difficult to understand. Most of Victor's assumptions collapsed in the face of Craig's forthright, intelligent and rational self-analysis. His middle-class parents had been affectionate, and had never beaten him. His father had had a small collection of guns, but had denied his sons access to them, other than when teaching them to handle them responsibly. There were no clues in Craig's sexual inclinations: his sexual fantasies displayed no sado-masochistic proclivities: he was aroused by nothing more sinister than breasts. The only identifiable reasons for his youthful violence were frustration at his illiteracy (probably dyslexic, but it bewildered his interlocutor) and hero-worship of his criminal older brother, whose own criminality was equally mystifying.

Prison and punishment also proved a troublesome area. Craig had experienced a great deal of kindness; his illiteracy had been cured; he had been reformed; the lavatories had not offended him; he thought it important that people be made to see they had done wrong — if necessary by forced confrontation with the wickedness they had perpetrated; during his homicidal period he would not in the least have minded being hanged and he would have preferred the cat o'nine tails to the boredom of church.

Victor clutched thankfully at the straws provided by Craig's conversion to liberal attitudes. He was now against punishment and believed that prison should be corrective in essence and kind in its methods. Indeed, he produced some exhilarating ideas for setting up proper communities in which offenders could live a relatively normal life. Alas, though Craig objected to many aspects of the prison system, and had sometimes met with brutality there, he had emerged after ten years articulate, humane and positive. That he attributed the beginning of his rehabilitation to the kindness of Gilbert Hare, a liberal Governor of Wormwood Scrubs, was some consolation, but Hare was a reformer, not a revolutionary like Victor.

It is clear from the conversations that Craig liked his benefactor. He strove to understand what Victor was getting at when he talked over his head — as, for instance, when he tried to explain the distinction between the essence and the *accidentia*. Victor's unfamiliarity with those ignorant of things he took for granted resulted in a great deal of hit and miss. 'Do you know Jung?' he asked in passing, before galloping on to explain what a Jungian had said to him the night before. Did Craig know what the word vocabulary meant, he enquired during one session, during which the younger man had cheerfully tossed out words like 'criticisms' and 'subjective'. And having ascertained at an early stage that Craig was still a very occasional and diffident reader, he later pressed upon him a copy of *Tim II*.

Craig had his problems with Victor's ignorance. It emerged during one session that Victor had never heard of parents killing their own children. He then assumed it must happen for sexual reasons, and had to have it explained that the most usual cause was blind anger. Craig, who was both imaginative and perceptive, had a great deal of sympathy for people who cracked under the strain of a baby incessantly crying, but found it hard to transmit the idea to Victor, who had never in his life had to tolerate continuously distressed and demanding infants or fractious toddlers.

Craig's sensitivity to others came out again and again. He had shown no qualms in describing the nature of his desire to kill policemen and his absence of remorse, and Victor was unshocked by any of it. But when it came to music and politics he grew hesitant:

'Tell me about your feelings about music. What music do you like?'
'Well . . .'
'Don't mind what you say to me.'
'I like rock and roll.'
'You like rock and roll?'
'Yes.'

He went on gamely to explain, as best he could in answer to Victor's probings, how rock-and-roll differed from jazz, why the Beatles were so popular and why he disliked classical music. That subject was abandoned in favour of politics, and a discussion of the relative merits of Alec Douglas-Home and Wilson brought Craig to reveal, apologetically, that he was a Conservative. 'Well,' said Victor robustly, 'we'll get you out of that quite soon.' Quite forgetting the purpose of the meetings, he went on to give Craig a long disquisition on the ideal society.

After having five reels of tape transcribed, Victor first postponed and then abandoned a project that was clearly hopeless. Although Craig had been anxious to have the book written, he evinced no resentment. Recognizing from the start the debt he owed Victor for his help and sympathy, at times he found the generosity overwhelming. Whenever he needed money, he was told, he was simply to write the amount required on a piece of paper and send it to Victor. Instead, he apologetically appended a note of appreciation.

Victor was thrilled that Craig settled back into society well and quickly found himself a wife. He did not worry about the abandoned biography, having found an excellent justification for dropping it. To an author who in 1966 asked if he would be interested in a book on Bentley, he replied that 'Craig is now out of prison: he is living a very decent life: and I think to stir the case up might make his complete rehabilitation more difficult. And you will agree, I am sure, that the living are more important than the dead.'

Scrapping books at the planning stage had become a commonplace with Victor. Some died within a month of conception, some lingered on. *The Sanity of Christ* was revived from time to time. Its thesis was occasionally explored in speeches or at the London Society for the Study of Religion, a group into which he had been invited by Edward Carpenter, then Archdeacon of Westminster. (Victor was a valued member of the LSSR, where he was considered a mystic rather than a metaphysician.) To some extent, his work on *God of a Hundred Names* had assuaged his appetite for religious composition, and dulled his evangelical edge. In his last years he had resolved once and for all his problems about Christ, who, it transpired, was not sinless, but all the more lovable for that. That position was fraught with difficulties that he preferred to gloss over. Moreover, Victor had made a gentleman's agreement with Hodder & Stoughton that he should publish *The Sanity of Christ* with them, and, had he ever written it, it would have broken his heart to let it out of his own hands. (Not surprisingly, he had assured David Higham, his agent on this one occasion, that he was 'the worst businessman in the world' and there would be no problems over terms. Equally typically, he had then indicated that when contract time arrived, he would require an unusually high royalty and a guaranteed print run of 15,000 copies.)

God of a Hundred Names had sold well for a book of prayers. It had arrived in its original form as an unsolicited manuscript from the unknown Barbara Greene. Having appointed himself a collaborator, Victor had set to vigorously, and had a much-enlarged version out in time for Christmas 1962. ('Give God for Xmas', ran one slogan.) But all the puffs and advertisements could not make more than a modest bestseller of a book that was out of tune with fashion. Victor's fury at unappreciative reviews ran true to form, and fuelled his determination to give the public what it needed rather than what it wanted. Pleas from British and American publishers for his publishing reminiscences fell on deaf ears (Little Brown offered an advance of $10,000) as Victor mounted a series of abortive assaults on the spirit of the 1960s. It was not until the end of 1963 that he hit on a subject that fitted both his inclinations and his gifts. At Bournemouth with Ruth for the hated Christmas period he began the manuscript for *Journey Towards Music*. Many commitments suffered throughout January and February as he worked frantically to meet another self-imposed deadline.

The genesis of the book is revealed in its prologue: an interview between Victor and Peter Heyworth of the *Observer*, which itself had stemmed from Victor's public statement that contemporary opera performances were marred by elaborate productions (Zeffirelli's *Falstaff* was the prime offender). Victor reminiscing about his musical life set rolling a wave of nostalgia which had to express itself on paper; quite suddenly, the most important thing in life was to tell the public what music had meant to him. His urgency made him furious with the *Observer* when the publication of the interview was somewhat delayed. There was a certain lack of perspective in a letter he wrote to the responsible features editor in January 1964, thanking him for a letter of apology for the postponement: 'The bit in the Supplement about guerrilla fighting among the Arabs, or something like that, fitted *exactly* the space that would have been occupied by the interview. It surely can't be suggested either that (a) this piece was of such crucial importance that it wouldn't brook a week's delay, or that (b) it would interest a vaster public than that stuff of Peter's and mine — whatever view may be taken about the relative importance of guerrilla fighting and the arts . . . '

In one essential the interview was redolent of his father's views 60 years before: 'there were', Victor explained sadly, 'many great singers when I was a boy: there is only one today [Callas].' Yet Victor had a passion for and knowledge of music that his father could never have comprehended. During the fifties and early sixties, he had gone almost full circle to his teens in the importance he attached to attending performances. Abroad, he took in as many concerts as possible; he attracted great attention when he stood at the Proms in 1963; he wrote to the press about particular performances; he made expeditions to Edinburgh for the joy of attending two or three concerts a day. The congratulatory post-bag after his knighthood was swelled by people such as Ernest Bean (who ran the Festival Hall), Yehudi Menuhin (whom Victor worshipped), Desmond Shawe-Taylor (the music critic) and Malcolm Sargent, and to all of them Victor wrote that it gave him special happiness to hear from his musical friends. Otto Klemperer was his god: after one of his seasons Victor despatched to him an enormous laurel wreath.

The passionate enthusiast of the 1960s was in one important respect very different from the child who had queued for hours in the hope of a gallery seat. Victor's need for comfort — especially after his accident — made excellent seats a prerequisite and worries about the availability of the right kind of tickets placed a great strain on him. Special pleading and influential friends ensured that he normally got what he wanted, and whenever he failed, aggrieved letters followed. Typical was one to the Manager of Sadler's Wells in 1962, when his request for tickets in row A of the Dress Circle had yielded two in row B.

> I have constantly noticed that, in the case of Sadler's Wells, I am given second-class treatment, and beg to enquire what the reason may be. I am, I suppose, far and away the oldest regular concert and opera-goer in the United Kingdom, my record as such going back to 1914; and Covent Garden and the Festival Hall invariably accord me not merely ordinary fair treatment, but (as is perhaps justified by this circumstance) specially favourable treatment. I ask myself, have I given some offence to Sadler's Wells?

It added greatly to Victor's joy that most of the people he met through music were in turn delighted by him. He was a lovable and knowledgeable eccentric, who revered their achievements and show-ered blessings on them in words, champagne and roses. When he clapped wildly, they were pleased. When he ominously withheld his applause they worried. The few who were less than taken with him personally still appreciated his presence in an audience. Lord Drogheda, Chairman of Covent Garden, found Victor too opinion-ated for his taste, but he recalled happily in his memoirs that after a performance of Schoenberg's *Moses and Aaron* 'the realism of the Golden Calf scene caused the venerable Victor Gollancz to demon-strate in the stalls gangway where he stood up at the end of the first night's performance, gesticulating wildly and shouting out, "Filthy brutes!" as though sacrilege had been committed.' Victor's anger against the production stemmed from his horror of the sight of blood, with which on this occasion the stage was liberally bespattered.

Similarly, he was greatly upset by a contemporary production of *Tristan and Isolde* in which Tristan's wound was made very obvious.

It was that vast store-house of passion that Victor tried to set forth in *Journey Towards Music*, and in many parts of the book he succeeded. The mixture of sensual enjoyment, intellectual understanding, enormous experience of performances to compare and contrast, and idiosyncratic reactions to individual composers and performers lent much of the book great appeal. The old man appraising the Klemperer of the 1960s still had the breathless wonder of the small boy who had rushed to performances straight from school. Victor was at his best in his expression of enthusiasm, and familiarity never made him blasé.

There were deficiencies in the book because there was no editorial control — no one to correct Victor's growing habit of copying long passages out of his earlier books because they seemed too good to be left out of his latest one, no one to edit the excursuses, no one to ensure adherence to his stated brief. Airily, he announced towards the end of the book that

> my secretary tells me that I have already written eighty thousand words, and my publisher warns me that I must not exceed ninety thousand. I disbelieve the first, and feel inclined to snap my fingers at the second. But it is clear that I cannot follow my original intention, which was that the second part of this memoir, designed to be about music other than operatic, should be as long as the first. . . . So I shall do this: I shall write the merest sketch of Part II as originally planned, and shall keep the real Part II for another volume, if I can ever get down to it . . .

'My publisher', who was of course himself (he had taken against bulky books), wrote a travellers' description of the book that must have had some of his colleagues squirming with embarrassment.

> This, we predict, will be the Christmas book of the year, and, after that, will be a perennial bestseller on a large scale just as the *Musical Companion* is . . . with Mr Gollancz's now enormous public, a bestseller sale is assured . . . The style, delightful throughout, is sometimes light and gay, and sometimes deeply serious . . . It is probably not too much to say that this is the most attractive book of the kind ever written in this country, as well as a unique one: and there can be little doubt that it will become a classic in its field.

It came out in September, and as so often of late, the advance puffs were much better than the reviewers' quotes. Victor bore the cross of the critics' stupidity, overjoyed as he was by the welcome the musical establishment had accorded the work. He and his new friends remained in harmony for the two years he had left. He was thrilled to be taken seriously as a music critic and to have his opinions canvassed on new artists and individual performances. No one could doubt his instinct for excellence. He travelled to Cardiff to hear the young Gwyneth Jones in *Fidelio* and discovered in her such promise that after the performance, and even before they were introduced, he rushed up to her to plant kisses on both cheeks. Janet Baker was a further discovery, this time rewarded with flowers and asked to keep him posted on dates and locations of all her performances. And in 1965 the *Observer* paid him another accolade by inviting him to be their critic at the Bayreuth Festival in July.

For Victor, this was an important opportunity to resolve the ambivalence about Wagner that had dogged him for decades. Although he could be enraptured by *Die Meistersinger, The Ring* — as he explained at length in *Journey Towards Music* — had long ago lost the attraction it held in his youth. In his *Observer* article he went to the heart of the problem. After an impressive analysis of the performances, he asked:

> Do I still find a fascist element in Wagner's mentality? Yes I do . . . And do I still find 'The Ring' as a whole, musically and otherwise, distressingly hypertrophic? Yes I do. I enjoyed a lot of it, of course, as much as anyone: but I came away from 'Götterdämmerung', as the audience were trampling their applause, with a sense of utter satiety, and without a trace of the spiritual peace and quiet exaltation that even an average performance of 'Figaro' or 'Cosi', 'Fidelio' or 'Pelleas', brings with it . . .

He was cross with Bernard Levin when he picked up these remarks in a *New Statesman* article, 'Wagner and I'. 'It is not entirely clear to me', said Levin, 'how music *can* be fascist, or communist or social-democratic or Agrarian Party for that matter, but when so redoubtable an authority as Sir Victor Gollancz (who, like me, has just paid his first visit to Bayreuth) suggests — in a very much more complex and sophisticated sense, of course — that there is something fascist about Wagner's music, we must consider the question seriously . . . ' On this occasion, Victor addressed his complaint to the writer rather than the editor: 'No, I have never said that there was something fascist about Wagner's music: I should regard that as a ridiculous statement. What I have said is that Wagner was in part of fascist mentality . . . '

Such perplexing distinctions were made clearer in the book, *The Ring at Bayreuth*, into which Victor expanded his article within a couple of weeks of his return. There followed a short lull in his writing projects until the next summer, when he undertook what was to form the main part of his posthumous *Reminiscences of Affection*. He began it after a long period away from the office. A tiring trip to America (he bought 22 books and wrote most of the travellers' publicity material himself) had been followed by a two-month visit to Italy, during which he had virtually no contact with Gollancz. He was no sooner back, his batteries recharged, than he was immersed in his new book, initially titled *Bits and Pieces*.

This time the inspiration was provided by the odds and ends on the shelves in the Gollanczes' beloved Bottom House. This weekend retreat, near Henley, which they had bought in 1960, was a charming small house which Victor usually described as a 'tiny cottage' (it was in fact converted from a pair of farm cottages), with a manageable garden which Ruth had made into a thing of beauty. As Victor scribbled away at weekends from July onwards, the book began to drift from the objects to the people associated with them. As he found *lacunae* in his memory, he despatched letters to friends, acquaintances and experts asking for clarification — usually by return of post. Lady Walton was asked what record Sir William had played him before *The Magic Flute*. Father Borelli of the Naples House of Urchins (whose cause Victor had espoused in England), was asked for information on the locality. The Italian Embassy was consulted about Sicilian folk art. Sir John Rothenstein advised on the history of scenic gouaches. Pearl Binder received a letter complaining about Harold Wilson's treatment of the railwaymen and asking 'what was the tune that was very much in vogue at the time when Elwyn was courting you and we were with you somewhere in the South of France (where?) and you used to dance to it. The rhythm was ta-ta-ta-*ta*-ta, ta-ta-ta-*ta*-ta, and every now and again there was a sort of whoop. What the hell was the name of it, and what were the words?' And the manager of the Hotel Restaurant Beaumanière was asked for the recipe of the *gigot d'agneau en croûte* and advice on what in 1963 was the best year for Châteauneuf-du-Pape.

By October Victor had written tens of thousands of words on things, people, food, drink, travel and other assorted joys. The old friends described had mostly passed beyond his ken, either through death or as a result of disputes. The 1930s figured most prominently. There was very little mention of the friends who now mattered to him most: the Collinses, the Walstons, the Watsons, Sheila Hodges, Rupert Hart-Davis, Nancy Raphael (a frequent bridge companion), Mariella Fischer Williams (a young doctor and amateur violinist). His mind was firmly focussed on happy days with Rose Macaulay, Pritt, the Lows and other pre-war literary and political friends, usually against the background of the Brimpton garden. Of course, some of the inevitable discursive passages dealt with aspects of the present. What was destined to be his last chapter ended thus:

> But I must not end, after all, on so solemn a note. Here at Bottom House, where I am happy to be writing this last chapter, we have put up with a single lavatory ever since we came here eight years ago; but we recently decided to indulge in a second . . . and the local builder . . . will have finished it by next weekend. I look forward to using it the moment we arrive, and meanwhile am having inscribed, to hang on the door, the Brocha to be said every morning on going to stool. I shall put it down here in English:
>
> Blessed art thou, O Lord our God, King of the universe, who hast formed man in wisdom, and created in him many orifices and vessels. It is revealed and known before the throne of thy glory that if one of these be opened, or one of these be closed, it would be impossible to exist and to stand before thee. Blessed art thou, O Lord, who healest all flesh and doest wondrously.
>
> Blessed art thou, O Lord, creator of man.

It was fitting that the last words Victor wrote deliberately for publication should concern the religious implications of one of the simplest acts of human existence — a telling testimony to his heritage and his love of life.

Desperate to add the finishing touches to his manuscript and feverishly awaiting replies from the laggards among those consulted, Victor was at a high pitch of nervous tension in the autumn. He was highly irritable by 6 October. His last dictated letter was conceived in a fit of ill-temper. He had been sent a cheque for over £30 for an interview with Rediffusion. Most days he would have sent it back and asked them to pay it to charity, but this time he sent it back complaining of being paid a 'paltry sum' for 'what took close on an hour of my time'. He demanded instead a fee of 100 guineas. On the morning of the following day, he had difficulty in finding a taxi to take him to the office. Arriving late, his anger was compounded by finding that Livia, who had assumed he must not be coming in, had opened and was going through the day's orders. Soon after, he fell off his chair and was unable to move except crabwise, round and round in a circle. Semi-conscious, he tried from the floor to dictate letters to his secretary, Joanna Goldsworthy, who stood beside him pretending to take down the garbled speech in shorthand. Livia and John Bush were summoned and they managed to heave Victor back into his chair where he even made hopeless efforts to relight his cigar. They tried repeatedly to persuade him to let somebody call an ambulance, but he kept repeating 'No!', the only word he could articulate clearly. Ruth reached the office just as Victor, by now almost unconscious, was being removed to hospital.

The seriousness of his stroke was kept quiet for some time. It was almost automatic for people to assume that any ailment of Victor's was of slight to middling severity. There were many light-hearted letters before it became common knowledge that he was paralysed down his right side, whereupon those who knew him well wrote to Livia of their concern at the suffering this must be causing him. Many who had been rather amused by the fuss he had kicked up over previous physical set-backs realized that here was something different. Victor had confided to people that the pain from his broken thigh had made him understand what Christ had suffered, and they had accepted this as a normal exaggeration. Now he was really suffering — conscious of his illness, his physical deficiencies, his mental deterioration and the likely imminence of death. Even those who had endured much at Victor's hands found the thought of him in that condition terribly poignant.

It was Livia who persuaded Victor that he should learn to write again so that he would be able to correspond with her during her impending visit to America. In hospital and back at home, he laboured doggedly to develop the skill in a left hand driven by an inefficient brain. From the early hopeless attempts to produce even an approximate version of his own name, he graduated to writing whole sentences, and then to keeping a diary. Hugely frustrated, he was sustained by Ruth's presence, by the daily visits from Livia and frequent ones from John Bush, both bearing determinedly cheerful news of office matters, by the attention of friends and relations and by music. The wireless and the despised gramophone became a lifeline.

The stroke dramatically changed his attitude to people hitherto the objects of contempt or indifference. His daughter Julia and her husband found him grateful for their company and pleasant to talk to. He welcomed Vita, praised a painting she brought to show him, and noted the event with pleasure in his diary. Livia, now running the firm with Bush, asked frequently for his advice and even arranged for the Thursday conferences to be held at Eaton Place in his presence. 'Poo [Livia] is an angel!', Victor wrote in his diary. And, by Poldi's account (probably exaggerated), when Diana last saw her father, she reported: 'This is the first time in thirty-five years that my father has held my hand and has spoken tenderly to me.' But then he had heard (from Poldi, and against Ruth's wishes) that she was dying of cancer. His reaction to the news was so distressing, said

Poldi, that 'the barren years of lovelessness' were 'redeemed in this one moment of grace. My heart went out to him.'

The profundity of Victor's mind emerged very clearly in the diary. Reflecting miserably on his inability to understand prose properly he wrote one day that 'I suppose I ought to be less ambitious: read only pappy things. Well, that is not my way. I'd sooner understand 25% of stuff that means something than 100% of stuff that means nothing. So I'll continue on my path: trusting that enlightenment will come to me. If it does not — well, so be it. At any rate I shall have tried.'

Music was the eternal solace. 'I find that music means more to me than it did. A thing I would pass over without a thought now affords me the utmost delight. The Unfinished Symphony, for instance, I used to listen to as something at best pleasant and rather stale: now it comes to me as a heaven-sent thing. And there's very little indeed that nowadays I don't like. It is as if everything nowadays had taken on a new and delightful meaning.'

Looking back on his musical past he concluded that 'By and large, then, I was first and last a musician. What, then, is a musician? I take it that a musician is a man who feels his whole being transformed when music is played. The great musician feels this transformation: whether he really understands what is happening to him is a different matter. He may not understand what is happening: for all that, it *is* happening.'

There is much in the diary about his illness from day to day, coupled with resolutions to stop writing about such mundane matters and concentrate on more important things. Particularly heartrending are his efforts to come to terms with Ruth's daily nap after lunch, which condemned him to an hour alone. He fought despair. 'Life absolutely lacks savour. It is about a quarter what the real thing ought to be. I don't think that this sort of life can ever be really worth living: it recalls too vividly just what one is missing. One lives in a sort of twilight world. And it's really awful to have to endure what one knows one is going to endure after lunch. In spite of that, the thought of suicide never enters one's head for a moment. I suppose the feeling for life is too indestructible.'

In this condition, with optimism and despondency alternating, Victor lived until February 1967. Livia had gone off to America some weeks before, having buoyed him up greatly with her inspired suggestion that he write to her daily to give her advice. She had also made him ecstatic some time before she left by telling him that some of his diary was almost publishable. Vita had stepped in and visited every day to help Ruth support him in his painful efforts to walk. His colleagues and friends had been assiduous, and none more so than a newcomer to his circle, the political commentator Conrad Voss Bark, who made him feel a part of things by keeping him up-to-date with political gossip. Victor had even managed, courtesy of a wheelchair, to cope with a dinner party given by Nancy Raphael. He had contrived to write in his own hand a couple of notes to friends: his last was one of sympathy to Rupert Hart-Davis on the death of his wife. On 3 February, he was upset by a note from his daughter Diana, whose handwriting showed how serious was the cancer in her brain. He tried to coninue normally and Ruth left him starting to write to one of his favourite authors — John Bingham — to congratulate him on an award for his latest detective story. When she returned, a few minutes later, he was in a coma from which he never recovered. Five days later, he died.

EPILOGUE

VICTOR DIED ON 8 February 1967 and was cremated two days later at Golders Green. His oldest friend, Harold Rubinstein, ended his few words of appreciation by calling on those present to remember Victor primarily as a Judeo-Christian: 'Thou shalt love the Lord thy God with all thy heart, and with all thy soul and with all thy might. And thou shalt love thy neighbour as thyself.'

The obituarists who knew Victor least had the easiest job. Untroubled by any knowledge of his faults, they gave their readers an account of the life of an unusually energetic saint. The better-informed wrestled with some of the contradictions between Victor's principles and his practice and found themselves devoid of satisfactory explanations. There was general agreement that he had been a phenomenon who, as *The Times* put it, 'would have made his mark in any age'. In support of that reading, there were the hundreds of messages of condolence across a spectrum from Konrad Adenauer to ex-convicts, which showed that many people — even such old enemies as Raji Palme Dutt — felt personally impoverished by his death. Many of those whose involvement with Victor had been only tangential lamented the passing of his vitality: life without Victor was going to be duller for everyone.

A memorial gathering was held at the Central Hall, Westminster, on 3 March. There the actress Jill Balcon read extracts from *A Year of Grace*, Diana Collins, Gerald Gardiner and Frank Longford paid tributes and the proceedings ended with an excerpt from the last movement of Beethoven's Ninth Symphony. Some of his friends, including Isaiah Berlin, Robert and Dorothy Mayer, Daphne du Maurier, Yehudi Menuhin and Sybil Thorndike wrote about him a few months later to *The Times*, remarking on the great gap he had left in 'our national structure. His wide-ranging contributions to the colourful mosaic of the British way of life were unique.' They proposed the setting up of an annual award to be presented to the 'Writer of the Year' of any nationality whose contribution was judged to have made the greatest impact in the campaign against world poverty; they hoped also to be able to build a rural college in India in his name. Ironically, the agency for the appeal was War on Want, the organization Victor had inspired but abandoned. The college was built, and the annual award continued until 1984.

Closer to Victor's heart would have been the memorial concert held in February 1968 at the Royal Festival Hall. The orchestra was the New Philharmonia, which Victor had supported as a member of its Trust with attendance, help and advice from its foundation in 1964. His last and greatest musical hero Otto Klemperer conducted, and his friend Peter Heyworth, the music critic, wrote a tribute for the programme, praising Victor's gifts as a judge of musical performances. He described memorably Victor's presence at previous Klemperer concerts: 'Well to the fore in the stalls, his shock of white hair bristling round a red shirt . . . his hands clasped over a stout stick, he sat in motionless concentration.' The programme, selected by Ruth and Livia, included works by Mozart, Schubert, and Berlioz, and the programme-book included Victor's comments on each of them. Appropriately, the second half of the concert was devoted to Beethoven and culminated with the *Leonore No. 3* overture from *Fidelio*, of which Victor had written, 'It is a work to be accepted as supreme, and that is the end of it: others abide our question, Beethoven is free.' One critic described the performance as 'great Klemperer, with the orchestra as eloquent in mysterious pianissimo as in blazing affirmation.'

Livia put together *Reminiscences of Affection* from Victor's last manuscript and the usable parts of *Tim III*, and his friends were pleased that his last book bore vibrant witness to Victor's extraordinary appreciation of sensual pleasures. She published it early in 1968, at a time when the firm's survival was still in doubt. James MacGibbon had left shortly after Victor's death, because, as he put it recently, 'I always respected Livia but I assumed (wrongly in the event) that in any discussion with her I would be arguing with Victor's ghost.' The publishing world, used to seeing independent firms going out of business or being taken over, waited for Gollancz to fold. Authors left and agents sent books elsewhere. The firm survived because many old authors stayed loyal, because of the dogged determination of Livia and John Bush, because with Victor gone it was possible to adapt to the new realities of the market place and because the firm brought in talent and gave it its head. Short of a catastrophe, Gollancz is set fair to remain one of the few major independent firms left in the United Kingdom.

Ruth, at seventy-four, had to face the death of her second daughter within two months of Victor's. She was deeply distressed when the announcement in *The Times* gave her name not as 'Diana Ruth' but as 'Diana Maria Faith', for she had not known of the baptism. She felt too betrayed to go to the funeral. Livia was also shocked and stayed away. (Their absence was retrospectively announced to the world in 1970 when Poldi published *A Time to Love — A Time to Die*, which put on record an account of the Gollancz parents that bewildered and horrified some of those who had known them. The treatment of the family in the book is in fact partial by both commission and omission.)

Ruth coped with widowhood with that same calmness and strength she had shown throughout. She had loved Victor and she missed him, but she admitted also that she appreciated being free to live her own life. She studied archaeology, spent a day a week on social work at Toynbee Hall and made new bridge-playing friends. She gave more time to her children than formerly, and offered Vita encouragement with her painting. At eighty, her cancer was diagnosed. A major operation failed and she died in April 1973, having endured with grace a long period of suffering.

Victor left behind him mixed feelings in many people's hearts. In her tribute, Diana Collins, who had no illusions about him, put the case for the defence:

> If you aim at the highest possible, you expose yourself to being shot at for not consistently attaining it. Of course, Victor did not always live up to his own professions, he had faults, he was a human being, and he wasn't always the loving, compassionate, unselfish, forgiving human being that he so passionately aspired to be — but he struggled continually, and it is a measure of his real goodness that he did so struggle, that he recognized when he failed, accepted himself, forgave himself, and went on. If ever a man hungered and thirsted after righteousness it was Victor.

NOTES AND SOURCES

From 1928–67 virtually all the letters Victor Gollancz received, and copies of those he wrote, were filed in his office. These have survived, with the exception of the bulk of his correspondence with individual members of the Left Book Club, which was destroyed, probably accidentally. Some of his news-clippings up to the late 1940s and most of those for the later period have also been preserved.

There are three main collections of Victor Gollancz papers:

1. His publishing papers are located at Victor Gollancz Limited;

2. Most of his private papers are in the Modern Records Centre at Warwick, where work is still in progress (1986) on the cataloguing. (Enquiries should be addressed in writing to the Archivist, Modern Records Centre, University of Warwick Library, Coventry CV4 7AL.) They form an archive of great importance for any researcher into twentieth-century intellectual, literary or political history.

3. Further private papers, including family memorabilia, are in the possession of Livia Gollancz.

To give chapter and verse for every fact or quotation would involve adding more than a hundred pages to an already long book. I have tried to make this section useful rather than pointlessly comprehensive. There seems little reason, for example, to note that the evidence for one of Victor's attacks of pseudo-angina came in a letter of 19 November 1958 to an author of a book on Indian philosophy. To save space I am adopting the following stratagems:

1. I list below the most important interviewees, grouped under the headings to which they made their major contribution: in most cases, that contribution will be clear from the text. In many instances, they could have been be cited two or three times. For example, Lord Walston comes under the category of 'politics' although he became a friend of Victor's and was illuminating about him from that standpoint. Similarly, Livia Gollancz is cited under the category 'family',

although of course she was an important source for politics and publishing.

2. At the beginning of each chapter I list the main sources. Thereafter, precise references are given only where a fact or quotation is controversial, intriguing, important or likely to be of interest to researchers and the source is not self-evident. I give dates of letters only when they are of significance. As Victor's memoirs are so unchronological and there is no index to *My Dear Timothy* or *More for Timothy*, I give page references for key passages in case any reader wishes to pursue an issue.

3. Where a particular book is under discussion, unless otherwise stated, related correspondence will be found in the relevant author/book file or box in Victor Gollancz Limited.

The following were key sources:

1. *Family*: The four surviving Gollancz daughters: Francesca Jeffryes, Julia Simons, Livia Gollancz, Vita Gollancz. Sons-in-law: Stuart Jeffryes and the late Harold Simons. Other Gollancz relatives: the late Marguerite Gollancz, Oliver Gollancz, the late Hugh and Florence Harris, Phyllis Simon. Lowy relatives: Daniel Lowy and family, the late Lily Henriques.

2. *St Paul's*: T. L. Martin, Harry Yoxall.

3. *University*: Lewis Denroche-Smith (by correspondence).

4. *Repton*: The late Sir Adrian Boult, Sir James Harford, Sir James Darling and John Handfield (by correspondence).

5. *Publishing*: Kingsley Amis, Betty Askwith, Glanvill Benn (interview and correspondence), John Bush, Anna Clarke, the late Norman Collins, Lettice Cooper, Joanna Goldsworthy, John Gross, Sheila Hodges, Dorothy Horsman, Elizabeth Jenkins, James MacGibbon, Walter Meigh, Elinor Murphy, Hilary Rubinstein, Daniel Shipman, Kitty Stein.

6. *Politics and Causes*: The late J. R. L. Anderson (interview and correspondence), David Astor, Pearl Binder, Lord Elwyn-Jones, Lord Gardiner, Lord Goodman, the late Arthur Koestler, Betty Lewis, Lord Longford, John Midgley, Lord Walston.

7. *Friends*: Sir Richard Acland, Canon Edward Carpenter, Diana Collins, the late John Collins, Constance Cummings (Mrs Benn Levy), the late Sir Robert Mayer, Jean MacGibbon (by correspondence), Graham and Dorothy Watson.

Files or boxes in the firm's possession are cited thus: Glaspell, BROOK EVANS. Material in the Warwick archives is cited thus: 157/3/DOC/1.

For full titles of works cited in shortened form, see the bibliography.

Initials used throughout mean as follows:

MDT   Victor Gollancz, *My Dear Timothy*
MFT   Victor Gollancz, *More for Timothy*
HFR   Papers of Harold Rubinstein, now in the possession of his son Hilary, which include all letters from Victor Gollancz to Harold Rubinstein
JC   *Jewish Chronicle*
JTM   Victor Gollancz, *Journey Towards Music*
LG   Papers in the possession of Livia Gollancz
REM   Victor Gollancz, *Reminiscences of Affection*
VG   Victor Gollancz
VGL   Victor Gollancz Limited

NB: Major sources used throughout the book have been VGL author, memoranda and staff files; 157/3/I (substantial files of correspondence with individuals), 157/3/M/1–675 (miscellaneous correspondence, pre-1940), 157/3/MI/1–4319 (miscellaneous correspondence, post-1945) and 157/10 (1951–60) and 157/10/Gen (1940–51) which contain large numbers of relevant press-cuttings

Chapter I: Childhood

Books: Hermann Gollancz, *Personalia*; VG, *MDT, MFT, JTM, REM*; Samuel Marcus Gollancz, *Biographical Sketches*; for the Jewish background I owe a special debt to several books by Chaim Bermant and a conversation with him.
Other sources: *JC*, LG

Page

23	'Thus instructed . . .' Bermant, *The Walled Garden*, p. 15
28	'zealously . . .' appreciation in *JC*, 25 May 1900
29	'an uneasy synthesis . . .' Bermant, *Troubled Eden*, p. 241
30	'and his clever little wife . . .' Herbert Bentwich, *JC*, 7 November 1930
31	'The whole complex . . .' *JTM*, p. 65
34	'I asked myself . . .' *MDT*, pp. 136–7
35	'Conscious suppression . . .' n.d. in response to letter of 27 September 1953 (in the possession of Oliver Gollancz)
36	'anything, any idea . . .' *MDT*, p. 189
37	'The arrangement . . .' *ibid*, p. 191
37	'My earliest recollection . . .' *ibid*, p. 191
38	'I remember standing . . .' *ibid*, pp. 21–22

38   'I would always . . .' *MFT*, p. 150
38   'for the search . . .' *MDT*, p. 175
39   'It was the world's . . .' *ibid*, p. 171
39   'I was looking . . .' *ibid*, pp. 33–4. The picture he described was
        'The Charge of the Heavy Brigade at Balaklava' by Stanley
        Berkeley, reproduced in Maxwell, *Sixty Years a Queen*
40   '. . . there was the . . .' *MDT*, p. 45
41   '. . . while in one . . .' *ibid*, p. 93
41   'took it for granted . . .' Daiches, *Two Worlds*, p. 140

Chapter II: Schooldays

Books: the autobiographies of Norman Bentwich, Compton Mackenzie,
Lord Montgomery and Ernest Raymond; biographies of G. D. H. Cole by
Margaret Cole, Lord Nathan by Hyde; Mackenzie, *Sinister Street*; Picciotto,
St. Paul's School; Raymond, *Mr Olim*, Salter, *St. Paul's School*; VG, *JTM*,
MDT
Other sources: *JC*; St Paul's School archives, particularly school reports,
class lists, and School Union Society minute books; the *Pauline*

Page
44   'Dirty and sordid . . .' *MDT*, p. 38
47   'It is an extraordinary . . .' *ibid*, pp. 173–4
48   'He worked hard . . .' *JTM*, p. 66
48   'For three or four . . .' *ibid*, p. 71
49   'understood, as by no means . . .' *ibid*, p. 201
50   'If *Aida* . . .' *MDT*, p. 162
50   'The exposure of . . .' *ibid*, p. 139
51   'and with a passion . . .' *ibid*, p. 138
52   'Sometimes, I am afraid . . .' *ibid*, p. 41
52   'nor from a dislike . . .' *ibid*, p. 53
54   'He was always . . .' *ibid*, p. 20
56   'It was in her study . . .' *ibid*, p. 196
56   'The ecstasy it gave . . .' *ibid*, p. 198
57   'It was precisely . . .' *ibid*, p. 199
57   'By my own deliberate . . .' *ibid*, p. 208
58   'To R. S. A.' HFR
59   'I wonder whether . . .' *MDT*, p. 212

Chapter III: University

Books: the autobiographies of Sir Ernest Barker, E. R. Dodds and Douglas
Jerrold; biographies of Monkton by Birkenhead, Hastings Rashdall by
Matheson and Spooner by Hayter; VG, *MDT*, *REM*
Other sources: *JC*; *Isis*; *Varsity*; HFR; LG (includes VG's *Daughters, Dialogue
on Socialism* and *Sonnets and Poems*); New College archives, particularly the

minutes of meetings of the Warden and Tutors and the minute book of the New College Essay Society; Oxford Union archives

Page
60   Spooner letter LG
61   ' "Mr Gollancz," he said to me once . . .' *MDT*, p. 235
62   'I was eager . . .' *ibid*, p. 243
63   'He came round . . .' *ibid*, p. 253
64   'It is the picture . . .' *ibid*, p. 263
67   'but when my own . . .' *ibid*, p. 236
67   'I was constantly . . .' *ibid*, p. 226
68   Joad in *Isis*, 26 October 1912
70   'my longing [for office] . . .' *MDT*, p. 227
71   'Cecil Chesterton . . .' *ibid*, p. 413–4
72   'Forgive me . . .' *Sonnets and Poems*
73   Both Joy poems HFR
74   'Harold Rubinstein is staying . . .' LG
74   'We ate salmon . . .' *REM*, p. 24
75   'As to Christ . . .' *MDT*, p. 395
75   'most hopeful of all . . .' *JC*, 3 January 1913
75   'As I sit here . . .' *MDT*, p. 394
76   'And when I say . . .' *ibid*, pp. 396–7
76   'I was selfish . . .' *ibid*, pp. 395–6
77   '(1) I have always felt . . .' *MDT*, pp. 397–399
78   ' "I love to see . . ." ' *Sonnets and Poems*
79   'I leaped at . . .' *MDT*, p. 404
80   'Once I *had* started . . .' *ibid*, pp. 220–1
81   'The bloods drank champagne . . .' *ibid*, p. 416
81   'To lie abed . . .' *Sonnets and Poems*

Chapter IV: Serving: A Soldier?

Books: VG, *MDT*, *MFT*
Other sources: HFR; LG (includes VG's *Sonnets and Poems*); New College and Oxford Union archives; *Varsity*, with which *Isis* was by then combined

Page
87   'I went up for . . .' *MDT*, p. 227
89   '[I] was among . . .' *MFT*, p. 21
90   Proceeded to Cambois . . .' *ibid*, p. 21
91   'My dear Golgotha . . .' printed in Laurence Houseman, *War Letters of Fallen Englishmen*, London, 1930
92   'My beloved Golgotha . . .' *MDT*, p. 415
92   'Oxford had won me . . .' *MFT*, pp. 144–5
92   'Mean and most vulgar . . .' *Sonnets and Poems*

93   '[I] borrowed . . .' *MFT*, p. 21
93   Birth certificate LG

Chapter V: Serving: a Teacher!

Books: Darling, *Richly Rewarding*; Purcell, *Fisher of Lambeth*; Thomas, *Repton*; VG, *MFT*, (ed.) *The Making of Women, Political Education at a Public School* and *The School and the World* (with David Somervell). Articles: Cranham, 'Victor Gollancz'; Markham, 'Victor Gollancz at Repton'; Smyth, 'The Boss and Repton'

Other sources: unpublished memoirs of Sir James Harford (in his possession); HFR; *JC*; *Jewish World*; LG (includes VG's *Sonnets and Poems*); *A Public School Looks at the World* (the *Pubber*); Repton School archives, particularly school lists and calendars and debating society minute books; the *Reptonian*; two unpublished memoirs of David Somervell (in the possession of his son Robert); VG correspondence with Somervell, past pupils and others in 157/3/LI/MFT/1 and 4 (*More For Timothy*)

NB: In *MFT*, Victor uses pseudonyms for some of the staff and boys: Cherry Ainsworth for James Darling, London for Brownjohn, Bob Orreys for Bob Watson and Pruke for Snape

Page
96   'I announced that . . .' *MFT*, p. 159
96   'Till then . . .' *ibid*, pp. 161–2
99   'I may add that . . .' *Sunday Times*, 30 April 1916
99   'We doubt not . . .' *Jewish World*, 3 May 1916
101   'Waves of laughter . . .' *MFT*, p. 170
101   'The Paddock is a cricket-field . . .' *ibid*, p. 150
101   'I was flabbergasted . . .' *ibid*, p. 178
103   ' "I must write a line to you . . ." ' printed in *ibid*, p. 184
103   'I refuse to write . . .' printed in *ibid*, p. 187
103   '. . .that business of "teachers" ' *ibid*, p. 189
107   'ON BEING INVITED . . .' *Sonnets and Poems*
110   'Poor pitiful old man . . .' *ibid*
110   'Why, then, did I want to win? . . .' *MFT*, pp. 349–50
114   'THE CINEMA' *Sonnets and Poems*
115   'So . . . the term ended . . .' *MFT*, p. 278
119   'with a singular unimaginativeness . . .' Smyth, 'The Boss and Repton'
125   'The thing that worries me . . .' Darling to the author

Chapter VI: Finding a Direction

Books: Jerrold, *Georgian Adventure*; Liddiard, *Isaac Rosenberg*; family biographies and memoirs by Margery and Norman Bentwich; Phillips, *Solomon J. Solomon*; VG, *Industrial Ideals, REM*

Other sources: diaries of Ernest Benn, now in Modern Records Centre at the University of Warwick; HFR; *JC*; LG; family papers in the possession of Daniel Lowy

Page
130   VG correspondence with his uncles 157/3/P/DOM/1 (Domestic and family matters)
136   'I accepted the invitation . . .' *REM*, p. 25
137   Ruth Lowy's letter and message LG
138   '. . . during the two . . .' *REM*, p. 26

Chapter VII: Publisher: the Young Turk

Books: Benn, *Happier Days*; Hodges, *Gollancz*; Jerrold, *Georgian Adventure*; VG, *REM*
Other sources: Benn Brothers catalogues; diaries of Ernest Benn; LG (including VG correspondence with Ruth); 157/3/PUB/i (Publishing)

Page
142   'Sir Ernest and I . . .' *REM*, p. 140
143   '[He] . . . was much . . .' Glanvill Benn letter to author
144   'partly for financial . . .' Glanvill Benn letter to author
150   'Unless Sir Ernest . . .' Glanvill Benn letter to author
151   'Hearing your still pompous . . .' 157/3/BR/3 (Broadcasting)
153   'by a hideous . . .' *REM*, p. 142
154   'My boy, then . . .' Yoxall in letter to Livia Gollancz
155   'We went off to . . .' *REM*, p. 27
156   'But contraceptives . . .' *MDT*, pp. 203–4

Chapter VIII: Publisher: the Independent

Books: for this and all other publishing sections, I have gained essential background and other information particularly from Barker, *Stanley Morison*; Higham, *Literary Gent*; Hodges, *Gollancz*; Howard, *Jonathan Cape*; Lusty, *Bound to be Read*; Morpurgo, *Allen Lane*; Warburg, *An Occupation for Gentlemen* and *All Authors are Equal*; VG, *MDT, MFT, JTM, REM*
Other sources: LG; 157/3/PUB/iv (Publishing)

Page
169   'Isn't the thing to do . . .' 7 February 1931 to Gerard Hopkins in his ANGEL IN THE ROOM
169   Priestley/VG correspondence February 1932 in Golding, MAGNOLIA STREET
170   Maurice Richardson, *Fits and Starts*, London, 1979, p. 203
174   Graves/Riding/VG correspondence in Wolfe, DIALOGUES AND MONOLOGUES
175   Watson, Graham, 'Sketches from Memory'

177   '. . . you must have noted . . .' W. Kean Seymour, TIME STANDS
185   'I am sorry . . .' quoted in Barker, *Morison*, p. 244
187   'a homogeneity, a cohesive policy' Hodges, *Gollancz*, p. 52
189   Ford/VG correspondence in Ford, RETURN TO YESTERDAY

Chapter IX: History Around Him

Books: As for chapter VIII. VG: *MDT*, *MFT* and for Brimpton parties and friends of the 1930s, see *REM passim*. For the political background, I owe a special debt to Caute, *The Fellow-Travellers*; Leventhal, *The Last Dissenter*; Pimlott, *Labour and the Left*; Wood, *Communism and British Intellectuals*
Other sources: LG; 157/3/P (Personal Affairs); 157/3/POL/1 and 2 (Political organisations 1931–9); 157/3/PUB/iii and iv (Publishing)

Page
195   'On the last . . .' interview with Norman Collins
196   For correspondence on attempted acquisitions of other publishers see 157/3/PUB/iii and iv/75
199   'In the early morning . . .' *JTM*, p. 179
200   'My parents first . . .' *REM*, pp. 16–17
203   'that I could not . . .' 157/3/P/CHI/1 (Children)
203   VG to chauffeur 157/3/MO/1 (Motoring)
204   VG's interest in the Brimpton house and garden is illustrated in 157/3/P/AN/i (Antiques and Works of Art), 157/3/P/BRI (Brimpton Lodge) and 157/3/P/GAR/1 (Garden at Brimpton)
204   'I am not thinking . . .' *MDT*, p. 279
205   'A line to bless you . . .' LG
205   Haile Selassie letter in the possession of Francesca Jeffryes
208   Labour Party and Ramsay MacDonald correspondence 157/3/POL/1
210   Correspondence with Temple and Dearmer in Dearmer, CHRISTIANITY AND THE CRISIS
212   '. . . There are days . . .' *MFT*, pp. 351–2
213   To Fleg 1 April 1933 in Fleg, JESUS
213   To Spender 21 January 1936 in his FORWARD FROM LIBERALISM
214   'You are, from . . .' to J. Hampden Jackson in his THE POST-WAR WORLD
214   VG/Brailsford correspondence in Brailsford, PROPERTY OR PEACE
215   Lipsey/VG correspondence in Orwell, DOWN AND OUT IN PARIS AND LONDON
217   VG/Strong correspondence in Strong, SEA WALL
218   Douglas Jay, *Change and Fortune*, London, 1980, p. 53
225   The confusion, inefficiency etc. of dealing with the Soviet Union is illustrated in the files for BOLSHEVO, Brontmann, ON TOP OF THE WORLD and for all volumes in the NEW SOVIET LIBRARY

226   'What precisely is the point . . .' to Ralph Fox in Vinogradoff, THE
           BLACK CONSUL

Chapter X: The Organizer

Books: As for chapter IX. For this and all LBC sections, I have gained
essential information especially from Lewis, *The Left Book Club*; Martin,
Harold Laski; Thomas, *John Strachey*; and from Neavill's and Samuels's
articles on the Left Book Club
Other sources: the *Bookseller*; *Daily Worker*; the *Left Book News*; the *Left News*;
LG; the *New Statesman*; *Tribune*; 157/3/POL/1; 157/3/DOC/1 (Documentary — largely to do with the Communist Party)

Page
228   I am indebted to Mr. F. Morton for information about the
           Progressive Book Society
232   'nine considerations impelled . . .' *MFT*, pp. 355–6
234   Lynd n.d. but March 1936 in Jellinek, THE PARIS COMMUNE
235   Strachey/Palme Dutt correspondence quoted in Thomas, *John
           Strachey*, pp. 154–5
236   VG/Strachey correspondence quoted in Thomas, *John Strachey*,
           p. 156
237   'The treatment should . . .' 4 February 1937 to Stephen Swingler
           in his OUTLINE OF POLITICAL THOUGHT
244   'to break down the vicious . . .' April 1937 in Farrington, THE
           CIVILISATION OF GREECE AND ROME
245   'I feel distressed . . .' in Webb Miller, I FOUND NO PEACE
245   To Pollitt, January 1939 157/3/DOC/1
246   VG/Harrisson correspondence in his SAVAGE CIVILISATION
250   'You remember . . .' in J. R. Campbell, SOVIET POLICY AND ITS
           CRITICS
250   'pointing out . . .' To Allen Hutt in Hutt, POST-WAR HISTORY OF
           THE BRITISH WORKING CLASS
251   'As it goes on . . .' in Mahon, TRADE UNIONISM
252   Pollitt in the *Daily Worker*, 8 May 1937
252   VG in the *Daily Worker*, 23 April 1937
253   Sherman, 'The Days of the Left Book Club'
254   VG interview in *Moscow Daily News*, 11 May 1937
255   'amazing that place . . .' 21 May 1937 to W. O'Sullivan Molony in
           his VICTIMS VICTORIOUS

Chapter XI: A Power in the Land

Sources: as for chapter X

Page
257   'the Left Book Club, with . . .' in Haldane, A. R. P.

259   'consist of waking . . .' Stuart Samuels, 'The Left Book Club'
262   'I can well understand . . .' 9 June 1937 to Donald Brace in Albert
       Rhys Williams, THE SOVIETS
263   Laski re Dalton in *Left News*, August 1937
266   VG/Postgate in Frank Jellinek, THE CIVIL WAR IN SPAIN
268   'When it came in . . .' 20 July 1938 in Amber Blanco White, THE
       NEW PROPAGANDA
269   'I should not myself . . .' in Orwell, AUTHOR'S MISCELLANEOUS
272   For the China Campaign Committee see 157/3/DOC/1/228 and
       389–401 and *REM*, pp. 134–40
274   'The applause by members . . .' *MFT*, p. 362

Chapter XII: Squeezed by Ideology

Sources: as for chapter X; *Forward*; VG, *Is Mr. Chamberlain Saving Peace?*

Page
277   'We discourage it . . .' to T. Francis Jarman in Koestler, SPANISH
       TESTAMENT
279   Brailsford to Foot, quoted in Leventhal, *The Last Dissenter*
280   'The Coles, Tawneys . . .' quoted in Thomas, *John Strachey*, p. 174
280   Letters to Attlee, Churchill, Citrine and Eden 157/3/POL/1/84–5
281   'I looked within . . .' *MFT*, p. 372
283   Strachey to Boothby, quoted in Thomas, *John Strachey*, pp. 179–80
283   'I see a future . . .' in Woolf, BARBARIANS AT THE GATE
289   'and saw the world . . .' *MDT*, p. 433
289   VG/Pollitt 157/3/DOC/1
289   'that some of Gollancz's . . .' to Leonard Moore 25 April 1939,
       printed in *The Times Literary Supplement*, 6 January 1984
291   VG/Dean of Canterbury in Johnson, ACT NOW
296   VG/Wilkinson in Wilkinson, THE TOWN THAT WAS MURDERED
299   'I refused to budge . . .' Woolf, *The Journey*, p. 13

Chapter XIII: Retreat from Moscow

Sources: as for chapter X; VG, *The Betrayal of the Left*, *MFT* (especially chapter II, 'The Communist Mentality, Conscience, and Treason' and pp. 357–377), *Where Are You Going?*; 157/3/DOC/1

Page
301   VG/J. B. Coates April 1960 157/3/PE/1/16 (Personalist Group)
302   'I have been talking . . .' in Rader, NO COMPROMISE
303   Lewis/Lynd/Reid/Strachey/VG correspondence in 157/3/DOC/1
310   All relevant correspondence is in VG, WHERE ARE YOU GOING?
312   VG/Inkpin 157/3/DOC/1/85, 87, 88

313	'So you have crossed . . .' 157/3/DOC/1/74
313	'No one, in my view . . .' to F. C. Cracknell 157/3/DOC/1/81
314	Orwell to Gorer in Orwell, *The Collected Essays*, vol. 1, p. 529
315	VG/Attlee/Morrison/Nicolson LG
319	VG/Lewis/Reid correspondence re Lewis's *Daily Worker* article 157/3/DOC/1/156–171
319	Treves to VG in Treves, ITALY, YESTERDAY, TODAY AND TOMORROW
321	VG/Nathan LG
321	*Cherwell*, 21 November 1940
323	*Daily Express*, 25 November 1940
323	*Truth*, 20 December 1940
324	Correspondence re proposed debates with CP 157/3/DOC/1/209–28
325	Correspondence with Hewlett Johnson and Hyman Levy 157/3/DOC/1/260–78 and 285–93
326	All relevant correspondence is in VG, THE BETRAYAL OF THE LEFT
327	VG/Pritt correspondence 157/3/DOC/1/260–78
327	'It's terrible . . .' 2 April 1941 157/3/DOC/1/278
327	VG/Mollie Pritt LG
329	VG/Jordan 157/3/DOC/1/295

Chapter XIV: Meanwhile . . .

Books: as for chapter VIII
Other sources: LG

Page

331	VG/Lofts August 1939 in her BLOSSOM LIKE A ROSE
333	'What a marvellous . . .' LG
335	Correspondence re telephone delays 157/3/DOC/1/190–9
338	'I was talking . . .' 157/3/DOC/1/120
344	'There was a perfectly shocking . . .' 'The Uncommon Commoner' in *Sunday Times*, 7 April 1963
345	'We were not very successful . . .' *REM*, p. 101
346	Macaulay letters LG

Chapter XV: War: Embracing Too Much

Books: Stocks, *Eleanor Rathbone*; VG, *MDT*, *MFT*, *Russia and Ourselves*. Pamphlets: Geyer and Loeb, *Gollancz in German Wonderland*; Vansittart, *Black Record: and Present*; VG, *Let My People Go*, *Shall Our Children Live or Die? A Reply to Lord Vansittart on the German Problem*
Other sources: Richard Acland's unpublished memoirs (in his possession); *Left News*; 157/3/ASP (Anglo-Soviet Public Relations Committee later Association); 157/3/JE/i (Jewish Affairs 1927–30) and 157/3/JE/1 (Jewish question in wartime)

Chapter XVI: War: Breakdown and Recovery

Books: as for chapter VIII; Addison, *The Road to 1945*; Fleg, *Why I Am a Jew*; Kingsford, *Publishers Association*; VG, *From Darkness to Light, A Year of Grace*.
Pamphlet: VG, '*Nowhere to Lay Their Heads*'
Other sources: *JC*; *LG*; *The Times Literary Supplement*; VGL Publishers Association files; 157/3/JE/1 (Jewish question in wartime), 157/3/LB (Left Book Club), 157/3/LI/NT/1,2 and 3, ('*Nowhere to Lay Their Heads*'), 157/3/PUB/1 (Publishing)

394   'immigrant peddling foreign dirt' correspondence of May 1945 re
          remarks of General Sir George Jeffreys MP, LG
394   Correspondence re standing for parliament August 1944 with Joad
          in VG, SHALL OUR CHILDREN? and February 1945 with Cole in his
          THE INTELLIGENT MAN'S GUIDE TO THE POST-WAR WORLD
396   'I believe, of course . . .' 157/3/LI/NT/1/118
396   'The victory of . . .' E. G. O'Brien quoted in the *Brentford and
          Chiswick Times*, 17 May 1945
397   Samuels, 'The Left Book Club'
398   A. J. Cummings 14 February 1947
399   'In the case of the last . . .' 19 September 1949 to Donald Bruce in
          Bruce and Foot, WHO ARE THE PATRIOTS?

Chapter XVII: Post-War: The Emerging Philanthropist

Books: Catlin, *Above All Nations*; Duff, *Left, Left, Left*; VG, *Our Threatened
Values*. Pamphlets: Duff, *Save Europe Now 1945–1948, Three Years' Work* (in
157/3/SEN/1); VG, *Europe and Germany, Is it Nothing to You?, Leaving Them
to Their Fate, The New Morality, What Buchenwald Really Means*
Other sources: LG (include incomplete file of VG's letters to the press);
Spectator; 157/3/PR/1–4 (Letters to the Press) include correspondence arising
from his letters; 157/3/SEN/1–4 (Save Europe Now) include administrative
papers and related correspondence including exchanges with government
ministers

Page
402   All relevant correspondence is in VG, WHAT BUCHENWALD REALLY
          MEANS
405   Correspondence with Kingsley Martin and others re Czecho-
          slovakia 157/3/DOC/1/369–81
405   'In the devilish . . .' published in *Manchester Guardian*, 15 August
          1945; related correspondence in 157/3/PR/3
406   Wittgenstein/VG 157/3/PR/4, which also includes a great deal of
          related correspondence
408   Browne/VG correspondence 157/3/LI/NT/1/115–6
410   'Correspondents in Berlin . . .' published e.g. in *Manchester
          Guardian*, 11 September 1945
412   Correspondence with Patricia Russell 157/3/SEN/1/9–16
414   Correspondence with Wilkes and Zilliacus October 1945
          157/3/SEN/1/17–18
416   'I couldn't possibly . . .' 157/3/PR/4/283
420   'Original Sin vs. Utopia in British Socialism' in *Review of Politics*,
          April 1956, Indiana University
421   Waugh to *New Statesman* published 1 June 1946
422   Fleg and Niemoller correspondence in VG, LEAVING THEM TO THEIR
          FATE

423   All relevant correspondence is in VG, OUR THREATENED VALUES
427   D. R. Davies in *Church of Ireland Gazette*, 26 July 1946
427   'Having done more . . .' *Birmingham Mail*, 20 July 1946
428   'In theological language . . .' 157/3/I/Acland
431   'It is, of course . . .' *ibid*
431   'It was not a conveyance . . .' *REM*, pp. 42–3

Chapter XVIII: Causes

Books: Collins, *Faith Under Fire*; Craig, *Longford*; Duff, *Left, Left, Left*; VG, *In Darkest Germany*. Pamphlets: Duff, *Save Europe Now 1945–8, Three Years' Work* (in 157/3/SEN/1); VG, *Germany Revisited, On Reconciliation*
Other sources: LG (include all letters to Ruth, an incomplete file of letters to the press and a small file of sample correspondence about post-war hardship cases); 157/3/GE/1–11 (German Visit), an enormous collection of correspondence and other documents relating to VG's 1946 visit, 157/3/GE/2 (Anti-letters), 157/10/Ger (press-cuttings relevant to Germany and including items on VG quoted in this chapter with translations where appropriate), 157/3/PR/5–7 (Letters to Press), 157/3/SEN/2 and 4 (Save Europe Now)

Page
433   'You may not remember . . .' J. G. Nicoll, 3 April 1959, 157/3/BR/1
439   'the almost unbearable . . .' *The Times*, 5 November 1946
439   'The most horrible . . .' *The Times*, 15 November 1946
440   'The shamelessness of . . .' *News Chronicle*, 13 November 1946
443   Letters from Brimpton: e.g. *New Statesman*, 30 November 1946, 7 December 1946, 14 December 1946; *Daily Herald*, 23, 26, 30 November 1946; *Observer*, 24 November 1946; *Manchester Guardian*, 6, 7, 8 December 1946; *The Times* 13, 29 November 1946; *The Times Literary Supplement*, 30 November 1946
445   All relevant correspondence in VG, IN DARKEST GERMANY
452   An account of the first meeting of Christian Action is given in the pamphlet, *A Call to Christian Action in Public Affairs* 157/3/I/Collins
453   VG speech at the Sheldonian printed in amended form in his *On Reconciliation*
454   'Many must have . . .' *Church of England Newspaper*, 5 December 1947
454   VG speech at Trinity College Dublin 157/3/PR/7/1
458   '*Good Deeds*' *Pinguin*, March 1947
459   '"You'll find me . . ."' *Heute*, 1 May 1947
460   '"Jewish Apostle"' — VG profile in *Newsweek*, 16 December 1946
461   'His room . . .' Hans Habe, 'Germany's Jewish Apostle', *Aufbau*, November 1947

463 "A Light for German Youth!" *Müncher-Merker*, no. 120, 24 December 1948

Chapter XIX: More Causes

Books: VG, *MDT* (especially Chapter XX, 'My Socialism'), *MFT*. Essay: VG, 'Personal Freedom' in *The Meaning of Freedom*
Other sources: *JC*; LG (unless otherwise stated, all the administrative papers and correspondence relating to the JSHS come from this source), 157/3/DH/1 (*Daily Herald* competition), 157/3/EM/1 (European Movements), 157/3/FE/1 (Federal Union Ltd.), 157/3/JS/1–2 (JSHS), 157/3/LP/1 (Labour Party), 157/3/LB/1–2 (Left Book Club), 157/3/PR/5–13, 15 (Letters to the Press), 157/3/UE/1–7 (United Europe Movement)

Page

494   'I speak as a . . .' speech in full in UEM booklet 157/3/UE/5/7/1
496   VG speech 6 February 1948 LG
497   Churchill to General Marshall 7 April 1948 LG
499   Young/Laski/VG correspondence 157/3/LB/1/54–5, 67–72
499   See 157/3/LB/1 for correspondence with LBC members
500   VG article in *Tribune*, 31 January 1947
502   *News Chronicle* correspondence 29 August and 1 September 1949
503   157/3/PR/8 contains extensive correspondence about the impris-
       oned German Field Marshals
504   'Those German Generals', *Tribune*, 10 September 1948
505   VG/Acland correspondence 157/3/I/Acland
507   'but you go fatally . . .' Trinity speech 157/3/PR/7/1
508   The text of 'Personal Freedom' was published (slightly amended)
       in *The Meaning of Freedom*, Supplement no. 7 to *World Liberalism*,
       1956
509   157/3/PR/12 contains the correspondence about von Weizsaecker
511   VG to Foot in Bruce and Foot, WHO ARE THE PATRIOTS?
513   VG/Strachey 25 October 1949 157/3/LP/1/29
515   VG to Pearl Binder 157/3/MI/2006
515   VG/Isobel Cripps LG
517   VG to Stafford Cripps 23 October 1950 157/3/MI/715–23

Chapter XX: Meanwhile . . .

Books: as for chapter VIII
Other sources: LG; 157/3/PUB/2

Page

520   Curtis Brown/VG correspondence in du Maurier AUTHOR'S MISCE-
       LLANEOUS
522   Elizabeth Jenkins/VG correspondence in Jenkins, THE TORTOISE
       AND THE HARE
526   'The day will come . . .' *Leader* magazine, 8 February 1947
526   'The cynics . . .' *Magazine Digest*, August 1947
527   VG/Nathan/Strawson LG
529   Cass Canfield, *Up and Down and Around*, London, 1972, p. 74
530   Sloane/VG in Crockett, POPCORN ON THE GINZA
531   'I have five . . .' from speech published in *On Reconciliation*

Chapter XXI: A Year in the Life

Books: Collins, *Faith Under Fire*; VG, *A Year of Grace*. Pamphlet: VG,
Christianity and the War Crisis
Other sources: LG (include substantial number of documents acquired by
VG during his visit to Germany); 157/3/CL/1–3, 5 (Civil Liberties), 157/3/
GE/3, 157/3/LI/YG/1–8 (*A Year of Grace*), 157/3/TR/2/1 (German Visit)

Chapter XXII: Apogee

Books: VG, *From Darkness to Light, MDT, MFT*
Other sources: LG (including the manuscript of *Last Words for Timothy*);
157/3/LI/DL/1 (*From Darkness to Light*), 157/3/LI/MDT/1–8 (*MDT*),
157/3/LI/MFT/1–5 (*MFT*), 157/3/LI/LWT/1 (*Last Words for Timothy*),
157/3/MU/B/1 (Music: Bookings)

Chapter XXIII: And More Causes

Books: VG, *From Darkness to Light, MDT*. Pamphlet: VG, *Christianity and the
War Crisis*
Other sources: Sir Richard Acland's unpublished memoirs (in his possess-
ion); LG (include the bulk of papers on the Association for World Peace);
157/3/JE/6 (Friends of the Hebrew University of Jerusalem), 157/3/PRI
(Prisoners), 157/3/WW/1 (War on Want)

628   *South Africa*, 9 October 1954
629   VG to *The Times*, 31 January 1952
629   Correspondence re overseas travel allowance 157/3/PR/16/6–37 (Letters to the Press)
630   'If, in defiance . . .' 25 July 1953
630   Correspondence re trade unions 157/3/PR/16/39–74
630   Correspondence re prison visiting and Ronnie 157/3/HL/21–37 (Howard League and penal reform)
630   'He always . . .' *MFT*, p. 333–4
633   'The only possible . . .' *MFT*, p. 336
634   VG/Acland correspondence 157/3/I/Acland

Chapter XXIV: The Absolutist Conscience

Books: As for chapter VIII; Abse, *Private Member*; Collins, *Faith Under Fire*; Driver, *The Disarmers*; Duff, *Left, Left, Left*; Hamilton, *Koestler*. Pamphlet: VG, *Capital Punishment: the heart of the matter*
Other sources: LG (includes press clippings and photographs relating to VG's 1960 visit to Germany); letters to Elinor Murphy (in her possession); 157/3/CAP/3 (Capital Punishment), 157/3/LI/DL (*From Darkness to Light*), 157/3/LI/DR/1–3 (*The Devil's Repertoire*), 157/3/GE/8 (Germany), 157/3/ND/1 (Nuclear Disarmament), 157/3/PAC/1–8 (Pacifism), 157/3/PR/15–16 (Letters to Press), 157/3/PUB/4, 5, 17–25 (Publishing), 157/3/TR (Travel)

Page
639   'I haven't the . . .' to A. D. Peters in Koestler, REFLECTIONS ON HANGING
642   VG address LG
643   'I don't know . . .' to Louis Marks 157/3/LI/DL
644   Correspondence with Gardiner, Koestler and Peters in Koestler, REFLECTIONS ON HANGING
645   VG to du Maurier in du Maurier, THE SCAPEGOAT
645   VG to Collins 24 April 1956 157/3/CA (Christian Action)
647   Correspondence re 'The Bridge' in 157/3/NB/1
648   'I have no solution . . .' in 157/3/CA
649   VG to Silverman 157/3/MI/3513
650   All material concerning JSHS in LG
652   *The Sanity of Christ* material in 157/3/LI/SC
653   'With the advance . . .' *Oxford Magazine*, 5 December 1957
654   VG to Pat Arrowsmith 157/3/ND/1/73–5
654   'I had the idea . . .' 157/3/CA/1/23
655   VG/Acland correspondence 157/3/I/Acland
655   'I hasten to let . . .' to Ira and Edita Morris 157/3/LI/DR/1/6–11
656   All correspondence re *The Devil's Repertoire* in 157/3/LI/DR
660   Correspondence with Duff 157/3/ND/1/142–56

Chapter XXV: The Generation Gap

Books: VG, *God of a Hundred Names, A New Year of Grace.* Pamphlet: VG,
The Case of Adolf Eichmann
Other sources: 157/3/BR (Broadcasting), 157/3/CAP/1–3 (Capital Punish-
ment), 157/3/LI/AE/1–3 (The Case of Adolf Eichmann), 157/3/CA (Christ-
ian Action), 157/3/PR/16–19 (Letters to the Press), 157/3/PUB/9 and 25
(Publishing), 157/3/RHO (Rhodesia)

702   Bentwich in *The Times*, 19 December 1961

702   VG/Longford letter in *The Times*, 2 August 1962

702   VG to *The Times*, 11 September 1962; correspondence arising 157/3/PR/18

703   'Apropos of yesterday's . . .' *The Times*, 5 December 1962; correspondence arising 157/3/PR/19. For VG and gentile condemnation of ritual slaughter see 157/3/JE/3 (Jewish Affairs)

704   VG/Bermant 157/3/JE/Misc

705   Correspondence re Defence and Aid controversy in 157/3/RHO/1 and 157/3/I/Collins

706   'All this, I fear . . .' 2 January 1963 157/3/CA/1/99

707   VG/Wilson in Wilson, AUTHOR'S MISCELLANEOUS

711   VG/Calder in *The Times Literary Supplement*, November 1963–February 1964

711   Correspondence re proposed letter to *The Times* re the Moors murders in 157/3/PR/22

712   Freeling, VALPARAISO

714   VG/MacGibbon/Rubinstein 157/3/PUB/9 and 25

715   Whitefriar, 27 January 1962 in *Smith's Trade News*

719   Correspondence re knighthood in 157/3/P/KN (Knighthood)

722   VG/Thompson 157/3/MI/3813–5

Chapter XXVI: Odes to Joy

Books: VG, *God of a Hundred Names, JTM, The Ring at Bayreuth, REM*
Other sources: LG (Craig/VG transcripts); 157/3/LI/GH (*God of a Hundred Names*), 157/3/LS (London Society for the Study of Religion), 157/3/MU/B/1–4 (Music: bookings), 157/3/MU/G (Music: general), 157/3/MU/K/1 (Music: Klemperer), 157/3/MU/NP/1 (Music: New Philharmonia Orchestra), 157/3/MU/O/1 (Music: *Observer* interview), 157/3/MU/OG/1 (Music: opera, general), 157/3/MU/RB/1 (Music: *The Ring at Bayreuth*)

Page

722   VG/Gibbon 157/3/LI/MFT/4

726   VG/Craig in Gollancz, LIFE OF CHRISTOPHER CRAIG

729   Correspondence re *JTM* in VG, MYSELF AND MUSIC

730   VG re Wagner in *Observer*, 8 August 1965

731   Levin, *New Statesman*, 17 September 1965

733   Letters of sympathy 157/3/P/ST/ (Personal: stroke)

735   Letters of condolence on VG's death 157/3/P/CON and LG

SELECT BIBLIOGRAPHY

1. Published writings of Victor Gollancz (in chronological order)

Dialogue on Socialism (the Chancellor's Latin Essay), Oxford, 1913
Sonnets and Poems, Oxford, 1917 (privately printed)
The Making of Women: Oxford Essays in Feminism, (ed. Gollancz), London, 1917
Political Education at a Public School, London, 1918 (with David C. Somervell)
The School and the World, London, 1919 (with David C. Somervell)
Industrial Ideals, Oxford, 1920
Is Mr Chamberlain Saving Peace?, London, 1939
Where Are You Going? An Open Letter to Communists, London, 1940
The Betrayal of the Left. An examination and refutation of Communist policy from October 1939 to January 1941: with suggestions for an alternative and an epilogue on political morality (ed. Gollancz), London, 1941
Russia and Ourselves, London, 1941
Shall Our Children Live or Die? A reply to Lord Vansittart on the German problem, London, 1942
'Let My People Go' Some practical proposals for dealing with Hitler's massacre of the Jews and an appeal to the British public, London, 1943
Translation of Fleg, Edmond, *Why I am a Jew*, London, 1943
'Nowhere to Lay their Heads' The Jewish tragedy in Europe and its solution, London, 1945
What Buchenwald Really Means, London, 1945
The New Morality: four letters, London, 1945
Europe and Germany: today and tomorrow, London, 1945
Is It Nothing to You?, London, 1945 (photographs with preface)
Leaving Them to Their Fate: the ethics of starvation, London, 1946
Our Threatened Values, London, 1946
In Darkest Germany, London, 1947
Germany Revisited, London, 1947
On Reconciliation: two speeches, London, 1948
A Year of Grace: passages chosen and arranged to express a mood about God and man, London, 1948
Christianity and the War Crisis, London, 1951 (with L. J. Collins)
My Dear Timothy: an autobiographical letter to his grandson, London, 1952
More For Timothy: being the second instalment of an autobiographical letter to his grandson, London, 1953
Capital Punishment: the heart of the matter, London, 1955
From Darkness to Light: a confession of faith in the form of an anthology, London, 1956
'Personal Freedom' in *The Meaning of Freedom*, Supplement no. 7 to *World Liberalism*, London, 1956
The Devil's Repertoire or nuclear bombing and the life of man, London, 1958

The New Year of Grace. An anthology for youth and age, London, 1961
The Case of Adolf Eichmann, London, 1961
God of a Hundred Names, London, 1962 (with Barbara Greene)
Journey Towards Music: a memoir, London, 1964
The Ring at Bayreuth: and some thoughts on operatic production, London, 1966 (afterword by Wieland Wagner)
Reminiscences of Affection, London, 1968

Additionally, he wrote numerous articles in the *Left Book News*, the *Left News*, the *Manchester Guardian*, the *News Chronicle*, the *New Statesman* and *Tribune*, contributed occasional articles and letters to a wide range of British daily and weekly journals and wrote some forewords to books.

2. *Other secondary sources*

I have confined this bibliography to published works mentioned in the text and those that I found especially valuable for background information.

ABSE, LEO, *Private Member*, London, 1973
ADDISON, PAUL, *The Road to 1945: British Politics and the Second World War*, London, 1975
BARKER, SIR ERNEST, *Age and Youth*, Oxford, 1953
BARKER, NICOLAS, *Stanley Morison*, London, 1972
BENN, ERNEST, *Happier Days*, London, 1943
BENTWICH, MARGERY, *Lilian Ruth Friedlander*, London, 1957
　　Thelma Yellin: pioneer musician, Rubin Mass., 1964
BENTWICH, MARGERY and NORMAN, *Herbert Bentwich: the Pilgrim Father*, Jerusalem, 1940
BENTWICH, NORMAN, *Wanderer Between Two Worlds*, London, 1941
　　My 77 Years. An account of my life and times 1883–1960, London, 1962
BERMANT, CHAIM, *Coming Home*, London, 1976
　　The Cousinhood: the Anglo-Jewish Gentry, London, 1971
　　The Jews, London, 1977
　　Point of Arrival: a study of London's East End, London, 1975
　　Troubled Eden. An anatomy of British Jewry, London, 1969
　　The Walled Garden: the saga of Jewish family life and tradition, London and Jerusalem, 1974
BIRKENHEAD, LORD, *Walter Monckton*, London, 1969
BURGER, FRANZ, *Gollancz's Buchenwald Never Existed*, London, 1945
CALDER, ANGUS, *The People's War: Britain, 1939–45*, London, 1969
CANNON, OLGA and ANDERSON, J. R. L., *The Road from Wigan Pier. A biography of Les Cannon*, London, 1973
CATLIN, GEORGE, BRITTAIN, VERA and HODGES, SHEILA, *Above All Nations*, London, 1945 (foreword by Victor Gollancz)
CAUTE, DAVID, *The Fellow-Travellers*, London, 1973
COLE, MARGARET, *The Life of G. D. H. Cole*, London, 1971
COLLINS, L. JOHN, *Faith Under Fire*, London, 1966
CRAIG, MARY, *Longford: a biographical portrait*, London, 1978
CRANHAM, PETER, 'Victor Gollancz', *Reptonian*, Summer and Michaelmas, 1975

CRICK, BERNARD, *George Orwell: A Life*, London, 1980

DAICHES, DAVID, *Two Worlds: an Edinburgh Jewish childhood*, London, 1957

DARLING, J. R., *Richly Rewarding*, Melbourne, 1977

DODDS, E. R., *Missing Persons: An Autobiography*, Oxford, 1977

DRIBERG, TOM, *Ruling Passions*, London, 1977

DRIVER, CHRISTOPHER, *The Disarmers. A study in protest*, London, 1964

DUFF, PEGGY, *Left, Left, Left. A personal account of six protest campaigns 1945–65*, London, 1971

FOOT, MICHAEL, *Aneurin Bevan*, vol. I, *1897–1945*, London, 1962, vol. II, *1945–1960*, London, 1973

GARTNER, LLOYD P., *The Jewish Immigrant in England, 1870–1914*, London, 1960

GEYER, CURT and LOEB, WALTER, *Gollancz in German Wonderland*, London, 1942

GOLLANCZ, HERMANN, *Personalia: the story of a professional man's career told in certificates, testimonials, congratulatory messages, letters and addresses, reports and presentations, etc., relating to Sir Hermann Gollancz M. A., D. Lit., Rabbi, Emeritus Minister of the United Synagogue, London, Emeritus Professor of Hebrew in the University of London University College*, Oxford, 1928

GOLLANCZ, SAMUEL MARCUS, *Biographical Sketches and Selected Verses*, (translated and edited by Hermann Gollancz), Oxford, 1930

HAMILTON, IAIN, *Koestler: a biography*, London, 1982

HARRIS, C. C., *The Family* (London, 1969)

HAYTER, SIR WILLIAM, *Spooner: a biography*, London, 1977

HIGHAM, DAVID, *Literary Gent*, London, 1978

HODGES, SHEILA, *Gollancz: the story of a publishing house, 1928–1978*, London, 1978

HOWARD, MICHAEL S., *Jonathan Cape, Publisher*, London, 1971

HYDE, H. MONTGOMERY, *Strong for Service: the Life of Lord Nathan of Churt*, London, 1968

HYNES, SAMUEL, *The Auden Generation: literature and politics in the 1930s*, London, 1976

JERROLD, DOUGLAS, *Georgian Adventure*, London, 1937

KINGSFORD, R. J. L., *The Publishers Association 1896–1946*, Cambridge, 1970

LEVENTHAL, F. M., *The Last Dissenter: H. N. Brailsford and his world*, Oxford, 1985

LEWIS, JOHN, *The Left Book Club*, London, 1970

LIDDIARD, JEAN, *Isaac Rosenberg: the half-used life*, London, 1975

LOEWENSTEIN, PRINCE LEOPOLD OF, *A Time to Love – A Time to Die*, London, 1970

LONGFORD, FRANK, *The Grain of Wheat*, London, 1974

LUSTY, ROBERT, *Bound to be Read*, London, 1975

McCULLOCH, GARRY, 'Victor Gollancz on the Crisis and Prospects of Labour and the Left, 1942', *Bulletin* of the Society for Study of Labour History, no. 44 (Spring 1982)

MACKENZIE, COMPTON, *My Life and Times, Octave Two 1891–1900*, London, 1963
Sinister Street, vol. 1, London, 1913

MARKHAM, J. V., 'Victor Gollancz at Repton', *Repton School Terminal Letter*, May 1967

MARTIN, KINGSLEY, *Editor*, London, 1968
Harold Laski, London, 1969

MATHESON, P. E., *The Life of Hastings Rashdall*, Oxford, 1928

MAXWELL, SIR HERBERT, *Sixty Years a Queen*, London, 1897

MAYBAUM, I., *The Jewish Home*, London, 1953

MONTGOMERY, LORD, *The Memoirs of Field-Marshal the Viscount Montgomery of Alamein*, London, 1958

MORPURGO, J. E., *Allen Lane, King Penguin: a biography*, London, 1979

NEAVILL, GORDON B., 'Victor Gollancz and the Left Book Club', *Library Quarterly*, vol. 41, no. 3, July 1971

ORWELL, GEORGE, *The Road to Wigan Pier*, LBC edition, London, 1937

ORWELL, SONIA and ANGUS, IAN (eds.), *The Collected Essays, Journalism and Letters of George Orwell*, vol. I, *An Age Like This 1920–40*, vol. III, *As I Please 1943–45*, London, 1968

PAKENHAM, FRANK, EARL OF LONGFORD, *Five Lives*, London, 1964

PERETZ, MARTIN, 'Laski Redivivus' (*Journal of Contemporary History*, vol. I, no. 2, 1966)

PHILLIPS, OLGA SOMECH, *Solomon J. Solomon: a memoir of peace and war*, London, n.d.

PICCIOTTO, CYRIL, *St. Paul's School*, London, 1939

PIMLOTT, BEN, *Hugh Dalton*, London, 1985
    Labour and the Left in the 1930s, Cambridge, 1977

PURCELL, WILLIAM, *Fisher of Lambeth: A portrait from life*, London, 1969

RAYMOND, ERNEST, *The Story of My Days: An Autobiography, 1888–1922*, London, 1968
    Mr Olim, London, 1961

ROLPH, C. H., *Kingsley*, London, 1973

ROTH, CECIL, *History of the Jews in England*, Oxford, 1964

SALTER, F. R., *St. Paul's School 1909–1959*, London, 1959

SAMUELS, STUART, 'The Left Book Club', *Journal of Contemporary History*, vol. I, no. 2, 1966

SHERMAN, ALFRED, 'The Days of the Left Book Club', *Survey, A Journal of Soviet and East European Studies*, no. 41, April 1962

SMYTH, CHARLES, 'The Boss and Repton: 1916–1921', *Repton School Terminal Letter*, May 1973

STOCKS, MARY D., *Eleanor Rathbone*, London, 1949

STRACHEY, JOHN, *A Strangled Cry, And Other Unparliamentary Papers*, London, 1962

SYMONS, JULIAN, *The Thirties: A Dream Revised*, London, 1960

THOMAS, BERNARD (ed.), *Repton, 1557–1957*, London, 1957

THOMAS, HUGH, *John Strachey*, London, 1973

VANSITTART, SIR ROBERT, *Black Record: Germans past and present*, London, 1941

WARBURG, FREDRIC J., *All Authors are Equal*, London, 1973
    An Occupation for Gentlemen, London, 1959

WATSON, GRAHAM, 'Sketches from Memory', *Bookseller*, 15 October 1977

WILSON, DUNCAN, *Leonard Woolf: a political biography*, London, 1978

WOOD, NEAL, *Communism and British Intellectuals*, London, 1959

WOOLF, LEONARD, *The Journey Not the Arrival Matters: an autobiography of the years 1939–69*, London, 1969

INDEX